GUARDIAN OF THE PROMISE

D0400927

Also by
Irene Radford

The Dragon Nimbus
THE GLASS DRAGON
THE PERFECT PRINCESS
THE LONELIEST MAGICIAN
THE WIZARD'S TREASURE

The Dragon Nimbus History
THE DRAGON'S TOUCHSTONE
THE LAST BATTLEMAGE
THE RENEGADE DRAGON

The Star Gods
THE HIDDEN DRAGON
THE DRAGON CIRCLE*

Merlin's Descendants
GUARDIAN OF THE BALANCE
GUARDIAN OF THE TRUST
GUARDIAN OF THE VISION
GUARDIAN OF THE PROMISE
GUARDIAN OF THE FREEDOM*

*Coming soon from DAW Books

IRENE RADFORD

GUARDIAN OF THE PROMISE

Merlin's Descendants:

Volume Four

DAW BOOKS, INC.

DONALD A. WOLLHEIM, FOUNDER

375 Hudson Street, New York, NY 10014

ELIZABETH R. WOLLHEIM
SHEILA E. GILBERT
PUBLISHERS

www.dawbooks.com

This book is dedicated to my patient husband, who promised me much and lived up to most of it.

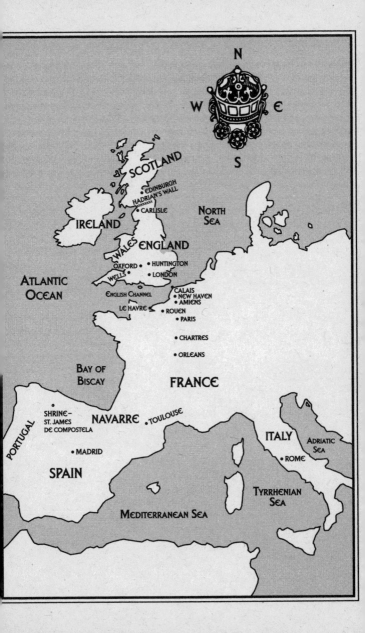

AUTHOR'S NOTES AND ACKNOWLEDGMENTS

When I embarked upon my journey into Elizabethan history, I had no idea I could produce two very large books about the Kirkwood family, spanning four generations. What is even more amazing to me, I still did not have a chance to go play with William Shakespeare. The Bard is probably the single most famous character to emerge from the long reign of Elizabeth I. Yet his life and work falls into the declining years of her era and overlaps with her successor, James I of England and VI of Scotland. This demonstrates to me just how important this queen was to history. She counted among her suitors Ivan the Terrible of Russia, two French princes, King Philip of Spain, and numerous others. In an age when women had little status she ruled alone, without a consort, without a man to make her decisions. She did it for forty-five years. The anniversary of her accession to the crown, November 17, was celebrated as a national holiday in England into the eighteenth century.

During her reign we see an explosion of creativity in the arts. The merchant class emerged as a power to be contended with. Commerce led to the growth of a merchant fleet, better ship designs, and professional sailors. Education became commonplace, the English language was codified, and people began to participate in government and religion rather than having it handed to them from on high. It was truly no accident that the English defeated the Spanish Armada; though even they admitted to a little help from God.

Elizabeth is a wonderful role model for modern women.

Historians have documented nearly every waking moment of the queen's life. Before her accession to the crown, there are gaps in the documentation of her life. Thus I was able to insert the character of Robin, a fictional bastard son born to Elizabeth and Robert Dudley. No proof of such a child has ever been found. Speculative historians suggest that descendants of such a child still live in Britain and still pass down the family lore of their most famous ancestress.

I must also confess to taking liberties with history in two other places. Mathew Parker, Elizabeth's Archbishop of Canterbury, died in his bed of old age. He was not murdered by a werewolf or anyone else as far as we know. Gilbert Gifford, the Catholic priest recruited (blackmailed) by Sir Francis Walsingham into setting the trap to expose Mary Queen of Scots' plots to assassinate Elizabeth probably carried through with the scheme as planned. But given his previous devoted service to Mary's cause, I thought it likely that he might have double-crossed Elizabeth's spymaster.

The existence of werewolves is no longer believed to be true. Lycanthropy is regarded as a serious psychological disorder that may be cured. In the sixteenth century, the best scientific minds began to look at shape-changers from this viewpoint. King James I of England, and VI of Scotland wrote a learned treatise on the subject. The Catholic Church, however, regarded werewolves as demon-infested beings in need of cleansing. Their favorite form of banishing the Otherworldy spirit was fire, burning at the stake. Reports of the number of executions of confirmed werewolves during the sixteenth century vary from three hundred to three thousand. I touched upon these contrasting views briefly in this book. For the purposes of the plot I chose the magical origin of werewolves and created Yassimine's culture. As far as I know, no society existed that worshiped the wolf as depicted. The ritual, of course, while using some historical elements, is the product of my imagination.

The title of *El Lobison*—or *El Lobizon*—refers primarily to a South American version of the werewolf. This can be traced to Spanish and Portuguese legends that depict a man cursed to pay for his sins by shape-changing on Good Friday. I needed a title for my Master of Werewolves and appropriated this one. Many of the early documents about lycanthropy refer to a Spanish princess as the mother of werewolves. This could be part of the propaganda against Spain during the period of the Spanish Armada and the Spanish Inquisition. I thought it fitting for my plot.

As in any project of this size and scope, I could not complete it on my own. I have to thank research guru Lea Day for the loan of books, her searching out of obscure facts, and for plowing through the ponderous first draft. ElizaBeth Gilligan gets virtual hugs nearly every day for her continual support, her ability to brainstorm ideas and make me think them through to logical conclusions, and her reading of early drafts of the work. Karen Lewis is also on top of my list for her unending care to make certain I write the best book I am capable of. Mike Moscoe, Reverend Richard Toll, and big brother Ed Radford also deserve many thanks.

Much appreciation to my agent, Carol McCleary of the Wilshire Literary Agency, for her faith in me, her shoulder to cry on, and a few well placed kicks to keep me writing when all I want to do is crawl into a hole and pull it in after me. My editor, Sheila Gilbert, falls into this category as well. She's the best in the business.

Finally I have to thank my husband Tim and our son Ben for giving me anchors into reality. Tim has been known to surgically remove me from the computer and force me to take breaks so that I can come back to the work with a clear head and fresh ideas. Ben keeps the computer operating and suffers through too many long distance phone calls at odd hours. You two make it all worthwhile.

And thank you, also, to you, the readers who give my stories and characters life beyond my hard drive.

Irene Radford
Welches, OR
November, 2002

Cast of Characters
*denotes historical figure

The Descendants of Merlin:

Donovan Kirkwood: b. 1535. Baron of Kirkenwood. Came late to his magical talents. Trustee for the heritage of the Pendragon. Counselor to Elizabeth I of England, spends much of his time in Scotland spying upon the court of Mary Queen of Scots.

Father Griffin Kirkwood: 1535–1563. Donovan's twin who became a Catholic priest. Referred to as Griffin the Elder to separate him from Donovan's son.

Meg Kirkwood: b. 1536. Sister of Donovan. Brutally raped by the Douglas clan in a border raid. Her mind never heals. She finds peace only in the seclusion of the Hermitage near the faery circle at Huntington.

Peregrine and Gaspar: b. 1551? Illegitimate children that may have been sired by either Donovan or his deceased twin brother Griffin the Elder. Accepted into the family at birth and raised at Kirkenwood.

Mary Elizabeth Kirkwood (Betsy): b. 1558. Donovan's eldest legitimate child by his first wife Katherine.

Griffin and Henry (Hal) Kirkwood: b. March 1561. Donovan's twin sons by second wife Martha. Griffin inherits the estates as the eldest, Henry becomes candidate to the Pendragon because he has magic.

Deirdre: b. September 1561. Daughter of deceased Pendragon Griffin the Elder (1535–1563) and demon possessed Roanna (1537–1563). Raised in seclusion by Meg until her father's death. Dame of Melmerby and Cross Fell.

Margaret Roanna Griffin (Maggie Rose): b. 1581. Daughter of Deirdre and Michael Maelstrom.

Baruckey: b. 1581. Son of Yassimine and Hal.

Their Familiars:

Newynog (Hungry): Familiar to Griffin the Elder.

Coffa (Remembrance): Unclaimed pup of Griffin the Elder's familiar Newynog. Goes to Deirdre.

Helwriaeth (Mighty Hunter): Male familiar given to Henry (Hal) from Coffa's first litter.

Brenin (King): Male familiar given to Betsy from Coffa's first litter.

Descendants of Henry Tudor—King Henry VII of England:

*Henry VII: 1457–1509. First Tudor King, grandfather of Elizabeth I and great grandfather of Mary Queen of Scots.

*Henry VIII: 1491–1547. King who implemented religious reform in England. Elizabeth's father.

*Edward VI: 1537–1553. Only legitimate son of Henry VIII by third wife Jane Seymour. Minor king 1547–1553 with several regents.

*Mary Tudor: 1516–1558. Henry VIII's eldest daughter by first wife Katherine of Aragon. Ruled 1554–1558.

*King Philip of Spain: b? Mary's husband, brought the inquisition to England. Suitor to Elizabeth and sponsor of the Spanish Armada.

*Elizabeth Tudor: 1533–1603. Henry VIII's middle legitimate child by his second wife Anne Boleyn. Queen of England 1558–1603.

Mary Queen of Scots: 1542–1587. Crowned Queen of Scots soon after her birth. Raised in France. First husband *Francis, Dauphin of France. Second husband *Henry Stewart, Lord Darnley. Third husband, *James Hepburn, Earl of Bothwell. Exiled to England in 1568.

Robin: Illegitimate son of Elizabeth and Dudley, adopted by Donovan Kirkwood.

Henry Stewart, Lord Darnley: 1545–1567. Grandson of Henry VII by Margaret Tudor's second marriage. Second husband of Mary Queen of Scots.

The House of Valois—Rulers of France:

Catherine de Médici: 1519–1589. Daughter of the Florentine family of bankers, married to *Henri Valois—Henri II. Mother of three kings of France, none of whom produced heirs. As Dowager Queen, she ruled as regent for all three of her minor sons.

Henri II: 1519–1559. Duc d'Orléans. Married Catherine de Médici 1533. King 1547–1559.

Francis II: b? Probably around 1542. King of France, July 1559–December 6, 1560. Raised with Mary Queen of Scots from age of five and married her.

Charles IX: 1550–1574. King upon Francis' death in 1560. On the throne at the time of the St. Bartholomew's Day Eve massacre.

Henry III: b? Duc d'Alençon. Youngest son of Catherine de Médici. Ascended throne of France May 30, 1574.

Henri Bourbon: b. 1553. King of Navarre, Huguenot. His marriage to a Valois princess precipitated the St. Bartholomew's Day Eve massacre. Became king of France in 1584.

The Stuarts of Scotland:

Mary Queen of Scots: see above

James Stuart: d. 1570. Earl of Moray. Illegitimate son of *James V of Scotland, premier lord of the land. Later regent for *James VI.

James Stuart: b. June 19, 1566. James VI of Scotland and I of England; Son of *Mary Queen of Scots and *Henry Lord Darnley. Crowned King of Scots July 24, 1567. Dismissed all regents in 1578 at age of twelve after murder of his Regent the *Earl of Morton.

Others:

El Lobison: The Master of Werewolves.

Yassimine: b. 1559. Slave of *El Lobison.* Born in the steppes east of the Ottoman Empire.

Earl of Morton: Replaced Earl Mar as regent for James VI in 1572. Strong enemy of exiled Mary Queen of Scots, the child king's mother. Deposed and murdered by Scottish Lords 1578.

Duc Henri de Guise: d. December 23, 1588. Cousin to *Mary Queen of Scots and Captain General of the Holy League.

Mathew Parker: d. 1575. Archbishop of Canterbury.

Dr. John Dee: 1527–1608. Preeminent English mystic, scholar, alchemist (scientist) of his day.

Robert Dudley: 1533–1588. The love of Queen Elizabeth's life. Master of the Horse, later elevated to the peerage as Baron of Denbigh and Earl of Leicester.

Douglas Howard: (pronounced Dooglass). b? Countess of Sheffield, Dudley's first wife. Marriage kept a secret and later renounced by both parties. One son born to them, *Sir Robert Dudley 1574–1649.

Lettice Knollys: 1541–1634. Dowager Countess of Essex. Mother of Robert Devereaux, 2nd Earl of Essex. Second wife of Robert Dudley. One son born to them, *Robert, Baron Denbigh 1579–1584.

Ambassador Fénelon: Representative of France to England in 1574.

Don Bernardina de Mendoza: Ambassador from Spain to England after the Treaty of Bristol in 1574.

Edward de Vere: d? Earl of Oxford. Secret Catholic. Declared his faith in 1580, seduced one of Elizabeth's maids in 1580, as well. An eccentric and free spirit. Married *Anne Cecil, Lord Burghley's daughter (she was fifteen).

Henry Hastings: 1536–1595. 3rd Earl Huntington. Descended from Edward III. Had a claim to the throne, but not ambitious enough to pursue it. Married to *Katherine Dudley, sister of Robert Dudley.

Katherine Dudley: d. 1620. Lady Hastings. Lady-in-waiting to Elizabeth I.

Mary Dudley: d. 1586. Lady Sidney. A favorite lady-in-waiting to Elizabeth I.

Thomas Howard: d. 1572. 4th Duke of Norfolk. Open Catholic who conspired with Mary Queen of Scots to depose Elizabeth I by assassination. Executed for treason.

William Cecil: d? Lord Burleigh. Elizabeth's Secretary of State and chief advisor.

Malcolm the Steward: 1525–1572. Steward of Kirkenwood killed by werewolves.

Thom Steward: 1530–? Steward of Kirkenwood, Malcolm's brother.

Bess Hardwick: Countess of Shrewsbury and mistress of Chatsworth Manor. Her husband was Guardian of Mary Queen of Scots for many years. Bess controlled who visited the queen. Married her daughter to *Charles Stuart—second son of Earl of Lennox and younger brother of *Lord Darnley, Mary's second husband. Granddaughter *Arabella Stuart became a pawn in the marriage market because she was a cousin of Elizabeth I.

Sir Francis Walsingham: Diplomat and spymaster for Elizabeth. Nicknamed her "Moor."

Sir Michael Maelstrom: b. 1554. Spy for Walsingham. Baron of Bobbington and Six Ashes.

Zella: b. 1564. Hedge witch with one blue eye and one brown eye.

Edmund Campion: Jesuit priest, largely responsible for success of the Jesuit mission to England and the upsurge of Catholic resistance.

Robert Parsons: Radical Jesuit priest, paired with Campion in Jesuit mission to England.

Gilbert Gifford: Sympathizer with Mary Queen of Scots, blackmailed by Walsingham to act as agent in final plot against Mary.

Sir Amyas Paulet: Puritan, final goaler of Mary Queen of Scots.

Thomas Phelippes: Code breaker for Walsingham.

Francis Throckmorton: Secret Catholic caught and executed in a plot with French Embassy to free Mary Queen of Scots.

Sir Nicholas Throckmorton: Uncle of Francis, friend of Leicester.

Master Burton: Brewer who delivers beer to Chartly Manor. Not privy to the final plot to implicate Mary Queen of Scots.

Anthony Babington of Dethick: b. 1561(?)–1586. Conspirator with Mary Queen of Scots in a plot to assassinate Elizabeth I.

GUARDIAN OF THE PROMISE

Merlin's Descendants:

Volume Four

Prologue

7 June, 1572. The fourteenth year in the reign of Her Majesty, Gloriana Regina, Elizabeth Tudor. The Kirk in the Woods, near Kirkenwood Manor, the North of England.

THE sun crept to the peek above the horizon, way to the north of due east. I sat on the lake verge watching the light grow and the shadows shrink. Faeries buzzed around my head, giggling as they tugged at my unruly hair. I laughed with them. The innocent laughter of the young.

'Twas the time betwixt and between, neither day nor night, here or there, real or unreal.

As I was betwixt a child and a woman.

Gently, I twined a wreath of magic around the flowers scattered at my feet. They wove into a living crown. I transported the garland to my head with a gesture of my finger.

The faeries tilted the bright halo so that it canted over my left eye.

We all giggled hilariously.

My aging wolfhound, Coffa, drowsed at my feet along with her unnamed pup. I could not remember a time before Coffa came to me as a familiar.

My three cousins and I were the only children of our generation of Kirkwoods to possess magic and familiars. We played with magic as toys with no idea of how to use it for any but our own pleasure.

The lake rippled. A disturbance at the center spread outward. I sensed a presence beneath the water. Who would inhabit the watery depths?

Could it be the legendary Lady of the Lake? I daydreamed a few moments that she rose from her mysterious home to give me the great sword Excalibur. I would travel

1

the world, wielding the sword for justice, righting wrongs, and defending the weak as my ancestor King Arthur had done.

Would you not rather be the Merlin? A tiny voice like the chiming of silver bells asked. The faery voice spoke with the resonance of an entire flight of creatures. *The Merlin carries history and news to the common folk, listens to their woes, and befriends them.*

I sighed. Of course I'd rather be the Merlin. As my father had been. In all things I wanted to be like my father, a man who was fast becoming more legend than memory.

Way off on the other side of the lake, the church bell tolled Matins. A raven launched himself from the rooftree with a noisy flap of wings. The dreams faded. I was just a little girl. The Lady would certainly never deem me worthy of the sword. I guessed she rose merely to play with the faeries on this warm summer dawn.

"Deirdre!" a voice called from the direction of the church. "Dee, where are you?"

The faeries popped out of this reality in surprise, then popped back in, giggling all the while at their own shyness.

" 'Tis merely my cousin Hal," I explained to them. "He's very protective of me and doesn't like it when I go off on my own." As much as I loved my cousin, sometimes I needed to explore these woods by myself. The faeries only came when I was alone. Hal was too impatient to let me study plants and flowers and insects to learn their secrets.

"Dee!" Hal's call echoed across the lake. He sounded urgent, worried.

I ignored him. My friends, the faeries and the Lady of the Lake, were much more important.

A cloud darkened the growing light. A chill breeze ruffled the lake water. The waves grew higher. The wind whispered with anxiety as it shifted in the tree tops.

Run, the faeries urged me. A bright green one nipped my ear.

Flee, the Lady added from beneath the lake waters.

"What?" I asked. I rose to my knees and got tangled in my skirts. Linen petticoats tore as I tugged them from beneath my feet.

A thrumming sound vibrated through the ground. I ripped the layers of fabric to free my feet. The moment I regained my balance the faeries left me for their own refuge. The Lady sank deeper into the protection of the water.

Coffa jumped up, snarling, teeth bared, ears flat. Her pup growled, too, but remained at my side.

A wolf as large as a man slunk out of the woods. Drool glistened on his yellow teeth.

His eyes glowed red with Otherworldly malice.

"Dee, we come!" Uncle Donovan, my guardian, yelled. He stood beside Hal on the church steps. His illegitimate sons, Gaspar and Peregrine, joined them, long swords still sheathed. Malcolm, the Steward of Kirkenwood, carried a crossbow and a quiver of arrows. They all ran around the lake. Hal leaped over rough ground. Gaspar slashed at low hanging branches that impeded him. Peregrine dove into the lake. He swam with long even strokes.

The wolf growled.

None of them could reach me in time.

Coffa lunged at it. The pup tugged on my skirts, urging me away.

Snap. Snarl. Yelp. Coffa and the wolf tangled, jaws clamped upon each other's throats. Clumps of fur flew.

Magic, Dee. Try some magic, Hal called to my mind.

Magic? What kind of magic could keep the wolf at bay. My heart cringed. My magic had attracted these beasts touched by the Otherworld.

Coffa's hind legs collapsed. She rolled, bringing the huge wolf with her. She should have outweighed the wolf by three stone or more. She should have stood head and shoulders above a normal wolf. This beast was as big as she.

A second wolf crept out of the woods. And a third. And then a fourth. Noses worked. Tongues flicked. Drool slid down in ugly poisonous ropes. Throats growled. Red eyes glowed.

The men fanned out, each aiming for a different wolf.

The pup pulled me behind a curtain of willow branches. Not good enough. The wolves would find me by scent.

Coffa's legs scrambled for purchase. Weakly. The wolf kept her down.

I looked for the armed men. Peregrine might get to me first. Not before four wolves ripped out my throat. Coffa was already dying.

I sobbed as I reached for whatever magic existed in the

air, in me, in the earth. Power tingled in my feet. Without bothering to breathe deeply and prepare myself, I drew the energy upward through my knees to my belly and outward to my hands. Rapidly I braided the willow fronds together. I wove and twisted them into a semblance of a wall. With gaping holes. There were not enough of them to make my shield impenetrable. Magic glinted in the dawn's light and the dew, weaving a web of power between the dangling braids.

Coffa whimpered once more and died.

The pup threw herself at my magical barrier and bounced back.

I gathered her into my arms, sobbing. "No. She can't die. She can't. She's all I have of my da!" I wailed.

The weight of my wolfhound pup drew me to my knees. I gathered more strength from the earth. I tried to replace my grief with anger. I wanted to tear the wolves apart with my bare hands.

Malcolm Steward aimed his arrow at the closest wolf and shot. Arrow sped. Wolf yelped and paused. It licked at the arrow protruding from its flank. Then with its teeth it ripped the arrow from its flesh. It came away bloody, dripping with gore.

The wolf barely paused to lick it clean. It sped to Malcolm and took him down. One bite ripped out Malcolm's throat.

I gagged in horror. "Malcolm!" I choked. As close as family, I'd known him all my life, trusted him as a beloved uncle. "Malcolm," I sobbed.

At last Peregrine climbed out of the lake, drawing his sword even as his feet touched solid ground. He met the four wolves with cold steel. They bit at his blade and danced away, stung by its edge. The wolf that had killed Malcolm joined them.

A raven swooped down and pecked at the lead wolf's nose. The beast turned and bit at the bird. It flew away with a sarcastic croak.

Peregrine lunged with his blade. I watched each slash in wolf fur close and knit within a few heartbeats. Malcolm's murderer had already healed.

"What creatures of evil are these?" I gasped.

The pup struggled to be free of my grasp.

Gaspar and Uncle Donovan joined Peregrine. Two of the wolves broke away from the attack on him. They crept up to my hiding place. They tested the barrier with paw and nose, jerking back from the flash of stinging light of my magic.

And then Hal was there. Barely a year older than I. Fire came to his hands with ease. He flung ball after ball into the fray.

The lead wolf's fur caught the fire. It screamed in pain, dropped, and rolled. The fire kept burning. Stubby paws transformed into human hands that beat at the flames. They kept burning.

Fire engulfed the wolf. From one eye blink to the next a man appeared beneath the fur. Skin blackened. An inhuman scream erupted from tortured limbs. He writhed.

Then stilled.

The fire ate at his skin until only bones remained.

A horrible stench flooded my senses. I gagged.

A second wolf caught fire and ran howling into the woods. The remaining two backed off, slinking, snarling, reluctant to continue, reluctant to leave their prey.

"Retirada!" a command came from deep within the line of trees. *"Retirada!"* An accent tinged the deep guttural voice. I had not the time to decipher it.

I did not even realize the man had spoken in Spanish rather than English.

The wolves turned and ran as one.

Through the mist of my barrier I glimpsed a short, wiry man clad all in black and silver. He loped away at the head of the pack. Something was wrong with his left arm. He cradled it close against his chest.

"Dee!" Hal tore at my barrier. "Open the wall, Dee, you are safe now."

I took a deep breath and then another. My mind unwove the willow fronds. One by one they parted. The magic collapsed. It slithered around me, becoming a tight envelope of mist, and then it disappeared inside me. The earth greeted the magic through my feet and gratefully accepted it back. The spell grounded successfully.

I collapsed into Hal's arms. Uncle Donovan rushed to enfold us both in a deep hug. "Werewolves. How could werewolves attack you this close to dawn!"

"Magic. They sought my magic," I stammered. I trembled all over. My knees wanted to collapse. I could not take my eyes away from the still form of Malcolm. Only Hal's embrace and the pup pressed to my side kept me upright.

"Powerful men know of the Pendragon. They search this region for signs of magic in hopes of finding, perhaps killing, the Pendragon," Peregrine reminded us all. He had no magic himself, but he'd lived around magicians all his life.

"What kind of spell did you weave to attract *were-wolves?*" Uncle Donovan leaned away from me and looked me sternly in the eye. "I have forbidden you to work any magic without my supervision." His attention strayed to the blackened form that had once been a man.

"I know," I replied meekly. Suddenly I could look nowhere but the grass at my feet. " 'Twas just a silly spell to entertain the faeries." And because of it, Malcolm, a good and honorable man, had died.

And another had paid the price for that death, most horribly.

"A very silly spell indeed. 'Twas stupid. Dangerous!" At last, Uncle Donovan looked at the horror that had once been Malcolm's face and neck. He gulped and bowed his head a moment. "I shall have to think on your punishment for disobedience, young lady." Uncle Donovan dropped his arms from my shoulders.

I suddenly felt cold and alone.

Hal tightened his grip on me in reassurance.

"They killed Coffa." I let a tear trickle down my cheek. I could not think on the man who was also dead.

"She was old for a wolfhound." Uncle Donovan sounded sad. "She was beyond breeding again. She left you another familiar. The pup will also be Coffa, Remembrance, so that you remember why a trusted retainer *and* your familiar died." He turned on his heel and marched back toward the church and Malcolm. He shed his doublet and placed it reverently over the face of the corpse. "Gaspar, Peregrine, fetch Father Peter. We need to burn the body to sanctify his unclean death."

We all gulped back sobs. Then my guardian returned his attention to me.

"Remember, Deirdre, you are not the only one with a

familiar. You are not guaranteed the heritage of the Pendragon, and therefore your use of magic must be circumspect and carefully controlled."

"Yes, Uncle," I replied meekly. My face flushed with guilt. I'd never live up to my father's legacy.

Chapter 1

24 August, Eve of St. Bartholomew's Day, 1572. Fourth year in the reign of James VI of Scotland. Fourth year of imprisonment of Mary Queen of Scots by Gloriana of England, Elizabeth Regina in her fourteenth year of reign. Edinburgh, Scotland.

"ARE you sure we should be doing this?" I asked. I reached for Coffa. She butted her head beneath my hand, eager for attention.

"Don't be a 'fraidy cat," Cousin Betsy scoffed. She looked down her nose at me in disdain. At the great age of thirteen, her body had matured into womanhood. This, of course, gave her elevated stature in the hierarchy among the children of the household. She assumed that this status also gave her increased wisdom.

Her dog, Brenin, or King, lounged at the foot of the staircase below the narrow landing where we stood. He was calmly chewing the decorative molding at the base of the stair rail.

Hal charged forward, ever ready to meet any challenge put forth by his older sister. He bent to peer through the keyhole into Uncle Donovan's private solar. His dog Helwriaeth, "Mighty Hunter," stood halfway up the staircase sniffing at the baseboard for traces of a mouse we had seen earlier.

The tall, narrow house in the heart of Scotland's capital offered little privacy. But it gave my uncle convenient access to Holyrood Palace where he attended court as a diplomat for Queen Elizabeth of England.

"What do you see, Hal?" Betsy hissed in a sharp whisper.

"Da, at his scrying bowl. He's using an ugly crockery bowl and an unpolished agate. He must be truly serious to revert to common tools of the Earth," he replied.

"Let me see." Betsy pushed him aside.

Hal stumbled against the banister. When he righted, he rubbed his back. Betsy's blow had bruised him.

I sensed a cloud of magic rising like a mist around her and nearly panicked. Betsy flung her talent about as if magic had no limits and no dangers. Since the attack of the werewolves last June, I hesitated to use any magic outside the lessons set for me by my uncle.

Hal walked a wary path between us. He had witnessed the attack. Indeed, his fireballs had killed one of the hideous creatures and driven another away.

As much as we wanted to forget that werewolves existed, we could not.

I spun around so my back was to them and made the sign of the cross. Uncle Donovan's household was not known for great piety. But my father, Uncle Donovan's deceased twin, had been a Catholic priest. Part of me clung to the idea that his intense faith offered me a morsel of protection.

Hal jostled Betsy away from the keyhole. She slammed against the wall, knocking her head. Surely Uncle Donovan must hear us!

I wanted to know what occurred on the other side of the locked door. But I chose a less violent method of finding out than Betsy and Hal had. Hesitantly, I touched Hal's shoulder. I fell into instant rapport with him. Our hearts beat to the same rhythm, we breathed in unison, and our thoughts aligned. I saw what he saw.

I could not perform this trick with anyone else. Betsy could not do it all.

Silently we watched as Lord Donovan Kirkwood, twenty-seventh Baron of Kirkenwood, took three deep, even breaths to clear his mind and his heart. As he opened his eyes, he dropped an agate into his scrying bowl.

"What does the bowl reveal?" Betsy asked. She clenched her fists as if preparing to knock Hal aside once more.

Hal hushed her with a wave of his hand.

"Mary. Show me how my cherished Mary fares," Uncle Donovan invoked.

"Not again." I sighed, releasing all of the pent-up tension in my shoulders.

"Why can't he ever scry for *my* mother?" Hal pouted.

"Because Martha died. Father can't scry for the dead," Betsy said haughtily, as if *she* could part the veils between death and life.

Uncle Donovan pressed the base of his palm hard against his forehead. I almost felt the sharp pain that stabbed him between the eyes.

He leaned his head back and removed himself from the spell.

The images would vanish. They had shown him nothing of the fate of Mary Queen of Scots. They never did. As much as he loved the exiled queen, his talent, not discovered until after the advanced age of twenty-five, could not overcome the distance. Or perhaps he could not overcome the coldness of *her* heart.

Catholic Mary had fled Scotland on the heels of rebellion by her Protestant lords. She presented a unique problem to Queen Elizabeth. She kept her cousin in ever closer confinement. English Catholics tried to assassinate Elizabeth and put Mary on the throne. Parliament screamed for Mary's execution. The English queen could not bring herself to fall into her father's habit of beheading queens. Henry VIII had rid himself of two of his six wives that way, including Elizabeth's mother. Elizabeth had settled for executing Thomas Howard, Duke of Norfolk, the chief conspirator in Mary's last major plot.

Confused and betrayed at the collapse of the plot for papal troops and European backers to invade England, Mary had wept copious tears and finally written to Uncle Donovan asking for counsel and solace.

If he had gone to her, he had managed to keep it secret from everyone, including us. He did not have permission from Elizabeth or from King James of Scotland's regent, the Earl of Mar to depart Edinburgh. Did he think his correspondence with Mary a secret? Not much remained secret from Betsy for long. And what she knew, Hal and I soon learned.

A terrible sense of wrongness possessed me. We'd eavesdropped on Uncle Donovan's scant privacy. I think Hal felt it, too. He reared back from the keyhole, rubbing his neck.

Before Betsy could dive into place to watch Uncle Donovan through the keyhole, I reached for the latch. The lock opened for me with a thought; no lock could detain a Kirkwood for long.

'Twas merely a trick, not true magic, I reassured myself.

"Uncle Donovan, what occupies you so that you cannot come riding with us?" I bounced into the room, followed immediately by young Coffa. My familiar was still an ungainly pup, but she never strayed far from me no matter what temptation she sniffed. Hal's Helwriaeth, and Betsy's Brenin, were much bolder and not so firmly attached to my cousins as Coffa was to me. They were also much bigger.

Uncle Donovan ruffled Coffa's ears as he drew me onto his lap.

I ran my fingers through Uncle Donovan's dark auburn hair. Threads of silver showed brightly in the candlelight. I did not know my guardian's age, only that he was adult and therefore *old*. My father would have looked like him. I traced the lines of his face, once more memorizing them, pretending that my own father still lived.

Hal had the same dark hair glinting with hints of red. Betsy was blonde. All three of them had piercing bluer-than-blue eyes. Mine were only a pale misty gray and my hair was brighter, redder. Every time I looked in the mirror, the differences between me and my relatives reminded me that my mother had been a demon-possessed witch who did not belong to this family.

But we all had the same determined thrust to our chins. I'd overheard the servants call us stubborn beyond belief.

I sighed wistfully. I so wanted to be like this family, wanted to be one of them rather than the orphaned, and illegitimate cousin. I always felt separate from them, an intruder.

Betsy and Hal crowded into the room with their dogs. The tiny chamber became redolent with the scent of three big dogs, growing teenage bodies, melting candle wax, and burning coal on the brazier.

The room grew warm with all our bodies pressed so close.

"We have to help Da find what he needs in the scrying bowl," Hal announced.

"And where is your twin, Griffin, Hal?" Uncle Donovan asked.

"Sleeping off his exertions on the training field. He takes this knighthood business far too seriously, Da." Hal sulked, thrusting out his lower lip and dropping his gaze to his feet. "He and Robin have no need of me in their jousts." He referred to Robin Kirkwood, the young man Uncle Donovan had adopted about the same time I came into the household.

"Griffin is older than you, Hal, by only an hour, I know. He will inherit Kirkenwood eventually, so he must learn the ancient skills of knighthood to protect our household from Scottish raiders. You, though, should inherit a far older and more important heritage. With your magical talent, you may become the next Pendragon of England."

"If I do not win the title first," Betsy insisted. Her chin came up and out so that she looked as if she peered down upon us all from a lofty height. Both Hal and his brother topped her by several inches. She still looked taller when she assumed that pose.

"I might win the title, too," I said meekly. Coffa laid her great head on my lap as if agreeing with me.

"Maybe, maybe not," Uncle Donovan reminded us all. "My Grandmother Raven promised me that my son will be the Pendragon . . . one day. She was never wrong in her prophesies, even if the dogs have become confused in choosing her successor."

The current dominant female wolfhound always bestowed a *female* pup from her last litter on the current or next Pendragon. No other wolfhounds had the intelligence of a familiar. I had received my first Coffa, a female, from my father's familiar Newynog. She, in turn, had given male pups to Hal and Betsy at the same time young Coffa came to me from her last litter. I was still her first choice, but either of my cousins could also become the Pendragon, magical Guardian of Britain and adviser to monarchs.

"Now, Da, what is it you were trying to scry?" Betsy took command of the session. She never liked anyone to question her superiority.

"What he always looks for: Mary," I replied. I tried to smooth the sadness away from his eyes with my fingertips.

"But you saw something different this time, Da?" Hal cut to the root of the problem as he always did.

"Something very different and very frightening," Uncle Donovan replied. He shifted me off his lap. I stood close by his left shoulder, cuddling into the curve of his arm. Betsy dominated his right. Hal moved around the table to face us.

The dogs plunked down where they could find room, easy in each other's company. One of them passed gas and all three set to sniffing out this marvelous event. Not for the first time, I wished our family had bred the ancient war dogs for smaller animals rather than these prized beasts that when fully grown stood taller than me at the shoulder.

"First you need more light." Betsy snapped her fingers. A tiny flamelet appeared at the end of her index finger. She touched it to the oil lamp beside the scrying bowl. The scent of smoked fish combined with the miasma of odors already filling the room. Then she placed her hand upon her father's shoulder.

"But the light must be balanced." Hal lifted with his mind a second lamp from a shelf above the chair in the corner. When it rested firmly on the desk, he blew a steady flame upon the wick—like a dragon of old. The Pendragon.

When his task was completed, he grasped the large crockery bowl in both hands and stared into it. I began a circle of protection with one hand on Uncle Donovan's shoulder, the other on Hal's.

Betsy fished the agate out of the bowl. She closed her eyes and passed her hand over the rumpled water surface. It calmed immediately.

The flower design in the bottom of the crockery looked fuzzy. I had to squint to decide what kind of flower. A rose? Mary loved roses. Her rival, Queen Elizabeth, hated them. This symbol should reach out to the woman Uncle Donovan loved.

"Breathe deeply," Betsy commanded. All four of us took three long breaths, counting the inhalation to match the exhalation. Then she fished Uncle Donovan's pen knife from the well of writing tools on the desk. She pricked her finger until it bled. Three drops of bright red landed on the agate before she stuck her finger in her mouth and sucked the wound closed.

"Betsy, no!" Uncle Donovan protested. He tried to grab the agate from her. She yanked it out of his reach. "You do not know what dark forces you unleash . . ."

"Pish tosh, Da. I'm only making the spell stronger so we can penetrate whatever barriers prevent your spell from reaching its target."

"Betsy, I know . . ."

"Your talent is weak, Da. I command this spell. Now all of you breathe."

She captured each of our gazes with her own. Her will became ours. We breathed again in unison. On the third silent count, Betsy dropped the agate into the water. Then she touched Hal's and her father's shoulders, closing the circle once more.

The water rippled outward from the agate's passage. Clouds roiled and obscured the painted rose. Clouds of greasy smoke.

The images in the bowl of water streamed outward, engulfing me. Mobs of men with cudgels, women with pitchforks, children with knives and stones ran through streets with foreign looking buildings. The mob screeched incomprehensible words. Blood spattered the cobbles, the people, the corpses that littered the streets.

France, a faded memory whispered to me. Or was it Uncle Donovan informing us. Did he relive the religious war that had cost so many lives ten years ago? He had not witnessed the atrocities. But his twin brother, my father, had. My father had worked very hard to end the wars.

And failed.

Betsy's blood had brought us vision of the violence and death.

I watched in horror, as a woman hacked at a child with a butcher knife. *"Huguenot chien!"* she screamed in French. "Protestant dog."

Each knife thrust stabbed into our group mind. Our eyes, ears, and hearts burned. I gasped for breath, trying to pull away from the obscene images. I could not. I reached out with my mind and melded with the child as he burbled away his life, blood frothing at his mouth. He could not be more than ten years of age—the same age as me. Dead.

Dead!

"Do not follow him, Dee!" Uncle Donovan shouted. He

turned his head to the side and broke contact with the spell. "Do not give any bit of yourself to death." He shook my shoulders. "Every time you guide a soul onward, a tiny bit of you passes with the reluctant soul."

"Betsy, why did your blood guide us to this vision?" Hal asked through gritted teeth. "Dee's father brought the wars to a close more than ten years ago."

Fresh blood stained the waters as it stained the streets of Paris. Innocent blood. Not Betsy's. My blood?

Every part of me wanted to jerk away from the hideous images of dead bodies strewn about as so much straw in the wind. Blood filled the streets. Stray dogs lapped it up. Rats feasted on the dead and staring eyes of a man cradling his young child in his arms. The babe whimpered for its mother, beyond squalling in fright. The living dashed about seeking more victims, so crazed by their bloodlust, they cared not who became their next victim, friend or foe alike.

Part of me remained locked inside the images we had watched.

"This is all wrong," Uncle Donovan choked.

With great clarity, I knew that we watched events in Paris as they happened, this day, this hour. With or without Betsy's blood, we were meant to see this for a reason.

"This is supposed to be a day of joy and celebration," Uncle Donovan gasped. "Catholic King Charles' sister marries Huguenot Henri de Navarre this day. 'Tis supposed to bring a peace between the Catholics and Huguenots, not this . . . this slaughter."

And then the images wavered, distorted, became shadows of wolves. Their eyes glowed red with the fires from hell. Behind them stood a slim, swarthy man dressed in black and silver who wore a hook to replace his left hand. "Werewolves," I whispered.

Betsy's face turned pale. She swallowed heavily and repeatedly as if choking back bile. "I did not do this!" she cried.

Hal's chin trembled and his eyes became huge. He breathed in short painful pants, never getting enough air. He, too, shared the deaths of those he saw in distant Paris, as Uncle Donovan had. And so had I.

"Werewolves," I said again. "The Catholics fear that all Huguenots are werewolves. The full moon approaches and it is a *blue* moon! The second full moon within a calendar month makes werewolves more powerful than usual. Parisians slaughter to protect themselves."

Uncle Donovan swept the bowl of water from the table with one long cast of his arm. The crockery shattered as it hit the floor. Water splashed. The dogs yelped and lunged to protect and support their chosen ones.

Coffa nipped at my arm, trying desperately to break the thrall that held me in the scenes I had witnessed.

I felt a bone break in my wrist. Blood flowed from bite marks, and still I saw the wolves coming for me.

"Run for your lives. They will kill us all!" I screamed and fell to the mercy of black nothingness.

Chapter 2

19 June, 1574. Sixteenth year of the reign of Gloriana of England, Elizabeth Regina. Sixth year of Mary Queen of Scots' imprisonment. Kirkenwood, near Hadrian's Wall, England.

I SORTED through all the fine gowns Uncle Donovan had given me. I kept looking over my shoulder to make sure Betsy and the others continued sleeping. None of the lovely silks and brocades I wore to the court of James of Scotland suited my purpose. I sighed my frustration. Perhaps the wools reserved for the coldest days of winter?

I tiptoed past Betsy's bed toward the laundry basket. Two days back at Kirkenwood after months in Edinburgh and we had just finished sorting out the clothes that needed cleaning before storing for the summer.

I paused by the narrow window. Below me stood the village of Kirkenwood. Sixty massive standing stones ringed the cluster of houses. Forty more stones had fallen over the centuries. Some remained where they had crashed to the ground and became a wall of a cottage. Other stones had broken up and become field walls or foundations. A few had found their way into the walls of Kirkenwood Castle.

Atop the center stone, taller than all the rest, was a lumpy shape that did not belong. Even as I watched, it stirred, flapped and resettled its wings, and became a familiar raven. A solitary, and very cranky bird, had always guarded Kirkenwood. No one knew if it was the same immortal bird, or if another replaced him in secret when he died. Usually he perched on the well, pecking any who dared disturb him. Why had he suddenly shifted his perch to the top of the standing stone as if he watched me?

I shuddered slightly and turned away from the silhouette

of the broken circle. Each stone supposedly captured a face within its granite grain. The faces of my ancestors. King Arthur, his mistress Wren, her father the Merlin, my great grandmother Raven who still haunted the halls of the castle. Each of them scowled at me in disapproval. I did not belong here. Their blood coursed through my veins, but my mother had been a foreign witch. She had harbored a demon and wreaked havoc in her wake, including her own death and that of my father.

How securely had Uncle Donovan sealed that demon behind his portal to the netherworld?

I'd be well rid of those faces in the stones and they of me.

Coffa nudged me from behind. I nearly yelped in surprise. I'd told her to watch the gallery for signs of any sleepless wanderers, not hover nearby with her disapproving sighs.

She did not like my purpose. She grabbed my wrist and tried to tug me back to bed. That same wrist had healed from the time she broke it in Edinburgh. I was wary of the pain she could cause me.

Yet I knew that if I returned to the massive straw mattress I shared with Betsy, Coffa would sprawl atop me to keep me there. I could not allow that.

I eased my arm free of her teeth and returned to my search. My fingers found a familiar weave. I pulled it free of the tangle of other clothing, careful not to tip the basket or make any undue noise. Betsy slept lightly, ever conscious of her responsibility as the eldest to keep me and three other orphaned girls of noble birth from running wilder than we already did when at home.

Coffa lifted her magnificent head and whined a question. I shushed her with a gesture. She turned three circles and lay down beside me, head up, ears cocked, and disapproval written all over her face. Finally, she laid her head on her paws, one eye closed, the other watching me warily.

We'll be gone soon enough, love, I promised my familiar. *Within the hour, you and I will be running across the moors toward the sea.*

She sighed on a snort as if she did not believe I'd really do it.

Brenin, Betsy's dog, snored lightly. He never stirred from his position, draped across Betsy's feet. If he awoke, then

Betsy would, too. As long as Coffa did not alarm him, I should be safe.

I donned the woolen gown along with thick stockings. Here in the north of England, where the constant wind whistled coldly around the castle ramparts, the heavy weave warmed me nicely. In the sunny countryside around Paris, its weight, warmth, and elegant cut would mark me as out of place. No noblewoman would travel alone and on foot. What else could I wear?

In the deepest recesses of my clothes press I found a faded russet gown. Not the green I favored, but eminently suitable for my quest. Simple. Serviceable. And only slightly too large. In another year, when I finished growing and my breasts filled out, it would fit admirably. The extra length I could tuck up at the waist.

Where had the dress come from? I did not remember seeing it before. It smelled . . . of rosemary and lavender and Aunt Meg. The only mother I had ever known. Mad Meg, Uncle Donovan's sister. Her mind wandered between reality and her own nightmares. She resorted to nursery rhymes and songs to cover her confusion. She also appeared and disappeared at will. No one knew for certain where she wandered in between. No matter. I needed the gown she had left. I discarded the forest-green gown and stuffed it into the bottom of my pack. The russet I threw on over my shift along with a sturdy leathern bodice that would serve as a corset—not that I really needed one yet. But Aunt Fiona, Uncle Donovan's other sister, widowed and needing someone to manage, insisted I learn to be a lady. She seemed determined to stamp out all memory of my mother's peasant heritage.

But my mother, Roanna Douglas, had another heritage that no one spoke of. Once and once only, Uncle Donovan had told me the terrible truth of how Tryblith, the Demon of Chaos, had dominated my mother her entire adult life. She had seduced my father—a Catholic priest and avowed celibate. She had finally regretted her alliance with the demon and crept off to Aunt Meg's hermitage in a faery circle. Mad Meg had woven magical protection around the circle that kept the demon at bay during my birth. As soon as my mother could, she crept away from Meg's protection and rejoined her demon. She loved me enough to leave me with Aunt Meg rather than risk exposing me to the demon.

Still, Uncle Donovan feared that I had been tainted by the demon during the months my mother carried me in her womb.

I feared it, too; often wondered if the demon in me had attracted the werewolves that killed Malcolm. I had given up wandering the woods around the lake and the kirk for fear the werewolves would come again to claim me. But I could not allow that fear to stop me now. I had a mission to accomplish. 'Twas my responsibility.

I shuddered once more, suddenly chilled, and dismissed the memory. I had more important things to do.

Satisfied that I had packed all that I would need on my journey and could safely carry, including my father's rosary tucked deep in the bottom of the pack because it was illegal to possess such a thing in England these days, I donned a simple kerchief wimple and sturdy clogs for my feet and hoisted the bag to my back.

At the doorway I hesitated long enough to look back, making certain that Betsy and Brenin slept soundly. I didn't need to check on Coffa. I knew she followed closely. Her presence was as constant as my own heartbeat and my lungs drawing breath. Somehow she managed to keep her claws from clicking on the stone flooring.

Satisfied, I eased the door closed, using both hands until I could drop the latch in place with my mind.

A ghostly hand rested lightly on my shoulder. I jumped and gasped. My heart beat double time. "Da?"

The preternatural touch became real. Not the ghostly presence of my father.

"Going somewhere?" Hal asked from right behind me. And right behind him stood Helwriaeth, a full hand taller at the shoulder than my Coffa and more massive across those shoulders.

Coffa, the traitor, wagged her tail happily at her littermate. She should have warned me that my cousin approached on silent feet.

"Wherever you are going, cousin, I go with you," Hal announced. He kept his voice down rather than invite Betsy's wild temper and viper tongue.

At thirteen, his voice sometimes cracked and deepened to adult tones. In the throes of excitement, however, he'd still break into a boy's soprano.

"No," I said, drawing Hal away from the doorway toward the gallery. The central keep of Kirkenwood still resembled a medieval hall, one huge dining chamber rising two full stories. The musicians' gallery overhung the back half of the hall. The lord's chamber and the girls' bedroom led off the gallery.

The gallery above the hall led other places than just the two primary bedrooms. I knew the secret of the hidden passages. Unfortunately, so did Hal.

"I have to do this alone, Hal," I insisted.

"No, you do not. We're cousins. We both have magic." He didn't say that we both had a claim to the title of Pendragon. But we would have to earn it first.

"This is my responsibility." I truly wanted Hal's company on this frightening journey. Of all of the family, he alone made me feel a part of the whole. But I could not expose him to the risks.

"You are only twelve, Dee. You cannot do this alone."

"Do what?" I stopped short of the hidden door, crossing my arms beneath the buds of my breasts. My women's courses had not yet started, but my body was changing, getting ready. I was an adult in body, mind, and spirit.

I could manage this task on my own.

So why did my knees and hands tremble in fear?

"You are running away to correct something your mother left undone." Hal's tone became fierce with anger or frustration, I could not tell the difference at the moment. I should have been able to.

Rather than crane my neck to look him in the eye—he'd be as tall as his da 'ere long—I stared at his throat apple, just above the top of my head.

"No, Hal, I'm running to Paris to correct something Roanna Douglas made very wrong."

He stared me down, knowing I could not withstand that midnight gaze as he probed deep into my soul.

"I have read some of my father's journal," I said quietly. Not that I had understood much of what I read.

"Da would never give you permission . . ."

"I do not need permission. I found them and read my father's thoughts and recountings as is my right! I am the daughter of the last Merlin of Britain. I need to know everything that happened to him, everything that led to his death. Including my mother's . . . Roanna's descent into madness and her congress with the demon."

"She didn't cause the St. Bartholomew's Eve massacre two years ago," Hal said gently. He had leaped ahead of my explanation. The rapport between us was strong. "She was nearly nine years dead when that happened."

"But she and her demon sowed the seeds of religious conflict so that they could reap chaos and more chaos. I think she left behind werewolves to perpetuate that chaos." I spoke the last sentence with both my voice and mind, the better to penetrate his stubborn head.

"The Duc de Guise is dead. Assassinated. Without him stirring up animosity, the Huguenot leaders came to accord with Queen Regent Catherine de Médici."

"*Roanna's* lover, the Duc de Guise, is dead. His son is even more rabid in his persecution of the Huguenots. And the new king of France is firmly under de Guise's control. Henri III returns to Paris from Poland any day now—probably with a pack of werewolves. He will end his mother's regency and her policy of tolerance. He will unleash another slaughter. I have to stop it."

"How?"

How indeed? I sighed to cover my frantic searching for ideas.

"I must get close to Henri III. Then I shall weave a protective barrier around him so that he sees and hears only the truth. De Guise will not be able to influence him anymore." I made up my plans as I spoke. "Then I shall work no more magic. You and Betsy must determine between you who is truly the next Pendragon."

"You can't do it alone."

"I won't risk you or anyone else. This is my responsibility."

"What sea captain will take a young maid alone across the Channel? What hostler will sell or rent a horse or carriage to a young maid alone? What bandit will allow a young maid alone to traverse France unmolested?" He lifted one eyebrow in imitation of his father. When Uncle Donovan faced me with that expression, he made me search my heart for the truth.

If I did that now, I would not follow through with my responsibility.

"Get out of my way!" I thrust him aside and lunged for the panel with the hidden latch.

Hal stumbled over Coffa's formidable body. As he righted himself, arms flailing and making a great deal of noise, I latched and locked the portal behind me. He'd not follow through this passage without waking the entire household and destroying much of the wainscoting.

But I did not count upon his ingenuity, or his willingness to enlist aid.

Chapter 3

"WAKE up, Griff." Hal shook his twin's shoulder. Urgency made him rougher than he intended.

In one smooth movement, Griffin grabbed a knife from beneath his bolster and pressed it against Hal's throat.

Then he woke up. "Sorry, Hal," he mumbled, ready to go back to sleep.

"Stay awake, Griff." Hal shook him again. "I need your help."

Griffin opened one eye. "Unusual. You needing *my* help." He pushed himself up, resting his back against the bolster. He stretched his arms wide, straining his shirt, an old one, across his chest and shoulders. All of his hours of practice in the tilt yard had built more muscle than Hal had. Griff's beard was also coming in darker and coarser than Hal's.

He knew a swift pang of jealousy. Unfair that his twin matured more rapidly than he.

"Can't you just wiggle your fingers and mumble some magic spell?" Griff yawned.

"Not this time." Hal fumbled lighting a candle. The flint and steel would not spark properly. After three tries he gave up, and snapped his fingers. A flamelet stood on the end of his finger. He touched it to the wick. It flared high. The only problem was he'd have to extinguish it with magic. The flame would be impervious to mundane smothering.

He held the light up to make the shadows retreat to the far corners. "It's Dee. She's running away. We have to make her take me with her."

"Easier to stop her." Fully awake now, Griffin rolled off the wide bed and pulled on sturdy riding breeches. "We need Betsy."

25

"Do you want to wake Betsy up out of a sound sleep?"
Hal shuddered. His sister might turn him into a rat or a
raven or a worm for such an affront.

"I'd rather fight off two dozen raiders of the Kerr clan
by myself. Without a sword." Griff shuddered, too. "But
there's no help for it. If we are going to deter Dee from
whatever she has set her mind to, we need Betsy."

"Together, then. You hold her hands, I'll stun her with
some kind of magic." Hal shrugged, wishing he had a better plan.

"Never confront your sister with only half a plan," Griff
warned him.

"Right. I'll hold a ball of cold fire beneath her nose. If
she tries anything, she gets burned. The threat of scars
should deter her."

"That's the only thing that might deter Mary Elizabeth
Kirkwood."

Together, Hal and his twin crept from their room at the
back of the Hall, up the broad staircase to the gallery. Together, as they had always been.

"If you go with Dee, I go, too," Griff whispered.

Hal eased a bit in the shoulders, relieved that he and his
twin would not be separated. But they already had begun
to drift apart. Hal spent more time studying his magic. Griff
nearly lived in the tilt yard or studying the Steward's led-
gers. Griff showed evidence of maturing physically. Hal
could not seem to grow beyond his skinny chest and hair-
less face.

"What if it doesn't work out that way?" Hal asked, afraid
of the answer.

"Then you and I will find other ways to keep our minds
in contact. You do it to me all the time, showing me my
opponent's next move, sharing your latest discovery from
deep in the woods, finding me when I'm out riding."

Hal grabbed his brother in a quick embrace, opening his
mind to communication. As long as they both lived, neither
of them would be alone.

"This isn't finding Dee," Betsy said from the doorway to
the girls' bedchamber. Fully dressed, she looked as if she
had arisen and groomed herself after a full night's sleep.

Her wolfhound, Brenin, still blinked sleepily, tail drooping. He rocked back, bottom up, head down, stretching his

forelegs. At the apex of the movement he yawned, showing his sharp teeth to one and all. Then he shifted his weight forward, stretching his hind legs, followed by another yawn. A brief shake all over and he looked as fit and ready as his mistress.

"How do we get past the guards?" Griff asked as the three trooped down the stairs. He sidestepped over the center of the third riser that always squeaked. Hal climbed onto the banister and slid downward to avoid the fifth step that groaned. Betsy glided down the far side, hugging the wall.

The dogs, of course, bounced down, letting their claws click against the wood. That was a normal sound. The dogs took turns prowling the castle at night, guarding against intruders.

"Haven't you boys figured out how to master the geas Father put on the guards and the gates?" Betsy returned once they were all safe back in the Hall.

Hal and Griffin shrugged in unison.

"You have not tried hard enough. Or thought deep enough. Go ready the horses. I'll tend to the guards." Betsy tossed her head in disdain.

"How?" Hal asked. He watched her eagerly for signs of the spell she must prepare for the onerous task of breaking through their father's magic.

Betsy smiled enigmatically in the gloom. Then she fished her eating knife out of her scrip, bared her arm, and sliced deeply along the underside of her forearm. "Easy," she replied.

Hal crossed himself hastily. "Da has forbidden you to use dark magic," he breathed.

"Da is not here," she spat back. "Now do you want to rescue our cousin or not?"

With my palm against the wall to guide me, I traversed the first quarter of my journey from memory. Coffa knew the way as well as I, and she trotted ahead of me, comfortable in the dark, but uncomfortable with the nature of my mis-

sion. I thought a ghostly hand guided me. At the fork in
the tunnel, the hand urged me to the left. So did Coffa.
Neither my familiar nor my da wanted me to go to France.

I had to do this. I could not live with myself if the St.
Bartholomew's Day Massacre repeated itself at Henri III's
coronation.

I called a ball of cold flame to my palm. It sputtered to
life reluctantly, not liking the stale air this deep beneath
the surface. But Pridd—Earth—was my element. With my
feet firmly grounded I brought forth the element opposite
to my own.

Tanio—Fire—gave me only a weak and flickering light,
enough to keep me from tripping over the rough passage
that led through the natural cave system beneath the castle tor.

"Good-bye, Da," I sighed. "I have to do this."

The presence faded into the stone walls. I turned right
and began the long descent down slippery stairs to the
caves beneath the castle.

Coffa protested. She wanted to continue on the familiar
route to the lair, the family archives of arcane history and
alchemy. I insisted and grabbed the thick ruff of her neck.
She sat on her haunches and stubbornly refused to consider
my route. I tugged again with both mind and hands. Reluctantly, she allowed me to drag her into the side tunnel. If
she had truly resisted, I'd never budge her bulk.

Uncle Donovan rarely, if ever, used the tunnels anymore.
The dampness in the stone walls bothered an old wound
in his left thigh. But Betsy, Hal, and I found infinite inspiration in exploring and believing we eluded our elders. Hal's
twin, Griffin, probably knew of the ancient escape route.
The laird of the castle must know these things. And Hal
could keep few secrets from him. But Griffin had no magic
and thus had little use for the hidden rooms with their
collections.

At last the ground leveled out. I caught glimpses of sta-
lagmites and stalactites, some grown into thick columns. I
wended my way carefully around the puddles and debris
from old rockfalls. Coffa splashed deliberately into the center of each depression, making certain I shared the water
with her.

Frequently, she planted her huge body between me and

my destination—often filling the only clear path between obstacles. She truly did not like this plan. Each time, I had to force her to move with a sharp probe from my mind to hers.

Each time she cooperated with less ease.

Then I reached the tombs. A huge cavern off to my right provided a last resting place for many of my ancestors. Hal and Betsy avoided this place. I had a unique affinity for it. Since Earth was my element, did I commune more easily with the deceased spirits that rested within in it? Without hesitation, I took the extra moment to pause beside the large sarcophagus in the center. It dominated all the others in size and importance. Centuries of cave drip had coated the carved figure atop the stone lid with a smooth coating as shiny as marble. But to me, the square and determined features of Arturo Rex stood out bold and clear.

I kissed my fingertips and placed them upon the mouth of the carved effigy. Then I repeated the gesture on the simple stone box beside him. His beloved Wren lay at peace to his right, his counselor and lover in death as she had been in life. But a small dark chasm separated them still. My ancestress had never been wife to the love of her life.

Silently I wept for their ancient tragedy, so close to the story of my own parents. Or so I liked to think. I slept more easily thinking that Roanna and Griffin truly loved each other despite his church and her demon that kept them separate.

Like Arthur and Wren, they lay together in death where they could not in life. But not here. Someday I would journey to Aunt Meg's hermitage and the faery circle where Uncle Donovan had buried them.

Actually, he had buried my father and left Roanna to rot. Meg had brought my mother to her final resting place.

Coffa licked the stone face of Arthur and the tiny etching of a wren on the companion stone coffin, making her own reverence to my ancestors and one of her own, rumored to rest at Wren's feet.

I bowed my head a moment in silent prayer for courage.

A sense of peace flooded through me. Ghostly light rose up around me. A huge cauldron floated in the chill air. Tendrils of colored life flowed out of its foaming depths.

The threads tangled and wrapped around each other. At the same time they reached out to embrace every living thing, plant, animal, tree, or lowly weed.

Bright points of light popped into view. They flew wild circles around the cauldron of life, the gräal of my ancestors, the Grail of legend.

"Faeries?" I breathed to Coffa. I had not seen my friends since that day two years ago when the werewolves had attacked us.

My dog danced about, trying to nip the creatures as they flitted about the tomb. The faeries tugged at her whiskers and sat on her nose.

I spun a circle in delight at the wondrous display.

Behind me stood a glowing image of a man in regal armor from a long forgotten century. He held up a magnificent sword. Red runes of power coursed down the blade.

"Arthur?" I gasped.

For answer, he dipped the tip of the sword, tapping each of my shoulders lightly.

I reached up to touch the points of honor he had bestowed upon me. A slight tingle coursed up my fingers. My mind filled with a glowing peace.

Then he smiled. I saw in that spectral expression traces of every man in my family.

"I pray that I have the courage to complete this quest with honor and dignity," I whispered.

He looked briefly at Wren's tomb, beside his own. *So like her. Godspeed, little one.* With those few words he vanished.

So did the faeries and the cauldron of life.

I heaved a sigh of regret that he did not accompany me. I would have to make do with the memory of this wondrous moment.

"We have his blessing on this quest," I whispered to Coffa, too awed to speak aloud.

She still did not agree with me and tried to go back the way we had come.

"I can't," I told her. A few sharp yanks on her neck ruff and she followed me with dragging feet.

From the tomb I hurried back into the main passage and into an anteroom. My witchlight faltered and died in my hand. I had to go slowly here, painfully stubbing my toes on the uneven ground. Here, so close to my goal of escape, I wanted to hurry. But Coffa stood in my way once more.

She enclosed my wrist in her huge mouth, urging me back the way we had come.

I sighed and carefully separated my flesh from her teeth before she became insistent and clamped down on me with the massive jaws meant to crush bones and tear the throats out of wolves.

"No, Coffa. We have to do this," I reminded her in hushed tones. I do not know why I didn't want my voice echoing around the cavern.

She shifted her grip to my sleeve. I yanked it free and stood my ground. She whined and dropped her head. I had won this confrontation, but I could envision others when I would not.

With as much determination as I could muster in the face of my dog's supposed wisdom, I gathered her neck ruff in my hand and proceeded.

At least Hal should not have caught up with me yet. The main gate of Kirkenwood was heavily guarded, and the men had orders from Lord Donovan himself not to allow any of the children exit past sunset, no matter what coercion we provided. My uncle had placed a magical compulsion or geas on the men so that they were immune to childish magical persuasion. Hal and I had tried and failed too many times to count to escape through the main gate.

At last, I smelled the fresh green of the bushes that obscured the narrow exit from the cavern. Hal and Griffin could no longer squeeze through the tiny crack. Betsy also had grown too much to use this route. They were condemned to pass through the crypt to an iron gate and exit through the church that stood at the base of the castle crag beside the lake.

Father Peter spent too many midnight hours on his knees in the church for me to risk passage past him.

Sharp stones scratched my back and threatened to trap my shoulders. But Earth was my element. I persuaded the bones of the Earth to let me pass with a minimum of damage. In another year, when my breasts filled out, I doubted I'd be able to manage this escape.

Coffa made it through the crack because she was one of the smallest females the family wolfhounds had ever whelped. And because I worked with Earth to help her through.

They were waiting for me. All three of them, Betsy, Hal, and Griffin, with the two wolfhounds, Helwriaeth and Brenin. Four horses dozed, hipshot, nearby.

"How did you get out the gates?" I heaved a sigh.

Then I saw the gash on Betsy's forearm. She had used blood to break Uncle Donovan's geas on the guards.

Chapter 4

DONOVAN opened his eyes abruptly. Something, some noise, some presence, had awakened him. He lay immobile while he extended his senses.

"Martha?" Sometimes the ghost of his second wife visited him, usually to reprimand him for something. But she always forgave him afterward. He smiled in memory at how well she used to forgive him in bed. But that was before her untimely death.

"Ah, Martha, if you'd only shown a little patience and not gone off to London where the plague could get you."

The sound came again. Not Martha's imperious sniff.

Did he hear a raven cawing in the distance?

Whatever had disturbed his restless sleep eluded him.

Perhaps he woke from worry over Elizabeth's latest missive. A straightforward summons written by a secretary and signed with Elizabeth's broad strokes. Below that, written in a coded and crabbed hand, Elizabeth had said Donovan must come to London immediately to help her deal with "five men/wolves who waited at her door."

Werewolves. The same ones that had attacked Dee two years ago?

He tried counting the children's different heartbeats. Betsy he found easily. Her heart had always been slow, calm, and strong. Griffin and Hal had faster rhythms, difficult to separate them from each other. They were too much alike. He had to listen carefully to make sure he heard two separate boys and not one. But tonight he heard only one. Which one was missing? A quick scan for Dee proved her missing as well.

Damn. If Dee was out prowling, then Hal was her companion.

He rolled to the side of the bed and grabbed his aching head in both hands. Too much wine last night. Wine to help him sleep when his thoughts looped obsessively around plans to break through Elizabeth's guards to see Mary.

He sighed, as deeply and expressively as Deirdre did, and threw off the counterpane. Rubbing his gritty eyes, he swung his legs over the side of his very large, very empty bed.

Since the death of his second wife, Martha, twelve years ago, he'd shared this particular bed with no woman. Something about its massiveness kept reminding him that this was the laird's bed and belonged only to the laird of Kirkenwood and his lady.

Martha reminded him of that with each ghostly visit.

He'd warmed other beds with other women, but only one woman drew his heart these days.

Mary.

He couldn't find her in any scrying bowl and Elizabeth refused him permission time and again to visit Mary's latest prison.

Had Elizabeth done something to hurt Mary? He had to know. The miscast love spell had died with Roanna, Deirdre's unlamented mother, but Donovan had discovered that his love for the exiled queen went deeper than the spell. Mary occupied all of his waking and most of his sleeping thoughts now. He sought refuge in wine to dull his mind.

He should check on the children. He rubbed his temples. The thought fled almost as quickly as it came.

Perhaps if he scried one more time he'd find solace in a glimpse of Mary. The water in the pitcher beside his washbasin was stale, the basin dirty. The good crockery bowls were all in the lair deep within the gatehouse foundations. Not a place he liked to trek to this late at night. He found an old doublet and trunk hose, stuffing his long shirt into them awkwardly. No matter that the tail hung out. He was only going to the well and back. In the dark hours after midnight no one should be about. Except perhaps the cranky old raven.

He considered lighting a candle. He did not need one. The night sky never turned truly dark this far north in June.

'Twas a night twixt spring and summer, the time twixt midnight and dawn. The time when ghosts caught twixt this life and heaven walked the halls of Kirkenwood.

Donovan shuddered and opened the door from his chamber.

You promised to guard her! A voice hissed at Donovan.

"Raven?" he whispered. He had feared his grandmother in life. He feared her more since her death.

Silence so heavy he could barely breathe.

"What must I do, Raven?" he whispered to his long dead grandmother.

Guard her!

"Which her?" His sister, Mad Meg, came first to his mind. But Meg required solitude to live with the hurts inflicted upon her during one of those horrible Scottish raids of their youth. She had retired to the hermitage below a crag where she could tend a very special faery circle and a tomb.

"Betsy?" Donovan asked his grandmother's ghost.

The heavy darkness of the gallery grew thicker yet. Like a soaking mist upon the moors. More like the miasma of a vision induced dream.

"Deirdre," he sighed. He should have guessed that troubled child first. Ever since he'd told her about her mother and the demon Tryblith, she had grown more defiant of his authority and more stubborn about discovering the truth about her parents. Some things a maid of twelve should not know.

The darkness lightened.

"What is she up to this time?" Then he remembered that he could not find Dee's heartbeat, nor Hal's among the children. How could he forget such a thing?

Too much wine, and too deep a loneliness for Martha. Or Mary. Or some warm and loving woman.

He called a bit of light to his palm. He'd best check the chamber next to his own, just to make sure he had not dreamed her absence from his magical count of his charges.

An almost physical yank pulled him away from the doorway of the girls' bedchamber. The little ball of cold light burned brighter, hotter. Donovan shook it free of his hand before his skin blistered. The ball bounced through the air.

Shadows faded before it. Dust motes gathered behind it, taking on the vague outline of a woman with intense blue eyes that snapped at him in impatience.

"Raven." He retreated slightly before the manifestation of his grandmother.

She pointed at the crack in the dark wainscoting that was the only indication more than stone walls lay beyond.

A tiny tuft of brindled gray dog hair fluttered slightly in the preternatural breeze that followed Raven's movements.

Donovan sucked air through his teeth.

"Tell me, Raven, that she has merely gone to the lair in search of her father's journals." He'd hidden them time and again and she always seemed to find them.

She has already read the scribblings of your twin, but she does not understand them.

"Then perhaps she wishes to experiment with herbals or alchemy."

You know she has not.

"Then where will she go?" He knew she'd easily traverse the tunnels to the crypt behind the church—the Kirk in the Woods that gave the barony its name. All of the children explored the tunnels. Just as Donovan had with his twin Griffin and their sister Meg. But he always made certain he knew when his children and his wards had sneaked away for their games and when they returned. Twice he'd had to rescue young Griffin and Hal from climbing dangerous chimneys within the caverns. The passage had narrowed abruptly and the boys had become trapped before they realized their predicament. He himself had got stuck in one at the age of nine. Raven and his brother had freed him.

You know in your heart where her conscience will lead her.

Donovan didn't bother to reply as he raced back into his chamber for his boots and coat. "I pray I'm in time to stop her."

"If you must go to Paris, Dee, we are going with you," Hal insisted. He did not like this one little bit. And neither did

Helwriaeth. The chill midnight air raised goose bumps on his arms. The dog clung tight by his heels and whined. This close to the family cemetery, inside and outside the caves, he envisioned all kinds of spectral interference.

He wished this midnight confrontation with only a sliver of moon showing could take place anywhere but near the cemeteries.

"If you all go with me, then Uncle Donovan will be forced to come after us," Deirdre said quietly. "Queen Elizabeth will throw him into the Tower for ignoring his summons to court and leaving the country without her passport. He is supposed to leave for London at dawn. He can't be allowed to follow us to Paris."

None of them could argue with her logic—though Hal wanted to. He could not allow her to be right this time.

Just because Uncle Griffin the Elder's wolfhound had chosen her to be the next Pendragon by bestowing a favored female pup upon her just before dying did not make Deirdre the only candidate for the position. Nor did it make her wiser than the rest of them put together.

"Deirdre is correct," Betsy confirmed.

Hal glared at her.

"One of us must go with her and two must stay," Betsy finished, completely ignoring Hal.

"I am the warrior. I shall protect her," Griffin announced. He partially drew his short sword.

"You are the heir, the one Da must retrieve if you disappear," Hal corrected his twin. "My magic will protect her better than your sword. What chance have you of holding off a dozen brigands with only a single sword?"

Griffin bristled with indignation. He looked just like one of the dogs when cornered.

"I am a more suitable chaperone," Betsy said. She rolled her eyes, as if all of the children in the household were a tremendous burden upon her. Betsy tucked a stray blonde curl back into her netted caul as if it were one of the offending children. Even at this midnight hour she appeared neat and meticulously groomed.

"You, Betsy, are also the most tempting target for brigands to ravish," Griffin said firmly. He faced his older sister, hands on hips, eyebrow raised in imitation of their father's sternness.

Hal had to hold back a giggle. A quick look at Dee and he realized that the heir to Kirkenwood was already a match for both Betsy and their father in stubbornness.

"If only Aunt Meg were still here. She'd go with me," Dee sighed. She edged deeper into the shadow.

Hal caught a glimmer of the enticement she spun into the mind of one of the horses. In the same instant he recognized her plan to escape while her cousins argued. He could not allow that.

"I'm going with you," he announced. He aimed a bit of compulsion in Dee's direction.

Her head reared back and her eyes widened. Coffa growled and raised her neck ruff.

"Don't you ever try to compel me again," she snarled.

"I'll do what I have to, to keep you safe. Nothing else is important," Hal confessed lowering his eyes.

"He's right," Griffin said quietly. "He is the logical one to go with you. Betsy and I will keep Da here and misdirect any agent he sends in your wake."

"Just do what you have to do and return to England quickly," Betsy added. "I do not like the feel of this. It's . . . it's as if someone . . . no some*thing* awaits you with bated breath, licking its chops."

"Werewolves," Dee breathed. She turned paler in the thin light.

A chill breeze smelling slightly of sulfur and blood turned Hal's skin to gooseflesh.

Chapter 5

A NEW scent overlaid the damp earth, horse, dog, and four teenage bodies. My sense of urgency increased.

"He's coming." I vaulted onto the nearest horse, not caring that I appropriated Griffin's blood-bay gelding. My own dun mare was not so fleet or strong of heart. I drew the scent of sweet hay and warm bran mash from the earth and reminded the horse of how good a gentle currying felt. He settled easily under my firm hands.

Griffin babbled a protest. No one but Griffin, not even the stable hands, dared ride the headstrong beast. They did not know how to touch the animal's mind. But I did.

Hal grinned hugely as he mounted his own golden bay gelding. His was equally headstrong but not nearly so mean.

Without further explanation or farewell, I rammed my heels into the horse's sides and touched his mind with my own sense of urgency. He leaped forward, as eager for the run as I.

"Hal and I need to be beyond pursuit by the time Uncle Donovan reaches you," I threw over my shoulder to Betsy and Griff.

Griffin continued to stare after us, mouth opening and closing in astonishment, like a puppet during the May Day festival shows.

A raven lifted from the rooftree of the church porch. It followed us a short way into the woods, then veered off to return to the castle well where it normally roosted.

Betsy assumed command, as she did so well. Within a few heartbeats, she had shoved Griffin atop my mare and mounted her own. Once seated in the saddle, Griffin regained his senses. They galloped around the lake heading south, Brenin leading the way. Hal and I rode due east toward the sunrise and the port at Tynemouth.

"I hope you remembered to bring some money for passage," Hal grumbled. He whipped his horse with his reins, leaning low over the saddle in an effort to keep up with me.

"Some," I replied. The wind caught in my throat, robbing me of breath as well as words.

"Enough?" he asked, drawing alongside. He showed his teeth in feral glee at the competition to pull ahead of my horse.

I knew he and Griff raced wildly across the moors. I knew the horses were evenly matched. But I could not risk a headlong race. There was too much at stake this night, too many miles, and too many challenges ahead of us.

"My father had the gift of visions," I said, reining in the horse a little. He did not want to curb his natural desire to stay ahead of his stable mate. I insisted with my mind as well as a shift of balance and tighter reins.

With a snort of disgust, the beast slowed a little.

Hal kept his own mount close beside me. "Complete the thought, little cousin," he said, a bit breathless from the wild gallop.

"I have had no vision, but I sense terrible danger ahead, Hal. I do not like that you will be at risk because of *my* quest."

"And I do not like that you will put yourself at risk. But I cannot stop you, so I will stay with you and protect you as I can."

"Noble thoughts, cousin. But will they hold when you face fire, pain, and terrible loss of self?" The words spilled out of my mouth unbidden. To my own ears they sounded as if uttered by an alien throat.

The sense that some other spirit used me as a vessel to impart a message made me shudder uncontrollably. Magic opened wondrous possibilities. It also tempted the wielders with power and made them vulnerable to other magical creatures—such as werewolves.

I sighed, knowing that in the days and weeks to come I would face dangers I could not imagine and power would tempt me sorely.

"Where have they gone?" Donovan asked his daughter and son. He had to clench his back teeth to keep from shouting. They would only see his loss of control as a weakness they could exploit. He had no illusions that he could overcome any spell Betsy cast. She'd been a stronger magician than he ever would be by the time she was three. Once she had moved through the torment of puberty, her talent had blossomed as well as her beauty.

He almost pitied the man she married. That choice would have to be hers. Any man he picked for wealth, status, or alliance of titles and lands, would end up on his butt in the midden. Betsy would marry only of her own choice at the time of her choosing.

If Martha had lived, she might have curbed Betsy's aggression. Though a mundane, without a scrap of magic, Martha had a way of maintaining control of one and all in her circle. But alas, Martha had left him and then died.

"Answer me, Griffin," Donovan stared at his eldest legitimate son. This boy had no magic. So unless Betsy had already tampered with his will, Donovan could still intimidate and dominate him.

The boy gulped. His throat apple bobbed, too large for his skinny neck. He'd grow into it eventually. Soon.

"Where have Hal and Dee gone?" He wound a thread of compulsion into his words. His magical vision saw the tendril of blue energy spiral down into the boy's eye.

Then it snapped abruptly.

Donovan jerked his head away as the magic backlashed into his own eye. He had to shake his head and close his eyes a moment to regain his composure. When the world righted again, Betsy smiled back at him sweetly.

"I ought to turn you over my knee and thrash you for that, young lady." Donovan clenched and released his fists repeatedly, knowing he'd never hit her, or any of the children entrusted to him. Other disciplines worked better than blows.

Betsy maintained her slightly jeering, knowing expression.

"Instead, I shall send you to your Aunt Meg."

"But . . ." Betsy gasped.

"A few months living off the bounty of the land, relearning the ancient rituals, tending your uncle's grave, and with no company other than your slightly mad aunt will make you think about the consequences of your actions."

"But . . ."

"Think about the danger Hal and Dee face. Think about the possibility that they will *die* while on this wild escapade. Think, child."

He gave them a moment for those thoughts to sink in.

"Now, where have they gone?" He turned his attention back to Griffin. He should react most strongly to the possibility of losing his twin, his other half, his other self.

As Donovan had lost his own twin, to long separation over a petty quarrel and then to death. The perpetual hole in his emotional gut gaped open.

I am here. A spectral hand seemed to touch his shoulder. The pain lessened a little.

I've had enough ghosts this night, Donovan whispered to his brother. *Go haunt your daughter and counsel her away from this insane quest.*

"F . . . France," Griffin stammered staring at his boots. "Dee feels responsible for the last massacre of Huguenots. She must prevent another from occurring at Henri III's coronation."

"Fool!" Donovan exploded with rage once more. He paced wide circles around the children. His left thigh ached in the perpetual damp and from the strain of tonight's upsets. But he could not remain still, nursing the old injury. He paced and trod uneven circles and loops, visiting each corner of the Hall as well as all the empty places between.

"How does she think she can do that? And what makes her think the first mob reacted to her?"

"Her mother's demon sowed the seeds of Chaos," Betsy replied. "Dee must counter the effects of that Chaos to keep it from invading her as well."

Did she sound smug? Or did she merely recite facts?

Donovan hadn't really expected an answer. Now that he had one, it made sense. Betsy's refusal to meet his gaze did not make sense. She knew something more. Or a different truth.

"You," he pointed to Griffin, "saddle my horse. You," he pointed at Betsy, "summon my secretary while I pack." He stomped toward the stairs to the gallery.

Griffin scuttled out.

"Da, stop and think, as you commanded us to do," Betsy pleaded.

Donovan halted, one foot raised to mount the first tread. He put it back down on the floor and turned slowly toward his daughter. All the while his mind worked furiously, planning his route, trying to outthink wild and precocious Deirdre.

"Da, Elizabeth will throw you into the Tower for leaving England without her passport. For ignoring her latest summons to London. You will lose what little chance you have of gaining Elizabeth's permission to visit Mary."

The last stopped him. He did not fear the Tower. Elizabeth needed him to spy for her in Edinburgh. She would not allow him to linger long within the fortress prison.

But Mary . . .

Donovan drew a deep breath and returned his wandering attention to the current problem. He had to stop his son and niece from falling into another tragedy compounded by innocent error.

"Send Robin, your secretary, after Hal and Dee. Do not go yourself," Betsy pleaded. She reached up on tiptoe and hung a golden chain about his neck. The weight of a heart-shaped locket suspended from it. Betsy applied a lingering kiss to his cheek. "Wear this in London. It contains a lock of my hair. Touch it and you will be in contact with me. I will keep you informed of what Dee and Hal do in France."

"Thank you, Betsy," Donovan said. "I shall send Thom Steward. He has more love and patience for those two than Robin." As useful, precise, and meticulous as Robin might be with documents and diplomatic details, he was a solitary young man, little older than Betsy. Nor did Donovan dare risk the well-being of the boy that Elizabeth Regina doted upon but could never acknowledge as her own.

Robin's parentage remained Donovan's secret now that his twin had died.

"But Robin has noble bearing and speech," Betsy protested. "He'd have much better luck . . ." She reached to press her fingertips against the locket.

Donovan backed away, unsure why.

"Do you wish Robin's absence more than the return of your brother and cousin?" he asked arching one eyebrow at his headstrong daughter. "Mayhap, dear Betsy, you are jealous that Robin's affections belong to the daughter of a glassworker. I believe you desire his absence merely to separate him from Faith."

Betsy buried her face in her hands and fled. Her shoulders shook with her sobs as she went.

"The course of true love never did run smooth, sweeting," he whispered in her wake. "I believe the time comes soon when I must send you to court as *my* spy upon Elizabeth. Time among the glittering popinjays will turn your head away from the one man I dare not allow you to wed."

He went in search of his steward, wishing he had the courage to pursue the errant children himself. "Best Gaspar and Peregrine go, too." His lumbering bastard sons doted on Deirdre. They would protect the girl with their lives.

He shuddered with cold premonition.

"Watch over them all, dear brother, Martha, Raven," he whispered to the ghosts that never left him. "Keep Dee safe. I love this little one almost more than my own children."

He heard Martha's distinct sniff of disapproval. She had given him sons. His concern should be for the twins.

Chapter 6

19 June, 1574. The cellars beneath the Spanish embassy, Paris, France.

"COME, *la lobuna*," the guard growled in Spanish.

Yassimine cringed. She did not understand everything spoken to her in this strange language. But that phrase needed no translation.

Grinding her resentment and anger deep into a corner of her heart, Yassimine calmly placed her sharp tambour hook and thimble aside. She rubbed her eyes free of the grit from peering at the fine work with only a single smoking oil lamp for light. Then she rotated her shoulders, relieving them of the hunched posture required for this needlework.

She hated leaving the fine embroidery in the middle of a section. She had learned early that life was perilous. Any task left unfinished might never reach completion. But completion and relief of boredom were all she sought from the work. Christian women hungered for needlework. They had nothing else to lighten their lives.

"*Vamos*," the guard snarled, impatient with her hesitation.

Yassimine rose slowly from her stool, careful to keep grace in each motion as her mother had taught her from an early age.

Move like water, smoothly, so that one drop blends with the next. Here and there are the same to the eye. She heard her long dead mother's voice in the back of her mind. That little bit of love was the only thing that had kept her sane since her capture five years ago.

That and her anger.

The guard who had spoken entered Yassimine's cell holding a whip in one hand and a torch in the other. She backed away from the implied menace in the weapons and in his eyes. A second guard entered the room holding a chain made of silver links. The guards always worked in pairs with a second pair watching from the narrow passage outside the iron door.

One of their tonsured priests also stood guard, carrying one of their hideous crosses showing their god dying most horribly upon it. She ignored the man and his talisman. They could not harm her unless she believed they could.

The Chain Man crossed himself, closed his eyes, and took a deep breath before snapping the silver links to the leather collar studded with iron around her neck. She bared her teeth and growled at him. He jumped back, crossing himself repeatedly.

Very briefly, she enjoyed his fear. Then the whip slashed at her arm, tearing the heavy black gown The Master insisted she wear. She flinched away, still snarling.

The Chain Man yanked her metal leash. She hoped his fear had made him soil his netherwear.

With heavy steps, she followed where they led her. She fought to hide her elation. Removal from the windowless cell deep underground could only mean one thing: The Master needed her skills.

Dozens of torches lit the passage, turning the darkness into day. Yassimine blinked rapidly, waiting for her eyes to adjust to the absence of shadow. The guards hated what their imagination put into those shadows.

Yassimine held her head high. Her mouth salivated at the scent of their fear.

The steep stairs to the ground level strained Yassimine's legs. Too used to sitting or pacing the confines of her cell, the unwanted exercise made her long to bend forward and use her arms to help lift her legs up each rise. The guards kept her leash too short. She bit her lip until it bled rather than cry out with the pains in her thighs. The men granted her a short reprieve at the landing while they checked to ensure the absence of the servants on the back stairway to the next level.

Surreptitiously, Yassimine rubbed the coarse wool of her

gown against her legs. The scratchy material brought her blood to the surface of the skin, easing some of the ache. Heightening her anticipation of what was to come. She breathed deeply of the air that did not smell of her own body, fishy lamp oil, and moldy earth.

She tasted life in that breath. Seven lives. Seven people inhabited the chambers surrounding the stairs. Servants probably, men and women who worked hard for their scant pay, but appreciated the luxury of a bed with blankets and enough food to keep their bellies happy. She, too, could appreciate those things. But she was not free to move about, to converse with others of her kind, to breathe fresh air. Her own fears made her realize she did not truly trust the freedom others took for granted. There was always a silver chain to pull her back into confinement.

Another painful flight left her breathing heavily. She resisted the urge to let her tongue loll. Panting would not cool her heated blood. Shedding this hideous gown and wimple might.

"What day is this?" she asked the guards in broken Spanish. She dug in her heels and refused to move forward until they answered her question, no matter how much pressure Chain Man put upon her leash and collar. The heavy silver links would separate before they defeated her strength of will.

"Nineteen June," Chain Man grumbled.

The words meant nothing to Yassimine. "How near the Summer Solstice?" She narrowed her search for information. She had been confined too long, her sense of season, and the movement of moon and stars across the skies had diminished. Once, she would have known precisely where and when she was without thinking.

"Three days."

Numbers, days, and weeks were words she had come to learn. Three days, less than one quarter of the moon phase.

"And the phase of the moon?"

"Dark tonight," Chain Man admitted on a grin, as if he knew her dependence upon the moon. He hauled once more on the chain.

This time she followed more willingly, understanding now the weakness in her muscles. A bit of her heart light-

ened. The Master must have wondrous tasks for her if he
brought her forth from her sensory deprivation at the dark
of the moon near the day of the shortest hours of darkness.

Still holding the cross as a kind of barrier between Yassimine and himself, the priest knocked upon an ornate double door inlaid with paler woods, mother-of-pearl, and bits
of gold leaf. Such a portal should adorn the palace of a
sultan. Yassimine had learned that The Master wielded as
much power over his subjects as a vizier, though he bore a
different title and different responsibilities. He reported to
a king and a high priest, but mostly he acted upon his own
authority, for his own purpose.

A muffled voice from within summoned the priest to
throw open the portal. The guards thrust Yassimine past
the opening and slammed the doors shut once more. She
heard their sighs of relief through the massive panels. She
almost rejoiced out loud at their fears.

But The Master did not want to see her tiny triumph.

"Come into the light where I might see thee," a disem-
bodied voice commanded roughly in her birth language.

Yassimine glided toward the blazing fire in the hearth.
Each step barely bent the nap in the thick carpet. She
longed to cast off the tight leather shoes with their thick
soles and allow the soft texture to caress her feet.

The Master snapped his fingers, ending her reverie.

Yassimine stepped into the garish light of the fire. Heavy
curtains blocked the natural daylight. She could feel the
allure of the sun through her heavy clothing. All of her
being needed to dash to the window embrasure and throw
open the draperies. It had been so long since she had felt
the sun's caress on her face, smelled the sharp wind as it
blew across the steppe unimpeded. At times she could scent
every life, every blade of grass, every tree, and stream the
wind had touched.

Now all she smelled was the reek of an unwashed male
body, stale wine, and air too long enclosed. Not much better than her cellar prison.

"Yes, Master." She knelt before the massive chair that
faced the fire, keeping her eyes lowered.

"I have a task for you, my demon." The man lisped in
his highborn accent.

Yassimine risked a glance through her lowered lashes at

his sallow face—pale, thin, and unhealthy. As always, his servants had perfectly groomed his pointed beard and mustache. A few strands of silver had crept into his hair and beard since last she had been summoned to his presence. His heavy-lidded eyes and pursed lips, painted to achieve the color of ripe strawberries, gave him the look of a weasel ready to burrow into her soul, leaving a trail of filth on its route.

He reached out with the hook that should have been his left hand and lifted her chin. Inwardly she smiled at the loss of that limb. He deserved the disability.

She forced any glee out of her expression and posture, concentrating instead upon the heavily jeweled cross he wore about his neck. The fire cast reddish tints upon the precious metal and brought the stones to life.

"How may I serve you?" she asked in her imitation of Spanish, his tongue. She thought she could speak it as well—if not quite so fluently—as he could. But if she ever dared hope for a future, that was one secret she must not reveal to him.

"The Holy League awaits the return of the new French king, near the night of the full moon."

A frisson of excitement and alarm coursed through her blood.

"You will, of course, be granted the freedom of the city for three nights, to honor the event." He smiled with half his mouth, the right side. The other half remained almost frozen. That side of his face rarely showed emotion. That side of his body rarely moved without a great deal of effort.

Still smiling, The Master rose and walked stiffly over to a brazier full of glowing coals. He opened a golden casket nearby and withdrew a large chunk of red meat.

Yassimine's mouth watered. Many moons had passed since she'd last tasted meat. The Master knew that meat sharpened all of her appetites and shattered the careful control he imposed upon her. Withholding meat and light, and dousing her with special numbing herbs allowed him to suppress her nature. Or so he thought.

The meat sizzled on the brazier. The scent made her nostrils flare and her blood run hot. She opened her mouth, the better to taste the air.

"Ah, I see that you long for this food as you long for

freedom. And so you shall have it. After I have tamed you."

"Anything, Master," Yassimine panted, not caring about the indignities he would require of her, just so she could taste the meat.

"Cast off your robes."

Yassimine made to stand, the better to shed the heavy wool that chafed her skin and constantly reminded her that she was this man's slave in all things. She endured it all for the rare taste of meat.

"No need to rise, my demon pet." His smile did not reach his eyes.

Still on her knees, Yassimine slowly unwound the wimple from her hair, freeing the heavy black locks that fell to her waist. Forcing herself to take her time, she began working on the ties at wrist and shoulder that bound the ugly gown to her form. She knew what this man liked, a slow and tempting revelation of the merchandise he had purchased at so dear a cost.

The heady scent of the meat made her fingers clumsy. But at last the voluminous folds fell away. Then she freed her feet from the heavy shoes. She no longer cared that The Master's eyes feasted upon her naked breasts, the smooth skin of her belly, and the luxuriant dark mound below. Silver chains burned slightly where they pierced her nipples and navel. Exposure to light and air increased the discomfort. The small pains unleashed a wave of desire. Heat and moisture sprang from her body in anticipation. She twisted slightly, making the chains dangle and sway, enticing The Master's eyes to follow their movement.

As always, the master's gaze fixed upon the bespelled links that bound her to him, body and soul.

"Bend over," he commanded her, licking his lips and swallowing hard.

She obeyed willingly. The meat, so close and yet so far, weakened her knees as well as her resolve. Just let him finish with her quickly so that she could eat the meat before the fire seared all of the blood and life from its juices.

He ran the tip of his hook the length of her spine. Arrows of pain shot throughout her body as he broke the surface skin and droplets of blood sprang free. She snarled at him, ready to attack her attacker with teeth and nails. He laughed at her protest.

Then he was inside her, thrusting deep and long. She forgot her resolve to feign indifference. A scream of pleasure erupted from her throat. Fire filled her loins and her breasts. Pleasure coursed up and down her spine replacing the sting of his hook. Intoxicated by the scent of fresh meat and the sensuality of her physical and magical chains, she abandoned plans to kill this man today.

Chapter 7

1 July, 1574. An inn on the road to London.

DONOVAN flung himself from his side onto his back. He stared into the darkness above him and tried to force his mind into blankness. Every time he flopped into a new position, he seemed to hear a raven croak a question, as if his movements disturbed its sleep.

He'd left the raven at Kirkenwood, more than a week ago.

He should make plans to deal with the bleak barley harvest. Worry about Hal and Dee kept him from thinking clearly. Worry would not help them. He had other children and responsibilities that required his attention.

"Oh, Martha, you always helped me keep my priorities straight. You made it easier to sleep at night," he whispered.

He fingered the locket Betsy had given him just before he left. Her eyes had been red from tears and sleeplessness. Still he held firm to his decision. She must go to Mad Meg. The locket contained a single lock of her golden-blonde hair. The same color as her mother's.

Slowly he allowed his fingers to make loving circles around the heart-shaped piece. He did not aim his thoughts in Betsy's direction. She knew nothing more than he did about Dee and Hal. Or so she had told him through the scrying bowl each morning since he had left home.

A rough edge near the catch of the locket scratched his fingers. He cursed and sucked on the offended finger. He tasted blood.

The wound healed quickly.

An image of Mary came to him, as she had been the one

night they'd slept together. He banished the memory. Both of them had aged and changed since then. Their relationship must change as well.

He breathed deeply and concentrated upon his responsibilities. The things he could act upon. Did he have enough grain in storage to see his people through the next year? Did he have enough gold stashed away to buy grain from richer farms to the south?

He should write letters of credit and recommendation on the morrow and send them with Thom Steward to the grain markets. . . . No, he could not do that.

Thom Steward, along with Donovan's illegitimate sons Gaspar and Peregrine, had followed Hal and Dee to France. He endured many anxious moments worrying about them all.

Nothing he could do about that now.

Who could he send in search of winter stores? Robin? His secretary had an authoritative manner—much like Robin's royal mother. But he had not yet the maturity in face or emotions to bargain hard and long for the best prices. Donovan might have to go himself. But he was needed in London. And what of his routine mission to Edinburgh? He needed to consult with the French ambassador to the court of King James. The Protestant lords who ruled Scotland in the young king's name anxiously awaited news as to whether Henri III would uphold his mother's policies of religious tolerance or side with the powerful de Guise faction and the Holy League.

The de Guise family had all but ruled France for the past three generations. Mary Queen of Scots was a de Guise on her mother's side. . . .

Mary.

He fingered the locket again, wishing it contained a lock of the exiled queen's red-gold hair. He had no keepsake from her. Nothing but memories.

"Oh, Mary, do you lie sleepless within your gilded prison this night?" he asked aloud. "Do you think of me? Do you even remember?" His mind drifted back to the early days of his mission in Edinburgh.

Mary had kept him close by her side as adviser and friend. She had even proposed to him at one point. He had to refuse because of his marriage to Martha, the mother of

Griffin and Hal. His frankness and honesty had prompted an intimacy unusual between a royal and courtier.

Then Henry Stewart, Lord Darnley, had entered Mary's life. From the moment he had ridden up to Holyrood Palace, Mary had been besotted by Darnley's golden beauty and words of adoration. Despite advice to the contrary, the young queen had taken Darnley as her husband on 29 July, 1565.

As soon as Mary had spoken her marriage vows, Darnley had shown his true face. A face of cruelty, ambition, and extreme vanity.

Donovan flipped onto his belly. His neck ached. The sheets were hot, his back itched. The stone walls of this inn seemed to press closer.

His heart ached.

He kicked off the covers and rolled to his other side. Ghosts and memories pressed against his eyelids. At last he drifted into a half-waking, half-sleeping state where his dreams became reality. Memories took over his dreams. . . .

Near midnight, 25 September, 1565. Edinburgh. Nine years before.

Donovan downed a full goblet of wine in one gulp. It did not cool his anger or his fevered thoughts. Once again, Mary Queen of Scots had blundered in council. They considered the illegitimate son of James V to be the true ruler of Scotland. Mary's Privy Council nearly ignored her at every turn. This afternoon she had dismissed them in a temper and flounced out.

"I tried to warn you, Mary," he muttered.

Too restless to sleep, he paced the confines of his narrow town house. He longed to ride through the hills on a fast horse with the wind in his hair and the stars shining brightly above him. 'Twas a rare clear night this eve.

Perhaps then he could relieve the prickles that ran up and down his spine.

If only he had thought to bring the children with him. His adopted son, Robin, had reached his ninth birthday. Perhaps 'twas time to start teaching him the fine art of diplomacy . . . Betsy, the twins, and Deirdre were all still too young to leave their nurse. He missed them terribly.

But the city was not safe by day or night for himself or the children. He dared not walk the short distance to the stable at the White Horse Inn for a mount without several weapons and more guards. Seemingly, the criminals of Edinburgh had as little respect for Mary's laws and authority as did her Privy Council.

He downed another goblet of wine. Finally, reality became a little fuzzy around the edges. "Martha, you would have eased my doubts and set me to making logical plans," he sighed, wishing his wife's ghost would help him now.

The house remained free of haunts.

Casting caution to the wind, he threw a short cloak over his doublet and strapped on his favorite sword. He clumped down the stairs to the nearest exit still buckling the sword belt about his hips.

The door flew open at a touch from his fingers. He stepped back, drawing his weapon in one movement.

"Stay your hand, milord," a husky voice commanded. A feminine voice deepened and made rough by tears.

"Mary?" He peered cautiously into the gloom. "Your Grace." He bowed to the woman who was Queen of the Scots by the Grace of God.

She stretched out her hand. Her long fingers gripped his wrist. They looked skeletal in the flickering light of an oil lamp. Under the pressure of her grip he let the sword slide back into the sheath.

"What brings you here, Your Grace?" Donovan drew her into the dim entry lit only by a single oil lamp. He checked the street outside his door for signs of an escort or clandestine observer. Empty. "Why did you come alone?"

"I . . ." She gulped and straightened her spine. "We have no place else to seek advice and . . . and solace." She meant the royal "we," of course.

"Come." Donovan took her hand and led her up three flights of stairs to his private solar. Without asking, he poured her a goblet of wine. He handed it to her and waited for her to finish it all before speaking.

The queen took several small sips. All the while she kept her eyes open and her gaze fixed upon Donovan.

"You are safe here," he whispered.

"He follows me everywhere."

Donovan did not need to ask who. Darnley shadowed

her movements throughout the day, jealous of any who
might influence her, diminishing his control and thus his
illusion of power.

"You can command . . ."

"I command nothing. He punishes me if I do not follow
his instructions." She nearly spat the words.

"Punish? How?" Donovan swallowed his disgust. "Only
a coward uses a woman so ill."

"Coward, yes. That describes my husband." She shrank
back within the folds of her cloak.

"Your Grace, how may I help?" He reached for her
hand, grabbing it before she could pull away. Once they
had been close, on the brink of an illicit affair.

But Martha had been alive then. He could not betray
his wife.

The untied sleeve of her shift fell back from his grip.
Bruises looked like dark smears of dirt all along her
inner arm.

Donovan drew in a sharp breath through his clenched
teeth. "Are there more?"

Her silence answered better than words.

"Put him aside before I challenge him to a duel!"

"Nay, milord. The bishops have warned me against ending a marriage so newly made. Barely two months' time.
Elizabeth will but laugh. She forbade the marriage."

"Elizabeth postured against the union knowing you
would jump into it to defy her. She wanted you married to
a bully and a fool. She has thus divided your kingdom."

"But the Church. Holy vows taken before God's altar . . ."

"Damn the Church!" Donovan slammed his fist into his
open palm. "What honor is there in a church that condones
this?" He swept her cloak from her shoulders. Through the
fine lawn of her high-necked shift, another bruise showed.
The man had left his handprints about her throat. "What
right does the Church have to allow the man to nearly
choke you to death?" He could not help caressing the ugly
marks on her throat.

She leaned her cheek into his caress. "Mon cher, I should
have married you."

"You still can, Mary. Annul the marriage or have it dis-
solved. Divorce Darnley if you have to. Do whatever you
have to do. Then we can marry."

"The bishops, the Pope, the sin of divorce . . ."

"Let the princes of your church object. Divorce is no sin if it saves your life." Donovan gathered her close and kissed her to stop her objections.

She melted into him.

His blood flared and his heart swelled. He deepened the kiss. Pressure built in his groin.

Her lips parted under his urging. She tasted of rosewater and wine.

"This is no true marriage, Mary. The Church of Scotland will give you the divorce," he whispered when they finally came up for air.

"The Church of Scotland is no true Church. An annulment must come from Rome." She ducked her face away from his probing.

"Then begin the negotiations." He lifted her chin with a gentle finger. "Put Darnley aside before he kills you."

"He would not. He has no power, no authority without me." She almost sounded as if she believed her words.

"Mary, Darnley is descended from your great grandmother, Margaret Tudor. He has royal blood in his veins. With you dead and Moray in exile in England, he will seize control."

"He has *English* royal blood, not Scots!"

"Darnley will oust the Privy Council and replace them with his catamites."

"The Scots will not allow it; I will not allow . . ."

"You will be dead. What could *you* do?"

"He will kill me?"

He watched the truth dawn in her eyes. They stood eye to eye, nose to nose for many long moments.

"I do not wish to die," she said barely above a whisper.

"I do not wish you to die." He kissed her again. Quickly. Gently. Fire ignited his loins.

But this was no whore to be rushed and forgotten.

He wrapped his arms around her to calm her shudders and just held her. So sweet. He savored the scent of her hair, the warmth of her body, the way she fit so neatly against him.

After many long silent moments he dared move his hands, running them the length of her spine.

She winced and drew back. He gentled her again.

"Let me ease your hurts, Mary. Divorce Darnley and marry me. I love you. I have always loved you. I will never hurt you." Warm moisture touched his hand where he had caressed her.

He swallowed deeply and closed his eyes a moment before he dared look. Blood stained the back of her gown.

"God's wounds, I will kill the man myself."

"Non, mon cher." She touched his lips with gentle fingers to silence his words. "I will not have the sin of murder on your head." She kissed him to silence his protest. Tears glistened in her eyes.

"Did I hurt you?" Donovan touched her back gently.

"Not you. Never you." This time her kiss was deep and passionate.

"Let me dress the wound. I have a healing ointment. 'Twill keep scars from forming."

"Please."

Carefully he loosened the laces on the back of her gown. She winced and cringed several times. But she did not cry out. The gown peeled away easily. But her shift stuck to the drying blood.

His own skin felt flayed in empathic union.

"He did this tonight," Donovan said flatly.

"He had one of his catamites with him in *my* bed. I screamed at him." Her voice shook with tears.

"Lay you upon my bed. I must bathe these wounds and dress them carefully." He pushed her into the bedchamber behind the solar. He gathered up the ointment and a small lamp to warm the stuff.

He found her stretched out, facedown upon the feather tick with her back bared, the shift bunched about her hips. She rested her forehead against her crossed arms above her head. Her long, golden-red hair she had swept over her shoulder. The long length of her back and a brief glimpse of the sides of her breasts excited him. He clamped down on his desire. Not tonight. She needed care and tenderness tonight, not passion.

"Oh, Mary, how could any man do this to you!" He eased a dripping cloth over the broken flesh. "What did he use? A walking stick?"

"He is no man. Not like you." She turned her head to face him.

An invitation glittered in her gaze. He ignored it, turning his attention to warming the salve. As he smoothed it into her wounds, his hands strayed to massage her entire back. Taut muscles released under his practiced touch.

"Love me, Donovan. Love me as a true man loves a woman," she whispered.

"Mary, beloved. Are you certain you want this tonight?"

"I need you to obliterate the memory of Darnley's touch. I need you to love me."

He needed no further invitation to gather her into his arms. She fumbled with the ties of his doublet. He kissed her nose and removed the garment himself. His shirt remained a great barrier between them. He discarded it gladly.

He cupped her pert breasts, relishing the creamy white skin. "If you only knew how long I have wished for this moment." He kissed the rosy tip until it puckered.

"I, too, have longed for you to touch me thus." She fumbled with the ties of his breeches.

"Easy, my love. Do not hasten our union," he chuckled at her eagerness. He guided her hands to his chest.

A quick student, she played with the line of hair that marched down his belly to disappear beneath his belt. An agony of pleasure.

Slowly he rained kisses all over her body, warming her, preparing her. Somehow, he divested himself of his breeches and hose. He tugged her shift free of her body and threw it elsewhere. Impatient now, he snugged her tight against him, letting her get used to the pressure of his erection against her belly.

Her hands found him. The hesitant touch nearly brought explosive heat. Not much longer. He promised himself. A few more moments.

With hands and tongue he opened her, moistened her. When she lay back panting for release he finally brought her atop him. Just the tip of him entered. She contracted, drawing him upward, inward. His hands found her full breasts and kneaded.

She caressed his beard with a gentle, wet fingertip. He drew it into his mouth and suckled. She gasped with pleasure.

Unable to hold back longer he plunged and withdrew, finding her rhythm. Surge and recede. Pressure/pain/joy/

release, love built within him. He became her, she became him. His magic reached out and twined around their minds, bonding them forever and a day.

"Mary, my love!" he cried as the tides took him and he spilled his seed deep within her.

When he awoke before dawn, she had already left him.

A year and a half later, Henry Stewart, Lord Darnley, consort to Mary Queen of Scots, died violently. His house on the outskirts of Edinburgh exploded. His naked body was found strangled at the edge of the garden.

Chapter 8

3 July, 1574. The outskirts of Paris, France.

I STOPPED in my tracks, too weary to take another step. Beside me, Coffa lowered her head to match her drooping tail.

The days and nights, the *weeks* on the road had become a blur of barns to hide in, meals begged or sharing what the dogs hunted, and cemeteries to sleep in. We sought the quiet resting places of the dead to avoid detection. Few sane people sought out a cemetery after dark. Hal had rarely slept in the burial grounds, shivering and starting at every sound. Once, he and I had stopped at an isolated farm and worked for our keep for a sennight to give Coffa a chance to rest a badly bruised front paw. He had slept then. I had never worked so hard in my life and hoped to never again. The true meaning of money was a hard lesson for two spoiled children raised in noble luxury.

"I have to sit." I sighed so heavily I wasn't sure there was any air left in me—or strength to draw the next breath. My knees wobbled and plunked me down on a boulder beside our path. The rock had no convenient smooth spots on which to place my bottom. No matter.

It glistened with moisture from the perpetual mist. No matter.

At least the mist was warm and caressed my skin lovingly rather than trying to tear holes in my face like the rains back home.

Coffa sprawled at my feet. Helwriaeth plunked down where he stood next to Hal.

For one hundred heartbeats I did nothing, moved nothing, thought nothing. Then the pains in my feet won over the bone-aching weariness. Listlessly, I tugged at my boots. They were overfull of feet and my hands slipped on the mist-slick leather.

"Let me help," Hal said. He trudged over from where he had ceased walking a few paces ahead of me. Collected moisture dripped from his forelock into his eyes. His hands slipped just as mine had.

We needed his strength combined with a lot of wiggling on my part to free my feet from their leather coverings. At last the light breeze and gentle mist cooled the sweat and eased some of the pain dragging my limbs down. I wiggled my toes and leaned back, lifting my face to the mist.

The dogs showed a little interest in sniffing my discarded boots. They did not rouse enough to tussle over them.

When Hal and I had started the venture, I thought my affinity with Pridd, the Earth, would invigorate me as long as I walked. What little strength I gained from my element faded soon after we crossed the Channel on a leaking fishing boat. Hal had been sick the entire voyage. I managed to keep my stomach from turning inside out—just.

Neither of us had regained full strength after that.

"I used to think riding a horse all day was tiring," I said on a sigh. "Walking is much harder."

"Walking is for peasants," Hal snorted.

"The Merlin always walked the length and breadth of Britain on his missions," I reminded him loftily. I could be just as much a snob as he, but in my own way. "If you hope to become the next Pendragon, you have to learn to walk." I wilted. "But walking would be much easier with a staff. My father had a marvelous staff topped by a black crystal as big as his fist."

"Da buried the staff with his brother."

"As was fitting. He was the last Merlin. The real Pendragon. I just hope I can live up to his legacy."

"If I don't claim the heritage before you." Hal eased himself down onto the wet ground heedless of the grass soaking his backside. He moved as if his back ached more than his feet. He'd shouldered a goodly portion of my burden as well as his own. Considering the miles we had traversed and the weight of his pack, he deserved to hurt all over. As did I.

"Or maybe Betsy will beat both of us to the title. She is

older, and a stronger magician. And she is at home while we trek through France on a useless mission." Hal sat with his knees drawn up and his hands dangling between them. He gazed into the distance dejectedly.

"But she is not as interested in learning the ancient languages or delving into the old scrolls. All she wants to do is experiment with new spells and alchemy. She dabbles in dark magic. She uses blood to fuel her magic." I had to find *some* fault with my older cousin lest I give in to my fears that Hal's statements were true. If Betsy grabbed the title of Pendragon while Hal and I followed my quest . . .

"But if her experiments produce the Philosopher's Stone, how can we compete with that?" Hal looked over his shoulder at me.

"She won't find it," I insisted. A long silence stretched between us, as long as the road we had traveled. I felt Hal withdrawing from me, taking on thoughts and ideas, plans and goals separate from mine. That distance frightened me. But one day we must take diverging life paths. Only one of us could be the Pendragon. My father and Uncle Donovan had discovered the tragedy of two rivals claiming the heritage.

"We still have a few hours of walking ahead of us. Do you suppose we could stay at an inn tonight? I would so love a bath." I had to change the subject before I started crying. Before I called off this journey and returned home.

Farther to home than to Paris, a voice behind my heart reminded me. The points of honor where Arthur had touched me with his ghostly sword burned, reminding me that he had blessed this venture.

I had to move forward, grow into my responsibilities, not retreat into childhood. This mission would make me a woman. I knew it.

It scared me.

"Oh, for a real bed with real sheets and dry blankets," Hal sighed. "But we can't afford it. You wouldn't let us sell the horses and you didn't think to bring extra money."

"The horses belong to Uncle Donovan. They were not ours to sell. And I brought all the money I had."

"You know where Da keeps a pouch of coins for emergencies. This is an emergency."

"The coins were not mine. My father did not need

money on his travels. The people of the road always cared for him."

"Because he was the Merlin and they loved him. We are just two children, with two oversized, overhungry dogs, trying to act like adults."

I glared at him for daring to voice my own doubts and inadequacies.

"Rain tonight." He lifted his head and sniffed the air, just as Helwriaeth did. "Hard rain, worse than this mist. We'd best be inside the city walls by then." Hal hauled himself up with a groan. He held out a hand to help me up.

I stared at my boots. They had collapsed where we tossed them. I groaned aloud at the thought of putting them on again. Resolutely, I tugged off my heavy stockings, rolled them neatly, and stuffed them into my pack. Then I picked up the offensive boots and began walking.

"Dee!" Hal protested. "Dee, you'll hurt yourself."

"Less than wearing these things one more minute. I've got blisters." With my feet bare, the Earth could renew me much better than if leather and wool separated me from true contact with my element. If I had to walk like a peasant, I'd best shed all traces of the lady Betsy and Aunt Fiona tried to beat into me. Only ladies wore shoes and boots.

Just over the next rise we spied the old pilgrim road from the north into Paris. We had avoided roads because of the mud and refuse collected there, as well as from the desire to travel secretly.

Dozens of travelers crowded the road, all headed toward Paris as if the cathedral on *L'Isle de la Cité* held out her arms to shelter and enrich them body and soul. Merchants with rich trains of wagons, simple people carrying nothing, lords and ladies on fine but impatient mounts, all sought one destination. Many of the people boarded the ferry across *La Seine* on foot or with their horses. The boatmen collected many coins for the passage. The cumbersome wagons continued down the narrower and much longer road alongside the river. They could enter *La Ville* from the south through St. Germain and the Latin Quarter.

Hal directed me toward the deeply rutted wagon road. Only partially recovered, I looked at the additional miles skeptically.

We heard snatches of conversation from our fellow travelers.

"People torn limb from limb."

"Terrible bite wounds."

"Anyone on the streets after moonrise."

"Tonight is the third night of the full moon. It will come again."

People crossed themselves at the end of each tale of woe. All of them were too similar to have strayed far from the truth.

"We have to hurry." Hal took my elbow and urged me to walk faster.

"We cannot spend a night without shelter within the *cité,*" I agreed with him. Ghosts and faeries, trips through the netherworld I could understand and had faced in reality and in my dreams. I had even conquered the occasional monster beneath the bed.

But this tale of a ravening beast loose on the streets of Paris held nothing of comforting familiarity. None of my magic could defend me against . . .

"Will we be safe or should we conclude our business and start for home before sunset?" a nervous merchant asked each person who passed him.

His concern echoed up and down the line of those waiting for a ferry. The unrest in these people irritated me more than their whispers of a monster, like an old briar scratch that refuses to heal.

Hal tugged on my sleeve, pulling me north and east toward the *Montmatre* heights. We didn't really need words between us. Still, I wanted a little sympathy, a little understanding for my abject weariness.

"You can sleep in a convent tonight, Dee. I'm sure the sisters will give you the bath you crave and tend your blisters," he said quietly.

I half-smiled at how he had read me and my thoughts. "And you, Hal? Where will you find your bed and bath and care for *your* blisters." I knew he had them from the way he walked, rolling his steps toward the outside.

"Convent guesthouse." He grinned back at me. Mischief danced in his eyes for the first time in weeks.

But we are not Papists! I almost blurted out the thought.

"We don't have to tell them that. We've been taught the

rituals. You have your father's rosary. You run the beads through your fingers every night as you fall asleep." He shrugged and continued walking downhill. He knew I had no choice but to follow.

"And the dogs?" Coffa butted her head against my thigh begging for reassurance that we would not be separated. I noticed Helwriaeth doing the same. "These are noble dogs of a noble breed for sale only to the nobility. Why would we, two peasant children on pilgrimage have them following us so faithfully and so obediently?" The beginnings of a story began to form in my head. After all, the original Merlin, from whom we claimed descent, was a bard, a storyteller who used music to accent and augment his tales. I could spin wonderful stories, even sing a little where necessary.

"Are we bastard brother and sister seeking our father in the crowd gathered for the coming coronation?" Hal quirked up his left eyebrow, just like his father. "Our da could have left the dam of these pups with our mother as part of his promise to educate me and provide you with a proper dowry."

The story began to take shape in my head. "He'll know us by the dogs, part of the litter born while he sheltered with a prosperous vintner during a fierce winter storm. He loved our mother and returned often over the years despite his existing marriage to a noble lady with rich dower lands. Now our mother and grandfather are dead and our uncle has thrown us out rather than share the inheritance with two bastards."

A common enough tale that was exploited with many variations by the companies of players sponsored by noble-men throughout England.

"But only if we speak proper French," I reminded him. I'd been speaking that tongue since we landed on the Con-tinent. Hal had clung to his native English. For the first time in a long time, I was grateful that Uncle Donovan insisted we learn other languages.

"You should be a playwright, Dee," Hal chortled in his badly accented French.

"And you, fine sir, my chief actor. I shall give you the pretty words to speak, you provide the emotion and the near tears to convince our audience of the truth of our tale."

"Or the universal truth."

We both nearly collapsed with laughter.

When we sobered, I said, "Mayhap we hail from Brittany. That will explain your terrible accent."

He shrugged his acceptance and we continued our journey, much lightened in body and spirit by our laughter.

By the time we reached the road, the morning mists had cleared and the soft sunshine broke the clouds. A gentle breeze stirred the grass and shrubs, still vibrant with spring green. The warm day caressed my soul and brightened my spirits as the harsh climate of Kirkenwood and Edinburgh could not.

Hal, however seemed to thrive in the chill winds we had grown up with. He drooped as the day and the warmth progressed.

We found our convent north of *La Ville,* the name given the quarters of Paris that had sprawled out from the confines of the large river island. The good sisters fussed and cooed over me, glared at Hal skeptically, and then accepted his promise of chopping firewood and drawing water from the well in return for our baths and a night's lodging. Travel grime embedded on our hands, faces, and hair would not succumb to the usual basin and ewer. We needed *baths.*

The dogs were banished to the stable. Both Helwriaeth and Coffa sulked and trudged off, their tails between their legs.

My heart nearly broke at the separation. My relief at being within stout walls before sunset shredded around the edges. How could I be truly safe without my familiar?

Then the sisters produced a bathtub. Mentally, I promised Coffa that we would be together again tomorrow, after we had both slept and eaten well.

Now that we need not sleep rough and eat rougher, with the dogs as our pillows and hunters, I took the time to listen carefully to the conversations of our hostesses.

They echoed the fears of the travelers.

"Good thing you found us before sunset, *mon enfant,*" Sister Marie Celeste clucked at me as she rinsed my soapy hair for the third time.

"And why is that, Sister?" I asked, eyes wide and looking as innocent as I could. The lies we had told to gain this night of luxury bothered me. The nuns seemed so terribly trusting and more innocent than Hal and I.

"*C'est trés terrible,* the crimes the Protestants inflict upon innocent souls. Not even enough parts of the bodies left to bury properly. Not enough left for God to recognize and bless as they enter the gates of heaven." She crossed herself. I mimicked her action hastily.

"None of the comfort of Last Rites." She dabbed at a tear with the edge of her veil. "As horrifying as it was, perhaps the mob knew best when they slaughtered the Huguenots two years ago on St. Bartholomew's Eve."

Sister Marie Celeste firmed her chin and scrubbed my back so vigorously with coarse soap and rough cloth she nearly tore through several layers of skin. She continued her litany of warning without pause.

I chilled in the warm bathwater, more frightened of her than of the monster that stalked Paris on the nights of the full moon.

Sister Marie Celeste ignored my unnatural stillness and kept talking. "Perhaps our new king will finally bring Frenchmen to their senses and consign all Huguenots and other heretics to hell where they belong."

I had to stop such a massacre before it happened.

Chapter 9

3 July, 1574. The English Midlands, approaching the village of Nether Pedley.

"KEEP up, Robin," Donovan called to his young secretary. "We'll stop at full dark. I know an inn about an hour from here." An inn within a few hours' ride of Mary's latest prison.

He wrapped his hand around the heart-shaped locket on his breast. Just touching the gold convinced him of the rightness of this detour.

Robin clung to his reins with quiet determination. Robin would rather walk than ride anywhere.

He had no reason to emulate Queen Elizabeth's or the Earl of Leicester's famed seat. Either of them could outride anyone in the kingdom. But then, Robin wasn't supposed to know that Elizabeth had borne him before she became queen. Robin knew only that Donovan had adopted him, the illegitimate orphan of a noble lord.

"I must remind you, sir, Her Majesty has not approved of this enterprise. Mary Stuart's visitors are strictly regulated by the queen." Robin said carefully between bounces.

"Mary's jailer, the Countess of Shrewsbury, makes those decisions, with or without Elizabeth's approval," Donovan tried to laugh.

Robin's face remained sober and disapproving.

"Your objection is duly noted, Robin." Donovan did not want to repeat this conversation. But he knew his secretary would continue to remind him of the folly of the journey. "If Her Majesty catches us, you may explain our position to her." He had no doubt that all Elizabeth had to do was look at the young man and forgive all. Young Robin resembled his mother in appearance, but he carried the flare and humor of his sire—when he wasn't trying to appear older and more serious than he was. Elizabeth had fallen in love with the boy's sire when they were both near the same age as Robin was now. She could not help but be reminded of that youthful passion just looking at Robin.

Robin "humphed" loudly. But he couldn't hide his grin. He knew how to charm any lady, from the pretty glassblower's daughter up to the queen herself. And Betsy in between. He'd broken more than one heart in his short career. But his heart belonged only to Faith, the glassblower's daughter and his dearest friend since infancy.

Donovan and Robin rode another hour in comfortable silence. The shadows grew deeper around them, enclosing them in a bubble of their own limited visibility. Donovan resisted the urge to bring a ball of cold light to his hand. Soon the moon rose, full and bright. The shapes and shadows on the face of the Queen of Heaven stood out in stark contrast to the clear sky. Dew glistened on the verge grasses like tears on a maiden's cheeks. By this silvery light Donovan could see the road ahead well enough to guide them another quarter hour.

He recognized a gnarled oak at a minor crossroad. One more hill and depression to cross.

Deep forest crowded the road at the bottom of the hill. Branches from trees on either side interlaced, blocking out most of the moonlight. A perfect haven for bandits, Gypsies, and vagabonds.

Donovan loosened his sword in its scabbard. Robin followed suit. They had both traveled this way before.

The evening breeze intensified. A new chill ran through Donovan's blood. Presentiment, not a change in the temperature. He slowed his horse. Robin reined in beside him. He withdrew his sword fully from its utilitarian sheath.

"I'm not certain cold steel will deter what waits for us," Donovan whispered.

"Creatures of the Otherworld fear iron. Steel is born of iron." Robin leveled his blade at a peculiar rustling in the underbrush.

"Not all denizens of the Otherworld fear iron. Some shy from silver, some from Holy Water."

Robin crossed himself.

Donovan heaved a heavy sigh. Holy Water only worked if the caster truly believed. Robin did. Donovan didn't know what he believed in. Most of his scattered faith had died with his twin brother, Griffin the Elder. He had steel in his sword and dagger. He had silver in his coins and buttons. They would have to do, no matter what they faced, mortal or eldritch.

"Ready, Robin?" He took three deep breaths, triggering heightened awareness in all of his senses.

Donovan might not have Hal's easy access to flames, or Dee's ability to shift the earth under an enemy's feet, or Betsy's affinity with storms to confuse and misdirect an attack, but he knew how to fight man to man.

"Aye, sir. I've only mundane senses and the strength of my arm. Should be enough to guard your back and send any lurkers retreating with their tails between their legs."

"Make your noble ancestors proud, son." Together they nudged their horses forward with a touch from their heels.

Shadows took form; moved into the center of the rutted road. Hulking forms with indistinct edges. Roughly the form of men, but . . .

Silver chains encircled their necks and pierced their ears.

"Wolves, sir," Robin whispered through his teeth.

"More than wolves. Less than men."

"How do we fight them?"

The strange creatures were upon them before Donovan could think. He slashed at grasping paws, jabbed at lunging forms, kicked snapping jaws away from his horse. His steed reared, rolling its eyes. Donovan clung to its back with his knees, wielding his weapons without interruption. Beside him, Robin employed the same tactics. He nearly fell twice, but kept his seat.

The lead attacker howled at the moon. His eerie call made Donovan's horse prance and plunge in terror. More shadowy forms gathered in the trees.

Donovan slashed at the howler. Its ear, studded with silver buttons and short chains, landed on the road. A deep gash in its neck spurted blood.

A man collapsed in the road, clutching his wounds and moaning in pain. All traces of the wolf vanished. Clearly a man, naked except for his silver adornment. He scrabbled desperately seeking the wolf's ear that lay beside him.

The other five howling attackers fell back, content to
wait for easier prey. Three bled heavily. Pale skin shone
through patches of dark fur. The rough lupine outline
shifted, became more upright. A man stared back at him
with glowing red eyes, filled with pain and . . . despair.

Donovan gulped and prayed for strength to whatever
God or Goddess listened.

"Werewolves," he hissed. "Solitary creatures hunting in
unnatural packs. First at Kirkenwood, then on the outskirts
of London. Now here. The same pack or different ones?"

As of one mind, Donovan and Robin jabbed their heels
into their horses' flanks and pelted through the dark reaches
of the road.

"Sweet Jesu! I saw them shift," Robin said quietly.

He might not have spoken at all. Still, Donovan heard
his fear and shaking faith.

"Aye. We must report this."

"Only a priest can deal with this abomination," Robin
agreed.

"I wish Dr. Dee were still in this country. He'd know
what to do." The foremost magician and alchemist in Europe surely had a spell or a potion to defeat or cure the
horrible creatures.

"Fire, silver, and Holy Water. The copse must be burned
and the wolves rooted from their foul nest." Robin crossed
himself again. "Mayhap Her Majesty will dispatch a bishop
to do the job."

"Whatever is done must be finished by tomorrow night,
or they will transform into ordinary humans until the next
full moon." Had they truly lain in wait specifically for him?
All the tales he had read indicated that werewolves were
solitary beings, outcast by both wolves and mankind. They
protected their territories fiercely. To find more than one
in a district was unusual, to say the least. To find five, possibly
more, spoke of great evil.

Which of his and England's enemies had the power to
control were creatures' base instincts and make them
hunt together?

He prayed that none of the forces of chaos surrounding
Mary directed such powerful beings tainted by the Otherworld. Spanish, French, Protestant, or Catholic, who would
dare? Who was so desperate?

"Surely their wounds will betray them," Robin suggested. "The local priest need only seek out those who bleed from knife and sword wounds on the morrow."

"The moon is still full. They will all heal by dawn, without scars. The lost ear will knit back into place. We must act tonight."

And he must postpone his visit with Mary. An extra day for news of his presence to filter south to London and the ears of the queen. He did not look forward to feeling the lash of her tongue, or possibly a trip to the Tower for the transgression of visiting the exiled queen.

"You ride to London and the queen at dawn," Donovan ordered. "Tell her what we encountered. She will draw her own conclusions. But she must have this news."

"I need not reveal to her why we ride through this district, milord." Robin grinned in conspiracy. His fine teeth gleamed in the moonlight.

"Intelligent lad. I value your discretion."

"The queen values yours."

Late evening, 4 July, 1574. The Convent of Montmatre north of Paris.

Hal jerked his head slightly toward the Lady Chapel as Deirdre passed him. He knelt in the back of the convent church in an attitude of prayer waiting for the Compline bell to ring. Dee nodded ever so slightly to indicate she understood the need for secrecy. A nun clutched Dee's elbow quite firmly as she escorted the girl to the choir. Clearly the archaic fear of males still lingered in this cloister.

Protestants firmly believed in marriage for all, including priests and other clerics. Since that time, men and women had become easier in each other's presence. Cloisters and celibacy had no place. Except in countries still dominated by the Church in Rome.

The Mass seemed to go on for hours. Hal's knees protested the extended time upon the cold stone floor. But he dared not wiggle about too much, or rise even slightly lest the sisters decide to throw him out for disrespect, or worse. He just could not understand why religious folk required a body to willingly endure so much discomfort to demonstrate his faith.

Back home, Father Peter and Da had formed a happy blend of the old pagan rituals with enough Christian gloss on top to satisfy the busybodies who thought they alone professed the correct religion. Hal had little hope that anyone outside Kirkenwood would adopt a similar attitude any time soon.

So he ignored the ache in his knees and lower back, and the restrictions imposed upon him and his cousin. For tonight. For the seeming safety of stout stone walls between them and the outside world and whatever stalked the city on the night of the full moon.

But he could not, would not, be separated from Dee, or the dogs tonight. Danger waited for them just beyond those walls.

He'd heard too many rumors to feel safe.

At last the sisters filed out of the church toward their solitary cells. Hal waited impatiently for the last of them to troop past him before he made his rounds with Helwriaeth and Coffa at his heels. Unbidden, he checked all of the latches on all of the gates, reinforcing even the stoutest bars with a magical thread. The doors must remain closed until sunrise when he, and only he, lifted the wards.

The rain continued pounding into the many puddles. No trace of the moon glowed to light his silent progress around the walled grounds.

The hair on his arms, his back, and his nape stood on end in anticipation. Someone, some*thing* awaited him beyond the protection of the convent.

Chapter 10

3 July, 1574. Nether Pedly, England.

LIGHT, song, and beer fumes poured out of the public room of the inn. Donovan dismounted and threw his reins to the reluctant stable boy who shuffled out to greet them. Robin slid off his own mount stiffly. The creak of saddle leather might have been his joints. He bent double massaging his knees and thighs. As he gradually righted, his hands kneaded his butt and back and finally he shrugged and twisted his shoulders.

"Feel better?" Donovan asked as his secretary sighed at the end of his ritual.

"Actually, yes, I do." Robin pasted a smile on his long face and preceded Donovan into the pub.

"Your parents would be proud of your fortitude if not your ability to control your horse," Donovan chuckled as he hoisted his bags to his shoulder and followed.

"You have never told me about my parents. Not even their names." Robin turned in the doorway, challenging Donovan to evade the issue once more.

"You are my son now. Adopted legally. And I am proud of you." Donovan pushed past him into the doorway. He had to stop thinking about his monthly reports to Elizabeth on Robin's health and well-being as evidence that the queen still had a claim on Robin.

Donovan paused in the entry a moment to let his eyes adjust to the smoky torchlight. His nose itched at the smell of warm, unwashed bodies, spilled ale, and rancid meat.

Two dozen men singing off-key.

Robin winced as a barmaid's voice soared above the cacophony and cracked on an impossible note. "Mayhap I

can teach these people true music while we reside here,"
he groaned. He had his mother's delicate ear and voice for
a tune. Donovan remembered the hours of Robin's youth
while the boy taught himself to play lute and timbrel. He'd
also pestered Donovan endlessly until he bought a virginal
for him to play as well. They'd both whiled away many an
hour at court in Edinburgh with music of their own making.

"Doubtful we can teach these yokels anything. They only
want to join in the crowd, not make music." Donovan allowed his bag to slip to the floor with a thump. "Besides,
you leave for London at dawn."

Robin looked as if he might protest.

Donovan waved away his objections before they were
voiced.

The music, if you could call it that, continued unabated,
but the landlord noticed them and ambled over, proffering
frothy mugs of the local brew.

Donovan accepted the tankard gratefully. He downed
half of it before speaking. "Where can we find the local
constable, mine host?" he asked at last.

"Why?" The landlord lost most of his jovial expression.
Not once had he shown any deference to the richly clothed
lords who stood before him.

"We were set upon by scoundrels just north of here,"
Robin supplied.

"In the dark patch of woods that crowds the road at the
bottom of the last hill," Donovan added. The hair on his
nape bristled. Something was wrong, and not just with the
landlord's attitude.

"Ah, milords, just some of the lads with a bit too much
of the drink in them." The landlord laughed shallowly. His
smile did not reach his cheeks, let alone his eyes. "Think
nothing of it. I can see they harmed you not. Come. I've
rooms to let and a fine supper laid. Ye'll not go to bed
hungry."

" 'Twasn't some of the lads," Donovan insisted. His voice
took on an edge that promised consequences with all the
weight of his title and wealth to back him.

Robin crossed himself.

"In the name of the queen, I raise the hue and cry for
the five men dressed as wolves who attacked me on the
road," Donovan announced.

The room suddenly grew still. Each of the raucous songsters halted in mid note.

"You do not truly want to do this, milord," the innkeeper said quietly.

"And why would I not seek to bring disruptive forces to justice for violating the queen's peace and jeopardizing innocent travelers?" Donovan turned icy calm around a roiling mass of magic that begged him for release.

"Withdraw your demands, milord. Please. 'Tis not wise." The landlord leaned forward. The garlic and beer on his breath nearly sent Donovan reeling.

Donovan stood his ground. In a fight he was taller with a longer reach than the landlord. And he was armed.

Robin edged closer, guarding his back against the mass of men who watched the confrontation with rapt attention.

Donovan resisted the urge to draw steel and be done with the affair. Sword and dagger did not close arguments. They tended to open them wider and cause more trouble. He pulled on every diplomatic skill he'd learned in his years at court: Elizabeth's, Mary's, and then James'. Calm resolve replaced the anger. But the magic still itched just beneath his skin.

"Think you, if we could rid those woods of the menace that stalks us, would we not have done so?" the landlord hissed. "Think you, this one small village could stand against the forces that gather there?"

"Why do they gather?" Donovan finally asked the question that had plagued him ever since he realized who—or rather *what*—had attacked him.

"Power attracts them."

"A magician lurks nearby," Donovan muttered. He should have sniffed out the presence of one who had been touched by the Netherworld.

"Nay, 'tis greater power than some woods witch or alchemist," the landlord sneered. " 'Tis the plots and turmoil over t' Chatsworth Hall that draws them. The Catholic devils seek to use demons and creatures of the night to free Mary." He spat into the floor rushes.

"No," Donovan gasped. "Mary would never . . ."

"Bah, the Catholic witch sits like a spider in her lair, spinning plots instead of webs." The landlord finally took his attention off Donovan and surveyed the room. With a wave of his hand the singing resumed, somewhat subdued compared to the joyous riot of sound from before.

"Why do they sing so loudly?" Robin asked. His long face grew longer with his puzzled frown.

"Easier to forget what waits outside on the nights of the full moon. Now do ye want the rooms or no? Supper at least."

"Yes, we'll sup in our room and be on our way in the morning," Donovan agreed.

His heart sank. Once again, outside forces sought to manipulate Mary, sully her good name with their own schemes to grab power. Who? The Spanish? The Pope? Or discontented Englishmen who resented Elizabeth's peace and prosperity simply because it came not from their own making?

3 July, 1574. Near midnight, Paris and environs.

Yassimine ignored the magical tug on her senses. The silver rings in her nipples burned slightly more than usual.

But a scent, a heartbeat, a presence demanded her attention. She had to find out what—or who—was so much stronger than The Master that its magic overrode his.

Was this her opportunity for freedom and power of her own? Or her doom? For good or ill, she had to know. For half a moon, The Master had carefully stripped away her controls, withdrawing the drugs of suppression, clothing her in sensuous silk, bringing her body alive with sex, and sumptuous meals consisting only of barely cooked meat.

But he'd given her a new piercing. A most humiliating ring burned her pubis. He'd waited until she was swollen from his sexual assault upon her. Then while she sprawled naked and relaxed, gnawing on a succulent bone, he had swooped down upon her with a white hot needle. She had screamed and fought. His control of the silver was faster.

She wished she'd eaten his remaining hand in revenge. Just thinking of the sweet taste of his flesh made the silver burn deeper.

She ignored the pains. Running naked through the streets alleys of the city on the nights of the full moon, she could rejoice in releasing her true self. She exulted in the freedom and the assault on her senses. *But you and your kind are not welcome here. You are not worshiped as gods,* a tiny voice in her head reminded her of the dangers that came with her freedom. Tonight she would live her destiny, despite the fears of ignorant Christians.

The muddy waters of the River Seine presented no problem to her. She swam them easily. The women of her clan had taught her early how to survive in water, how to escape marauders by using the water to mask her scent and provide her with secret hiding places. Now she entered the river without a splash.

The current was stronger than she expected. The water deeper. The streams that crisscrossed the broad steppes of her home did not often grow to these proportions. She could not let the surprise overwhelm her. She lengthened her strokes, using arms and legs equally. The fretful moon tried to slip free of its cloud cover and failed. Still, it commanded her senses. Pockets of mist enveloped her, then evaporated, as did the silvery light.

Barely chilled, she climbed the opposite embankment easily and shook all over, shedding extra water. Her chains chimed delicately with the movement. Once hot and demanding, the water had cooled the silver links as well as her body. Curiosity cooled her never-ending appetite for meat, hot and bloody. She set off at an easy lope, casting about for some clue to her destination.

Due north. Beyond the city. She ran lightly, barely touching the ground, leaving few prints.

She stopped short, digging in her heels. The chains grew hot where they pierced her skin. The collar about her neck tightened. The Master was not pleased.

"I am stronger than this," she growled to herself and continued her search. Her steps dragged now. Her chains burned wherever they touched her. Still she could not stop.

A scent came to her strongly, four sources of magic blended into two, then to one. The magic nearly matched her own. One of her own!

Home and freedom called to her. She loped on, oblivious to the angry welts growing on her nipples, navel, and pubis.

She slowed to climb the heights above the city.

A stone fortress loomed atop the hill before her. Moonlight glittered on flecks within the stone walls. The one who called to her sheltered there. No mundane could keep her out with a full moon giving her power beyond her ken. She dashed across the open space to the front gate. It resisted her touch. She leaned against it with all her weight and strength. A slight shift of the wooden panels rattled the crossbar. Another shove. The gate remained impermeable.

3 July, 1574. Approaching midnight, the Convent Montmatre.

With the convent as secure as he could make it, Hal tiptoed into the Lady Chapel behind the high altar of the convent church to warn Dee.

"Did you hear?" Dee asked in French the moment Hal poked his head into the tiny chapel filled with lit prayer candles. She knelt before the little altar as if keeping an extended prayer vigil. Coffa sprawled in the shadows by the north wall. Helwriaeth joined his littermate.

The smell of burning candle wax and incense made him sneeze. He held his breath lest the explosion of air waked someone in the dorter and they came to investigate.

Hal decided he'd best kneel beside Deirdre in case some prowling warden came looking for them, no matter how much his knees ached.

He had to adjust his thinking for a moment before the French words came to him. "About the murders?" Hal whispered back as he crossed himself and bowed before the altar, all the while keeping his senses extended for any sign of intruders.

"Yes. Last night when the moon was full and the night before. Probably again tonight if the pattern holds true."

"What pattern?" Suddenly Hal wished he'd made the effort to study as much as Dee did. He'd spent too many hours sparring with his twin in the practice yard and not enough of them reading. Still, a Pendragon needed strength in his body as well as his mind.

"Supernatural predators," she hissed back impatiently. "Those who use the full moon to hunt are active on the night before and the night after as well."

"Then why didn't we sense anything last night? We were camped barely ten miles from the city."

"This beast seems confined to the old city on the *Isle de la Cité* and within the neighborhoods, the quarters, in close proximity to it."

Something about Dee's silence at the end of that statement said more than her words.

"I take it supernatural predators do not usually confine their hunting to one small area?"

"*Peut-être* it finds the hunting too good in the crowded confines of the *cité* and the Latin Quarter."

More silence. Hal used the time to cast about with his hearing and sense of smell augmented by his contact with Helwriaeth. The dog remained alert but easy in the shadows. He sensed that all others within the convent slept. Deeply.

Too deeply.

With a thought, Hal commanded Helwriaeth to patrol. The dog lumbered to his feet, resentful that he must perform this chore alone.

"What?" Dee asked, alarmed by Helwriaeth's departure and the sudden lifting of Coffa's ears.

" 'Tis passing strange that none of the nuns, the lay sisters, the lay workers, or the guests so much as stir. Not for a drink of water or a trip to the privy. Not even shifting position because they dream. Helwriaeth does not believe they dream."

Dee lifted her head and sniffed the air, much as Coffa would. Her eyes narrowed as she concentrated on the augmented senses that bombarded her. Hal knew what she experienced, knew the incredible bond with a familiar. Suddenly he had to join Helwriaeth. He couldn't be without the dog for one more moment.

Then he heard it. A rattling at the front gate of the courtyard. Someone . . . Some*thing* wanted to gain entrance to the convent.

Chapter 11

FRUSTRATED, Yassimine circled the entire fortress twice, pounding on every gate. All of them resisted her. She slammed her fists against the main gate whimpering her disappointment.

Why did one of her own call to her so strongly and then reject her?

She tried again, putting all of her strength, her magic, and her will into the blows.

At last she howled her frustration, crying real tears for the first time in five years.

"Did you hear that?" I stopped Hal from leaving my side in the Lady Chapel with a trembling hand upon his arm. My other hand tangled in Coffa's ruff. Her guard hairs bristled, and a low growl rumbled through her throat.

"What is that unearthly howl?" Hal asked. He broke free of my restraint and ran to the low postern door behind the altar of the Lady Chapel. I stayed close upon his heels. A slight shiver ran through him as he peeked out the door to survey the convent grounds. He wrapped his arms about himself as if suddenly chilled. Helwriaeth loped back to him, pressing his considerable bulk against Hal.

"An unholy predator of the night," I breathed. The phrase echoed with the resonance of an ancient scroll. Which one? What had I read about such creatures?

Fear put a lock on my memories. I could only react.

Coffa wanted to retreat to the safely of the church. So did I. But if I was to be the Pendragon, I had to face this creature and divert or destroy it.

I could do this. I was an adult. At least I felt like one sometimes.

"We have to do something," Hal reminded me.

"What?" Something about silver tickled my mind.

"Doesn't silver control it?"

"Silver wounds some nether creatures." I remembered a small book, heavy in religious philosophy denouncing such creatures with little useful information about defeating them. Except for one fact. "Ordinary iron or steel wounds and causes pain, but the creatures heal quickly. Sometimes the wound only lasts a few minutes. Then the creature bounds back stronger than ever. We saw it happen . . . that other time." That was why Malcolm's arrow had only slowed the attacking werewolf. That was why Malcolm had died under the savage jaws of the ravening beast.

"A silver cross?" Hal asked.

Barely pausing to think, we both reached for the rosary I kept in my scrip.

"Gold," I said, disappointed at the wealth represented by the gold cross and decade beads. The rest of the chain was yellowed ivory beads. All of them needed replacing. Only the cross with the circled arms remained from the original. I'd seen its ghostly reflection upon Arthur's breast.

Memory of his blessing did not bolster my courage or improve my thinking.

"I don't know what to do, Hal." Defeat dragged at my shoulders. All the sleep I had missed in the last weeks piled heavy weights on my feet and hands.

How could I expect to follow in my father's footsteps if I could not think beyond the mournful howl outside the gates?

"Stop, please!" I held my hands over my ears, trying to block out the eerie call of the beast. The noise ran through me like tiny knives had entered my blood. My skin wanted to burst to be free of the sound. I needed to join it, run in circles, chase my own tail.

"We retreat," Hal replied sadly. He grabbed Hel-wriaeth's ruff and tugged the dog away from the gate. He could only tug and hopefully guide. A wolfhound with the scent of prey or danger in its nose made its own decisions.

Helwriaeth decided to stay and challenge the monster awaiting entry. Coffa ignored my suggestions to return to the cell assigned to me. She stood stalwartly between me and it. A deep growl rumbled in her throat and her fur stood up all along her spine. Her bushy tail grew to twice its normal size.

"Can that thing break through your wards?" I asked.

He shrugged. "The gates won't open."

The pounding on the outside grew more fierce and demanding.

"But that thing could break them to pieces." He turned wide and frightened eyes to me.

"Why did that thing venture outside the *cité* tonight?" I edged back toward the church. Once before, werewolves had roamed outside their normal range to find me, attracted by the magic I wove for the faeries. I had not worked any magic today. Not consciously.

Did I ooze magic from my pores as sweat?

I did not want this responsibility, or to carry on my heritage. I only wanted to be safe, at home, with Uncle Donovan protecting me. My lower lip trembled, and moisture burned my eyes.

If I used my magic to keep the creature out of the Convent of Montmatre, would it then kill more innocents closer to Paris?

If I did nothing, it would certainly kill me, and Hal, our dogs, and the good sisters.

"What would your father have done?" Hal asked.

Several moments passed before his words penetrated my loop of self-doubt and misery.

"Think, Dee." Hal shook my shoulders. His voice took on a desperate note. The gates had begun to buckle. "What would your father have done? You've read his journals. You know him almost as well as if he'd raised you."

But I did not know my father. The script within the journals was encrypted. Gibberish to my untrained eye.

I knew a few of the stories, however, passed from the Gypsies, through Aunt Meg, to me. My father had faced Otherworldly creatures and survived. He'd also saved an entire camp of Gypsies from the enchantment of an Elfin Wild Hunt. That story was a favorite around the fire on cold winter evenings.

I almost felt my da and King Arthur and all of my ancestors who had been Pendragons make the decision for me.

"Circle. We need to draw a circle." My da had used his staff to draw his circle all the way around the camp. I had no staff, no tools, nothing but myself and my dog.

I moved out into the courtyard of the convent. A modest open space stood between the imperiled main gate and the stone buildings of church, dorter, guesthouse, stables, and cloister.

"You go right, deasil, I'll go left, widdershins. Cover the entire courtyard so that the beast has no space outside the circle to get to any of the buildings. Use your heel to draw the circle, and keep a hand on Helwriaeth the whole time," I instructed him.

Hal nodded once, grabbed his dog, and began the task, starting at the center of the gate. I followed, going in the opposite direction with Coffa firmly in hand.

Exhausting work. The magic flowed out of me into the line I drew by dragging my heel. I dared not think about how tired I would be at the end. I dared not think what would happen if either of us faltered. Half a spell was worse than none at all. Instead of creating a barrier between us and that thing, a broken circle would invite it in.

A gate panel splintered. I'd worked only a quarter way around the cloister. I couldn't protect the entire convent; with all the outbuildings and gardens it covered acres.

Hal and I met in front of the church. We crossed our circles and continued on. Coffa whined. She wanted to dash out and sink her teeth into the throat of the enemy. I needed her beside me, giving me strength, guiding my path so that I did not falter.

One board on the gate broke in two. Pieces flew across the line of the circle. The circle was not yet complete.

A hairy fist (paw?) followed the broken wood into the cloister.

I shuddered, paused, swallowed hard. How could I continue? My nearly thirteen years might be enough for my body to believe itself an adult, but inside, I was just a child. I could not challenge that *thing* physically or magically.

"Keep going, Dee," Hal insisted.

I gathered the shreds of my strength and my resolve and continued on. Past the stable, past the gatehouse. Blindly I continued to draw a circle. Step. Drag. Step. Drag. Sweat poured into my eyes and down my back. Coffa leaned heavily against me. Her whines turned solicitous.

Something solid bumped into me. I screamed. A hand clamped over my mouth.

"Easy, Dee. We're done. Easy," Hal whispered.

Then I looked down at the line we had drawn. Our heels met.

"Not quite done. We need to cross the path." The words came out on a choking cough.

One last push of strength. One more step.

A shimmering wall of power snapped into place and rose up and over us in a perfect dome. I sank to the ground, too tired to even think about moving. Hal plopped down beside me. The dogs nosed the edge of the double circle around its full circumference.

"They're inspecting the work for imperfection," Hal told me.

I didn't care.

We huddled together for hours, listening, waiting. Praying. The moon set.

The pounding on the gate ceased. The creature loosed a mighty howl of despair.

I almost felt its very human heart break.

4 July, 1574. Past midnight, the Convent of Montmatre outside Paris.

"'Tis gone," Hal breathed.

"Are you sure?" Dee asked.

He traced the dark circles shadowing her eyes with a gentle finger. She needed sleep and food. They had both expended a lot of magic this night, she more than him.

"I am sure. 'Tis gone." Hal stirred, hoping to find enough strength to rise and break the circle of protection before stumbling to his bed.

"How do you know?" Dee made it to her knees, then slumped.

Hal knew how she felt. "I just know. Something here." He touched his empty belly with a clenched fist. Chills began to rack his body.

Helwriaeth ambled over, offering his shoulder for Hal to lean against. He did so, grateful for the dog's massive strength and loyalty. A sloppy tongue across his face helped restore him a little.

"Me, too," Dee replied. "I feel it, too. A terrible emptiness that wants to shatter me. But I did not know if I could trust it."

"We are both too tired to think. Go to bed, Dee." For the first time since leaving home, they would sleep separately. She wouldn't wrap him in her arms to ease the nightmares that tore at his sanity when they slept in cemeteries—the only place safe from prowlers and watchmen. The convent graveyard was too close to the guesthouse for comfort. He knew the ghosts of the dead would find him tonight. He knew they'd remind him of all the things he should have done, needed to do, the responsibilities he shrugged off, the dangers that awaited him and he postponed.

"Help me break the circle," she said listlessly. Coffa offered a shoulder as a brace to help Dee rise.

"We created it together. We have to break it together," Hal echoed her. "Do we have to do it at the starting point?" He looked across the courtyard, not certain he could walk as far as the gate. It looked a mile away and getting farther by the minute.

"I don't think so." She swayed on her feet. Her eyes locked onto the gate. "It was human once," she whispered. "Part of it still is. It's more lost than we are. My mother . . ."

"Nonsense. You're just too tired to think it through." Hal shivered at her words. He didn't dare believe them. If he did, then he might understand too much of tonight's adventure. All he wanted was to sleep long and hard. When he woke, he would attend Mass, eat a hearty breakfast, and then he would lead Dee into the city where she would complete her quest.

Determinedly, he smudged the marks of the circle he had drawn. Only the outside line dissipated. The shimmering dome of power faded to half its original light. Dee's imprint remained as firm as the dome.

"Dee?" he reminded her of her task.

She continued staring at the broken gate as she stumbled to the edge of the circle. A halfhearted swipe of her foot banished the magic that protected them and kept them confined. He stepped to the other side. Dee didn't move.

He reached back to grab her arm and shake her out of her reverie. Coffa growled and shifted closer to her mistress. Helwriaeth responded with a deeper warning and a nip to Coffa's ear.

What was happening? The dogs always got along.

"Dee?" Hal sent a tendril of magic into his cousin's eye to reinforce his question. It cost him dearly. He swayed with dizziness.

Finally, she shook herself free of her thoughts with a visible effort.

"Go to bed, Dee. We'll talk more about this tomorrow."

"Yes," she promised. Without looking at him she trudged toward the dormitory, Coffa at her heels. Three times she stopped and cast her gaze back to the gate. He thought he saw her mouth the word "mother." Then she shook her head and plodded on, only to stop again after a few steps.

"What is the matter, Dee? We banished that thing," Hal challenged her.

"No, we didn't. We only stalled it. We will meet it again. Soon. I do not think any of us will come through the confrontation whole or unchanged."

A chill of presentiment ran up Hal's spine. He knew he would not sleep this night. Or any other night soon to come.

"Was it a werewolf?" he asked finally. He'd seen werewolves before. Two years ago. Magical fire had banished them. But they looked like oversized wolves. Except for their red eyes. The creature that hunted them tonight had used its paw like a human fist. "What was it?"

Dee raised her shoulders in a shrug. Her chin trembled and a tear slid down her cheek. "I don't know what it was. I don't know how to fight it or protect us from it."

"Neither do I," Hal muttered. He kissed the top of her head and pushed her toward the dormitory and sleep.

Slowly, dragging every step, he began a prowl of the entire convent. Better to walk in agony than sleep tonight and dream of that *thing*.

Chapter 12

4 July, 1574. The Convent of Montmatre.

THE nuns fussed and cooed over me the next morning. Sister Marie Hope stuffed extra bread into my pack and totally ignored Hal and the dogs.

"Now remember, little one, you may return to us any night you cannot find safe lodging in the *cité*." Reverend Mother chewed her lip, then spoke again, patting my head. "*Peut-être* you should return to us each night. The *cité* is not safe for a maid."

"The dogs and I will protect her," Hal insisted. He scowled with his fiercest expression.

I was too tired to say anything or cringe away from Sister Marie Celeste and her violent prejudice against "nonbelievers." In her way, she was as dangerous to me as the monster who'd tried to break into the convent last night.

Long after I had retired to my bed, I had lain awake, fearing to dream of the beast Hal and I had barely held at bay. If the beast was the instrument of the Protestant faction and preyed only upon Catholics, then why had it come for Hal and me last night? Neither of us professed the Catholic faith. Neither of us professed much of any faith at all.

I suddenly felt empty. Bereft. Faith had sustained my father through many trials and tribulations. I would need faith of some kind in the days to come. I knew it deep in my bones.

If only I could read and understand his journals I might catch a glimpse of true faith.

Papa, help me! I prayed to the only source of comfort I knew.

A ghostly hand rested upon my shoulder in support.

I smiled my thanks to the sisters. Coffa led the way through the gate, more eager for the next adventure than I. Hal followed me. Strangely enough, Helwriaeth trailed reluctantly behind, tail between his legs. He knew something . . . something terrible but important. What?

By daylight, no one questioned our entrance into the *cité*, though many people shied away from the dogs. We listened to the whispers in market square after market square. Speculation about the monster who terrorized the city passed from merchant to housewife to servant to tavernkeeper in hushed tones accompanied by wards against the evil eye and frightened peeks over the shoulder.

Out loud, the Parisians spoke excitedly of the festivities when Henri III returned from Poland. They wanted pageants and masques, processions and tourneys. The coronation itself was for the nobility alone inside the cathedral, though.

We skulked and eavesdropped until well after noon waiting for someone to say something that might reveal strong prejudice for or against the Huguenots.

"I'm hungry, Dee," Hal announced as he tore a baguette in half and handed me the slightly smaller portion. Both dogs sat prettily, begging for their share of the bread.

"You ate last night," I admonished Coffa. She stared back at me all hungry innocence. I broke off a small portion of the soft bread and proffered it on my palm. My dog nibbled it gently from my hand, her teeth never touching my skin.

"Sacre bleu!" a woman gasped, holding her hands over her heart. "It did not savage you!" Then she fanned herself with her apron.

"The dogs are pets," I replied, keeping my eyes cast down. On my travels I'd learned that adults responded better to shy children than to bold ones.

"Noble pets. Too noble for one dressed in threadbare clothes and dirty bare feet." The woman moved closer, peering at me intently.

Hal tugged on my sleeve. I sensed his anxiety to avoid confrontation, to be gone from this overly curious woman.

"Mayhap you be a *Huguenot sorcière* and the beast your familiar. Many have been savaged, killed, dismembered by such a beast!" She grabbed my sleeve before I could dart away.

Coffa growled. The woman clung tighter.

"Nay, Madame," I protested, turning my eyes up to her. I put all the innocence and horror I could muster into my gaze. "I but came to the *cité* this day in search of my noble father!"

A crowd began to gather. Their murmurs rose ever higher, approaching shouts.

"Death to all Protestant dogs," a voice rang out from the back of the crowd. It tolled through the increasing noise like a bell calling the faithful to Mass.

Coffa pressed tighter to me. Her sides rumbled with her protests. Helwriaeth joined her, adding his deep bass tones to the rising turmoil.

Run, Hal commanded me with his mind. *We've got to get out of here.*

Where? Where can we go that is safe? Panic sent my mind in circles. I could see no farther than the hate and the fear in the eyes of the woman who held me.

My father had never run from a fight in his life. His faith had sustained him. I believed in nothing.

"Papa help me!"

"Show your rosary," Hal commanded loudly as he grabbed my other arm. The dogs wiggled in front of me, pushing the woman away. She let go of my sleeve to cross herself.

Her movements gave me enough time and space to fish the chain of gold and ivory beads from my sleeve.

"Protestant witch, how dare you brandish holy relics!" The woman grabbed for the golden cross. Greed now lit her eyes rather than fear.

Instinctively I moved my hand to grasp the cross, protect it from those who did not know its true significance. King Arthur of legend had owned this circled cross. The rosary beads came later.

The woman's hands claimed the beads and yanked.

I tugged back.

The chain broke, beads spilled over the cobbles. Several people dropped to their knees to claim the precious gold and ivory for themselves.

I ran.

Hal led the way. Coffa made a path for us. Helwriaeth

guarded our rear. The crowd fell away from the dogs' dripping teeth and angry snarls. Their brindled fur stood straight up the full length of their spines and tails, making them seem even larger than they were.

Sobbing in fear and bewilderment, I stumbled in their wake. Tears blurred my vision and made me clumsier than before. The third time I fell, or was it the fifth, Hal hauled me to my feet and kept his arm around me. "A few more steps, Dee. Just a little way to go," he murmured encouragement to me.

I looked around. We passed beneath *Le Châtelet,* and onto *Le Pont Notre Dame.* Shops lined either side of the bridge. Vendors called out their wares and prices. Shoppers raised their voices to bargain. Scholars gave lectures to robed students. The cacophony grew. The dogs dropped their ears in confusion. They lifted their noses and whined, unable to detect our enemies among the mass of people.

"Where?" I asked, looking around, as confused as the dogs.

"Church."

Peace descended upon my rampant emotions. Of course. The sanctuary of the church, still held sacred in this Catholic country. Only one remained in England, the old freedom of Whitefriars where my father had taken shelter among the glassblowers. But it was abandoned now to pigeons, an occasional vagabond, a few madmen, and ghosts. We could shelter in any church in France, free from persecution, until a new plan came to mind.

Church. The place my father always sought when troubled.

The thought of a dim nave, made mysterious and glorious with stained glass and candles, soft music, and a gentle God straightened my spine and firmed my steps. With my newfound assurance I spared the time to listen for signs of pursuit.

We stepped onto the *Isle de la Cité* just as the mob pursuing us took possession of the bridge. Stones hit the cobbles around us with force. Angry voices grew closer. The crowds on the bridge parted. I sensed massive numbers of people joining the original throng. The irate people of the market square had raised the hue and cry.

Part of me wondered if that was the proper term for the mob that followed us. Did French law define the duty of a neighborhood to pursue criminals en masse? I did not know.

I hastened my pace up the steps of the massive stone edifice before us. Hal kept his arm about me, urging me to greater haste.

A stone hit Helwriaeth's haunch. He yipped in pain even as he turned to face his attackers.

Somehow Hal ushered me up the stairs and marshaled the dogs into the narthex of the cathedral. Somehow we stayed ahead of the mob.

A shadowy black form loomed ahead of us, blocking access to the nave.

With my heart in my throat and footsteps ringing loud and close in my ears I choked out the one word that would save us. *"Sanctuaire!"*

"For people, not for beasts," the shadow growled in tones akin to the dogs he condemned.

"Try keeping them out," Hal muttered. He shoved aside the shadow that proved to be nothing more than a black-robed and cowled man.

The mob pelted up the steps in our wake, unheeding of the sanctuary. My memory of the vision of the St. Bartholomew's Eve Massacre two years ago flashed across my mind's eye. Once their bloodlust was up, these people would stop at nothing.

"The crypt," I ordered Hal.

He did not hear me. Or did not heed me. He and Helwriaeth aimed straight for the high altar—the traditional place of sanctuary.

"Hal!" I insisted in tones that mimicked Aunt Fiona. I did not need magic to command attention. "We need to go to the crypt. It's the only safe place."

He followed me then. I closed the gate at the top of the stairs just as the first of our attackers came through the narthex into the nave. The cowled man had disappeared. I didn't know where and didn't care as long as he did not interfere.

The mob aimed for one of the side doors, convinced we had escaped them by that means. Their noise dissipated and quiet reigned. I did not trust the quiet. Coffa kept sniffing at the closed gate. Someone awaited us there.

Carefully, I made my way down steep staircases set into

stone, through damp passages and finally to the place I had only read about in arcane documents about the pilgrimage route of the mystery cults. But I remembered as clearly as if I had been there. A small chapel opened up at the end of a long tunnel, hewn out of solid rock, cramped and dripping. Only one small vigil light, encased in red glass, burned above the altar to light our way.

Hal sank down to the floor, eyes closed. Helwriaeth stood over him, fur still bristling. "Are we safe here?" he asked. He sounded exhausted. His eyes darted back and forth seeking the ghosts he always feared near cemeteries.

I lit a votive with a spark from the flint and steel left by the previous worshiper. I would not use magic in this sacred place. A place made sacred by the spring that still kept it cool and damp. People in need of spiritual guidance had come here in respect and awe with offerings to their goddess or gods long before Romans had brought their church to this place.

"We are safe here. Here is the beginning and the end of time. Here is where I will find some answers."

Some answers. Not all. Never all, my father's voice whispered to me from across the grave.

Goose bumps climbed my spine. But they were the good kind, the welcome-home kind, not the beware-danger-lurks kind.

4 July, 1574. The village of Nether Pedley, near Ashbourne, England.

Dawn came bright and early for Donovan. He'd sat up most of the night listening to the late night rain drip from the eaves of the inn. He remembered nights when he and Martha had stayed awake listening to the rain, talking quietly, loving each other.

The locket on his breast seemed to burn. He clutched it and his memories eased to the night he had spent with Mary. One night of loving. All he wanted was a lifetime of loving the exiled queen.

Water droplets glistened on the ends of maple leaves and turned spiderwebs silver. He was amazed at the perfection of the gossamer creations, as beautiful as his love for Mary.

But all of the beauty of the morning did not lighten his heart. Two of his children were missing. Mary had involved herself in—or been manipulated into—another plot to grab power from Elizabeth. The likelihood of charming his way past Bess, Countess of Shrewsbury, for an interview with Mary seemed unlikely. He fingered Betsy's locket and drew comfort from it.

The beginnings of a plan tickled his brain.

"I have ordered breakfast and the horses, Father," Robin said quietly from the doorway. He alone of all his children used the formal form of address to Donovan—though Betsy resorted to it when she wished to show her disapproval of her father. The others used the familiar "Da."

Donovan wished Robin would remove that barrier of formality.

"Will you have eggs with your beer and cheese or perhaps kidney pie?" Robin refused to look him in the eye.

"Neither," Donovan wanted to say. He had no appetite. But the day would be long and hard. "Eggs," he said aloud. "And ale, not beer."

Robin raised his brows at that. Since the importation of Flemish hops a generation ago that allowed the fermentation of beer, Englishmen, by and large, had nearly forsaken the traditional ale. They could not get enough of the stuff and complained bitterly if the brews were late, too new, too old, or flat. Beer seemed to have become a right more than a beverage.

"I ride alone to the manor," Donovan added, stretching up from his seat by the window. "You must hie to London with reports of the wolves we encountered."

"Lord Shrewsbury is more likely to respect your request for an interview with his . . . ah . . . guest if you arrive in a state worthy of your title and position at court," Robin reminded him.

" 'Tis Lady Shrewsbury who rules that household!" Donovan spat on half a laugh. Strong men trembled in their boots when Bess confronted them for perceived minor offenses. Even Elizabeth Regina walked warily around that lady's goodwill.

Elizabeth could not have contrived a surer guardian for
Mary.

Robin put on his winsome smile, the one he usually reserved for Faith the glassblower's daughter, his beloved.
His entire visage changed from sober clerk to handsome
lover.

"Perhaps you had best ride with me." Donovan changed
his mind. "I rely on your charm and your youthful fair
visage to win Bess' favor." He clapped his ward on the
shoulder. The boy's long face, sallow skin, and dark hair
would remind Bess of *someone*. She might not make the
connection of his parentage right away. But the puzzle
would intrigue her.

Bess loved nothing more than secrets. Secrets gave her
power over the powerful. She treasured them, hoarded
them, and wielded them prudently. She would love Robin
and the secrets he represented.

Would she be intrigued enough to allow Donovan a few
moments alone with Mary?

Before the dew had dried on the grass, they headed east.
Donovan liked riding cross-country, allowing his horse to
pick its way while he sorted his thoughts and settled his
emotions. On horseback he could find the inner stillness
necessary to working magic.

Today that stillness deserted him. Even touching Betsy's
locket did not soothe him. He could think of nothing but
Mary.

Something else nagged the back of his mind. He needed
to be doing something else, worrying, planning . . . what?

Visions of Mary banished all else from his mind. His
excitement rose with each passing mile. He'd see Mary
again, even if he had to climb up the outside of her tower
prison. His imagination ran rampant with his gallant actions
and a dramatic rescue of his love.

Robin left him in peace to daydream.

And then the sprawling manor of Chatsworth Hall rose
before them. Not a formidable prison after all. Just a magnificent home designed to keep a family and its guests
comfortable.

"Only one more dragon to vanquish," he muttered.

"Did you say something, Father?" Robin peered at him
queerly.

Had Donovan been talking to himself the entire ride? If so, the boy must doubt his sanity. Donovan must doubt his own sanity.

What had he forgotten?

"Bess will be like a dragon guarding the castle gates," Donovan explained.

"Yes. Quite." Robin pursed his lips.

Donovan shook his head. How could he have raised a child who preferred literal and precise words rather than mystical metaphors? The life of Kirkenwood Castle and all of the Kirkwoods revolved around Otherworldly concepts and symbolism.

Queen Elizabeth, beneath her literary allusions and fondness for masques and plays was a logical, determined (stubborn), practical thinker. Who else would think to pay off England's debts by revamping the coinage and changing the sumptuary laws, encouraging people to spend money and generate trade rather than strict economies and frugal living? She would love this young man if Donovan ever gave her the opportunity to know her natural son. If he ever told Robin the truth of his parentage.

Polite and efficient grooms took their horses at the main entrance to Chatsworth. An officious steward announced them. Bess received them in a small solar that caught the morning light. She did not stand to greet them or put aside her needlework. (Donovan noted that her stitches were not as fine or even as Mary's work.)

"Lady Shrewsbury," Donovan gave his best imitation of a courtly bow. But the old injury in his left thigh chose that moment to lock his knee. Robin had to haul him upright again by grabbing his elbow and pushing on his waist. "Haven't had that happen in a while," he muttered his apology.

"I know all about your gimpy leg, Milord of Kirkenwood," Bess replied harshly. Her sandy blonde hair had grayed considerably since Donovan had seen her last. She had put on weight, too. But the added roundness to her round face did not soften her expression or enhance her fading beauty—if she'd ever had any.

Donovan had loved one strong and determined woman. His second wife, Martha, had an inner core of steel that she had earned through many years of making hard decisions in a world that did not respect a woman's right to decide her fate. She had learned to work with men. Most of the time Donovan shied away from women with wills of their own. Too often they had adopted the manners of their queen without the strength of personality to back them up. Those women tended to bludgeon a man with their willfulness.

He preferred women more willing to defer to him. Women who needed his protection and advice. They were easier to figure out.

Bess would not be easy to read or to work with if she took a dislike to him or his request.

"My secretary and I journey to London to make report to our queen. We wished to pay our respects to you and your noble husband as we passed," Donovan explained. God's teeth, couldn't she offer a man a place to sit? His leg throbbed and threatened his balance. Robin hovered too close, trying to protect him when he least wanted protecting. He wanted to get through this interview quickly so he could see Mary.

"Chatsworth is too far off the main roads for casual visitors and acquaintances. You have come with a purpose. State it." Bess didn't need her steel corset to keep her back straight and stiff. She had her determination to be as unpleasant as possible.

"Then I shall be as blunt as you, milady. I have acquaintance with your guest from my years at court in Edinburgh. I wish to pay my respects to *her*. I have news of her son, King James of Scotland."

"No. You may not pay your respects to my guest."

Chapter 13

4 July, 1574. Chatsworth Manor.

DONOVAN seethed, seeking a scathing retort to Bess' dictate.

"My Lady Shrewsbury, I heard riders approach. Oh!" a soft voice with a lilting French accent said from the doorway.

Donovan turned as quickly as his painful leg would allow. His heart lodged in his throat, making it difficult to breathe. It pounded so loudly in his ears he could hear nothing else. "Your Grace." He bowed from the waist, not trusting either knee to support him in anything more elaborate.

"Your Grace." Robin managed a sweeping courtesy worthy of the courtier he was born to be.

"I told you to keep to your rooms when visitors come," Bess said, a harsh edge in her voice. No polite titles or courtesies. She must hate the exiled queen Elizabeth had put in her charge—or rather in her husband's charge, as if Bess herself were not a worthy guardian of the diplomatic nightmare named Mary Queen of Scots.

Mary seemingly did not hear her hostess' rudeness. Her gaze and attention belonged only to Donovan.

"My Lord of Kirkenwood," she said breathlessly. "Your unexpected visit brings joy to my heart."

"I have waited long and long to gaze upon your lovely countenance once more, Your Grace," he replied. He could look nowhere else but at her.

She remained tall and graceful. Gone was the laughing girl who loved to dance and delighted in her gardens, hunting, and the gossip of court. A mature woman who had known hardship, buried two husbands, married a third under duress, fought a war of rebellion and lost, and given up her son as well as her kingdom stood before him. She'd put on a little weight, enough to fill out the sharp edges of her face and figure. Her slightly out-of-date cream-colored gown embroidered with blood-red roses emphasized her dignified height and regal posture. But her once red-gold hair had faded, and her eyes looked puffy as she strained to see beyond the end of her nose.

"Still the most beautiful woman in the world," Donovan thought out loud.

"Best my cousin not hear you whisper such sweet compliments to another woman," Mary laughed.

Light bells rang in the back of Donovan's mind, like faeries giggling on the wind.

"Good Queen Bess is as blindingly beautiful as sunlight on water, sparkling and awesome. You, though, sweet lady, are the elusive moonlight glistening on faerie wings, flitting through the woods. Never captured, only glimpsed, and ever more beautiful because of it." The pretty words of a courtier tripped from his tongue. He'd heard players say much the same in some whimsical theatrical. But he meant the words, every one of them, with all of his heart.

"Walk with me, milord. The roses are most lovely this year." Mary held out her hand in invitation.

"I did not give you permission to walk out of doors today," Bess protested.

"Be sure to report my infraction of the rules to your husband, mistress. And to *your* queen. I am certain they will devise some punishment, though how much more they can contrive to curtail my freedom, I do not know." Mary tossed her head in disdain.

Donovan offered his arm. She placed her white hand with its almost preternaturally long fingers upon it and smiled at him. They stood nearly eye to eye, nose to nose, lip to lip.

No. They must not indulge in such intimacies while Bess and Robin observed.

Behind them, Donovan heard Robin ask something inane and polite of Bess. She replied. More words that drifted past his ear like so much moondust. He cared not. He was with Mary. In a moment they would be alone. He asked nothing more of life or the gods at this moment. If all they had was this moment, then this moment must be made wonderful.

"The morning light brings wonderful highlights to the colors of this rose," Mary gushed over a deep red blossom. Dewdrops kissed the petals.

Donovan wanted only to kiss *her*.

"Mary, we must talk," he sighed. Daydreams of recapturing the rapture of their one night together must wait.

"How fares my son? Our son," she asked, still bent over the rose.

"Young James, King of Scots, is growing up as determined as you. He has a prudent head on his shoulders. I foresee a time in the not-too-distant-future when he will dismiss his regents and rule on his own." One piece of firm evidence lived to confirm that Mary had come to his bed one night. James. The son they had conceived in a few moments of wild passion never to be repeated.

"But he is so young!" She straightened up to make her protest the stronger.

"Old enough to listen and know that his counselors all have hidden motives and goals that do not necessarily coincide with the best interests of the kingdom. He will rule with care when the time comes."

"I can only pray that he has listened to the priests and tutors I have sent to him. Scotland cannot prosper until She returns to the proper faith."

Donovan made no comment on that. James' regents and counselors had outlawed Mary's Catholic faith and turned back at the border or the harbor every priest no matter who sent them. Mary would not listen to the truth if she did not want to hear it.

"Mary, beloved, I have come to warn you that evil forces gather round you once more. Men who lust after power but want none of the responsibility of ruling fairly or justly, seek to use your name to further their own ends." Images of the werewolves who hunted as a pack sent a frisson of warning up his spine once more.

He had to hasten to London and consult with Elizabeth. Together they should be able to devise a plan.

There was something else he needed to . . .

"If these men will help me regain my throne . . ."

"The Protestant barons of Scotland will not have you back as their queen, ever."

"But the people of Scotland, my Highland clans . . ."

"The clans of the north do not command enough troops to conquer the rest of Scotland." Nor could they put aside clan rivalries long enough to work together for a common good.

He took her hands and forced her to look him in the eye and know the truth. "The clans are poor in land and in spirit, though many cling to the old faith. The rich lowlands that feed all of Scotland are almost completely Protestant. The barons *like* ruling Scotland without interference from a monarch. They will not have you back even to try you for the murder of your husband Lord Darnley."

Protests died on her lips. Tears welled up in her eyes. She gulped a moment and closed her eyes. When she reopened them she had regained control over herself. "Then I will have my other throne—the throne of England, denied me by my illegitimate, heretical cousin Elizabeth."

"By English law, Elizabeth is neither illegitimate nor heretic. To call her either is considered treason." Donovan allowed that message to sink in. "Mary, please reconsider. Elizabeth is prepared to hold you prisoner for the rest of your life. Thomas, Duke of Norfolk, and many others have already died trying to remove her from power in your name. Will you be the cause of more useless deaths?"

Her chin remained firm and stubborn.

"Your only hope to escape the bonds of Elizabeth and her dragon Bess is to publicly renounce your claim to England, as you abdicated Scotland."

" 'Twas not a true abdication, forced from me upon the threat of my life. Pope Pius V and now Pope Gregory XIII have declared it invalid."

"Your only hope is to accept it as valid, along with your resignation of England for yourself and your future children."

"And what of my existing husband, Bothwell? Do you think the Danes will release him from prison if I remove myself from Elizabeth's list of heirs?"

"You were prepared to annul your marriage to James

Hepburn, Earl of Bothwell in order to marry Norfolk. Neither Pope Gregory, nor the Archbishop of Canterbury, nor the Presbyters of Scotland will force you to remain married to the man who kidnapped and ravished you if you truly choose to be rid of him."

"And why should I do that, Donovan Kirkwood, Baron of Kirkenwood?"

"To marry me. You would be free to return to any of my homes, or we could settle in France. You could help me raise a passel of motherless children, perhaps bear more bairns of our own."

"I must give up everything I hold dear to follow my heart. I am a queen, milord. Queens do not have the luxury of marriage for love. Elizabeth will not allow me my freedom, no matter what, unless I turn Protestant as well. The price is too high, Donovan." She turned from him, hanging her head.

"Think on these matters, Mary. Please." He let go of her hands reluctantly.

"I hold you in my heart, Donovan. Along with our son James. My memories must be enough. I could give up my crowns if I thought either Scotland or England would benefit from my actions. But I cannot give up my faith, and I cannot believe that either country is safe from evil until they return to the true Church of Rome." Holding her head high, she strode purposefully toward the manor house.

"Beware, beloved. You refuse to see that peace under any faith is preferable to war and persecution under yours. Unscrupulous men already gather with plans to use your blindness. I fear you will be victim rather than victor." Darkness crowded his vision. His inner sight sparkled with the conviction of the truth of his prophecy.

"Gods forgive us both." He hastened after her. "Mary, wait, please." He caught up with her under the little overhang of the postern door. "At least grant me one kiss. I cannot bear it if we part with bitter words. One last kiss is all I ask."

"Oh, Donovan," she sighed and melted into his arms.

He met her warm and soft lips with the heated demands of his mouth. His arms wrapped around her lush body, drawing her closer, and closer yet. His hunger for her rose.

After a moment of listless compliance, she returned his embrace with fiery passion. Thus had they come together once before. Needing each other, drowning in each other.

"Would that we had more privacy," he panted when he finally allowed his lips to leave hers.

"Would that you could creep into my bedchamber tonight," she sighed, resting her head on his shoulder.

"You have but to point to the proper window and no walls will keep me out." He kissed her temple gently. The fierceness had not left him yet. He dared not unleash it with Bess and her bevy of servants and retainers likely to come looking for them any moment.

"Must I truly give up everything I value to be with you night and day?" she asked wistfully.

"I fear 'tis true, sweet Mary. Ours is a love not meant to be." As his brother's love for Roanna was not meant to be in their lifetime. Griffin the Elder and Roanna the Highland Rose could only be together in death. Donovan prayed to every saint and god that might listen that such was not the case between him and Mary.

"I cannot do it, Donovan. My loyal and trustworthy knight. I must stand for my rights, my church, my lawful inheritance."

"You sound like my brother," he said bitterly. Just once, he wished he could believe in something bigger and mightier than himself.

You believe in the family. Is the leap to belief in God so much longer? His brother's voice, overlaid with Grandmother Raven's voice, with Martha's voice, with all the voices of the ancestors back to King Arthur's Merlin haunted him.

With effort, Donovan closed his ears and his mind to the ghosts.

"If I sound like the twin you lost and still mourn, then you must understand why I cannot renounce my claims or my faith, even for a love as great as ours." Mary turned away from him and reached to open the postern door. Her hand lingered in his, fingers twining.

Donovan pulled her back for one last embrace, regretful, bittersweet.

"My head understands, but never my heart."

The sound of horses' hooves treading on the graveled drive tore them apart. Two plodding animals, large, well-shod, and placid, Donovan decided from the loud, slow crunch approaching from the other side of the rose garden's defining hedge.

"We found you at last!" came the bright giggles of his daughter Betsy. "Robin, do help me dismount."

"Curse it. Must that girl defy me at every turn? She refuses to see why I must keep them apart."

"As we must ever be apart," Mary reminded him.

"Politics be damned. I'll not be kept from you forever." Donovan stole one more kiss before heading toward his errant daughter.

Chapter 14

4 July, 1574. Paris, France. The crypt of Notre Dame.

I AWOKE with a start in the cold and damp crypt of the cathedral. Coffa warmed my back, snoring lightly and kicking in her dream of chasing rabbits. My chest and face were cold. Had I dreamed of Hal's feather-light kiss upon my brow? I almost remembered words accompanying that kiss. What had he said?

Even if the memory was only a dream, I needed to pay attention to it. In my family the gift of portent through dreams ran strong. My father had it. Upon occasion I had glimpses of it, too.

Hal kissing me good-bye. I sat up, eyes darting about in alarm. The vigil light beside the altar cast more shadows than it banished. Coffa roused, ears cocked, nose working, wary but not overly concerned.

I trusted her to know if anyone or anything threatened me.

"Hal?" I whispered into the darkness.

Only my personal ghosts and fears answered me with silence.

Drawing upon the Earth beneath me for strength, I brought a ball of cold witchlight to my hand. The shadows retreated. I was truly alone.

Where had Hal gone? I searched the memory/dream images for clues. Something about information and food.

My stomach growled to let me know my body agreed with his mission even if my mind and heart did not.

The chill of the crypt and my own fears set the hairs on my arms and my nape on end. I had to find Hal. I needed his physical strength as well as his constancy (bullheadedness I often called it) to keep me from abandoning my quest when fear and difficulty assailed me.

"Coffa, come." I rose stiffly and made my way back the long passage to the steep spiral staircase. Years of accumulated damp made the metal treads and railing slick. Coffa did not like the idea of climbing, though she'd trotted down them willingly enough with a dangerous mob on her tail.

The dangerous mob. Gone elsewhere for now. Simmering and seething. Waiting for a single spark. Paris was ready to explode with hatred, fear, and blood. Just as it had two years ago. I did not believe that the mob of its own volition had slaughtered ten thousand people in three days simply because their princess married Protestant Henri de Navarre. Someone had provoked the violence for his own evil purposes. I had to stop it from happening again.

The new king, Henri III, was the key. If he vowed religious tolerance as the law of the land at his coronation, then the de Guise faction, the Holy League, Rome, must bow to his will, even if they disagreed.

Before I could intervene with Henri III—and I did not yet know how I would gain his presence—I needed information and food. Hal had gone for both. Should I wait for him or go in search?

Curiosity, stubbornness, and a need to be out and *doing* something propelled me upward. My dog was left to follow me as best she could. I knew she would come after me. She always did. Her sense of duty to me was stronger than my own sense of caution.

At least I had enough sense to stop and listen with all of my senses extended to the far reaches of the cathedral before stepping into the nave. A few lay servers bustled about preparing for Matins. They barely acknowledged my passage through a side chapel and out into the drizzle-wet streets. Only normal traffic outside the cathedral. The mob had not gathered to wait for me.

The underlying violence remained in the air, heavier than air, almost tangible. I had to hurry and complete my quest.

I hoped the mob had not cornered Hal somewhere without me to help him. Briefly, I cast about for a sense of my cousin's presence. Coffa and I could not see, hear, or smell him on the wind. My dog tried following their scent trail.

We headed for *Le Pont St. Michel,* across the Seine to the south. At the beginning of the bridge the tramp of many people obliterated the trail.

I had to resort to magic though my stomach protested in hunger and a pain behind my eyes made it difficult. Our enemies might find us by tracking my magic. I had no choice. I had to find Hal.

Carefully, I sent threads of magic out in every direction. All but one withered and died before they found their target. The last one, traveling south and west, beyond the Latin Quarter toward St. Germain met a wall.

I'd never known Hal to erect such a strong shield before. Usually, he left at least one tiny chink for me to penetrate. Betsy could break down any barrier he erected if she added blood to her casting. I doubted even Betsy could find a way around or through this wall.

But it was more than a wall against penetration by magic. This wall was also a core of malevolence, fear, and lust. It radiated uneasiness. Everyone in Paris was susceptible.

A very powerful magician manipulated the mob from a power source nearby.

"Oh, Hal, stay away from there. You can't handle it alone." I stopped thinking a moment, only trying to *feel* where Hal might be. But the irritation built into that magical wall got under my skin. "I'm not sure I can handle this magician alone. I'm not certain the two of us combined can do more than protect ourselves from him. We need your da, and Betsy, and my da, too!"

4 July, 1574. Spanish Embassy, Paris.

Yassimine heard the whip snap. Almost simultaneously burning pain erupted across her bare back. It stung. She felt a welt rising, red and raw. The lash had not broken her skin. Even though she had not fed last night, she had gorged herself, as instructed, the two nights before. Her body was strong and resistant.

She jerked and moaned anyway. The Master expected it. The Master enjoyed it when she writhed in pain. The sooner he perceived her as humiliated and penitent, the sooner he would send her back to her subterranean cell. Only there in the dark solitude would she have the clarity of mind to think hard about the presence of the *other*.

She had to know if she could use this new power to defeat The Master and form her own pack.

A meneur des loups, the French called this new presence. One who tamed the wolves that were not true wolves. The Spanish called The Master *El Lobison*. She liked the French phrase better, and intended to claim it for her own.

The whip snapped again. This time the leather snaked around her neck. Yassimine held her breath against the burn of the lash. The Master tightened it, just a bit, just enough to let her know he could choke her if he chose.

She rattled the chains that bound her wrists. The manacles slid slightly on the single hook set into the wall. Neither the hook nor the chains would last long if she exerted her full strength. Ordinary iron. She could break them if she chose. But that would alert The Master that she used him as much as he used her.

She arched her back and moaned again.

Her plans for escape were not yet complete. She had to endure him a little longer.

"Pay attention to your lesson, Yassimine!" The Master commanded. His voice sounded very like the whip—his favorite toy next to the hook that replaced his left hand.

She savored the memory of the taste of that hand. She'd savaged him the first full moon after he bought her at a slave auction. But his magic was stronger than she. He had beaten her senseless while still bleeding. Then he had staunched the wound and raped her again.

Eventually, he would pay.

"I must obey," Yassimine recited the litany he had screamed at her since moonset.

Another crack of the whip. This one was not so fierce. Yassimine rotated her hips as much as her back.

The scent of The Master's arousal came to her, sharp and urgent. He'd finish with her soon.

"I must not stray so far from you that the silver chains burn. I must not stray beyond the limits of the city," she continued reciting the words.

His scent came closer. She heard The Master coiling the whip.

"You will remember your instructions from now on?" The Master whispered harshly in her ear. He ran the butt of the whip handle down her spine to rest just above her bottom. There he traced a delicate circular design.

She swayed in rhythm with his ministrations.

"I will remember," she said on a long exhale.

"I do not wish to force another chain upon you, Yassimine." The whip clattered to the floor. He grabbed her hair and yanked her head back. His tongue mimicked the circular pattern below her left ear. He buried his face in her hair as his hook snaked around to lift her breast.

Yassimine leaned back against him. Her nipples puckered in anticipation of the savage joining to come.

"You are mine, Yassimine. Mine to command. I paid a great deal of gold for you. You must obey me." He spun her to face him. The chains of her manacles twisted upon the hook, straining her arms above her head. Her breasts thrust outward. His teeth captured one nipple, not quite biting, more intense than a suckle.

"Yes, Master." The scent of her own moist need combined with his.

"Why did you disobey me last night? You knew I must punish you." He panted the words as he fumbled with his codpiece.

She breathed in sharply, not wanting to answer him quite yet.

"Answer me!" He slipped the tip of his hook into the silver ring that pierced her pubis. Gently, at first, he tugged.

Pain. Pleasure. Excitement shot sharply upward and outward. Her veins filled with anxious heat.

"Answer me." He tugged again. Harder. "Why did you disobey me?" He twisted the hook in the ring so that it pressed against her opening.

Another sharp singe of pleasurable pain rammed the core of her femininity. She gasped.

Then he thrust his swollen cock deep inside her, strong and hard. She rode the waves of heat that coursed up her spine. He filled her. Her power over him grew. He needed her.

His breath mingled with hers, spicy, sweet. She sucked him in, deeper and deeper until he exploded.

And then she bit him. A taste of his blood flowed over her tongue.

Just a little nip to the side of the neck. Enough to warn him of the dangerous path he trod. Enough to gain a little control over him. He bit her back, harder. She, too, courted danger.

But his teeth did not break her skin. She half smiled at his human weakness.

Then he sagged against her, spent and gasping for air. She answered his question. "There are others, like me in Paris. Wolves and yet not wolves. Two, I think. I sensed them. And then I smelled them."

The Master reared his head away from her. His cock popped out of her. He fumbled to control and conceal his organ, and his lack of control, once more. "That is impossible. All of your get are elsewhere. I control them. Better than I control you." He righted his clothing, his posture, and his dignity. "There are no other *lobunos*. Werewolves. You are too strong. Your scent permeates the city. No other would dare trespass on your territory."

The absence of his hot body pressed against her left her chilled. Her nipples puckered more tightly. His eyes narrowed their focus upon her. Desire flared once more.

"This *other* is not one of my get. I did not bring about the change in him. He . . . he is *other*." She feigned a loss of words, letting him question her intention before he could recover and engage in another bout of sex.

"Where did he come from? How did he get past my barriers around the city?"

"I do not know, Master. I know only that he is here."

"Where are they?"

She shrugged. The movement lifted her breasts. The chain between them swayed. The Master grabbed her, lifting, pushing. He rubbed his rising cock against her once more.

"Where are they?" he repeated baring his teeth. He held his hook at her opening, ready to tear her apart.

"One of the *others* is female," Yassimine gasped. Excitement sent a flood of moisture over the tip of his hook.

He began to rub her with the blunt curve. "What is the significance of that, my pet?" He licked the side of her neck.

She moistened her lips, ready to bite him once more. "Female is unusual. *Les loups-garous,*" she used the French term for one of her kind, "are solitary hunters. Even during mating season. We do not travel together unless controlled by you. And we respect another's territory. Either one of these *others* is formidable. Together their power is . . . great. Greater, perhaps, than yours."

"Impossible!" The Master spluttered. His erection faltered. "No magician is stronger than I. I control all of the werewolves. *All* of them!"

"Not these. These are so powerful I can smell the wolf in them even now in broad daylight. And the moon is no longer full. I should not be able to smell them at all unless they are within arm's reach. My need to protect my territory flares. *La lobuna* in me refuses to fade with the moon in response to their smell." To emphasize her point, she pulled on her manacles. The hook pulled out of the wood paneling. With another quick twist and tug she broke the wrist shackles as well.

The Master took one step back, away from her.

"Only a mage as powerful as I can force your kind to hunt together. I must protect my territory, as well as yours. I will have to kill these *others*. That will weaken the mage who controls them. Then I will hunt him down and destroy him as well. My plans have come forward too far to allow a rival to destroy them now."

"Only I can kill the *others*. They will not succumb to magic or mundane weapons. Especially when they are together, combining their powers. Only one of their own can kill them."

The Master had to give her the freedom of the city again tonight. If she could find the others, they must help her break the magical chains that bound her to The Master. Then she would gather together all those *lobunos* she had helped create. Five in England. Seven around Rome. Three in the Germanys. No power, political, spiritual, or physical would resist her then. She would rule the world and, once more, people would bow down and worship the wolf within her.

Chapter 15

4 July, 1574. Chatsworth Manor, England.

"YOU should arrange their betrothal," Mary Queen of Scots said quietly to Donovan. They strolled toward the main drive where Betsy continued to gush news of her adventures with her Aunt Meg to Donovan's secretary.

"The girl is besotted and the boy is obviously from a noble family. An advantageous match." Mary's hand brushed Donovan's. A signal of her own affection that must remain secret.

"Elizabeth will never allow them to marry," Donovan returned. Martha would not have approved either. She would have pointed out how unsuited were their personalities, their expectations, their place in society. But then his second wife had never approved of anything about Betsy, the product of Donovan's first marriage.

Warm tingles ran up his arm from Mary's touch. Her presence seemed to remove the guards on his tongue.

"Elizabeth? Why should she object? None of you are of royal blood." Mary eyed him sharply.

Donovan clamped his mouth shut on the obvious retort. Robin, when just an infant, had been the object of Norfolk's plots to assassinate Elizabeth and set himself up as Robin's regent. The Kirkwood family could not allow the boy to become an innocent pawn in another scheme to wrest power from Elizabeth.

Elizabeth ruled England with an iron fist, cloaked in a velvet glove. She held England united, stable, peaceful, and prosperous. Could Mary do the job half as well?

Mary continued to look to Donovan for an explanation. She narrowed her eyes in speculation. The longer he kept quiet, the more she must probe the secrets surrounding Robin's birth.

"Elizabeth has plans for my family," Donovan finally stammered. "The border march guarded by Kirkenwood is very valuable. Our heritage is more valuable. She wishes to control our breeding as she controls everything that touches her or her realm."

"Does she know . . . ?"

Another secret that must be guarded. "No. Elizabeth does not know that you and I . . . that James VI of Scotland might be . . . is my son. James does not know either." Of all his extended family and political contacts, only Mad Meg had guessed the truth. She spoke in such convoluted riddles, however, that no one took her prattling seriously.

Bess approached them, obviously curious about the newest visitors to her palatial home. Donovan said no more. Too many secrets. Too many hearts broken by politics and religious differences and fate.

A gifted playwright could make a compelling drama of this.

Donovan took a deep breath and prepared to face his daughter and his sister. Only something of dire importance would drag Meg out of her seclusion near Huntingdon and away from the shrine of their brother's grave. He dared not speculate on the nature of the latest disaster.

As the groups converged, Meg stepped away from her niece directly into Mary's path. The queen either had to stop or step around a very determined obstacle.

Robin opened his mouth to reprimand Meg for this serious breach of royal protocol.

Donovan gestured for quiet. Meg always had a purpose. Once set in her mind nothing deterred her, not common sense or manners, or incredible distance. Years ago, she had left Kirkenwood alone, traveled all the way to London on her own, merely to set her brother, Griffin the Elder, on the quest to rescue Robin from the machinations of the Duke of Norfolk. At the time, the duke had been the most powerful noble in the land. London had been hundreds of miles to the south, and she had no guarantee except her own inner visions that she would find Griffin at all. Donovan smiled. Meg might be mad, but she always got results.

Blonde curls dangled messily over her deep blue eyes. Kirkwood eyes. Her simple kirtle and skirt were threadbare and patched. As usual, she wore no shoes or kerchief.

Betsy, though dressed simply, maintained her impeccable grooming and sense of fashion. Neither probably thought about their own safety long enough to even consider an escort of armed men.

But then, both had weapons few men could match.

"He's quite mad, you know," Meg said without preamble or introduction. She took the queen's hand and pressed some crumbled leaves into it. "He doesn't remember you, or your love. He'll die soon, alone and forgotten by all but you."

"Rosemary," Mary whispered, raising the little sachet to her nose. "Rosemary for remembrance."

"Who?" Betsy breathed the question on everyone's mind.

"Get away from her, you filthy peasant!" Bess tried to shoo Meg back toward the horses. Meg stood firm, never taking her eyes off of Mary.

"Madam, control your servant!" Bess ordered Betsy.

Betsy had the grace to blush. So did Robin.

"You must excuse my sister, Lady Shrewsbury," Donovan apologized to his hostess. "Her mind does not work along conventional patterns." He took Meg's arm and tried to turn her back to Betsy.

Meg planted her feet and refused to budge. "Best you remember *his* fate. You can still change yours, but not his." She continued speaking to Mary.

"What is she talking about, Lord Kirkenwood?" Mary asked Donovan.

"I think you know, Your Grace. Meg always makes certain at least a portion of her messages are understood."

"Bothwell," Meg and Mary whispered together. James Hepburn, Lord Bothwell, was Mary's third husband. He had fled to Denmark during the last war of rebellion against Mary in Scotland. Instead of allies he had found a prison.

Mary gasped and fell silent.

"Your sister?" Bess humphed and flounced back to her salon in a flurry of skirts and fluttering lace handkerchief.

"Green does not suit her," Meg giggled, looking pointedly at Bess Hardwick's expensive brocade gown.

"Ah, but green suits Queen Elizabeth, and yon Bess wishes to make herself another sort of queen," Donovan replied around a smile.

"Green suits you," Meg looked at Mary. "But you refuse to wear it because it is your rival's color. Best you stick to gold, or mayhap a blue if it is deep enough in hue." She cocked her head prettily as if she had nothing more important to do than discuss fashion.

"What brings you to Chatsworth?" Donovan asked his daughter. He made no move to escort her into the manor or find hospitality for her. "I did not give you permission to leave the hermitage." He tried to look stern. How could he with Betsy looking so hopelessly at Robin? He could almost hear her heart breaking as the young man turned his attention to the exiled queen, offering to escort her inside the manor.

Donovan fingered the locket with a lock of Betsy's hair in it. She should have given it to Robin.

Once more the rough catch pricked his finger. A drop of blood smeared upon the silver.

Betsy smiled. She took her father's finger and sucked on the wound as would a lover. "There, Papa, all better."

"Why have you come?" Donovan's attention kept wandering back to Mary. He had to concentrate hard to question his daughter.

"Meg had a vision," Betsy said succinctly. Her eyes turned in the direction Robin had taken.

"Meg has visions nearly every day. What in this one brought you down a dangerous road alone? You have no protection, few supplies. Probably no money. How could you be so foolish, Betsy?"

"Hal and Deirdre are in Paris. They need help. I will go to them," Betsy announced. "You will not stop me." She almost chanted the last words.

"No, you will not go!" Donovan forced the words out. Why could he not concentrate on what he must do? All he could think about was Mary.

"What kind of help do they need, Meg?" Donovan's protective instincts leaped to the fore. Plans for the journey to the foreign capital formed in his mind, even as he spoke. "You, Betsy, will remain in England under your aunt's protection." He pointed his finger at his daughter. It shook with anger and anxiety.

Betsy looked down her nose at his hand in disdain.

He did not remove it.

"Magical help. They face monsters," Meg replied. "Men who are not truly men, animals that are not truly animals, magic that is not the magic we know. Enemies to peace. Enemies of life."

4 July, 1574. Near sunset, Paris.

Hal scrunched lower in the shadows where he and Helwriaeth watched and listened.

A swarthy man wearing garish yellow-and-pink balloon trousers that ended at his knobby knees, with a contrasting doublet, paced in front of the gate to the Spanish Embassy. His companion stood a little taller; also dark-haired but fairer of skin. He waited, patiently leaning against the wall to the forecourt. He, too, was dressed in the latest of fashion, but in more subtle and complementary shades of brown and rust. He either had well turned calves or padded his hose better than the flamboyant one.

Hal instantly labeled them as a Spaniard and his French compatriot. Both had plans that did not bode well for the peace of the city.

"We cannot wait until the next full moon. The city is ready to explode now. In another month fears will abate and tempers will cool," Señor Flamboyant spat in an atrocious accent. Even Hal spoke better French than he did.

"In another month, summer will be at its peak, water will taste flat and barely quench the constant thirst. Only the poorest and most desperate will remain in the *cité* then. Tempers will flare even without our prompting," Monsieur

Subtle replied. He inspected his fingernails idly rather than watch his companion's restlessness.

"*El Lobison* informs me that his . . . ah . . . slave is still primed to work with us tonight."

Who, or what was *El Lobison?* Hal wondered. Once more he wished he'd studied languages better. The word had no correlation to English that he could think of.

"The slave? She works again tonight?" Monsieur Subtle stood up straighter, no longer needing the wall to hold him up. "But I thought . . ."

"So did I. Apparently, our friend has worked his magic too well." Both men grinned evilly.

Hal listened closer. He'd smelled no magic around this place. Helwriaeth had led him here, following a scent of his own, one that made him growl deep in his throat and keep his nose in the air working constantly.

Any strong magic needs investigation, Hal told his familiar with his mind.

Helwriaeth snorted and rotated his ears, seeking more information. His nose still bounced up and down, constantly seeking whatever had brought him here in the first place.

"Are the men ready?" Señor Flamboyant stopped his constant prowl for a moment. But his fists clenched and his toes tapped impatiently. He was not one to abide stillness long.

"*Mais oui,*" Monsieur Subtle replied.

Hal did not like the way his eyes glittered. Greed or lust drove him now, not indifference.

"I have gathered two hundred mercenaries. They are bored sitting in their camp all day, every day. They drink too much and whore too little. One word and they will begin the slaughter."

"I have a list of targets." Señor Flamboyant handed a folded and sealed parchment to the Frenchman. "They are to start in the Latin Quarter, then move north of the river to the warrens of streets and markets where the Huguenots infest. Let the slave slash the throats of a few loyal Catholics first. Then once our men begin retaliating against the Huguenots, the rest of the city will join the slaughter, as they did two years ago on St. Bartholomew's Eve."

Hal fidgeted. He needed to get this information to Dee. Together they might come up with a plan. Together they might be able to stop this atrocity. Then they would not need to risk forcing a foreign king to listen to two children.

But he also needed to neutralize the "slave." A female who slashed throats on command. What kind of hideous creature could she be?

Then he knew. A creature of the night who had prowled the convent grounds by moonlight. A creature who was neither human nor beast, but both. Memory of the hairy paw smashing through the wooden gate turned his blood cold.

"Somehow we have to stop this beast, Helwriaeth," he whispered.

Helwriaeth liked the idea of killing the slave. He had a personal grudge against that one.

But the emotions and sensory perceptions Helwriaeth fed to Hal were fuzzy, as if the dog were not quite certain when the grudge began—or would begin.

Hal shuddered with premonition as well as indecision. He weighed his options and didn't like any of them.

"Follow Monsieur Subtle, Helwriaeth," Hal whispered with mind and voice. "I'll keep my mind open and find you later, with Dee." He ruffled Helwriaeth's ears. His familiar leaned into him for a long moment of shared warmth and love. Then, with a quick tongue across Hal's face, Helwriaeth turned his attention back to Monsieur Subtle and Señor Flamboyant.

Hal crept away. He had to open his senses to Dee and at the same time keep part of his mind tuned to Helwriaeth. Double images assailed his eyes. He saw what his dog saw on top of his own perceptions. A third point of view layered on top of that. The cobbled street seemed to shift and heave. He stumbled over his own feet. "Slow and steady," he told himself.

A headache stabbed him in the back of the neck and deep within both his eyes. He squeezed them closed trying to concentrate.

Then he caught a magical whiff of Dee. She was headed in his direction. He sent her a brief image of a pub he'd passed earlier. They would meet there. Then he closed down his contact with her. One layer of perception lifted away from his eyes. He breathed a sigh of minor relief and listened more keenly to the two conspirators outside the gates to the Spanish Embassy. Their conversation came through garbled. Only a few stray words, meaningless, out of context. Unfortunately, Helwriaeth did not understand the conversation without Hal's mind to interpret for him.

The two men embraced with a kiss of peace to each cheek. Monsieur Subtle departed toward the east and Señor Flamboyant sauntered back into the embassy compound.

Helwriaeth lumbered to his feet, stretching his back and his hind legs, then rocking back and stretching his chest and forelegs. Hal shared the lurch and stretch of muscles. His spine seemed to settle into place.

Only then did Helwriaeth amble in the wake of the conspirator. He kept a fair distance between them, letting the man's scent guide him.

Then the man's body odor filled Hal, an exotic oil laced with spices. The perfume covered but did not hide rancid sweat, laden with garlic. The man had used the heavy perfume for many days rather than take the time to bathe. Both Hal and his dog wrinkled their noses in distaste. They shared a brief moment of humor at some half-thought joke.

"What's so funny?" Dee asked.

Hal almost stumbled over her. His vision fractured. A new layer of perceptions crowded out reality. He saw Dee as she would become: two inches taller, fuller breasts, tinier waist, a more slender face dominated by her big eyes, gray tinged with blue around the edges, more perceptive than ever. She looked into his heart and . . .

And turned away.

He shook his head to clear it. But the memory of how beautiful Dee would grow lingered. He needed to enfold her in his arms, protect her, share his life with her.

The forbidden nature of his thoughts sent a shock of guilt through him. His head cleared and he saw the world as it was at this moment. Dee was his cousin, more like half sister. Their fathers had been identical twins. He and Dee had been raised together as brother and sister. He must admire her from afar.

"Uh, is Coffa in heat?" he asked, still staring into her eyes.

Dee looked at her dog. She tilted her head as if listening. "I don't think so," she murmured. Her inflection rose into a question.

"Just wondering. Helwriaeth has been acting strange. Thought maybe . . ." How did he finish the thought?

"Where is Helwriaeth?"

Then he told her what he had discovered.

She took a deep steadying breath and exhaled on one of her expressive sighs. She had reached a conclusion she did not like.

"Simple. We put the mercenaries to sleep with a spell. Then we hunt this 'slave,' " she said with decision and began walking in the direction Coffa indicated Helwriaeth had gone.

"But how do we deal with this monster once we find it?"

Dee shrugged. "We'll think of something. We always do. My head will be clearer once we eat."

"Are you sure we'll think of something?"

For the first time she hesitated.

And he saw impending disaster hidden deep within her eyes.

Chapter 16

5 July, 1574. Spanish Embassy, Paris.

YASSIMINE curled up on the pile of silk cushions The Master kept in a corner of his salon. Her eyes drifted closed for a much needed nap. Her knees twitched. She shifted to her back with her knees drawn up. Better. Now her lower back curved down into the crack between two cushions. Back onto her right side facing the room. That position twisted her neck. She rolled onto her left side with her back to The Master and one of his lieutenants—the one who dressed in the height of fashion but his colors clashed so violently they almost hurt her eyes.

Ah, much better. Perhaps now she could sleep off her exertions of the past three nights and this morning. Her body still wanted to retract into her wolf form. The nearness of the *other* nagged at all of her senses.

The Master's words drifted across her ears demanding she listen. Not now. She needed to sleep.

Her eyes shot open. She could not sleep while an *other* prowled her city.

"Unleash the men tonight," The Master said quietly.

"*El Lobison,* the moon is no longer full. We agreed to wait another month. Henri will have returned by then. We will draw him more fully into our cause if he sees firsthand . . ." the lieutenant protested.

"Tonight," The Master insisted.

"Will she be able . . . ?" the lieutenant asked.

Yassimine's back itched. They talked about her. She needed to know more.

"She will transform tonight. There is another of her kind within the city. Possibly two others. Find them and kill them before moonrise," The Master stated very calmly. As if other creatures of the night happened upon them every day.

Yassimine could not allow The Master to kill the others. Only they could free her from the bonds of magic that chained her to The Master. She'd need more help than just removing the physical chains that dangled from her pierced body. Until the chains were broken or removed, she would know no freedom, taste no true power.

"How? How can one tell a werecreature from an ordinary man except on the full moon?" the lieutenant asked.

"You know." The Master held up a silver medallion in an ornate pattern. He turned the thing so that the red jewel in the center faced Yassimine. It began to glow and pulse. The light faded and died when he pushed the talisman into the lieutenant's hand, the jewel facing the window now.

The garish one shuddered. "I shall send out men to listen in the marketplaces. Someone, somewhere, must suspect a neighbor of being infected." He kept his eyes lowered and his hands clasped. His knuckles turned white and his knees trembled beneath his padded breeches.

Yassimine wondered how she could use his fear to her own ends. If she could make him report to her rather than The Master, then perhaps she could slip out early and make contact with the *others,* have them free her before the change took over her reason and her need. If she confronted them after the change, then they must kill each other. Nothing could stand between them and death.

Unless . . .

Was death preferable to endless years of slavery by The Master?

No. She must prevail. She had seniority of wolf form. Her people had worshiped her as a god. So, too, would these *others.*

5 July, 1574. A ruined chateau northeast of Paris.

I draped one arm over the neck of each of the wolfhounds. Coffa gave me nearly complete pictures of the men camped inside the grounds of an ancient and nearly ruined castle a few miles east of the city. Helwriaeth supplied me with sounds ranging from belches and scratches to snores and quiet conversations. Between the two, I probably knew more about the two hundred mercenaries camped within the walls than their own commander.

If anyone truly led this mob of greedy, drunken brigands.

Boredom gnawed at them. Drink aggravated their uneasiness. When the order came for them to move into the city and begin murdering the populace, they would go willingly. The problem would be to direct their slaughter.

My problem was to bleed off their restlessness and prevent them from going anywhere.

"Can you do it, Dee?" Hal asked quietly. He stood behind me in the little copse at the foot of the chateau hill. Strangely, he did not touch his wolfhound. I'd never known him to stand separate from Helwriaeth if they could touch. Not since they had bonded on the day of the dog's birth, the same day my young Coffa came to me.

"I think I can put them to sleep. But the spell will take time. The sun drops rapidly." Doubt bounced around my stomach. A night's sleep and a few hasty meals scavenged from street vendors was not enough to ferment ideas or brighten my confidence.

The magic I intended to work would attract the power behind the wall of evil I had sensed earlier. There had to be another way to divert the mercenaries from their assigned job.

If there was another way, I could not think of it.

"What do you need?" Hal paced restlessly. Like his father always did.

I was afraid the thrashing underbrush would alert the sentries to our presence.

Hastily, I pawed through my scrip looking for packets of herbs Aunt Meg had taught me to carry. I devised and discarded a dozen combinations before I found the little bit of ghostweed reserved for emergencies. It was the best remedy when someone was in great pain or their internal humors were so unbalanced only a deep sleep would restore them.

But the plant could only be used in minute amounts.

Uncle Donovan had added his warning to Aunt Meg's. His words held the weight of authority. Did he have firsthand experience of the drug?

I had nothing else with me. But I need not take much of the drug myself. Sympathetic magic was the key to this spell.

"Hal, go to the far side of the camp. Be careful no one sees you or hears you. When you are directly opposite me, build a small fire. I will signal you when to light it. At the precise same moment as me, you must drop this leaf into the fire."

"It will work better if we have connecting fires at the North and South of your spell, as well as the East and West." His eyes lighted with hope.

"We have no one to light those fires, or drop the leaves into them."

"A progression. We both walk the full circuit and light each fire in turn, returning to the East to close the circle. Like we did last night with the—at the convent." He shied away from mentioning the beast.

I felt the same reluctance to confront the memory.

"I have something else in mind, Hal. Please, I know more about ritual than you do. Just do as I ask."

"I don't like being separated from you, Dee." His hands trembled as he spoke.

"That did not stop you from leaving me in the crypt this afternoon."

"You were safe there."

"I shall be safe here. You are the one who courts danger. You will be moving around the camp." The world spun around me. Abruptly, I had to sit.

Something was wrong. What?

If I believed in something, someone greater than myself, I might have prayed.

Believe in yourself. Believe in the family. They will lead you to God. Remember, that no matter what name you give to God, she is listening, my father's voice came to me as clearly as if he stood at my side directing the spell.

What will be, will, little one. Do what you must to stop the violence before it begins.

Hal trudged off, Helwriaeth pressed tightly against his side.

Bit by bit, I stacked my own kindling and firewood. I named the construct "Tower." Then I drew a circle around the entire thing with a stem of the ghostweed plant. This I named "Wall." Little twigs scattered about became "Men."

My concentration was absolute. I heard nothing, saw nothing but my work.

When I lifted my head to seek Hal's progress, it was like coming awake after a long nap—the kind where I had slept too heavily and awoken too abruptly—that left me quivering inside. I wondered how much of me I had put into the ritual. Certainly, there was a big enough hole in my mid-region to account for that.

Then Coffa's stomach growled. Mine answered. I understood the emptiness.

"Soon," I promised myself and my dog. "Soon we will all sup and sleep. All four of us. Hal and Helwriaeth, you and me. Then we can go home." I breathed deeply as I pictured the weathered keep of Kirkenwood atop the massive tor, the village at its eastern base, surrounded by a circle of standing stones, the little kirk hidden in the woods by the lake at the southern base of the tor, Uncle Donovan, my cousins, the other fosterlings . . .

A tear dripped from my cheek to my chin. Another hole opened in my middle.

I needed to be home.

Coffa lapped my face clean. I hugged her close. She wanted to go home as much as I.

Hurry. Hal's mental voice intruded upon my misery. *I hear someone coming. Dee, not all of the mercenaries are inside the camp. Hurry!*

I groped for flint and steel. Hastily, I struck them together. *Fire, now,* I nearly shouted to Hal. My first spark died, but the second caught the tinder. A delicate breath to the base of my kindling tower sent greedy Tanio, the element of Fire, reaching for more and more wood.

"Ghostweed, now." As the last syllable dropped from my mind and voice, I let go the leaf and stem, into the heart of the fire. It floated listlessly. Awyr, the element of Air, akin to Tanio, caught the plant, played with it slightly. But then Pridd, my own element of Earth, grabbed the thing and drew it relentlessly into the heart of the fire.

At the first touch of flame to the dry stem, I recited the words that would bind them all together and project the magic into the Real Tower, contained within the Real Wall, and affect only the Real Men.

> *Tanio, Fire, bring light to darkened minds.*
> *Awyr, Air, breathe life into my spell.*
> *Pridd, Earth, ground us all in your Goddess' love.*
> *Dwfr, Water, blend my words with the Elements;*
> *With the Symbols;*
> *With life;*
> *With Peace.*

Then I chewed up the last little bit of the ghostweed, and spat it into the center of the flames and symbol of the Tower.

Magic connected my fire to Hal's with a snapping sound like a twig breaking.

A lopsided dome shimmered into place over the entire castle and grounds.

My mouth grew numb.

Smoke rose and swirled; formed an arrow and sped toward the Tower.

My mind followed the visible tendrils of my spell as the smoke whipped through the castle ruins, permeating every nook and cranny, invading every mind within the walls.

My mind drifted. I almost followed the smoke, almost became a part of the sleepy peace that brought every drunken mercenary to his knees and then dropped them all into the waiting arms of Morpheus.

The same peace descended upon my shoulders. My body grew as light as the smoke. My mind lost the drive to complete the spell. I smiled and lifted my arms.

I drifted upward, uncaring for anything but to be home. If I peered very closely into the distance, I could see Kirkenwood atop its tor. The village and standing stones. I could hear Uncle Donovan call to me. He needed me. I had to go to him. He held out a hand. I reached to grab hold of it.

"*DEE,*" Hal called to me with mind and voice. *Help me!*

Helwriaeth added his mournful howls to Hal's plea.

Kirkenwood's pull was stronger. Home. Family. My connections to the past and present.

I forgot Hal and my mission. I even forgot dear Coffa.

Chapter 17

5 July, 1574. A ruined chateau outside Paris.

"HURRY, Dee." Hal cast about him with every sense available. Three men—no four—crept toward him. Two came from the south, one from the north, and the last from the east, behind him.

Helwriaeth stood on guard, growling. Drool strung from his half-opened jaws. The guard hairs all along his spine stood up. His tail jutted out, long and straight and still. He'd allow no man to attack Hal while he lived.

Fire, now, Dee commanded.

Hal snapped the fingers of his left hand. Flame shot from the index finger into his kindling. Tendrils of smoke drifted upward. A tiny glow brightened, burst into flame.

He breathed a brief sigh of relief.

Helwriaeth's growls grew deeper, ended on half a bark.

Hal hovered over the little fire, sprig of ghostweed in his hand.

Waves of malice rolled before the approaching men.

Hurry, he pleaded.

Dee did not honor him with a response.

He knew the spell could not be rushed. He knew that only Dee had the strength, concentration, and familiarity with ritual to do this.

But he needed to be gone from here.

A string of whispered Spanish words came to him on the breeze. He needed to concentrate, puzzle out their meaning.

"Look at the fire and the circle and the dog. This is the magician who challenges The Master's authority," said one of the two men approaching from the south.

"We must capture him alive," a second voice replied. He

sounded very much like Señor Flamboyant. "The Master
will wish to question him."

"But he is only a boy," the first protested. How can he
wield so much power as to challenge *El Lobison?*"

"A great concentration of power in one so young does
not bode well for The Master," Señor Flamboyant said.
"Capture him alive!" he called across the woods.

More thrashing in the bushes. Grunts and curses in Spanish and in French.

"Now, Dee. Now. We have to finish this now!"

Helwriaeth leaped. A man gargled and moaned. Hal
smelled hot blood from the great vein in the neck. He felt
Helwriaeth's triumph at felling an enemy.

A shot rang out.

"Yiikkkkkeeee!" Helwriaeth screamed.

"How dare you hurt my dog!" Hal sprang in the direction of the gunfire. He landed upon the shooter before he
could reload. They both fell to the ground. The shooter
tried to bring his weapon around to club Hal behind the
ear. Hal let fly with a fist to the man's jaw. His head
rammed backward into a rock with a satisfying thud.

Hard hands yanked Hal back onto his feet.

He flailed. His elbow connected with a shoulder. Señor
Flamboyant grunted. He did not relinquish his grip. His
companion wrenched Hal's left hand around behind his
back and pushed upward. His shoulder felt ready to dislo-
cate. Hal still held the sprig of ghostweed, the key ingredient in the spell, in that hand.

The spell had to work.

"Ghostweed, now, Hal. Now!"

The fire lay three paces behind Hal and to the left.

"And now my young friend, who are you and what do
you plan with that ritual fire?" Señor Flamboyant asked in
French in his horrendous accent.

"It isn't a very big fire," his companion commented.
"Looks like . . ." His eyes opened wide and he bit his lip.
"There is another fire and another magician."

"Sí," Señor Flamboyant snorted. "I thought him too
young to have any effect upon a magician as powerful as
The Master. Where is your Master?"

The man holding Hal pushed harder upon his arm. Something tore in the joint. Hot pain dribbled down his arm.

NO! They couldn't go after Dee. Hal had to stall, had to divert them until Dee finished. She couldn't finish until he dropped the leaf into his own fire.

Hal dug in his heels, flexed his knees and reared backward. His captors struggled for balance. He wrenched around, trying desperately to shake them off.

Now, Hal.

He dropped the sprig. He forced his thoughts to direct it into the dying flames. The pain in his shoulder nearly made him pass out.

The two men wrestled him away from the fire.

Helwriaeth groaned and thrashed. Blood spurted from his side.

Hal went limp. "Helwriaeth," he breathed in despair.

"The other magician. Where is he?" Señor Flamboyant insisted. He drove his fist into Hal's gut to emphasize his words.

"There is no other magician," Hal gagged. He needed to double over, clutch his middle, contain the pain. He fought for breath and consciousness.

His captor maintained his rigid grip on Hal's arm, forcing him upright.

"How can there be no other magician," the man behind Hal sneered. "You are but a beardless boy."

Only one thing would keep them away from Dee.

Forgive me, Da, for usurping Dee's heritage.

I need no other. I am the Pendragon of Britain!"

"I have heard of one such as you." Señor Flamboyant gasped and backed away. His eyes flicked from the writhing form of the wolfhound and back to Hal. Hastily, he crossed himself.

"You will pay for the injury to my familiar, Dago worm!" Hal cursed. He allowed his eyes to cross and he began mumbling nonsense words in Welsh. Anything to make the man believe.

Run, Dee. Run away now. And never look back. They'll catch you. You must run back home and never set foot in France again.

"The Master will be most interested in you and your dog." Señor Flamboyant smashed his fist into Hal's jaw.

Stars burst before his vision, then blackness.

Run, Dee! Even if the spell did not work, you must run.

The ghostweed hallucination continued, more real than reality. Dimly, I heard commotion. I pushed it aside. Uncle Donovan was so sad. I had to reach out to him, comfort him. I needed to be home. And the ghostweed took my spirit there.

Just as my fingertips brushed Uncle Donovan's, he faded into mist. The ever-present wind of northern England stirred his phantom image and dissipated it to the four cardinal directions. Kirkenwood suffered the same fate.

Frightened, I looked down. I still thought I was flying. But the Earth rushed toward me at an alarming speed.

I landed back in my body in a heap. Every joint in my body ached from the shock. I continued to jerk about when all I wanted was to still every muscle, still every thought, still this aching fear in my gut until I knew where I was. Who I was. Why I could not reach my beloved uncle.

"Lady Deirdre," a man said urgently into my ear.

"Deirdre." I rolled the name around my mouth with my tongue. It fit. Better than the acrid aftertaste from the ghostweed. "Yes, I am Deirdre. But I do not believe I am a lady."

"That's our Dee," another man said with a chuckle. He sounded familiar.

I forced my eyes open. Grit and a sticky film made them too heavy. Still, I concentrated on blinking them open by stages. Eventually I could focus. The broad face of my cousin Gaspar, Uncle Donovan's illegitimate son, swam into view. Shorter and stockier than the rest of the men in the family, with a tangle of blond curls, Gaspar was by far the gentlest and calmest. He moved and thought at a slower pace than most of the Kirkwoods. But he understood people, took their emotions into himself, and made them his own.

He could not lie and gladly protected all of the younger children with pride.

I trusted him.

I reached up to cup his face with my hand. He did not dissolve. Nor did he shy away from my touch.

"Gaspar." My voice sounded weak. And dry. I tried to swallow. That much of my body worked.

"What ails you, mistress?" the first man asked.

"Is that you, Thom Steward?" This time, my words sounded a little stronger. Who else would Uncle Donovan send in search of two errant children but his trusted steward and the steadiest of his older sons?

Then I remembered why I lay on the damp ground with an evening breeze chilling me to my bones.

"The spell. Did we complete it? Where is Hal? Coffa!" I rolled over and onto my knees in one motion.

My head threatened to remain on the ground. But eventually it caught up to me.

Gaspar's restraining hand upon my shoulder kept me on my knees.

"Coffa!" I called, long and plaintively.

"She took off, east, the moment she recognized us," Peregrine, Uncle Donovan's other illegitimate son, said from the edge of the copse. He seemed to be scanning the ruins of the castle with a small spyglass. Tall, dark-haired, with a long nose and sharp cheekbones, and restless, he looked and acted more like a Kirkwood than Gaspar did. Keenly intelligent, he could have been Uncle Donovan's heir except for his bastard birth and the fact that he had no magic in his soul. Not a scrap. And he resented the rest of us for it.

"Where is the young master?" Thom Steward asked. He left his hand on my shoulder, anchoring me to the earth. His touch was a terrible presumption of his class.

I leveled a withering gaze upon his restraint.

He did not flinch away or offer apology.

Gaspar chuckled. "He's more afraid of Father, if he should lose you again, than he is of your witchcraft, Dee."

"Hal is at the other side of the castle. He watches a secondary fire to complete the spell." The words tumbled out as strong as a river in spate. In moments, my "rescuers" knew as much about my current situation as I.

"Coffa?" I finished my narrative.

"I don't like the fact that the dog left you, Dee." Peregrine folded his spyglass. "Even if she did wait for us to reach you first. I'm going to find her and Hal. I can only presume Coffa went to help him in some manner. Looks like your spell worked. No one stirs inside the wall." He stalked off, heading north and east around the ruins. He walked deasil, along the lucky path of the sun, instinctively.

I would have gone south first, widdershins, along an easier path. Cold dread climbed my spine as if the direction my cousin walked could change the outcome.

Suddenly I was up and running, despite Thom Steward's protests. Gaspar ran alongside me. I spared him but a glance. He was as worried as I.

Thom followed as best he could, stumbling over tussocks, roots, and displaced stones from the castle ruins. He was no longer young and had never been as agile as the members of my family.

We met Peregrine at the remains of the fire. There was no sign of Coffa, or Helwriaeth, or Hal.

"Where?" I asked everyone and no one as I circled the area.

"Blood here. Trampled undergrowth. A struggle took place here." Peregrine knelt by the broken fronds of a stand of ferns.

"More blood here," Gaspar said. He crouched over a sharp rock protruding through the turf.

Reluctantly, I edged toward the ferns.

"No, milady." Thom held me back.

"I have to touch it. I have to know." I wrenched away from his grasp.

Peregrine backed away, willing to give me clear and untainted access to the site. Neither he nor Gaspar had any magic of their own, but they both knew a great deal about it after living all of their lives in a household of magicians.

My fingers came away from the blood, sticky and red. "It's fresh. Less than an hour old." My skin tingled beneath the blood. A sensation akin to running my fingers lightly over the tips of guard hairs on a dog's back.

"Whose, Dee?" Peregrine asked.

"Helwriaeth," I sobbed. Too much blood. No dog, not even one as mighty as our wolfhounds could survive long after losing this much blood. "Hal will be devastated."

"And this blood?" Gaspar asked, still hovering over the rock.

I crawled over to him, not trusting the strength in my knees. The loss of a familiar was too horrible to contemplate. I did not know how I would live without a Coffa in my life. She had yet to whelp and give me a replacement as her mother had. Hal had no promise of another pup upon the death of male Helwriaeth.

The blood on the rock felt different, heavier. It burned slightly where it touched me. "Human."

My breath caught in my chest. Black spots burned before my eyes ere I remembered to exhale.

"Whose?" Gaspar whispered. He held my hand gently in his. His eyes implored me to tell him that his half brother yet lived.

"Not Hal," I choked out. "Thank the Gods, this is not Hal's."

"He's alive!" Joy burst all over Gaspar's broad face.

"We do not know that for certain, sir," Thom reminded us all. "He did not shed blood here. But they still have a head start upon us. Anything could happen in just a few moments."

Chapter 18

5 July, 1574, Paris.

I CALLED to Coffa with mind and voice. Over and over I summoned her. Slowly, my cousins, Thom Steward, and I trudged back the miles to the northern quarters of Paris.

We came abreast of the heights of Montmatre off to our right, nearly back to the *cité* and still Coffa did not respond to me.

Never had my dog disobeyed me so willfully. Nor had she ever tolerated my absence for this long.

Something terrible must have happened to Hal and Helwriaeth for her to defy my summons.

Everywhere we passed, the locals shied away from the blood on my gown and the scent of magical herbs that permeated my clothes, my hair, my skin. Some made the sign of the cross to ward themselves from strangers in their neighborhood. Some made the sign against the evil eye. Many just slammed doors or shutters to keep us out.

The entire city waited for moonrise and the next assault on their souls and bodies.

Finally, as we neared the Seine and the bridges to the *Isle de la Cité*, I felt a whisper across my mind that might have been Coffa whimpering in loneliness and confusion. We picked up our pace and followed my sense of her.

We found Coffa south of La Ville near St. Germain, pacing a relentless circle around the Spanish Embassy and its environs. The palais of the wealthiest of nobles, of several embassies, and of church princes defined St. Germain. Each had extensive grounds, walls, and guards. Heavily armed guards, and they watched us warily.

Every time Coffa passed them, they tried to shoo her

139

off with clubs and stones. Intent upon her purpose, my dog ignored them and managed to stay just beyond their reach.

Gaspar crossed himself and backed away from the embassy gate. My cousins and I settled within a copse one hundred yards from there. Peregrine pulled out his spyglass and peered at the building and its walls. Gaspar followed my dog around and around.

I sat upon the grass, a towering oak to my back, too exhausted to think, and much too worried to do more than pull at my hair and twist my skirt hem into knots. Questions plagued me, yet I could not find answers with logic or magic or in my heart.

After two more circuits of the embassy, Coffa plunked herself down beside me. She sighed deeply, as if her heart would break, and laid her massive head in my lap. We both began to shiver with fear.

Hal was in serious danger. And he did not have Helwriaeth to help him.

"What do you see, Peregrine?" I asked.

My cousin collapsed the spyglass and joined me on the grass. He stretched his long legs out onto the graveled drive that led to yet another palais. If a fast moving carriage or troop of riders rushed past, he risked life and limb.

"I see closed shutters on all of the windows. I see armed guards prowling the courtyard. With every other step they cross themselves and mutter. Prayers, I presume. Something unholy transpires inside the residence tonight. They know it. And they fear it. But they must obey," Peregrine recited his conclusions.

"We must capture one of them and find out what is happening," Gaspar said. He pounded his right fist into his opposite palm.

"They will not talk," I said quietly. "They fear the one called The Master and his slave more than they fear God. We'd have to torture them to gain information." I did not know how I knew this. "I will not stoop to their methods.

"But Hal . . ." Gaspar protested.

"There is another way. I need quiet and privacy."

"She'll scry for him." Peregrine nodded his approval.

Seeing the present, past, and future in distant places while peering into a bowl of water or dancing flames was my strongest talent. Hal had command of fire, could breathe it when required, snapped it to life with his fingers most often. Betsy tuned herself to the wind.

Together, we could control nations if we chose. The awesome power at our fingertips chilled me. I did not want the responsibility that goes with power. I wanted only to go home and hide beneath the covers.

And never work magic again.

I could not do that. Hal depended upon me.

"The sun sets. Best we find rooms at an inn," Thom said. He patted his purse to let me know he had funds.

"I know a better place." A sanctuary more ancient than the Roman Church; more ancient than the gods of the Celts. As ancient as mankind.

Deep within the earth, Pridd, my element, would guide me, nourish me, console me.

"Hie yourselves to the inn close by the cathedral. Keep Coffa with you," I ordered them.

My dog whined in protest and pressed herself close against me.

I petted her, crooning reassurance. She did not like the slick metal stairs that spiraled downward to the crypt and the chapel. I had best go alone.

"You will eat 'afore you begin this business, milady," Thom insisted.

"Aye," Peregrine agreed. "You'll eat and rest. I will stand guard over your chosen place."

"As will I," Gaspar jumped up, eager for the next phase of this adventure.

"One only," I insisted. "The other two must keep Coffa close. She wants to rescue Hal. She must not be allowed to break into the embassy grounds. They will kill her for the sport of it."

"As they will kill us, if we linger much longer." Peregrine ushered us to our feet and along the road that led back toward the Latin Quarter and thence onto *L'Isle de la Cité* and the cathedral.

6 July, 1574. Past midnight, the Crypt of Notre Dame.

Food and an extra blanket from the inn finally stopped my shivers. The cool, damp air of the crypt lingered on my cheeks. The musty smell of old, old earth and bones anchored me. All I wanted to do was sleep and awaken in the morning back in my own bed in Kirkenwood.

Peregrine paced the crypt near the entrance to my hidden chapel. He carried a shielded lantern. Its flickering light sent shadows dancing high upon the walls. I shared the chapel with ghosts from another time, another god. I had the sense that once before, in another lifetime, I had prepared this same spell, in this same place. Then I was ancient but just as worried as at the present time in my youthful body.

Coffa's distant anxiety intruded upon my mind, kept me aware of the dangers my cousin faced with every breath.

I could delay no longer.

This spell needed strength and focus. It required more than just a glance into times and places far removed from me.

A plain crockery bowl represented Earth, Pridd. It cradled Water, Dwfr, Her opposite element. I lit Fire, Tanio, with flint and steel into the kindling beneath the bowl, fanned the spark to life with my breath, Awyr. Then I moistened my finger and drew a circle around the whole on the clay tiles of the floor.

I chanted ancient words that fit the antiquity of the place.

Ghosts crowded 'round me. They represented and petitioned ancient gods that the Roman Church had never been able to banish from this place. My breathing became heavy in my chest. Hardly enough room or air was left here for me with all these personalities leaning over my shoulder, watching, listening, waiting.

And then one of the shades separated itself from the others. A gentle hand touched my shoulders. Warmth and love flooded me.

I could begin now. My da had joined me.

I dropped a pebble into the water. Ripples blossomed outward. I kept my vision slightly unfocused on the ripples rather than the pebble.

Darkness tainted with blood roiled up from the bottom of the bowl. I heard screams in my head. Screams of anguish, of grief, of despair.

No identity attached itself to the screams.

And then the vision vanished, as the tide washes away scribbling in the sand.

6 July, 1574. The cellars of the Spanish Embassy, Paris.

Hal scrunched his fingers together and tucked his thumb tight against his palm. With his hand as small as possible, he slipped it downward, trying desperately to free himself from the shackles that bound him to a stone wall. The iron band did not give. Neither did the bones in his hand. When the pain became too intense to continue he relaxed a moment.

Then he concentrated on the keyhole of the shackles. Da had a trick—learned from his late twin brother—of moving the little metal pieces until they released the lock.

Nothing happened. In frustration he twisted and yanked against his restraints for the hundredth time. They held. And so did the hook in the wall that held the chain.

Off in the corner of the small, windowless room, Helwriaeth whimpered and thrashed. The light from a single lantern high up in the corner above Helwriaeth gave just enough illumination to reveal the awful damage inflicted by a single bullet.

Hal's own thigh burned in sympathetic pain.

He forced himself to still his struggles. He reached out to his familiar with all of the love and comfort he could muster.

Deep inside he ached with grief. His dog might survive the bullet wound in his flank. But Hal had to balance the evil humors from the bullet *now*. Before the damaged flesh turned septic.

He flailed again against the chains. The sound of metal clanking against stone almost masked the rattle of a key in the lock of his prison door.

Helwriaeth tried valiantly to rise and growl a warning. He fell back against his straw nest with another whimper.

Hal held his breath. What did his captors want of him?

Had they found Dee?

He bit his lip to keep the questions from tumbling out of his mouth.

The door creaked open. The bright flare from a torch nearly blinded Hal. He blinked furiously, trying to force his eyes to adapt to the change in light.

When he could see again, the door was firmly closed and locked. One slight man with swarthy skin and a neatly trimmed dark beard stood before him, arms crossed beneath a short cloak that draped mostly over his left shoulder, legs braced apart in an aggressive stance. His black doublet and trunk hose laced with silver, with a small silver lace ruff was the height of fashion. Behind him stood a burlier man clad all in black, right down to the hood that masked his face.

The torturer.

The blood drained from Hal's face. His skin felt icy cold. At the same time heat flashed up and down his limbs. His knees wanted to buckle. The chains held him upright.

"Ah, I see you do not relish pain," the shorter man said in heavily accented English. He stood slightly to one side of Hal. The top of his head just reached Hal's nose. A small and slender man by English standards.

"You speak my language?" Hal had to change the subject. He couldn't think about what these men planned to do to him.

"When necessary." The man shrugged.

"What do you want from me?" Hal wondered how long he could keep from telling everything he knew. Would he lie, or make up stories just to get relief from the torture?

Looking into the hard black eyes of the short man and the eager, pale blue gaze of the hooded man told him they would stop only when they wanted to, not when Hal revealed what they wanted to know.

"The moon wanes. Therefore, the ritual requires a certain amount of time to complete," the short man said, ignoring Hal's question. "The . . . ah . . . discomfort will be more tolerable if you cooperate."

"Why?"

The short man raised his eyebrows in question.

"Why have you brought me here? Why won't you let me care for my dog?"

"I have brought you to this place for the ritual."

"What ritual?" Hal nearly screamed. "Just let me tend to Helwriaeth's wounds."

"Helwriaeth? What an interesting name. A ghost from hell?"

" 'Mighty hunter' in the old tongue."

"Ah." The Spaniard tapped his chin with one finger with blackened fingernails. Grime or an affectation? He kept his left hand behind his back and beneath the cloak. What was wrong with it?

"Most interesting. The dog will be more useful in the ritual than I expected. Kin to wolf and yet not a wolf. Too bad he has to die."

"No!" Hal fought his shackles. They rattled uselessly.

Helwriaeth lifted his huge head, teeth bared. But no drool hung from his beard. He needed water. He needed help.

Hal licked his lips. He needed water, too. And help.

The torturer stood mutely against the door.

"The bond between you is strong."

Hal did not dignify that statement with a reply.

"The dog would die for you, no?"

Hal concentrated on the locks rather than answer his captor. If only he could see the mechanism, he would know which piece to move with his mind.

The little man's neck would snap quite easily under Hal's hands.

"You may wish my death all you want. Many desire the same end." The little man beckoned the torturer forward. "I have many enemies. Most of them are powerless against my magic. They must sit mutely and wait for one much stronger than you to breach my defenses."

The torturer proffered a dagger to the little man. Light flickered upon the keen edge, turning it red, as if it were already blooded. Red runes marched up the ebony hilt. An athame, or ritual knife.

Hal swallowed. A lump in his throat nearly gagged him.
Helwriaeth growled feebly.

"Your dog must watch. Blood is required for the ritual.
Yours and his, my Pendragon Niño." The little man
laughed.

"What . . . what did you call me?"

"What you claimed to be. The Pendragon of Britain. But
you are still but a niño in magical maturity." The man
beckoned the torturer forward. "The face first. Teach him
to shave."

The hooded man planted himself so close to Hal's chest
his shirt laces tangled with the ebon beard that fell below
the black hood. Hal smelled garlic on his breath and
recoiled.

His head banged against the stone wall. Black stars burst
before his eyes.

And then came the icy sharp pain as the knife sliced
his cheek.

He screamed.

Helwriaeth yipped.

Hal opened his eyes just in time to see his beloved dog
gather the last of his strength. Clumsy with pain Helwriaeth
braced his three good limbs beneath him. In one mighty
burst of energy, he lunged.

The torturer raised his hands to protect his face. He still
held the long dagger.

Helwriaeth clamped massive jaws on the man's throat.

Blood spurted.

Growls and howls.

A tangle of limbs and fur.

The torturer slammed the knife blade into the dog's
throat.

They both gagged and crumpled to the floor, dead.

Chapter 19

6 July, 1574. The cellars of the Spanish Embassy.

"HELWRIAETH!" Hal's anguish ripped through his throat like the dagger ripped through his dog's.

The short man let loose a string of Spanish curses. Hal translated one as "Son of camel dung." He did not want to translate the rest. The man wrenched Helwriaeth's corpse off of his torturer, using the hook that replaced his left hand. The dog's death throes had clamped his jaws tighter on his victim's neck. When the Spaniard finally freed the dog from the torturer, he came away with a chunk of flesh still clamped in Helwriaeth's jaws.

"Farewell, my noble friend," Hal murmured. Grief alone kept him from cringing at the sight of the hook upon the man's maimed limb. That hook could inflict worse wounds than the athame.

Emptiness. Loneliness.

And then a flood of love washed over him.

We are with you, heart-son of the Merlin. Have courage. We will give you what strength we can.

A deadly calm spread through him. Hal knew he now had Helwriaeth's courage, dignity, and nobility to help him withstand the coming ordeal. He prayed the best of his dog would linger long enough.

The Spaniard yanked the dagger out the dead dog's neck. "You will pay for your animal's foolish gesture."

"A noble gesture." Hal stood as tall and straight as his shackles would allow. "My familiar chose to die defending me rather than wait for you to use him in your obscene ritual."

"So, my Pendragon Niño has a spine after all." The Spaniard ran his hook along Hal's ribs.

Hal flinched. His flesh crawled at the touch of the sharp metal.

Pain. The knife slashed across Hal's ribs.

He inhaled sharply. The ritual knife, not the hook. Why? The hook would have been more personal.

"You may as well give in to your desire to cry out."

More pain. Down the length of Hal's left arm. Sharp. Demanding of attention. Then a flow of hot blood welled out of the wound.

"Give in to the pain," the Spaniard said. "Learn to love the pain, make it your own, and draw power from it!" He raised his eyebrows in a weak imitation of Da's single, intimidating lifting of one brow in query or sarcasm.

Remembering his father's strength and the travail of Uncle Griffin in his role as the Merlin, gave Hal the courage to fight this man with his only weapon. Silence.

But, oh! It was hard to hold back the burning tears.

Helwriaeth dead!

Empty loneliness warred with his need to keep silent.

His left arm grew weak. The shackles kept it raised.

This would be so much easier with Helwriaeth beside him, giving him strength.

We are with you. The voice in Hal's head sounded like Da, but different.

"Uncle Griffin?" he asked, blinking blood out of his eyes. Mist seemed to gather over Helwriaeth. Hal could not see well enough to know for certain if the ghost of the Merlin had come to help him in his ordeal or guide him to the other side.

Another icy hot slash on his upper chest.

Hal bit back his gasp. He tried to breathe through the pain. Every movement of his lungs made the new wound burn.

"Your blood must mingle with the wolf inside and outside your body. Let the blood flow!" the Spaniard chortled.

More cuts in rapid succession. To Hal's legs and face. He grabbed the chain above the shackle on his right arm to relieve pressure on his left. That single limb free of pain was all that kept him from collapse.

Cling to the pain. Make it your own. Possess it. Master it. Use it as a weapon against him.

"Scream! If you do not scream, you do not release your humanity! *By the king,* you are stubborn." The Spaniard lashed out again. This time his blade cut Hal's right arm.

Hal barely felt it. The voice in his head kept talking, reminding him how much magic came from pain.

"You are but Niño!" the Spaniard protested. "You will be difficult to control once this is finished. But I will control you. I am The Master. The Master of Wolves. *El Lobison.* You will be my prime wolf in Britain. The Protestant dogs will no longer undermine my mastery with *science.*" He spat the last word.

Hal needed to think on that. But he could not move beyond the pain to concentrate on mere ideas. Only the pain mattered. Only the pain was real.

"This would have been easier with the dog still living. His foolish but willing sacrifice to save you will give this spell a similar strength." The Master of Wolves nearly chortled as he turned his wicked blade and his hook to butchering Helwriaeth.

Hal sagged in momentary relief that there would be no new pain. He had a few moments to master the pain.

El Lobison shouted and proclaimed ritual words in a language Hal did not know. Each syllable sounded alien, almost forced from the throat. Nothing he had ever heard resembled those words.

Each hack and slash into the dog's carcass reminded Hal that the knife inflicted no new indignities on his own body. How could he feel grateful and guilty at the same time?

Then the Spaniard—Hal would not call him The Master even in his own mind—lifted a bloody mass from the corpse. He cradled it lovingly; his hook did not penetrate it. Then he pressed it to his lips.

Hal gagged.

But the Spaniard only kissed the gore with reverence.

"Keep your Bloody kisses to yourself," Hal intoned. Outrage grew in him. The pain leaped into his mind, as powerful as any spell or ritual he'd ever experienced.

The shackles flew away from his wrists and ankles.

Hal lunged. He grasped the Spaniard's throat with murderous intent.

"I am your Master!" the man spat. He shoved the bloody mass of offal into the profusely bleeding wound on Hal's chest. "The spirit of the wolf in your dog's heart will invade your body. Your spirit will bind with the nature of a wolf. Wolf blood must mingle with yours. Accept the primitive lusts within the blood!"

Fire lanced through Hal.

He tightened his grip on his enemy's throat.

New flames ignited the wound across his abdomen. He doubled over, still clinging to his torturer.

"You shall die with me, *bastard of camel dung.*" He threw the man's own curse back at him in Spanish.

Hal's knees gave way under the new onslaught of pain. Blackness crowded his vision.

The Spaniard only smiled. A death grimace.

The blackness overwhelmed Hal. He felt his grip slackening but could do nothing more.

"I am stronger than you, Pendragon Niño. I am Master of the Wolves."

6 July, 1574. Greenwich Palace, London.

"I beg Your Majesty, grant me passport to France." Donovan shifted uneasily from the prolonged time Elizabeth kept him on his knees. The cold tiles on the black-and-white marble floor of her audience chamber reminded him of a chessboard. He was merely a pawn in the queen's greater game of keeping England safe, strong, and at peace.

Elizabeth Regina, Gloriana of Britain, looked down her long nose directly into Donovan's eyes.

"Why, my Wolfhound, do you not just hie yourself over the Channel on the family broomstick as did your children?"

Donovan winced at her sarcasm. But the twinkle in her brown eyes warned him of her jest.

"My children took themselves to France on a personal quest without my knowledge or permission. Now I hear they face terrible danger. I must have your leave, Majesty, to go to their aid."

"I would keep my Wolfhound close." She caressed his hair. Elizabeth's longtime friend and lover, Robert Dudley,

Earl of Leicester had transgressed recently. Elizabeth indulged in these meaningless gestures simply to inflame his jealousy.

"There is a private matter we must discuss, as you mentioned in your summons, Majesty," Donovan whispered.

"You are away from court too much." Elizabeth said aloud, continuing her display of affection. "We will send for you later," she whispered.

"May I remind Your Majesty that I must endure long spells of absence from your beauty at your behest? Edinburgh is cold, drafty, and lonely without your shining presence." Donovan used the flowery court language as expected of the queen's courtiers.

Finally, Elizabeth gestured for Donovan to rise.

He stumbled. Elizabeth caught his arm and steadied him.

A gasp ran around the assembled courtiers at this familiarity.

But then the Earl of Leicester was currently out of favor. Rumor had it that Dudley's current mistress—possibly a secret wife—Douglas Howard, Dowager Countess of Sheffield, was heavy with Dudley's child.

Elizabeth's courtiers could afford to waste no affection or attention on their wives and children. Unless Elizabeth herself arranged the match for her own devious reasons. And then she wanted the man back at her side as soon as a son and heir came squalling into the world.

She'd done that for Donovan. His second wife, Martha, had been picked for him by Elizabeth for the sole purpose of begetting an heir to Kirkenwood. Now that Donovan had an heir, Griffin, and a spare, Hal, Elizabeth saw no reason to mourn Martha's death from the awful plague of 1563.

If the queen even suspected Donovan had turned his affections to Elizabeth's rival, Mary Queen of Scots, she could easily throw him into the Tower and restrict Mary's freedom even more than she already had.

"Majesty, my *heir* is involved in this misfortune." Donovan pressed the advantage of Elizabeth's closeness, keeping her hand on his arm and his mouth close to her ear. "I fear he faces the same dangers of which you wrote to me. Werewolves threaten the peace of Paris."

"You have two heirs," Elizabeth turned her back on the

mass of courtiers and began walking toward a tiny antechamber. Not everyone in her entourage would fit there.
"We will discuss the other matter privately. Later," she
hissed.

"I have two heritages to bequeath," he replied quietly.

Damned if she didn't set a purposeful stride. Most of the
courtiers would have to scurry to follow at her pace.

"Which boy has gone to France?" Elizabeth stopped
abruptly, just inside the door to the chamber.

"Henry, Hal we call him, named for your father."

"The second son. The eldest is always named Griffin."

Donovan nodded his head.

"In your generation, both heritages would have gone to
your elder twin, Griffin."

"If he had not gone to France to become a priest."

"But he came back and became the Merlin."

Again, Donovan nodded.

"And which of your sons looks to follow your twin?"

"Hal shows signs of controlling a great deal of power
when he has matured enough to understand it."

"Is there another heir to this power? Another to help
combat the Otherworldly forces that gather at our door?"

"Aye."

"You become more like Griffin every day!" Elizabeth
slapped his forearm with her fan. "Speak, man. I'll not
tolerate silence in you as I did in your brother."

"My daughter Betsy, named for you, Majesty. And my
niece Deirdre, named for a long-dead relative."

"From which branch of your sprawling family does this
Deirdre hail?"

Donovan swallowed. He did not know why he was reluctant to reveal Dee's parentage. But he knew he had to
tell his queen the truth. She'd find out eventually. She was
determined in ferreting out the secrets of her courtiers as
well as her enemies. Knowledge was her tool and her
weapon. With knowledge she could balance the forces that
would drag her into war, or scandal, or economic ruin. With
knowledge she could keep herself and England safe.

"Before his death, my brother Griffin engaged in a brief
affair with . . . a fatherless woman I never met." But he
had. He just had not known her name or the role she and
her pet demon would play in the religious wars a decade

ago. "Roanna was her name. Of Clan Douglas. She birthed a single girl child from that brief union and entrusted her upbringing to me and my sister Meg." He recited the facts as if reading an accountant's ledger.

Elizabeth hissed as she drew a sharp breath through her teeth. "Griffin?" she mouthed the name of the man she had befriended.

"Aye, madam."

"I did not think he had the stones . . . Never mind. This child interests us. Hie yourself to France and rescue both these errant children. And when you return, we will interview the girl. Mayhap find a place for her in our household."

"My daughter, Betsy, is more of an age to attend you, Majesty." Donovan remembered his earlier plot to distract Betsy from her infatuation with Robin.

"We will receive her as well. But not until Griffin's daughter comes to us. Present them both to us when you return." She tapped her chin with her fan. "We shall hold the other wolves at bay at little longer with the help of our spymaster, Francis Walsingham, and the alchemist, Dr. Dee." The queen dismissed him with a flick of her hand and returned to her milling crowd of attendants.

"Milord of Kirkenwood," Elizabeth called over her shoulder.

"Yes, Majesty?"

"We would know the nature of your frequent correspondence with Mary Stuart before your escape to France."

A muted gasp passed from mouth to mouth of the queen's ladies-in-waiting.

"I pass news of her son, Majesty. The heart of a parent yearns for such things. Especially the heart of a mother." He narrowed his eyes, wondering which of his letters Bess Hardwick had passed on to the queen. How much of his heart had he revealed?

"What sort of news? Word of diplomatic envoys petitioning James? Or perhaps word of plots against the boy's regents?" Elizabeth returned to his side. She snapped her fan open and closed again several times.

"I send news of King James' progress in education, how tall he has grown, how his health fares. Is such trivial information forbidden to a mother separated from her only

child, Majesty?" A subtle reminder of the similar letters
Donovan conveyed to Elizabeth in code with news of Robin's education, health, and growth.

Donovan opened his eyes a little wider, hoping for a
mask of innocence.

"Such news is not forbidden. Yet. Tread warily, Wolfhound, should your letters contain protestations of love or
coded plots for our guest's escape." Elizabeth tapped her
folded fan repeatedly against her palm. "You leave for
France with your word of honor that you will return to us
with the children."

"I do not write in code to anyone but you, Majesty. I
have no need to. And you have my word of honor that I
will bring my children home to the safety of England or
die trying." Donovan bowed from the waist, keeping his
eyes upon Elizabeth's expression.

"Prettily said, Wolfhound. Remember that you are our
subject, not Mary Stuart's. Go now, fetch your errant children and bring them back to us. Perhaps we can teach them
manners and obedience at court. You seem to have failed
in this, Milord of Kirkenwood." She cupped his face briefly,
then turned back to her ladies and courtiers.

Chapter 20

9 July, 1574. Paris.

FOR three days I searched for Hal in my scrying bowl. I sought him from deep within the Earth in the safety of the crypt. I sought him in the open air of the park before the embassy. I sought him in a puddle of ale on a tavern table.

All I saw of my cousin was the cloud of darkness that cried tears of blood.

While I cast this small magic, my cousins and Thom Steward appealed for an interview with the Spanish ambassador. They sought the help of the English ambassador but he had left Paris, escaping the heat and disease and evil humors of summer. The Spanish guards turned my family away at the door. Thom Steward wrote to the Spaniard directly, using Uncle Donovan's name. They pounded on the gates in the name of the Pendragon.

Always they were turned aside.

Coffa refused to eat. I had no appetite. We both spent long hours staring into an empty distance. We wasted and we pined.

Instead of enhancing my magic, the ghostweed seemed to have drained it from me. The one time I truly wished to use my magic it would not heed my call.

While my mind roiled, the city quieted. The mercenaries slipped away from their camp and did not regroup. The monstrous deaths around the cathedral ceased. The heavy pall of dread left the Parisians and settled upon my shoulders. All of it.

My spirit nearly broke under the weight of it.

For three days I accepted this as my cost for the spell I had worked.

On the third day I awoke knowing that the heavy cloud of despair originated not with myself, but from an outside force. A very powerful magician controlled me, kept me from seeking Hal directly.

The time had come for action. I shrugged off the nearly overwhelming dread, ate a hearty breakfast, and went in search of the components of my next spell.

9 July, 1574. The cellars beneath the Spanish Embassy, Paris.

Hal breathed deeply, willing the lingering aches and cuts to fade. At least the Spaniard had moved his chains and shackles to a lower hook that allowed him to recline or sit on the straw.

Cold seeped into his butt and lower back from the stone floor. Dampness from the ancient cellar walls invaded his shoulders. The cuts on his back eased briefly with the cool contact. Then they hurt more from being too cold.

He did not know how long he had lingered here, half conscious. *El Lobison* came and went at irregular intervals. Sometimes he burned incense, drew arcane sigils in the air, leaving trails of fire, and chanted in some guttural language. Sometimes he rubbed part of Helwriaeth's rotting corpse into Hal's wounds. Sometimes he just stared at Hal with malicious gloating.

Hal understood none of these rituals.

He drew in another long breath, held it, released it on the same count. His mind drifted toward home. Kirkenwood. The castle atop the tor, the village, the standing stones.

But the faces in the granite stones closed their eyes and turned away from him.

He jerked awake from the half dream. Why would his ancestors shun him?

"Ah, you are awake," the Spaniard said from the doorway.

How had he entered so silently? Or had he been in the cell all along?

"I asked the English ambassador about you last night," the Spaniard continued with only the briefest of pauses. He kept his arms folded so that the hook was masked by his sleeves.

Hal turned his head away, gesturing his refusal to listen.

"Does it surprise you that I should dine in such august company?"

"Why did the ambassador not leave Paris for the summer?"

"He came back at my behest. We had much to discuss."

"I am surprised that a *civilized* man would receive you." Hal could not help replying. He put every ounce of contempt he could muster into his words.

"Ah, but the noble and powerful of Paris do not openly acknowledge who I am. Just as they do not acknowledge you or the heritage you claim."

"I *am* the Pendragon of Britain. There is no one else to challenge me."

"Do you protest too much, Pendragon Niño?"

"There is no one else." Hal hung his head as if in sadness.

"We are much alike." The Spaniard, too, dropped his gaze. Possibly he grieved for lost family. Possibly he lied with every word and breath.

"I will never be like you!" Hal spat.

"But you already are." The Spaniard gestured with his hook, looked hard at it, then tucked it into the folds of his short cloak. Out of sight, out of mind. "I have asked many questions in the last three days. It seems many people know the legend of the Pendragons of Britain, but no one knows for certain that you exist, or perhaps you lived long, long ago." The Spaniard cocked his head and considered Hal for several moments.

Hal would not dignify his statement with a comment.

"I heard rumors that your family pays lip service to the dominant religion of the day, but secretly you maintain a reverence only for the old gods, the old ways, and the old magic. You keep them alive when all others turn their backs."

The Spaniard ceased his examination of Hal and sorted through a pile of rags and herb packets beyond the brazier in the opposite corner of the cell from Hal. He emerged from the shadows with a heavy fur pelt draped across his arms.

Hal gasped in revulsion that the man had skinned Helwriaeth and now displayed a trophy.

But the coloring was wrong. And the animal had been much smaller than a full grown male wolfhound.

"A wolf pelt," the Spaniard explained. "A fresh one. I had to send my men deep into the forest to hunt it. A used pelt will not do for you, my Pendragon Niño."

"I do not belong to you."

"But you will." The man grinned, showing his yellow and pointed teeth.

Hal shuddered at the pain he must have endured to file his teeth so they resembled the wolf's.

"My family, like yours, traces our ancestry deep into the past. Long before Christian or Muslim came to Spain, we ruled as magician kings. With each wave of conquerors, we have . . . adapted. I and my family have become the most trusted advisers to the new men who call themselves kings and emperors. I believe your family serves the same function. We both whisper into the ears of politicians. We spy for them, and we manipulate our country's enemies. But our memories are long. My family, too, worships the old gods, the old ways, and the old magic in secret."

"Black magic," Hal muttered.

"Perhaps. Who can define magic? It is a part of life if we but embrace it."

Hal could not argue with that. Instead, he kept his eyes on the wolf pelt that the Spaniard stroked with his fingers. What could be the purpose of the pelt? He could think of no means it could be used to continue the torture perpetuated by the man.

"What you call white magic is but a weak attempt to bend the forces of nature. I use magic more thoroughly. I do not merely bend, I change and control to my own needs."

"You pervert the talent granted you."

"No. I embrace it. I utilize my gifts to the fullest. You will not. Therefore you will never have enough power to defeat or even escape me." The man sounded so calm, so rational.

A great trembling began in Hal's gut. If what he said
was true . . .

"Now for the next part of the ritual." The Spaniard
draped the pelt around Hal's shoulders. He patted it into
place with his right hand, keeping the wickedly sharp hook
behind him. The skin beneath the fur was still raw and
bloody.

Hal nearly gagged at the smell of blood. At the same
time his body betrayed his sensibilities by snuggling into
the instant warmth generated by the fur against his skin.

The Spaniard drew the muzzle of the wolf and the tail
together across Hal's chest. He chanted again in that bizarre language. An old language, older than Latin, Greek,
or Welsh. Perhaps older than time itself.

A strange sense of the world falling away cleared Hal's
mind. He saw, heard, felt, and smelled only this cell, the
man before him, the fire glowing in the brazier.

Suddenly his skin itched all over his body. The pelt
blasted new heat into his bones. He needed to fling it off.
The chains kept his hands immobile. He wiggled his shoulders, trying to shrug it away. It seemed to nestle more securely about his neck and across his chest.

A howl threatened to erupt from his throat. He clamped
down on it before it was fully born.

"Ah, you are nearly ready to take on the form of the
wolf. The pelt merely dictates which form you will take at
transformation."

"I will not succumb," he said to himself over and over.

"Ah, but you will succumb, because I am the greater
power," the Spaniard said. He dangled a new item from
his stash beyond the brazier from the hook. A richly jeweled and furred belt with silver fittings and buckles.

"What . . . what is that?" The heat and the itch had
almost become a part of Hal. He practically welcomed a
continuation of the discomfort.

He had to remind himself that he was stronger than he
seemed. He had the spirit of Helwriaeth and all of his ancestors to help him.

He just wished they would give him some ideas of what
he could do to stop this obscene ritual.

" 'Tis a girdle most ancient and powerful," the Spaniard

said. "I liberated it from a primitive tribe that lived on the
steppes of the Silk Road. It cost me dearly. I lost many
mercenary troops defeating their warriors and enslaving
their women. They bungled more than the attack. They
lost their booty and I had to buy the women at auction in
Byzantium. Beautiful women. Women most skilled in ancient arts lost to the chaste and boring females of Chris-
tendom and Islam." He licked his lips.

Hal could not help but feel a searing thrill of excitement
at the picture the man painted of the delights these exotic
women promised.

"Yes, this girdle cost me dearly. But it has gained me
much. A priestess of these people wore it, and nothing else,
on the auction block."

The image of the nearly naked woman sprang into Hal's
mind. Pressure increased in Hal's groin. The heat and itch
increased, almost pleasurably. What was happening to him?

"You shall meet this priestess tonight. She shall teach
you many delights when she places this girdle about your
hips."

"Wha . . . what is the purpose of this girdle?" Hal looked
at it as carefully as he could before *El Lobison* put it away.
The rough-cut sapphires, rubies, and diamonds winked at
him in the dim light. They seemed to invite him to gaze
into their inner depths and lose himself there.

He ripped his gaze back to the Spaniard.

"You will see, my Pendragon Niño. You shall see. Soon
enough. Until then, cherish your freedom of will. This is
the last you will know of it. I promise." The Spaniard
exited. His hysterical laughter echoed throughout the dungeon long after his footsteps faded.

Chapter 21

9 July, 1574. The cellars beneath the Spanish Embassy, Paris.

YASSIMINE sniffed around the edges of the heavy plank doorway. "A halfling," she whispered. Excitement made her heart pound and moisture flood between her legs. She licked her lips and flexed her fingers.

"You know what you must do." The Master played with the ends of the silk veils he had draped around her. Usually, he reserved the right of her removing the translucent layers one by one for himself. Tonight, he meant for her to seduce another. And in the seducing she would work the final magic to change the halfling into one of her own kind. This was the task for which she had been born. This ability had made her a priestess.

"The moon is not full," she stated around her need to pant.

She feared she had not yet gained enough strength to finish the task; no matter how much she wanted to do it. Nor had she drained enough magic from The Master to wrench power from him at the crucial moment of the ritual. The last three times he had used her body she had bitten him and drawn blood. Just a drop or two. In licking the bite wound clean, taking his blood into her, she had absorbed a little bit of his control. Made him more of a wolf and less of a man.

She would not have been able to run so far from him the night she sensed the *others* across the river had she not done this. The chains of silver and magic had burned her, weakened her. But they had not broken her.

Now she knew the *others* she sensed were this halfling

161

and his wolfhound. Their bond and their magic mimicked the scent of her own kind.

She needed more time and more of The Master's blood—given to her voluntarily. Already his teeth resembled fangs. Next time he would sprout more body hair.

"Not tonight," she repeated. "The moon is too far past full." Perhaps, if she forced The Master to wait, she could gain enough strength to bring him down and regather his pack around her.

She would control the wolves then. She would have the responsibility of their actions. And her own.

She would have no one to blame.

"We are not yet at the dark of the moon," The Master insisted. He circled her breast with the tip of his hook. Her nipple puckered in automatic response to what he promised her. "You still pant for fresh meat. You still crave to run free from sunset to dawn hunting your prey. Your prey is in that room. Tonight he will become your mate, your lover, and your son."

His breath fanned her neck and ear seductively. Just his words melted her bones, made the change begin in her.

He unlocked the massive door with a wave of his hand and three magical words—locked to keep their victim in or her out?

The scent of the half man, half beast flowed out of the dungeon like a river once the weirs had been removed. Her nostrils flared. Lust, thick and heavy, weighted her loins and her breasts.

She had no more excuses.

The Master gathered his magical paraphernalia and her bejeweled girdle and strode into the cell with the same jaunty sureness with which he greeted ambassadors and princes of the Church. Yassimine followed more meekly. She looked at the naked form huddled in on itself in the corner through lowered lashes. Naked except for a fresh wolf pelt around his shoulders, he shivered. A pathetic bundle of skin and bones. She looked away. The Master would punish her if she examined the halfling too closely. Her place was not to know the men she transformed. Or to want their touch ever again. Her place was only to do the deed.

By morning the halfling would be one more in The Master's army of werewolves that wreaked havoc upon the lands of the Spanish Empire and nibbled at the peace of Spain's enemies. All at The Master's direction. He needed only a few more of her get to rule the world—or so he claimed.

She could not allow that to happen. She had to wrest control from him before he conquered the last bits of the known world and the world beyond the seas.

The Master lit a brazier in the corner of the dungeon with a snap of his fingers. He chanted words that were close to the language of her birth, but more ancient, not quite the sounds she expected. By now she had the syllables memorized. Meaning was not important, only that the words came from the mouth of a magician in precise order.

The same ritual had been done to her by her sire during her twelfth summer, when her woman's courses had begun. Among her people such a getting was worshiped.

They had bestowed the precious girdle upon her as symbol of her priesthood.

Yet her people still hid on the nights of the full moon. They still feared what she and her kin did. Everyone wanted the honor and the power of becoming one of the Were. No one wanted to be the victim of their bloodlusts.

The people of these strange Christian countries feared becoming a creature of the Were almost as much as they feared dying at the jaws of one.

The Master sprinkled fresh herbs upon the fire. The smoke grew acrid. It filled her lungs and made them itch. Her skin crawled in preparation for the change.

The halfling would feel it, too. He'd start to thrash in a moment under the intense irritation of the smoke. Her blood heated in anticipation.

She took up the girdle and slung it about her hips.

Chanting his arcane words, The Master plunged tongs into the midst of his glowing coals. He retrieved a small pottery crock. The fired clay glowed red beneath its glaze. Power symbols etched into its round sides flashed white and then darkened to black as the pot cooled slightly.

Still muttering his words—Yassimine had never fully heard this part of the ritual and wondered if The Master continued the incantation or merely uttered nonsense sounds to please himself—he dipped his hook into the pot and scooped out a green paste that dripped like demon ichor.

Yassimine shuddered in the first throes of sexual pleasure. The herbs and the heat would burn the victim's skin until he felt as if it had shrunk and become too small for his muscles and bones. In a way it would.

The Master daubed the thrashing form in the corner almost gleefully.

The halfling screamed.

Her breasts became heavy and her knees weak.

Soon. Soon he would transform and then she would take him inside her. With one such as he, she would achieve true satisfaction. Something The Master could never give her.

But something about the skinniness of his legs and arms, the high pitch of his screams alarmed her. He came upright and threw himself against his shackles.

Her head jerked in his direction of its own volition. She opened her eyes wide and gasped.

Very little body hair covered him. Just the bare beginnings of dark shadows around his privates.

"He's but a boy!" A great trembling invaded her muscles. Her voice caught and wavered. Finally, she choked out, "Master, you have to stop now. He's but a boy. You don't need *children*. You need men. He will not be able to fulfill his role." He might not have the maturity to achieve full erection and penetrate her.

"This one will grow to his full potential soon enough. And when he does, I shall have the last kingdom that defies my control," The Master spat. "Cease your qualms. You have a task to perform." He reached across the small room and dropped a glob of the green paste between her breasts.

It burned through her skin and spread its irritating poison into her blood. She squirmed against the powerful itch and backed against the door. She had to get out of here. She could not allow The Master to do this to a *child*.

On the other side of the door she heard two guards chuckle at her discomfort. They did not open the latch, and she had not the magic to do it from this side.

A whimper escaped her throat.

The boy echoed her cries of pain.

He thrashed and tried to free himself from the constricting

wolf pelt. His chains rattled like bells tolling a death knell. But only followers of the White Christ rang bells to signal a death. And The Master did not follow the White Christ—no matter that he went through the motions and mouthed the words of their rituals.

The Master worshiped older gods. Gods older than even those of Yassimine's people. Gods that demanded blood sacrifice and sent demons to powerful magicians as their messengers.

Power rippled out from the boy's naked body. Magical power akin to The Master's, and yet different. For a brief moment she caught his gaze. He pleaded for mercy with her in that brief look. Pleaded for death rather than to lose his soul to the wolf.

This boy/man was someone special. Someone who could lead the pack. But when he emerged from the ritual, he would be The Master's creature. He would lose his power.

She could not use him to overthrow The Master.

A tear escaped Yassimine's eyes as she watched the boy struggle against his fate.

Even as she mourned the loss of his magical power, she triumphed at the murder of his humanity. The enchanted smoke, the scent of the wolf pelt, and the unmistakable odor of a male nearing arousal sent hot blood to her belly and breasts. Moisture dampened the silk that wrapped her loins. Heat filled her being. Even the soft silk became too heavy on her body and irritated her inflamed skin.

The change began in her. Muscle expanded. Bone grew denser. Fur thickened.

She would not completely transform this night. The moon was past full. Her skin showed through the fine fur that thickened slightly. A dim part of her remained human.

The Master thrust a fine needle into the coals in the brazier. He waited only a few heartbeats—heartbeats that thundered in Yassimine's ears—then he drew it out. The tip glowed red. With a smile on his face he whirled and plunged the needle through his victim's earlobe.

The boy screamed and wilted a little.

Yassimine's own piercings, in nipple and navel and pubis burned as well. But they burned with lust, not pain.

In seconds The Master inserted a tiny silver ball earring into the hole he'd made in the boy's flesh. Then he secured

it with a fine chain and stud. The loop was just long enough
to brush the boy's jaw every time he swung his head from
side to side.

She wanted to lick away the drops of blood that lingered
on his face, soothe the wound with her own special healing
and utterly possess him. She swayed slightly and her own
chains moved sensuously across her body beneath the concealing silk. She had much to teach this boy and only regretted he was not old enough to truly appreciate the gifts
she gave him.

"Now, my dear Yassimine, work your magic on him."

She gulped back the last of her misgivings.

One by one she dropped the silken veils. As she rotated
her head, freeing her hair from the confines of the veil she
drew the fabric under the boy's nose. His senses must be
heightened by the smoke and the stimulating herbal paste.
He'd have no choice but to smell her perfume that clung
to cloth as it did to her body.

Her thick black mane became a new veil. She loosed the
first scarf that bound one breast, making certain her bared
nipple alternately hid and peaked out from beneath the
shielding hair.

The boy kept his gaze cast down. His body did not stir
in interest. But he had to know what she was doing. His
nose worked much like that of a wolf catching a scent on
the wind.

She spun, pivoting on one foot, propelling herself with
the other. The veil covering one hip flew out and away. It
landed at the boy's feet.

He looked up then, eyes glazed, face red with embarrassment.

The Master laughed and rubbed himself.

The boy looked away again. His budding interest in her
shriveled. He held up his hands as if begging for mercy.

She should have stopped. She should have found the de-
cency to spare him at that point.

But the heat of the cell, the drumming of her heart, and
the sinuous dance she wove compelled her to finish. She
had to work a little harder for this one. Once started, she
could not stop. She'd never tried to before. Never needed
to. Even now, when she knew she should, she had to con-

tinue. Another of her get to fill her loins, to perpetuate her race, to fill the aching need The Master had created in her.

Another veil came off and draped across the boy's raised hands.

She ran her fingers along his chin. The faint dark shadows on his upper lip and along his jaw were still silky. Not yet as coarse as a man's beard. That would change very soon. The magic of the change would quickly bring his body to adulthood. She needed to feel his rough beard scratch her breasts raw.

She flung her hair back, exposing her naked torso to his troubled gaze.

He stirred again. Manly desire flickered across his eyes, banishing the filmy glaze of drugs and bewilderment and pain.

"Release his shackles now," she whispered to The Master as she passed him, draping yet another veil over his shoulder.

"No." The Master's voice came out slurred and heavy. His eyes drooped and he licked his lips. He was more aroused than the boy. But he'd wait. He had the maturity to wait until the ritual was finished.

"The magic does not work if he's chained." Yassimine continued to dance and entice. She cupped The Master's cock through his still-laced codpiece. He swelled immediately.

"He must come to me of his own free will."

"As if any of this is his will?" The Master laughed with heavy sarcasm. He fumbled with the ties of his piece.

"Release him."

"He has magic. Powerful magic that will overcome the spells if I open his bonds."

"His magic will blend with mine. The wolf will enter him more completely. You will not have to wait for the next full moon to bring him under your control." She removed the next to last veil. This one she twined through her fingers, letting it drift and float as she circled round and round, sending her balance and her senses outward and upward.

"Do it," she commanded her Master with all of the lustful compulsion that drove her.

His eyes glazed as he took the tiny silver key from his belt. Two steps brought him within reach of the halfling. Two heartbeats and the key was in the lock. Two circles and the chains fell to the straw along with her last veil.

Yassimine removed her girdle, her last vestige of clothing. She wrapped it around the boy's waist. It clung to him, molded to him, barely needed the clasp. A true symbol of the gift of godhood she gave him. Together, priest and priestess, they must now worship the wolf.

"And now you are mine," Yassimine growled into the boy's ear. She rubbed her breasts across his chest and down, down to his nearly full arousal. Her tongue followed, down the length of his body until she took him into her mouth and made him ready.

Then she pulled them both down into the straw and abandoned herself to her need. She took him into herself greedily. With her last coherent thought she bit his neck until he bled. She took his blood into her mouth, savoring the hot sweetness of his youth and innocence.

He answered her with a bite of his own. His elongating teeth broke the skin and lapped her blood.

Chapter 22

10 July, 1574. The cellars beneath the Spanish Embassy, Paris.

HAL awoke instantly with none of his usual drifting in and out of nothingness that could last an hour or more. His eyes opened and he knew instantly where and when he was and what had transpired.

He'd become a man last night. Even his twin Griffin, the heir to Kirkenwood, had not yet tasted the delights a woman had to offer. He wiggled his head a little where it rested upon the woman's belly. A smile grew on his face of its own volition.

Dozens of scents assailed him, sweet and acrid. He stroked the bejeweled girdle now resting comfortably around the woman's waist.

His memories of pleasure vanished in the face of new dread. More had happened than just a warped seduction by a woman of experience, witnessed by a depraved enemy.

He stiffened his muscles and joints with fear.

A small hand touched his hair gently, stroking him. "Hush," a feminine voice whispered. "We must not disturb *him* yet."

Hal had no question as to the identity of "him." A quick glance into the corner where the man rested, as naked and spent as Hal and the woman, revealed a black aura covering him in a shadowy mist. Hal shuddered at the evil within the man that could generate such a blanket of evil energy.

"He will sleep for a time. He always does after . . ."

"Wh . . . what did you do to me?" Hal fingered the spot

on his neck where the woman had bitten him. "It should be sore, bruised, weeping." He found no evidence of violence.

"You heal very quickly. Even for one of us," the woman said.

"And who is 'us'?"

"One of the pack."

He did not like the sound of that word at all. "I am human, not some crazed beast."

She did not answer him.

"What did you do to me?" he asked on a sigh.

"I have made you what your inner being craved to be."

The moment of silence drew out. How did he answer, or question, such a statement?

The woman sighed. "You do not embrace the wolf within you. Your familiar made your spirit strong and receptive."

Hal almost gagged as he remembered Helwriaeth's death, the man smearing his blood and organs into Hal's open wounds. The mingling . . .

"There are things you can do to reduce the risk to those you love," the woman whispered hastily. "But you cannot directly break his control over you." Her hand brushed the dangling silver the man had pierced his ear with.

The man who had arranged this ritual stirred from his place beside the brazier. He sprawled his limbs and lay on his back. A loud snore escaped his mouth.

Hal reached to yank the earring free, even at the expense of a torn lobe. At the first brush of silver his fingers burned as if plunged into the heart of a fire. He yelped and sucked on the new wound.

"How do I break the spell you have cast upon me?" he asked at length. Every bit of magic had an opposite. One could break any spell, if one only knew the components. So Da and Dee had taught him.

Oh! God. Dee. What had happened to her? Had he kept the Spaniard from finding her? Had her spell succeeded?

Hal braced his arms to rise from the decadent sprawl across the woman's lap.

"Not yet, my pup." She held his neck in place with surprisingly strong hands. "I will help you escape. But you must promise me, on your word of honor as a *loup-garou* as well as the *meneur des loups* you were before."

Why did she use the French words instead of the Spanish? He struggled to find meaning in them. Something about wolves. . . . Then Dee's impatient face appeared in his mind.

"A tamer of wolves, you silly boy."

He heard her say the definition of the second term as clearly as if she were in the room.

Then he knew the first term. Knew it in his gut before his brain registered the words. *Loup-garou.* A werewolf. He ran his hands over his body, seeking evidence of the change. His beard and mustache seemed heavier, coarser. Hair sprouted on his chest and loins. His chest. Was it broader, more clearly defined as well as hairier? The beautifully exotic woman had turned him into a *werewolf.*

Goose bumps broke out all over his skin. He sweated and shook. His teeth rattled together.

"Devil's eye was part of the salve. You must make a similar paste of ghostweed and spread it across your shoulders every day to counter it. Small amounts only. The weed will give you delusions of power otherwise. You must never wear fur because a wolf pelt was used to invoke the creature already within you. You must never eat meat. On the three nights of the full moon, you must separate yourself from men. And above all else you must never engage in . . . be with a woman who is not one of our kind." Agitation entered the woman's voice. Still, she kept a firm hand on his neck anchoring him in place.

"These practices will give you a measure of control. Nothing can cure you."

"Why do you help me?"

"I have never turned one such as you before. You need to grow a bit before embracing your true nature. Then you will come to me, share my power, and together we will bring down *El Lobison.*"

"What do you mean by 'my true nature?' Do you mean only certain people can be . . . become . . ." He swallowed heavily, forcing down the lump in his throat.

"Anyone can be turned. You are a wolf, as am I."

"Why? Why do you do it?"

"Because it is part of who I am, what I believe, the gods I worship. Our gods, our nature. Once the ritual begins, we become trapped in the magic. I could not stop even when I realized your youth and innocence."

"Why does *he* do it?"

"He seeks to control through terror. You stopped the terror he wished to invoke in the streets of this city. Now he must control you to break others."

"But . . ."

"Go now, quickly. Before The Master wakes." She shoved him off her lap. "Remember the gift of freedom I have given you and return to me when the time is ripe to overthrow his control of the pack."

"He will punish you if I leave. You must come with me." Hal grabbed the shreds of his clothing and tugged them on haphazardly. His shirt strained across his shoulders. His breeches had become a tight fit about his hips.

"I have endured punishment before," she said. Her voice sounded as if she anticipated the punishment with excitement rather than dread. "I can give you time. Obey me in this. Obey me when you return."

One look into her dark eyes convinced Hal. He rose to his feet and tiptoed to the door, careful not to brush loose straw into the man's face as he passed him. He paused only a heartbeat to close his eyes and bid silent farewell to Helwriaeth's corpse, crumpled into the far corner of the dungeon cell.

"It's only a husk. The true spirit of my Helwriaeth lives in me," he muttered.

"Quickly. He stirs." The woman crawled over to the man. Her Master rolled onto his side and reached out. She took the hand and began stroking his palm in sensuous circles. "I can distract him only a short time before he discovers your absence. Go!"

Hal faced the door. The latch lifted easily at the briefest touch of his mind. Da had promised him that little magics would come more easily with maturity. He certainly *felt* older today. As old as myth and more tired of life than a ghost.

And yet strength coursed through him. He had to move. Had to keep moving or he would howl his distress with Helwriaeth's mournful voice.

"I would know your name." He did not turn to face her. Somehow he knew she could banish him with a mere glance and no more information.

"Would you know it to curse me before your god?" A tremolo entered her voice.

"I know not if I will curse you or thank you for my escape. What are you called, in the language of your heart?"

"Yassimine."

"Yassimine," he breathed. "I will remember."

"One more thing. Until you learn to exult in the wolf you must pray every day and every night to whatever god you believe in. Pray long and hard. The deep meditation will calm the wolf for a time, give you a measure of control."

"Trouble is, I do not know that I believe in any god."

"Then find one you can believe in; even if only the wolf within you."

Outside, he found the guards asleep on their feet.

Only as he ran past them did he realize the woman had been conversing in a foreign language. Very alien syllables. Yet he had understood her.

The changes within him must be profound. He had the better part of three weeks before the full moon. By then he must understand all that she had done to him.

10 July, 1574. An inn near Notre Dame de Paris.

I needed a magical cannon. Something strong enough to blast a gaping hole in the wall of despair my enemy hid Hal behind. As much as I wanted to haul a real cannon off the walls of Paris and drag it to the Spanish Embassy, such a mundane weapon would not work.

No mundane plan or tool would work.

My enemy was formidable. Magic ruled his life.

I had to be stronger to free Hal from his clutches. I, a girl child of twelve. But I was a Kirkwood by birth and upbringing. I had to do this.

The magical references I would have consulted remained locked away in the lair of Kirkenwood. The family stash of herbs, minerals, and arcane tools remained there as well. I had to make do with what I could buy or scrounge.

Fortunately I had Thom Steward and my cousins, Gaspar and Peregrine, to help.

"Gunpowder," I had told them firmly last evening. "A small amount."

"How small?" Peregrine eyed me skeptically. More and more he looked like Uncle Donovan with his dark coloring, high cheekbones, and piercing blue eyes.

"The amount needed to fire an arquebus."

Thom Steward blanched at the suggestion. "Our purchase will be questioned. The authorities . . ."

"Then steal it," I insisted.

"And the arquebus?" Gaspar asked.

I found comfort in his blond bulk. He did not condemn or judge, only asked the questions necessary to carry out my requests.

Or were they demands?

"I do not need the weapon itself, only the powder."

I rattled off the list of other ingredients. Peregrine nodded sagely as if he understood why I wanted such bizarre things as the hair of a Spanish guard, a lodestone, and a bit of bone from a cat. Gaspar merely looked happy to finally be doing something.

"The myrrh to break a hex will be expensive," Thom Steward finally said. He hefted his purse. Not as many coins as only a few days ago.

"I will procure myrrh," I said. "As I will find the mistletoe to open doors and angelica to clear a path. I must gather them myself." Fortunately, I had found an apothecary in the city who had much the same philosophy for magic and healing as myself. I could only pray that the apothecary had or knew a hedge witch who would part with some ghostweed. It alone was strong enough to sympathetically lull the suspicions and close the eyes of those who guarded Hal.

I resigned myself to substitute deadly nightshade for the ghostweed. Not as effective, but adequate.

I buried my face in Coffa's ruff, hoping to share in her strength and courage. I feared my entire spell would be merely adequate. I needed spectacular to break the locks and get through the magical barriers erected around the palace of my enemy.

Hal's enemy.

More than that.

King Philip of Spain spearheaded the Catholic campaign to bring about Elizabeth's downfall in England. And along with her death he intended to restore the Roman faith. Spaniards held Hal, an heir to the Pendragon. Was this part of the plot? Was I next on the list for kidnap and possibly death?

Thom Steward, Gaspar, and even Peregrine looked to me for final orders.

"I must counter the forces of darkness with light. I begin the spell at first light in the glade across from the postern gate of the Spanish Embassy."

We had only a few hours. With money, with wiles, and with stealth, we gathered all that I must have. Coffa created distractions when money and sweet words did not garner what I needed. Thus I accepted the unknowing donation of the myrrh and a censer full of incense from the sanctuary of a church and the chaplet of hydrangea from the gardens of the palace of *La Louvre* at midnight.

The mistletoe and angelica had come from the apothecary—at the cost of letting him see and touch my budding breasts. Hal's safety was worth more than the brief humiliation.

We gathered in the park outside the Spanish Embassy as the first rays of dawn crept above the horizon. I drew a small pentagram around the censer with gypsum and magic. Coffa stood guard over my spell along with Thom Steward. They prowled a wide circle around us, adding another layer of magic to mine, though they did not know it. Gaspar and Peregrine each kept a hand on my shoulder, lending me strength and courage. I pulled energy from them ruthlessly. To blast through the barriers around the Spanish Embassy, my magical cannon needed every bit of power I could pour into it.

To my sensitized eyes the lines of the five-pointed star within a circle glowed an intense blue, almost the color of charcoal. I poured the measure of gunpowder in the bottom of the censer. I followed that with nightshade, angelica, and mistletoe. Mystical and ancient words of invocation accompanied each herb into the pot. By then, my words sounded slurred and my body slumped with fatigue.

Before I could balk, I sliced my finger with my little eating knife. I counted nine drops of blood added to the mix. My blood. My link to Hal.

My first step toward the dark magic Betsy loved.

"Like to like," I murmured with each drop.

Gaspar blinked frequently, trying to keep his eyes open. Peregrine breathed deeply, exhaling on long sighs, as if his lungs had grown too tired to work.

I had to continue. Without completion, the spell would scatter aimlessly, infecting innocent parties in unexpected ways. All kinds of barriers would dissolve. I did not want to break down the barrier of a priest's secrets garnered in the confessional, or open the locked doors of a royal *palais* to a thief.

Gathering the last of my reserves, I rolled the ball of cat bone in the myrrh and placed it on my open palm.

"Fire," I whispered.

Peregrine handed me a lit candle. The spell would be stronger with fire from my mind. I had not Hal's talent with it, or the strength to conjure it.

> *Clay from Mother Earth's bones,*
> *Blood from my Life to Water this spell,*
> *The Breath of the Gods fills the Air,*
> *Fire bright to light the Way.*

I touched the flame to one of the holes in the bottom of the censer. It lit the gunpowder. At the moment of the powder flash, I hurled the bit of cat bone into the postern door across the alley.

The earth shook. The door imploded. Two guards flew from the walls. I heard their screams. Then I heard the crunch of their necks breaking.

I could not breathe. Once more, innocent bystanders had died as a result of my magic.

My spell backlashed against me. It threw me backward. My head cracked with a dull thud.

Black smoke rose all around. I coughed. I gagged. I ached. I cried. Coffa nudged me, urging me to get up, to finish.

Limply, I recited a few words to dismiss the elements and ground the spell.

My tears would not stop.

"They come. We have to leave now!" Thom Steward shouted.

Coffa pelted for the now open gate.

"Coffa! Come back."

"We have to leave, Mistress," Thom Steward urged me upward. Ten men threw open the main gate. They emerged cautiously with pistols and swords held defensively before them.

"I won't leave without Coffa."

Peregrine lifted me into his arms and ran. We retreated without Hal or my dog.

Chapter 23

10 July, 1574. The Spanish Embassy, St. Germain, Paris.

HAL paused at the steps leading up from his cellar prison. He looked over his shoulder toward the closed door of his cell. Grunts and moans emanated from behind that door.

He closed his ears and mind to what must be occurring there. But he could not close his nose. Yassimine's perfume overlaid the scent of a man's sweat and spilled semen.

Some of that scent came from himself.

He hurried up the steps, away from his memories of torture and ritual. Away from what he feared he had become. Away from himself.

At this early hour before dawn, only a few servants stirred. He heard/smelled/felt them moving about the kitchen to his left at the first landing of the stairs. He stood hunted still, back pressed against the wall beside the door.

Two men, dressed in rough shirts and breeches and carrying pitchers of steaming water, slammed the door open as they tromped toward the next flight of twisted stairs. The broad and heavy portal swung toward Hal, blocking his view of the men and their view of him.

He held his breath for several moments, waiting to see if others followed the men with wash water for the nobility above. He heard rude shouts and muttered curses in Spanish, male and female, within the kitchen. But the people there seemed inclined to stay within.

With a gentle push the door began to close, as if moved by a gentle draft. No one came to investigate it.

Hal waited a few more moments for signs of movement up and down the stairs. With half of his attention on the activities of the servants he scanned his immediate envi-

rons. A change in the air currents from below alerted him
to the next source of danger. The Master stood by the open
door of the cell, adjusting his trunk hose and doublet while
he spat a stream of Spanish curses into the dim interior.

Breathless with panic, Hal bolted for the next landing
and the door to the outside. He did not pause to consider
the direction of his flight until cool morning air brushed his
face. He turned his nose to the wind and caught . . .

A blast of magic full in the face. The ground shifted
beneath his feet. He struggled for balance. Black mist rushed
toward him, enveloping him. Blinded and reeling, he fought
to grasp the doorjamb.

His hand encountered only air. Flailing about, he stumbled forward.

Coffa stood squarely before him, growling and dripping
drool from her exposed teeth.

Puzzled by her aggression, he held out his hand, palm
down. Fighting his instincts every moment, he avoided looking
directly into her eyes. He must not challenge her. She could
kill him with a single clamp of her jaws to his throat.

She backed off a step, whining. Hope flared briefly in his
heart. If Coffa was here, then Dee could not be far away.
Dee would help him unravel the puzzle of his capture and
the ritual he had endured. "Dee?" he asked the dog.

He needed to grab hold of her ruff and let her sturdy
strength balance him.

She snapped at his hand and renewed her growling
warning.

"Easy, girl," Hal said quietly. "You know me, Coffa.
Smell my hand. Remember who lies beneath the surface
smells you do not understand." He approached her slowly,
cautiously even though the hairs along his spine stood
straight up in warning of danger from behind.

Shouts of alarm erupted all over the *palais*.

Coffa worked her nose and curled her lip.

Frantically, he searched the rear of the walled compound
for inspiration. He had to get out of here. Now. Before
The Master sounded the alarm.

A guard, armed with a heavy pistol and a number of
blades looked down from his post upon the wall. He
blinked his eyes in confusion then opened them wide at the
sight of the wolfhound and the man she had cornered.

"Coffa, heel," Hal commanded in his most authoritative voice.

She dropped her ears and whined in bewilderment. But she kept her teeth bared. Her growls continued to rumble in her belly.

"Take me to Deirdre." Hal continued to push his authority over the dog, all the while keeping a picture of her mistress in his mind. He projected the image as completely as he could.

The door burst open behind him, nearly knocking Hal flat.

"Ring the bell, damn you!" The Master yelled. "Sound the alarm. He must not escape."

Hal wasted no more time on the dog or caution. He ran full out for the nearest exit. The narrow pedestrian door in the wall lay on the ground, splintered and broken. Beyond it, the manicured park and freedom beckoned.

He ran with Coffa nipping at his heels.

A large bronze bell began clanking from the corner tower.

10 July, 1574. An inn near the Cluny-La Sorbonne, Paris.

Donovan rested his head against the shoulder of his horse. The beast he'd hired in Calais had served him well, if not as swiftly as his own bloodstock, and deserved his rest. This quiet inn near the Pont St. Michel in Paris offered clean stables if not much else.

He thought the vicinity of the University would have more amenities for traveling scholars and church leaders. But the rabbit warren of streets in the Latin Quarter limited the space available to this establishment.

The dull ache in Donovan's left thigh began to burn. His mad dash from London to the coast, the rough voyage across the Channel, and then the long ride inland to the city had cost him more than he liked. Who knew what dangers his family faced in this foreign land? He needed to be fit and strong to protect them.

His sturdy sword rested comfortably and easily in its sheath at his hip.

"Gods, I hate getting old," he muttered.

What evil but Tryblith, the Demon of Chaos, could have caused Meg to have such a dramatic vision?

"I thought I sealed that devil's spawn behind its portal!" he muttered. Perhaps his magic had been as inadequate in that endeavor as it was in scrying for Mary.

He grabbed the panniers behind the saddle.

The earth rolled beneath his feet. An explosion sent him reeling into the timbered walls of the stable. He fought for a precarious balance. Black smoke gushed toward him. His horse rolled its eyes and reared.

Donovan covered his nose and mouth with his sleeve as he searched for the source of the menace. Other than the prancing steed, no one else in the busy forecourt seemed aware of aught but their own business.

"Magic," he whispered. The horse nodded its head as if agreeing with him. "What have the children done now? Wish I had one of the dogs with me. They could root out the source."

He straightened away from the wall, surprised to find he still clung to his saddlebags.

A tousle-headed boy peered at him from behind the watering trough. His eyes narrowed, calculating and curious.

"Stable the beast. Fresh grain. And procure me a room," Donovan ordered in French. He tossed the lad a coin and his bags. "I'll return before sunset."

He took off at an ungainly trot. His senses reeled, distorted by the blast of magic

His children needed him. He kept moving, righting for balance with each step.

All around him, people went about their business, blissfully unaware of the awesome power behind the smoke and the trembling ground. At the marketplace he paused to sniff the air. As rapidly as it had come, the black smoke dissipated. Or rather retreated in a roiling mass. Donovan followed it.

A few streets farther and he ran headlong into a small band in flight. Three men walked as rapidly as they could without attracting undue attention. They looked over their

shoulders anxiously. The tallest among them carried a limp
form in his arms. His sons and his steward.

"Where is Hal?" Donovan asked, rushing up to Peregrine.

He took Deirdre's limp body gently from Peregrine. His
son appeared dazed but whole. He'd recover, given the chance
to be quiet internally while locked away from the turmoil
of the mundane world.

Gaspar, on the other hand, looked as if more than his
wits had been rattled. A black smudge marred one pale
cheek and the tips of his blond hair appeared singed. By
the magical black smoke or something less arcane?

Donovan cradled his niece close to his chest while he
waited for the others to form answers in their addled
brains. Dee's eyes were scrunched closed as if shutting out
the world.

Swiftly, he checked her for the awkward posture of a
broken bone or cowering away from internal injury. She
did not thrash, just lay there limp and withdrawn. He dared
a brief probe to her mind and met a roiling mass of black—
like the retreating smoke.

Or the cloud of confusion around a demon.

"Jesu, I hope it's not Tryblith again."

"We failed, Uncle Donovan," Deirdre whispered weakly.
Her voice sounded as if she had to drag it out of some
dark recess in her soul.

Her words and her pinched face threatened to drive a
stake into Donovan's heart.

"Not total failure," Peregrine choked out.

"She put a band of mercenaries to sleep before they
could start a massacre," Gaspar added. He seemed to be
regaining his senses a little faster than the others. He had
a reputation for having fewer wits to lose. Donovan knew
that to be a mask. Gaspar played at innocence and stupidity
to disarm people. They spoke freely of private things in
front of him, believing him incapable of understanding.

"The dogs?" Donovan asked. He didn't dare yet ask
what had become of his son. Hal, the hope of all his ancestors to become another Merlin, a Pendragon worthy of
dealing with Elizabeth Regina, Mary Queen of Scots, religious wars, and other diplomatic tangles, not to mention
the day-to-day welfare of Britain.

For a few heartbeats Donovan was able to numb the

pain that threatened to grow outward from his scarred thigh to envelop his entire being.

"Coffa!" Deirdre's eyes widened, and she reached back the way they had come.

"Last I saw of her, she ran into that door you knocked down," Gaspar said.

"Into the thick of the smoke," Peregrine added.

"Mayhap she seeks her littermate and Hal," Gaspar said. He spent a lot of time in the kennels at home and understood the dogs nearly as well as Dee, Hal, and Betsy.

"Let's get you all back to the inn. You need quiet, food, and drink to sort this through." Thom Steward finally found enough courage to organize them, as he organized Kirkenwood and all of the people who lived there.

"Coffa!" Deirdre cried. Her sobs reached right down into Donovan's heart and threatened to rend it in two. "I can't hear Coffa."

"Whst, Little One." Donovan crooned as he pressed Deirdre's face into his chest. "Whst. You need quiet to listen for her. Quiet to soothe your aching mind."

"I never needed quiet before." She wriggled to get down. Donovan held her tighter.

"Coffa will come back on her own. You must be patient and call her. Call into the quiet in the back of your mind." He murmured to her all the way back to the inn.

Deirdre was safe. But Hal.

Hal! He stretched his mind as far as he could to reach his son.

Silence.

Chapter 24

The inn near Cluny-La Sorbonne.

DONOVAN retraced his steps with Dee clutched tightly in his arms. All around him, the early morning activity had increased. He sensed urgency and anxiety in the whispered gossip that passed from merchant to merchant, student to scholar, housewife to barmaid, and back again.

"I failed. I did not have ghostweed. Only deadly nightshade," Dee mumbled over and over.

The innyard remained open and welcoming. He hastened there with his sons close against his heels and his niece pressed against his heart. Thom Steward came last, guarding their backs.

The stable boy had taken care of Donovan's horse and procured rooms—the best in the house for a man wearing noble dress and throwing coins about.

Donovan tucked Deirdre into the bed. She continued to thrash and moan. He retired to the minuscule sitting room and set about mulling some wine in the hearth. This, he could do better than some serving maid. He kept a few essentials in his scrip like nightshade for use as a sedative. He added a pinch to his concoction, hoping it would calm Deirdre enough to make sense of her ravings.

But he needed to be out, tearing Paris apart, looking for Hal. He needed to know what sense of urgency flew on the breeze into the hearts of the locals.

He chewed on his lip while he brewed his potion. Peregrine gave a brief sketch of what had transpired so far.

"She only knew Hal was in the embassy because she could scry all of Paris except inside those walls," the young man concluded.

"A logical conclusion," Donovan agreed. But what the hell was Hal doing in the Spanish Embassy?

England and Spain were moving toward a trade treaty and exchange of new ambassadors. Elizabeth prepared to slight France if persecution of Protestants continued or escalated. He'd met with Elizabeth's team of diplomats to discuss how such an alliance might affect England's relations with Scotland.

Would the magical turmoil in the Spanish Embassy in Paris affect the treaty? Did it have something to do with Mary Queen of Scots?

"The magical cannon broke something," Gaspar insisted. "The earth rolled beneath my feet and the backlash wind nearly toppled me."

Donovan raised his head abruptly from stirring the wine. "Did you sense the magic because you were connected to Deirdre or because it is in your nature to perceive such things?"

Donovan himself had had little or no sense of magical talent until well into adulthood. This illegitimate son, Gaspar, might be another late bloomer.

Gaspar shrugged.

"I was connected to Deirdre and felt no earth movement, but I saw the smoke," Peregrine said. He stood with his hands on his hips and chin outthrust. He might look exactly as Donovan remembered his twin at that age, but Peregrine had not the finesse, or talent, or calm of Griffin the Elder. Just the intelligence. He'd make a good secretary for Donovan when Elizabeth called Robin to court—as surely she must.

What about Gaspar?

"Have there been any more attacks from this flesh-eating monster? I need to know about it. Was it a werewolf?" He'd had the unnatural creatures on his mind since the attack outside Nether Pedley and the one two years ago at the kirk near Kirkenwood. Was this the same pack Elizabeth reported menacing London, or a different one?

"No more attacks since we found Dee," Thom Steward replied. "But the full moon is past."

"And the people have not risen to massacre each other." Donovan almost sighed. He had too many questions, too many problems.

"No," all three responded.

"The city remains uneasy but not violent," Thom concluded.

"I presume the mercenaries have disbanded."

"Aye, sir," Peregrine answered. "They crept away when they awoke from Dee's spells. Nor have they returned. I have checked the ruins every day. I have heard no rumors of other gatherings."

"Then Deirdre's first spell succeeded. The Demon of Chaos was not loosed upon the city." Thank the stars and moon above for small favors.

"The populace move uneasily by day and bar their doors at night. Priests are busy blessing those doors to keep evil at bay. But the spell that put the mercenaries to sleep led to Hal's capture," Deirdre said from the doorway to the inner room. Her face was very pale and her gray eyes looked huge in their sunken sockets. She seemed taller and more mature than the last time Donovan had seen her, back at Kirkenwood.

He shuddered to think about the massive amounts of magic that had coursed through her young body.

"I failed to protect my cousin, Uncle Donovan. I failed in the one thing the Merlin must do at all costs, protect those she loves." A dull cast covered her eyes.

"You are not yet the Pendragon, Deirdre." When had the two titles become inseparable? But they weren't. The Pendragon, the title Donovan's family guarded jealously meant the guardian of all Britain who must deal on a broad political, diplomatic, and economic scale. The Merlin was a popular leader, a spiritual being, a kind of shepherd who held in trust the fragile hearts and hopes of the people.

Anyone could become a Merlin. Only one of the Kirkwood family could become the Pendragon.

Donovan's twin, Deirdre's father, had been a Merlin as well as the Pendragon.

"I cannot hope to achieve the heritage bequeathed to me by my father until I find Hal." Resolutely, she stalked out of the rooms.

"Deirdre, 'tis not safe!" Donovan grabbed for her on the landing above the common room. She eluded him without breaking stride. His two sons and his steward stood aside to let her pass, then grimly followed her.

Would Martha have been able to control any of them? He doubted it.

Cursing in several languages, ancient and modern, Donovan had no choice but to become yet one more in Deirdre's devoted entourage.

His only option in protecting her.

And to find Hal.

Suddenly everyone stopped, halfway down the rickety stairs to the common room. Others crowded around them headed upward, rapidly, driven by something they feared. Donovan pressed himself against the wall.

He reached for his dagger.

"Coffa!" I cried, wrapping my arms around my dog's neck. "Where have you been, my love?" A quick look around showed me only the faces of strangers. No sign of Hal. I buried my face in my dog's fur.

Dimly, I knew that a great many people flowed around us, up and down the stairs. They cursed and shoved but did not touch me or my dog.

Coffa drew a large sloppy tongue over my face. I didn't bother to wipe off the slobber. Her return was too important. Too precious.

Doggy breath accompanied images in my mind. Strange colors floated around the edges of a long and narrow courtyard made of stone. Walls crowded in on her. Loud noises and unfamiliar smells confused her. Damp earth beneath her/our paws. Strange tingles on the edges of her/our fur.

"She brought me back to you," Hal interrupted the series of memories.

Hal. And not Hal. The changes in his voice, deeper, more melodic, without a trace of cracking or boyish hesitancy made me look up. Some trauma haunted his eyes. He smelled of foreign magic. Not his own.

Coffa whined. I hugged her again. The changes in my friend, my cousin, my beloved companion, frightened us both.

Immediately, my eyes latched onto the silver chain dangling from his left ear. The lobe showed no signs of redness or swelling, as if the piercing were old and well healed.

Yet three days ago he'd not worn that ornament and had shown no signs of wanting to sport the courtly fashion. This earring dangled sensuously, not at all the simple gold ring made popular by the queen's sometime favorite, Robert Dudley, Earl of Leicester.

I searched further for the source of the changes I sensed. His posture, the set of his jaw, the dark shadow on his cheeks and upper lip that mimicked Uncle Donovan's beard in shape and color, and the sadness in his eyes told me more than a thousand words. Magic had aged him from a boy into a man.

Everything about him seemed bigger, more decisive. Except for that earring. My eyes kept returning to it as if bespelled.

I heard Uncle Donovan slam his dagger back into its sheath. A sigh of relief escaped us all.

"Coffa found me. She and I escaped together with the Spaniard raising a hue and cry," Hal continued. He set his shoulders and gazed clearly and levelly into his father's eyes. "Helwriaeth is dead." He clamped his jaws shut.

I gasped and clutched my chest in grief. "Helwriwriaeth." The rest of my words choked on a sob.

"He died trying to protect me." The set of Hal's chin told me he had already grieved and no further discussion would be tolerated.

"And you, my boy, how fare you?" Uncle Donovan reached out his arms as if to embrace his prodigal son. Something in Hal's gaze made the father retreat in confusion.

The press of people on the stairway shifted from fear of Coffa to curiosity. I had the dog under control. She made no signs of menacing the strangers.

Too many strangers. We needed privacy to plan our next move. I rose and gestured upward to the men of my family.

We all retreated back to the rooms up the stairs.

I reached a hand to my uncle in comfort as soon as the door closed behind us. I was as bewildered as he.

"We have to leave Paris today. Now. This instant," Hal said flatly.

"I just arrived. I've not had a bath and my leg aches

abominably," Uncle Donovan responded with equal steadiness. His stiff spine told us all of his determination.

"Then stay and face . . . 'Tis not safe anywhere in the city. Anywhere in France for those of our blood. We have to leave. Dee and Coffa and I at the least. The rest of you should be safe. You have not . . ."

Hal swallowed deeply and clamped his jaws closed once more. I heard his teeth grind together.

"We have not 'what'?" Uncle Donovan asked. He clenched his fist and took a step closer to his son.

Hal replied with silence. Not even mental images of the danger leaked from him.

The moment stretched and stretched again until I could bear it no longer.

"Have we time to retrieve our belongings from the other inn?" I asked, thinking of the clothing and dirty laundry strewn about by Peregrine and Gaspar. Thom and I had given up trying to enforce neatness.

I had almost all of my meager belongings on my person.

"No. We must hire horses and be gone. Now." Hal turned on his heel and marched back down the twisting stair to the common room. "My enemies, enemies of England, enemies of the Light, follow me. They cannot allow me to escape them and live."

A string of curses issued from Uncle Donovan's mouth. The air around his head began to turn blue.

Coffa enclosed my wrist in her massive jaws. Her teeth did not prick the skin, but she exerted enough pressure to convey her own sense of urgency. She tugged me to follow Hal.

"We have to go, Uncle Donovan. Something terrible awaits us if we linger. The people who held Hal still pursue him."

"I smell magic," he said quietly. Uncle Donovan's nose worked as if he fought a sneeze. "The air reeks of sulfur and ghostweed and arsenic." Even as he spoke, he shouldered his saddlebags.

Gaspar nodded in mute agreement with his father. Peregrine and Thom looked at each other in confusion.

Down in the stable Uncle Donovan pressed a large number of coins into the hands of the chief groom. Within heartbeats, five prancing horses were saddled and led out to us. My uncle threw me up behind Gaspar. I wanted a mount of my own. I could control the most stubborn of beasts.

"Don't even ask," Uncle Donovan glared at me as if he had read my thoughts.

He might have. With all of the questions and sense of urgency flowing through me, I had not considered shielding my mind from those I loved.

"But . . ."

The sound of galloping horses and crazed shouts cut off my protest. I heard a horse skid on the uneven cobbles as it rounded a tight corner in the narrow back streets of the Latin Quarter. Hal's enemies had found us already.

Uncle Donovan vaulted onto his horse like a man half his age without old injuries to slow him down.

"Hold tight," Gaspar said through gritted teeth. We bolted out of the stable yard and down the first alley to our right. Five armed horsemen came into view. A gun fired. The bullet whizzed past my ear. We all ducked low. Our mounts whinnied in fear and galloped. Coffa kept pace beside me. She grinned and drooled into her beard, eager for the run and the adventure.

I thought I'd had enough adventure this past week to last me a lifetime.

Behind me I heard many voices raised in anger. In fear. And a howl akin to Coffa's. A howl from the throat of something large and monstrous. A howl straight from the bowels of hell.

I shivered and clung more tightly to Gaspar's waist. He kicked the horse into greater speed. Ahead of us, Hal's shoulders shook and his spine seemed to collapse. He bent over, wrapping his arms around his mount's neck. His entire body seemed to shiver in dread. Or was it grief?

Behind us Uncle Donovan herded Peregrine and Thom Steward toward the bridge.

Coffa snapped at a man who stood in the street. He jumped away from her teeth into the midden at the verge, yelping and flailing. We thundered past. Others who lingered in our path scrambled out of the way.

They also cleared a path for our pursuers.

Hal held out his hand, palm up. I supposed he prepared a ball of cold fire to hurl back to the mounted men who led the hue and cry. Already his hand glowed.

No! I screamed at him with mind and voice. *You must . not reveal to the masses that we are witches.*

Hal dropped his hand. He chanced a look over his shoulder. His face blanched.

I looked, too. The lead rider, clothed in black and silver, had closed the distance by two horse lengths.

We have to make the mob believe that man is the enemy, I sent to Hal, still looking over my shoulder.

"Allow me," Uncle Donovan replied instead with a grin.

I must have lost control if my uncle overheard my mental statement.

Uncle Donovan scrunched his eyes closed in deep concentration. His hands went slack on the reins. He bowed his head. Then he reared upright, spine stiff and fists clenched.

The ball of fire Hal would have cast at the men now appeared in the hand of the leader. He stared at it with dark eyes wide and unbelieving.

The crowd of people gasped as one. They ceased their mad pursuit and stared at the manifestation of witchcraft in their leader. Not at the supposed witches they pursued.

With a shake of his hand, the ball of fire left the leader's palm and flew over our heads. It landed in a refuse heap perilously close to the wooden sides of a tavern.

About half of the crowd rushed to douse the fire that now licked at the building.

But it was witchfire. Only more magic would douse it, unless they managed to totally drown any and all fuel it might touch.

The other half of the mob closed in on the mounted men. They pelted our pursuers with offal and pounded them with clubs and tools. One horse screamed and went down. Other mounts collided with it, stumbled and crashed against the cobbles.

Unhindered, we cantered beyond the city walls and into more open country.

Hal slumped over his mount, shuddering and gasping for breath.

"Pull alongside of him," I urged Gaspar, wishing I had started this journey behind Hal and not my older, more stolid cousin.

Gaspar nodded mutely as he maneuvered his horse to match gaits with Hal's.

"Stay alert," I commanded Hal. "You mustn't fall off now."

"What? How?" he stammered, coming upright again.

I nudged Hal's horse with my mind. I made the beast think that safety and comfort lay in keeping pace with Gaspar's mount.

"Let me worry about the horse. You talk to me. Tell me what ails you and what I must do to cure you."

"There is no cure," he said on a sob. "No way to mend this. No way to . . ." He took a firmer grip on the reins and wrested control of his horse away from my mind. "I'll not have you tainted by my curse."

"Hal, but . . ." Tainted? Curse? What was he talking about?

"Just stay away from me until I have sorted this out."

"No one loves you more than I do, Hal. No one understands you better than I do. Let me help."

"I don't want your help, Deirdre Rose. Not now, not ever. Just leave me alone!"

My cousin, no, this strange man called me "Deirdre" not "Dee." He hadn't used my full name since we were infants teething on my dog's ears.

Chapter 25

13 July, 1574. The road to Calais.

OUR journey home was swift and, for the most part, uneventful. My anxiety for Hal and the dramatic changes in him overshadowed the lessening sense of dread as we moved west. Each night, he sought out graveyards and crypts for our camping places. He argued that the locals were less likely to stumble upon us accidentally there because they never habituated the homes of the dead after sunset. I had used that same argument on our long walk from Calais to Paris. But just those few short days ago—it seemed a lifetime—he had shied away from burial grounds, sleeping restlessly if at all, clinging to me the while. Now, he chose to stand guard all night, prowling around the tombstones, touching them almost affectionately. His night vision had improved one hundredfold, and he never tired.

"We will reach Calais 'afore noon tomorrow," Uncle Donovan said as he dismounted stiffly. He bent over his knees rubbing his thigh for a long time. "We sleep tonight on real beds with a hot meal to fortify us."

I smelled salt on the air and welcomed the evidence of the end of our journey.

The rest of our party also slid from their horses, groaning and aching from the punishing ride from Paris. Three long days, sleeping rough and eating little, and then only what we could manage in the saddle. We'd changed horses six times, never all of us at the same inn.

Every few leagues, Uncle Donovan or I had cast spells scattering our tracks to the four winds and erecting fields of confusion that would divert any magic that sought us.

Hal alone remained ahorse in the innyard. The beast

moved uneasily beneath him. He mastered it with firm
hands and more than just a touch of magic. "We can be in
the harbor by midnight," he protested. The lantern light
from the nearby inn reflected redly in his eyes.

I wanted to cross myself in superstitious fear. But our
family no longer adhered to the superstitions of the Catholics. Instead, I fingered the cross from the broken rosary in
my pocket.

"We rest tonight. Our pursuers are far behind." Uncle
Donovan shouldered his saddlebags and marched toward
the inn.

Hal continued to look anxiously over his shoulder. Then
up to the waning moon. He seemed to sigh in relief. Then
he touched the silver earring and stiffened again.

"He is right. We have seen no sign of the riders from
the Spanish Embassy for a day and a half," I tried to console him. "I cannot sense them or smell any seeking magic.
It reeks of sulfur." I shuddered at the shadow memory of
the demon that had haunted my mother. It, too, had reeked
of sulfur and tainted all it touched with a black aura.

"You can't understand!" Hal swung his right leg over the
saddle and jumped to the ground, as limber and sprightly as
he had been this morning. The silver earring glinted in the
lamplight. He seemed very conscious of it, touching it frequently, and shifting his neck so that it brushed his cheek.

"Why did you pierce your ear?" I asked the question
that had burned within me for days.

"I—ah—" Hal fingered the chain of the jewelry that dangled below his earlobe, not touching his skin at all.

"Perhaps you did not make the choice?" I chanced at
the only explanation I had for his nervousness.

"Forget it, Deirdre. Let me worry about it. You should—
just forget everything that happened these past few weeks."

"You no longer call me 'Dee,' " I accused.

" 'Tis no longer fitting to give you a childish name," he
retorted. He jerked his saddlebags free of his mount and
handed the reins to the hovering stable boy.

"Then tell me, Henry, why did you pierce your ear?"

"I—I told you to forget it." He stalked into the stable.
The horses shifted restlessly, snorting their wariness.

"Are you going to sleep in there?"

"What if I am?"

"Will you continue to sleep outside—in the family cemetery—when we return home? Or perhaps in Arthur's crypt?"

He opened his mouth as if to reply, then snapped his jaws shut. "What I do is no concern of yours." He turned his back on me.

Inside, I wept for the loss of his love. What had I done to offend him? I suddenly knew myself to be alone. I loved no one as I loved Hal. The rest of the family, I cared for. But only Hal had full command of my heart.

"Perhaps he merely grieves for the loss of Helwriaeth." Uncle Donovan came up behind me and slipped his strong arm around my shoulders.

I leaned into him, welcoming his warmth and his solid steadiness.

"When Coffa whelps, we'll have to make certain Hal bonds with a new pup."

I allowed his words to push aside my worries. For a time.

That night I crept out and followed Hal as he wandered the local churchyard. Clouds moved in and blocked the moon and stars. Little if any light filtered out from the closed shutters of the houses. Still, he moved effortlessly while I stumbled over every patch of uneven ground.

He reached a clear spot, leaned back his head, and let loose a mourning wail. The eerie sound echoed around the trees and the stone walls of the church.

Coffa backed away from the noise. She tugged upon the hem of my gown, urging me back to the safety of the inn. When I resisted, she shifted her grip to my wrist. Her teeth came perilously close to breaking the skin. My bones ached from the pressure she put on them.

I looked at her, wondering at the sense of desperation spilling out of her. I had not enough light to see more than a vague outline, her fur slightly lighter than the surrounding darkness.

"We'll go back soon," I promised her in a whisper.

Hal whirled around to face me.

A normal person could not have heard my quiet words, little more than a breath.

I rushed up to him and wrapped my arms around his

shoulders. He returned my hug, fiercely, for a moment. Then
he pulled my arms from around him and placed them at
my sides.

"Go away!" he said wistfully.

I sensed his gaze resting on me, peering through my surface thoughts, into the depth of my loneliness.

"Let me help you, Hal."

He sighed and turned his back on me. "*El Lobison* will
not allow me to get away from him. I must watch that he
and his minions do not creep up upon us."

"*El Lobison?*" I rolled the name around my mouth,
seeking a definition. It matched nothing I understood.

"His aura is black. Entirely black with evil, no other colors.
No light. No forgiveness. He pierced my ear. Through the
silver I know where he is and that he still hunts me."

"I can remove the earring. It's bespelled. That's what
worries you. I know I can take it out." I reached for the
silver. My entire hand burned at the first brush of the delicate chain against my fingers. The ache spread up my arm
to my shoulder before I could pull away.

The pain fled as soon as I retreated.

"No one can remove it." He turned his head so that I
could no longer see the jewelry. "No one can help me."

"How do you know that if you won't tell me what troubles you? We used to share everything, Hal. You are my
closest friend. I love you."

"Not anymore."

"How do you know that? If you would just talk to me. . . ."

"You are very good at listening. I know. But listening
won't help. Trust me in this. But do not trust me in anything else. Now just go away, Deirdre. Go back to my father. Let him lull your suspicions with his half promises,
and his half talent, and his half beliefs."

"Helping you is my responsibility, Hal."

"No, 'tis not. You are not the Pendragon. Not yet. Go
away and let me mourn in private."

"Uncle Donovan says you are to have a pup when
Coffa whelps."

Hal snorted with a hint of mirth. "I don't have to mourn
Helwriaeth. He is a part of me still. I mourn something
else. Something more precious."

"What could be more precious than your familiar?" I

knelt and wrapped my arms around Coffa. She continued to urge me away from this place. Away from Hal.

13 July, 1574. The Spanish Embassy, Paris.

The Master waved his hand over his scrying bowl. He looked up and smiled at Yassimine.

She cringed deeper into her corner under his measuring gaze.

"He cannot escape me, no matter what obscuring magic he casts," he said, baring his teeth.

Yassimine decided to ignore him. Maybe he would leave her alone. Every part of her body ached from his repeated beatings. No rape. Just physical torment.

"Don't you want to keep your pup close so you can train him properly?" The Master asked. The smoothness of his tone warned her of the lulling spell just beneath his words.

"My kind hunts alone," she replied.

"Why did you help him escape, my pretty wolf?" He darted across the room with the speed of the Were. Before she could prepare for pain, he twisted his fist into her hair and yanked her head backward.

Her head flew back, exposing her neck. Her eyes opened wide in alarm.

He laid the tip of his hook upon the great vein in her neck.

"Answer me, bitch! Why? I needed another day to anchor my control of him, make him grateful for the changes we wrought in him."

Yassimine swallowed deeply. The skin on her neck stretched painfully, making it difficult.

"He was too young," she gasped.

"We have converted the young before." He pulled tighter against her hair. "You enjoyed the half-grown ones almost more than the big men."

Her scalp burned with the strain he put on her. Still, the words would not come to her.

"Do I have to beat you yet again to get you to talk?"

He kissed her savagely, bruising her already swollen and cut lips, maintaining the pressure on her hair and scalp.

Yassimine willed herself to respond to him, control him with her body as she did so often. Her mouth lay inert beneath his. She had nothing left to give him.

"I could take you here and now. With or without your consent. But then it never is truly rape with you, Yassimine." He kissed her again, hauling her upright.

"Give yourself to me!" He slammed his fist into her eye. His heavy ring sliced the delicate tissue above her cheekbone.

She cried out and covered her face from this latest insult. Her fingers came away bloody. Her entire face throbbed. Tears started in her eyes. The cut burned.

"Bite me, Yassimine. Bite my neck and force yourself upon me!" he screamed.

She slumped back into her cushions, too tired and sore to do aught but cry. The beatings used to lead to sex. No more. After three days of beatings, little food, and less water, her body had nothing left to give.

She pulled the rough woolen cloak tightly about her shivering body.

Why couldn't The Master return her to her cell and let her pass her days in silent solitude? She needed to think and plan for the time when she killed him and assumed leadership of the pack. She needed to know more about The Master's magic to maintain control over the normally solitary wolves. She needed to lessen the pain he delighted in inflicting upon her.

"Bah." He released her hair with a frustrated toss. "The boy worked his magic on you. But it will wear off. All magic has its limits."

"Does it?" she asked quietly.

He ignored her and returned to his bowl. He began to chant a new spell. "I do not have to *find* him. I need seek only the earring. He can't escape me. And neither can you. His early departure just means a little more effort to remind him of where his loyalty resides now."

He threw a handful of aromatic herbs on the closest brazier. The smoke rose in a choking cloud. Yassimine covered her mouth and nose with her cloak. She watched him carefully for hints to the source of his magic, waiting for his next assault. There was always a new assault.

The Master breathed deeply of the smoke. His eyes glazed. He murmured words in an ancient language she almost understood. Then he bent over the bowl of water.

He smiled. What he saw must have pleased him.

"He goes to England. Just as I had planned. He shall take command of my pack already there. No one shall interfere with my plans now. No 'scientist' shall relieve the horror my wolves inflict by claiming creatures of the Were do not exist."

The Master rose gracefully from his crouch over the bowl. "Señor Ruiz," he called into the anteroom. "We go to England as soon as I can arrange a passport. Begin preparations."

Yassimine breathed a sigh of relief. He would leave her. She could go back to her cell.

"I hope you do not suffer from seasickness, my dear wolf. I want you feeling your best when we land. You and the boy will have much to do if we are to bring Elizabeth down and place Mary upon the throne. Mary is malleable. She listens to any man with a breath of logic, no matter how twisted. Elizabeth listens to no one. She has to die so that I can rule England through Mary, as I rule Spain and her vast colonies through Philip and the power of my werewolves. Soon I shall rule France as well. Protestants do not fear my wolves and will not bow to my regime of terror. Protestants try to *cure* them."

Cure? Yassimine listened more closely. A *cure?* Suddenly, she feared everything about England and these terrible Protestants, whatever they were. A cure defied everything she believed in.

Chapter 26

15 July, 1574. Dover, England.

"WE will stop in Ide Hill long enough to fit court clothes, then we must hie to London." Uncle Donovan did not look as if he wanted to hie anywhere. He moved stiffly. The grueling ride from Paris had taken its toll on the old injury to his leg. "I must report to the queen that magic is afoot in France and must be tended to," he continued wearily.

"I will not join you on that journey," Hal said quietly. Then he collapsed half in and half out of the surf. He returned his dinner to the sea.

Peregrine and Gaspar looked a little green as well. Our crossing from France had been rough. The small fishing boat we had hired had nearly foundered. Even now, the captain and his men pushed the vessel back out into the deeper water. They could not get rid of us fast enough. Or was it me and my wolfhound they considered the Jonah of the journey?

I thought longingly of a hot bath, and sleeping in the same bed more than one night. Preferably one that did not move beneath me.

We had half a dozen court costumes stored at Ide Hill, the family residence outside of London. My uncle had inherited it from his second wife, Hal's mother. One day it would go to Hal. Kirkenwood was entailed to Griffin as heir to the barony.

Coffa pranced in the waves, biting at the ever-moving water and getting in the way of the work of relaunching the boat.

Only Thom Steward looked as if he was ready to follow my uncle any farther.

"I must return to Kirkenwood," I said. My father's journals were there. I needed their wisdom to find a way to discover and solve Hal's problems: his sudden preference for solitude, his yearning for cemeteries—and most of all—a bespelled earring. Perhaps now, after my experiences in Paris, I had the magic and maturity to decipher my father's writings.

But I really wanted to retreat to Aunt Meg's hermitage at the foot of the tor in Huntington. There I could tend my father's grave while I thought and planned and figured out what I should do next. There his ghost could help me read the journals.

"I presume a seamstress can cobble together something acceptable for both of you to wear before Elizabeth learns we have returned and demands our presence at court," Uncle Donovan said. He tromped up the strand toward the nearest village. Peregrine, Gaspar, and Thom followed unsteadily. They probably never considered defying him.

"No," Hal and I replied together.

"I don't want to expose you to the politics and vanities of court any more than you want to be there, but the queen has commanded an interview with you both. I dare not defy her." Uncle Donovan turned his back on us and continued his march away from the sea.

"Hal is too sick to travel," I protested.

Hal looked as if he would contradict me, thought better of it, and dropped to his knees again. His skin looked only a shade less pale than the sea foam. He winked at me before coughing and convulsing his mid-region.

"You can recover at Ide Hill. A nice walk on dry land that does not shift beneath your feet is the best cure for *mal de mer*." Uncle Donovan returned to grab Hal's arm and haul him to his feet.

I was surprised to see that Hal now stood nearly as tall as his father's shoulder, maybe a bit more. He'd grown a handspan on this journey.

"But what about Deirdre? She's suffered a lot on this journey. A day or two is not enough time." Hal had recovered some of his habits of defending me, but not enough to shorten my name. Or let me help him.

"There is nothing wrong with Dee that a few days with Betsy and your Aunt Meg won't cure. She's been too much

in the company of rough menfolk. She needs a bit of gentil-
ity, is all."

I opened my mouth to protest. Then I saw the stubborn
set of my uncle's chin. He'd not budge on this issue.

A bright giggle snapped my senses into full alert. A dozen
specks of colored light circled Uncle Donovan's head.

Faeries! They blessed us with their presence. All the while
in France I had not heard their laughter, like the chiming of
tiny silver bells. I lifted a hand out for one to land on. They
circled away from me in another cloud of giggles.

On the night I had sneaked out of Kirkenwood, I had
seen them in Arthur's crypt. They had blessed my journey
to France.

Now they blessed my return.

My sense of the world shifted suddenly and settled more
comfortably on my shoulders. I smiled.

Coffa raised up on her hind legs to snap at the flitting
creatures. They dove across her head, pulling on her whiskers. My dog whirled and bit at the air. She exuded mirth
after weeks of concern, anger, and depression.

Go, the faery voices urged me. *Visit with our lady in the
palace. She will care for you. We will see to that.*

Then they popped out of view.

A little heaviness returned to the air.

"Yes, Uncle, we must hie to Court. The queen has commanded," I said, and began the journey.

"What are you up to, Dee? You never agree so readily."
Uncle Donovan narrowed his eyes.

I knew he searched my aura for signs of deceit.

A shrug of my shoulders and determined steps were my
only answer. I could send for my father's journals. Perhaps
the queen would like to study them with me. After all, she
had made a pet of my father for a time. When he was an
outlawed Catholic priest, in need of friends.

Hal and I needed a friend right now.

16 July, 1574. Ide Hill, southeast of London.

Ide Hill welcomed me with gentle air, soft rain, and lazy breezes. I forgot the bone-chilling rains and howling winds of Kirkenwood. I embraced the south.

The faeries agreed with me. They followed us all the way to the yellow stone manor atop a slight rise.

Hal sulked every step of the way to the home he would inherit. "I want to go to Kirkenwood. I need Kirkenwood," became his litany. He was irritable and broke out in sweat through most of the warm days. His nose rose to the faint breeze, sniffing for . . . something familiar?

"My mother died here," Hal muttered as we rode into the forecourt. "Mother, the servants, everyone from here abandoned me," he added bitterly.

"They did not abandon you," I replied. "They *died.* Then my father found you and cared for you until your da came for you and Griff."

He glared at me. "Everyone always abandons me. Even you, Deirdre. You will desert me in the end." He jumped off his horse and stalked toward the lush parkland beyond the manor.

A dozen servants rushed to take the horses, help us dismount, just welcome us. They wore uniforms in the family colors, royal blue on black with a dragon rampant emblazoned on sleeve or shoulder. Betsy and Aunt Meg awaited us in the foyer. They wore fine clothing in light colors and cool linen. Meg hugged me and clucked over my rumpled gown and tangled hair. Betsy turned up her nose at the smell—covered as I was in travel dust, salt spray, and sweat.

Then Meg stood back and gazed at me fixedly. A glance flashed between her and Betsy and they knew as well as I did that my breasts now filled the gown that had been too big for me when I departed from them mere weeks before. We three women knew that my woman's courses would begin any day now. I was almost surprised they had not already.

Aunt Meg never stood on ceremony. She marched out
to where Hal hovered at the edge of the tree line, threw
her arms around him, and began to cry. Hal leaned in to
her and dropped his head onto her shoulder. His back shivered and he gulped.

Gently, Meg kissed his temple and brow. Without a
word, she took his hand and led him into the formal gardens at the side of the house.

My chin quivered and my eyes burned. I'd not had the
courage to embrace him. He'd talk to Meg. But I had always been his confidante. He should have talked to me!
The bonds of friendship and love stretched thin at that
moment.

"A bath first. Then we decide what to do with you."
Betsy gestured me up the stairwell. She followed at a distance safe from me, making certain I did not contaminate
her lovely gown and her oversensitive nose. At every step
she smoothed the embroidered underskirt at the front of
her gown. Not a bit of dust marred the hem or her soft
indoor slippers.

"I'm to go to court," I announced to her. The only words
that came to me around the lump in my throat.

"So am I. I hope you will not interfere with my life there
any more than necessary." She tucked a stray curl into her
cap with a sharp, almost angry motion.

"Hal doesn't love me anymore." The words came out in
a gush along with a spate of tears. I could control them
no longer.

"Who could love you, smelling as you do? Let Meg deal
with him. She's probably the only one who can. You will
have to give up running wild with the boys and spend more
time with civilized women, like me. Women have secrets
men refuse to acknowledge. I will explain a few things to
you. After you are clean and rested." She wrinkled her
nose and backed away another step. "You smell like the
sewers of Paris."

Chapter 27

19 July, 1574. Richmond Palace, near London.

"OUR Wolfhound has returned!" Elizabeth exclaimed, throwing open the doors to her salon.

The sweet sounds of lute strings wafted softly through the antechamber of Richmond Palace. A man's tenor voice soared in harmony with the instrument.

Donovan listened closely, trying to recognize the voice. He could not place the man who could reach such high notes and maintain a richness to his tone. Someone new. Someone to delight and distract a restless queen.

"Majesty, the light of your smile rivals the sun," Donovan bowed deeply, clenching his fist against his chest.

The girls sank into deep curtsies, as they should.

He did not want to leave either of the girls in London when he returned to his post in Edinburgh. Donovan did not trust the queen to keep the girls out of mischief.

Hal . . . where had the boy got to? He had managed to make his new doublet and trunk hose look rumpled and ill-fitting, though they'd been made to measure just yesterday. He'd lost his feathered cap before they'd traveled a league from Ide Hill.

Ah, Martha, what kind of barbarian have we begotten?

Donovan shifted his eyes as much as possible from his awkward pose. His son had managed to disappear. His son who needed to learn the protocols and the machinations of court. His son who must one day step into the role that had not adequately been filled for two generations . . . and more.

You are needed here, Donovan said directly into his son's mind.

A mental barb punched back at him, stabbing him in the back of the eyes. Hal's shields had grown stronger since . . . since France. A lot of things had changed since France.

We need to talk, Donovan said, seeking Hal with his extra senses.

"No, we don't," Hal replied sullenly, appearing at Donovan's elbow. "I need to talk to my twin. At Kirkenwood."

"Stay beside me," Donovan whispered, grabbing his son's arm in a tight grip.

Perhaps he should have made arrangements for Robin to accompany them today. Robin could persuade Hal to stay.

"Present these two charming women to us, Wolfhound," Elizabeth said through a smile. A genuine smile? What kind of trap had she laid?

The queen presented her hand for Donovan to kiss. He breathed a caress across her rings and came upright.

"Which one of these young women is the child of Griffin, our Merlin?" Elizabeth shifted her attention from Donovan to his charges before he'd finished straightening his back.

Deirdre popped up from her curtsy. "You knew my father, Majesty?"

"So, you are the child of our Merlin and Roanna, the Highland Rose?" Elizabeth belatedly presented her hand for Deirdre's obeisance.

"Yes, Majesty." Deirdre kissed the ring properly. But she returned her eyes too quickly to capture the queen's gaze. Hunger crossed Dee's face. "I would speak with you at length about my father. Your Merlin." A never sated hunger for information about her father.

"Bold brat," Elizabeth laughed. "Very like your father. We see you have his wolfhound." The queen ruffled Coffa's ears. The dog leaned into her caress, soaking up the attention like a cleaning rag.

"Coffa is the granddaughter of my papa's Newynog," Deirdre replied. "And that one is Coffa's brother, Brenin. He belongs to Betsy." She pointed to the well-behaved male dog who stood guard behind his mistress, where he should be. Unlike Coffa who always surged to the front.

Beside her, Betsy waved an anxious hand. She retained her curtsy according to protocol.

"Then you must be Mary Elizabeth." The queen gestured to Betsy to rise.

"Yes, Majesty," she replied prettily.

"Very like your father." Elizabeth appraised her. "Except for the blonde hair, of course. You have the look of the Kirkwoods. But you, daughter of Griffin, you must take after your mother."

"So I am told, Majesty. I never knew either of my parents. Uncle Donovan and Aunt Meg raised me." Deirdre turned a sidelong glance toward Donovan.

His chest swelled with pride and love.

"Meg?" Elizabeth turned an inquisitive gaze toward Donovan.

"My sister, Majesty."

"Ah, yes, Mad Meg. We remember our Griffin telling us about her. A prime example of why we must keep a strong defense along the border."

"Yes, Majesty. I have reports on the raids we repulsed this past winter. I also have reports on my work in Edinburgh. *And what we discovered in France.*" Donovan tried to turn Elizabeth's attention away from the girls.

"Later," Elizabeth dismissed him with a wave of her hand. "I will interview our new ladies."

"My son is also come to court, Majesty." Where had the boy gone *this* time! "The son who will inherit a part of my heritage." By tacit agreement they never mentioned the title Pendragon aloud. He could never be certain who listened at the keyhole even if the queen should be alone.

The queen stilled. "'Tis my understanding the dogs choose . . ."

"Both Hal and Betsy attracted familiars," Deirdre prattled as if the queen were her new best friend. She edged very close to overstepping the bounds of protocol. "We do not know yet who will be the Pendragon. But Hal lost his dog in France. He doesn't want another one. Not yet, anyway," Dee continued.

Perhaps Deirdre's bright freshness was exactly what the court needed to lift it out of the dark machinations of power hungry courtiers and international intrigue, Donovan speculated silently as he observed his queen and Deirdre.

"Come, all of you, we will walk in the gardens," Elizabeth commanded. She limped slightly, spoiling her otherwise elegant glide through the anteroom to the large reception chamber. She had limped for three years now from an ulcer on her leg that never truly healed. "Milord of Kirkenwood, your arm." She returned to her usual imperious tone.

Donovan offered his right arm for the monarch and then escorted her through the next crowded chamber and the next to the queen's private salon and an exit to the gardens.

Betsy and Deirdre trailed behind with their dogs.

"Your son, milord? I do not see him with you." Elizabeth said when they were clear of the gaping and whispering mob of courtiers, ambassadors, and governmental officials.

"Henry—Hal, we call him—has not been well since our return from France," Donovan replied. Not exactly a lie. The boy who had not been himself, now chose solitude out of doors rather than hours closeted with Deirdre and Betsy experimenting with magic.

Off to his left he caught a glimpse of crimson. Hal had worn a red doublet today.

"We will have your report now, in this semiprivacy. "Tell us, Wolfhound, do the girls listen with your—ah—peculiar acuteness?"

Donovan nodded. Both Betsy and Deirdre had the ability to eavesdrop on thoughts as well as words.

"Good. Later we will interview the two children in private about what they discovered in France. Children no longer, I suspect," the queen mused.

"Adversity tempers us all, some more hastily than others."

Perhaps that was all that troubled Hal, an awkward and abrupt growth spurt had sent him into maturity before his mind and emotions had a chance to catch up. Deirdre certainly had transformed from girl to young woman in a matter of weeks.

A nagging knot at the base of his skull told Donovan differently. A frisson of atavistic fear sent the hair on his arms standing on end and warned him that Hal was near. He had to get to the bottom of this, and quickly.

"We shall enjoy having Deirdre at court. Perhaps young Henry needs more time before waiting upon us beyond an occasional report," Elizabeth patted Donovan's arm.

Donovan grimaced.

"Never fear. We shall protect Deirdre's and Betsy's virtue as we protect our own." The queen nodded knowingly.

Donovan almost snorted. Elizabeth had borne her lover

a secret child before ascending to the throne. Robin was constant evidence to Donovan of just how chaste the queen was not.

"The girls' reputation is not what concerns me, madam. Both girls are more than capable of defending their honor by themselves. I have seen to that."

His fears centered on Hal. Hal who might never become the Pendragon.

You promised me, Grandmother Raven. My son will be the Pendragon.

The ghost of his grandmother, the last fully acknowledged Pendragon of Britain, did not answer.

Chapter 28

HAL pressed his back against a towering oak. He needed more air to light the fire in his lungs so he could run all the way home to Kirkenwood. He longed to hear the raven caw a greeting to him. He had to banish the dream of the standing stones turning their faces away from him. At Kirkenwood, the familiar would enfold him and let him shed the alien wolf that had invaded his being.

That would not happen for another two weeks. The dark of the moon had just passed. The tiny sliver of a new moon sapped his strength, his agility, and the keenness of his mind.

Keeping his da out of his head, and thus keeping him from discovering the truth of Hal's time in Paris, took all of his concentration.

For the first time since the ritual in that Paris dungeon the earring did not burn. Nor did the jewelry drag his senses away from the here and now to another place, to another man's commands.

Did the Spaniard's power over him wane with the moon? He needed to talk to Dee. If anyone could help him, she could. He had to forget his embarrassment and humiliation and tell her all.

He peered around the tree trunk. Da and the queen walked the graveled path a few paces from his hiding place. Dee and Betsy glided along behind them in silence. There seemed to be a wall of animosity between them. Their dogs gamboled behind them, snapping at insects and tussling together in immature friendship. Not at all reflective of their mistresses' hostile silence.

For a moment, the pain of Helwriaeth's death stabbed him in the heart. He scrunched his eyes closed and pushed the ache away.

Hal looked again for a chance to spirit Dee away from the others. Just for a few moments. His imagination lay inert. He could not think what would engage them so. How could anything be more important than his problem?

Coffa leaped off the path to chase a stray scent.

Dee stopped to call her back.

Hal waved to her, gesturing her toward him.

"Come, Deirdre, you must learn proper attendance if you are to stay at court," Elizabeth called to her sharply.

Dee shot Hal a regretful glance. "Later," she mouthed, then hurried to catch up with her elders. Coffa stood for a long moment between Dee and Hal. The dog looked from one to the other. Then she performed the canine equivalent of a shrug and returned to her mistress.

Hal retreated behind his tree. He sighed from the bottom of his aching soul.

Dee to stay at court.

He'd waited too long to speak to her. He'd allowed his hurt and confusion to become a barrier between them. Now he had to wait until . . . until never. Once Elizabeth got her clutches into someone, she never let go. Dee was lost to him. He had to find his own solutions.

Stealthily, he made his way back to the stable. Tomorrow he'd leave for Kirkenwood, no matter what Da said. Kirkenwood. He turned his face to the north, sniffing for a trace of home.

21 August, 1574. Hatfield House, England.

"What gossip have you heard at court regarding this new treaty with Spain, Deirdre?" Queen Elizabeth asked me one morning as we sat in her study.

Sixteen other women, including my cousin Betsy, littered the room, some doing needlework, some reading aloud to each other, others merely gossiping. Lady Dudley, sister-in-law to Robert, the queen's longtime companion and friend—and rumored lover—played the virginal.

Elizabeth sat at a writing desk cluttered with documents.

"There be little love for Spain among your courtiers, Majesty." I looked up from the seam I had mangled. "They ask is it wise to invite them to send an ambassador and therefore his spies from the Society of Jesus into the heart of our land?" I reported what I heard. Listening closely did not require magic.

My own thoughts I kept to myself. I knew the importance of the treaty in balancing power between France and Spain. I knew, because Elizabeth had told me, that the treaty sent a message to Henri III and his regent mother, Catherine de Médici, that England could withdraw trade from France if they continued to persecute Protestants.

My memories of the Spanish lord chasing us from Paris to Calais still made me shudder. I could never approve congress with Spain after that.

I also wondered why *El Lobison* had broken off the pursuit so abruptly when he obviously wanted Hal quite desperately.

"Ah, the matter of the Jesuits." The queen tapped her chin with her quill. A tiny smile tugged at her mouth. "Is the Society of Jesus truly the menace we have labeled them?"

"The Jesuits have not the control of a monastic order, Majesty," Betsy reminded her. She had studied the Jesuits closely, reading every document she could find about their training methods and the rumors of the dark magic they employed to return lapsed Catholics to the fold.

I suspected much of their "magic" was nothing more than brutal torture.

"The Dominicans and the Franciscans are limited in their activities by the Rule set down by their founders. The Society of Jesus answers only to the Pope," Lady Dudley jumped into the conversation. She frequently recited facts Elizabeth, and all of us, already knew simply so the queen could hear them in a new light.

"The Bishop of Rome has excommunicated you—as if he thought he had authority over you—and declared it the duty of all Catholics to remove you from your throne at all costs. Spain is very closely tied to both the Bishop of Rome and the Holy Roman Emperor. We need to fear both the Treaty of Bristol and the Jesuits who must surely come to our shores in the wake of the new Spanish ambassador," Lady Hastings, sister to Lady Sidney, continued the reminders.

I drew a deep breath. All this was information Elizabeth knew. She often challenged us with questions about well-known political subjects, always seeking new ideas, new perspectives on old issues. Her councillors advised her. We offered new perspectives on the issues.

She also allowed others to talk long and hard through an issue while she waited for new developments, more information, for her enemies to reveal their plans.

"French Ambassador Fénelon has already protested this treaty most strongly," Lettice Knollys, Countess of Essex, chimed in.

As the most junior of the queen's attendants, I was content to let my elders speak. 'Twas not my position to offer advice. I only reported what I had seen and heard.

"Yes, yes," Elizabeth dismissed the countess' comments with a flip of her long fingers. "And Ambassador Fénelon has warned us that the new Spanish ambassador Mendoza will instigate trouble."

"Receiving this man and his credentials may not be wise, Majesty." Lettice shook her head. As the most senior among us, she had the right and the duty to speak her mind.

"How shall we counter this man, Deirdre?" Elizabeth dismissed Lettice. She turned her attention to me in a complete breach of rank and protocol. But she was the queen. She could do that with impunity.

I shrugged and shifted position. My corset chafed through the layers of undergarments. The heavy white velvet gown made me perspire in the late August heat.

"Sit still, child!" Elizabeth reprimanded me. Her stern scrutiny made me want to fidget more.

"Your father had an amazing quality of stillness about him. You need to emulate him. Especially if you are to take his place in the world." Most of the women presumed that Uncle Donovan was my father as well as Betsy's. They accepted my illegitimate status without question. Few highly placed lords of the realm did not have at least one "extra" child.

"I would know more of my father, Majesty," I said quietly, hoping only she would hear. "No one has ever told me about *him*. Only about his deeds."

"Well, now you know one more thing about his disposition than you did moments ago," Elizabeth snapped. "Think on his stillness. His ability to listen."

I closed my eyes and stilled the center of my being as if preparing for magic.

"Now tell me what you would do about Ambassador Mendoza," Elizabeth commanded.

"Overt action will be taken as hostility, possibly negate the treaty. He must be watched, his acquaintances noted and followed. Suspected Jesuits among them must be removed from England whenever possible," I replied.

"Sir Francis Walsingham has already implemented those actions," Elizabeth said impatiently. "Suggest something new."

"A spy in the embassy? Or possibly in the taverns and theaters frequented by the Spanish retainers?"

"The taverns," Elizabeth mused. "We must think on this."

She gathered up the pile of documents and rose to her commanding height. Instantly, all seventeen of her attendants rose with her. The soft background buzz of the conversations ceased. We looked like a chessboard, a backdrop of black and white against which the powerful queen blazed in a gown of emerald green bedecked with jewels and long ropes of pearls.

We lined up in order of seniority to follow Elizabeth wherever her ceaseless energy led us.

As she passed me, Lettice, Lady Essex, pinched my arm hard enough to bruise. "Yours is not the place to engage the queen in important conversation!" she hissed.

I kept my silence. Who could I complain to?

Betsy rolled her eyes and pursed her lips in silent agreement with Lady Essex.

But Elizabeth had asked me specific questions—the kinds of questions she would ask the Pendragon as one of her advisers. The order of seniority among her ladies meant nothing to her. Except possibly the opportunity to divide us with jealousy. Elizabeth observed friendships and alliances closely and manipulated them to suit her own private agenda.

I wondered if she needed me excluded from the society

of her ladies so that I might move among the court, listening covertly, unquestioned by friends and allies.

That evening I wrote a long and pleading letter to Aunt Fiona, Uncle Donovan's widowed sister and chatelaine, back in Kirkenwood. I begged her to send me my father's journals. I hoped for insight into Elizabeth.

I also vowed to practice listening more closely to the plots and machinations that swirled around the queen like mayflies—or faeries. Griffin Kirkwood the Elder's stillness would be harder to find.

21 August, 1574. Kirkenwood.

Hal slammed the door to the lair firmly in place. He breathed deep and long. Every portion of his being demanded he run free among the moors, feasting on hot flesh, shunning the restrictions of men.

He grabbed his knees fiercely, with his butt planted against the stout wooden planks. Still, his blood sang with heightened awareness, with the howling of his kind begging him to join them in freedom.

He reached shakily for the flagon of wine he'd stashed here earlier. The cool sweetness slid down his throat, easing the itch beneath his skin. For a moment.

"I am a man, not a beast." He repeated the words over and over. The itching ache did not dissipate. He reached for more wine. That only dulled his mind.

The moon touched the horizon. He knew it in his bones and his blood. A howl lodged in his throat begging for release. He swallowed the urge.

His hips and shoulders shifted. His arms grew longer and his legs bent into a different shape. The hair on his arms grew darker, coarser.

Sudden heat flooded through him. He tore at his shirt and hose. His toes burst through his boots. Drool ran in thick streams onto his hairy chest.

Then his vision narrowed, faded to shades of gray, sharpened within his tight focus.

"I have to stop this," he moaned. The words sounded more like a growl than human speech.

He dropped to all fours, bounced up again. "I. Will. Not. Succumb," he said through bared fangs.

His knees gave out. He dropped and rolled, sat up and scratched his back with one of his hind paws.

A low growl rumbled out from his belly. He snapped at the air. The taste of fresh meat, hot and dripping with blood tantalized his memory. Nothing else would satisfy him.

The stone room offered only a few roots to chew upon. Not enough. Never enough. He tore at the tapestries on the walls. He dug at the wooden door.

Trapped.

A niggle of sanity reminded him that he was safe here. The people he loved were safe as long as he stayed here.

He paced a while, sniffing anxiously at the door. Then he settled upon a nest of torn blankets. Best to sleep through the hours of the full moon. When it set near dawn, he could . . .

Footsteps echoed in the stone passageway outside this hidden room.

"Hal? Are you in there, Hal? It's me, Griff. What's wrong?" Hal's loving, meddling twin banged on the door. "I'm worried about you. You didn't eat any supper."

Hal snarled. His heart leaped in his chest. Energy pumped through his veins.

Freedom. Griff offered freedom to run, to mate, to hunt . . . to kill.

He had to stay. He could not endanger Griff or any of the others in Kirkenwood.

"Hal, I'm coming in." The latch lifted. The door creaked open.

Hal stared in horror at the moving portal. In his haste to reach the safety of the lair, he'd forgotten to bolt the door!

Fresh air wafted across his muzzle.

Freedom! His thoughts narrowed to the opening. Food.

Hal wedged his nose in the opening then darted free. He had to ignore Griff. Else he'd rip out the throat of his twin, his littermate. His otherself.

The scent of the blood of dozens of lives scattered through

the entire castle called to him. Any one of them would taste sweet. All of them might satisfy his appetite.

He prayed he could control himself until he broke free of the castle. How could he live with himself if he ate someone he knew?

Chapter 29

Late autumn 1574. The Moors beyond Kirkenwood.

"HAL, where are you!" Griff called. His voice faded in the mist.

Hal heard him with the clarity of his wolf senses. Three full moons had waxed and waned since he'd left Paris. Each month more and more of his heightened senses lingered. Each month his control over the beast within him lessened.

Now the moon came full again tonight. The sun set early here in the north. He had not much time.

He huddled beneath an undercut of dirt and roots on a creek bank. Today there was only a trickle of water. With the next rainfall it would swell to a torrent. He resisted the urge to lap up a mouthful. He must only drink from cups and eat with a knife and spoon.

"Hal!" Griff called again.

"Go away, Griff. Please," Hal whispered. But he knew his twin would not give up the search. Griff was as determined, relentless, and stubborn as any Kirkwood.

"Da is ready to leave for London," Griff continued. He was close. Too damn close. "He wants us both to go with him. We'll see Betsy and Dee."

Ah, Dee! Hal's heart ached at her prolonged absence. He missed her almost as much as he missed talking to Griff, sorting out his problems with his twin, sharing his life with him.

"I can't go," Hal whispered to himself. "I can't take the chance Dee will see me like this." The last came out on a sob.

"You can't hide it forever," Griff said from right above Hal. "Mayhap Dee could help you." He jumped down, splashing in the creek as he found his balance.

"How did you find me?" Hal asked. He remained in his hidey-hole, pressing back as far from Griff as possible

"Why can't you trust me anymore, Hal?" Griff reached out his hand to Hal in entreaty.

"Stay away!" Hal turned his face away. "I'll not let my curse taint you."

"You won't. I'm your brother, Hal. Your *twin!* Trust me."

Hal clamped his mouth shut on the torrent of words that wanted to spill forth.

"Very well. I must remain here with you until Da gives up and leaves without us." Griff hunkered down and squeezed into the undercut beside Hal. Griff draped his right arm around Hal's shoulders so they fit.

"You have to go. You miss Betsy and Dee almost as much as I do," Hal said. Grudgingly, he accepted the warmth and comfort Griff offered and slid his left arm around his twin's waist.

"I miss Betsy not at all," he spat.

"What did she do to you?" Hal growled.

"I escorted her to Aunt Meg's hermitage last summer. On the way there, I caught her twice scrying for you and Dee. Both times she cast curses through the bowl of water—spells fueled by her blood, ghostweed, and sulfur. She wanted both of you to die on that trip and leave her claim to the Pendragon uncontested."

Hal caught his breath in sudden conviction that his sister—*his sister!*—had made him vulnerable to the Spaniard and the perverted ritual. If Betsy had not cursed him, would he have been caught by *El Lobison*'s minions? Would Helwriaeth still live?

"I miss you, Hal. You never speak to my mind anymore. Now tell me why you stand an inch taller than I and have more muscle, though I'm catching up since my voice stopped cracking." He grinned as they had when small children plotting new mischief.

"Griff, you must be back inside the walls of the castle before moonrise." Anxiety quivered in Hal's belly.

"I know. We have hours yet. I have to wait long enough for Da to leave without us. He won't do that till near noon."

"How . . . how do you know about me?"

"I made some guesses that fit what I have read and seen since your return from Paris."

Hal shifted to his knees, the better to watch Griff's expression. "What have you guessed?"

"That the full moon calls you in dangerous ways. Beastly ways." Griff dropped his eyes as if embarrassed.

"Say it!" Hal commanded. He could have compelled his brother to speak. Since Paris, he had not the courage to open communication with him. He could not risk sharing the terrible ritual and transformation. Could not risk harming Griff.

"Werewolf," Griff whispered.

"You know?"

"I know."

"I am dangerous, Griff. You cannot be with me once I begin . . ."

"That first full moon after you returned from Paris, I saw you go into the lair. Only a wolf came out. You did not hurt me then. You will not hurt me now."

"You cannot be certain. I am not certain."

"Hal, I know you. You will not hurt me. Now tell me everything. Together we will think of something, some way to help you control your . . . appetite."

"Oh, Griff, it was awful." Hal slid back into the undercut, resting his head on his twin's shoulder, letting the words and tears finally come forth.

Yuletide 1574. London.

The minor fasting and solemn penance of Advent ended with a joyous candlelit Anglican Mass on Christmas Eve. Elizabeth joined in the festivities in the days before gift giving at the New Year with an almost desperate abandon.

Her beloved Robert Dudley, Earl of Leicester, had secretly married Douglas, Lady Sheffield, and begotten a son. Though the earl had returned to court, groveling and fawning over the queen, she had not forgiven him. Though he denounced the marriage and declared his son illegitimate,

Elizabeth snubbed him often. She danced with other court-iers, including Uncle Donovan. She feasted with the entire court and whispered beguilingly to the Spanish Ambas-sador.

As a lady-in-waiting, I was expected to stand by and watch, observe without comment, and listen carefully to all of the gossip.

Ethics hammered into me by both Uncle Donovan and Aunt Meg, as well as my own reluctance to work magic, kept me from probing minds and memories. So I learned to read the small nuances of posture and inflection, to watch eye movements and read lips. I crept around the edges of the merriment with all of my senses open.

Ambassador Mendoza leaked rumors of Leicester's sup-posed marriage to Elizabeth. His retainers spread gossip of an empty treasury, of Elizabeth indulging in orgies. From the French Ambassador I heard rumors of a Spanish inva-sion fleet just off the coast.

I kept Elizabeth informed of *all* I saw and heard.

As much as the revelry bored me, I thrived at court. Elizabeth's intellect challenged the entire court. I learned much of history, languages, economics, diplomacy, and life from proximity to her.

And the weather! Deep winter in London was like spring in the north country. For the first time in my life I did not shiver from constant wind and rain. Occasionally the sun peeked through the clouds—even in dark December.

I did not want to go home. And though I missed Hal terribly, I knew he would not welcome me until he over-came the hardship of our journey to France.

Betsy threw herself into the week of masques and ban-quets, musicales and flirting. She had little patience for Elizabeth's intellectual challenges and long discussions of politics.

"What will you do when Elizabeth catches you?" I whis-pered to Betsy angrily one morning when she crept into the bed we shared just before dawn. My duties to Elizabeth required I rise long before the sun to attend her. The queen rarely slept and required her ladies at odd hours.

Coffa snapped at Brenin as he leaped upon the bed to curl up with Betsy.

Brenin growled back at her.

I grabbed my dog's collar and hauled her away from her littermate.

"Elizabeth will send you home in disgrace and me with you. I do not wish to go home." I sounded very like Coffa in my resentment of my cousin.

"Elizabeth will send me home in disgrace without you. You, cousin, are her pet. She loves you as a substitute for your father." Betsy almost spat the last word.

Resentment boiled in me. But I held my tongue as Elizabeth had taught me. Let others reveal their weaknesses through their emotions. I, like my queen, must remain silently strong.

"Once I am free of Her Majesty's tyranny, I shall convince Papa that Robin must marry me to save my reputation." Betsy shrugged and yawned.

"And what if you conceived?"

"I shan't until I want to." She snuggled into the warm covers for a few moments' rest before Elizabeth demanded her presence. "I learned the practical side of being the Pendragon. Magic." She circled one finger. The pitcher and basin on the washstand spun and rocked, sloshing water.

"There is more to being the Pendragon than magic," I countered by pulling all of the covers and Brenin off the bed with a blink of my eyes.

Then I silently cursed myself for succumbing to my anger with this ostentatious display.

Betsy scowled and drew the blankets back over herself with a more elaborate gesture of her hand. Then she flounced onto the bolster and turned her back on me.

"Who were you with?" I asked with a sigh.

"Does it matter?"

"Of course it matters. Is he of good family? Will your father allow the match? Are his intentions honorable? All the court knows you went off with *someone* after midnight."

She pulled the coverlet over her head in an attempt to silence me.

The silver bell in Elizabeth's chambers ended my interrogation. I departed with the vague uneasy feeling that Betsy had won this confrontation.

I hurried through Elizabeth's private study and solar to her bedchamber. Lady Mary Sidney—sister to the partially disgraced Robert Dudley—held up two different sleeves for the queen's selection. Elizabeth chose the silver embroidered white to go with her sapphire gown.

"Where is Mary Elizabeth?" the queen asked me sharply.

"My cousin is still abed. Last evening's revelries taxed her mightily," I demurred with a deep curtsy.

"More like one of the Hastings brothers taxed her!" she roared with mischievous delight.

I kept my eyes down and my knees bent.

"Fetch her now. Her father joins us to break our fast." The queen dismissed me with a wave of her hand. "Deirdre?"

"Yes, Your Majesty?" I halted with my hand on the latch.

"I would that your uncle does not take his daughter home quite yet. I have a use for her. And for you."

"Yes, Majesty." I dipped another curtsy and hastened away. Strange that Elizabeth tolerated Betsy's promiscuity when she closely guarded the virtue of the rest of her ladies.

Betsy's eyes and face were puffy from lack of sleep when I led her into the solar, despite the rosewater I had given her to bathe with. Our dogs stayed at our heels, ignoring each other. Uncle Donovan rose stiffly at our entrance from his place beside the queen at her small dining table. His eyes narrowed knowingly as he looked at his daughter. I did my best to remain unobtrusive in the shadows.

"Your father had a trick of stillness, Deirdre," Elizabeth said around a mouthful of smoked fish. "He wrapped the shadows around him like a cloak. No one could find him if he did not want to be found. You do not yet have the trick." The queen beckoned me forward.

Coffa moved before I did. She planted herself beside the queen and openly begged to share the fish.

Uncle Donovan surveyed his daughter with a critical and criticizing eye.

"Who?" he asked through gritted teeth.

Betsy merely smiled at him with wide eyes. "Whatever do you mean, Papa? Did Robin come with you?" She looked around her father, searching for his secretary.

Uncle Donovan snorted and returned to his place. "We will discuss this later. In private."

"We have need of your daughter all week, Milord of Kirkenwood," Elizabeth countermanded. "Enjoy her company now before you hasten back to Edinburgh with letters and reports to our ambassador. You must leave right after gift giving and Mass at the New Year."

"Yes, Majesty." He nodded his head and drank from his tankard of beer to hide his expression.

But I knew that hardness in the lines around his eyes. He would make time to catch Betsy alone for a serious discussion of her behavior.

"We, too, note the absence of your secretary, Milord of Kirkenwood," she added.

"My adopted son has duties at Ide Hill," Uncle Donovan replied curtly.

He and Elizabeth stared at each other silently. The queen looked away first with a sigh.

This was a mystery that intrigued me. Robin always avoided court. Why?

"Sit, ladies," Elizabeth said after many long moments. "Break your fast with us."

Betsy made a point of placing me and both our dogs between herself and Uncle Donovan.

We chatted idly for several moments. Betsy ate little and kept darting fearful glances at her father. I ate heartily, knowing Elizabeth's schedule would tax my strength before she remembered to eat again.

"Give it to Deirdre, milord," Elizabeth whispered very loudly. She prodded my uncle with a her long, beringed fingers.

I looked up sharply. Coffa's ears pricked, and she nuzzled my hand. Then she parked herself beside the queen again. Elizabeth dropped an idle hand to ruffle the dog's ears. She never treated Betsy's Brenin with affection; barely tolerated him. But then, Betsy's familiar was more aloof, reserving all of his attention and affection for his mistress.

"Your Aunt Fiona sent this for you along with her letters to me," Uncle Donovan said. His face was tight, slightly disapproving as he handed me a square parcel wrapped in silk.

I knew what the package contained the moment I touched it.

"My father's journals," I gasped as I cradled the bundle next to my heart. At last. No more furtive glances at a paragraph here and there. The entire journal at my fingertips whenever and wherever I needed it.

"Some of them," Uncle Donovan replied. "My sister could not find the later volumes."

I looked at him suspiciously. My father had not died at home. He had entrusted his few belongings, including his journal, to his twin. Uncle Donovan knew where the last volume lay.

"You have passed your thirteenth birthday. You are mature enough to understand much of your father's early life," he said succinctly. "Will you excuse me, Majesty? I have duties."

"Yes, begone, milord. I, too, would know of Father Griffin's early life."

With one last disapproving glance, Uncle Donovan exited the room.

Betsy sighed in relief.

"We keep you here, young woman, only because your father insists that we cannot have Deirdre without you," Elizabeth said sharply. Her fingers clenched into a fist. "You will mend your behavior as of this moment."

"Yes, Majesty," Betsy replied, not at all repentant.

"Mind our words, Mary Elizabeth. Or you will spend your days emptying our chamber pot!" Elizabeth rose to her impressive height.

Betsy and I fumbled upward as protocol demanded.

"Majesty, if I may be so bold?" Betsy interjected. She kept her gaze steadily upon the queen, no trace of meekness or demure shyness.

"What?" Elizabeth retorted.

"Majesty, if my behavior offends you, perhaps you should find me a husband who will control me. My father's adopted son and secretary has never tolerated my independence and willfulness."

"Robin?" Elizabeth looked intrigued.

I held my breath waiting.

"Aye, Majesty. Robin." Betsy continued to stand boldly between Elizabeth and the doorway.

"An interesting idea, Mary Elizabeth. One we shall have to ponder. Write to your father at Ide Hill. Command him in our name to present his adopted son to us before the New Year." The queen gathered her fan and one last bite of bread. Then she turned to me.

"You are free for the rest of the day, Deirdre. We expect you to read the journals. We shall share insights about Father Griffin with you after supper. Mary Elizabeth, attend us. But leave the dog with Deirdre. We do not like him."

I clutched the books to my heart as I retreated to my chamber as hastily as I could and not trip over my own feet. My father's journals!

Chapter 30

New Year 1575. Whitehall Palace, London.

"WHATEVER happens, Robin, keep your mouth closed and your cap on," Donovan said. He adjusted the soft red brocade so that it obscured one of Robin's eyes and shadowed most of his face. "*Jesu,* I wish Martha were here. She would find a way out of this interview."

"I know the etiquette, milord," Robin insisted. He righted the cap so that he could see. The feather had seen better days—before Hal had worn the cap and discarded it in the mud. "And your beloved second wife would probably not have the artifice to beguile Elizabeth into ignoring me."

"You may know the etiquette, young man, but you do not know how vicious court can be. Martha knew . . ."

"I know the intrigues and jockeying for power in Edinburgh."

"A game of bowls compared to Elizabeth's collection of popinjays."

"Yes, milord."

"Why can't you call me 'Da' like the others? I adopted you when you were but five. You've known no other father, Robin."

Robin shrugged and looked away. "Does not seem fitting."

"Very well. Let us get this over with and hie out of London afore nightfall."

Donovan had little patience with the intricacies of court. Hal had disappeared onto the wild moors rather than spend Yuletide anywhere but Kirkenwood. Griff had followed his

twin rather than be separated. Donovan worried over both
of them.

He needed to be home, ferreting out the cause of Hal's
continued distress. What had happened to him during those
three days in the Spanish Embassy?

Donovan nodded to Elizabeth's page that they were ready.
The boy slipped into the small audience chamber behind
him and closed the door. Seemingly only a heartbeat later,
he reemerged and flung the portal wide. He announced
Donovan and Robin in a deep bellowing tone that belied
his youth and scrawny frame.

Elizabeth wore gold and green. Her veil shimmered with
diamonds or crystals. She played with three long strands of
her famous pearls. Her graceful fingers twitched with nervousness.

"Your Majesty." Donovan made a deep bow. One step
behind him, Robin made a more graceful flourish with his
hat.

Damn! Donovan cursed silently. He had told the boy to
keep his hat on. No sense in gossip mongers getting a close
look at him and Elizabeth in the same room. And—*God's
wounds*—Dudley was here too, temporarily forgiven for his
misalliance with Douglas Sheffield.

If Elizabeth desired secrecy or privacy, she had chosen
the wrong company.

Behind the queen, Betsy preened, touching her hair,
smoothing her white gown, batting her lashes at Robin.

Deirdre and Coffa sulked in the far corner. Brenin sat
beside them, alert and ready to jump to Betsy's side at the
least indication he was needed, or wanted. Most of the
other ladies scattered about the room engaged in quiet
conversation.

The queen, of course, dominated the room. She seemed
to consume all of the available air and light, leaving nothing
for the others.

"My Lord of Kirkenwood, you may present your ward,"
Elizabeth commanded. She kept her gaze upon Robin,
greedily drinking in every detail of his appearance.

"Majesty, Sir Robin, Knight of Kirkenwood," Donovan
mumbled.

"You knighted him?" Elizabeth asked as she extended
her hand for Robin to kiss.

"Aye, Madam. Seemed the fitting thing to do."

Robin blushed prettily as he pressed his lips to Elizabeth's coronation ring. He lingered too long, his eyes fixed on Elizabeth's face.

"A most noble countenance. And pretty manners. You have done well in raising him, milord." Elizabeth gestured them both to stand straight beside her. The three of them stood at nearly equal height. With an impatient wave of Elizabeth's hand, courtiers and ladies drew away, giving her the semblance of privacy. But all attention remained fixed on Robin. Most, if not all the watchers leaned just a little toward the queen, desperate to catch any fragment of the ensuing conversation.

Robert Dudley, the Earl of Leicester, approached. Elizabeth did not shoo him away, though she must have seen him. He lingered behind Elizabeth, an unacknowledged participant in this introduction.

Betsy, too, kept close to the queen. Too close. Elizabeth glared at her. She backed up one step, no farther.

Donovan gestured to his overbold daughter to retreat with the other ladies. She did not.

"We would hear of your adventures in Edinburgh, young Robin," Elizabeth said. She took the boy's arm and paraded around the reception chamber. Dudley and Betsy stayed a bare step behind.

All eyes in the room followed the queen's progress. Donovan closed his eyes a moment for calm.

Now Elizabeth paraded him before the court with a very possessive air. Every lady they passed simpered and preened before him, this latest favored courtier. Betsy glared at each with menace. Only two had enough sense to back away and lower their eyes at her implied threat.

When the queen and her little entourage had made a full circuit of the room, they paused near the dais.

"We find this young man most learned and astute, Milord of Kirkenwood," Elizabeth pronounced her blessing. The best compliment of all from her.

"I have often wondered why you did not send your adopted son to Oxford," Leicester said.

Donovan eyed the man narrowly. University was often the destination for illegitimate sons. Before Henry VIII broke with the Roman Church, men who attended Oxford or Cambridge usually took orders in the church and became celibate clerics: a safe fate for those who might challenge a title or pollute a bloodline.

Even now many university scholars remained celibate, more in love with books and learning than with a woman.

If any knew Robin's true bloodlines, they must hope and pray that he, too, would retire to the dust and mold of a library somewhere. He could become the focus of a rival claim to the throne too easily.

"My adopted son is too vital and intelligent to cloister. He has been most useful as my secretary. I have deliberately kept him close." Safe was the proper word, but not necessarily the politic one.

Elizabeth nodded her understanding. "We would keep this young man close to court for a time," she added.

"Please, Majesty, I have need of Robin in Edinburgh," Donovan pleaded with his eyes as well as his voice.

"Surely another could be trained to take his place at your side, milord. You do have other sons," Leicester reminded him. "Other sons who have more to inherit than this boy."

Donovan gulped. Certainly, Hal should be the one to accompany him to the Scottish capital, to learn politics and diplomacy as well as how to deal with royalty and courtiers.

Ever since Paris, Hal had become indifferent to all but his own solitude and running free across the land with the wind in his face, like one of the great wolfhounds the family raised.

"Robin has a maturity and steadiness the other boys have not yet developed," Donovan stated flatly.

"If I may be so bold, Your Majesty?" Robin asked. The queen's hand still rested possessively upon his arm.

"Speak." The queen smiled into his eyes, so like her own.

"Majesty, I am useful in Edinburgh with Milord of Kirkenwood. I do not wish to be just another decoration."

Everyone in the room gulped at his lack of courtly discretion. Elizabeth had imprisoned men for less grave insults.

"Are you saying that Gloriana's Court is nothing more than . . . decoration!" Leicester's dark face flushed and his full sensuous lips thinned to a rapier frown.

"Forgive my blunt words, milord." Robin bowed slightly toward Elizabeth's favorite, not at all nonplussed. "In

Edinburgh, I have employment and a function that suits me. Employment and a function that I know benefits Her Majesty."

"Still, we regret that you will not be close to us." Elizabeth fussed with her pearls and withdrew her hand from Robin's arm. But instead of moving away, she beckoned Betsy forward. "We would know that you are well placed and cared for by a loving wife."

Betsy curtsied prettily.

Blood drained from Donovan's face, leaving him cold and weak-kneed.

"Thank you, Majesty." Robin bowed slightly. From the cover of his lowered head he shot Betsy a venomous glance.

She ignored him.

"But I am not prepared to make a match." Robin stiffened his spine and held his chin up.

"And if we command?" Elizabeth narrowed her eyes.

The court withdrew a pace.

"Useless. I am already married."

Absolute silence rang around the room.

"You dare . . . !" Elizabeth thundered.

"Who?" Betsy squeaked.

"I have taken a woman of good family as my bride."

"Faith!" Betsy's anger rose as quickly as the color in her face. Her fists opened and closed repeatedly. She closed her eyes and breathed deeply. Did she prepare a spell?

Donovan stepped between her and Robin.

Deirdre crept out from obscurity. She reached a hand toward her cousin as if to cast a calming spell.

"You lowered yourself to wed the glassblower's daughter!" Betsy screamed. Her eyes took on a wild and disordered glaze. She reached her hands to her temples and grabbed long tendrils of hair. He'd never seen her with a single hair out of place, not even upon rising in the morning.

Donovan jumped to her side and captured her hands before she tore her hair or threw devastating magic. "Control yourself, daughter."

"You forsake *me* for a peasant!" Betsy ignored her father, the queen, and the court. All of her being seemed centered on Robin.

"We will annul this misalliance," Elizabeth said. Her

calm voice belied the agitation of her hands among the pearls. "Any marriage contracted by you without my permission is invalid."

"Forgive me, Majesty, but the marriage took place in Edinburgh last summer. Your laws, and your church have no authority there. I am well and truly married to a woman I love with all of my heart. We took binding vows before God's altar. We have conceived a child in lawful wedlock. Would you cast another child to the wolves of society with the taint of bastardy?"

Betsy screeched and lunged for Robin, fingers extended to claw at his face and eyes.

Excited jabbers burst out among the court.

"You defy us?" Elizabeth looked close to fainting. Her white face paint did nothing to hide her near collapse.

Leicester wrapped his arms about her, literally holding her upright.

"I follow my heart, madam. As did you once." The last was added on a mere whisper.

Donovan doubted any heard beyond the queen and her paramour.

"Get out!" Elizabeth snarled. "Ungrateful wretch. Leave us this moment. As long as your wife lives and this marriage lasts, you may never return to court. Never!"

She turned her back on the entire room and stalked into her private solar. She slammed the door on all but Leicester.

Donovan thrust Betsy into Deirdre's care, grabbed Robin, and exited hastily.

Robin, the audacious brat, whistled a jaunty tune.

"Why did you not tell me?" Donovan asked through gritted teeth.

"That I had married Faith? I thought you knew. We have made no secret of it in Edinburgh."

"Keep your bride and your child in Scotland. Away from Elizabeth's assassins. If any of Elizabeth's enemies suspect your lineage . . ." Donovan swallowed hard and fought for calm.

"Why did you not tell me you knew Elizabeth and Leicester to be your parents?" he continued after a long moment while they mounted their horses and fled the palace grounds.

"The subject never came up." Robin shrugged non-chalantly.

"When did you find out?"

"I have always known, as if the message was whispered to me in the cradle. The ghosts of Kirkenwood have much to say if one but listens."

Chapter 31

Spring 1575. London.

MY father's words within his journals remained elusive. I picked out more of the text than I ever had before. Most of it read as gibberish. I finally realized he had encrypted the pages with magic.

Elizabeth's vigilant gaze had shifted focus from me to Betsy since she had banished Robin from court. Therefore, I had more free time to slip away and haunt the booksellers of London. The penny presses that hawked pamphlets and bulletins at St. Paul's Square served me not. I needed the dealers in ancient and rare texts.

After many months of searching, I found an aged scholar tucked away in a dusty cavern of a shop in East Cheap. He had traveled far and wide in his youth as a wine merchant on the continent, collecting verbal lore and ancient texts. Though he professed Christianity now, I suspected he had been born a Jew. He knew far too much about their ways and their writings for a Christian. Over the months he became used to my inquiries and finally allowed me to wander through the collection of bound books, scrolls, and loose parchments. I learned to trail my fingers along a stack of works. When a tingling crept up my arm, I paused to investigate.

I found many interesting discussions on the origin of magic, the Mystery School Cults, and explorations of ancient holy sites. Few of these I could afford to buy. But I read them often enough in the shop to nearly memorize them. The scholar knew every word in every text and engaged me in many a lively debate.

I learned almost more from him than from the books. I

think he allowed me free reign because he was lonely, and hungry for another keen mind to match his own.

At last I found a folded sheaf of parchment written by my father during his years in Rome as a Vatican scribe. He outlined clearly the method he had used for encrypting works that needed to be preserved. Many of these manuscripts were in jeopardy of being burned as heretical material. Too much ancient knowledge had been lost already.

The scholar bargained hard for the folio. I paid every penny I possessed for it and promised him more from my next allowance. He winked at me, knowing I must return because of my own hunger for knowledge. We both knew he made the deal because he wanted an excuse to send for me if I did not return on schedule.

Perhaps I read the folio too quickly. Perhaps I lost a key secret in a missing page. Only a few more passages in the journals swam free of the concealing magic.

The last entry in my father's earliest journal stopped my reading and my thinking for many long moments.

21 June, 1558: The vision that has haunted me for years felled me once more. Mary Queen of Scots and her husband the Dauphin of France witnessed my seizure and heard my words. The assembled court witnessed my humiliation. Only my faithful familiar Helwriaeth stood by my side to support me in my hour of travail.

I do not remember the words I spoke. A warning certainly. The images, however, remain clear in my mind. Towering waves frothed with blood. Many ships broken and sinking. Men screaming and dying. And the young queen, headless, walking across the waves leading a long line of men in her wake.

I feared the same future as my father's vision. The woman who had captured Uncle Donovan's heart was the center of much of the politics of Elizabeth's court. She was the center of divisiveness. Her name cropped up in rumors almost every day. Usually I heard her name spoken with derision, fear, and anger. Sometimes I heard men speak of her in awed whispers.

Those men I followed and listened to more closely, suspecting secret Catholics among them.

Sir Francis Walsingham, the queen's spymaster, set his agents to follow me, knowing I would lead them to secret plots against the queen.

My father's vision told me how enduring the problem of Mary was, how much a threat she was to England. An invasion fleet was coming.

When?

From where?

England had many enemies. Elizabeth had more. Nearly all of them were Catholics.

I sought out my queen.

Elizabeth reclined on her bed, a huge pile of pillows and cushions propping her up while she read and translated a ponderous text by Plutarch. Betsy dressed the ulcer on Elizabeth's leg with a foul-smelling poultice. I detected essence of mummy beneath the mint and sulfur. I'd have chosen beer as the mixing agent, Betsy preferred a child's urine. Since Betsy had begun tending the queen's ailment, Elizabeth limped less and danced more. The queen had found a use for my cousin after all. She kept Betsy close and treated her as an innocent victim since Robin had confessed his marriage to another woman.

Betsy thrived under the attention.

"We knew of your father's visions, Deirdre," Elizabeth said after reading my copy of the passage in the journal. I knew she would not be able to decipher the actual journal. "We had not been made privy to the details, however."

She scanned my closely written script again. "This cannot be a true vision. We have vowed not to execute our royal cousin." She shuddered slightly.

"I understand, Majesty. To take the life of an anointed monarch sets a precedent no one wishes to see established," I replied.

Betsy finished tying a bandage on Elizabeth's leg and peered at the little book I carried. "May I read it, Your Majesty?"

Much of my cousin's behavior had tempered over the past few months. She no longer stayed away all night, nor did she look for reasons to argue with me or belittle me. I could only guess that she plotted something new since Robin had escaped her.

Our dogs still walked warily around each other, nipping occasionally, but mostly ignoring each other.

Elizabeth gestured that I should hand Betsy the journal. She peered at it closely, sniffed it, held a page to the light. "I find nothing hidden beneath his words. Not even a spell," she announced at last.

I held back my snort of derision. I had detected no magic in it either, until I had removed some of it.

" 'Twas written while my father was still a new priest. He had renounced his magic," I told them both. I had read of my father's agonizing decision to renounce all he held dear, all that was familiar, in order to become a priest. His wolfhound was all that had followed him into the new life. I had wept with him as I read of his heartbreak and loneliness.

But I did not understand his reasons for throwing away his heritage. My faith was not as strong as his. I wished it were. I wished I could believe in something, anything, as strongly as he believed in God. I wished I could love someone with the intensity he loved God. Someone other than Hal.

He had applied the magical encryption to his writings later, when he knew the sacrifice he must make to secure peace in Britain.

"Father Griffin Kirkwood, the Merlin of Britain is dead," Elizabeth said with a sigh. "His visions died with him. Our cousin escaped death at the hands of her Scottish barons. Therefore the vision of her death has been averted."

Betsy closed the journal with a snap and returned it to me. "We need fear this vision no longer," my cousin pronounced on a smirk.

Our rivalry was not yet finished.

"But, Majesty, blood on the waves clearly is a symbol for a great battle at sea. The Scots have not a fleet. The danger must come from France or Spain, or possibly the Pope will unite the powers of Europe to sail against you," I protested.

"The fleet could be symbolic of the civil war in Scotland that preceded our sister queen's escape to our custody." Elizabeth returned to Plutarch.

I curtsied my acknowledgment of her dismissal. I did not accept it. Mary would die and a fleet would sail to punish her executioner.

The journal and the spell to remove the cloaking magic on it had come to me at this time for a reason. 'Twas my responsibility to seek out the danger and stop it before England suffered an invasion.

"Deirdre," Elizabeth stopped me at the door—as was her wont.

"Yes, Majesty?" I turned and curtsied to her once more.

"Milord of Kirkenwood has requested that both you and Betsy return to Kirkenwood this summer while we progress through the southlands. We would abide by your wishes in this matter."

"Oh, yes, please, Majesty," Betsy gushed. "As much as I love your royal personage and the honor you have accorded us, I do miss my home and family. Please allow us to return for the summer."

Elizabeth peered down her long nose at my cousin in speculation.

"And you, Deirdre? What are your wishes?"

A sense of urgency from the journal made me think twice. If I stayed with the queen and her court I might learn something, overhear plots, intercept letters . . .

But Hal was at Kirkenwood. I missed him and longed for his council. The other volumes of my father's journals were at Kirkenwood.

Other arcane texts were stashed at Kirkenwood. I could learn from them, perhaps release more of the journals to my eye.

"I wish only to please you, Majesty." I bowed my head. Fate had placed the journal in my hands, let fate determine how and when I would need that information.

"You may both attend Milord of Kirkenwood for the summer." Elizabeth scowled at the Latin text she translated. With a few curt words and gestures, she dismissed Betsy and me to our duties.

I decided to seek out the French and Spanish Ambassadors and listen closely to their secret conversations.

Over the next month, as Elizabeth and her court prepared
for a summer progress to visit loyal barons and woo recalci-
trant ones, I spent much of my time creeping through the
shadows. I witnessed secret notes passed between lovers. I
heard gossip about gambling debts. I learned the breeding
secrets of stable masters.

But my quarry, the foreign ambassadors, eluded me.
They were never alone and never lingered. Their secrets
remained in the embassies.

And while I spied upon powerful men and the women
who slept with them, Betsy made many plans for the journey home and packed and repacked her clothing. I resigned
myself to the journey. I convinced myself that I pursued a
fool's errand in London.

The day before the court removed from Whitehall for
the hot, disease-ridden months, I sat with Lady Sidney and
Lady Hastings with a pile of the queen's mending. By rights
of seniority, they should have supervised the packing indoors. But they had chosen to sit outside in the silver knot
garden where we would not disturb the bustle or be interrupted by demands for our helping hands. All attempts at
conversation had faded in the warm sunshine with only the
drone of bees among the flowers to entertain us.

My skills with a needle had improved over the months,
but still I managed to confine my work to sewing on loose
buttons and ties. Both tasks that required sturdy work
rather than neatness.

Coffa drowsed at my feet beneath the stone bench I had
chosen. She kept her head pressed comfortably against my
ankle. Every once in a while I felt her ears prick at some
sound or scent beyond my senses. I tuned into her perceptions, as much out of boredom as a need to keep her close
in my thoughts.

A muted conversation blended with the soft sounds in
the garden, the rustle of petticoats, the buzz of insects, the
heavy breathing of my dog. I distinguished no words, just
the concept of phrases, questions, and replies.

A quick glance at my companions showed Lady Hastings dozing over a rent seam. Lady Sidney still plied her needle, but her eyes drifted closed. Neither spoke. Nor did they snore—a trick learned early in Elizabeth's services. If any of her ladies needed to catch up on sleep, as we often did, the trick was to do it quietly, preferably with the eyes open.

I listened more closely, extending my magical senses rather than filtering them through Coffa's limited perceptions.

Three men stood just opposite the brick wall among the roses and graveled pathways. Elizabeth hated roses, almost feared them, and never ventured into that garden. The men's words took on the cadence of French.

"*Sacre bleu!* The air in Paris is easier to breathe with *him* gone," one man said with authority.

"No more the reek of sulfur and wet wolf fur," a second man chortled.

"But where has *he* gone? At least when *he* was in Paris we could set our spies to watch him. Now *he* works his mischief elsewhere. We have no warning, no information."

I crept closer to the wall, abandoning my mending.

"Would *he* dare bring his wolf here?" the first man said. He sounded older, firmer than the others. But I did not recognize his voice. If only I could see.

I edged toward the corner of the garden, careful not to let tall foxglove brush against my clothing and betray me with the rustling of my petticoats. I found a low door there. The gardeners used it to move freely between plots. The planks had warped, leaving gaps for me to peer through and listen.

Ambassador Fénelon's secretary stood with his right side to me. He, then, was the authoritative speaker. The two younger men, one stout, the other quite lean, stood with their backs toward me. From their stance and clothing I recognized them as two among the many members of the French Ambassador's household.

"*Le meneur des loups* goes where he wills," Monsieur Stout snorted. "Who questions the one who commands *les loups-garous?*"

The tamer of wolves! Could this be the one who directed the monster who had savaged Paris and kidnapped Hal? I had heard little more of werewolves since averting the massacre in Paris last summer. Only the occasional report of remote villages quaking in fear when they found a dead body savaged by wild animals. A common and ordinary occurrence. Except . . .

The few reports that made their way to London mentioned packs of men in the guise of wolves. Had I not read that werewolves hunted alone?

"If *he* has come to London, *he* probably hides in the depths of the Spanish Embassy, as *he* did in Paris," Monsieur Secretary remarked. The three men ambled away from me.

I needed to follow them.

I needed to search the Spanish Embassy.

I needed to talk to Hal.

The men moved out of earshot.

I fumbled with the latch, trying not to let the rusty bolt scrape too loudly.

A large masculine hand covered my own. Before I could gasp, another hand silenced my mouth.

Chapter 32

"WHO are you and why are you always one step ahead of me in spying on these men?" a rough voice demanded.

Where was Coffa to defend me?

He pulled me back from the gate into the shade of a yew tree. His hand over my mouth prevented my reply.

Lady Sidney and Lady Hastings continued to doze over their sewing.

I remained still, wary, and ready to bolt the moment he loosed me even a little.

He eased the pressure of his fingers on my mouth, but not his hand around my waist that held me tight against his chest.

I could scream. Lady Sidney and Lady Hastings would come to my rescue, or summon the guard.

Where was Coffa?

"Answer me, wench," he whispered harshly.

Curiosity won over caution. I turned as much as his restraining arm would let me. A man no more than two and twenty, with sandy blond hair, restrained me. The top of my head reached his chin, making him a handspan or more shorter than Uncle Donovan. He wore well-cut but sober clothing. I saw nothing remarkable in feature or form; neither handsome nor ugly, a pleasant face devoid of emotion. I would have trouble picking him out of a crowd.

"And who are you that you spy on the queen's ladies in the queen's private gardens?" I tried for a touch of Elizabeth's imperious tone.

"You answer my questions and I'll answer yours," he replied on a chuckle.

"I am Deirdre Kirkwood, lady-in-waiting to Her Majesty's Bedchamber."

"I know that. But you are also more. You spy for the queen about the court. You are over young for the honor of your position. And a noble wolfhound follows at your heels everywhere you go. Now tell me truly. Who are you?"

I answered him with silence. If he knew of the Pendragon, then he was a dangerous man who knew too much. If he did not know, then I was not the one to enlighten him.

"Perhaps I should ask who are your parents?"

"I am the bastard of Father Griffin Kirkwood."

"Ah, the Merlin. That answers many questions. Including the wolfhound. Yours is daughter or granddaughter to his beast."

"You knew my father?"

"Knew of him. The queen's pet, never seen without his wolfhound. She always met him in private; a Catholic priest who hid from the law in the sanctuary of Whitefriars and had passport written in the queen's own hand. A man of contradictions loved and revered by many."

Just then Coffa ambled over to us, sniffing the path, the flowers, and finally the man's boots before she sat and begged for pets from him.

"Thank you for protecting me," I snarled at her.

She looked up at me through sleepy eyes as if to ask whom I needed protecting from.

"Good dog." The man chuckled and loosed me so that he could caress Coffa. She leaned into him with a sigh and drooled.

I stepped away from my captor. Reluctantly?

"You have not answered my question, sirrah," I demanded.

He laughed again. "You sound just like your mistress in high dudgeon."

I raised one eyebrow—or tried to. I had not Uncle Donovan's trick of intimidation.

"Sir Michael Maelstrom at your service." He swept me a deep bow while keeping one affectionate hand on Coffa. She nosed his padded breeches for a treat.

Ah, she knew him then and he had bribed her goodwill with food.

I tried to find a deep anger against him. And yet . . . That dimple when he smiled made the sun shine just a little brighter.

My instincts wanted to trust him. Cold logic told me not to.

"That cannot be your real name," I accused him.

He shrugged. " 'Tis the name I was given."

"By whom?"

He shrugged again but did not speak this time.

"And your purpose in following me and coercing my dog into silence?"

"You noticed." He fished a strip of dried meat out of his pocket and held it out for Coffa.

She nibbled it daintily from his fingers. Anyone else would lose half a hand to her voracious appetite.

"I noticed. Who are you?"

"I already told you . . ."

"You gave me a made-up name only."

He sighed. "Very well, I work for Sir Francis Walsingham."

"The queen's spymaster!" He had not been following me about, merely following the same people I followed and listened to.

The perfect spy. No one would notice him in a crowd. Except me. I would know that dimple anywhere now. And I would be on the lookout for him.

To avoid him? Or to attract his attention?

Coffa trusted him. I had always trusted my familiar's ability to read people.

"Those men are getting away. They have valuable information. We need to follow . . ."

"I need to report back to my master." He grabbed my arm and dragged me from the shelter of the yew tree toward a recessed doorway opposite the gate corner.

"But they know of The Master," I protested. "We have to find out how much they know. We have to find out how long he has been in England."

"The Master? Whose Master? Certainly not mine."

"Um . . . You would not believe me."

"Try me. I have seen many strange things in my years with Sir Francis." His grip threatened to bruise my arm.

"A man hides within the Spanish Embassy. We believe he controls a monster."

"What man? And who is 'we'?"

"I do not know the man. Spaniards refer to him as *El Lobison*. His monster savages people on the three nights of the full moon. He used this beast to brew fear of Protestants in Paris. He wanted a repeat of the massacre on the eve of St. Bartholomew's Day. These Frenchmen called him *le meneur des loups*."

A sudden chill washed over me. I remembered the night my cousins and I had scried for Queen Mary and had seen death and destruction instead.

Another memory hit me between the eyes. A blow that nearly sent me reeling. A pack of oversized wolves with red glowing eyes attracted by my magic at the lake below Kirkenwood.

If I pursued *El Lobison,* the *meneur des loups,* would I become a victim of his monsters? Or become one of them?

Was I vulnerable or immune to his monster because my mother hosted the demon while she carried me?

"Who would have the power to control such a one? Surely Sir Francis and his troops know of him." Sir Michael moved faster, nearly dragging me off my feet.

"*El Lobison* is a great magician. He must be. How else could he control a *loup-garou?*"

"A greater magician than Dr. John Dee?"

I shrugged. I knew the name of Europe's most renowned astrologer and magician. I had never met him to judge his magical talent. My father's later journals might tell me more of him.

I had so much to learn about my father before I could . . . what? Become the Pendragon? Feel whole? Love a man other than Hal? Someone like Sir Michael perhaps?

"Come." Sir Michael Maelstrom yanked open the doorway. He did not release his grip on my arm.

"Where?" I dug in my heels.

He shifted his grip to my waist and lifted me off the ground. "Sir Francis needs to know what you know. All of it."

Coffa trailed at our heels, meek and eager to please.

"But I do not know all of it." I pounded upon his restraining arm.

"Then we will discover the rest together. After we report to *my* master."

June 1575. The Spanish Embassy, London.

Yassimine stood on the little balcony outside The Master's bedchamber. The nearly full moon made her long for the right to run, free of the fetters of restrictive clothing, to feast on hot, fresh, bloody meat. Tonight.

The sun set late in these northern climes. The moon rose later still. She did not want to wait.

The cool dampness of the city repelled her. She longed for the hot dry steppes of her birthplace. There she could separate individual smells and know each one intimately. The moisture in the air and from the sluggish river blended the scents and bound them together in a potpourri that remained elusive.

When the moon commanded her body, would The Master loose her on the city? Or would he chain her in the dungeon?

The stiff brocade of her black gown rustled. Her petticoats and farthingale chafed her skin. The stiffening in the ridiculous lace ruff that framed her face masked the scents she sought in the city.

Surely her errant pup, the English lad she had converted in Paris, had sensed her arrival half a moon cycle ago. She indulged in a daydream of hunting across the steppes, a full moon lighting the heavens, with a pack behind her. A pack entirely of her get. The youngling, Hal, at her side as her chief mate.

Soon, she promised herself.

Her other get had gradually found their way to her and The Master. The Master's control of them had been ruthless and demanding. Little of their humanity showed through their unkempt clothing, matted hair, and tangled beards. Even now they resided in the dark and damp recesses of the cellars, hidden from the view of ordinary mortals and from the realization of what had become of them.

The morsel of hope she nurtured in the back of her heart prayed to a myriad of gods that the young one, Hal, had not yet sunk to the same level as the others. She needed him strong, clear thinking, and occasionally human to satisfy her.

"You call him?" The Master asked, coming up beside her. He handed her a black lace veil. The silk threads felt as fine as a spiderweb, like the webs of power The Master wove through every country. "Cover yourself. Someone might see you."

"It interferes with my summons." She let the lace drift through her fingers like cool water.

They stood together silently for many long moments. Yassimine's heart beat loudly in her ears. Gradually, she became aware of another heart, distant, faint, resistant, pounding a counterrhythm to her own.

"Why does he not come, Master?" Her voice sounded almost panicky. More than that, sorrowful and afraid.

Afraid for her pup and for herself.

"He will come. He is new to our pack. His humanity is still strong and resistant. But he will come."

"Perhaps he is too far away. I can barely sense him."

"Can you sense the men I have selected to sail to the New World? Many of them are sailors who will take over the ship once they sate their appetites on the rest of the crew. Can you smell their eagerness to rampage through the cities of gold, striking at Spaniards and Indians alike so that none of them are sane and they blame each other for the many deaths?"

"Yes. Their musk is strong. They wish to mate and create more of their kind. Yet I know them to be sterile."

"They are farther away than the pup. He will hear you and come, as a child comes to his mother."

I do not think so. Something in him allows him to resist you, Master. Once she killed The Master, she did not want the strongest of her get to turn on her for revenge.

"You shall have the freedom of the city tonight," The Master promised.

" 'Tis not time, Master."

"Yes, but I would have you learn your way through the maze of streets. You must find three specific locations tonight while you have your intelligence. You will mark them so that you will return to them when the wolf rules your instincts."

"There is something you must know, Master. This is the last full moon I will be able to hunt with a plan."

"Do you defy me?" The Master twisted his fist into her unbound hair and yanked it back hard.

"No, Master. I do not defy you. But my body obeys older instincts."

"Explain." He pulled harder, forcing her head back. Her throat was fully exposed and vulnerable to his all too sharp hook or his bite. In the past months his canine teeth had become longer, more pointed, closer to fangs. But he would never become a full wolf. He had not undergone the full ritual. Instead she drained him of his humanity while leaving him in his human body.

"My get are sterile, both as wolves and as men. I am not."

"Eh?" He loosened his grip on her. "How can that be?"

"When I endured the ritual, I was meant to be mother to my people as well as priestess." For a moment she dared remember the intensity of that first coupling, the joy of her people as they watched and cheered. Then nine moons later they again watched and cheered as she birthed a son. They fed him blood before he tasted his mother's milk. In that moment he became a god to the nomads of the steppes.

But nine days later, her people sacrificed the child rather than allow it to rule over them. They allowed the birth only as proof of a successful ritual for Yassimine.

She wept each year on the anniversaries of the babe's birth and his death. At all other times she hid her grief. 'Twas the way of her people. She knew it, understood it. Accepted it.

And hated the loss of her child.

"And now?" The Master prompted her.

"And now I have conceived. As the child grows within me, my wolf will become dominant. I will have no control over it. It will emerge at odd times and refuse to come forth at others."

"Is it mine?" He grinned, baring his large white teeth.

"Of course. I have been with no other since the ritual in Paris, nearly a year ago." But The Master had not a wolf form to take while fathering the child. Would it be human or wolf? A monster or a loving child?

"Then you must feast well this full moon before you are forced to endure confinement again."

"Who must I target, Master?"

"Three powerful men who impede my domination of England. You may take out as many of their households as you like, as long as these three die."

"Which three?" She panted in anticipation of hot blood on her tongue.

"Sir William Cecil, Lord Burghley, Secretary of the Treasury and mastermind of the queen's politics; Sir Francis Walsingham, the queen's spymaster; and Lord Robert Dudley, Earl of Leicester, the queen's lover and favorite courtier."

Chapter 33

June 1575. Kirkenwood.

"YOU will place this missive in Her Grace, Mary Stuart's, hands directly," Donovan instructed the courier. Bernard was just one of many refugees from Whitefriars who had found a home and employment with Donovan. Father Griffin, Donovan's priest brother had sent them here from the last remaining sanctuary in England when war and plague threatened them more than the law. In honor of Father Griffin the Elder, none of them had reverted to a life of crime. Honest men and women, they worked willingly for their keep.

"Aye, milord. Her Grace knows my signal. I will pass it to her in the garden, away from prying eyes." The young man's own eyes danced with mischief.

"The Countess of Shrewsbury has become quite cunning in keeping Her Grace under close surveillance," Donovan warned.

"Her Grace is in love. She, too, has become quite shrewd in evading the old harridan's ploys."

"Just be careful. The old harridan is quite capable of having you thrown in the Tower if you are caught."

"Aye, milord."

"Be off with you now." Donovan held the horse's bridle while his trusted retainer mounted. "Complete this task and return alive, boy. I just might knight you for valor when you do."

"I can't afford a knighthood, milord." The boy leaned down and spoke confidentially. "The brewmaster charges knights more than common folk for a tankard."

"Well, we can't exactly go to the queen with explanations

when asking for an income for you. We'll see what I can come up with. When you return safely. Successfully."

"Then I am off!" He took control of the reins and spun his horse about. With a kick of his heels he spurred the horse into a gallop out the gate of Kirkenwood.

The raven took off from its perch on the well and escorted the boy as far as the standing stones, cawing raucous complaints. Then it returned and settled on its customary perch.

"Another letter to Mary?" Hal came up behind Donovan.

Donovan started. "You have inherited my brother's ability to creep about on cat feet."

Hal lifted his lip at one corner, baring a very pointed canine tooth. "That must mean that I have improved my mental shields. You cannot detect my mind from a distance."

"Is that it?"

Hal shrugged.

"You did not answer my question, Father."

Donovan winced inwardly at the formality. For an entire year the boy had remained aloof, never corresponding with the family, rarely dining with them, usually roaming the moors the entire night. Many nights he slept in the family cemetery.

At least he'd stopped growing long enough for his twin to nearly catch up with him. Quite unsuitable for the older boy to be the slighter.

"What was your question?" Donovan looked down his nose at his son. Not nearly as far down as he would have liked. He was losing his ability to intimidate either of his sons by size alone. A little voice in the back of his head reminded him that he controlled Hal not at all and Griffin only when it pleased Griffin.

Had he and his twin been much different at the age of fifteen?

With a chuckle he slapped his son on the back. "Yes, I sent a report to Her Grace on how well her son grows."

"And how much you love her and miss her." Hal ducked out from under Donovan's embrace. "Did you ever write such love letters to my mother when she took herself off to Ide Hill without you?"

Donovan repressed the stab of guilt. He and Martha had quarreled often, made up often as well. But that last time . . . that last time he had allowed the demon-born love spell for Mary to come between them.

" 'Tis a private letter, Hal." Donovan frowned. "I need you to run the stud dogs today. They are getting fat and lazy."

"You pay servants to do that." Hal turned his back on his father.

"One of the responsibilities of the lord of the manor is to supervise the staff, set an example for them."

"Then Griffin should do it. He will be lord of the manor."

"I told you to do it. You need to spend time with them against the day you attract a new familiar."

"I will muck out the byres or the kennels. But I will not run the dogs." Hal stalked toward the stable.

"Hal, come back here!"

Hal ignored the summons. The raven reached out to peck his hand as it ran along the cool stonework. Hal jerked his hand away with a curse. Then he ran into the dark stable, as if chased by a raven demon.

"Henry Kirkwood!"

Donovan stomped after him. The time had come to find out what the hell had happened to the boy in France.

Hal searched the stable for a place to hide from his father. The solid stone construction of the building atop the rocky tor proved a more formidable barrier than the dimness of the interior. If he slid beneath a pile of straw in the loft, as he had when he and Dee had been young, his father would find the spot sooner or later. In his current mood, Da was not likely to give up his pursuit.

The silver earring burned. It urged Hal to follow the summons.

But he would not.

"A full year I've done as you told me, Yassimine, and it makes no difference. No meat. Long meditations. Longer hours underground in the lair. Sedating potions. Nothing works. I am still a beast. Still a danger to my family and my people. The moon still commands me." He pounded his fist into a supporting beam. It splintered.

A horse whinnied in fear in the next stall.

The other mounts took up the nervousness and began to shift restlessly. Da's big stallion kicked at his loose box.

"Hal!" Da called from the yard.

Griff? He called to his twin with his mind. *I need you to divert Da's attention.*

Griffin did not reply verbally. Hal had only an impression of clanging swords and sore shoulder muscles. Weapons training was a constant occupation on the border with Scotland. Landowners on both sides earned their living by raiding. 'Twas a time-honored profession, not likely to end soon.

Mary Queen of Scots' exile in England only added fuel to the feuds. Strangely, the tragic queen had more supporters in England—mostly Catholics living near the border—than in largely Protestant Scotland.

"Son, we need to talk," Da said. He stood in the doorway blinking, waiting for his human eyes to adjust to the gloom.

Nothing for it but the postern. Years ago, during a vicious winter storm, much of the hillside outside the postern had broken away and slid into the valley beside the kirk. Now the exit from the stable opened onto a sheer cliff rather than a safe pathway for men and beasts. On this day at the beginning of the full moon, the barricades presented no problem to Hal. With his preternatural strength, he ripped at the stout boards nailed across the door.

The sound brought Da deeper into the stable.

Hal kicked at a reluctant slab of wood. It splintered and hung drunkenly from the jamb.

"What are you doing, Hal?" Da came up behind him. He placed a gentle hand on Hal's shoulder.

"Go away, Father. Get away from me before I hurt you!" Hal slammed his shoulder into the door. It creaked open on rusted hinges. He nearly fell through it from the momentum. Only Da's hand upon his arm kept him from flying down the cliff to certain death.

Perhaps 'twould be better than this half life.

"Talk to me, son!" Da swung him around, anchoring him

to the stable floor. "Ever since France you are different. What happened there? What is wrong with you? I can't help you unless you tell me."

"You would not understand."

"Perhaps. Perhaps not. We cannot know unless you tell me."

Hal could not bring himself to form the words. Instinctively he fingered the hot earring.

"That bit of jewelry is only the most obvious change in you, Hal."

Silence stretched between them a long moment.

"I am not a slave to fashion myself, but I find this a distasteful display in one so young." Da grabbed the chain. "Yiee! That burns." Immediately, he yanked his hand away and sucked on his fingers. "The thing glows. What magic do you possess?"

Hal ducked under his father's restraining hand. In a heartbeat he was out the main door of the stable. Another heartbeat took him through the bailey and out onto the moors.

June 1575. London.

Sir Michael reported to his master, Sir Francis Walsingham, in concise and accurate words. Within moments, the queen's spymaster knew as much as Sir Michael did about the conversation I had overheard.

Throughout the recital he kept a heavy hand upon my shoulder to force me to remain in the narrow chair before Sir Francis' writing desk.

"You and your spying upon the ambassadors to Her Majesty's court present a problem to me, Mistress Deirdre Kirkwood," Sir Francis said. He stared at me and Sir Michael Maelstrom with a disapproving frown. His dark eyes and swarthy skin had earned him the sobriquet of "Moor" from the queen. I knew his value to her by the nickname. Elizabeth bestowed them only on her pets. Robert Dudley, Earl of Leicester was her "Eyes," Walsingham her "Moor," and Uncle Donovan her "Wolfhound."

Sir Michael squirmed under his employer's scrutiny. I

practiced some of the patience Elizabeth had forced upon
me.

"I will happily return to my duties at Whitehall." I put
on a smile. I hoped it would disarm him rather than give
him a clue to my sarcasm.

"You also present a solution to a problem."

"I had no choice but to bring her to you." Sir Michael
belied his nervousness with the haste of his words.

"Her Majesty will question my absence."

"Her Majesty expects you to depart her court on the
morrow and return to your uncle's estates," Sir Francis
countered.

"Tonight she will expect me to serve at table." Not precisely true.

"As most junior of the ladies-in-waiting, your duties are
confined to the bedchamber."

"Check, Sir Francis." But not a checkmate. I bowed my
head.

"Sir Michael, parchment and pen." Sir Francis snapped
his fingers and pointed to a cupboard behind him.

More obedient than Coffa, Sir Michael fetched the required items.

"Prepare a missive for my signature. Explain to Her Majesty that Mistress Kirkwood possesses information and talents I require. I will return her to the palace unharmed
before dawn."

"The queen guards the virtue of her ladies closely. I must
return to my chamber 'unharmed' before she retires for the
night." Check.

"Which will be a few hours before dawn." Check. "Your
dog protects you better than I could hope to."

"My dog has been corrupted by your agent." Coffa sat
beside Sir Michael, resting her head on his knee. He
scratched her ears absently with his left hand while he
penned the letter.

"Your dog shows good taste. Sir Michael is most loyal
and trustworthy."

The object of our conversation blushed to the tips of his
ears. An endearing trait.

"Now, Mistress Kirkwood, I need to know what you
know about a man with no name who keeps a slave inside
the Spanish Embassy, first in Paris and now here."

"Before I can tell you anything, I need to know what you know about my family and our long heritage."

"Sir Michael, please fetch us wine, the burgundy in the cellar."

Sir Michael rose and left the room without protest. He did lift his eyebrows in speculation. I returned his gaze with a bland countenance—another trick I'd learned while attending our queen.

"So you are one of *them*," Sir Francis stated.

I met that statement with silence.

After a moment, he sighed. "Very well. Her Majesty has informed me that one among your family inherits special qualities that allows him—or her—to become a protector of England. I believe that protection extends beyond normal senses."

"Magic."

"Magic, if you will. Though I have yet to witness any act of true magic that cannot be explained by tricks and machines and science."

I decided not to enlighten him.

"You do not need to believe in magic," I said after a moment's reflection. "Sufficient that the Spaniards do believe and fear the powers of this man with no name. They call him The Master. Or *El Lobison.* He controls a monster. I believe the monster is a werewolf. I cannot know for certain until I return to Kirkenwood and consult the family library of rare texts on matters arcane."

"Dr. John Dee, the queen's astrologer, has proved that lycanthropy is a disease of the mind. Curable." Sir Francis dismissed my comments with a wave of his hand.

"Catholics, and the Spaniards are almost all Catholics, believe that lycanthropy is possession by a demon or a curse of the devil," I countered. "They burn convicted werewolves at the stake by the hundreds. Nearly three hundred in recent decades."

"So why is this man in England?"

"I do not know."

"Guess."

"To create more werewolves. To create chaos through terror as he did in France." And then I told him about the deaths and dismemberments in Paris, how the city was ready to rise against Protestants with extreme violence, how a band of mercenaries lay waiting to lead the next massacre.

But I did not tell him that The Master had held Hal captive for three days. The Master's werewolf had been in the same household. Hal had emerged from his imprisonment changed . . .

In that instant I knew what had happened to Hal. I had blocked the possibility from my mind. Unthinkable.

But it was the only answer to the troubling changes in his personality.

Hal had told The Master that he acted alone in subduing the mercenaries in order to protect me. He told the Spaniards that he was the Pendragon.

Now The Master sought to control the Pendragon of Britain and thus shatter our magical protection of England against invasion.

The fleet my father saw in his visions was coming from Spain.

When? After Mary Queen of Scots lost her head.

Mary still lived. If the vision was to be believed, as long as her life tormented Elizabeth, England was safe.

'Twas my destiny to make certain she lived for a long, long time. But I also had to make certain none of her plots to overthrow Elizabeth succeeded.

Chapter 34

That same evening. London.

HAL was a werewolf. The realization sank in my belly like a heavy stone.

Oh, Hal, why did you not tell me?

"Sir Francis, I must return to Kirkenwood. Immediately." In my distraction, I rose and began to pace restlessly about his study.

"Impossible. I need your expertise to ferret out this Spaniard and his slave," Sir Francis said firmly.

"You do not understand." I stopped my prowl long enough to brace myself against his writing table and leaned over. I caught his gaze with my own and willed him to open his mind to my urgency. He blinked and looked away.

God's Blood! The man was stubborn.

"Sir Francis, I will be of much more use to you in the autumn when I have read every text in Kirkenwood's library on lycanthropy. I will also study Spanish more closely so that I can understand what I overhear."

"Sir Michael's knowledge of Spanish is sufficient. He will accompany you to Kirkenwood. You will share your research with him. This summer is the ideal time to employ your talents. Elizabeth has already agreed to part with you for some months."

Coffa streaked back into the room. She leaped at the window. Her weight broke the latch and opened the doors wide to the night air. She growled and snarled.

I lunged to grab her collar, fearful that she would tumble over the balcony.

"What?" I asked her. Her senses came through a garbled mixture of scents and images of another dog.

Not a dog. She would never bother challenging any mere dog except another wolfhound.

"The werewolf is out there," I whispered to Sir Francis.

Sir Michael, who had come in on Coffa's heels, crossed himself. Sir Francis shook his head and closed his eyes.

For the first time his mind opened, and I heard his disgust at Sir Michael's superstition. "There is no such thing as a werewolf. Only a person sick in the mind."

"Sick mind or unnatural beast, *it* watches this house." I hauled Coffa back into the room and slammed closed the doors. "You must return me to the palace and seek lodging elsewhere. No one is safe in this house."

Shudders of cold inadequacy racked my body. Once more I had to work magic. Strong magic. Would someone die because of the spell?

"Mistress Kirkwood, Sir Francis is protected by a legion of his people. I assure you, we are all well armed and well trained," Sir Michael said. He rested his hand on the hilt of his short sword.

"Are you willing to go out in the night and face a werewolf?"

He swallowed deeply, settled his shoulders, and nodded.

"You have courage, Sir Michael. I hope it does not make you foolhardy."

"Send three men to follow whoever watches this place," Sir Francis commanded. "Take the dog, if Mistress Kirkwood will allow. Let it sniff out your quarry."

Coffa liked that idea. I did not. But I allowed her to go.

"Tell them to keep a fair distance. Stay downwind of the beast and its Master."

Coffa fairly ran out of the room and down the stairs. Sir Michael nearly fell headlong down the stairs trying to catch up with her.

"Clearly, our interview has ended, Mistress Kirkwood. I shall send you back to the palace with an armed escort." Sir Francis rang a little silver bell. In another time, in other circumstances I would think it sounded like faeries laughing. Not tonight. Not with the threat of the wolf out there.

"I will leave when my dog returns." I plunked down in my chair. "While we wait, I will set out whatever protection I can." I rose again before I'd barely settled.

I had no scrip with me. Ladies of the court did not carry

their belongings about with them. Perhaps the kitchen
would have some of the common ingredients I needed. Simple wards against magic and things Otherworldly.

"Fennel!" I cried with delight as I entered the kitchen.
Cook threw up his hands and backed away from me.

"Give me all of it," I demanded.

Sir Francis, hard upon my heels, shrugged and rolled his
eyes upward.

"Milord?" The cook looked skeptically first at me and
then to the stalks of the plant hanging upside down from
the rafters above his worktable.

"Give it to her. 'Twill make her happy and keep her
busy for a time," Sir Francis replied.

I glared at him but scrambled up on the table and retrieved the six long stalks of fennel. The seeds fell into my
kerchief with a brush of my hand.

"Each person within the household should carry a few
of these in his pocket." I should have thought of this before
Sir Michael left with my dog.

Then I separated out the stalks. "How many windows
and doors do you have, Sir Francis?"

"What does that . . . enough of this nonsense, child."

"Do you wish to become the werewolf's next meal?" I
returned his stare for many long moments.

He looked away first. Then he turned on his heel and
retreated upstairs to his office.

"Were . . . werewolves?" Cook asked anxiously. He
looked in despair at the haunch roasting over his hearth.
Not enough to satisfy a monster and keep it from ravening
the household as well.

"Aye, a werewolf. Cross two twigs of the fennel, tie them
with red thread, and hang them in each window and upon
each door on this level."

Anxiously, he grabbed a handful of fennel stalks and an
equal measure of the seeds.

I took the remainder to protect each opening on the two
floors above with the same remedy. I had not enough of
the herb to extend to the upper stories and doubted a wolf
could scale the walls higher than the first balconies.

When I had finished, I walked the house, deasil, from
room to room, touching each hanging charm and infusing

it with whatever power I had. A few ritual words set a tiny glow about the plant that only I could see.

By the time I finished, fatigue dragged at my limbs. Grit crusted behind my eyelids. I yawned hugely as I plunked down in the chair beside Walsingham's writing desk.

The safety of Kirkenwood and my family had never seemed farther away than it did at this moment.

But at Kirkenwood, another werewolf awaited me.

"This is the home of Sir Francis Walsingham. Of the three men we mark tonight, he is the most dangerous," The Master said quietly.

Yassimine scanned the outside of the fine brick home near the river. The trim had been recently painted, the forecourt was neatly swept, even the flowers in the window boxes looked orderly and organized.

"This man is intelligent and logical," she replied, no louder than a breath.

"Yes." The Master looked at her with something akin to respect. Or was it only fear?

An armed man strolled past the front door of the house; a guard who pretended to be a casual visitor. Yassimine spotted his sword, dagger, pistol, and a short club. He could well have more weapons hidden on his body. Five more guards patrolled the area within a few heartbeats. They moved at intervals so that they could see at least one other guard at all times.

She counted stories and windows, judging the distance from the ground to the first balcony. Most people locked and barred doors. Few bothered with windows, especially above the ground level. She searched to see if Sir Francis Walsingham had set traps to prevent an enemy from climbing the walls. She searched for vines and trellises to aid her. A walk around the building revealed a lone rambling rose climbing the back wall to a balcony, larger and deeper than all the rest. This must lead to the lord's bedchamber.

She returned to the front of the house and watched the

guards and their patterns for many long moments. The guard sidestepped an animal trap beneath the first window.

Yassimine shuddered at the thought of catching one of her limbs in the wicked teeth of the trap. What other snares lay scattered about the grounds?

"He has laid traps for the unwary. Entering his home will not be easy."

"I trust you to accomplish your mission, Yassimine. His death is essential to my plans."

The breeze shifted direction for a brief moment. For half a heartbeat she did not smell the river. She smelled the *other*. The same scent that had taunted her in Paris just before The Master brought the boy to her for transformation.

Was Hal here? Strange that she did not sense his presence. She sniffed the air warily and quickly sorted the components of the scent. Like the boy and not the boy. Lighter. Feminine. With a wolfhound at her heels. The female and her familiar merged into one scent, one essence, one magic more powerful than either of them alone.

"We must forget this man as a target." Yassimine turned away from The Master. Already her skin itched and her bones ached with the need to transform. The scent of the *other* and the wolfhound called to her. The allure of this *other* was stronger than Yassimine's lust for Hal; stronger than the burning chains that pierced her body and demanded obedience to The Master.

"No, we will not find another target," The Master said. "Walsingham must die. His death more than any other will send the message to the world that Elizabeth's reign has loosed dark forces upon England. The Catholics will see that she and her Protestant scientists are deposed." He kept Yassimine from retreating with a firm hand on her arm.

She glared at his restraining grip. He did not release her.

"This man Walsingham is protected. I cannot break through the layers of spells and barriers."

"Guards have never stopped you before. What kind of spells and barriers?" The Master glared at her. His gaze darkened. "Who protects him?"

"A sorceress of great power who keeps a wolfhound familiar. I cannot do your deeds until you remove her."

June 1575. London. The first night of the full moon.

Yassimine waddled warily toward the mansion near the Strand. Low growls erupted from her throat at every step. Something, *someone* within threatened her. She had to hunt that *one* tonight. Eliminate this rival for power and control.

She knew deep within her belly that once she had eaten this *one* all of that *one's* power and control would enter her. She would at last have what she needed to break The Master's chains and run free. The pack was gathered. All she needed was to remove her chains and assume command of the chains that bound the others to The Master.

The moon rode high in the night sky, banishing shadows. Yassimine moved closer to the mansion. She welcomed the obscurity in the lee of the building. Softly, she crept around the place, circling, seeking her mark, avoiding the mundane traps.

Her nose found the wisp of scent from her perfume. Here she had easy access to the house and her quarry.

The Master wanted her to kill the dominant male of this household. Yassimine had other plans. Sweet feminine flesh alone would satisfy her appetite.

Once more she circled the building. Each step came faster, more sure. Each step brought the scent of her quarry closer. When she reached her mark again she flung herself at the wall.

Her claws tangled with the thorny vine that climbed toward a vulnerable balcony. In the next heartbeat she bunched her muscles and bounded over the iron railing. She landed heavily upon the flagstones of the balcony. The sound grated on her ears.

Movement and shocked cries from within. Shouts.

And then . . .

Begone foul spirit
Be quit this secured place.
Begone creature of the night
Begin your egress flight!

Waves of magic repulsed Yassimine, burning her flesh through her fur. Only the silver chains and piercings remained cool and immune to this spell.

She fought for balance against the pressure of magic crushing against her chest. With a mighty effort she lunged forward. The glass and wood of the balcony door jolted her back into the iron railings.

Her breath came quick and shallow. She had no strength. She had no will. She had to yield to the pressure and the energy that banished her.

Jumping back to the ground jarred every joint and muscle, but the pain was less than staying upon that balcony.

Her stomach growled. She needed fresh, hot blood to feed herself and the pup growing within her.

She would find prey this night. But she would not vanquish the *other*.

The magic pushed her back to the Strand. As long as she ran away from her Enemy, she had speed and strength.

A man came into view, walking slowly. An old man. His flesh would be stringy, but his blood would fill her. He wore black and carried a walking stick. A bit of white from his shirt showed through the high collar of his robe.

A priest! He would taste almost as sweet as the *other*.

Yassimine lunged for his throat.

Chapter 35

Whitehall Palace, Westminster, England.

SIR Michael and Coffa had lost the werewolf's scent at the river and never found it again.

Each hour during that long night I renewed the spells of protections at Sir Francis Walsingham's doors and windows. At dawn, Sir Michael escorted me back to Whitehall.

I stumbled with fatigue. When I entered Elizabeth's privy chamber, I found the room a study in chaos. Ladies threw garments about, packing and unpacking at the same time. Servants scurried to and fro with hot water for baths, trunks filled and empty, furniture in various stages of construction and dismantlement.

I slipped through the tangle of feet and petticoats to Her Majesty's bedchamber. Elizabeth slumped in her favorite chair beside the window. Alone. Red-eyed from tears.

"Majesty!" I knelt beside her in alarm. "How may I ease your pain?"

She sobbed heavily and tangled her long fingers—for once devoid of her myriad rings—in my hair.

"Sweet Deirdre," she wailed. "What would your father have done in this crisis?"

"What crisis, Majesty?

"You do not know? All of London knows."

"I have been closeted with Sir Francis Walsingham all night, Majesty. We have exchanged much information."

"So his note said." She stared out the window for a long moment, making no move to finish dressing or to prepare for the day to come.

I kept silent, knowing instinctively that she needed to gather her thoughts and contain her emotions.

"We remove to Windsor within the hour," she said at last.

"You have delayed your progress, Majesty?" I sat up a little straighter. Elizabeth often changed her mind without warning; the better to keep her enemies off-balance and test the flexibility of her allies. But something was different about this shift in policy.

"We do not progress through the lands this summer. We must remain close at hand." She sighed deeply. I knew how she enjoyed traveling about from manor to town during the hot months when the city became a breeding ground for pestilence. Coming close to her people, watching various masques and fetes, hearing petitions and pretty speeches enlivened the queen and reaffirmed her priorities. The annual progress also made her visible, approachable, beloved by the masses.

"What has happened?" I asked, afraid to breathe.

"His Eminence Mathew Parker, the Archbishop of Canterbury, died during the night."

"Wh . . . where was he?" I prayed silently that he had died in his own bed of natural causes in distant Canterbury. The Primate of the Church of England had been an old man. Still, the timing. . . .

"At his London residence. He'd taken a stroll after dinner to settle his digestion . . ." Elizabeth broke off with a sob.

"The beast attacked him," I finished for her. My heart stuttered. A hole in my gut told me that in protecting Sir Francis last night, I had sent the wolf elsewhere to kill an innocent.

"You know!"

"I guess. The beast watched Sir Francis' house yesterday. My dog chased it off. It returned later. My wards repulsed it."

"A different beast?"

"I cannot know without more information."

"We find your presence comforting, Deirdre. Stay with us this summer."

"I need to consult the family library about this beast." I could not be as forthright with her as with Sir Francis.

"Send for the texts."

"They are old and fragile. They will not travel well. And

I do not know which ones I need. Sometimes a most important sentence fragment is buried in a discussion of something else." Sometimes the proper text was obscured by magic. A spell for improving the fertility of the sheep might be hidden in an accounting of the wool harvest. Or a demon's name might be encrypted in a receipt for mulled wine.

"We cannot bear to part with you. We need the Pendragon to advise us on the selection of a new Archbishop."

"Majesty, think, please. You have surrounded yourself with the wisest men in the kingdom, Burghley, Walsingham, Dr. Dee."

"We need your magical insight . . ."

"Then send for Dr. Dee. Have him gaze into his crystals or read your horoscope. He has much more experience than I in looking into men's hearts. Please, Majesty, allow me to retire to Kirkenwood for the summer. When I return to you after the first frost, I will be much better equipped to assist you in these matters. Surely you can delay appointing the next Archbishop until then?"

"And if the monster kills again?"

"When you quit London, so will everyone who can afford to. The city is not healthy in the summer. The Master—*le meneur des loups*—seeks to evoke terror in the hearts of the mighty. As near as I can guess, he wants chaos among those who govern. So he strikes at the wealthy and the powerful. He will find little fodder for his campaign this summer."

"Very well," she sighed heavily. "You may quit the court until October. But we insist you write reports every week. Couriers will burn a path between Kirkenwood and our residence."

"Thank you, Majesty." I curtsied deeply and backed out of her bedchamber. I needed to be quit of London before she changed her mind.

As much as I loved the southlands, I needed the resources at Kirkenwood.

Coffa agreed with me.

Sir Michael awaited me at the door to my own chamber.

"I am dispatched to Kirkenwood," he said through a scowl.

"Who sends you?"

"Both of them. Elizabeth and Walsingham. They exchanged letters yesterday and made the decision for us. For some reason they think you and that damnable dog of yours are indispensable to the kingdom. I am commanded to protect you with my life."

"What about your immortal soul? Will you risk that as well?"

He crossed himself hastily.

"Will you?"

"If I die in Her Majesty's service, then my soul is not at risk. If I deviate from my chosen path, I expect you will send the dog to take me down before I am beyond forgiveness." He quirked a half smile at me.

I wished I could return his humor. Instead, I sighed and nodded. All the while I hoped this journey would be less adventuresome than Paris. For both our sakes.

Early summer, the Spanish Embassy, London.

Yassimine flung the heavy covers off her bed. Fever made her limbs heavy. Sweat drenched her shift.

Dreams clouded her reason. The huge wolfhound lunged for her throat. The boy sneered at her as she reached out to him in love. The Master whipped her mind and her body.

She could not tell dream from reality.

An unknown woman bathed her brow with tepid water. The midwife. Sanity returned for a moment. She recognized the stark walls plastered white with colorful flowers painted in a symmetrical arching pattern. Above, heavy ceiling beams in some dark wood clearly defined the confines of the room. The Master had given her a tiny windowless anteroom for her private chamber. Both doors—one to his bedchamber, the other to a salon—were bolted from the inside.

He could not come to her without permission. Unwelcome petitioners had to go through her to reach *him*.

But today the bolt and crossbar were not in place. *He* stood in the doorway, looking at her with haunted eyes.

He said something in French, a language that flowed but

did not sing as did the Spanish, and did not stab at her soul with understanding like her native tongue.

Yassimine did not need to know the words to understand. He asked the midwife if she would live.

The woman grunted a reply. Noncommittal. Life was up to Yassimine and the gods.

A mighty cramp grabbed at Yassimine's belly. She moaned and clutched at her middle.

The woman muttered something.

"She said you are to push," The Master translated.

Every instinct in Yassimine warred with each other. The human part of her wanted desperately to preserve the child, give it another chance to grow inside her. The wolf within needed to expel the unwanted and diseased mass so that it could start over with a new mate and a new child.

A new mate. The next child must be conceived by a man in wolf form. Not The Master, a magician who mimicked the wolf. But all of Yassimine's get were sterile.

Except perhaps . . . Could a magician turned werewolf retain his virility?

"The silver," Yassimine panted. "The silver kills the child." Vaguely she pointed to the chains that hung from her breasts and navel, the others that decorated her pubis and ears.

The Master shouted something to the woman in rapid anxiety.

She shrugged and commanded Yassimine to push once more.

Another cramp clutched at her insides like tongs left too long in the fire.

With a gush of blood, it was over.

More conversation between The Master and the midwife.

"She says you will live, but your recovery will be long. My plans for bringing Elizabeth down must be delayed." The Master spat, as if the setback were her fault entirely.

"I want to see it," Yassimine whispered.

The woman shook her head. *"Non"* she repeated over and over.

"I must see it! I have to know."

The Master shrugged and gestured to the woman.

Reluctantly, muttering strange phrases all the while, she lifted a bloody lump wrapped in soiled linen.

Yassimine lifted a weak hand to push aside the covering. All she saw was blood and fur.

A child sired by a werewolf would carry human features, the beast from both parents hidden behind the strength of both.

This child's human father had failed to keep her wolf under control. The warring spirits of human and wolf had killed the child before it was fully formed.

Yassimine lay back upon the bolster and stared at the beamed ceiling.

Next time. Next time the child would live.

And she knew the werewolf who must sire it. The only one capable of matching her in strength.

Chapter 36

Mid-June 1575. Kirkenwood.

UNCLE Donovan greeted Betsy and me with open arms.

"At last, we all are together again," he whispered with moisture in his eyes.

I threw my arms about both of them, anxious to be part of the family once more. I needed their strength, their understanding, and their insights to help Hal. The family would never be complete without him.

The raven on the well remained silent at my homecoming, as if he knew something terrible must come of this reunion.

Uncle Donovan squeezed me tight and then disengaged from the hug.

Sir Michael hung back from the exuberant greetings. He acted embarrassed. Our family had always expressed our affection physically. Not for the Kirkwoods the common practice of ignoring, and often neglecting, children until they emerged from the care of governesses and tutors, fully formed and civilized adults.

After exclamations over the changes in Betsy and me since our last meeting, half a year ago, Uncle Donovan turned his attention to my escort. He studied them all with a practiced eye. The queen's guards, he dismissed to the kitchen by way of the stable for their mounts and the barracks for their own grooming. Sir Michael, he continued to appraise.

"I have reports you may carry back to Her Majesty on your return journey," he said as he finally dismissed the young knight.

"My orders are to remain as bodyguard to Mistress Deir-

271

dre Kirkwood until she returns to court in the autumn."
Sir Michael stiffened his shoulders in as stubborn a gesture
as my uncle's outthrust chin.

Betsy and I exchanged mirth-filled glances. Each man
had met his match. I decided to let them circle and sniff
and decide territoriality, like any two male dogs sharing
a kennel.

"I'll not have a queen's spy in my household. I have
proved my loyalty time and again." Uncle Donovan turned
on his heel and stalked back into the manor.

"I extend my protection to you as well as to your niece,"
Sir Michael replied. He followed the laird, close on his
heels, not about to be dismissed.

"And you and your mistress think I cannot protect me
and mine? Have I not done so for nigh on twenty years?
Without any aid from Her Majesty."

"That may well be, milord. But I have my orders. I'll
not disobey while I have breath in my body."

"You may tell the queen that *she* may have chosen an
heir to my brother's place as her secret adviser, but the
choice is not hers. You have only yourself to protect and I
have no need of you here."

"I know nothing of your brother's place with Queen Elizabeth. Her Majesty values both Mistress Deirdre and Mistress Betsy. She parted with them reluctantly and only with
the promise of my protection of them from those who have
grief with your household."

"We have no idle hands in this household, sirrah. If you
choose to stay, you'll shear the sheep, and harvest the barley like the rest of us."

"If Mistress Kirkwood shears sheep and harvests the barley, then I will do so at her side. And, like your men, I will
keep my weapons close by. The Scots are not the only
raiders we have to fear this summer."

That stopped my uncle.

"It comes so soon." A deep sigh escaped Uncle Donovan.

Suddenly I feared what these two men knew. More than
I did.

"Something comes. When, we do not know."

I'd had enough of cryptic statements and half truths. If

disaster came, I wanted Hal, my cousin and best friend, at my side. I had to break the spell put upon him by The Master and his slave before the next disaster.

"Where is Hal?"

"Hal is wherever he chooses to be." Uncle Donovan retreated to the Hall, Sir Michael at his heels.

"He's probably in the lair," Betsy said upon a sigh of disgust as she, too, retreated to the interior of the castle.

I looked to Coffa for help. She pricked her ears and lolled her tongue. No help there.

"The lair is too obvious," I said to myself. "The moon is past full. He doesn't need to hide underground."

Coffa liked the idea of a romp on the moors. Even after weeks of travel she had energy to spare.

"Come, Deirdre," Betsy called to me from the top of the steps. "Hal will wait. We need to wash off some of this travel dust." She looked as clean and well-groomed as the moment before we departed Whitehall.

I, however, needed a bath and clean clothes.

How did she do it? As I gnashed my teeth in frustration, I wondered if she had found a spell to repel lowly dirt from her noble person.

Sir Michael gestured me indoors with a slight hand motion. "I will seek out your cousin with your dog," he whispered as I passed.

He returned without Hal just before the supper bell rang.

Uncle Donovan merely shrugged his shoulders in defeat and began the meal without him. Betsy lavished attention and affection upon her father. She shoved Griffin away from the honored place at Uncle Donovan's right. My cousin settled next to me at the end of the high table, excluded from the intimate conversation between the laird and his daughter.

Sir Michael barely squeezed onto a bench at the other end of the table.

"Where is Hal?" I hissed at Griff under the cover of a raucous laugh among the retainers below the dais.

"Seeing to his own business." Griff clamped his teeth shut.

"Griff, do not keep secrets from me. I know most of them anyway. Hal needs me and my help."

"You don't know all of our secrets."

A page replenished his tankard just then. He hovered so long I wondered who had set him to eavesdropping.

I replied to Griff's comment with an arched eyebrow rather than words that could be overheard.

"I knew he'd not keep it from you for long," Griff said. Then he near emptied his tankard in one gulp. "Look for him in the one place Betsy will not go."

Extra people crowded the Hall this evening. The armed escort from London, troubadours, traveling merchants, and farm workers. But they were all intent on the meal, the ale, and themselves. No one seemed to notice when I slipped away with Coffa to seek Hal.

Shadows cloaked me. My plain dark gown reflected no light. Even Coffa's claws remained silent on the stairs and in the gallery. I felt safe using the passage through the castle walls.

An oil lamp lay ready in its niche inside the passage with flint and steel beside it. I waited to light it until after I had closed the door behind me.

Coffa led the way. She seemed eager to explore our old haunts and did not object when I turned right toward the caves. Memories of our last journey through these walls nagged at me. So much had happened since then. I had grown. Hal had changed. Helwriaeth had died. Coffa had matured and passed through two heats. At the next she would breed.

Would one of her pups replace Hal's lost familiar? Doubtful if he remained a werewolf.

I entered the first echoey cave with its dripping walls and growing columns of limestone. My footsteps sounded loud in my ears and repeated themselves over and over. Shadows from my little lamp danced against the walls and ceiling like the troubled ghosts of the pain and loneliness Hal and I had endured since the last time I had passed this way.

I hurried along, for the first time in my life frightened of what surrounded me.

At the entrance to the crypt I paused and blew out my light. I thought I heard a muffled curse, but the echoes within the cave distorted the sound of my breathing and my heart beating loudly in my ears. After a moment, my eyes adjusted to the darkness. A sliver of light showed at the narrow cave exit (sunset came very late this time of the year at these northern latitudes). A broader expanse of gray came from the gateway up to the sacristy of the kirk.

"Hal?" I whispered.

Not so much as a shift in the air.

"Hal!" I called somewhat louder.

Hal, al, al, al, replied the echo.

Still no reply, no sense of another presence.

I eased through the crypt, wending my way through the tombs. The gate to the church opened with a touch. Someone had come this way since Father Peter had said Vespers. At the top of a long flight of stairs, I paused once more to orient myself. The red vigil light drew my gaze to the altar.

On impulse I knelt in prayer before the altar. My father had spent many long hours here in his youth before greater things called him away from his family home.

My education had included the forms of religion, but rarely the substance. Other than obligatory attendance at Anglican Mass—the fines were prohibitive to abstain—we did not include religion in our daily lives, even so far as to take the Lord's name in vain as lightly as did our queen.

"Papa, guide me," I prayed. "Show me the way to do what I must do."

Follow the light in your heart.

I needed more than that. I wanted answers—not cryptic philosophy.

I forced myself to fold my hands and bow my head. I breathed deeply, seeking the calm before wielding magic. My heart continued to beat rapidly. My breaths came short and shallow.

I could not find the peace or answers in prayer that my father did.

A shift in the air. Not so much movement as a shrinking away from me.

"Hal, I know you are here." I stayed on my knees, not wishing to frighten him away.

No, I am not. His mental voice came strong and clear. Either his power had grown tremendously in the last year or he was very close, within line of sight.

"If you are not here with me, then where are you?"

Nowhere.

"You have to be somewhere, Hal."

Neither here nor there, neither real nor unreal.

"I think I know what happened in Paris, Hal. I need to remove the earring. We can break this thing if we work together."

"Is it possible?" he breathed.

I had him now. He crouched in the doorway, on the porch of the little church.

I rose and faced him. He shrank into a tighter ball but did not move. Inch by inch I crept toward my cousin, as I would a wounded and frightened dog.

"I've done a lot of reading in the last year, Hal. I think I can break the spell cast upon you. We have to start with the earring."

"It burns, Dee. Waking and sleeping, it burns."

"The Master calls to you through the earring," I guessed. "I think he is gathering his wolves to him in London. He has already killed Mathew Parker, the Archbishop of Canterbury. Sir Francis Walsingham is on his list. Possibly others." Three more steps. I was almost close enough to touch him. "We can't allow him to manipulate you, too, Hal."

Tentatively, I reached out a hand and brushed his cheek.

"Oh, Dee, I have missed you so." He rose and pulled me into a fierce hug.

I leaned into him, cherishing the strength of his embrace. With Hal's arms around me, I could find the peace to pray.

But first I had a chore to finish.

While Hal clung to me, I reached up to touch the earring.

> *"Silver chain, bright as a star*
> *Send your message from afar*
> *Back to the sender alone*
> *Gone away, no one home."*

With the last word I yanked at the chain.

Molten metal seared my finger. I yelped and jumped. Sucking the burn only controlled the pain, but did not banish it.

"Oh, Dee, I'm sorry. I knew it would not be this easy," Hal sobbed.

"Step away from the girl," a cold voice said from the stairwell to the crypt.

"Sir Michael, you have no right to follow me in my own home," I snarled.

"My duty to protect you gives me that right. Now, sir, step away from her."

"Who is this interloper?" Hal bared his teeth. But he kept me enfolded in his arms.

"Sir Michael Maelstrom, this is my cousin, Henry Griffin Kirkwood. Hal. He is closer to me than a brother. You may sheath your sword."

"He is an agent for the Spaniard." He leveled his sword and approached us. "Now stand aside, Mistress Deirdre, while I deal with him."

"Your weapon is not silver. You cannot harm me."

"But I can separate you from Mistress Kirkwood. *En garde.*"

Hal batted aside the sword with one hand. In the same gesture he kissed me quickly on the mouth and disappeared into the dusk. In a heartbeat, the trees and the tombstones of the cemetery had swallowed him whole.

"Where did he go?" Sir Michael rushed to stand between me and the door. "I've never seen anyone move so quickly." He pressed hard upon his right shoulder with his left hand and gasped. His lips thinned and he swallowed hard. His grip upon his sword hilt loosened.

"Let me see." I replaced his massaging fist with gentle but questing fingers. "Everything is in place. Bruised perhaps. I'll make a poultice for you later."

Hal had merely batted the sword aside, but the strength behind the gesture nearly dislocated Sir Michael's shoulder. He'd be sore for days.

"Sheathe your sword," I advised him.

"I have to go after him. He is dangerous."

"He has gone where you and I cannot follow." And taken my heart with him.

While Sir Michael nursed his arm, I touched my mouth in wonder where Hal had kissed me. His caress had burned me as deeply as the silver chain had seared my fingers.

But I felt no pain from his kiss. Only love. I nearly wept at the wonder and the sadness of loving a werecreature of the darkness.

Chapter 37

Summer 1575. Kirkenwood.

FOR the next three months Hal avoided me. I avoided Betsy. Robin remained in Edinburgh away from Betsy's vindictive vows. Uncle Donovan prowled Kirkenwood like one of the dogs. He took to arguing with the ghosts of his family on sleepless nights. He wrote daily to Mary Queen of Scots, begging her to abandon whatever plot swirled around her.

Coffa selected a mate within days of our arrival. She became fat and lazy while the pups grew in her belly. We all rejoiced when she whelped a dozen bundles of wiggling fur. She kept them close to her, reluctant to wean them, as if she knew that soon she would have to part with all of them forever.

Sir Michael dogged my heels as closely as Coffa did. I think he slept outside my door at night. I could not keep him out of the lair, so I put him to work. Together we searched the extensive shelves of family records and arcane texts. I sought references to werewolves. He looked for my father's journals. The volumes I had read and not understood as a child had disappeared.

I learned more than I wanted to know about the habits of werewolves. And I wondered that no tales of human mutilation had cropped up around Kirkenwood through the last year. No one whispered about demons or witches slaughtering livestock for bloody rituals.

How had Hal controlled his wolf for this long? Did he chain himself to some dark dungeon for the three nights of the full moon? Or did he roam the moors so far afield that his kills were not noticed by the locals?

Sir Michael often lost himself in some of the more mundane journals. Uncle Donovan maintained an extensive correspondence with Dr. John Dee, the queen's astrologer and alchemist. Occasionally, Sir Michael tried an experiment or two with noxious herbs, ground minerals, and open flames. He succeeded only in driving us from the lair, choking and laughing and stumbling over Coffa.

His arm about my waist as he helped me up the stairs only added to our camaraderie. Here was a friend I could trust in many things.

But I could not tell him everything. Not yet. He still believed in evidence, science, and practicality. Magic meant nothing to him.

Could I find comfort and happiness with this man? He was not Hal. But then, Hal was my cousin. He still had a wolf within him. We could never be together.

I sighed, letting my emotions and questions leave me with that long breath of air. Too much work lay ahead of me to worry about myself.

As the days marched toward the Equinox, the raid by Scottish border lords came. We had waited all summer for the enemy to ride over the border, howling for revenge and booty. As usual, it came right after harvest, when the lambs were weaned and the stock fat for the lean winter months.

They came on the night of the dark of the moon when we could not see them approach across the hills. But the dogs smelled them and warned us well in advance.

We repulsed them as we always repulsed them, with minimal loss of stores and no loss of life. They took several dozen sheep and a few cows. In a week or a few days, our men would ride back across the border to retrieve the lost livestock and take part of their stores as punishment for the raid.

Thus life had always been on the border. We lived with constant war. We died from it.

When it was over, I helped the women bathe wounds and bind broken pates. Nothing major. Almost as if the heart of the raiding had dissipated with Queen Mary's imprisonment. The lairds led sorties against each other more out of tradition than need.

Uncle Donovan led the chase to punish the raiders. Hal, Griffin, Caspar, and Peregrine joined him. Surprisingly, Sir

Michael was the first to mount and ride at Uncle Donovan's shoulder. Coffa gamboled ahead of them leading the pack of war dogs. They always needed to run off an excess of restlessness. The raven followed a short distance and returned. I had never seen it fly farther than the standing stones.

The moment the men rode out the gate I abandoned my duties and began a search of Uncle Donovan's chamber for my father's journals.

I needed to know, for his sake as well as my own, more about Griffin Kirkwood's vision of an invasion fleet prompted by Queen Mary's execution.

Secret compartments in the walls and floor of the laird's bedchamber revealed a strongbox with more gold coins than I thought the family had ever possessed. I found another secret compartment with Uncle Donovan's diplomatic papers for his work in Edinburgh. They told me much of his life outside of Kirkenwood that I did not know.

Enough speculation. I had to find the journals before the men returned from their retaliatory raid.

Finally, exhausted by a sleepless night and a fruitless search, I flopped upon the large bed I shared with Betsy. As I rolled over to my side in the center of the bed, a lump in the mattress pressed against my breasts. At first I dismissed it as a clump of straw. But it did not give way to my prodding fingers.

Curiosity overcame my fatigue. Before I could think better of my actions, or even check to see if Betsy approached, I crouched beside the bed and stuck my arm up to my shoulder under the mattress. My fingers brushed against something hard. I had to shift about and ram my arm deeper, clawing with my fingers against the rope frame.

A step sounded in the gallery near the door. I jerked my arm free and rolled under the bed. I did not want to confront Betsy with my long absence from aiding in the cleanup after the raid. She took her duties as chatelaine far too seriously. Those duties truly belonged to our Aunt Fiona, but Betsy fancied herself more capable than any of her relatives, especially those without magical talent.

I just fit beneath the frame of steps that allowed us to climb up to the high mattress. A few more pounds or a more ample bosom would have prevented me from entering the hiding place. Once beneath the frame, I encountered the musty rope work that supported the mattress, half an arm's length from my nose.

I recognized Betsy's shoes as I peered out. She groaned wearily and climbed atop the mattress. It sagged dangerously close to my chest. Dust and mouse droppings plopped onto my face. A sneeze demanded exit from my nose.

I held my breath.

Betsy rolled again and flung her arms about. She was always a restless sleeper.

The ropes bounced. More dust and droppings cascaded into my face.

I gasped and choked, holding as much of the sound as I could within my throat.

"Who dares!" Betsy clambered off the bed. She shoved aside the blanket chest at the foot.

Light penetrated to my hiding place. And there, a scant finger's length from my nose I saw the books. Bound in red leather, the slim volumes of my father's journals. All five of them.

"You!" Betsy grabbed my foot.

I clung to the rope frame. A strand snapped into my face. I exploded with sneezes.

The books slipped from their resting place to my chest. I clung to them fiercely as Betsy tugged at my leg.

"How dare you!" I screamed as I slid from beneath the bed. "You stole them. These are mine." I was on my feet, brandishing the dusty books in her face.

"They are mine," Betsy protested. She grabbed hold of my treasure and tried to yank the books out of my possession.

"You have no right to them. They are mine by right of inheritance." I jerked away from her, turning my back.

"You? You have no rights. You are a bastard." She leaped upon my back, pulling my hair.

I gave her an elbow in her belly as we toppled to the floor.

"And you are a harpy and a whore." I bit her hand as she tried to scratch my eyes.

"I am the heir to the Pendragon. Not you. You have no right to anything, bastard. Give me those books."

"Never. The dogs have chosen me. The queen has chosen me."

"I also have a dog. And the queen does not choose the Pendragon." She reared back, ready to fling a punch.

I rolled away and stumbled to my feet.

"Come back here!" she commanded. "Thief! Traitor! *Usurper!*"

I ran down the steps, across the Hall and into the bailey.

The guards hauled open the gates for the men to ride back through. I stepped aside just in time to avoid being trampled.

Sir Michael wheeled his horse to the side. It pranced about until he mastered the reins. He jumped off his saddle beside me.

"Where have you been, *ma petite?*" He brushed a cobweb out of my hair.

Hal scowled at us both and rode back out the gate.

Uncle Donovan called after him. Something about walking the horse cool and rubbing it down.

Hal ignored him and angled a path away from the tor and the village at its foot.

I knew he headed for the crypt. Right now, I had more important things on my mind than his sullen mood.

"We leave for London at dawn," I told Sir Michael. "Pack your belongings and keep these safe." I thrust the precious books into his hands.

"What?"

"What we have been looking for these past three months. Whatever happens, give them to no one. Not even my uncle, or my cousins. No one is to read them but me."

"As you command, Mistress Kirkwood."

"Kirkwood no longer. My mother was Roanna Douglas. My father never married her. Her name is mine and I wear it proudly. I am Deirdre Douglas, Pendragon of Britain."

"Are not the Kirkwoods a prouder family this side of the border?"

"Not to me. Not any longer."

"I forbid you to depart." Donovan glared at his niece. What was she thinking?

She returned his stare levelly, calmly, with absolute defiance.

"You have no right to keep me," she finally said in that chillingly calm voice of hers that reminded him of the depths of hell fostered by her mother's demon. A demon he had sealed behind its portal in a remote cave many leagues from here.

He resisted the urge to make the sign of the cross.

"I am your guardian."

"Her Majesty, Queen Elizabeth, is now my guardian. She has been since the day I became her lady-in-waiting." Still no emotion out of the child.

"You damage your reputation and therefore the queen's by traveling alone with Sir Michael."

"Hardly alone with ten armed guards."

"You will wait and journey to London with Betsy. If I allow her to go at all. I do not like the way London and court influence you both." Martha had said those exact words to him once. Now he understood them.

"I go nowhere with your daughter. She is a thief."

"You have no say in this matter. The queen may have merely loaned you to me for the summer, but while you are here, you are as my daughter."

"I am your brother's nameless bastard, got on a peasant witch. A demon-infested witch."

"Your father entrusted you to me with his dying wish. And he married your mother in a magical ceremony just before . . . just before . . ." He could not bring himself to tell her of that bizarre ritual that required the lovers to kill each other in order to send the demon back behind his protective portal.

She shivered once, then mastered her fear of the demon.

"Your father wanted you here." Donovan appealed to the one thing guaranteed to strike a spark in her. "He knew that only I could protect you, cherish you as my own."

"I am a bastard. I belong to no one. The queen has chosen to favor me. Therefore I go to her."

"And what of us? What of the love and shelter and education I have lavished on you?"

"And sanctioned, by your neglect of Betsy, the theft of the one item that truly belongs to me." She began to shake.

Guilt flooded through Donovan, burning his ears and surrounding his heart with ache.

"Deirdre, daughter of my heart, you are too young to

understand those journals. My brother was a complex man, driven by forces even he did not comprehend. . . ."

"But he was my father! I have nothing else of him, not even the startling blue eyes of the entire family. His journals are mine, to study, to try to catch a brief glimpse of who he was and what he wanted for me, for Britain."

"I would have made Betsy give them to you when you are older, more mature."

"You cannot *make* Betsy do anything." Deirdre fled the Hall in a rush of tears. At the doorway she caught hold of Sir Michael's arm and dragged him toward their saddled horses.

"You did not appeal to her need to ease me out of my strange moods," Hal said. He leaned casually against the stair banister, half hidden by the shadows.

"Are you so important to her?" Donovan could not face his son. Every time they confronted each other, it ended with Hal running away, disappearing for days on end.

"She came here to cure me, and failed."

"Betsy and I together . . ."

"Haven't a clue where to begin."

Only the barest whisper of footfalls indicated that his son deserted him also.

"We are better off with both of them gone, Da," Betsy whispered. She floated down the stairs with Brenin beside her. She was clad in simple black—no lace, no hoops or extensive petticoats—and carrying a staff. For a moment the stark features of his grandmother Raven shone through her serene countenance. "Together, we shall preserve and protect Britain as our family always has."

Then she emerged into the shaft of sunlight from the high windows. Her dark-blonde hair shone gold like her mother's. The same gold as the locket she had given him so lovingly. For a moment he could almost believe in the halo of light surrounding her.

Then that same sunlight glinted off the gold of a heavy ring on her left thumb. The red enamel of a dragon rampant on the crest glinted like a drop of fresh blood.

"You have not the right to wear that ring or carry that staff."

"There is no one else, Da. Just you and me. The dogs did not choose you. Coffa did not bestow one of her pups on Deirdre or Hal. And I have seen in a scrying bowl that the wolfhound familiar will never return to Kirkenwood to breed. Helwriaeth is dead. Only my Brenin lives to sire the next batch of pups in direct descent from the first familiar. The dogs have chosen me as the next Pendragon."

He wanted to protest. She held his gaze. His arguments evaporated as mist at dawn. Perhaps if the raven commented on Betsy's announcement . . .

The raven remained silent.

Betsy kissed her fingertips and pressed them against the locket containing a lock of her hair. The locket with a drop of Donovan's blood marring the catch.

"There is only you left," Donovan agreed. The words sounded hollow in his ears, as if someone else said them for him. "You, Mary Elizabeth, must follow in Grandmother Raven's footsteps. You must be the Pendragon of Britain. Only you."

She smiled and released the locket.

Chapter 38

September 1575. Harvest moon. The Yorkshire Dales.

YASSAMINE ran, eating up the miles with a long lope.

Behind her, The Master sheltered with a Spanish agent near the great Cathedral of York. Even at this distance, she sensed him crouching over a scrying bowl.

They sought the same quarry in their own manner. She drew closer to the boy. Ever closer, and yet he remained elusive. She needed to broaden her search. Go north. Ever toward the cold northern wastes.

Her senses maintained loose contact with the other wolves of The Master's pack. They were scattered around England, all seeking one of their own who had refused to join them. They hunted in twos and threes, quartering the land, sniffing every corner for sign of the lost one.

Cold burned through Yassimine's thick fur. She hated this country. By morning, frost would glisten atop the harsh grasses that fed only sheep.

Sheep, bah! These British breeds were more wool than meat. Not worth the trouble of killing them for food.

Her silver piercings tingled, reminding her that The Master watched her. Only with his permission did she roam so widely and so free. He'd removed the heavy chains but left the little rings. Her skin never quite healed around the silver.

She reached the top of one of the craggy hills. Her stomach growled, reminding her of why she felt compelled to run so far and so fast. No prey out on these barren reaches. No human prey. But a great stag rested off to the west by a cascading rill. It would do. Yet only human blood truly satisfied her. She'd had none since the priest in London.

The turmoil that hunt had caused made him sweet meat indeed.

The Master tugged at her consciousness. Once she fed, her imperative to run would diminish. He wanted her to wait.

She stalked the stag. They'd not find the boy this night. Hunger tugged at her sanity. Hot blood pulsed in the animal's great neck vein. Fresh meat. Its life pumped into her as she tore at the heart.

And then she caught a whiff of the boy.

September 1575. Full moon. The North Midland Downs.

The silvery light of the full moon glinted on frost crystals on the sedge grasses and gorse. Our path lay clear and slick with ice ahead of us.

"Shall we continue until moonset?" Sir Michael asked around a yawn. The ten men of our guard mimicked him. We were all tired.

We'd seen no signs of an inn or a village or even a farmhouse on this deserted track. And no signs of pursuit from Uncle Donovan or Hal. For two weeks we had traveled barely a day ahead of them. Now, at last, as we neared Sir Michael's native Staffordshire, we had left the main travel routes behind and lost our pursuers.

Or perhaps the full moon had loosed Hal's wolf and Uncle Donovan had been forced to stop and restrain him. I shuddered and almost cried at the agony of mind and spirit that must possess Hal. He had been so gentle as a boy, eager to study the creatures of the wild rather than hunt them. The swordplay and warrior games that fascinated Hal's twin had bored Hal. Now violence must have become an inherent part of his life.

My father's journals called to me with a siren song. I needed to read them, know the secrets of his life and the faith that had driven him into exile from his family. My actions, if not my convictions, had brought about my own exile from the family.

"Is there shelter ahead?" I thought longingly of the warm bed and crackling fire at last night's inn. Tonight I would have to make do with Coffa as my pillow and blanket. She would warm me better than any campfire.

Sir Michael shrugged. He hadn't said much during these past two weeks of grueling travel. I had told him a little of the complex tensions among my family. But not all. Not about the magic.

"I know of a rocky overhang near a rill about half an hour ahead," the sergeant at arms suggested. "We could build a fire and find shelter from the wind. It is near the main road but not easily found unless you know what to look for."

And the rocky outcropping would hide the light of our fire from those who sought us.

"Yes. I prefer an overhang to a cold night exposed on the hilltops." Sir Michael kicked his horse into a brisk trot.

I followed, too tired and cold to protest. But *something* about the clarity of light in the night prickled the hairs on the back of my neck and along my spine. That *something* urged me to keep moving.

We found the overhang easily enough. Dried gorse and a few scrubby trees provided us with fuel for a small fire. The guards went about the business of setting up camp with quiet efficiency. I knelt by the trickle of water and splashed my face free of some of the travel grime. Then I filled the leather flasks with water to heat with whatever journey food we could cobble together from our packs. Surely Coffa could add a rabbit or grouse to the mix.

Sir Michael stood over me, sword half drawn, alert to the tiny nuances of life moving through the night.

"You feel it, too," I said as I lifted a dripping flask from the water.

"Gypsies have been reported in this area. They'll kidnap you, steal our horses, and leave us stranded—if they don't cut our throats."

"Why would they do that?"

" 'Tis in their heathen nature."

"If they offer me a hot meal, a cheerful fire, and soft blankets, I just might take up with them."

"Don't ever say that, Mistress Kirkw . . . Mistress Douglas."

"Then do not entice me . . ."

"I seek to warn you only. We shall post guards tonight. Two at all times. Two-hour shifts. We shall keep you safe. But please, Mistress Deirdre, do not wander off on your own. Even if you . . . um . . . need a few moments of privacy, one of the men will walk with you and turn his back." His eyes wanted to say more.

Rather than explore his unspoken thoughts, I smiled slightly and returned the few steps to the fire.

We made a cozy meal with dried meat and bread broken into the stew. I added a little parsley from my scrip for flavor, and some roots gleaned from the creekside. And then two of the men came in from hobbling the horses with a rabbit they had trapped. Coffa found her own dinner in a grouse. Not enough to truly fill our bellies, but we eased the worst of the hunger pangs and made merry company with stories of past campaigns and exploits.

As the tales wound down, I ventured forth with my own tale. I spoke of King Arthur in the early days of his reign.

Similar tales circulated through the court, and troubadours carried the myths and legends of my ancestors far and wide. They'd all heard versions of this story; some only brushed at the facts. They had no way of knowing I told them the truth, as reported in my family's archives.

"And as the Lady of the Lake rose up through the depths of the waters, she thrust her hand through the ice, clasping the hilt of a mighty sword."

Sir Michael sat a little straighter; listened a little more closely.

All the while I spoke, creating images and emotions with my words, I watched Sir Michael. Somehow it became important to me that he understand how truly I spoke, how close I was in blood and spirit to the actual events.

"At the Merlin's urging, King Arthur walked warily upon the ice, ever watchful for a crack or hint of thinning that would give way and plunge him to his death in the frigid depths.

" 'Hurry, boy,' the Merlin urged him. 'The Lady will not wait forever for you to seize your heritage.' "

One and all, the men nodded as if they knew the capriciousness of the dwellers of Otherworlds. Their own queen was often likened to the faeries.

"And then King Arthur, of fame and legend, reached out his fingers and claimed the hilt of the sword. The Lady proclaimed to one and all, 'I gift to thee Excalibur!' and she sank once more back into her watery world."

Awed silence rang in the clear night air.

"Bravo! Mistress Deirdre. You tell the story as if you were there." Sir Michael clapped his hands once.

"Perhaps I was," I whispered.

If he heard me, he did not deign to answer me.

We all shifted and settled, eager for whatever ease we could take this night in our rough camp. Muted conversations drifted toward me.

"Hush!" Sir Michael quieted us all with a gesture.

We all heard the muffled cadence of song in the distance. An eerie tune accompanied by soft bells.

Faeries? I had never known the Otherworldly creatures to remain in this world after sunset.

Though the full moon might entice them.

And then the breeze shifted direction slightly. The tune in the distance took on an exotic lilt. The words became clearer and lost meaning entirely.

"Gypsies," Sir Michael said quietly.

"Up there," the sergeant at arms mouthed as he gestured to the plateau above us.

"Awroo roo roo roo," a wolf howled in the distance.

"Awroo!" Coffa answered. She heaved herself to her feet and stood between me and the outside world, braced for attack.

Sir Michael thrust me up against the back wall of the overhang.

Two more creatures yipped in the distance, from a different quarter.

I knew deep in my gut that these were no ordinary wolves.

All of the men drew their swords.

Once more, I knew I must work magic to save myself and my men. Who would die in recompense?

Chapter 39

September 1575. Full Moon. Staffordshire, England.

HAL crouched in a ravine watching a seep become a trickle, then swell into a stream. Easier to watch the water flowing than to observe his own body. The change became easier each moon. Less painful. Less of a shock to his mind and senses.

Each time he remembered less of the hours he spent transformed into a ravening wolf.

The light paled. The buzz of insects jumped to a louder level. He sniffed the dampness of dewfall, the crushing of grasses beneath his feet, the human scent permeating the clothing he had neatly folded and sat upon. Excitement coursed through his veins. His vision dimmed with the light, losing color definition. He cursed this one failing of the wolf within him. Shades of gray told him many things. Human color told him more.

The bite of frosty air on his naked skin gave way to an enticing freshness as his body hair thickened.

Da and the others were tucked up nicely in their snug inn two miles away. They'd not follow or interfere with him tonight. He could not smell Dee and her champion on the wind. They must have diverted off the main road. No matter. They were too far ahead for him to invade their hiding place tonight.

Gradually, the details of the moonlit scene around him became sharper—scent and hearing augmenting his eyesight. Like it had when Helwriaeth was still alive. As if Helwriaeth still lived within him.

A moment of bone-wrenching agony. His skin crawled with fire.

He loosed a howl. A primal sound.

He heard the echoes of his cry repeat in the distance.

Hunger gnawed at him. The memory of hot meat dripping with blood sent him slavering.

The ground flashed before him as he loped across the rolling hills onto a high plateau.

Fire! He smelled burning wood, sensed the variation in temperature.

And then he smelled the people who huddled around the fire. They laughed and sang together, chasing away the shadows of their fears with companionship. Two males. Their musk burned his snout with an acrid taste. Five children, barely worth smelling. Three females of varying ages. One was in heat. Hal's member responded.

He'd satisfy his lusts with that one just before he ate her.

The hunger propelled him forward. At the last moment he dropped to the ground and slunk forward on his belly. His nose sorted out the males and the females; the stringy, tough, old ones from the tender youths.

The wind shifted quarters. The cart pony pawed the turf restlessly. The men looked up from the fire. They turned outward, blinking and shielding their eyes.

Hal slunk lower, stilled. He observed them closely with the remnants of his human knowledge. Swarthy skin and black hair, oiled and curled in strange arrangements. Tattered clothing in contrasting shades. He guessed that there were many bright colors. The women wore their wealth in bracelets, belts, and coins dangling from their caps and ears. The men had the heavily callused hands and the curving backs of hard laborers.

Gypsies! Illegal wanderers who worshiped pagan gods and respected no laws but their own. No one would miss them. At last he could sate the hunger that never quite left him, though he'd eaten his fill of game and livestock.

The wolf in Hal decided to taste the blood of all of them.

One man stood and shouted into the night air. The human words passed beyond Hal's understanding. He crept closer. Only inches before he could leap and tear out the man's throat.

The wind shifted again.

A soft sound. A crooning voice soothing a fussy baby.

He knew that tune. His mother had sung that lullaby to him.

Revulsion racked his body and his mind. He shuddered and howled. His nose and ears went numb. Every joint and muscle wrenched. Cold night air bit at his naked skin. Color returned to his eyes.

Sobs tore at his throat. He dug at the turf with aching fingers, fighting to remain hidden until he could creep away unnoticed, alone, no longer hungry.

A lone wolf howled off to our left. Another to the right, and yet a third let loose with a mournful yip from the plateau above us.

And then I heard the most heartrending cry of all. A young child, frightened and alone.

"Sweet Mary, Mother of God, give me strength." I borrowed a prayer from my father. Calm settled on my shoulders and in my gut. I could manage this crisis, if I but concentrated.

A horse screamed in fright. Its hooves thudded against the turf. I heard it break its tether and gallop off into the distance.

Coffa growled and snapped her massive jaws.

Another creature answered her. Close. Too close.

Sir Michael circled the tip of his sword, seeking an adversary.

"Let Coffa take the first one. She is bred for this," I said to him quietly.

"I'll protect you with cold steel, Deirdre."

"Cold steel will slow them down but will not harm these creatures, Michael."

He chanced a glance at me over his shoulder.

"We need silver and fire." Memories of another attack by wolves superimposed themselves upon my vision. Was I here or beside the lake? Would Hal come to my rescue, or must I kill him?

I shook all over.

"We have no silver but a few coins."

"But I have fire." I hoped. Fire was Hal's element. Earth mine. Water and wind answered to Betsy.

In rare times of desperation I had called all four.

Coffa lunged. Frantic yips and growls and snarls came from just beyond the light of our tiny campfire.

Michael and his sergeant engaged the second creature. Where was the third?

No time to think on that. Find the calm. Keep faith in myself and my father's god. Let the magic flow through me, do not command it.

And pray that Hal was not among the attackers.

> *"Pridd, Awyr, Tanio, Dwfr*
> *Earth, Air, Fire, Water*
> *Elements combined to give us life.*
> *Elements combined in fiery death*
> *Protect us from this Otherworldly strife."*

Cold fire gathered in my hand. It blazed high, casting light in a broad circle.

My stomach lurched at the sight of the overlarge wolves with unnatural five-fingered paws and clear, intelligent eyes that glowed red.

At that moment Coffa took command over her duel with the wolf. She gained her feet, jerked her head, and tore open the throat of her opponent. Blood sprayed high. It splashed my hands and face. Where it touched me, it burned hotter than the fire I commanded.

The other wolf, enraged by the death of his partner dove past the guard of the soldiers. His jaw latched onto Michael's wrist.

I heard bones snap.

I flung the ball of light into the wolf's face. "Burn, damn you. Burn all the way to hell."

With a yelp, it broke off its attack. Tail tucked between its legs, it tried to run. The fire consumed its head. It ran in circles, yipped once more, and collapsed.

The second wolf's throat began to knit before my eyes. As it scrambled to its feet once more, I caught it with another ball of fire. It died more quickly and cleaner than the first.

The men sagged, resting heavily upon their swords as if they were canes. Several trembled with fear and exhaustion. The sergeant cradled his sword arm in his left palm. Michael bit his lip and tried to direct them to alertness once more. They both looked overly pale in the uncertain light.

I had no time to deal with them yet. I had to be certain the werewolves would not rise again. Had to be certain neither of them were Hal.

Before our eyes the fur faded. Limbs lengthened and straightened. Snouts and teeth retreated. They stretched and paled into the bodies of naked men. Their faces were so ravaged by fire, no one could identify them.

Coffa nosed each and turned away, satisfied that her duty was complete.

I knelt and examined the men more carefully.

"Come away, Deirdre." Michael touched my shoulder with his good hand. "The living need you."

"I have to know," I sobbed as I ran my hands down arms and across torsos seeking some identifying mark.

"They are both dead. We need fear them no longer."

"There was a third wolf. We all heard it on the plateau above."

"Coffa does not smell it."

"One of them might be . . . might be . . ." How could I tell him that he had lived with a werewolf all summer? That my own cousin . . .

"Neither of them is Hal," Sir Michael said with authority.

"How . . . ?"

"Their hair isn't dark enough. Their shoulders not broad enough and their legs not long enough. Trust me, Deirdre. You did not kill your cousin this night."

"But another night I might have to," I sobbed.

Chapter 40

September 1575. Full Moon. The North Midland Downs.

DONOVAN watched in horror as his son changed from a beautiful young man to a ravening wolf. Bile burned Donovan's throat and gullet.

He was glad Martha had not lived to see this terrible thing. The knowledge of Hal's bestiality would have killed her as surely as the plague had.

How had Hal become . . . this . . . this thing? Why?

What had either of them done to deserve this terrible punishment?

Paris. It had happened in Paris. That much was certain.

Before he could ponder their dilemma further, Hal loped away.

Donovan followed. His aching left leg slowed him down. But Hal was in no hurry, and the bright moonlight revealed his dark silhouette as he wandered the hills, nose in the air.

The scent of woodsmoke awoke a new terror in Donovan's heart. People camped out on the downs. People. The natural prey of shape-shifters. He had to catch up to Hal and stop him before he killed.

But how could he stop a preternaturally strong werewolf?

He only knew he had to try. He had to stop this madness before the family fractured any further. Bad enough that Deirdre had run off with her knight errant. Bad enough that both Donovan's wives had died; that his twin Griffin the Elder and Roanna had killed each other; that Mad Meg preferred to live in the hermitage than at home.

"I made promises to preserve and protect the family," Donovan muttered. "By God's wounds, I shall keep that promise."

Hal dropped to his belly and slunk forward.

The laughter and songs of Hal's prey drifted on the breeze along with the scent of smoke, and cooking, and horses.

Hal crept forward stealthily on his belly.

Donovan climbed as quickly as he could. His old wound sent jolts of burning ache up and down his leg to his hip and lower back. Desperation pushed him on and on until the leg gave out. Then he crawled.

He heard a lullaby crooned in a clear sweet voice. A familiar tune. One that his wife Martha had sung often, as had Donovan's own nurse and grandmother. His pain and confusion became a sob of sweet memory.

At the top of the hill he froze. Hal was nowhere in sight. The benighted travelers—Gypsies by the swarthy look of them and their clothing—huddled together, clutching their few children tightly.

A pale form ran past Donovan going back the other way. More than a ghostly figure. A man. A naked man.

Hal.

Filled with even more questions, he stumbled after his son. He caught up with the boy, shivering and sobbing, at the seep where Hal had shed his clothing.

"We're going home," Donovan said. "Tonight." He turned his back and handed Hal his shirt.

Hal said nothing. His breathing remained ragged and he swallowed heavily, as if a lump of phlegm clogged his breathing.

"You could have told me, boy."

"No, I couldn't."

"You should have!"

"To what end?"

"We could find a cure together. Some of the best doctors in England have addressed the subject of lycanthropy."

" 'Tis a curse and a spell, not a disease."

"We don't know that. These doctors . . ."

"Those doctors were not there."

After a long moment, Donovan swallowed his fears and tried a different tactic. "Explain to me in detail what they

did to you. If we know the original spell, we can find a way
to reverse it."

"I can't go home with you, Da. Next time I might not
be able to control it. Next time I might kill someone we
both know and love. Best if I go now."

"You can't. The family . . ."

"I must."

" 'Tis illegal to be homeless. You'll be branded, enslaved,
like those Gypsies back there."

"Better that than I kill one of the family. The family will
find a way . . ."

Hal turned away and ran down the hill into the darkness
of the setting moon.

Donovan ran three steps after him. His leg collapsed
under him. He could go no farther.

Early October 1575. Woodstock Palace.

The squat silhouette of Woodstock Palace never looked
quite so inviting as after the long flight from Kirkenwood.
I had fled the refuge of my childhood into a vicious attack
by werewolves. The spots on my face and hands where the
wolf blood had sprayed me remained burned and sore.

Michael's wrist was swollen and useless despite my splint
and bandages. His flushed face, sleepiness, and disorienta-
tion revealed fever from the wolf bite.

We arrived in the palace forecourt a sorry sight: weary,
ill, and disheveled.

I clung to the saddle many long moments after my feet
touched ground. Weak knees and aching shoulders made
walking even a few steps difficult, beyond thought. Michael
braced me with his good arm about my waist. We leaned
into each other, unsure of our next step or if we could
make it unaided.

The house steward cleared his throat noisily behind us.
"Excuse me, sir, madam. The queen requires your presence immediately."

"As soon as we have settled and washed away the travel dust," Michael replied.

"Immediately, sir. You do not wish to provoke the queen's displeasure."

So, Elizabeth was not in a good mood. And she wanted to speak to us—more likely reprimand us—for having arrived before our reports.

With no further fuss or ceremony, Michael and I trudged into the queen's presence in one of the small receiving rooms, despite our appearance and what had to be an offense to the royal nose.

Sir Francis Walsingham stood beside the queen, dark and brooding and not at all happy.

"What happened to you?" he nearly shouted as he thrust us into chairs without the queen's permission.

Michael and I looked at each other for a long moment. Finally, I blurted out our predicament. "Werewolves. Attacking in a pack. Unnatural."

"When? Where? The same pack as a year ago? You should have sent word to me," Elizabeth demanded.

"First report," Michael said. His voice was weaker than it had been just a few moments ago. His inner strength was draining. I had to get him to bed and poultice his wounds immediately.

"Is The Master behind this?" Walsingham asked. He took a step away from us, keeping his hands well away from any chance of contamination from a casual touch.

"We think so. Werewolves are usually solitary. Very territorial. For three to be within a mile of each other should have set them fighting for dominance, not hunting together," I choked out the words. We had never found the third wolf. Had it been Hal?

Michael nodded. He almost swayed in his chair.

"What else have you learned to help us track down this menace?" Elizabeth leaned forward, peering at me intently.

"Majesty, please, may we be excused? Sir Michael needs medical attention. Now."

This seemed to shake the queen out of her single-minded examination.

"Of course." She waved us off. "Sir Francis, see to it. Drag as much information out of him as you can before he succumbs to the fever. And you, Mistress Kirkwood, you shall return to me as soon as you are clean."

"I no longer answer to that name, Majesty." I stood up as tall and straight as my weary and aching body allowed. "The Kirkwood clan is no longer my family. I have taken my mother's name. I am Deirdre Douglas."

"No." She narrowed her eyes. "You are more valuable to me than the bastard daughter of a Scottish peasant. I give you the name your family favored long ago. Deirdre Griffin. An honorable name for the Pendragon who must stand at my shoulder, even if it is from behind a curtain or a veil of mystery." She half smiled at the images she presented. Her humor was returning.

"Majesty." I dropped a deep curtsy. Coffa braced my shaking knees with her massive body. "Thank you for the honor, but the Kirkwoods will fight me for the title. I do not bring to you the staff or the ring of the office."

"Unnecessary. You have the dog." Another wave of her hand. Jewels glittered on her fingers, including her coronation ring. Michael and I retreated. He leaned on me heavily, and I used Coffa unmercifully as a crutch.

At the door to Walsingham's suite, Michael clung to me. Neither of us seemed inclined to trust the other's safety to anyone else. But servants separated us and led me away to my own bath.

Coffa elected to stay with Michael. Years ago, Uncle Donovan had taught me that the first rule of accepting a familiar into my life was to trust my dog.

I trusted Coffa to care for Michael when I could not.

I thought the servants would lead me to the chambers reserved for Elizabeth's ladies-in-waiting. Instead, they took me to a private room. My sense of direction was distorted from fatigue and worry. The maze of rooms twisted me about. But I thought I ended up adjacent to Walsingham's rooms. Michael might be only a few feet away on the other side of a bolted door.

I leaned against the paneling that separated us. "Heal," I implored him. "Heal well and quickly."

The servants led me away to my bath.

Hours later, in a borrowed black gown, minus farthingale and ruff, I rejoined my queen. I had dressed my burns with a salve and a spell. Lady Mary Sidney herself had brought me food and ale. I even had time for a short nap before the summons dragged me back to the private audience chamber.

On the way, I pushed into Sir Francis Walsingham's quarters. Retainers and soldiers alike tried to stop me. With a wave of my hand, their weapons froze in scabbards. A few whispered words of a spell kept the tall warriors from approaching me.

Sir Michael, the object of my quest, lay moaning on a great bed. A physician bathed his broken wrist. His assistant ground roots for a salve in a mortar. I sniffed the ingredients and inspected the bandages. He was in good hands.

"Dee," Sir Michael called weakly.

I rushed to his side, clasping his uninjured hand.

"Dee, be careful." His hand grew limp and his eyes closed.

"Care for him well," I admonished the physician. "You have me to answer to if he dies."

My tone and posture must have alarmed the man. He nodded so briskly he almost lost his black-tasseled cap.

Satisfied, I continued my journey to the queen.

I was not surprised to find Michael's employer absent from this audience. Instead, Robert Dudley, Earl of Leicester, stood beside the queen. His hand rested familiarly on her shoulder. She clasped it there, their fingers entwined. Several of the ladies hovered around the fringes of the room.

I made my curtsy on steadier limbs than the last time. My mind focused acutely, memorizing every detail of the room and its occupants. I noted three avenues of escape. I assessed the readiness of courtiers to draw their weapons.

Most of all, I watched my queen, trying to judge her mood and her thoughts.

Moments later William Cecil, Lord Burghley, bustled in. He rubbed his hands together, yelled for parchment and pen, dispensed hurried instructions on a diplomatic missive, and demanded an accounting of expenditures by a minor official before he reached the queen. He brushed a hasty kiss across the back of her extended hand and finally paused long enough to scan the room and its occupants.

"Where is the . . . what is his name?" Lord Burghley

snapped his fingers. A clerk thrust a scroll of parchment into his hand. "Ah, Sir Michael Maelstrom. I was told he would be here."

"Sir Michael sustained serious injury. Sir Francis is informing him of this meeting as we speak," Leicester said quietly.

Elizabeth squeezed his hand.

"Very well. Has anyone spoken to the girl?" His eyes slid right past me, as if I did not exist or were as invisible as a servant.

I sought to slink farther into the shadows. Somehow I knew this gathering was about me and Sir Michael. Decisions had been made without me. I bristled inwardly, determined to guide my own destiny.

Leicester nodded in my direction. Burghley finally looked directly at me. "Oh," he mouthed the word. "I expected someone . . . someone . . ."

"Taller? More imposing? Less human?" I asked. Indignation stiffened my spine and flamed my courage. If Elizabeth expected me to become her Pendragon, then I would have to assert myself when I'd rather slink in the shadows and listen.

"Er . . ." Burghley's eyes clouded.

Elizabeth's eyes lit with merriment. Not many people could discomfit Burghley, the formidable Secretary of Treasury and former Secretary of State who had weathered many stormy diplomatic seas and kept England afloat over the years.

"Get on with it, Burghley. The young woman is tired and wounded herself." Lady Sidney, Leicester's sister and Elizabeth's favorite Lady of the Privy Chamber, prodded the man with her fan.

"Very well. Lady Deirdre Griffin of . . . of . . ." He consulted the parchment. "Dame of Melmerby and Cross Fell, Her Majesty Queen Elizabeth is pleased to post the banns of your marriage to Sir Michael Maelstrom of . . . of Bobbington and Six Ashes. The marriage to take place at Yuletide." He allowed the parchment to roll closed with a snap. "Now, Your Majesty, if you will excuse me, I do have other duties."

Without waiting for permission he stomped out.

I think my jaw gaped. Lady Sidney pushed it closed with a finger and a whisper, "You'll catch flies."

"But . . . but . . ."

"God's wounds, child, are you not pleased?" Elizabeth exploded with one of her frequent oaths.

" 'Tis a surprise, Majesty." I sank into a deep curtsy and bowed my head so I would not have to look at her while I thought.

Did I want this? What was the queen's motive? She did not like her ladies or courtiers forming alliances on their own. She controlled this marriage.

Did I love Michael? Did he love me? I hated the thought that our friendship might be jeopardized by a forced marriage.

"Come, child. We have much to discuss." Elizabeth rose, keeping Leicester's hand tucked neatly in her own. "We shall retire to our chamber. The rest of you are free to seek your beds."

I followed in her footsteps, too confused to do anything else.

Upon the queen's instructions, Leicester closed the door behind us. None of the courtiers or ladies accompanied us.

"Why, Majesty?" I asked as soon as Leicester threw the bolt, guaranteeing us a modicum of privacy. Elizabeth's ladies would make their way to other chambers with other doors that opened into this one. When Elizabeth was prepared to disrobe and seek her bed, then and only then would she call for them.

"Be happy, child, that we have granted you the one thing we could never have." Elizabeth looked directly into Leicester's eyes. I could not be certain if she used the royal "we," or referred to herself and Leicester. Their love affair had been the gossip of the Western world for almost two decades. Yet they'd never been caught, never acknowledged the love that was so obvious between them.

Now that they both aged, scandals had been forgotten. Former alliances were long dead or cast aside. They could marry if she chose. But her courses no longer ran regularly. There would be no children of the union. Why else would she, the most powerful woman in the world, make herself subservient to any man, even her longtime lover?

"You would force me to marry against my will—something you avoided most adroitly."

"Now in my old age I frequently regret not taking the love of my life to the marriage bed." Another long glance between them.

In that moment I knew that Sir Michael Maelstrom might be my friend forever. But he was not the love of my life. Hal was.

I knew that the moment he kissed me outside the kirk.

But Hal was lost to me. The curse of the wolf claimed him.

Even before Paris, our close kinship proscribed our union.

With a sigh, I realized that Sir Michael and I would deal well together. In friendship but not in passion.

"I will consent to the marriage if you tell me why you arranged it so hastily."

"You and Sir Michael have much work to do together for Sir Francis. As a couple you can move through the world nearly unnoticed. As a single woman, you cannot. Best if you are wed since you will be thrown together so much."

"Then I am not to be your lady-in-waiting?"

"That, dear child, is too low and visible a position for our Pendragon."

"My uncle and my cousin will object." In my mind's eye I saw Betsy conjuring up a great storm of mischief. Especially if she returned to court.

"Let them. You are our ward. We have granted you two small estates as dowry. More than Milord of Kirkenwood would give his niece. More than your father possessed. The documents are signed. You will wed on Yule Eve. Now leave us. Go to your knight and nurse him back to health."

Chapter 41

Late October 1575. Kirkenwood.

"I DO not believe this to be a good idea, Betsy." Donovan pulled his daughter back from her headlong plunge down the path to the kirk.

Brenin growled a protest at the roughness of his grip. He glared at the dog, and the beast backed down. Not a good sign for the strength of will of this wolfhound familiar.

" 'Tis the only way, Da. We have to prove to Elizabeth that I am the only candidate to be her Pendragon."

"There has to be another way."

"No. She is blind to all but her own wishes. We have to cut through the veil of darkness her courtiers place in front of her." Betsy's bluer-than-blue eyes stabbed right through his objections. Kirkwood eyes. All of those truly born to the clan had those eyes.

Deirdre did not. Bastard born of a love that should never have been. Deirdre had the magic and the education. But she did not have the right.

Absently he fingered the heart-shaped locket Betsy had given him.

The chain of logic for Betsy's claim to be the Pendragon wound through Donovan's mind without interference.

And yet he wanted to refute the argument. How?

So much had changed in just a few months. He had only Betsy and Griff to hold close as family now. Once he had had a very large and extended clan plus numerous foster children. All had grown and fled.

He had to do everything possible to keep Betsy from running off as well. Even if it meant violating every tradition he knew.

"I have to have the sword," Betsy insisted. She pulled out of Donovan's loosening grip and proceeded down the narrow path. She placed each step carefully, twisting her feet right or left to fit upon the steps worn by centuries of Kirkwood feet. In many places her feet almost did not fit. She had big feet, like a man. And she was tall for a woman, but not as tall as Elizabeth or Mary. And like both queens, Betsy was determined and aggressive. All qualities she would need if she shouldered the responsibilities passed down through many generations from King Arthur's Merlin and his daughter Wren.

"If the Lady grants you the use of the sword, you must learn to use it; take training with Griffin." Donovan could only follow her and that lumbering dog of hers.

"I have anticipated you there, Da. I began sparring with my little brother months ago."

And why had Donovan not heard of it? He had been home the entire summer, an unusual occurrence. As laird of the castle and Betsy's father, all of her activities fell under his direction. He shook his head in regret. The year she had spent at court had given her an independent streak. At seventeen, she should have been more concerned with finding a husband than playing with swords, let alone the weapon she sought.

" 'Twould be very nice if the faeries blessed this event," Betsy said. She stepped off the steep track into the strip of forest. A few more steps took her to the verge of the family cemetery. "I have not seen faeries in many long years."

"A raven would be more appropriate," Donovan muttered.

Donovan caught up with her. "Proceed carefully, Betsy. We do not wish to frighten the Lady." He stayed her with a gentle hand.

For once she obeyed him, walking slowly, touching the gravestones with respect, cautious not to step upon any of the graves. Even Brenin ceased his playful bounds. He moved as carefully as his mistress. She kept a hand on his ruff.

The lake was quiet today. The constant breeze up on the castle tor did not reach this secluded vale at the base. A cascade of water chuckled down the cliff face to feed the lake. A constant flow, never varying by season or rainfall.

No one had discovered the source of the spring deep within the bones of the earth that thrust upward so sharply. But the same spring fed the well within the keep.

The kirk off to the right looked abandoned. Like Mad Meg, Father Peter came and went with the wind. Either of them might suddenly turn up when least expected and most needed.

A hush fell over the forest, stream, and lake. Birds ceased their chatter. The wind above held its breath. The water lapping at the shore stilled.

Donovan forgot to breathe.

A single raven, perched atop the church porch, croaked harshly, a herald who commanded attention.

"She comes," Betsy whispered. Awe tinged her voice. "I can feel it."

Then there was a burst of sound like a million tiny silver bells all chiming at once.

He looked around. Something tugged his hair followed by a bright giggle.

"Faeries," he mouthed. He whirled about to watch their aerial acrobatics. They flew so quickly he could not keep up with them. As he turned dizzily, he felt the weight of the locket thump against his back. He started to reach for it. Decided to wait as he watched.

Brenin rose up on his hind legs nipping at a red-and-orange being. The faerie lighted on his nose, taunting him. The dog looked crosseyed, trying to figure a way to bite it. With another shower of giggles the Otherworldly creature took flight. The dog followed it to the edge of the water, snapping all the while.

Donovan watched the faery's progress across the lake to an overhanging fern where it bounced up and down, daring the lake to dampen its showy wings.

The raven took off with a loud flap of its wing and another croak, this one sounding like disgust.

" 'Tis a blessing, true as true," Betsy exclaimed. She, too, bounced up and down in excitement.

A disturbance in the center of the lake, the deepest part, sent ripples outward in ever expanding circles.

"Watch." Donovan quieted his daughter with a touch.

Her eyes followed his pointing finger.

A feminine form, clothed in white samite, bejeweled with

droplets like diamonds and crystals, rose to the surface. She
lay just beneath the water, stern, and chill. Her hands
clutched the jeweled hilt of a long sword tightly against
her breast.

Betsy crept to the water's edge.

The Lady continued to float just out of reach. She did
not raise the sword.

"I have come for Excalibur," Betsy announced in an authoritative tone.

Donovan shook his head. The Lady responded more to
politeness and respect.

You are not worthy! The Lady's words rang around the
lake. And she sank out of sight, still clutching her fabu-
lous sword.

"No," Betsy breathed. "No!" she wailed. "You can't do
this to me. Do you want my blood? Blood always makes
the magic work stronger." She brought her eating knife
from her scrip and held it up against her palm prepared to
slice it open.

Donovan grabbed to stay her hand. She evaded him. He
saw numerous scars on all parts of her hand. Revulsion
nearly choked him.

"I'll give her the life of a serf if that is what she requires!" Betsy's eyes grew wild, unfocused. Her gaze darted
about.

Donovan needed to flee this woman he no longer knew
before she fixed upon him as her sacrificial victim in her
mad quest for magical power.

He could not run. He had to stop this. Now.

Presumption, the faeries chimed in chorus. They swooped
and dove about the lake. The last of the autumn sunshine
shimmered in their wings. *Presumption must be repaid
with humiliation.*

Insect-sized beings tugged on Betsy's hair and nipped at
her nose. She batted them away.

Brenin snarled and leaped to catch the tormentors. He
managed only to send the faeries into even more intricate
patterns of attack.

Donovan had to work at holding back a laugh.

"Do not be disappointed, Betsy," he said when his voice
would no longer betray his mirth. "Clearly, the mission
ordained for you does not include demonic battles."

"What do you mean?" She turned on him, eyes wild, hair in disarray. "We are beset by werewolves in the family. They hunt in packs throughout the country. Clearly, I am ordained to battle them into submission."

"Perhaps that is another's battle." Donovan dusted off his hose and headed toward the path and home. And his mind cleared. A glaze he had not known existed lifted from his eyes.

"You have manipulated my mind, Betsy," he gasped, too astonished to be angry.

" 'Tis my prerogative as Pendragon." She pouted.

" 'Tis no one's prerogative to control another's mind. Not even in self-defense." He turned to face her, wanting very much to slap her.

She glared at him in defiance.

After a long moment of stalemate he thought better of hitting her. More like she needed to be turned over his knee—something he should have done more often in her willful life.

But now it was too late. She was too old and too strong. And he feared her.

"The Lady is correct. You are not yet mature enough to shoulder the responsibilities you crave." He turned on his heel and marched back toward the path.

"Where are you going?" Betsy demanded—as if she had the right to command his actions.

"We are off to Edinburgh on the morrow."

"I do not wish to go. My place is here. I have much to study." She plunked herself on the grassy verge, chin thrust forward.

"The place of the Pendragon is in the world, learning the ways of people and the intricate weave of politics. You will accompany me if you truly wish to be Pendragon. Or do you merely desire the magical power?"

"Robin resides in Edinburgh. I shall be humiliated if I must face him."

"That I doubt. Robin has a new babe to occupy his thoughts. He will hardly notice you."

"Babe?" Betsy sobbed. "You allowed the child to live?"

"I do not condone murder—especially of an innocent child."

"Does Elizabeth know?" Betsy's confidence, indeed her

entire being, seemed to wilt and shrink in the face of this
new disappointment.

"The queen will know when Robin chooses to tell her.
Perhaps on our next visit to London."

"I hope she throws him into the Tower! The glassblower's daughter and her babe as well."

The faeries seemed to think this statement the height of
hilarity. They took off in new spirals and swoops above the
place where the Lady had lain.

But wait. She was still there.

"Methinks the Lady has a message for you, Betsy. She
has not sunk back into the depths of her watery home."
Donovan came back to his daughter's side.

The battle is not yet determined. Excalibur sleeps!

Late autumn 1575. Woodstock Palace, outside London.

For weeks Sir Michael's fever raged. The magical nature
of the creature that had bitten him defied my mundane
cures. My poultices drew out pints of green ichor from the
wounds. But the source of the infection kept producing
more. The essence of mummy sent to me by the local
apothecary looked suspect. He had probably coated the
corpse of a criminal with pitch to make it look like the
essential ingredient. So I wrapped the site of the werewolf
bite in tobacco leaves. A very expensive cure. It helped
a bit.

Sir Michael roused a little with this new treatment.
Enough to take a little broth and to hold my hand.

"They told me our future," he whispered through
cracked and parched lips. "Do you agree to this, little
one?"

"Aye," I said shyly, blushing. "We deal well together."
Before he could say more, I spooned some broth into him.
I could not bear to hear his words of love.

Soon he slept again.

While I waited out his illness I studied my father's journals. The lines of closely written script still meant nothing

to me. Only a few words leaped out at me with any meaning.

I cried. This one last link to my father defied me. I could not reach him through his own words.

I fell asleep in the chair at Michael's bedside. Dreams and reality merged. I think I was reading a page of the journals. Suddenly a few words came into focus. I heard my father's voice read them aloud to me.

> *"My brother's wound festers. It defies mundane cures. My sisters urge me to use my powers to heal him.*
>
> *"I cannot.*
>
> *"Magic is forbidden to me, a priest, an emissary of Monsignor Eustachius du Bellay, Bishop of Paris.*
>
> *"Only God can help my twin now. I trust in Him."*

A break in the script, then on a new page:

> *"I took my brother to the family chapel. There I placed him before the altar and knelt in prayer. I recited the prayers for the sick. I recited every prayer I knew and made up some more. I prayed the rosary through several times. I prostrated myself. I gave everything I am to God for the sake of my brother.*
>
> *"Hours? Days? I know not how long I prayed. Perhaps I slept, perhaps I fell into a trance. I awoke to a touch from my sister Fiona. She claimed that the chapel had been flooded with an eldritch blue light for a day and a night.*
>
> *"Donovan's fever has broken."*

A little of my father's love and trust for his God crept through me. I tried to pray. Words failed me. Michael's fever did not abate.

Perhaps I did not love him enough. I began to understand a little of what made my father so beloved of the people of England. He gave everything he had for those entrusted to his care. Gypsies and wanderers still made pilgrimage to his grave. I vowed to do the same, as soon as the weather opened the roads again and Sir Michael, my Michael, recovered.

Aunt Meg still tended the grave from her Hermitage. I had never been allowed to visit her there.

As if my thoughts of Aunt Meg conjured her, she appeared at Woodstock three weeks after my arrival. No one attempted to stop Aunt Meg. She walked past stupefied guards with twigs and moss sticking to her hair and her gown. She looked like a wood nymph stepping out of a legend into reality.

She hummed an almost familiar tune under her breath. Servants and armed guards followed in her wake. They walked as though in a trance.

Fresh air smelling of dew and evergreens and fresh grass growing filled the air around her.

I felt the elements gathering to her in preparation for the magic she needed.

The moment she appeared at the door to the sickroom faeries popped into this world in a bright halo around her head. I had never heard of the tiny beings deigning to grace the interior of any building.

Hope brightened within me. The dark room suddenly seemed lighter, my future less lonely. Mad Meg had come to help.

"Poultice, then infusion," she said as she thrust a nosegay of tiny white flowers, their petals forming stars with a pale blue/yellow/pink center, each blossom no larger than the nail of my littlest finger. As I stared at the unfamiliar posies, the colors seemed to shift and my vision blurred a little.

"Faery stars," Meg informed me.

Ah, that explained the presence of the faeries. Legend claimed they were drawn to the flowers and could be summoned by them. If you could find the plants. Incredibly rare, they hid from the most ardent seeker. I had heard that one found them only by chance when needed the most. Even then, attempts to transplant failed and the blossoms withered before they could be used.

Under my aunt's watchful eye I prepared the flowers. Half went into my mortar with various astringents, moistened with a bit of distilled wine. Together, we invoked the elements in balance and the healing properties. Then I plunged a hot poker into the concoction. When it steamed, I slathered it onto a clean bandage and laid it atop the unhealed werewolf bites.

Michael bucked and swore and tried to wrench his arm away from the burning cure. But Meg held him with hands strong beyond their seeming.

A faery settled upon the poultice, studying it intently. Its presence seemed to quiet Michael a little. He still writhed beneath Meg's hands.

Coffa jumped on the bed and added her weight to help keep Michael from heaving off all restraint.

While Michael wrestled with the new pain of the poultice, I poured boiling water over the remaining flowers. I let them steep for several minutes. A sweetness more delectable than honey wafted across my nose. Faeries giggled drunkenly as they, too, drew in the fragrance.

"Do I need to add anything to this?" I asked Meg.

"Just your love."

That was the hard part. I knew I did not truly love Michael. Not as I loved Hal. Not as I longed for him to stand beside me night and day, guiding me, humoring me, sparking my mind and body with his insight.

I had to forget that love. Hal and I could never be together as lovers, or as friends.

Did I love Michael enough to infuse this cure with the last essential ingredient? I thought of long lonely days ahead without him. I tried to imagine myself alone as Meg chose to be alone.

I would miss Michael sorely. He listened to me. He supported me without question. He learned my secrets and kept them. He had proved himself a worthy knight and fine friend. Yes, I did love him in a way.

I prayed to the faeries and the elements and my father's God that it would be enough.

Chapter 42

A BRIGHT green faery landed on my shoulder and whispered secrets to me in a language I could not fathom; in a voice that echoed the combined thoughts of the entire flock of faeries. Aunt Meg cocked her head and listened. Her eyes brightened.

"They will help." She nodded once in affirmation.

Then the green fellow swooped over to Coffa's head. He wobbled and nearly ran into the headboard before he found a perch.

We had to move quickly and get the infusion into Michael before our otherworldly helpers became too drunk on the fumes to do aught but fall asleep.

I held the steaming goblet to Michael's mouth. He inhaled deeply and relaxed his struggles.

Coffa scooted back a bit to relieve her tremendous weight from the patient's chest. The green fellow had to cling to her fur to keep from falling off. His wings fluttered in an irregular and asymmetrical pattern.

Meg giggled at the sight.

I had to smile. But until Michael was free of the infection that ate at him, I could not indulge in mirth.

One by one, the faeries settled onto the bolster and counterpane in a showy display of shiny colors borrowed from flower and field, but more intense, too bright to be real.

"Gently," Meg cautioned me. "It needs to be hot but not burn his mouth so he can take no further nourishment."

"Maybe you should do it."

"Nay. It needs to come from one he loves and trusts.

Else the wolfbite will not retreat. The wolves prey on the loveless and the lonely."

Hal had not been lonely when The Master converted him. Had he?

I shuddered a moment.

Then, resolved not to allow Michael to suffer the same fate as my cousin, I blew a cooling breath across the top of the goblet. More of the steam wafted up Michael's nose. He lifted two fingers, all the strength he could muster.

I placed the cup near his mouth, then with my free hand lifted his head and shoulders. None of the precious brew must spill from his mouth.

He sipped once, twice, and turned his head away.

"All of it, Michael!" I pressed the cup to his lips once more.

He complied for two more gulps and refused the medicine again.

"Michael," I said sternly.

"You, too," Meg whispered. "You have to take it, too."

I looked to her for confirmation.

She nodded sharply and refused to meet my eyes.

"What will it do to me?"

Silence.

"Meg?"

" 'Twill bind you . . . your magic into the cure." She refused to say more.

Hurry, the faeries urged me. *The flowers dissipate. You must drink or lose his soul as well as his life.*

I inhaled deeply and took one long swallow of the infusion of faery stars. Sweetness burst upon my tongue. Lightness possessed the top of my head. I might have sprouted wings and floated.

Michael smiled. Much of the strain in his neck and shoulders melted. I pressed the cup to his mouth once more. He drank the last of the potion.

Sleep claimed him. A deep, healing sleep that left a smile on his face and an apprehensive lump in my gut.

November 1575. Just after a full moon. Kirkenwood.

Hal ran. His heart pounded in his ears. Hot pain lanced up his thighs to stab him in the groin and the side. Chill air bit deep inside his lungs. Still he ran.

Some of his preternatural strength from the full moon lingered. So why could he not outdistance the men who chased him on horseback?

They'd found him as he patrolled the fringes of his territory, protecting his boundaries from other predators—especially The Master who continued to call to him. The villagers had ridden hard and caught up with him just before midnight.

A half-hidden rock tripped him. He tumbled down the side of the moor into a stream in spate. Icy water poured down the neck of his doublet. Holes in his boot sole exposed his tender toes.

Without thinking, he rolled to his knees and was on his feet and running again. This time he thrashed through the water, letting the liquid take his scent. Two dozen long paces and he leaped out of the little river and circled back the way he had come.

Dogs bayed uphill from his position. They plunged down the hillside along the path of his fall. Noses to the ground, they did not sense him yet.

Hal continued uphill. He needed to get behind his pursuers.

Why had they chosen to hunt him down tonight? He'd killed nothing in two days. The three sheep and the milch cow he'd slaughtered at the height of the full moon had sated his wolf.

In all the months he had hunted this precinct, not once had he taken a human life or threatened one. Something deep within him cringed at taking another soul into his body through the act of cannibalism.

Helwriaeth's spirit gave him enough wisdom, patience,

and, he prayed, nobility. He needed no victim's soul in an endless quest to replace the one stolen by The Master.

And he had never hunted near Kirkenwood. Neither man nor beast endangered his lair.

The village reeve from Kirkenwood paused before taking his horse down the steep slope after the dogs. He peered into the distance, watching for movement in the fitful light of the waning moon.

Then Hal saw *her*. Betsy rode slightly behind the hunters. Did she quest for his blood tonight? What new spell did she need to fuel with death?

Why had Da left her at Kirkenwood, unfettered in her pursuit of power?

Hal dropped to the ground. Color and movement would betray him. Staying where he was made him vulnerable to the dogs. Could he run back to the crypt beneath Kirkenwood before they found his hiding place?

Not with the limitations of a human body.

He knew that strong human emotions could draw him out of the wolf body on the night of the full moon. Could the strong wolf instinct for preservation dominate over his human body as the moon's light and strength waned?

Only one way to find out.

Creeping on hands and knees along a circuitous path, he sought a fold in the hillside that would block the reeve's view. And elude Betsy's magic. Gorse tore at his clothing. Stones scraped his knees and palms. Blood oozed from a slash on one shin.

A dog caught the scent of blood and bugled his triumph to the others. Betsy squealed in delight to match the dog's enthusiasm.

Hal had to hurry.

Shivering with cold and fear he shed his clothing and bundled it with his belt. He slung the makeshift pack over one shoulder and crouched deeper into the shadows.

"Concentrate," he told himself. "Concentrate on running away on all fours with the wind in my face and my tail held high." He pictured himself as a wolf.

Betsy would not expect him to transform tonight. Not with the moon waning.

The dogs came closer. Horse hooves thundered against

the turf behind them, so close he could hear their murmurs and their thoughts.

"The bitch will have our ears if we don't catch him tonight," one man hissed to his neighbor. The two were at the head of the pack of hunters out of earshot of their mistress. Betsy rode well to the rear; eager to watch the kill but not to perform the deed herself.

"Seen too many ears and hands decorating the gatepost since her da left her in charge," a hunter murmured back.

"She quotes ancient law for the least infraction." The reeve crossed himself. "She exacts the maximum punishment—an ear for the sin of gossip, a hand for failing to fulfill her wishes. Worse than when Bloody Mary was on the throne trying to make us swallow the Church of Rome."

"Tongues, hands, ears." The second man made an ancient gesture to ward off evil. "They's but trophies to her."

A number of people had disappeared from Kirkenwood of late. Hal had thought they crept away in the night, fearing less the dangers of life on the road than living under Betsy's cruel dominion. Rumors persisted that Betsy had enticed men to her bed, then murdered them as an extension of her pleasure.

She had sunk lower than The Master.

"You aren't fit to be the Pendragon, Betsy," Hal whispered to himself. "I'll do everything I can to keep you from it."

With that thought he knew what he had to do.

"Concentrate."

He dared a glance over his shoulder. The silhouettes of his pursuers grew larger, darker. The dogs bayed.

Hal's muscles wrenched and his bones melted.

"Concentrate. Awroo-roo-roo." And he was off.

Tongue lolling, drool dripping from his beard, he loped easily. Each long stride ate the furlongs. Fur and muscle kept him warm. He was the wind. He was the hunt.

His pack bobbed against his back, a reassurance that when the chase was done, he could once more become a man.

He did not think how his half-existence on the fringe of life bespoke of his diminishing humanity. He had one more act of defiance to accomplish. Then he could let the wolf rule him.

But he would never heed the call of The Master. He would never stoop so low as to kill other humans at that man's bidding.

"Griff, wake up!" Hal crawled beneath the warm coverlet beside his brother.

Griff rolled to his side and mumbled. He sprawled over the large bed. Then he rolled away from Hal, thrashing. Hal had to duck away from flailing arms.

Before Hal had moved to the crypt, his twin had been a neat sleeper, ever conscious that he shared the bed as well as his life with his brother. Now he slept restlessly, uncomfortable alone.

"Griff, wake up," Hal said a little louder, shaking his brother's shoulder.

"Wha . . . ?" Griff half opened one eye. "Hal?" He opened both eyes and sat up.

"Listen carefully, Griff, I haven't much time."

"Hal, are you all right? Let me look at you?" Griff grabbed Hal's shoulders. "Light a candle, twin. I need to see you."

"No time. Can't take a chance."

"Is Betsy prowling the castle? I swear that woman never sleeps." Griff shoved hair out of his eyes and dropped back against the bolster. "Talk, then. 'Tis a relief just to hear your voice and know that you live."

"This is the last time, Griff. I have to leave Kirkenwood tonight. Life is too dangerous for me here."

"No, Hal. You can't leave me alone with Betsy."

"I have to. But you have to assert yourself, take back control of Kirkenwood from her."

"I can't do that alone. I need you and your magic to counter her, Hal."

"My magic isn't strong enough to counter hers." Hal hung his head. "I'll not spill blood to . . . I won't do it.

But listen, she expects magical attack. She wards herself and the castle against it."

"She kills people to get enough blood for her wards and her spells." Griff shuddered and pulled the counterpane higher.

"She does not expect a mundane attack," Hal said quietly.

"But . . ."

"Hear me out, twin. She sleeps late. You must rise early. Take control of the mundane tasks of the laird. Give orders to the steward, supervise the pickling and salting of meat, lead patrols. Take charge. Tell everyone to avoid Betsy at all costs."

"And when she begins killing every retainer for the sin of disobeying her?"

"She can't. Not now."

"Why not?"

"I stole this from her." Hal folded back the silk wrappings around a knife. The blade glowed with magic, making a candle unnecessary.

"Her athame!" Griff gasped through clenched teeth. The ritual knife she used for each of her mutilations and murders.

"I'm throwing it into the lake. The Lady won't give it back to Betsy."

"Betsy will just use a new blade." Griff scrunched lower beneath the counterpane.

"Not if she can't find one."

"What?" Griff sat up straighter again.

"I have taken every sword, dagger, scythe, and carving knife and hidden them in the crypt. Inside Wren's tomb, beside Arthur. Betsy doesn't dare go to the crypt. The ghosts there frighten her. I've sprinkled them all with horseradish and the ashes of broom. The blades are purified and useless to her."

"We need those blades, Hal."

"Dole them out, one at a time as required. Return them to the tomb after each use. Renew the horseradish and ashes daily."

"Is that enough?"

"If the opportunity presents itself, force her to confront the standing stones. Our ancestors have a few things to say to her." Hal covered the blade again. The glow disappeared. Under cover of darkness he slipped out of the room. "Good-bye, Griffin. I'll miss you."

"Hal, come back. I need you. If we neutralize Betsy, you'll be safe here."

"Not anymore. The villagers know me for what I am now. They'll not let me live."

Hal fought tears of loneliness as he turned his back on his twin, on Kirkenwood, on life as a normal man. But first he had one more chore.

Chapter 43

Advent 1575. Edinburgh.

"WHAT troubles you so, My Lord of Kirkenwood?" King James VI of Scotland spoke with his careful enunciation as he looked up from his studies. His soft brown eyes reflected his mother's intelligence.

"A missive from my queen, Your Grace." Donovan tossed the folded parchment on the table where the nine-year-old king could read it or not, as he chose. The boy managed to read every letter that came into or left the Palace of Holyrood whether intended for his eyes or not.

Donovan had learned to either leave his papers lying about or take private communication verbally in another part of the city. Inwardly, he smiled at this child's resourcefulness. He'd need it to stay alive amidst the volatile and violent politics of Scotland.

" 'Tis marked private." James did not even look up from the text on geometry. He loved mathematics, especially when he could apply it to a study of the stars and their movements. Were he not a crowned and anointed monarch, he'd make a formidable astrologer.

"Elizabeth invites me to attend the nuptial mass for my niece, Deirdre." Donovan wasn't certain how he felt about the news.

His hand reached for the locket about his neck without thinking about why he touched it so frequently.

He had to forget both Deirdre and Hal. As far as he and Kirkenwood were concerned, they had both died.

And yet . . .

Despite the formal language of the letter from Elizabeth, he knew that both his queen and his niece would welcome him warmly. He truly wanted to stand beside his niece on her wedding day.

"Will you go?" James asked, lisping a little. He frowned. A dimple appeared in his cheek. The same dimple Donovan had witnessed in his own mirror every morning while he shaved.

"With your permission, Your Grace." Donovan bowed slightly. He had one chance to mend the breach with Deirdre, to bring her back into the family.

"You belong to Elizabeth. You do not need our permission to come and go." Was that a bit of a tremble in the boy's chin.

"Your Grace, I value the trust and friendship you have granted me. I would never betray you by leaving without your permission and knowledge." Donovan dropped to one knee beside the boy, putting him at eye level. He presumed to take James' hand and hold it tightly, lovingly.

Oh, how he wished he could tell the boy that he was not an orphan, had a parent who truly loved him. But to acknowledge the one night he had spent in Mary's bed would destroy James' legitimacy and his right to the throne. Might very well destroy his fragile sense of self.

As much as Donovan wanted to gather this boy king into his arms and whisk him back to Kirkenwood, he knew that England needed Scotland as a strong Protestant ally on its northern border. If England invaded and tried to absorb this small impoverished kingdom, all of Europe would declare war against England. If France or Spain, or—heaven forbid—the Holy Roman Emperor tried to restore order in a warring Scotland, then England was threatened by Catholic armies poised on its borders. For now, Scotland needed to remain independent and at peace under James and his regents.

James could keep Scotland strong and independent, as Elizabeth kept England out of war. Mary could not do that for either kingdom.

"You will not leave me, Lord Donovan?" James asked, very much a little boy in need of a friend.

"I'll stay by your side as long as you need me, Your Grace."

James nearly fell into Donovan's arms. His small arms encircled Donovan's neck and held on fiercely.

A tear touched Donovan's eye. His family had shattered. All of his children were now self-sufficient, independent, and had little use for him. But James needed him.

For a time he could think of the boy as family, the only family he had left other than ghosts.

After a moment James sat up in his tall chair again. He firmed his chin and dashed moisture from his eyes and his large nose with the back of his hand.

"We must preside over a trial two days hence, My Lord," James said, returning to his careful enunciation and formal address. "We wish you to sit beside us in guidance."

And won't the regent and Privy Council love that!

"What is the nature of this trial, Your Grace?"

"A witch was caught right here in Edinburgh. She was putting curses on the ale at the White Horse Inn." James bounced a little, excited by the scandal.

A chill ran up Donovan's spine. He had to put a stop to this.

"We devised the trap that caught her," James prattled on. "She put something in the ale that made our trusted earls and knights speak out of turn."

"But, Your Grace, that is the nature of ale when drunk to excess." Donovan's mind spun with ploys to free the supposed witch. No legal way existed for her to prove her innocence short of death.

"Ale is a staple of the diet. Strong men do not loose their tongues upon a single drink."

"Not a single drink. But what about five or ten or more? Surely these men merely sought an excuse for their own drunkenness."

"Nay. We questioned them closely. The men are innocent. 'Tis the woman who is guilty. 'Tis always a woman who is guilty. Like my lady mother." James closed his mouth resolutely.

Donovan knew he'd not persuade the boy now. Perhaps on the morrow.

But James never changed his mind. Not even when proved wrong.

Donovan had best forget about a trip to London for Deirdre's wedding. He'd best forget about leaving Edinburgh at all for a long, long time. James needed his guidance more than any of the other children. Scotland and

England needed Donovan beside the young king, moderating the poison whispered in his ear by his superstitious, fanatical, and power hungry Privy Council.

His sense of family, the close gathering of all of his children shattered. A gaping hole opened in his heart.

Yuletide 1575. Greenwich Palace, London.

On the morning of my wedding, I cried. From first waking before dawn, through the long ritual of bathing and dressing until I stood outside the royal chapel, tears flowed without stop.

"Whst, child. No need to be afraid. Sir Michael is a gentle man. He'll not hurt you," Lady Sidney said as she bathed my eyes with rosewater.

Too choked with tears, I could not reply that I did not fear the man the queen had selected for my husband.

"Hush, now," Lady Hastings added her own soothing. "You'll stain the fine gown the queen has given you. Such a fine green brocade, all decked in tiny garnets. You look like a sprig of holly. Fitting for the Yuletide celebrations."

"And the petticoat your uncle sent, all embroidered in gold and green. Truly a wondrous wedding ensemble," Lady Sidney echoed her sister.

At this new reminder that Uncle Donovan had not totally exiled me from his family, I let loose another spate of tears. He'd also sent an expensive set of plate. But the petticoat, a lavish luxury and an intimate gift, said more than all the money he had spent.

Elizabeth's ladies cooed and clucked over me until I managed to control myself enough to walk to the chapel.

Elizabeth met me there. She pressed a stiffly embroidered handkerchief into my hands—white on white with just a touch of green needle lace around the edges.

" 'Tis not a disaster, this marriage," she said, spine as stiff as the starched ruff around her neck. " 'Twill work out for the best all around." With a little huff she flounced into the chapel ahead of me.

I could only follow. Momentarily, my tears dried. In the face of Elizabeth's near contempt, I found the courage to face my groom.

Throughout the long Mass, punctuated with Elizabeth's favorite polyphonic music sung by her privately endowed choir, I concentrated on Sir Michael's handsome face and the adventures we would face together in Her Majesty's service. We were friends. Comrades-in-arms. We laughed together.

For a short space of time I pushed aside Uncle Donovan's absence. Betsy's and Griffin's silence—not so much as a single note of congratulation or condemnation—my youth, the abruptness of this wedding, Michael's near miraculous cure. All the reasons for my tears became insignificant.

Except one.

Michael was not Hal.

Hal held his breath beneath a yew tree. A wolfhound lounged on the ground beside him, oblivious to the weather. One of the regular patrols passed them by without a second glance. Even the scent of a very wet dog did not alert the man huddling beneath his cloak.

Beyond the yew tree stood Greenwich Palace, Elizabeth's favorite domicile during the Yuletide season. Candlelight sparkled inside the many glass windows. Raindrops on the outside refracted the light into tiny rainbows. Sprightly music drifted through the air. The scent of roasting meat, candied fruits, and mulled wine made Hal's mouth water.

Inside all was warm and joyous.

Outside the weather was cold and wet. Damp seeped through Hal's leather doublet and trews. He'd forsaken boots for rags and strips of leather. He'd rather hole up in a lair with a fire and a scroll of ancient text, than be here, but he had a mission. If ever he was to stop Betsy from becoming the true Pendragon of Britain, he had to do it tonight.

When the guard rounded the corner of the palace, Hal moved in the opposite direction. He'd watched the palace for days and found a postern door used by servants and couriers. Once he had even crept inside to find the rooms he needed. Now he must deliver his package, tonight, while all inside reveled and the guards had taken extra tots of beer to warm their bellies against the drizzle.

The dog trotted obediently at his side. Hal missed Helwriaeth more than ever at this moment. The dog at his heels had not the intelligence, nor the psychic bond of a true familiar. Still he would serve his purpose admirably. The family kept only the best dogs in their kennels. All the others were culled or sold to the nobility of Europe and England as fully trained hunters. Much of the family fortune came from the excellence of the kennels.

At every shrub in the geometrically symmetrical gardens, the dog lifted his leg. Hal paused and rolled his eyes upward at the delay. Good thing the moon was dark or he'd probably feel the urge to mark territory atop the beast's scent.

Eventually they came to the door. Locked, of course. The latch presented no barrier to Hal's mind. He and the dog slipped inside a cloakroom. Warmth blasted his face and hands and knees. Sleepiness made his eyes heavy.

More than the sudden change in temperature lay hidden in the warm air. Dee had set wards. He smelled her distinctive brand of magic in the magical deterrent. An ordinary thief or intruder would suddenly feel too tired to complete his nefarious deed.

The dog dropped his nose to the corners, sniffing. His ears and tail drooped. Must be strong wards if they affected the dog as well as men. Perhaps she had set them against werewolves.

He swallowed a sudden lump of sadness that threatened to choke him.

Hal pushed on. The cloakroom led to a small receiving salon. That room led to a larger room. That one in turn offered three choices: a staircase going up, or two bedchambers.

He tightened his hold on the dog's leash and headed up. The dog resisted. Raised in a kennel, he had never climbed stairs before. They presented an unfamiliar barrier to him.

He did not like the worn wooden surface that smelled of too many strange people. His claws clicked loudly on the polished wood. Hal dragged him by brute force to another series of dressing rooms and bedchambers.

He paused at the top of the stairs listening. 'Twasn't yet midnight. All of the revelers should be in the other wing, dancing and singing and drinking.

The dog rushed eagerly to the next door, nose to the crack of light beneath it. He let loose a slight whine.

Then Hal heard the attraction. Another dog snuffled the same door from the next room. Beyond the dog, he heard the deep rumble of a male voice speaking softly followed by a distinctly feminine sigh. That sigh held a world weariness and sadness.

Only one woman in the world could say so much with a sigh.

Dee.

Who was the man who spoke to her in such an intimate tone?

Sir Michael Maelstrom. It could only be him. She'd not allow any other so close to her.

Jealous fury boiled through Hal. He yanked the door open. Two wolfhounds blocked his way as they sniffed ears and tails and made small growls of greeting.

"Hal?" Dee jumped away from Sir Michael, holding her right sleeve, untied from the bodice.

Sir Michael gathered her close with his left arm while he searched for his discarded sword with his right.

"Deirdre." Hal tried hard to fill his voice with contempt. Suppressing his anger at the sight of them in the early stages of dishabille made his hands and knees tremble.

"What brings you here?" Dee took one step toward him, her hand held out to him. Her left hand now sported a heavy ring—the family ring Sir Michael usually wore.

Sir Michael restrained her from venturing farther from the protection of his arm.

Hal cursed under his breath. He should have known.

"I've brought you a wedding present." Hal shoved the male wolfhound into the room. Coffa still worried at the creature's ears.

"But . . ."

"No buts about it. Betsy isn't fit to be the Pendragon.

You need to breed Coffa to keep the line of familiars viable. 'Tis the dogs that choose the Pendragon. Not the queen, or Betsy, or even my father." He almost choked on the last word. He hadn't seen his father, even from a distance, since that horrible night on the moors when they faced each other with certain knowledge of Hal's terrible curse.

"Will you return to claim one of the pups?" Dee knelt beside the dogs, one arm draped around the neck of each. The beasts licked her face and nuzzled her hands for caresses.

Her sleeve lay forgotten on the floor. Mute reminder of the intimacy of the embrace Hal had interrupted.

"Nay. I'll never have another familiar. Helwriaeth wouldn't like it."

"Helwriaeth is dead, Hal."

"Not entirely." Hal turned on his heel and marched back the way he had come. Alone except for the lingering light of humanity behind his heart where Helwriaeth's spirit had lodged. 'Twas that spark that allowed him to resist The Master. 'Twas Helwriaeth who kept him from sinking totally into the bestiality of his curse.

"Hal!" I cried.

Michael held me back. "Let him go, Deirdre. He's lost to you."

My husband tried to pull me into his embrace.

"Hal!" I wrenched away. Tears flowed once more. I thought I had no more to shed. The door resisted my attempts to open it. What had Hal done to it?

"Give it up, Deirdre," Michael said gently. He held my shoulders, quieting my sobs.

Still I played uselessly with the latch. No magic sprang to my fingers or my mind. It all seemed to flow away with my tears.

"He's so lost and lonely," I wailed, turning my face into Michael's chest. I needed his strong body to shield me from my own fears and aloneness.

"Your cousin is cursed, Deirdre. There is nothing you can do about it. But he gave you a magnificent gift, the opportunity to become what he can never be now." Gently he rubbed my back and neck, crooning as if to a child.

As if to emphasize Michael's words, Coffa crowded close to me, supporting me with her strong back and intense love.

At last I gained a modicum of control. "I would mourn him as if he had died." Instinctively, I reached into my pocket for the cross from the broken rosary that was never far from my fingers.

It wasn't there!

I pulled away from Michael, searching frantically for the talisman from my father.

"Is this what you are looking for?" Michael held up a long chain of gold beads marked with pearls at the decade. A golden-circled cross dangled from the ends. It spun, glinting shades of sunshine and brightness in the candlelight.

"My cross!" I gasped, reaching for the rosary. "You had it restrung."

"Aye. I know how you treasure it." He held the present just beyond my reach.

"Michael, please," I asked, feigning meekness.

"Here. Keep it hidden. The rosary is still illegal." Suddenly he sobered. "But I know you are not a Papist."

"I thank you from the bottom of my heart." I clutched the precious relic to my bosom. "I can never repay you, Michael. I have no gift for you. I have nothing of my own."

"The queen gave you a magnificent dowry. Two estates."

"Small ones with no revenue. I come before you with little more than what I wear and these two dogs."

"Yes, the dogs. The symbol of your magical heritage." His fists tightened and his shoulders slumped. In resentment?

We had never discussed that part of my life. He had guessed some of it. I was certain Sir Francis Walsingham had told him more. Did he know the dangers he faced married to one of my family?

"Michael . . ."

"No. Say nothing more. I know your heart belongs to another. This marriage is merely for the convenience of respectability." He turned and walked sadly toward the outer door. Coffa followed him. The male followed her.

I felt suddenly cold, more alone than ever. I lifted a hand in entreaty. Only my shift clothed that arm. We'd begun the process of a true marriage.

"Michael. It does not have to be that way."

He paused and looked over his shoulder at me. Hope flitted across his eyes. He masked it quickly and skillfully.

"Please, do not leave me alone." With a quick flick of my fingers I opened the ties on the other sleeve. They tangled, knotted. I tore at them, frustrated and frightened.

"Here, allow me. 'Twill be no end of teasing on the morrow should the others notice broken ties." His gentle fingers unraveled the troublesome knot. He held my gaze while he stripped off the sleeve.

" 'Twill be no end of teasing on the morrow no matter how chaste we appear," I said on a breathy whisper. "I want to be a true wife to you, Michael."

"And your cousin?"

"We had no chance to be together even before . . . before Paris. We both always knew we had to wed elsewhere. I would wed a friend, a man I can laugh with. A man with common goals and interests. A man I love enough to cure with magical flowers and the help of drunken faeries. 'Tis more than most maids can hope for."

" 'Tis more than Hal can dream about now." He hugged me fiercely. "I want to like the man, Deirdre. But I can only fear him and the hold he has over you."

"No more than I fear what he will do to himself, alone. Without even a dog for company."

"You and I are bound together now, Deirdre. For better or worse."

For all the love in his words, his voice sounded flat, as if he spoke to reassure himself more than me.

"Then best we make it for the better."

He kissed me tenderly. It lacked the joyful intensity of his previous caresses.

I returned his kisses and hoped the power of the faery stars we had drunk during his cure was enough to hold us together.

Chapter 44

MUSIC, laughter, applause, all the sounds of revelry grew louder in the long silence between Michael and me.

"Are you certain you want this?" Michael put a vast two inches between us. But he kept his hands on my shoulders.

I drew a deep breath and firmed my chin.

"Yes, Michael. I want to be your wife. I want to work at your side and I want to *live* by your side. I can think of no man I would rather be with."

"Not even Hal?"

"Not even Hal. As much as I love my cousin, I fear him. I fear what he has become as well as what he might do."

"Do you fear me?" His hands tightened on my shoulders. Only the thick brocade of my bodice kept bruises from forming.

I leveled my gaze to him.

"Never. Though I fear for your enemies—I have seen you in battle—I know with all of my being that you would never hurt me."

"I might if you ever try to leave me." His fingers tightened once more and inched closer to my throat. But he did not close the distance between us.

Clearly, the next move was up to me. I had to take the initiative.

I rose up on tiptoe and kissed his chin. "Why would I try to leave my faithful knight who saved me from were-wolves?"

"I didn't . . . you saved us all." Again that reluctant distance between us.

"Hush. We worked together. Very well." This time I kissed his cheek, just to the left of his mouth.

He moaned slightly and turned just enough to capture

my mouth with his. "Oh, Deirdre." He dropped his hands from my shoulders to gather me close to his chest. We stood quietly for many long moments with his cheek resting atop my head.

I let my arms creep up and around his neck. "Call me Dee. Like the rest of my family. You are my family now. My husband."

"I like the sound of that word," he murmured, kissing my hair. "And the word 'wife.' "

"Wife." I could not help the sigh that accompanied the word. A sigh of satisfaction without a trace of regret.

Michael's hands began to explore. He nibbled my neck. Hesitantly, I caressed his shoulders and ran my hand through his fine hair.

"Do you think we have too many layers of clothing between us?" he mumbled.

I almost couldn't hear him over the shouts of renewed mirth at the Yuletide gaiety of Elizabeth's court. How much longer before someone noticed our absence? How much longer before some drunken courtier moved the celebration from the Hall to outside our bedroom door? 'Struth, we should have waited for their escort to our bridal chamber.

Suddenly anxious to be under the bedcovers and away from prying eyes, I nodded and began working at the laces of my bodice.

"Here. Turn around." Michael pivoted me and covered my hands at my nape. His fingers worked slowly down the length of my spine, loosening the bindings. At each crossing he caressed my spine. At first I jumped and started at the unfamiliar touch. By the third release my shoulders relaxed.

The noise below moved closer.

"God's blood! I thought we'd have more time," he cursed as he yanked at the last bit of restraint. "I'd have thought they would put the laces up the front of a wedding garment. For easy access."

"Three women took two hours to dress me," I giggled. "You'd think they did not want us to consummate our union."

"They thought wrong." The bodice hit the floor, along with his doublet.

I began working on the skirt, petticoats, farthingale . . . far too many layers of clothing.

Michael shed his boots and trunk hose much more easily. He stood back, clad only in his shirt, which covered his netherwear completely, watching me with a silly grin on his face.

"You could help," I admonished him, with more than a bit of frustration.

"Oh, but that would deprive me of this most beautiful vision." The laughter was back in his voice and his stance.

"Do you want them to find us still clothed?" I jerked my head toward the doorway. Outside the noise of drunken men and a few tipsy women came closer.

"Come to think of it . . ." Michael found his eating knife amidst the scattered clothing. A few flicks removed the formidable barrier of my corset and reduced my covering to my shift and my netherwear. I'd worry about replacing the laces tomorrow.

"Into bed with you, wench." He slapped my bottom.

"Wench, is it?" I returned the slap.

He grabbed my hands. We tussled a moment and collapsed onto the bed, giggling and kissing and groping.

I stilled as he found my breast, squeezed, and molded it to fit his grasp. The incredible intimacy of his touch surprised me. Never had anyone . . . And then his mouth replaced his hand. He tongued and suckled through the fine lawn of my shift. Intense pleasure heated my veins, radiating out from his tender ministrations. I think I gasped. He looked up at me.

"Liked that, did you?"

"Michael, I . . ."

"Hush. We need no words." He placed one finger against my lips.

I wrapped my tongue around it and sucked. His grin spread. A new pressure asserted itself against my leg where his belly pressed alongside me. An uncontrollable trembling came over me.

And then the chill winter air wafted across my breasts. My nipples drew into tight knots as I realized Michael had pushed my shift off my shoulders, exposing me to his admiring gaze.

"It's better this way." He returned his attention to warming my left breast with his mouth while his hand took care of the right. I gasped once more.

A fierce knocking on the door panels set me to scrambling for my shift, the coverlet, Michael's body, anything to cover my nakedness.

"Go away!" Michael called to the revelers.

"She got tits big enough to see?" A drunken voice replied, slurring even those few words.

"Oh, yes," Michael whispered.

I blushed furiously.

He laughed silently.

"I'm tired. We need to sleep now," he called back to the mob who continued to knock and crack rude remarks about various body parts and what to do with them.

"Finished already?" another voice asked on a hiccup.

"Sssh," Michael pressed his fingers to my lips once more. "If we are quiet, maybe they will go away."

I couldn't help rolling my eyes upward. I knew how rowdy a wedding party could become. I just hoped they did not decide to break the door down and inspect the sheets for evidence that the marriage had been consummated.

The longer we lay quietly, the harder it became to suppress my laughter.

Michael's belly rippled with his own mirth. This brought a new reaction from the mysterious part of him that pressed so insistently against my thigh.

Michael waggled his eyebrows at me, then continued his assault on my nipples.

The crowd quieted. I sensed several of their number drifting away.

"You are no fun!" one complained. After one last bang on the door, footsteps retreated.

Coffa and the big male snored by the hearth.

"Alone at last," Michael sighed as he worked my shift lower, trailing kisses in its wake. He lingered at my navel.

My belly contracted in pleasure. Pleasurable sensations I never knew existed exploded within me. I kneaded his shoulders. Of their own volition, my legs parted.

He drew the shift and my nethergarment away. Part of me wanted to protest this last exposure of my modesty. And then the last of his garments fell away. I could not take my eyes off his smooth skin and well defined muscles. A thin line of hair, a shade darker than on his head, trickled down to his belly and . . . lower.

"Oh, my."

"Oh, my, indeed." He kissed me long and hard. His fingers fumbled ever lower in his quest to explore every inch of my body.

I think I returned the favor. Too much of my attention belonged to how delicious and warm and loved I felt with each new probing, each caress, and each wild kiss.

At last he shifted on top of me. I welcomed his weight as an extension of myself, a covering against the storm of sensations I barely understood.

We joined in mutual frenzy. The barriers of my mind shredded with my maidenhead. His love wrapped around me, enfolded my doubts, and twined with my own emotions.

Stars burst behind my closed eyes. I arched and drew him deeper into my mind and body.

We collapsed together, spent, replete.

A loud banging on the door startled us. Michael rolled off of me. The comforting haze of our joining faded.

Someone strummed an out of tune lute. Someone else sang a ribald ditty, off-key and out of tempo.

"Time to rejoin the party!" a third voice called. "Come out, come out, or we come in!"

Chapter 45

20 April, 1577. Chatsworth Manor, England.

"HE'S dead," Mary said. Her voice sounded flat and emotionless to Donovan's ear.

But he knew Mary Queen of Scots too well. The whiteness of her knuckles on her Breviary. Her plain wooden rosary that dangled from the book of prayers swung slightly from the tension in her hands.

And she had known the news he had to impart before he told her. How? Had she had something to do with it?

"James Hepburn, Earl of Bothwell, died on the fourth day of April of this year, in the dungeons of Dragsholm Castle in Denmark," Donovan reported as if reading the news from a penny broadsheet. He did not tell her that her husband had been chained to a pillar for years, quite mad. He did not want to think about the depths of bestiality the man had sunk to for the Danes to believe him a danger to himself as well as to his guards.

"I . . ." Mary stiffened and regained her composure. "We had heard that our husband was an honored guest of the king of Denmark."

"At first, Your Grace. Ten years ago, the Danes gave him refuge. A pawn to be played should you regain your throne."

"But as the years passed and the chance for our escape dwindled, he became less important to them than their treaties with England." She nearly spat the words.

"He is gone, Your Grace. No man stands between us now." Donovan took a presumptuous step closer. The heart-shaped locket seemed to burn through his shirt, begging him to touch it.

"No man stands between us, Donovan." She leaned her head upon his shoulder. "But one formidable woman does."

"Elizabeth," they said together on a single breath.

Then Mary straightened.

"If you would but give lip service to Elizabeth, tell her privately that you renounce your faith and your claim to her crown, she will allow us to marry." Donovan tried to hold her close.

She stepped away from his embrace.

"We could retire to Kirkenwood, or France, or Italy, live quietly, put politics and dynasties behind us," he pleaded.

"We would have a few moments of privacy, milord of Kirkenwood, to mourn our husband." Mary turned her back on him and his solution.

"Mary . . ."

She glared at him for his presumption.

"Our faith and our true right to the English throne are all that have sustained us these ten long years of imprisonment. Do not broach this subject again, milord."

"Your Grace." Donovan lowered his eyes and bowed slightly. His stomach roiled with disappointment. He had come here with hope in his heart and plans in his mind.

"We thank you for being the one to bring us this grievous news," Mary said on a softer tone. "We could not have borne the gloating in the demeanor of our jailer."

Donovan chanced a glance into her eyes. Tears brimmed there.

"Did you love him so much, Your Grace?" He relaxed a little. He still had a chance.

"Bothwell was strong. An exciting man." Her face became dreamy with memories.

"A dangerous man."

"Aye. That, too." She smiled in memory. Her open hand went to her breast as if reliving the enthrallment of his nearness. "He promised me much."

"And broke his promises in cowardly flight."

"Judicious retreat," Mary insisted. "I could not protect him from the ravening mob at the gates of the castle. They respected my position as their queen. I was safe. He would have hung before sunset had I not offered him escape through secret tunnels and passageways."

"And so he lingered ten long years alone in a solitary

dungeon. Had he seen his future clearly, he might have chosen to hang."

"Never," Mary gasped.

" 'Twas what I would choose," Donovan said quietly. His own future looked just as bleak and lonely. His family had shattered. Griff ruled at Kirkenwood. Betsy . . . Betsy ruled herself. The two made him feel most unwelcome. His diplomatic work for Elizabeth no longer satisfied him. He had nothing left but his memories.

Suddenly he could no longer tolerate the meager crumbs of love Mary doled out to him. The locket burned for him to touch it. He ignored the compulsion.

He and Martha had had a troubled marriage, but at least he had known she loved him, and he loved her.

"I leave you to mourn your husband, madam." He bowed himself out and fled down the stairs from her suite to the Hall.

Bess Hardwick stood there. She had read the official letter addressed to Mary before allowing Donovan to present it to the exiled queen. She sneered at him, gloating at this latest grief to descend upon her prisoner's shoulders.

Wordlessly, Donovan retreated. A bitter taste refused to leave his mouth.

Late spring 1577. The Mendip Hills near the Welsh Border.

Would this rain never end? Hal slogged through yet another swollen rill. The gorse drooped from the weight of water upon the budding tips of branches.

He lifted his nose, seeking prey. All he tracked was more rain upon the wet grasses and scrubby bushes. And mud. Lots and lots of mud.

His stomach growled in protest. A wave of dizziness weakened his knees. Not so much as a rabbit or squirrel stirred in this storm.

He trudged on, vaguely aware that his path carried him uphill.

A sudden itch between his shoulder blades made him

look about. His feet drifted off the vague game trail he'd been following. He'd walked three long paces before he realized he was stepping over shrubs and clumps of grass rather than around them.

"What?" He spun around, wary of danger.

Nothing was visible between the sheets of rain. Nothing could he scent other than universal wet. Nothing could he hear but the roar of the wind.

Still, something called to him.

"Why not?" He shrugged his shoulders and followed the subtle directive. "I've got nothing to lose. And whatever it is can't make life more uncomfortable than it already is." Hal touched the bruise on his jaw.

Last night, at the dark of the moon, he'd taken the chance to beg for a hot meal and a cup at a tavern on the old Roman road north of Wells. The landlord had promised him the meal and a cozy bed in the stable in return for heavy chores.

After chopping wood, hauling barrels, full and empty, and washing mountains of dishes, Hal had settled into a quiet corner of the taproom with his plate. The meal was hardly half eaten before a brawl broke out among the local patrons. Hal had dodged a series of blows while gulping as much food as possible.

Someone took offense at his neutrality and slammed a fist into his jaw. The sudden attack had raised the wolf in him. Snarling and biting, he'd fought for exit before the transformation took him. Fortunately, the cold rain had brought him to his senses before he sprouted fur or seriously hurt someone.

He'd been walking ever since. East and slightly north.

The land beneath his feet began to vibrate. Anxious. Eager. Excited. He sensed all those emotions and more. The rain eased a little. Visibility increased.

What was that atop the next ridge? Not a true ridge, more like a small plateau before the next soaring cliff face. Something stood up like . . .

"A faery ring," he breathed. Shelter of a sort.

The closer he got to the ring, the more distinct became the rough boulders that formed it. It was small. Well, most any ring of stones was small compared to the one that protected Kirkenwood Village, almost a mile in diameter.

The original one hundred stones had each stood taller than three men. Only about sixty of the Kirkenwood stones remained, and not all of them upright. Those that fell often became a wall of a cottage.

These stones barely reached Hal's waist. The circle enclosed land only a little larger than a good-sized farmhouse.

"Just a small ceremonial ring," he said. He talked to himself just to remind himself of his humanity. Like so many such rings, it stood isolated from any trace of civilization. No village or farm to welcome him. Not even an abandoned shepherds' cot to hide under until the rain eased.

Hal shook some of the wetness out of his eyes as he crested the hill. He examined the ring closely. Green fire still connected the stones. Powerful wards had activated the place. It guarded something.

It guarded a cave.

Hal shifted his attention to the narrow opening on the adjacent cliff face. Men had dressed two upright stones to frame the portal.

What lay within that it needed a faery ring to ward it?

"Only one way to find out." He set one cautious foot inside. A second step repulsed him with a slight burn.

"Magic!" Strong magic. He pushed against the barrier with his hand. It slid through with only slight resistance. Fading magic, he decided.

He pushed his entire body into the cave. Once he'd cleared the uprights, a blast of dry warmth replaced the damp chill of outside. He basked several moments in the relative comfort. Warm and dry only by contrast with the outside world.

Another barrier, not as strong as the first, made him pause a few steps farther along. Absolute blackness lay beyond. An atavistic dread made the hair on his back and nape stand up. A low growl rumbled from his throat.

He pushed himself onward once more. He burst through the magic and stumbled into a wide room of a natural cave. Looking back over his shoulder, he could see the outside quite clearly. Deeper in the interior remained devoid of light.

Remnants of a campfire sat in the exact center. Above it, a kind of chimney twisted toward the outside. Stashed against the sloping wall to the left of the fire were blankets, dried food, firewood and tinder, and torches. All were dusty and musty. No one had been here for a long, long time. Yet the supplies were perfectly preserved.

He fell on the jerked meat and dry cheese ravenously. He did not even think of poison or magical traps until the first pangs of hunger had eased. A thought brought fire to the tinder and wood. Soon he was warm and at least partially satisfied.

The torches beckoned to him. They teased him to explore deeper.

"Maybe I'll find more stores," he mumbled around a hunk of journey bread.

He'd lived in fear for so long now, he ignored the sense of dread that leadened his footsteps and made the darkness within so thick he felt as if he parted curtains. Cobwebs caught fire from the torch, flared briefly, then withered. The residents scuttled to the wall, away from the killing fire. So the magic barrier did not keep out spiders but kept the stores fresh and free of mold for human rather than animal consumption.

"An interesting spell."

He reached a fork in the tunnel. Two moldering skeletons lay together in the intimate dance of death. Hal did not bother to examine them. He'd seen enough death to last him a lifetime. These two ancients and their feud had nothing to do with the present.

All of the past influences the present, a feminine voice said softly into the back of his mind. He looked all around for the source. Nothing. No living being shared the air of this cave. Any ghosts that might dwell here had nothing to do with him.

Was that a chuckle from his unseen companion?

He shrugged it off and took the left-hand fork in the tunnel. It soon ended in a small room with ledges cut into the walls. More skeletons. The bones were broken and pushed aside. Any kind of grave goods had been looted centuries ago.

Hal returned to the fork and took the right-hand tunnel. Did the blank eyes of the skeletons follow his progress?

He made a quick ward against the evil eye, index and little finger extended from his clenched fist. He'd given up crossing himself before he left Paris. The Christian God would not protect him.

Then he saw it. The torch illuminated a round door made of bronze, hinged and bossed with iron. It looked like a giant targe—one of the round shields carried by Scots raiders. Taller than himself by two handspans, a man could easily step through it. A foolhardy man.

"What lies behind you?" he asked as his fingers traced the dragon's head at the center.

I can grant you great power, endless riches, and magic beyond your dreams if you only release me, a quiet voice said, deeper and harsher than the ghost who had taunted him earlier.

"Who are you?" Hal asked warily. He had a suspicion, but wanted it confirmed.

Your fondest dream and your greatest nightmare.

"A demon, I suspect."

The greatest of all demons. Your blood calls to me. You can break the seal and release it.

"No." Hal's breaths came rapid and shallow. Cold sweat broke out on his back. He needed to grow fur and run far from this place.

You must release me!

"I have no need of more demons in my life." Resolutely, Hal turned his back on the portal.

In the big room he gathered his meager possessions, two of the folded blankets, and as much food as he could stuff into his pockets and pack. The magical barriers offered no resistance to his exit.

Outside, the rain had stopped, and the sun peeked through fitful clouds. The green fire linking the stone circle seemed to flare in greeting.

"Hellfire and damnation, this is a good place to shelter." He dropped the pack.

"I can live with you, demon. But I won't even try to release you. I know what happens to your victims."

He marched back into his new home. It was warm and dry.

But was it safe?

As safe as any place else in the kingdom for a werewolf on the run.

Chapter 46

Summer 1578. Mortlake, England.

"DO you know anything about werewolves, Dr. Dee?" Hal asked Europe's foremost alchemist and magician.

The scholar peered over the top of his spectacles at Hal. His stringy brown hair fell forward, almost masking his eyes. But his overlarge nose broke through the veil of hair like the prow of a ship.

"Werewolves?" The scholar asked. A puzzled looked crossed his watery eyes. "As in lycanthropes?"

"Aye." Hal fidgeted with his cap. He did not like the man's intense scrutiny. Who knew how deep his probe might go.

"Many learned physicians have written about shape shifters. A most curious disease, they call it."

Hal sighed inwardly. He had been afraid of this. He needed help, not a lecture. While hunting, this last full moon he'd come upon benighted travelers. Almost, he'd succumbed to the lure of their hot sweet blood pulsing beneath all too fragile skin. The effort to run away and hunt elsewhere had cost him dearly in strength, control, and self-confidence.

"However," Dr. Dee continued without pausing. "I have come across many curious things in my travels." He rummaged through the crates and piles of books, minerals, drying herbs, and alchemical equipment for several moments.

Hal barely dared breathe.

"Ah, I knew I had unpacked it." He held up a girdle of blue-green satin, coarse wolf fur, and rough-cut gems.

"Where . . . where did you get that?" Hal's lungs hurt. His heart pounded loudly in his ears, and his knees shook. He groped for the high stool behind him and sat before he dropped to the floor in weakness.

"In Vienna. A Turkish artifact, I believe. Do you know it?"

"I have seen one very like it." Yassimine's girdle had yellow satin in it.

"I was told it plays an essential part in the ritual for making a werewolf." Dr. Dee laid the thing on a worktable at Hal's elbow. He stroked it lovingly.

Hal made certain no part of him touched the piece.

"The colors and combination of gems have an arcane significance I have not deciphered yet."

"So does the fur." Hal felt like he had to say something. "That is wolf fur. The girdle will make a werewolf. A lion's mane will make a werelion."

"Curious." Dr. Dee looked up at Hal. A smile brightened his countenance and cleared his eyes. "Have you seen the ritual?"

"No." He had not "seen" it. He'd been the object of it. But he could not tell Elizabeth's astrologer this. The good doctor was not known for his discretion.

"Pity. I would so like to know how it is done. Perhaps, if you know of a true werewolf, you could introduce me. I have many questions."

"You do not want to meet a true werewolf, Dr. Dee." Hal plunged into his planned speech. "We are plagued by one near Wells. So far the beast has eaten only sheep and deer. An occasional cow or pig. But just a few weeks ago, it threatened three travelers. They warded it off with a cross and Holy Water."

"I have heard that a silver sword will kill the beast."

"We think we might know the man. We would rather cure him of this curse."

"That has never been done, to my knowledge. All of the learned men who lay claim to cures admit that most, if not all, are only temporary."

"Is it possible the girdle could be used to reverse the ritual?" How does one reverse the sex act? Hal wondered. Perhaps if a man and woman lay together fully clothed and chaste?

But the woman would have to be a werewolf at the beginning of the ceremony, else she'd be one by the time it was finished.

"An interesting theory. I shall have to research it." Dr.

Dee scooped up the girdle before Hal could snatch it away from him. He folded it neatly and tucked it within the folds of his scholarly robes. "I should like to study this more under better light. The gems have many mystical properties."

"How will you research the topic? Few are willing to discuss it other than the physicians who insist lycanthropy is but a disease of the mind. And you report that most of them fail in their cures."

"I shall ask the angels," Dr. Dee said blandly. "I don't suppose you speak Enochian?"

"I am not familiar with that dialect." Hal peered at the alchemist skeptically. He'd heard a few things about the doctor's obsession with angels.

" 'Tis a most wondrous and complex language. My former partner, Mr. Kelly, was most fluent in it. We had many long discussions with the angels." Dr. Dee sighed.

Hal had heard a few things about the charlatan Mr. Kelly as well.

"Ah, well, the information will come when I need it. Will you stay to supper, Mr. Griffin?"

Hal shook his head, resigned to searching elsewhere. Not even the girdle could help him without a female werewolf willing to help him.

Summer 1578. Windsor Castle.

"What does she want with us this time?" Michael grumbled.

I straightened the pleats in the narrow ruff at the collar of his doublet. He immediately tugged at the starched lace.

"This is too tight," he complained.

"You are too used to the rough clothing we wear whilst traveling fast and hard." I tweaked my own ruff, grateful for the low-cut bodice of my court gown. Nothing enclosed my throat. Michael's tight male doublet rested around his.

"You are one to talk," Michael groused. "You walk as if you had just dismounted from a fortnight in the saddle."

He swatted my bottom but struck only petticoats and hoops.

"I did just dismount from a fortnight in the saddle. Last night."

"As oft as we travel from one end of Europe to the other at breakneck speeds, you'd think we'd be used to the sore muscles."

"And the scrapes and chafes and bruises," I sighed. This latest mission for Sir Francis Walsingham had taken us from Rome to Vienna to Madrid, all on horseback at bone-jarring gaits. Then a mad dash to Lisbon where we had taken ship for home. We had traveled faster than any courier. Surely Elizabeth had not yet had word of our return in the wee hours of the morning.

"You'd think Elizabeth would leave us alone to do our work!" Michael began pacing as I applied the white face powder expected of ladies at court.

"You sound more and more like Sir Francis every day."

"Well, 'tis the truth. Elizabeth knows nothing of spy work. She should leave it to the experts."

"She does. Then she demands our reports. She knows more than she lets the world know."

He handed me a light shawl. "I must say, I find your journey leathers more attractive than that contraption." He swatted the farthingale once more.

I smiled slightly.

"Although, this dress delights my eye." He ran a delicate finger along the neckline of the bodice, across the tops of my breasts.

"Later, Michael." I rose up on tiptoe to brush a kiss across his bearded cheek. He never bothered to shave while we traveled. Lately, we'd spent more time on the road than at home, so he had left the beard. "Her Majesty demands our presence forthwith."

He mumbled something. I did not catch the words, but I understood the content of complaint.

A footman awaited us outside the door of the retiring chamber assigned to us at Windsor. I gestured Coffa and her mate Mawr to remain stretched out on the cool stone floor by the balcony where they could catch the breeze off the river.

Deep clouds pressed the air into thick and sultry waves of heat. They also foretold a summer thunderstorm. But the rain and wind would not bring relief for some hours yet.

Neither dog seemed inclined to move anyway. Coffa was pregnant again and preferred her rest. I did not expect to need her keen hearing and scent to magnify my own observations. Mawr either slept or ran. No alternatives. His presence at court would be more a hindrance than a help.

We came into Elizabeth's presence in the gardens. She strolled the winding pathways, waving a silk-and-lace fan as she talked to Burghley; Walsingham; Christopher Hatton, Vice Chamberlain of her Household; and other high ranking members of her government. The usual mob of courtiers, diplomats, and ladies-in-waiting trailed behind her, anxiously awaiting a summons to her side.

The moment I saw Elizabeth, I knew something was wrong. A thousand worms crawling up my back could not have made me more uncomfortable.

"What," Michael whispered. He scanned the crowd, instantly alert. Three years of marriage and working together had taught him to be wary of my instincts.

"I do not know," I replied, also scanning the crowd for a face or form that did not belong.

"Look with your magic," Michael suggested.

I glared at him. He knew how many spells of mine had led to the deaths of innocents. Still he asked me to use it whenever his own keenly trained but mundane senses failed him.

I needed to think about the magic, calm, and prepare myself to use it. I quickly turned my head away from him. In moving so quickly, I caught a glimpse of something unnatural out of the corner of my eye.

A black aura.

Reading auras wasn't really magic, I told myself. No one would know that I did it. Even another magician. For surely the slight man had to be a magician to produce such a densely dark cloud of mist about him.

I did not allow my glance to linger on the man, or the woman beside him who was engulfed by the black miasma.

Michael spotted the man almost at the same moment as

I, more for his newness to court than anything sinister in his appearance.

"Who?" he whispered.

"Spanish by his dress."

"And the beauty beside him?"

Her thick black hair and swarthy skin, along with dainty features and deep, dark eyes, made her stand out in the crowd of sun-starved Englishwomen. The cut of her bodice above an ample bosom drew the eye of every man around her. If she breathed hard, she'd pop out of the restraints of black-and-silver fabric. From the panting looks of the men around her, all were hoping she'd do just that.

She walked with the fluid confidence of a woman aware of her femininity and willing to use it to gain her ends.

"Courtesan," I spat.

"Obviously. But who is she?" Even my own husband fell victim to her exotic sensuality.

I tugged at his sleeve to draw him back toward Elizabeth and Walsingham.

"Lady Deirdre!" Elizabeth nearly fell upon me from her discourse with her Vice Chamberlain on whether the newly imported love apple growing at her feet was indeed poisonous. She embraced me warmly the moment I rose from my curtsy. "You live. We were so worried about you." The queen placed my hand within the crook of her elbow.

"You look tired. Your journey was long and difficult. You must rest more," she continued walking. The crowd of officials and retainers flowed and shifted to accommodate me and my husband.

"Sir Michael and I returned late last night, Your Majesty," I explained. "We did not expect a summons so early this morning."

"But you are safe. That is the important thing," Walsingham said. He seemed to breathe a little easier than he had a few moments ago.

"Aye. We suffered a few cuts and sprains along the way. The agents of the Bishop of Rome are most persistent," Michael explained.

"We will have your report in detail later." Walsingham kept a possessive hand upon Michael's shoulder.

Another day, I might welcome this obvious show of affection from the queen and members of her council. Today, the slight man and his swarthy mistress kept moving closer to us. My skin itched with the need to run from him.

Why had I not brought the dogs with me? They could sniff the man and inform me of everything he had touched or eaten in the last week. Coffa could let me know if he had worked magic in that time as well.

The conversation drifted over my head while I concentrated upon the Spaniard and his mistress. I learned little from mundane observations. With reluctance, I loosed a little magic probe toward the man's mind.

It shattered.

Pain lashed my eyes like a knife blade.

I reared back.

Michael kept me from collapsing. I leaned into him, just a little until my balance returned. The pain did not go away.

No one seemed to notice the short interplay between us. We'd become practiced at avoiding attention while I probed as part of our work for Walsingham.

"What?" the spymaster asked.

I should have known I could keep nothing from Sir Francis.

"The Spaniard with the exotic lady clinging to his side? Does he have a hook to replace his left hand?"

"One of Mendoza's minions." He mentioned the Spanish ambassador. "Yes, he does use a hook instead of a left hand. Come to think on it, I do not believe his name has ever been given."

"Try . . ." I swallowed hard. "Try calling him *El Lobison*."

Both Michael and Walsingham looked at me strangely.

"At our court?" Elizabeth hissed. She must have overheard our whispered conversation.

"Aye, Majesty. I have encountered the wall around his thoughts before. No two magicians could erect the same barrier. And I would know him by the hook that replaces his left hand."

The queen chanced a glance over her shoulder. Her eyes narrowed in speculation. "Hatton," she called to her Vice Chamberlain, "inform Señor Mendoza we wish an interview in private. Within the hour." Immediately, she ceased her leisurely stroll through the gardens and marched toward Windsor Castle.

The rest of us hastened in her wake.

Once inside, Michael and I were ushered into one of the smaller salons. Only Walsingham and Hatton joined us. Leicester seemed out of favor again or away from court.

"Tell them, Sir Francis," Elizabeth ordered the moment she was seated.

"Yester eve, I received a . . . most interesting package."

The air in the room suddenly grew heavier. I knew I would not like the news.

Michael and I remained silent.

"An unseen, unannounced visitor left a jeweled box upon my doorstep. A thing of beauty and great value." He cleared his throat.

"Tell them!" Elizabeth almost screeched.

"Inside the box, wrapped in gold tissue cloth was the severed head and hand of . . . of Jimmie Henderson."

The world went white around me, and my knees buckled. Michael fared no better.

"We worked with him in Vienna. He gave us access to many important men close to the Holy Roman Emperor," Michael choked. I feared he would faint before I did. "Jimmie was supposed to meet us in Madrid. We had to leave before he arrived."

"Clearly, he arrived before you did," Walsingham said.

"The box was a message," Elizabeth spat the words, more angry than grieved. "Henderson was betrayed. King Philip, uncle to the Holy Roman Emperor, wishes us to know that he found one of our spies."

A moment of silence followed while I daubed my tears and Michael mastered his emotions.

"Read them the note," Elizabeth commanded when I finally turned dry eyes to her.

Walsingham drew a roll of parchment from his sleeve. He read a long passage in Latin.

I did not need to hear the words to understand the message. It implied that Michael and I had been revealed as Elizabeth's spies and would receive the same horrible fate soon.

" 'Twas not King Philip who sent you the box," I said quietly. "He would have executed the man publicly."

"Mendoza?" Elizabeth asked.

"The ambassador would be more subtle. 'Twas The Master of Werewolves. His slave probably ate the rest of the body. The next full moon she will be loosed again. This time in London." I gagged. So did the others.

Chapter 47

Summer 1579. La Palais de la Louvre, Paris.

I CANNOT believe I have returned to Paris without The Master leading me in chains, Hal thought as he adjusted his tightly fitting crimson doublet one last time. He doffed his hat and combed the long white feather. The last time he had worn crimson and a feathered cap he had been presented to Queen Elizabeth. Today, he made the acquaintance of Queen Regent Catherine de Médici and her son, King Henri III of France. He hoped this interview would fare better than the one with Elizabeth. He needed to keep his head, for Walsingham, for England, and for Elizabeth.

He needed to do this to prove his own worth to himself. And to Dee.

Hal's hunger for a cure had led him to ask one question too many. An agent for Walsingham had overheard him. The spymaster had sought him out, with a job that just might lead him to *El Lobison* and a few answers. But this time, Hal might approach from a position of power rather than vulnerability.

A page signaled him forward, through the long line of courtiers. Hal drew a fat roll of parchment from his sleeve. His credentials, provided by Walsingham.

Feeling awkward and uncertain, he swept a deep bow before the French royals. Henri gestured Hal to stand with a graceful hand. The young king surveyed Hal's face and figure, finishing with a smile. Catherine held out her stubby fingers for Hal's kiss and then for his papers. She looked like a fat, dark spider, crouched upon her throne, waiting to devour whatever hapless fly encroached upon her web.

Her small, beady eyes looked right past Hal as if he did
not exist.

"Majesty," Hal addressed Henri, "I must inform you of
the death of my grandfather, Le Conte de Loup-Blanc."
Not exactly a lie. Walsingham had coerced the ancient
Frenchman to adopt Hal in exchange for an undisclosed
amount of cash. The old man paid his debts and spent the
remaining few sous on a cask of wine, which he proceeded
to drink in copious amounts until his death—within a
fortnight.

"A sad loss for France and yourself," Henri said with
some feeling. He, too, extended his hand for Hal's kiss. He
allowed his fingers to tighten around Hal's for just a fraction of a minute. An invitation or a plea?

"You never met the old reprobate. He drank himself
useless for the better part of forty years," Catherine spat
at her youngest and least favorite son, the only one of three
kings she had birthed who looked to live long enough to
sire an heir. Assuming Henri, previously le Duc d'Anjou
and betrothed of Elizabeth of England, found a wife who
interested him more than his male playmates and friends.

"The deeds and will are in order." Catherine handed the
documents back to Hal.

"Henri Loup-Blanc, we will confirm you in the title at
noon on the morrow," the king said quickly, before his
mother could contradict him. "You will dine with us after."

"*Merci,* Majesty," Hal replied, hoping his accent had improved over the last two months of tutelage at the Chateau
Loup-Blanc. He hoped he never had to return to the crum-
bling country house. Best to let the roof fall in and leave
the rest to the rats and bats that already infested the place.

Catherine lifted her hand in signal to the steward. Her
servant grabbed Hal's elbow roughly.

Hal's upper lip curled, baring his teeth. He quickly covered his lupine response with an openmouthed smile.

"Move along, you are not the only petitioner today," the
steward said, tugging on Hal's arm.

"*A demain, Majesties.*" Hal bowed again, sweeping his
cap low until the feather brushed the parquet floor.

"*Un moment, Monsieur le Conte,*" Henri stayed his departure. "Do you fence, perchance?"

Walsingham had told Hal to make Henri a friend; to

become his confidant; wean him away from dependence upon his mother *and* the de Guise faction.

"*Mais oui, Majesty.* I am expert in both rapier and saber." A slight exaggeration. Hal knew the forms and rules of swordplay. No lad growing up on the border between England and Scotland completely avoided the lessons and drills. He had not wielded a weapon since . . . since his last journey to Paris.

"Join us now." Henri jumped down from the dais. "*Maman,* you can deal with the rest of the petitioners much better than we can."

"Majesty. . ."

Henri forestalled his mother with a casual salute. Then he grabbed Hal and nearly ran for the nearest exit. He led Hal through the maze of rooms to an inner courtyard. Half a dozen young men, already there, had stripped off doublets and cloaks to engage in contests with naked blades. A few sported bloody streaks upon sleeves and ribs.

The smell of blood sent Hal's wolf senses pounding through his veins; the smell sweeter than spun sugar.

"Beautiful, are they not?" Henri asked. He gazed at the duelists with longing. A different kind of lust fueled the king than Hal.

"*Mon dieu,*" Hal breathed. "They are sweet indeed." Inwardly, he cursed Walsingham. The spymaster had to know the hungers that drove Henri. So why had he sent Hal into this nest of catamites?

Because Hal dared not indulge in intimacies with anyone, male or female. Males presented less temptation to him.

Henri turned a brilliant smile upon Hal. "Sweet, indeed. Come, let us join them." He shed his doublet and cap and dropped them upon the ground. A servant grabbed them before they touched soil, folded them, and placed them neatly upon a bench beside the weapons cache.

Hal cared for his own clothes, using the homely movements to inspect each young noble in the yard, their weapons, naked sabers mostly, and their fighting style. Muscles rippled, smooth skin glistened with sweat. They breathed deeply in rhythm with their strokes, each movement timed and executed with precision and grace. "Saints preserve me, I'm in trouble," he muttered.

Henri selected a weapon, a rapier thankfully, and flexed

the blade. It bent and sprang back with a sharp twang. Apparently the king did not like the sound or the tension or the dullness of the tip. He tried another and another until he found one to his liking.

Not knowing what else to do, Hal reached for a talent he had used rarely these past years. He opened his mind to the king's thoughts. At first, he caught only a hint of satisfaction with the rapier.

Hal picked up a weapon, one that Henri had not discarded. He, too, flexed the blade. The tension felt fine to him. He discarded it anyway. He picked up approval from Henri and the idea that the blade had bent too much. The third rapier Hal handled seemed to meet the king's exacting standards. Hal could sense no difference between it and the others, but he settled for it.

"Engagé!" Henri shouted without waiting for a salute; a complete violation of the polite rules that governed nonlethal combat.

Hal parried sharply. Too far, he left his chest open. The sharp tip of Henri's blade came at him. Hal's wolf reactions kicked in. He leaned back and evaded the hit with the width of a hair to spare.

Black frustration shrouded the king's aura. He wanted the win at all costs. Rules meant little to him. He needed to establish superiority from the onset so he could dominate the relationship and dictate the terms of surrender.

A surrender Hal had no intention of giving him.

Suddenly he knew why Walsingham had sent him, in particular, on this mission. Henri needed to be beaten for his own good. Walsingham knew that Hal's wolf instincts would always demand that he remain on top in any battle.

Before he could think about it, Hal circled Henri's blade in a classic riposte. Senses wide open, he knew his opponent's next move. Parry, counterattack, evade, *pres,* remise. With the movements came a sense of familiarity. He'd done this before.

On and on they engaged, pressing each other forward and back. Hal's focus narrowed to Henri's hand, his eyes, and his thoughts. Awareness of the king's blade came last, secondary to foreseeing the next move. The sounds of other duels around them faded, then ceased. The two of them might be alone on some isolated moor fighting over sheep or barley. Those were battles Hal understood.

Circle, *pres,* attack, parry, evade.

Sweat dripped into Henri's eyes. Hal ignored the perspiration soaking his back and chest. His blood sang with the exultation of matching wits and weapons with an equal.

A door slammed. Henri's attention wavered. He broadcast a fear of his mother encroaching upon the exclusively male activity.

Hal pushed forward. "*Touché,* Your Majesty," he said quietly. A spot of blood appeared on Henri's shirtsleeve.

Around them a wave of applause drowned out Henri's curse.

Hal withdrew one long stride, politely waiting for Henri's next move. The crowd pressed closer.

Henri surged forward without an *en garde* or *engagé* thought to warn Hal. His slim blade slid between ribs and penetrated Hal's chest beside his heart.

Blood shot forth from the wound. Cold air whistled in Hal's throat. Pain seared outward.

The crowd fell silent, then gasped as one.

Hal's knees buckled. He went down, holding the blade. Every bounce of the thin sword sent new waves of pain through his chest. His arms grew weak. Blackness encroached upon his vision.

But the blade was steel, not silver. Hal jerked the blade free of muscle and bone. The fire in the wound robbed him of balance. Before his hands touched the ground, he felt his pierced lung seal. Breathing became easier.

"*Mon Dieu,*" the king whispered. He dropped to his knees. "*Mon ami,* speak to me." He tore strips along the hem of his shirt, wrapping the fine lawn about Hal's wound with enough pressure to crack a rib on a normal mortal.

"I shall live." Hal made his tone breathier and fainter than he needed to. Already the bleeding slowed to a seep.

"*Oui,* you shall live, here in the palace until you recover. We will tend to your hurts ourself." Henri signaled for his comrades to fetch a litter.

"Nay, Majesty. I thank you for your concern from the bottom of my heart. 'Tis only a flesh wound along the ribs. I shall mend on my own, quite well." Hal had no intention of allowing the man's clumsy efforts to discover how unnaturally Hal healed.

"We will send for the royal physician." Henri snapped his fingers. A servant disappeared into the palace.

The litter arrived. Hal allowed the men to tend him. As they lifted the litter, Henri grabbed Hal's hand with both of his own. "We must make amends. What do you wish? More land? A vineyard?"

"I ask only your friendship, Majesty," Hal said quietly.

"Granted. You will remain at court as long as you like."

"I must return to my own lands, soon, Majesty."

"When you are well. Only then, *mon ami.*"

Hal nodded his assent. By morning Henri would spill all of his secrets, personal and political to Hal. The day after, Hal planned a whispering campaign against de Guise and the Holy League.

Walsingham would be pleased.

But Hal was no closer to *El Lobison* and a cure.

Chapter 48

1580. The Crown and Anchor Tavern, London.

ELIZABETH had a raging session with Ambassador Mendoza and exiled the Master of Werewolves and his slave. Rumor placed The Master and his shape-changing slave in Spain, in Italy, in Austria. Everywhere but England.

I had heard that Sir Walsingham had headed the troops who escorted *El Lobison* to his ship. They all carried crosses, swords coated in silver, and flagons of Holy Water.

Reports of werewolves attacking in packs dwindled. I heard only occasional reports of a single livestock kill. I prayed that *El Lobison* had taken his creatures back to Europe with him.

Had Hal followed him?

Sir Walsingham and Elizabeth decided that Michael and I should adopt a more normal life. A visible life that pretended we were not spies.

As soon as Coffa whelped again, we sold her puppies for enormous fees. None of the little ones came to me as a familiar, and I breathed a sigh of relief at this sign that Coffa would remain with me for a time. The money bought The Crown and Anchor Tavern in Westminster, not too far from the Spanish Embassy.

All of our employees came upon Walsingham's recommendation. They all spoke at least one foreign language, usually Spanish.

Once we had settled in, I vowed to visit my father's grave. Perhaps there I could unlock the mysteries of his journals.

Somehow Michael, Elizabeth, Walsingham, and fate kept me from traveling to my father's grave, alone or with an escort. My craving for a connection to the man who had sired me smoldered in the back of my heart. I felt incomplete.

Perhaps if I had conceived in the next few years, I could have put aside my loneliness for family. Every time Michael and I departed our snug tavern for a spy mission, I thanked fate that no children encumbered our travel; not for lack of trying. Michael and I always found good excuses to go off by ourselves, under a haystack, in a faery circle of mushrooms, or in our bedroom. If we had had children to leave behind, I would worry constantly about them and possibly endanger ourselves through lack of concentration.

Many employees of the Spanish Embassy gathered at the Crown and Anchor Tavern, our tavern. Michael and I played host and serving wench there whenever Walsingham did not command us to travel on the queen's behalf. Another of Walsingham's trusted employees managed the place for us when we were required elsewhere. We all spoke and understood Spanish, French, and Latin. We overheard as much of what went on in Ambassador Mendoza's household as the ambassador himself.

Most of his correspondence to Mary Queen of Scots passed through our hands first. Not all of it continued on its way to the exiled queen. The single letter that mentioned Milord of Kirkenwood—my Uncle Donovan—as a possible coconspirator did not reach either Mary or Elizabeth. Not even Michael saw that letter. I consigned it to the fire.

Our tavern became a hotbed of gossip in several languages. Michael and I listened carefully to it all; sorting the truth from the chaff became our greatest challenge.

We learned that Leicester had begun an affair with a maternal cousin of Elizabeth, Lettice Knollys, her chief lady-in-waiting, and the wife of the Earl of Essex, long before the earl himself discovered his wife's infidelity. The affair had been going on since 1576.

No one dared tell Elizabeth, even Leicester's enemies. The bearer of bad news might suffer the same punishment as the offender.

When Essex died in Ireland, Leicester hastened to marry his new love—in secret—completely abandoning Douglas Sheffield and his son by her. The legitimacy of the son was debated hotly for many years.

Elizabeth threw her former lover into the Tower when

she finally discovered what he had done. She wept for days that her own refusal to marry him had finally driven him into another's arms in his desperate quest for an heir. A crisis in the war in the Netherlands ensured Leicester's release from prison. Elizabeth sent him to aid the Dutch in their rebellion against Spanish domination.

Uncle Donovan wrote to me often about his work in Edinburgh—never a word about Griff or Betsy or Kirkenwood. Hal disappeared, as if he had dropped off the face of the Earth.

Big dogs do not live long, ten to twelve years at the most. Rarely do they successfully breed after the age of six. Coffa had already reached that age.

My beloved dog did not come into heat again for two years. I feared that this meant not only the end of the line of familiars and the Pendragons they chose, but my end as well. I would die with my dog; both of us heirless.

My heart filled with fears and disappointments I could not impart to Michael, or Elizabeth, or even to Uncle Donovan. Our letters kept us in each other's hearts, but the distance of time and place stretched intimacy and trust. I needed Hal. Only he would truly understand my frustrations and inadequacies.

Michael pretended that nothing had changed between us, that we were still best friends and comrades. But I saw the pain in his eyes when he looked at me. I sensed his heartache that I did not love him as I loved Hal.

At last, in 1579, at the great age of nine, Coffa came into heat for the last time. She sought out Mawr with desperation and mated. Sixty-two days later she whelped five pups. Four males and one female runt who did not look to live long. After several long nights of sitting up with Coffa and her babies, the little female, mostly black in coloring with only a little brindled brown in her beard and ears, broke through her lethargy and began to thrive. On the day she opened her eyes, Coffa brought her to me and dumped her into my lap— as if she rid herself of a troublesome burden. She then waddled off to sulk in a corner, refusing to nurse her pups for several hours.

I went to her and held her great head in my lap for a long time. Her mind and emotions remained closed to me. She had already given up.

I thought my heart would break that day.

Coffa survived only long enough to wean her pups. Mawr died soon after. He had reached the great age of eight. His heart could no longer support his massive body.

I cried myself to sleep every night for a month afterward. The new puppy licked my tears dry and snuggled into my heart as my husband, my lost cousin, and my family had not.

She became Coffa, Remembrance, as well.

From my father's journals I had managed to glean that the Earl of Oxford was a secret Catholic. Elizabeth would hear none of it. She loved the flamboyant earl and bet heavily on his triumph of arms in the tournaments.

Then, in 1580, Michael and I discovered a plot.

One night in early spring, while thunderstorms raged and lightning cast eerie shadows with its too-white light, a stranger entered our little establishment.

A knot of theatergoers sang the latest bawdy song that night. Their voices rose above the constant noise of rowdy voices, clanging tankards, and many feet stomping on the rush-covered floor.

> " 'Tis sweeter far than sugar fine
>   And pleasanter than Muscadine.
>   And if you please, fair maid, to stay
>   A little while to sport and play
> I will give you the same, Watkins ale called by name,
>   Or else I were to blame, in truth, fair maid.
>
> " 'Good sir,' quoth she again. 'If you will take the pain,
>   I shall not refrain, nor be dismayed.'
>   He took his maiden then aside
>   And led her where she was not spied
>   And told her many a pretty tale,
>   And gave her well of Watkins ale."

They hushed at sight of the man. I knew all the sounds and moods of this place intimately. This quiet came out of respect rather than fear or surprise.

The stranger held his hands clasped before him as he paused in the doorway, dripping with rain. I knew that gesture from my travels on the continent. He was a Catholic priest. Probably a member of the Society of Jesus. Only the Jesuits traveled incognito. All other ordained clerics were required to wear a cassock and carry a rosary at all times.

Catholic priests were forbidden in England. Only Jesuits came here disguised.

Shy Coffa poked her head into the great room from the kitchen to see what caused the disruption.

A new clap of thunder shook the foundations of the tavern. It seemed to startle the patrons out of their stupefaction and back into the normal rhythm of sounds. The normal smells of spilled beer, cooking meat, sweat, and wet wool rose up from the rushes in a comforting miasma. They seemed to have been missing along with the sounds as we took the measure of the stranger.

They did not resume their raucous rendering of their song.

I hurried to the side of my husband for fresh beer for the newcomer.

"Society of Jesus," I mouthed the words.

Michael half nodded. Not much of a gesture, but enough for me. He signaled for one of the other wenches to cater to our regular patrons.

For the past six years a number of Englishmen had returned home after taking orders in the Pope's private order of priests and lay soldiers. They had a secret printing press and dispensed inflammatory pamphlets against the queen and the Church of England almost at will.

One of Michael's missions was to find that press and burn it.

I plunked a new tankard of beer in front of the man. "Welcome, stranger," I said in the rough accent of the streets.

He barely looked up at me. "Have you food this night, good madam?"

"Aye. There's a haunch roasting, and a pudding. Warm your belly good on a night like this. Not much in the way of greens. Too early." I prattled on about the wet weather and the late sowing, and the storm, much as any other wench would.

"Just bring me a trencher." He cut short my river of words. "And another pitcher. I expect a friend."

"Will he be wanting a trencher, too?" I stared at him with a surly frown, hands on hips, and chin thrust out belligerently. He'd insulted the ritual of tavern patrons in these parts by not sharing in the gossip. I knew him then for newly come from the Jesuit college in either Douai or Rome. (They never did teach those men common manners and the art of blending into society. Always considering themselves above such things.) He'd have to speak a few more words for me to detect the subtle inflection of French or Italian that might invade his speech to know which college produced him.

Before I could serve up a platter of food, another stranger entered the Crown and Anchor.

A tall and well-made man with broad shoulders and well-turned calves. An active man. Medium coloring, medium blue eyes, a patchy beard that looked as if it would peel off if he spilled his beer on it.

Not a stranger to Michael and me, despite his rude clothing, stooped posture, and fake beard. We had spent too many hours skulking around the edges of Court to mistake Edward de Vere, the Earl of Oxford for anything but the queen's champion in the last tournament.

I prayed that he would look past my kerchief and simple clothing. Most nobles viewed tavern denizens as peasants and therefore beneath their notice.

I consigned shy Coffa to the kitchen with a thought. My wolfhound was too unusual to be overlooked, even by Oxford. Coffa's mental snort of resignation seemed almost audible. Michael delivered the wooden plate with a half-loaf bread trencher heaped with pork and drippings. The yellow round of baked pudding was squashed into a corner. A sloppy presentation typical of other taverns, but not ours. He kept his head bowed and his mouth closed.

Oxford and the stranger dismissed him curtly.

Neither of them drank very much. I had no excuse to refill their beer. Any time one of us came within eavesdropping distance, they ceased speaking.

Other patrons came and went. They grew loud again, singing and slapping the wenches' bottoms.

Oxford and the unknown Jesuit lingered long, nursing their single tankard apiece.

"You have to do it, Deirdre," Michael whispered to me.

He grabbed my arm just above the elbow and squeezed hard. I could feel the skin bruising beneath his fingers.

"Michael, no, I . . ." I never had a good reason for not working magic. But I always hesitated, remembering the innocent lives lost when I wove spells.

The Pendragon is given gifts for a reason.

Finally, I did what I hated doing. I had delayed almost too long.

I concentrated hard on the flow of silent words coming from the men's minds.

At first I heard only an occasional vowel sound. Then the consonants began to fall into place. Words became sentences.

"In answer to your question, the Pope writes, 'There is no doubt that whosoever sends Elizabeth out of the world with the pious intention of doing God's service, not only does not sin, but gains merit,' " the Jesuit said softly.

"Then there is no sin in this murder?" Oxford almost beamed with joy.

"None. Fear not. Our plans may move ahead," the Jesuit reassured him.

"A ship awaits just offshore. At the dark of the moon, a launch will beach just north of Great Yarmouth at midnight. They will wait only until midnight the next night for you to bring her," Oxford said.

"Will our coconspirator provide the troops to storm the manor at Sheffield?"

"Aye. We will have Mary free from her jail three nights hence."

"Her uncle and cousin in France have gathered an army to mount the invasion in her name," the Jesuit continued. "The Papal Bull reconfirming Elizabeth's excommunication is ready to publish." His eyes gleamed with fervor.

"I must know the name of your coconspirator," he continued. "His Holiness must have only true Catholics involved in this Crusade."

"Milord of Kirkenwood requests that his name be withheld from the official report."

Chapter 49

"DEE!" Michael nearly screamed in my ear. "Dee, wake up." He shook me harshly.

I risked opening one eye. The great white light and roaring in my ears had subsided a mite. Enough to concentrate. I assessed my body and my senses with slow deliberation. All the while Michael fussed over me, dabbing cool water on my temples and chafing my wrists between his two hands.

Around us, the tavern crowd, much diminished with the waning of the storm, carried on their usual evening ruckus.

"Oxford?" I asked quietly.

"Gone for the nonce." Michael reached an arm around my shoulders and helped me to sit.

Apparently, I had collapsed behind the bar where we tapped the kegs.

"His companion?"

"Still here. Nursing another tankard."

I roused enough to peek around the end of the bar. Sure enough, the stranger sat at the same table near the back wall, drinking long and deep from his cup.

Stranger no more. I knew his name and his origin.

"He is Robert Parsons, newly come from Rome. A Jesuit as we supposed. He has a mission. Pope Gregory has not sanctioned the details of the plot, only the general purpose." How could I reveal my uncle's contribution to the new conspiracy?

I did not even think to discount his involvement. His love for Mary Queen of Scots had smoldered long and deep in his heart. He had taken great risks before just to visit her. What would he do for the opportunity to free her?

"We have to stop them." I struggled out of Michael's grasp to stand.

He held me back. "Easy, love. What is so important to raise you from a deep swoon?"

I wanted to throw my arms about his neck and hold him close to my heart. Would he still love me if I told him of my uncle's involvement in the face of the brewing conspiracy?

Coffa eased out of the kitchen and tried to nose her way between us. I batted her aside, keeping my eyes on Michael's face and my emotions under control. My familiar dodged my waving hands and slipped to the opposite side. She added her rough tongue against my cheek and hand to help rouse me.

I tolerated her ministrations because that was easier than making her cease.

"Oxford and Parsons seek to infiltrate Sheffield Manor and free Mary. Though I doubt Oxford will participate directly. He is too fond of his own skin to take such risks. The conspirators will spirit Mary to France where de Guise and the Holy League will proclaim her queen of England. The Pope will reissue his predecessor's Bull of Excommunication for Elizabeth. France will have its excuse to invade England."

"When?" Michael stood, bringing me with him. He kept an arm about my waist.

"Three nights hence, at the dark of the moon."

Hal would be at his weakest. I could not count on him for help, even if I could find him.

Betsy? She resided closer to Uncle Donovan than I. Would she intercept her father—if I could break through her magical barriers? My memories of her made me think she would reject my pleas simply because they came from me.

Still, I had to try.

"We must alert Lord Burghley and Sir Francis," Michael said. He still held me close. Under the cover of a marital embrace, our employees could not overhear us.

"No!" I could not take the chance the Secretary of Treasury and the queen's spymaster would learn of Uncle Donovan's involvement before I could extricate him.

"Lord Burghley will want to counter the plot with an army. A pitched battle will only publicize the attempt and make martyrs of Mary and any killed in the fight. The plot must be thwarted silently, secretly." My determination banished the last of the dizziness.

"Are you certain?" Michael looked at me skeptically.

I pressed myself against his chest and clutched the hand that wanted to explore above my waist.

"Yes, I am certain. You and I alone, together, must do this."

Coffa leaned into us both, drooling to join the affection.

"Not alone." Michael ruffled Coffa's ears and she rumbled with doggy bliss. "Never truly alone." He sighed.

"Lately, she has taken to sleeping in the kitchen. She prefers the warmth of the fires." I snuggled against him.

He kissed me then, in full view of the few lingering patrons. They applauded and cheered.

"Don't you men have homes to go to?" Michael called, reaching for the closing bell.

Grumbling and laughing at the same time, the men cleared the great room.

"We should be on our way," I said hesitantly.

" 'Twill wait an hour." He nuzzled my neck.

"We need to talk, Michael."

"On the road. An hour hence." Michael grabbed my hand and dragged me up the ladder to the loft above the kitchen.

March 1580. East Midlands.

Hal lifted his nose to scent the air. Clean cold air filled with moisture and not the odor of another human for many miles around. So much more pleasant than the warmer, more crowded atmosphere of Paris. For nearly a year he had moved back and forth between the village of Loup-Blanc and court, always timing his absence from Paris at the full moon.

During his time in Paris he had eased Henri III of France toward independence of thought and action. No longer did

Catherine de Médici, or Francis Duc de Guise dictate the young man's actions without question.

For nearly a year Hal had listened closely for any hint of a rumor about *El Lobison* or werewolf attacks.

Nothing.

Now he planned to sped a few precious weeks of solitude in his lair in the west of England. He could loose the tight controls of his wolf that civilization enforced upon him. Walsingham could wait for his reports.

He caught a taste of the newcomer on the wind.

Wariness raised the hair on his spine and arms. Territorial imperative roared through his blood.

Come! A compulsion swirled around him.

The Master and his slave had returned to England after nearly five years absence.

Come to me, now, my baby Pendragon.

Hal had never questioned the magic within the faery ring that protected the lair. This summons by The Master was the only magic that penetrated the circle.

Hal grew wary of the magical allure tinged with the scent of Yassimine's musky perfume.

Once and for all, he would end *El Lobison's* tyranny.

Two days past the full moon, he packed a few belongings and a purse full of coins. He set off at an easy lope. His wolf senses ebbed. Still he followed the call with ease. And determination.

Three days until the dark of the moon. Hal's strength neared its weakest. The Master's summons was at its strongest.

He stopped in his tracks, holding his breath. After one hundred heartbeats, the urgency of the call waned. Hal proceeded forward, measuring each step carefully. Too easy to run into The Master's waiting arms.

His waiting trap.

Hal aimed his steps a little to the north. He wanted to circle around the source of the call, take its measure, learn its weaknesses. Then he would attack. From the back, as a coward, if necessary.

Anything to rid himself of The Master's insidious demands.

A new scent wafted on the wind. Hal jerked his head right and left seeking the source, seeking an identity.

Fast upon the heels of the odor came a sound. Soft at first, then louder. The faint tinkle of bells, silver bells singing sweetly. The tune . . .

He tried humming it, almost recognizing it from his childhood. Sort of like a lullaby, but more, richer, fuller, more complex.

Compelling. More compelling than The Master's call.

Hal dug in his heels. He had a lot of practice resisting magical compulsions. All he had to do was wait for the conjurer to take a breath.

The sound of bells following on a subtle aroma increased. He began to sort the components of the smell. Old dust. Mold, cinnamon, mint, and . . . and . . . not sulfur but something sharp, from the Otherworld.

Hal's heart thundered in his ears. His feet itched to move forward, ever closer to the wonderful sound of silver bells singing in the wind.

His mind told him he had to flee, as fast and as far as possible. He'd never encountered anything stronger than The Master's summons through the silver earring. Even now the bit of jewelry burned all the way through his skull, stabbing him behind the eyes.

But this other . . .

The sweetness of the chiming bells could not have been born of this world.

Elves! The knowledge of the origin of the compulsion snapped into his mind with an almost audible pop.

And with the knowledge came the strength to resist the allure. With resistance came the need to know why the Otherworldly creatures chose this night to gather, this close to that other summoning.

Slowly he recited a cantrip he'd devised to aid in his resistance. He turned deasil three times, each time reciting the words anew, first in English for his own understanding, then in Spanish for The Master, and finally in Welsh for the elves. Then he spat three times.

A wall of magic rose around him, molded to his form, and became a part of his being.

Protection in place, Hal eased forward once more. He followed the sound of the bells without hearing the urgent summons behind them.

He climbed and descended two hills, leaped across a rill, and finally at the crest of the third hill sensed his quarry. He dropped to the ground and crawled the last few yards to a tumble of boulders.

In the distance, to the northwest, he sensed a gathering of anger and violence around Leicestershire, several days' hard run away. Somehow, he must be connected to the people involved with that violence. Else he'd not notice it so far away. But he couldn't attend to it until after he had dealt with The Master and this magical disturbance.

Eerie green light glowed across the plateau that stretched before him. Seemingly without a source, the radiance ceased abruptly mere inches from Hal's nose. A line of deliberately placed boulders defined a faery circle.

At the center of the circle, three boulders marked a spring that grew quickly into a creek. It flowed eastward to tumble down the side of the tor. Very close to where Hal crouched on the western side of the circle stood a solitary dressed stone. A grave marker. Its back was to him and he could not read the inscription. But he thought he knew who was buried here and why Otherworldly forces had chosen this place for a ring of power.

Inside the dome of light, a dozen elves wound a slow circle, arms linked, around a silver cauldron placed upon the center of the three stones by the spring. The fire beneath did not blacken the shiny metal or the fine granite of the boulder.

Bells on old-fashioned elvish caps and shoes and points on their doublets created the gentle music that lured unsuspecting strangers into the spell.

Hal could not see the contents of the magical pot, but it shot tendrils of bright scarlet light straight into the air. When they reached the roof of the green light dome, they frayed into a thousand threads that pierced the dome and spread out. They quested in all directions. One of the fiery threads snaked around Hal's envelope of protection.

He held his breath.

Eventually the thread slid away and continued its seeking elsewhere.

Questions filled Hal. Elves had no need to cast this kind of spell. All they had to do was mount a hunt; ride through

the night on ghostly horses chasing a phantom fox. Unsuspecting mortals had no choice but to join the hunt and ride
to their deaths in the wake of the elvish magic.

He worked his way slowly around the dome of light.
Every few feet he had to stop and wait for one of the
scarlet threads to decide he would not fulfill its quest.

By the time he reached true north, he sensed the shadows of Others creeping up the hill. Some came willingly,
some struggled against the scarlet bonds of elvish magic.

Ragged and unkempt, they appeared to be impoverished
outcasts. A dozen men. All men, no women came to the
edge of the elves' circle. There they waited, as servants wait
for instructions when summoned by their master. Or beg-
gars wait for scraps.

Hal peered closely at the others. Something in their bearing and scent told him they were not ordinary men. He
sensed a kinship with them.

A chill ran down his spine.

He turned his attention to the east, the source of the
other summons that never truly left him no matter how he
guarded against it.

Two more figures emerged from the shadows cast by the
waning moon. Male and female. Small, dark people wearing
foreign clothing, walking hesitantly, almost fearfully.

Even the darkness of the night could not hide these two
from Hal. He'd know them any place, any time.

The Master and his slave Yassimine.

The others could only be werewolves sired by their obscene ritual.

As Hal had been sired.

Why had the elves summoned the werewolves of England
and their Master?

Chapter 50

YASSIMINE tugged on The Master's arm, urging him to retreat.

"No, Yassimine. We must see this through. We must end this challenge to my authority."

"The dark of the moon nears. My powers dim," Yassimine protested. "I cannot save you if they attack directly."

"But you will save me, at the cost of your own life. You owe me my life, Yassimine."

I owe you nothing but death, she wanted to say. But could not. Instead, she bowed her head in acquiescence.

If The Master died tonight . . . She had not learned enough magic from him. She did not know how to control her get in a pack. Without the magic, they would become solitary hunters and lose their usefulness to her.

"There!" The Master pointed to the opposite side of the circle of elves. "There he is. If nothing else good comes of this night, at least we will have retrieved this lost member of the pack."

"The boy?" Yassimine dared not believe they had found the lost one. The one who could be her salvation or her ending.

"He still wears the earring. He is a mighty magician to have resisted me so long, but not as mighty as I. He cannot break the hold the earring has on him. I have mastered the Pendragon of Britain," The Master chortled.

"Gather and listen, ye foreign devils!" a voice boomed out from the core of the light dome.

Yassimine covered her ears and cowered from the voice that was all of the elves combined into one.

"This land belongs to us! Only we of all the denizens of the Otherworld are allowed to march across these lands.

We are one with the land. The temporal queen has granted
us sanctuary. You do not belong here. Leave now or face
our wrath."

"How dare they!" The Master nearly choked on his
anger. "I claim this land for my own as I have claimed
many others. These men answer only to me and I tell them
to kill each and every one of you," he proclaimed. And
with his words he pulled a silver amulet from beneath his
doublet. He held it up a moment so that all could see.

His minions stared fixedly at the talisman. They began
salivating.

The Master rubbed the silver and chanted in the ancient
language of the desert.

Yassimine, too, felt the slight burn in her silver piercings.

A dozen werewolf eyes glowed red. They took on the
hunched posture suggesting they were about to change. But
slaves to the moon, they did not sprout fur or snouts or
paws. They snarled and moved forward, mere men with the
hunger of wolves. The dome of green light repelled them.
They yelped and whined and clawed at the magical barrier,
torn between their compulsion to kill and the burning glow
that urged them to run.

Yassimine agonized with them, feeling the same compulsion but to a lesser degree. The Master did not want her
to soil her fine gown with elf blood.

All of the werewolves were trapped between the two
forces. All except Hal, the boy. He stood straight as a man
and calm. He moved with a deliberate grace around the
circle.

Murder glowed in his eyes. But he never once looked at
the elves. He stared only at The Master.

"Stop him, Master!" Yassimine screamed. "He'll kill
you." She pulled on his arm. "We must run."

"Nonsense. He cannot harm me. I am his sire. He heeded
my call at last. Now he must obey me." The Master stubbornly continued his chant with the silver amulet.

"I do not think he heeded your call, Master. I think he
followed a different summons," Yassimine said quietly.

The Master did not seem to hear her.

"Your wolves cannot break through our magic. We draw
power from the Earth. We are of the Earth. You are an

abomination, welcome not in this world or the others," the elves proclaimed in a single voice that boomed across the hilltops and returned triplefold.

Yassimine cringed under the power of the voice. Her sensitive ears shrank and rang. She cowered behind The Master.

Hal just kept walking toward them. He heeded not the commands of the elves or The Master.

All of the Otherworldly creatures atop this hill seemed to hold their breath in a moment of expectant silence.

"You command me to kill. In five years I have not killed a man. Beasts of the field I have ravaged and eaten. Never a man. Tonight I will kill a man. That is if you are indeed still human," Hal snarled. He reached clawed hands for The Master's throat. His teeth elongated. His legs shortened and his shoulders hunched. He began the change. Three days before the dark of the moon!

"How can he do this, Master?" Yassimine asked from behind the man who had commanded her existence for ten years and more.

"He is a powerful wizard," The Master whispered. For the first time shivers ran up his spine.

Now Yassimine knew true fear. Hal would release her from The Master's tyranny, his abuse and rape, his commands to create more and more pups for his arcane purposes.

She almost tasted that freedom on her tongue, felt the wolf within her stir in response to the one who neared.

"Restrain him!" The Master commanded Yassimine and all of her get gathered around the Elvish circle of power.

"They respond not to your call," the elves shouted.

With a sound of ripping flesh and the clatter of untuned bells, all of the silver fell from the werewolves.

Yassimine's own piercings tightened and pulled but did not release her flesh. The Master protected her.

If Hal killed The Master, who would protect her? Who would console her when she remembered the terror of mounted men pursuing her with fire? Who would tell her what to do?

Three heartbeats of indecision. Then she knew what she had to do. She needed The Master alive a while longer.

Emboldened by her need to keep The Master alive, Yas-

simine stepped in front of the man who had sheltered and
defined her all these years. The wolf within her responded
to the wolf in Hal.

The change came over her more quickly and gracefully
than over him. He still fought the violent nature of his
inner being.

Her clothing fell away. The last vestige of her humanity
shed with it. She snapped her jaws in warning.

Hal completed his transformation and returned her snarl.
His rough clothing fell away from him in a puddle of shredded leather and linen.

The world faded from her consciousness. She saw only
this threat before her. Fur stood up along her spine. It
tingled with anticipation for the coming battle. Her loins
grew heavy and her limbs light. Vanquishing this male
would satisfy her quite nicely.

He lunged for her throat. She dodged and rolled. Her
paws scrabbled for purchase on the rough slope. Gobs of
dirt and grass clung to her pads. She flung them free. The
scent of uprooted grass and dirt clung to her fur.

She found her balance and lunged in return. Her aim fell
short of his throat. A long gash appeared on his shoulder.
She tasted blood and fur.

He backed off a pace. But he did not pause to lick the
wound clean and speed the healing. He turned on her, committed to continuing the battle.

A new savagery rose in her. Drooling, teeth bared, she
threw her entire weight against his wound. He collapsed
under her. She locked her jaws around his throat.

And froze.

Suddenly his death and capitulation was not enough. She
needed him powerless, unthinking, driving his seed into her.

Pain jolted her joints. Fur retracted. Her muscles shifted
and bones lengthened.

Beneath her Hal emerged from his wolf persona. He
clamped fierce arms around her.

She nipped his neck and transferred her attention to his
mouth. Sensuous lips beneath his beard sought hers.

Moisture warmed the tight darkness between her thighs.
Her breasts grew heavy with longing. She shifted until the
tip of his erect shaft brushed against the core of her need.

"My wolves! Thieving elves, you've stolen my wolves."
The Master's cry startled them both out of their need to
complete the coupling.

Yassimine scuttled off of Hal. In one swift movement she
lunged upward and grabbed her gown. She held the sensuous velvet so that it covered most of her nudity before
assessing what troubled The Master.

All dozen werewolves fled. They scattered, each in a different direction, no longer bound together as a pack.

"We free them of your unnatural control," the elves
chanted. "We free them of their curse."

"You can't do that. I forbid it!" The Master darted in
the wake of the slowest of the running men. He stumbled.

Yassimine dashed to catch him before he fell. She abandoned her modesty along with the cumbersome gown.
Enough of the wolf remained in her to protect her naked
skin from the chill March air.

"Free me, too!" Hal yelled. He pounded upon the dome
of green light. Gooseflesh rose on his bare back. The bite
on his shoulder oozed blood, closing as she watched. "Take
this earring and my curse," he sobbed.

The elves ignored him.

"Please. In the name of the Pendragon of Britain, I beg
you to release me, too."

At last, one of the elves turned and faced him. The others kept their attention on maintaining the dome and the
fire beneath the cauldron in the center of their circle.

"The last time we faced the Pendragon of Britain, he
defied us and robbed us of the souls of two families of
Gypsies. He denied us recompense upon his death. Be careful, Pendragon, lest we exact vengeance upon you." The
elf turned his back.

"Your spell was broad and indiscriminate. Why did it
not affect me?" Hal continued to claw at the dome of
power.

"The second skin of magic you weave around yourself
repulsed our magic as we repulse your pleas."

Hal dropped to his knees. He pounded the Earth. He
cried and he cursed.

From one eyeblink to the next the Otherworldly green
light disappeared. The elves shrank to the size of insects

and popped out of sight. The cauldron lingered a moment then faded and drifted into the far distance, trailing scarlet strands of magic.

"All is not lost." The Master ceased his pursuit of his lost minions. He shook himself slightly as if ridding himself of troublesome thoughts or fleas. "I have brought you under my control at last, Pendragon Niño."

Hal did not respond. He slumped in the dirt at the edge of the circle of boulders.

Yassimine hastened to him. She wrapped his torn shirt and her arms around his shivering shoulders, cradling him against her naked breast. Gently she rocked and crooned to him as she would to a child. The child only this man/wolf could give her.

The Master pulled a length of silver chain from a pocket hidden inside his doublet. "This should bind you to me quite nicely."

In two swift movements he had pierced Hal's navel and slipped a link into the torn flesh.

Hal screamed and sat bolt upright.

Yassimine restrained him with the lingering strength of her wolf. "Easy, my son, easy. The pain only lasts a few moments." But the inner agony would never leave him.

"Dress him and yourself, Yassimine. We have an appointment at Sheffield Manor. The Earl of Shrewsbury is too ill to remain jailer to the Scottish whore. His successor, Paulet, is younger and no fool. He will not be easy to trick into releasing the queen into my custody. We must make certain that the exiled queen either escapes cleanly or is martyred to the cause of Spain. And when Spain dominates the world, so shall I."

Chapter 51

The next night. An isolated manor farm outside Sheffield.

A TINY sound woke Hal from a nightmare. Grateful for the end of reliving his desperate pleas to the elves, he lifted his head from his nest of blankets before the fire. He'd slept in worse places than the hard flagstone floor of a farm kitchen. At least he was warm on this rainy March midnight.

The ease of the warmth had not soothed his troubled spirit. If only he had not protected himself with magic, the elvish spell would have released him from his curse. If only he had fought Yassimine to the end rather than succumbing to her femininity, he would have robbed The Master of his most powerful weapon.

If only . . .

His nose worked when his eyes and ears failed him.

"Yassimine."

"Yes," she whispered in that slightly lisping accent. She spoke Spanish slightly better than English. Neither tongue came easily to her.

But Hal needed no language to understand her words. She spoke to the wolf within him and he comprehended more than mere words.

She padded into the large kitchen on bare feet, wearing only the thinnest of linen shifts. The faint musk underlying her perfume awakened his body.

"Leave me." He flopped onto his side with his back to her. He knew what she wanted and hated himself for wanting it, too.

If only he had stolen the magical girdle from Dr. Dee, he could use this moment to reverse the curse. But the scholar had guarded the piece closely for many days after

Hal took his leave of the man. As if he knew Hal intended to spirit the magical girdle away.

A new thought sprang to life fully blown. He rolled onto his back and stared at her.

The faintest of blushes flushed her bosom above the loose ties of her shift.

"We need to finish what we started, Hal," she said. She slipped closer to him. The low flames from the fire played with the shadows beneath her shift.

His body stirred. He no longer fought the lust she aroused in him.

"And what would that be?" he asked, keeping his eyes on the crests of her breasts. Under his gaze they peaked into tight knots.

"This." She shrugged out of the shift. The fine linen dropped to the floor in a shimmering puddle. Firelight turned her swarthy skin to rosy gold. Long legs enticed his gaze upward.

She stood before him, unashamed, bold, brazen, and eager.

He rose to his knees. The blankets fell away from his own nude body. He pressed his lips to her thighs and higher, tasting her need. His tongue flicked out across the dark triangle at the junction of her thighs.

She groaned. He cupped her bottom with his hands and drew her closer. His tongue probed deeper.

"Slower, my love," Yassimine whispered. She dropped to her own knees and kissed him deeply, cradling his head with both her hands.

He explored her breasts with sensitive fingers.

They collapsed onto the blankets, mouths still locked together.

The burning itch at his groin grew and built. His entire body felt on fire. Every touch inflamed his skin, made his joints ache.

They tangled and rolled among the blankets.

He needed to transform.

As if he had spoken of his need, he felt fur sprout from her golden skin. She snarled and nipped at his shoulder. He let the wolf take him. One nip to her chest and she flipped over, tail tucked along her back.

No more time for play and preparation. She wanted him. Now. He needed to bind her to him.

Some small sense of humanity urged him to prolong the experience, drive her near to desperation.

He licked her back and ears while pressing one paw at her opening.

She snarled for him to get on with it.

He worried her ear with tongue and teeth.

She wiggled to press against him.

He raked his claws along her belly, felt her teats swell beneath his touch. Then he drew his tongue along the inside of her back legs.

She whimpered.

The need pressed against him. The last of his humanity faded as he plunged into her.

The moment he withdrew, sated and tired, yet eager for more, she pulled away from him. In one blurring motion she transformed, gathered her shift and ran back to the bedchambers above.

Hal fell back onto the blankets, in his human body once more, with a smile on his face. On the morrow he'd maneuver The Master to visit Dr. Dee. The first ritual had needed one girdle, one for the werewolf to give to the victim. To reverse the spell, Hal needed two. He and Yassimine must exchange them and then cast them off, symbolically rejecting their wolves.

He had not Deirdre's fine touch with devising spells, but he knew the elements and the manner. The next time Yassimine came to him, he'd be prepared to reverse them both back to humanity.

March 1580, the night before the dark of the moon, north by northwest of London.

From London, Michael and I rode almost due north to Cambridge. With prime horseflesh between our knees, the miles dropped behind us with ease. A little compulsion touching the minds of our mounts kept them running happily far longer than most steeds. At Cambridge, we stopped for the night and rested our horses.

We spent the hours in each other's arms, tender and companionable.

Then we turned northwest and rode cross-country toward Sheffield. Coffa ran ahead of us, sensing the way. She kept our course true with the single-minded obstinacy that only a wolfhound can demonstrate. She had our quarry in mind and nothing would deter her. Her resentment piled on top of me in layers of guilt whenever we paused to water the horses or stretch our cramped knees. We wasted time and daylight. The hunt was up.

"Why is it that your dog is the shiest and meekest of animals back home, but turn her loose and she becomes a mightier huntress than Diana?" Michael quipped with a broad smile.

We dared not stop in the tiny hamlet near the manor. Upper Snivelton, a few miles up the road, offered a larger, more comfortable inn and anonymity.

Or so we thought. Milord the Earl of Oxford had the same plan, along with his coconspirator Robert Parsons.

The two arrived within half an hour of us. Coffa's fur bristled along her spine and she pushed the shutters open in the tiny window of our attic room. She growled to alert me. I dragged myself off the bed, half-clad, to see what alarmed her. One glance into the forecourt and I knew we must walk warily. Oxford might dismiss us as beneath his concern, but Parsons had observed Michael and me at close hand. Jesuit trained, he would remember everything and everyone he encountered in fine detail.

The landlord escorted them to the large parlor room on the first floor above the taproom. The moment they closed the door, Michael and I scuttled down the creaking staircase to the kitchen. We ordered journey food instead of our supper and departed quickly.

By sundown we dismounted in the shadow of the isolated castle. Lights glinted beneath the shutters of the tower rooms. A fine drizzle masked our presence.

"Do we wait for the attack?" Michael asked. He scanned the landscape with a soldier's eye to tactics. "Oxford will use his title to gain entry for himself and a small troop. Then he'll lower the drawbridge for the rest of his men."

"I would rather divert the small army before they arrive." I still had not told my husband that the leader of the army was my own uncle.

"How? They have a quest fueled by fanaticism."

"I'll think of something." I'd use magic to put them to sleep, no matter the consequences.

We tied the horses and struck out on foot. Michael wanted to go south and then east because the path was gentler. I tried to explain that he chose to walk widdershins. Unlucky. Counter to any magic I might need to work.

Reluctantly, he followed me on the deasil path; north and then east. We stumbled through heavy brush, making so much noise our quarry must hear us from a mile away.

The rain came heavier, soaking through our coats and turning our path into sticky mud.

"We should have gone the other way," Michael grumbled. He tripped on something and grabbed an overhanging branch to keep his balance. His grip sent a shower of collected drops down on his head. He cursed in three languages.

I glared at him.

Coffa ran back to lick his face. I felt her mirth at Michael's discomfiture. He only cursed more.

Then Coffa pricked her ears and looked into the near distance. She lifted her lip in a silent snarl.

I shushed Michael with a gesture.

He cut off his stream of invective in mid-word.

Instinctively, I tapped into Coffa's greater sense of smell and hearing. Horses. Many horses. Barely one hundred yards ahead and to our right. Between us and the manor.

Michael had come up beside me and touched my lips with his fingertips. I placed my own finger on his mouth "Many horses. Too many," I mouthed the words. He would understand. We had communicated like this many times in our travels. We had tried telepathy. But he could not read my mind as I did his.

So we read with fingertips the silent words formed by our lips.

"An army," he replied silently.

"Why so many?"

"Escape or rebellion?"

"Escape." I prayed I was right.

I did not believe Uncle Donovan so desperate to be with Mary that he would sacrifice all that he held dear, and betray his queen and his birthright. If my uncle had been so inclined, he would have done so years ago when Mary was held closer to Kirkenwood and the border of Scotland.

"We need to separate the troops from their leader." Without waiting for my husband's agreement, I crept forward. Coffa's nose guided me to the fringes of the armed escort.

We had expected twenty men—two dozen at the most. Nearly one hundred awaited orders. They stood at attention beside their horses waiting for orders to mount. Stern Northmen one and all. They wore steel breastplates and helms. They carried broadswords in utilitarian leather sheaths, not the ornamental toys worn by courtiers. The horses still carried the shaggy coats of harsh northern winters.

Many of the men openly wore crosses on thongs around their necks or painted on their armor. Catholics.

A casual observer would assume these men were Scots ready to restore Mary to her throne or conquer England in the name of their church.

One hundred men could protect a queen as she fled to some safe haven. They had not enough numbers to mount a revolution.

Frantically, I sought their leader. Uncle Donovan must truly be desperate. Or deluded by Oxford's pretty promises.

None of the men in the deep ranks stood out as a leader. Coffa had never met my uncle, could not pick out his scent among so many strangers. Daunted by their numbers, my familiar cowered behind me. She'd been trained for spying, not warfare.

The Kirkenwood dogs were all bred and trained for hunting and war. I could not imagine Uncle Donovan marching with an army without dogs. One dog for each ten men. We trained them that way.

But the lieutenants, Uncle Donovan's closest aides might have dogs as well.

I set Coffa to searching for a concentration of dogs. She found three toward the back of the ranks where the land rose slightly.

Following her line of scent, I cast out my own senses sniffing for the presence of magic. There! Very faint, but definitely my uncle working a scrying spell. I presumed he looked for Mary within the rambling manor. He needed to locate her before he stormed the walls.

Michael followed me without question as I worked my way around the army. I had to stop or divert my uncle before Oxford arrived. Before he committed himself to treason.

I sent out a mental probe. Uncle Donovan should have had enough magical talent to receive.

Instead, I hooked Hal.

Chapter 52

THE magic probe spun around Hal's head so quickly he almost missed it for what it was.

Tell me, the probe whispered seductively. *Tell me all that you know.*

Dee! His heart leaped in exultation. Rescue. He could think of nothing else. Not even the burning silver chain that now encircled his waist.

"Into fur. Now. Both of you," The Master commanded. He whipped out his spyglass and scanned the landscape around the stately manor near Sheffield.

Hal looked to Yassimine for explanation. She shrugged. Her gaze never left the Spaniard.

Hal ground his teeth in frustration even as he dropped to all fours. But he delayed letting the wolf take him.

Two days now he'd tried to push The Master toward Mortlake and Dr. Dee. Every time he tried, the new piercing at his navel burned so deep he needed to double over as with cramp.

During one episode, when he'd been too weak to resist, The Master had clamped a new silver chain around his waist and anchored it to the ring at his navel. His next act of disobedience had him rolling on the floor in agony.

And Yassimine had not returned to his bed. Not even when he tried to steal The Master's own bespelled girdle to reverse the ritual.

He needed to change his plans.

"Transform, now. The others await us." The Master kicked Hal in the ribs. "I shall carry your clothing."

Hal snarled and bit at the man's ankle. But he obeyed, letting his anger and frustration fuel the wolf. His nose told him where Deirdre and her wolfhound stood, behind a fold in the next hill. She scouted an army.

The smell of horses and men who had not bathed in many days assaulted his senses.

Only the burning chain about his waist kept him from running to Dee's side.

"Heel!" The Master commanded.

Yassimine trotted obediently behind his left foot. Hal followed. He made certain his path wavered behind and to the left of her. He ranged farther away from The Master every tenth stride. He came back periodically, close enough to reassure the man that he obeyed the burning chains if not the verbal command.

They paused at the crest of a hill. The Master raised his spyglass once more. How could he see with only mundane senses on this murky night of rain and heavy cloud cover? Not a single star shone to reveal the way.

"Ah, the army is in place. They have a magician with them. I sense his magic. The manor is poorly guarded. The Earl of Shrewsbury ages and ails. He grows negligent in his duties," he commented.

Hal snarled at him.

He knew the plan now. To liberate Mary Queen of Scots. What could he do to stop it?

The Master led them on a circuitous path that brought them behind the collection of men and horses and . . . and dogs. War dogs. Wolfhounds.

He stopped short, growling a warning.

A hound caught his scent and howled. Others took up the trumpeting call.

Every instinct in Hal urged him to run, to shed the fur and become a man.

Hal? What? Why! Dee called to him.

He breathed deeply for calm.

A small circle of torchlight awaited them. The Master ignored the baying dogs and the heavily armed men who challenged him. He waved his hand in front of the first guard's face. The man blinked several times and stood aside.

Yassimine snapped at his ankles but did not draw blood.

Suddenly, the hounds quieted. A tall man stepped out of the darkness and confronted them. Hal blinked his wolf eyes and nearly shed his fur.

Da. He wanted to cry out, to run to his father for protection; to rip out his throat; to run away and hide.

Instead he searched the myriad body scents for other family. He knew Dee was here. What about Betsy, Griff, Gaspar, and Peregrine? He would run from Betsy. As for the others, he'd wait and see what they planned.

A brief conversation ensued between Da and The Master. Both seemed wary, grudging of their trust. Yassimine circled them constantly, her nose working for signs of danger.

Hal sat on his haunches at the edge of the circle of light. Dee approached. He intended to divert her before she came afoul of The Master.

She burst into the circle of light, her wolfhound and her husband close on her heels.

"Uncle Donovan, turn back now before it is too late!" she cried.

Hal tried to stand before her. She neatly avoided him, intent upon her mission. The wolfhound, not one he knew, growled and bared her teeth. Hal growled back at her. She slunk behind the husband.

"Deirdre, get away from here. This has nothing to do with you," Donovan tried to block her. Peregrine backed him up. Robin stood behind them, silent, frowning, present but not participating.

Hal could not find Griff or Gaspar or Betsy. Da must sense the need to leave some of the family home and free of the taint of treason.

"This has everything to do with me. Do you know who this man is?" Dee took two steps forward and pointed accusingly at The Master.

"Get out of the way, Dee." The husband raised a wheel lock pistol.

Hal lunged. He connected to Dee with all four paws. They fell to the ground and rolled.

The pistol fired.

The Master yelped.

Yassimine screamed and flew through the air. Her jaws locked on the husband's throat.

Chaos erupted around them. Men shouted. Weapons fired. Dogs barked. Da drew his sword.

Hal disentangled himself from Dee. He grabbed Yassimine's flank, trying to pull her off her prey.

She had tasted blood.

Dee screamed and ran. Fireballs flew from her hands. She flung them wildly.

Yassimine turned on this new enemy.

Hal threw himself onto Yassimine's back.

Dee cradled the dying man in her arms. Tears flowed freely down her face.

Hal's heart nearly broke. He had not the time to think on this. He had to keep Yassimine from killing again.

Come! The Master called them.

The magical compulsion snared in Hal's mind, nearly blinding him. He had to run away. He had to make certain that neither Yassimine nor The Master returned to menace the family. His family. His only hope of salvation shattered with them.

The three of them loped off into the night, trailing blood from The Master's arm and Yassimine's teeth.

I ran. Coffa and my horse appeared out of the growing darkness. I mounted and galloped off heedless of direction.

A deep pain lodged between my heart and my throat. I could not swallow, barely breathed, choked on my tears.

Once again, I had worked magic and an innocent had died. I had read Robert Parson's mind without his knowledge or consent. I knew I should not have. And yet I had let Michael persuade me otherwise.

Michael, I cried over and over.

The emptiness in my mind was nothing compared to that in my soul.

Michael!

How could we have just found each other again and then . . . then . . . I could not even think what had happened to him. Over and over I saw the blood. The terror on his face. The blood. The light fading from his eyes. The blood.

The blood.

Coffa ran blindly. The horse followed. I cared not where
so long as it was away.

Agonizing hours later the sun rose in my face. I gathered
enough sense to let the horse stop. I walked him a mile or
so to let him cool, then led him to a peaty rill. He curled
his lip at the brown water and rough verge grasses at first.
Eventually, thirst and hunger overcame his dainty tastes.

I drank, too, knowing I needed to in order to survive.
Appetite deserted me. Even the water made me want to
retch in the grass.

An oak tree loaded with mistletoe clumps gave me a
backrest. I sat there a long time, not thinking, not sleeping,
not truly awake.

The sun rose higher. I had only one thought, one refuge
that called to me.

"Oh, Michael, I need you with me." My tears flowed
freely. My body convulsed with a new round of sobs. I
cried so hard I retched. And still I cried.

No beloved hand touched my shoulder to ease my sorrow. No one called to me across the void of time and death.

I was alone.

Perhaps I could find a measure of peace at the grave of
my parents. I had no one else to turn to. The rest of my
family had betrayed me.

"Michael!"

Chapter 53

HAL raised his head from his instinctive retching. He'd run only a short distance before the wolf deserted him and all of his human sensibilities took over. The smell of blood, the hideous sight of Sir Michael, his own sense of guilt made him gag.

He reached a longing hand back toward the scene of the disaster. "Forgive me, Dee. I never meant this to happen."

"Away. Now." The Master made the chain around Hal's waist burn.

Hal doubled over with the intensity of the pain. He fell to his knees and crawled a few paces in Deirdre's wake. He had to make her understand.

The pain increased. More than he thought possible. More than he could bear.

The Master yanked him to his feet and thrust a wad of clothing at him. With a mighty shove he propelled Hal toward the east.

Hal stumbled.

Yassimine called to him. Her love for him became a gentle tug on his earring. He hardened his heart to her call. She had betrayed him and his family and all that he held dear. She had no reason to murder Sir Michael. At the dark of the moon, the wolf in her should not have been strong enough to compel her to violence.

He thought himself the only werewolf capable of transforming at the time and place of his choosing. What made Yassimine different?

"Deirdre. I'm sorry," he sobbed.

He heard only her blind thrashing through the woods followed by her dog.

"Deirdre." Then he shouted to the highest heavens. *"Dee!"*

"We have no time for this," The Master rubbed his silver talisman and chanted something in that arcane language of his.

Hal nearly fell forward in his physical need to comply with the compulsion. As he regained his balance, his mind opened to a new perspective. He saw things more clearly than ever before.

If ever Britain was to be rid of The Master, Hal had to kill him. He had to swallow his revulsion against taking a human life. The Master wasn't human anymore. He was as vile as the demon that had haunted Deirdre's mother. He was evil incarnate.

He'd kill The Master. Steal his girdle. Then he'd drag Yassimine to Dr. Dee and the second magical girdle.

The Master rubbed the talisman once more to compel more speed in all three of them.

"You die," Hal whispered. "Maybe not tonight. But soon you die, and when I am done with her, so dies your murdering bitch."

But first they had to learn to trust Hal enough to turn their backs on him.

"After them!" Donovan ordered.

"Milord, the signal from the manor." Robin pointed to the lantern passing before a dark window in the west wing.

Donovan forgot to breathe. Mary. His Mary was waiting for him to rescue her.

His son and the vile Spaniard had escaped after committing foul murder.

He reached for the locket out of habit, paused with his hand halfway to his chest. Then he thrust his hand back to the hilt of his sword.

"Mary will have to wait," he sighed. "We cannot allow that man to escape."

"I agree." Robin leaped astride his mount.

Peregrine and Gaspar followed suit.

Donovan struggled into his own saddle. "Someone has to stay and . . . and tend him." He couldn't bring himself to look at the mangled corpse of Deirdre's husband. "Someone needs to go after her."

Robin saw to it. As he always did. Peregrine led ten men to wrap the body and take it to London and the queen with . . . what kind of report?

Donovan could not think. Every last hope of keeping his family intact had shattered.

"Tell Sir Francis Walsingham that a report will follow. You know nothing more than that Lord Donovan's men were attacked on the road. Nothing more," Robin directed. He even chose the men individually for the task.

"Robin, you must go after Deirdre. She trusts you more than me at this point. She might stop running for you. And Gaspar. Take Gaspar with you," Donovan said quietly.

"Where will she go?" Robin asked. Already he searched the ground for traces of her trail.

"I don't know. Back to London perhaps. To Kirkenwood. I do not know."

"To Huntington and her Aunt Meg?" Gaspar asked.

Donovan exhaled loudly. "Of course. 'Tis her only refuge."

"But that path is in the same direction as the Spaniard and . . . and his slaves."

"Then we ride a parallel course. Take twenty men. Stay as close to Deirdre as you can until it is safe to approach her directly."

"Safe? I have known her since she was born. What harm can she do me?" Robin raised his shoulders in a gesture that mimicked his mother.

"In her grief, Deirdre's magic will run wild. Her dog will respond savagely to any perceived interference. Walk warily, but let no harm come to her."

"A messenger to Kirkenwood?"

"Betsy will see what she needs to in her scrying bowl. But I need to disperse this army. We travel openly now. I have no reasonable excuse for this many men. Another twenty men to ride back to Kirkenwood and secure it. We cannot spare more if we hope to capture *le meneur des loups*."

With that statement a measure of calm settled on his shoulders. His mind cleared of the passion that had driven him here to Sheffield, to agree to Oxford's wild plan, to betray his queen and his family.

"Martha, forgive me," he begged the ghost of his wife. She did not answer him this night.

He had a mission. He knew what he had for do. He did not need Martha's guiding hand to know what was right.

Slowly he breathed in three counts, held it on three, exhaled. Power began to tingle in his fingertips. He breathed again on the same controlled count. His vision shifted. Bright halos appeared around his men. If he concentrated, he could read each man's emotions through those auras.

One more breath and . . .

The ghosts of his ancestors gathered around him.

"Ride with me?" he asked the wraiths of Grandmother Raven, his twin Griffin, and a dozen others. He could never be certain if King Arthur's Merlin and his daughter Wren haunted him or not. He thought he sensed their benevolent presence.

But King Arthur never revealed himself. His time was not yet come.

"Help me bring this evil to justice and banish *El Lobison* from the shores of Britain for all time," he prayed.

Still they held back. There was something more they wanted.

"Help me return my son to the bosom of the family."

A sigh of assent drifted on the wind.

"I will restore my family. Only the family is important," he said to himself through gritted teeth.

The wraiths gathered close, pressing him to continue the thought.

"And that means Deirdre as well."

At last the ghosts of his ancestors moved forward in pursuit of the werewolf master, his slave, and Hal. Two of them—possibly Griffin and Grandmother Raven branched off along the trail Deirdre had taken.

Donovan kicked his spurs into his horse's flanks and set off with murder in his mind and bewilderment in his heart. He took one last longing look at the blank windows of Sheffield Manor and his lost love.

If he brought Hal and Deirdre back to Kirkenwood, Betsy would give them all hell.

"This family was not meant to stay together," he muttered. "But I shall try. Even if I have to send Betsy to a convent on the Continent to control her."

"Loose the hounds!" he called back over his shoulder. "The bastard and his wolves won't elude us for long."

"You must use your magic to hide us," Yassimine hissed at Hal.

The ground beneath her vibrated with the thunder of half a hundred horses galloping after them. The huge hunting dogs trumpeted to each other in an eerie chorus.

Gooseflesh broke out on Yassimine's human flesh. The sound brought back flashes of memory from the time strangers had invaded her home village, killing all of the men, raping the women, and burning their yurts.

She shivered and nearly sobbed in terror.

The look Hal turned on her at the request made her crouch lower beneath the fallen log that hid them.

"Do it," The Master said. He reached for the silver talisman around his neck.

"I can veil the sight of the riders. I cannot mask our scent from the dogs," Hal replied. No emotion colored his tone or animated his face.

"Then find a way." The Master looked deep into Hal's eyes.

Yassimine knew he used magic to compel Hal.

"Do it yourself. You are supposed to be the greatest magician of all time." Hal maintained his blank expression as he stared back at the man who controlled all their lives.

The two men did this often, challenging the magic in each other for control.

"I do not waste my magic on such things," The Master snarled. He lifted his lip in a lupine snarl.

These contests made Yassimine nervous. More nervous than the army behind them with their bloodlust up.

"Please." Yassimine touched Hal's arm. She tried to convey all of her affection for him as well as her sensuality in the gesture.

Calmly, he lifted her hand from his arm and dropped it

away from him. The absolute coldness in his eyes made her womb shrink within her into a hard knot of despair.

"Very well," Hal sighed. He drew in a long breath and exhaled on the same slow count. His eyes glazed over. He dropped his head until his chin rested upon his chest.

When he looked up he seemed to glow with an eldritch orange light, akin to fire licking at tinder.

Yassimine reared away from him in fear. Even The Master recoiled.

"Remain perfectly still. Barely breathe," Hal whispered. He shifted around until he faced in the direction of the hounds howling in the distance. His hands wove a quick gesture and flame shot from his fingers.

A wall of fire sprang up across the path that had led them here.

Horses screamed in fright. Dogs yelped. Men cursed.

The flames arrowed off to the north, taking on the outline of a human figure with two wolves running at his heels.

"After them!" a man shouted.

The horses veered off to the north, nostrils dilated, the whites of their eyes showing bright in the dark night.

Hal remained rigidly upright, glowing brighter by the moment.

At last, the fire in him extinguished all at once, as if someone had dumped a bucket of water over him. He sank to his knees panting. His shoulders drooped and he breathed raggedly.

"Come, we must flee now," The Master commanded. He stood up, brushing leaf debris from his pantaloons.

Hal sagged. "I cannot. The spell . . ." His words trailed off in an exhausted moan.

"Carry him." The Master glanced briefly at Yassimine and strode off to the east, surefooted and authoritative.

"Lean on me." Yassimine inserted her shoulder beneath his arm and heaved upward.

Hal tried to recoil.

"Do you wish to stay here and die? If the army does not return and find you, then surely The Master will kill you to keep you from falling into their ungentle hands." She wrapped one arm around his waist. His scent filled her head with images of the night she had gone to him by the kitchen fire. And of the night when he first met the wolf within him.

Never before had she reached such heights of ecstasy while converting a pup or with The Master. But Hal had reached deep inside her being and touched the essence of her. Her heart had reached out to him, binding her to him in ways The Master could never understand.

Hal allowed her to drag him a few steps. He resisted touching her in any way other than that required for propping him upright.

"What ails you, pup?" she asked, trying to get him to let her take more of his weight. The wolf was still strong in her. She could lift him easily and carry him if she had to.

"You killed," he muttered. His words were slurred, but she understood.

"You knew the man."

"Knew him. Liked him. Respected him. He cared for my beloved and she loved him."

A long moment of silence as they stumbled along.

"You did not have to kill Sir Michael. You do not need to kill humans at all."

"But . . ."

Another long moment while he withdrew his thoughts and his words from her.

"He would have killed The Master."

"You should have let him."

"But . . ." She could not complete her protest.

Hal said nothing. His balance seemed better. The strength of the wolf replenished his body rapidly.

If she had let the man murder The Master, how would she convert new pups and gather them into a pack?

Then a new thought intruded upon her fears. Who would make decisions for her? Who would direct her actions?

You would have to take responsibility for yourself, Hal said directly into her mind.

Chapter 54

Lost in the Midlands of England.

I DO not know how many days I wandered. Eventually, I roused myself from the blinding grief. A terrible hole remained in my middle, but I knew I would go on living. In order to give Michael's death meaning, I had to live. I had to continue the work that had sustained us for all of our years together.

First, I had to figure out where I was. Then I had to find The Master and remove him from England once and for all. And if I killed the werewolf bitch along with him, so be it. I would avenge Michael one way or another.

First things first. I needed a meal, a bath, and true sleep. None of those things nor the hope of them appeared nearby. Where had I wandered to?

A pile of ruins south of me showed where someone had once lived. A castle meant a village. The lord had probably moved from the damp and drafty fortress to a more comfortable manor. Did he rebuild the village at the new location, or leave it and its people to rot?

Often, when the village followed the lord to a new location, one or two old-timers remained because of ill health, a peculiar tie to the location, or out of sheer stubbornness. I hoped to find at least one of them.

I crept downhill, leading the horse, letting Coffa sniff the way. She stayed close, shifting her nose from the air back to the ground frequently. As we neared the tumble of dressed stones, she began wagging her tail. A path wound away from the castle, back to the west. My dog waited for me at the head of the trail, eager, joyous. She drooled happily into her beard.

"You think this is the best way?" I paused to tap into her senses—difficult because I was so hungry and tired. A few crumbled huts in the opposite direction looked interesting if not particularly promising. No smoke rose from tilted chimneys or gaping smoke holes in the roofs.

Coffa bounded back to me and then bounced onto the trail.

I shrugged and followed her, picking my way more carefully through the litter of broken walls and gouged earth. Before long the path forked. One branch led forward up a hill, the other to the right toward a creek. Both of us drank eagerly from the creek. Then I looked around again.

Something odd about the shape of the land at the base of the tor intrigued me. But Coffa wanted to climb. I trusted my familiar to lead.

We climbed up a twisted path that wound around the hill and doubled back upon itself half a dozen times. Something I had read about such paths . . . I could not remember. So I concentrated on placing one foot in front of the other and not listening to the growls in my stomach.

At last we crested the hill. A ring of boulders defined a faery circle that covered most of the plateau. The air inside the circle looked hazy, out of focus. Filled with magic.

Shots of deep blue lightning darted from stone to stone and then into the center of the circle where they were lost to my sight because of the haze.

"Halloo?" I called.

My own voice answered me in echo. The sound took on an eerie tone as it repeated itself over and over, circling me, chasing itself around the faery circle.

I tried to follow my voice, round and round. Blue light flashed across my vision. It led me up and over the hills and back down on the other side. Nothing fit, direction became meaningless. My head wanted to float free of my body.

"It's about time you showed up," a voice reprimanded me. A sane voice, rooted in the depths of the earth that reverberated along my spine. A voice that would never get lost in the echoes. But it might open doors into the Otherworld.

Perhaps the Underworld where Michael walked. Perhaps I could walk with him a ways, ask his forgiveness for not protecting him from the werewolf. Forgiveness for not loving him as much as he deserved.

"Where am I?" I called into the haze. "Who are you?"

"The question is who are *you?*"

A vague outline of a human form appeared just inside the faery ring. I thought I should recognize the person, but . . .

"I am Deirdre, Lady Maelstrom."

"That is your name now. But who are you?"

That made me stop. All of my life I had taken my identity from those around me: Uncle Donovan, Hal, Queen Elizabeth, Michael. They gave me a place in society, and a placement within the family.

Who was I without them?

I had a feeling I needed to know. Not just to learn the identity of the questioner, but to know how I thought of myself without Michael, how I moved within the family and society henceforth.

"I am Deirdre Griffin, heir to the Pendragon." No one else would acknowledge my right to the heritage. But I did. And I knew that I must grow into the role. Betsy would not. Hal could not. There was no one else.

"Then find the entrance and welcome." The voice took on feminine tones and lost the awesome resonance.

I began walking the circumference of the circle. Widdershins, to my right, seemed the easiest route.

Coffa had other ideas. She enclosed my wrist in her massive jaws and led me in the opposite direction. I should have guessed I would not find the gate walking toward the darkness. I needed to follow the light on the path of the sun.

Very shortly, I stumbled into the creek before it tumbled down the tor in a series of chuckling cascades. Coffa splashed happily in the cold water. She shook water from her fur, joyous that she could share it with me. Droplets pelted my eyes.

The shimmering haze fell away. I focused my gaze and saw the interior of the circle.

"Aunt Meg!" I cried as I stumbled up the creek toward her perch on the center of three stones at the source of the spring.

The only mother I had ever known gathered me into her warm embrace.

"My lost chick," she whispered.

Our tears mingled. I poured out my sorrow to her. She rubbed my back and cooed soothing nonsense phrases.

A great weight lifted from me even as I emptied myself of emotion.

"Come, there is something you must see." Meg took my hand. Together, we rose from the nest of three rocks around the spring.

Then I saw it. A grave marker in the shape of a circled cross. Celtic knotwork adorned each of the four arms and the circle that joined them all like a sun rising behind. And it faced east so that the morning light would kiss it as soon as it topped the horizon.

"My father," I said quietly. Suddenly I was reluctant to approach. I had dreamed of this moment most of my life and never had the courage to face the truth of my beginnings.

"Your mother as well. Donovan did not want to bury her here. But Father Griffin would have wanted her by his side. They died together, bound by love and magic and destiny. So they lie together. Forever."

More tears choked me. Different tears. This grief was for the lives these two had sacrificed to end the tyranny of the Demon of Chaos.

"You were born here." Meg indicated a place between the graves and the central stones. Altar stones they must have been at one time. "Your Da celebrated Easter Mass here for the homeless and the Gypsies and the outcasts. He welcomed them all, and loved them all when the world rejected them."

I fell to my knees beside the grave, wishing I had known the man the people of the road still called the Merlin.

"How . . . how did my mother come here to give me life?"

"The demon was tied to her. She could not escape it. She loved you too much to allow him to taint your innocence. So she came to us here for help. To me and the keeper of this place before me. Deirdre, she called herself. Deirdre, we called you. We sheltered your Mam with love and with magic. While you were only hours old, she crept away. Old Deirdre and I kept you for over a year, along with Robin. Then Donovan brought your da here for burial. I took you and Robin back to Kirkenwood then. And Hal and little Griffin. Donovan let me be mother to you all then. I loved you best, though. You were mine from the moment of your birth. The others all came to me later, when they'd already known another mother."

Her voice trailed off. She gazed into the distance, lost in her memories.

The whole tale was the longest coherent speech I'd heard from my aunt. Mad Meg they called her. Often, she resorted to the mind and sensibilities of a child. Escape, Uncle Donovan called it. Escape from the memory of a cruel rape during a Scottish raid many years ago.

"I can't read his journals. They are shrouded in magic," I said, still kneeling by the grave. Wildflowers outlined the length and breadth of his final resting place. I wondered briefly if they grew that way naturally or if Meg had transplanted them.

"You can read them now. You have the maturity and strength to understand them. You have learned the discretion to use the information in them wisely."

"Have you read them, Aunt Meg?"

"A, B, C, D," she sang the nursery tune taught to children to aid them in memorizing their letters.

"Aunt Meg?"

"One, two, buckle my shoe, three, four," she continued. Her eyes glazed over, and I knew I'd get no more information from her.

After a long time, the needs of my body overcame the turmoil of my emotions.

"Aunt Meg, I need to eat," I said.

She shook herself and roused from her self-induced trance of nursery rhymes. "The stew should be ready." She rose and brushed her skirt and apron.

I stood as well, suddenly conscious of the male riding leathers I wore. For all of her madness, Aunt Meg always wore a skirt and bodice, sometimes cleaner than others, but for all of her grass stains and twigs in her hair, she remained feminine. She trekked over half of England at will, appearing barefoot at the precise moment she was needed, with whatever herb or flower or sympathetic tears one required.

Suddenly I wanted nothing more than to be like her.

"Then you must listen to the wind and the stars and the creatures of the wild," she replied to my unspoken thoughts.

"I am needed in London."

"But you will return to birth your baby here. Fitting that she will be born in the same place as you. The wolves will not find you here. Their curse shall never taint you or the babe. You will call her Rose, after your mother."

"A baby?" Awestruck I could say nothing more, could barely think. A child. "Michael's baby. Are you certain? How do you know?" Once the dam of wonder broke words flooded out of me.

"I just know. I always know." Meg shrugged and stepped into the creek. She glided through the water, or perhaps atop it, I could not tell, toward the entrance to the circle. One had to step into the water to enter or leave. A ritual cleansing I supposed.

A piece of Michael lived on. In me. In my baby.

I sat abruptly. Half in and half out of the water, I sat and stared off into the distance.

"A baby."

"A baby who needs her dinner. Come along." Meg hauled me to my feet and led me down the tor to her hut. Strange I hadn't seen it on the journey up. It stood solidly beside the last waterfall before the creek leveled off.

But then I hadn't needed to see the place before.

"A baby. Michael's baby." A measure of joy edged some of the sorrow out of my heart.

"A baby to live for. A baby to focus your goals. You need to protect her as you protect all of England. Think on what you must do," Meg whispered.

I must rid the world of *El Lobison* and his slave.

Chapter 55

The Midlands.

"YOU can change shape at will," Hal said to Yassimine. In the five days he had been captive to The Master and Yassimine, he'd not had a chance to ask questions. He needed to know their vulnerabilities before he acted.

He and Yassimine trudged behind The Master, who rode his fine Andalusian stallion across the hills. With every step, the silver chain around Hal's waist chafed and burned.

"Sí," Yassimine replied in strangely accented Spanish. She seemed more comfortable in that tongue than English or French. Her native language was totally incomprehensible to Hal. But he had understood that tongue the morning after his conversion in the Paris dungeon. Why not now?

Probably because the magic of the ritual had lingered. Now the magic was gone, leaving only the curse.

"Why are you not governed by the phases of the moon?" he asked again.

"I must change when the moon waxes fat with new life. Other times I can shift when I need to."

"How can that be? You are a werewolf." He feigned ignorance.

"I am . . . the mother of werewolves. A priestess of our kind."

"And that gives you more power and more control."

Interesting that werewolves had a kind of society that required a priestess and therefore a belief system. Hal had no idea the society was that extensive.

How much of it did The Master control?

"Sí. The others are governed solely by the moon. They are less human at all times, though."

"Am I a priest of your people?"

"You are but a pup. Barely weaned," she snorted on a short sharp laugh. "But a handsome pup, ready for more manly things."

Hal jerked away from her fluttering eyelashes and the gentle rubbing of her bosom against his arm. His revulsion for her brought a sour taste into his mouth. He wanted to spit and run away. How could he have enjoyed sex with her so short a time ago?

But he had to stay, had to earn her trust so that he could betray that trust and kill The Master. Once free of The Master, he would use Yassimine to regain his humanity. Then he would kill her, too. The thought of betrayal sickened him as much as her touch.

"Not here," he said quietly. "The Master is most jealous of your affections."

Even now the Spaniard looked back at them from atop his spirited horse. "Hurry along," he commanded. We must reach Great Yarmouth before the pack finds our trail again."

"Boston is closer," Hal offered. Anything to end this journey and remove The Master and Yassimine from England.

"Great Yarmouth is in Norfolk, inhabited by many Catholics still sympathetic to their late duke and his loyalty to Mary Queen of Scots." The Master spurred his horse forward. "Catholics listen to my cause."

More likely the Catholics did not question the superstitions The Master pressed upon them. They would also more likely believe his lies about helping Mary Stuart. He hadn't wanted to free the exiled queen at all. He wanted only to kill her and then blame her martyrdom on Protestants. Terror through death and blood increased his power.

Hal and Yassimine had to lope to keep up with him. They had no more chance for conversation for a long time.

But Hal had learned something. He was special or, at least, different among the wolves. He could control when and if he shape-changed. The urge simmered strong in him during the three days of the full moon. His strength ebbed and flowed with the phases of the moon, being strongest at the full, and quite ordinary among men at the dark. But he could resist the moon at the full and did not require a full moon to change.

Why was he different?

How could he use that difference to end The Master's tyranny?

"It is good you seek to know more of our kind," Yassimine said as they started downhill and could catch their breath. "I told The Master that you were too young for the conversion. Now you have grown into your manhood and your wolf. You are ready to join us completely."

"Join you in what?"

"The Master has not told you?"

"He has said remarkably little to me."

"That is because you are also a powerful magician. You could lead the pack in his stead, control them as he does. He does not wish you to know too much."

"But you do wish it."

"You would be a more gentle consort to me. More understanding. You could father true werewolves since you are one yourself. You would not need the ritual."

The idea tempted him. He, as Pendragon of Britain . . . of all Europe, with a network of informers, ordinary folk with the extra power of werewolves. No one would challenge him.

He could do it. All he needed was a little time and the death of The Master.

Memories of Dee and her gentle approach to magic, her reluctance to use it if another solution presented itself, reminded him of what the Pendragon stood for. What the Pendragon aimed for. Peace—not power. Protection—not domination.

"What does *El Lobison* mean among your people?"

"It is his name. I know no other. I do not know what this means in his tongue. I have never needed to know more than that he is The Master of werewolves."

Hal had read the name in an obscure text in the Kirkenwood archives when first he became a wolf. *El Lobison* was the title granted to the designated assassin of the most powerful international merchant family in Spain. A family backed by the Spanish Inquisition and the crown. A family notorious for murdering their rivals—openly. And getting away with it because no one dared challenge them.

Hal was about to step on their very sensitive lupine paws.

"I smell the sea," Yassimine said. She lifted her nose to the air.

"The port lies just ahead. We catch the evening tide," *El Lobison* said. He spurred his horse along.

Hal paused long enough to sniff the air, mimicking Yassimine. But he turned his senses behind him. Just a whiff of tired men, sweating horses, and flagging wolfhounds came to him.

Hurry, Da. Hurry and help me kill El Lobison.

Two days later. The port city of Great Yarmouth, England.

"Don't let them get away!" Donovan urged his horse to even greater speed with spurs and whip. The tired beast responded with a surge of speed and then faltered.

They had ridden hard from Sheffield to Great Yarmouth. Despite a little detour following a magical phantom, Donovan's magic told him the Spaniard and his werewolf bitch had never been more than two hours ahead of them. Donovan had sensed the magic in the figures that moved north and thought perhaps it was only the Spaniard or—worse—Hal blurring their trail.

But the scent of magic had faded too quickly. The dogs had scented nothing along the path and pulled against their leads to return to the easterly road. In less than half an hour Donovan and his army had returned to the chase.

Halfway across England they had run. A night and a day and well into the next night they had followed, taking only brief rest—a third of the men at a time—changing horses when and where they could. Several times they had caught glimpses of the fleeing quarry. And each time they had eluded him.

As Dee had eluded Robin. His secretary had returned to the main force less than a day after separating. Dee's trail had disappeared as if she had taken flight.

Donovan's heart ached at the thought of the grief she

must endure. Alone. "Go to her," he begged the ghosts that haunted him.

He did not know if they responded or not. He had the Spaniard to deal with.

At the edge of the sprawling harbor town the scent of their quarry became confused with the masses of people still mingling on the streets around the taverns and warehouses. But there was only one place they could go in a port city.

"Prepare my pistol, Robin," Donovan called as he slid off the exhausted horse. He grabbed the animal's reins, forcing him to walk and cool down.

Robin dismounted as well and fished for the weapons stored in the panniers. They were too cumbersome to carry outside their waterproof wrapping on the jostling ride; too dangerous and unreliable to leave loaded. In a matter of moments he had primed and readied both weapons. He handed one to Donovan and kept the other.

His stony expression belied the deep anger simmering within him.

Behind them, several more troops readied wheel lock weapons.

The streets narrowed. Mounted travel became impossible.

Donovan detailed a few men to continue walking the horses. He ran with the rest down the last few streets to the dock.

In the dim light Donovan made out the silhouette of a vessel anchored in deep water. Splashing sounds told him that someone rowed out to meet it.

He breathed deeply. "Give me sight," he begged of whatever powers listened to him. "Banish the darkness that separates me from mine enemy."

Nothing changed.

Donovan breathed again, careful to measure each breath in and out. He fought to ignore the urgency churning inside him. Bit by bit, he stilled his entire being. The world opened for him, banishing shadows and revealing the hidden things around the dock and out in the water.

The small boat jumped into focus. Four figures, Hal and the woman in the rear, a man at the oars, and the Spaniard in the prow.

Silently he brought the pistol to bear, sighting carefully

along the barrel. He held the Spaniard's head in his sights.
Then correcting slightly for distance and wind he pulled
the trigger.

A mighty blast and the acrid smell of burning powder
jolted him out of the magical trance. Darkness surrounded
him once more.

A dozen weapons fired to his right and left. Then quiet
resumed as men peered toward the silhouette of the ship.

Donovan detected the sounds of the oars splashing in the
water, farther away than before, and . . . and a soft moan
of pain. Deep pain.

He had hit someone in the boat. Who?

The faery circle near the castle ruins of Huntington.

Three weeks passed in the protected quiet of Aunt Meg's
Hermitage. I spent hours kneeling beside the graves atop
the tor. Did I pray? I am not certain what I did, only that
I held my father's rosary in my hands, counted the beads
over and over, and tried desperately to touch some part of
him, or my mother, or Michael who had had the beads restrung. No ghosts visited me.

But a constant stream of the living made pilgrimage to
the simple shrine. Common folk, Gypsies, glassblowers, the
poor and dispossessed. Many of the pilgrims remembered
my father and spoke of him with affection and sometimes
awe. Nearly twenty years since his death and their memories had not dimmed. Nor their respect.

They gave me a closer look at my father than any of my
family was willing to impart.

As I sat by the grave, running my fingers through the
wildflowers, plucking at the grass, I came across a hard
object lodged in the dirt, right above where I guessed my
father's heart would have been. Curious that any stone
should intrude upon the carefully tended plot, I rooted
around until I worked it free. A black crystal as big as my
fist warmed to my touch.

Many washings in the creek did not change the color.

The sun played interesting games with the crystal. Fire seemed to dance in its interior. If I looked long enough and hard enough into the heart of the stone, I might see the mysteries of the universe unfold.

Ruefully, I shook my head clear of such fantasies. An interesting piece only. Not the Philosopher's Stone of fame and legend.

I pocketed it against a time when I might want it for some arcane purpose.

At the end of the third week enough time had passed that my body confirmed Aunt Meg's prediction of pregnancy. I left the shrine. My heart was full of grief and loneliness but also a determination to continue the work of my father and his predecessors. The staff and the ring would never be mine, but I had my dog. I needed no confirmation from the family that I was my father's only and true successor.

On the road back to London, the people who had visited me at my father's shrine did not leave. Out of respect for my father, they kept me company. They protected me, a woman alone barely disguised by my masculine clothing. The one time armed men challenged me, the bandits backed away from the ragged and fierce entourage I had gathered. Only when I found lodging in clean and secure inns did my people fade into the distance. I met them again on the road the next morning just after dawn.

Each day I listened more closely to their tales, their woes, the laws that made being Gypsy illegal. I learned to call them Rom, for they called themselves the Romani and not Egyptians at all. I learned how their men were often killed outright and the women branded and enslaved; how having no home or allegiance to a lord made them the enemies of England and Queen Elizabeth.

I could offer no words of wisdom or advice to the people of the road. I gave them my sympathy, my loyalty, and my discretion. They gave me much, much more.

They told me more about my father and his simple message of faith. I fingered the rosary almost constantly. Faint glimmerings of belief began to warm my heart.

But a coldness lodged there. In order to take up where my father had left off, I needed to confront Betsy.

Rumors of her open claim to be the Pendragon had reached me in London. Elizabeth scoffed at the rumors, convinced that only the queen could confirm or deny the title. Other rumors reached me through the dark and secret ways of my world of espionage and duplicity. Rumors of Betsy's sexual exploits with any man of noble blood or bearing who presented himself at the gates of Kirkenwood. Rumors of strange-smelling smoke seeping out from the walls of the castle; of people in trances performing demeaning chores just to please Betsy; of unnatural births among the livestock, strange mixtures of wolves and sheep, of cows and horses.

These last I dismissed as too cruel and fantastic for even Betsy's experiments. More like, she sought the Philosopher's Stone, the source of all magic and key to the secrets of the cosmos.

The rumors had nothing but praise for my cousin Griff. He acted the laird in his father's absence and tried hard to mitigate Betsy's cruelty. The collection of ears and tongues hung by the gate had disappeared.

Two days south of Huntington, the horse went lame. I made provisions for his care at the next inn. Then I joined my new friends on the road and walked to London. At the time I had no sense of delay. The journey became more important than the destination. We camped at night, telling stories around the fire, singing and sharing whatever provisions came to hand.

I found a walking stick, nice sturdy oak with an interesting grain. At night I stripped off the bark to expose the beautiful golden wood. One of the women gave me a bit of leather from a rabbit skin. We stitched it around the stick as a cushion for my hand. Then we shrank it to keep it in place. When cured, the grip blended perfectly with the wood.

At the top of the staff, a knot worked loose, leaving a deep hole. Barely thinking, I tried the stem of my black crystal in the hole. The wood seemed to accept and enfold the crystal as a part of itself. Bindings of deer sinew and a good soak shrank the wood to hold the crystal snugly.

"Now you are a proper Merlin with a staff and a ring," Micah, the head of the Gypsy clan proclaimed.

I looked at my left hand where Michael's signet ring rested, a winged griffin rampant cut into a blood-red garnet. Not exactly the sigil of the Pendragon but close enough.

My father had walked and lived amongst these people for many months. This was how he came to learn the heart of Britain, through her people and not through politics, and monarchs, and international relations.

At times I almost believed he walked beside me on that trek.

I made many new friends on that journey. I also increased my spy network tenfold.

By the time I passed through Smithfield to Newgate, I had been gone from home more than a month. The everyday problems of running a tavern crept into my mind. I sorted through my priorities and wondered how I would manage without Michael. Then I began to plan my next interview with Sir Francis Walsingham.

At last, I entered the tavern yard. A dozen of the queen's guard stood in a rigid semicircle before the doorway. Uncle Donovan braced himself in the doorway, denying them entrance.

Flitting between them, eagerly adding to the conflict on both sides was Betsy Kirkwood, brandishing a staff and the ring of the Pendragon.

Chapter 56

Summer 1580. The Crown and Anchor Tavern, London.

DONOVAN stared at his niece at the edge of the crowd that watched the confrontation so eagerly. So young. She'd been so young when last he saw her. Still young. Too young to be a widow, to have watched her husband murdered so brutally.

Now she stared at him with the worries of the entire world in her eyes. Those huge gray eyes, so like her mother's. But the stubborn thrust of her chin she had from her father. She had aged in the past month. Matured as well.

Where had she been? Every attempt he made to find her had failed. He had not even found Mad Meg's Hermitage. It was as if the entire place had disappeared into the mist of another world. So he had hastened to London to see to the proper running of her tavern, knowing she must return there eventually. And so she had. Betsy had arrived, unbidden, on a similar mission.

She had suddenly decided to take a more active role in England's politics, seemingly through this very tavern located within a stone's throw of three embassies and a major ferry point on the river. Patrons of the new theaters on the south bank of the Thames would find this place very convenient to slake their thirst after an energetic afternoon of throwing catcalls and rotten fruit at the players. Much of London had an opportunity to visit this place. It must be a fount of gossip.

And very valuable to Elizabeth.

Dee carried a staff and wore a heavy ring, so like Betsy. Yet unlike Donovan's daughter. This beloved niece—daughter of his heart— carried a staff that fitted her height and nestled comfortably in her hand. And the ring she wore fit as if made for her.

"No wonder the Lady refused to gift the sword to you," he said quietly to Betsy.

"What?" Hair in disarray, eyes wide and wild, she had not heard him.

He cringed at the memory of the last time Betsy had found fault with him. She'd loosed a spell that mimicked a thousand ants crawling over his skin. He still itched at times in the most embarrassing of places.

"Too bad you do not remember your Grandmother Raven," he said as he stepped away from the door of the tavern. "She was the perfect image of the Pendragon."

When Betsy was five long paces behind him, he called to the knight and ten men-at-arms who sought possession of Deirdre's property. "Gentlemen, our dispute is now moot!"

"I do not know you, sirrah. Why should I believe your claims?" The knight, a barely-bearded youth, struck a silly pose made popular among actors, with one leg extended and the opposite arm raised with one finger pointing at the sky.

"The theater serves no good purpose if it makes asses like you think they are sophisticated," Donovan muttered sotto voce.

A tiny smile flickered across Deirdre's face. She quickly swallowed it. But she had heard his comment.

"New come to the court, are you?" Donovan asked the knight in a louder tone. Donovan had not attended Elizabeth since she had confronted Robin all those years ago. His reports to her had been written and channeled through Walsingham.

"The theater offers many services, Milord of Kirkenwood," Deirdre called from the edge of the crowd. "It keeps many troublemakers occupied and off the streets. It gives malcontents something to talk about other than mischief. The theater increases the business of taverns such as this where the gallery may gather to discuss the day's performances at length."

Having spoken her piece, Deirdre stepped forward, staff in hand, followed by the magnificent dog.

Betsy's dog had died a few years ago and never been

replaced. None of the litters Brenin sired had produced a familiar.

Deirdre's female obviously had.

Betsy would never forgive her that.

"Milord of Kirkenwood," Deirdre continued, emphasizing the title for the crowd that had gathered to watch the fun of a brawl. "Meet Sir Sydney. You might have made his acquaintance the last time you were at court. I believe he was a page then. Her Majesty knighted him less than half a year ago. About the time she last found quarrel with Milord of Leicester. She sought a new favorite."

"And did Her Majesty instantly regret her actions?" Donovan quirked an eyebrow at the young man.

"Oh, he has his uses."

"And who might you be, madam?" Sir Sydney asked. His voice rose on a squeak. He swallowed to keep it under control. His throat apple bobbed nervously. He shied away from her and wrinkled his nose.

"Deirdre Griffin, mistress of this establishment." She moved forward, through the press of her neighbors and friends. They all greeted her with warmth and familiarity. Many of the women hugged her and the men grabbed her hand. She and Michael had lived among them many years in geniality.

"Michael is dead," she told a plump woman. "We will all share a cup in his honor tonight. Pass the word."

A gasp went up among the neighbors. Then anxious murmurs. More hugs and tears impeded Deirdre's progress toward the front door.

By now the crowd filled the street, completely blocking it to other traffic. Carters and tradesmen alike set up a protest.

Donovan sensed a renewed violence rising among them. He needed to calm these people before blood was shed.

Then Dee moved forward, separating herself from the her friends and neighbors. She emerged from the crowd, maintaining her grip on her staff and on her calm. She seemed to radiate goodwill.

Donovan had to blink back tears at the brightness of her aura.

"I was told . . ." Sir Sydney's voice squeaked again.

"Before you say more, sir," Deirdre interrupted the knight, "let us withdraw to the taproom. We can discuss your orders over a long mug of brew."

"I was told," Sir Sydney resumed on a deeper note.

"What you were told need not be broadcast to the world." Dee grabbed his elbow and urged him indoors.

As soon as the darkness enfolded their little party, Dee dismissed all of the employees to the kitchen. Donovan moved behind the bar and drew four tankards. He passed them to Sir Sydney, Betsy, and Dee. His niece downed half of her drink in one gulp. She set the near empty cup back on the bar and sighed.

"Now, Sir Sydney, what were you told?" Donovan asked.

"That the mistress of this place was Lady . . . Lady Deirdre Maelstrom." He looked her up and down, curling his lip at her masculine riding leathers that had been worn too long. Twigs and grass peeked out of her mass of autumn leaf-red hair as it curled about her delicate face. Her eyebrows canted upward at the end in a perpetual expression of sarcasm. And mischief glinted in her haunting gray eyes. Obviously, no lady would appear in public attired thus.

"And . . . and Her Majesty commanded me to take possession of this tavern in her name because the Lady Deirdre was dead. This property reverts to the Crown."

"Maelstrom is . . . was my husband's title. And he is dead. I was only . . . lost."

Betsy clomped over to Dee and thrust her face forward until she stood nose to nose with her cousin.

"How dare you come back! I had everything under control." The scent of ghostweed gushed from her mouth.

Donovan gritted his teeth at the haunting odor. He'd tried the drug several times until he had nearly thrown himself off the ramparts of Kirkenwood under the delusion the weed gave him the power to fly. Even today, nearly twenty years later he still longed for the rush of power that ghostweed gave him.

Martha had left him after that first episode. He'd been too deep in the drug's thrall to stop her.

A terrible sadness engulfed him. Obviously, Betsy had succumbed too often to the craving from ghostweed. He'd lost her to the dark forces of magic a long time ago. When had she become insane as well?

"Give my good wishes to Her Majesty and tell her that I shall supply her with a full report on the morrow," Dee informed Sir Sydney. She ignored the fuming Betsy who loomed over her, magic nearly sparking from her fingers.

"I . . . I . . ." Sir Sydney stammered.

"Trust the good neighbors outside if not your own judgment, sir," Donovan said. He added a touch of magical persuasion to his words. "They know her for the owner of this place."

Through the open door, he saw how the men-at-arms rested their pikes. One of them was watching the activity of the crowd. He nodded to Dee in recognition. "Milady," he murmured.

"You know her?" Sir Sydney marched out and dragged the man back inside.

"Aye, sir. She be who she says she is. Escorted her to the queen's private solar many a time. Just took me a moment to recognize her in them outlandish clothes."

"Oh." The bluster and confidence seemed to drain out of the young knight.

"Report to Her Majesty all that you have seen here today, Sir Sydney, and tell her that my niece and I will attend her on the morrow." Donovan encouraged them to leave the tavern and yard.

"And what about your daughter?" Betsy managed to hiss even without any sibilant sounds in her sentence. "I am the Pendragon. Do I not deserve inclusion in your audience?"

"Elizabeth will dispute your claim," Deirdre said with a tired shrug. She edged toward the back rooms of her tavern, obviously anxious to seek reprieve from the rigors of her travels.

The crowd surged forward, eager to learn more from Dee.

"Elizabeth has no say in this. This is a family matter." Betsy rounded on her cousin, staff raised.

The crowd hissed and grumbled at the armed men outside. Betsy's anger fed their mood.

"Would you listen if I disputed your claim?" Deirdre turned her back on Betsy.

Betsy raised her staff, ready to strike her cousin. But Deirdre paid her no mind.

Sir Sydney and his men moved off. Haste bit at their

heels. They had no more purpose in this neighborhood and clearly wanted no part of the volatile emotions brewing.

"Go home now, good folk. We will raise a cup in Michael's honor tonight," Donovan called to the simmering crowd.

A few mumbles and protests followed his words. Mostly from men who had picked up loose cobbles and tools as potential weapons. The women scuttled away in tight knots of gossip.

The first of the stalled carters slammed his way through the lingerers. They shouted at him and he cursed back.

A stout woman in an apron pulled her man away by his ear. Jeers and taunts followed him. A few more men drifted back to their daily tasks.

Then a mounted courier bearing Leicester's bold purple livery pushed through and traffic took on a more normal pattern.

"Ladies, we need privacy," Donovan commanded. He closed the door and lowered the crossbar. With the words, he spun tiny webs of compulsion. Something he should have done more often when they were younger and more suggestible.

Both women reared back as if he had slapped them.

Donovan exhaled much of the tension that had built steadily in his body since Deirdre had ridden off, nearly mad with grief.

Two barmaids burst from kitchen and began fussing over Coffa by the fire. They offered her a bowl of water and a meaty bone. They petted her vigorously, picking burrs out of her fur. The dog, of course, basked in the attention as her due. The bartender took his place behind the taps. He played at rearranging his tankards while his eyes constantly swept the taproom.

Betsy and Deirdre stood dead center, staffs planted, eyes locked upon each other. Donovan could barely breathe from the weight of the violent tension between the women. Their auras nearly crackled with power.

"You have had plenty of time to read the journals," Betsy said. A hard edge crept into her voice, despite the outwardly calm words. "Perhaps you should share them now."

"*My* father's journals belong here with me. If you can read them, you are welcome to try. But they may not leave the premises," Deirdre replied. She had better control over her voice. But not her eyes. Anger, malice, grief, loneliness all poured forth in her gaze.

Betsy narrowed her eyes in speculation.

"Deirdre." Donovan enfolded his niece in his arms. "I am most glad to have you back among the living, hale if not happy. You gave me quite a scare, running off like that."

"Best she stayed lost," Betsy muttered. "You've always loved her more than me."

Donovan chose to ignore Betsy for the moment. He had no idea how to deal with his strong-willed daughter.

"What prompted you to desert your family in your time of need?" Donovan continued to hold Deirdre, as if he expected her to run away again.

"Treason." Deirdre slipped out of his embrace as water through an open hand.

Chapter 57

The Crown and Anchor, London, England.

"TREASON," I repeated on whisper. "I ran away from my family because of treason."

Everyone in the room stilled. They seemed to cease breathing as they listened.

"Harsh words," Uncle Donovan said. His eyes narrowed and his aura shrank. He measured his breaths as he gathered himself.

I braced instinctively for a blast of magic from him. Or from Betsy.

But my cousin seemed more curious than angry.

"Did Da try to slip into Mary's bedchamber again?" she asked. Mischief danced in her eyes.

"Out!" I commanded my employees. They hastened into the kitchen and solar behind the taproom. But I knew they listened at the keyholes.

Coffa lifted her great head from her paws, but she did not stir from her position by the hearth.

"Will you include me in your report to Walsingham?" Uncle Donovan shifted restlessly from foot to foot. From my youth in his household, I knew he fought to calm his instincts to pace or ride or slam his fist into something.

"Why did you do it?" I asked. My heart was torn between love for him and loyalty to my queen and country.

But did Uncle Donovan love anyone as deeply as he loved Mary? Would he sacrifice us all for the exiled queen?

"You know why," he said grimly. He began to pace. Coffa heaved herself to her feet and followed him. He'd have to go through her to get to me.

Betsy remained rooted in the center of the room, watching everything, weighing her observations, calculating how to use them.

"I know that you love Mary Stuart and want to be with her. But do you love her so much you would risk the assassination of Elizabeth and the return of the Catholic Church to England once Mary is free?"

"Mary would never . . ."

"Mary has plotted all those things and more. Which do you love more, Mary or England? You have to choose, Milord of Kirkenwood. Choose now." I had to remain firm. My future and my baby's future depended upon him. We would survive no matter what he chose. But would England? I did not like the feeling of dependence and vulnerability.

"I had planned to take Mary back to France, marry her, and live quietly there."

"Mary would not allow that," Betsy and I said together. One thing we had in common was an honest evaluation of the woman who had bewitched Uncle Donovan.

"I will not allow you to desert the family for a life in exile," Betsy continued. "I am the Pendragon." She glared at me in defiance.

She was not worth my time. I had to concentrate on Uncle Donovan.

Did Mary truly love him? Dozens of men worshiped her. Many, like Thomas Howard, Duke of Norfolk, had gone to their deaths for her already. Or had someone else cast a spell upon him?

I closed my eyes and concentrated a moment. When I opened them again, I saw new layers in his aura, subtle changes here and there and something quite alien sitting on his left shoulder, right next to the black spot where death lurked on everyone.

"Someone put a love spell on you," I blurted out.

"Your mother. It died with her."

"No, it didn't." Betsy adopted a bland and innocent face. She would not look me in the eye.

" 'Tis born of the demon, not Roanna. The demon still lives," I said, barely daring to breathe. I did not like the direction of my thoughts. For now, I allowed the demon to take the blame for the spell. For now; until I had proof otherwise.

"I sealed the demon behind his portal," Uncle Donovan insisted.

"Trapped between two worlds, but still alive. As long as the Demon of Chaos exists, so will your love for Mary." Betsy reached out to touch the layers of energy surrounding her father. Then her hand plunged through the aura to grasp the heart-shaped locket he always wore.

Had Mary given it to him?

I wondered if she could actually feel his emotions through the locket. Her talent was wild and strange. She had nurtured it with many alchemic experiments over the years. I had no way of knowing precisely what she could and could not do.

Mayhap, I needed to study her more before I dismissed her claims to be the Pendragon.

"The spell is unbreakable," Betsy announced.

I did not like the satisfied smirk or the set of her shoulders. She lied.

"For you, perhaps," I countered her. A little bit of magic trickled down my arm into my hands and fingers. I had to catch and backlash any spell she threw at me.

"Can you break it?" Donovan ceased his pacing and whirled to face me.

"Possibly. If that is truly what you wish. You have to truly wish to rid yourself of the curse." More power spread outward from my belly, enveloping my womb in a web of protection.

Betsy glared at me. After a long moment, while we all thought through the possibilities, she said, "I could break it if I had access to your father's journals. The key to the spell must be there. Your father found the Philosopher's Stone, the key to all magic and to understanding the universe. I am positive of it. How else could he be the only one who understood Roanna or her demon?"

"I doubt *you* will find anything in the journals." I still did not know if I would be able to read them. Though Aunt Meg thought I was ready. I had to read them with love not greed or desperation.

"But you can?" Betsy arched one fine blonde eyebrow as if she questioned my ability to tell the truth. Her aura thickened as power built within her, too.

I smiled rather than answer.

Betsy arched her fingers like a cat extending her claws. A draft swirled about her feet. The door was closed tightly, the windows shuttered. There was no place for the wind to enter.

"This is not about ending your father's obsession with a woman who will be his downfall, Mary Elizabeth," I said calmly. Names had power. By invoking her full name I hoped to unnerve her. Pregnant and exhausted, I could not hope to match her, let alone defeat her in a magical duel. "This is about you finding the Philosopher's Stone." Carefully, I kept my gaze away from the black crystal atop my staff.

She did not deign to answer, so I knew I had struck the truth.

"Ladies. Please," Uncle Donovan tried to intervene. He even took a step toward us.

I waved him away. "In my experience, the only people who think they need the Philosopher's Stone are those who do not have the talent or discipline to find answers within themselves. Best you seek out Dr. John Dee if that is your desire, Betsy. He claims to have found it. I do not make such a claim, and neither did my father."

We continued to stare at each other, never letting the other make an unobserved move.

"Betsy, Deirdre! We still have much to discuss. Many important issues." This time I did not try to silence my uncle. I had said my piece. It was time Betsy thought about it.

"I will tell Walsingham that I sent for you as backup for Michael and me, if—*IF* I can remove the love spell and you give me your word of honor that you will never again seek out Mary Stuart. Never again write to her. Never again join a plot to free her from Elizabeth's custody." This time I turned my full gaze upon Uncle Donovan with all of the power that had been building in me for my own defense against Betsy. I had to unleash it somewhere.

He flinched and touched the locket at the center of his chest. I sensed his attention wandering. A dreamy glaze came over his eyes. The spell sought to protect itself by distracting him with memories of his love for Mary.

"Do I have your word of honor?" I nearly shouted.

"But . . ."

"Then you go to the Tower with Oxford and the Jesuit

conspirators." I slammed my staff into the floor and turned to retreat into the kitchen. "I presume Oxford aborted the plan when you did not storm the gates. He should be holed up in his manor, shivering in the dark, waiting for Elizabeth to arrest him." I took two steps in my planned retreat.

"Do not turn your back on me!" Betsy screamed.

A rush of wind spun me around to face her, pushed me against the nearest wall, and pinned me there. I gasped for air, struggled to break the invisible bonds.

Betsy laughed. She did not bother to confine several curls that had escaped her cap. A touch of hysteria hinted at the insanity I suspected lurked in her mind.

I fought for calm and breath.

"Betsy, release her," Uncle Donovan said. Too weak. Too hesitant. Betsy would never listen.

"Not until she gives up the journals." The pressure upon my chest increased.

I fought it. It increased until I relaxed. Then it eased off. Inwardly, I smiled. Betsy conserved her own strength by setting her guiding element to feed off of my struggles.

Breathe in three counts. Hold three, out three. I calmed my mind and body. With each lessening of tension in my muscles, the wind backed off. Not enough to free me, only to breathe strongly and gather my strength.

"The journals can wait, Betsy," Uncle Donovan said. His voice took on an oily note of persuasion. He fed his words with a bit of magic.

Betsy sloughed off the worm of compulsion in her father's voice. "It is all about the journals and the secrets your brother hid from you. He was the last true Pendragon. The only way to succeed him is to understand his secret writings." She turned her attention back to me, noticed my stillness, and increased the pressure.

Outside, rain fell in torrents. Water was also her element. With a few words in Greek and a stabbing gesture she opened a leak in the thatched roof. First a few drops, then a trickle, and then a steady stream of water pooled upon the stone floor of my tavern. Very shortly, the puddle might begin to flood.

Was Betsy so insane she'd drown herself as well as her father and me in her mad fixation upon the journals?

"You can have the journals. If you can find them," I said

quietly. In my mind I saw them beneath the mattress of the big bed I had last shared with Michael. A sob of grief caught in my throat. Had my baby been conceived on that last evening together?

Ruthlessly, I shook off my sadness and replaced it with determination. I had added my own cloaking spell to my father's original fogging. A casual observer would not see the little leather-covered books unless looking directly at them.

"Where are they?" Betsy approached me with her right hand raised, fingers extended like talons.

Instinctively, I turned my face away from those long fingernails that could easily gouge out my eyes.

"Answer me!"

I firmly fixed the picture of them beneath the mattress in my mind, carefully avoiding where I had truly hidden them.

Coffa growled at Betsy's tone. My familiar stalked forward, teeth bared, drool gathering in long ropes from her beard.

Betsy backed off one step and lowered her hands.

Coffa maintained her defensive stance.

"Look within yourself," I replied. "That is where you will have to look eventually for answers to your dilemmas."

"Riddles! You speak in riddles, just like the writings of Grandmother Raven."

"I told you she was like her grandmother," Uncle Donovan said. "Do I need to flee to the Continent, Deirdre? Or may I remain in England a free man, loyal to my queen?"

"Are you truly loyal, or will your love for Mary overshadow your sense of duty and honor?"

"If it could, would I not have stormed her previous, less well-guarded refuges? Would I not have been part of Norfolk's crusade eight years ago?"

"You could not join with Norfolk because he intended to wed Mary as part of the plan. He wanted to rule England and Scotland in her name," I reminded him.

"If I loved her more than my honor or duty to Elizabeth, would that have mattered? Mary could not keep England peaceful and prosperous. Mary could not hold the people of England united. I sought to marry her, love her, protect her, not to put her upon the throne."

"Enough talk of politics. I need those journals, Deirdre," Betsy interrupted.

"I told you. You have to find them for yourself."

"You are no relative of mine, bastard bitch. I will find the Philosopher's Stone on my own." With one final push of wind against my chest Betsy stormed out of the tavern into the rain. The wind retreated with her.

I breathed deeply.

"Your report to Walsingham?"

"I have not decided. Best you retreat to Kirkenwood. You are not welcome in my home now. Perhaps not for a very long time. And, this time, curb your daughter's insane pursuit of power. Magic alone does not make a Pendragon."

He nodded. "The Lady of the Lake said much the same thing without words. I suspect you would receive a different answer than Betsy did if you sought Excalibur." He retreated as well.

I sagged against the wall. Coffa offered her shoulder as a brace.

My employees rushed into the taproom, questions falling from their tongues.

"Ready the place for business. The roof needs a patch now. Open the doors and welcome our patrons with smiles. Open that cask of beer and offer the first mug free to each. Fetch me quill and paper. I must send to the queen, requesting audience." I set my shoulders and prepared myself to face the rest of my life alone, without family.

Without Michael.

Without Hal.

But I had friends here in London and on the road. I had my baby.

And I had a mission. I alone could protect England in the crisis I knew must come. My father had predicted it.

Chapter 58

Summer 1580. Coast of Cornwall, England.

HAL looked up to the sharp angles of the castle atop the coastal promontory. Cornish summer, hot and moist, had come early to this region. Sparse sea grasses clung green and vibrant in rocky crevices. The setting sun added golden highlights to the scant life on this shore.

Life. Hope. A chance. Hal grasped those fragile concepts and kept them close to his heart.

The castle above them fell into shadow and took on the black hues akin to evil that Hal knew must dwell here.

The rowboat rose up and down in the slight ocean swell. The ship from which they had just debarked already hoisted sail and retreated from local fishermen and Elizabeth's customs agents. The boatman who had rowed Hal, Yassimine, and *El Lobison* out to the vessel in Great Yarmouth Harbor had died from the wound inflicted by a magically directed and propelled bullet. Word of the man's death spread rapidly through their destination port. No captain had wanted to transport *El Lobison* back to England. One captain had finally capitulated under heavy threat of being forced to become a werewolf. They made a very fast passage across the Channel and over to this coast of Cornwall. The captain of the vessel wanted to be quit of the Spaniard as soon as possible.

At each rise from the ocean swell Hal glimpsed a tiny crescent of shale beach beneath the castle.

Hopefully, the local boatman who manned the oars now knew the tricks of the local currents and rocks. Else they'd have a long cold swim.

Could The Master swim? Yassimine probably could, as

could Hal. The wolf instinct in her was strong. It would
find a way to keep her out of the treacherous unseen depths
of the ocean.

But *El Lobison?*

Hal shifted his weight in the back of the skiff. The boatman compensated deftly and kept the next wave from slop-
ping over oarlocks. The man frowned severely at Hal, as if
he knew his thoughts.

Hal shifted again, pretending restlessness and a lack of
control of his wolf.

The Master gasped and clung tightly to his seat in the
prow. His knuckles turned white. A torrent of words in
a harsh language Hal did not understand flowed from *El
Lobison's* mouth.

Instantly, the sea calmed. Not even the slight swell of
a slack tide on a still day marred their progress toward
the beach.

The boatman snickered at Hal.

"He's too smart for the likes o' you, pup," the man said
quietly. His accent was so thick Hal had to strain to understand him. *El Lobison,* with his limited knowledge of English, would probably comprehend less.

Inwardly, Hal seethed at the Spaniard. For more than a
month, Hal had tried again and again to find the man's
vulnerability.

The Master was indeed a master sorcerer with multiple
layers of defense. Casual spells of irritation tossed by Hal in
The Master's direction backlashed threefold. More serious
spells conjured in front of the fire in various manors and
castles on the way here, with Hal well armored against a
backlash, merely dissipated as if he'd never sent them.

But here, at The Master's local base of power, he might
let down his guard long enough for Hal to find a way to
terminate him and his obscene quest to control the world
through the terror of his werewolves.

The elves had freed The Master's pack in England. He
needed to rebuild it.

Hal needed to keep him from doing that.

In moments the boatman had run the little skiff up onto
the shale. He and Hal jumped out to push it higher onto
the slick rocks. When it was safely free of the waves, the
boatman leaped to assist The Master out of the boat.

Under the scrutiny of both men, Hal had little choice but to offer Yassimine his hand. His skin crawled as she closed her fingers about his palm. The invitation was there in her eyes, and in her pouting lips, and the way she squeezed his hand.

Hal had no interest in this woman who smelled of blood and death even when her wolf was least strong at the dark of the moon. Every time he looked at her, he remembered Deirdre cradling the lifeless body of Sir Michael Maelstrom in her arms; how she cried and moaned as if she, too, must follow him into death rather than face the future alone.

With another spate of words in The Master's arcane tongue, a cave revealed itself, tucked into a fold in the hillside.

Hal forced himself to listen to every syllable The Master uttered. He repeated each word silently, keeping the emphasis and phrasing identical. His life might depend upon learning The Master's secret spells.

"I do not like the smell of this place." Yassimine shied away from the dark cavern.

Hal did not like it either. Unlike the cave and tunnel of Kirkenwood, this place smelled of fear and blood and death. Unnatural death and black magic born in chaos.

"Swallow your fears, slave!" The Master snapped. He proceeded into the darkness without looking back. A few steps in from the entrance he snapped his fingers. A green flame shot from his hand into a waiting torch. The boatman lifted the torch out of its wall bracket and led the way.

Yassimine followed them reluctantly. She looked back constantly over her shoulder toward the diminishing pool of natural light at the entrance.

Hal brought up the rear, more curious than afraid. The Master kept secrets here.

They climbed steadily. Small passages veered off from the main passage. Hal slowed his step long enough to sniff each one. People had been imprisoned there. The smell of fear and pain was strong.

The Master never looked back. Nor did he pause.

At last they encountered a bolted wooden door, bound and hinged with iron. The Master opened it with a pass of his arm and no words. The bolts slid back without a hand touching them.

"I can do that. If I put my mind to it," Hal muttered to himself. He'd make quicker work of destroying the door with Fire.

Beyond the door lay the first of the undercrofts. Neat stacks of barrels filled the space. This castle was stocked to withstand a siege of many months.

Hal counted four levels of cellars above the dungeons. A castle needed foundations that deep to support the twenty-foot-thick walls and a massive keep.

The last of the undercrofts opened into the sunken kitchen. From there, they had to climb once more to the open bailey of the castle. The castle tower rose above them seven stories at least in height. The top arrow slit windows offered views of the entire countryside and far out to sea. The primary building had been set atop a mound, the motte, to elevate it higher yet.

Centuries of weather and sea spray had blackened the original stones. A dark lichen had attached to much of the walls, especially those exposed to the sea damp. In all, it looked as black and menacing close up as it had from a distance.

The hairs on Hal's spine and nape stood on end. He did not like this place at all.

The interior walls of The Master's private quarters on the third floor of the keep were covered in rich rugs woven in exotic swirls and abstract patterns. The colors nearly vibrated within the wool.

"I could get lost trying to trace one of the designs in my mind," Hal muttered to himself, suddenly dizzy. More rugs covered the floors. Huge cushions replaced chairs and silk draped the bed and partitioned off sections of the chamber for privacy. Dozens of branched candle holders brought light to every corner. Three braziers made the place seem cozy, almost intimate.

"Food and wine." The Master clapped his hands and spoke.

A scurry of footsteps behind one of the gauzy curtains indicated that an unseen servant scuttled to do his bidding.

Yassimine flopped down on a nest of cushions in the corner farthest from the six arrow slit windows—three in each of the two outer walls of this corner of the keep. She sprawled her limbs and reclined indolently.

Hal stood uneasily in the center. He did not know what was expected of him.

"Now we will plan." The Master rubbed his hands together as he approached a massive table made of some dark wood alien to England. He sat in the high-backed straight chair of the same wood. Thin cushions in yet a different abstract pattern of red and blue and yellow, nestled against his back and butt, molding to his slender frame as if bid to do so by magic.

"Plan what?" Hal asked.

"How to rebuild my pack of wolves here in England. You shall be instrumental this time, pup," he said with a sneer. A half smile flicked across his mouth and then vanished.

"How?"

The Master tugged on the bell pull above the table. A guard appeared in the doorway. At the same time a servant dressed in a grease-stained, rough linen tunic and wool breeches scuttled in. His tray was laden with a wine decanter, cups, a loaf of new-baked bread, creamy cheese, and thick slabs of barely cooked meat with a crisp crust of fat on the edges. Probably beef or mutton. Venison would be leaner. Yassimine did not like pork or fowl. Hal had never seen The Master eat those "lesser meats" either.

Hal's mouth watered at the scents rising from the tray.

"Bring our guests," The Master commanded the guard, totally ignoring the servant.

"All of them, sir?" the guard asked.

"Yes. Bring all of them. The full moon approaches. We need to evaluate each of our . . . guests."

Hal guessed the people were more prisoners than guests.

The Master waved permission for Hal and Yassimine to partake of the food.

Yassimine lunged upward from her nest of pillows and grabbed most of the meat. She tore at it hungrily. Fat dribbled down her chin. Hal lost his taste for the meat. He contented himself with the bread and cheese. The Master raised an eyebrow at him in speculation. The guard returned with three more armed men and about a dozen ragged and filthy peasants. An equal mix of men and women. They trudged into the room, all chained together with heavy iron. None of them looked anywhere but at their feet. The youngish men had not shaved in weeks. The women—barely mature—had not seen a comb or a hairpin in a very long time. They all needed baths and clean clothes without tears and split seams.

The Master stood up and circled the troop, inspecting each of them from crown to toes. Yassimine eyed them curiously. Hal cringed in disgust and fear.

He had a sudden and terrible suspicion of how the Spaniard intended to rebuild his pack of werewolves.

Hal caught the eye of the blonde girl at the front. She was taller than the other women, a tad neater, and stood straighter. She had a fine figure, not yet fallen into emaciation. Most startling of all, she had one blue eye and one brown.

Superstition would follow her wherever she traveled.

Undoubtedly, she would be The Master's first victim.

Her gaze betrayed her desperation.

"They are not all men," Yassimine spat. "I will not enter into the ritual with women."

"No, my dear. You shall not have to. We have the pup over there to work with the women," The Master replied, more interested in soothing Yassimine than observing Hal's reaction to this news.

"Is this necessary?" Hal asked, trying to keep the squeak out of his voice.

"Yassimine can convert only one man each of the three nights of the full moon. You shall convert a woman at the same time, thus doubling the number of wolves at my behest." The Master concluded his inspection and returned to the high-backed chair by the table.

Hal gulped. Hazy memories of his own conversion ritual lodged in a huge lump in his throat. Blood and incense. Helwriaeth leaping to save Hal and dying on The Master's knife. Torture and rape. And, finally, the all important bite to the throat.

It had taken three days to infect him with the wolf because the moon had not been full. Yassimine had needed the power to build slowly for her part of the ritual.

The thought of doing that to a young woman . . .

"Do you have two girdles?" Hal asked. What would happen if he stole a girdle and seduced Yassimine? Could he reverse the ritual before the Spaniard discovered his plot?

"Unimportant question. All of these candidates are virgins," The Master said, as if discussing the breeding of a dog or a horse. "Male and female. Virgins convert so much more quickly and completely than experienced lovers. They have no expectations. Can you detect if any of them have a magical talent as well as strength?" The Master continued.

"No." Hal's voice wavered.

"I'm told these shores abound in hedge witches. No formal training, of course, just instinct, and a ruthless desire to succeed or survive. That is all I need."

"No," Hal said. Louder this time.

"Of course, since I insist on virgins, I shall have to make do with the very young. You English are much more open to experimentation than Spanish peasants. You do not fear the Church as do they. But then, the young are much easier to train."

"No!" Hal shouted.

"But yes," The Master narrowed his eyes and stroked the silver talisman around his throat.

Hal's silver chains twisted and burned until he dropped to his knees from the pain in his head and his gut.

"You will obey me, pup. You have no choice."

Chapter 59

July 1580. The night before the full moon. The wine cellar of The Master's stronghold, Cornwall, England.

"YOU must not do this!" Yassimine grabbed Hal's hand before he could open the bung of a wine barrel and pour straw-colored wine into The Master's favorite decanter.

"Why not?" Hal's hand tensed under hers. He seemed too calm in the face of the terrible deed he was about to enact.

She watched with fascination as his muscles flexed. Such beautiful hands. She longed to have him touch her with those long, elegant fingers again. They could find such ecstasy together, touching, exploring, discovering.

She shook off her reverie about making love with this man. Since the fight near Sheffield he had not looked at her with lust or longing. Only with disgust and contempt.

"The wine for the ritual must be red. The color of blood," she said. She licked her lips in anticipation of the proceedings tonight, the night before the full moon. She had already picked out the first man who would undergo conversion with her.

"The wine will be red by tonight," Hal said. He kept his hand poised upon the tap, holding the decanter beneath it. She would have to remove his grip on one or the other to prevent his actions.

"But the color will be artificial."

"The entire ritual is unnatural."

"But necessary."

"No, it is not necessary. It is a perversion. Obscene. It must be stopped. The Master must be stopped." He spat upon the stone floor.

"But without the ritual there will be no more of our kind!" Horror made Yassimine swallow deeply. She had not thought before about living without her wolf. Her people worshiped the wolf. They vied for the honor of becoming one. On the nights after her conversion they had elevated her kind to near godhood. In times of bad harvest her people offered up one of their own to feed her wolf in appeasement to the gods. She was a priestess of her people, meant to lead them. She had a duty to ensure that others followed in her wake.

"*Our* kind should be eradicated. The Catholic Church seeks that end with burnings." Hal snarled. His own wolf was very close to the surface.

Yassimine shuddered and made her own ward against the evils perpetuated against her kind by all the churches, crossing her right wrist over the left and flapping her hands. Three hundred convicted werewolves had been burned at the stake in the last two decades in France, Germany, Italy, Austria, and Spain. The Inquisition actively sought the end of her people.

"The Protestant Church sees our curse as a disease. They seek to eradicate us through a scientific cure. Either way, they are both right," Hal continued.

"Never!"

"I will gladly die if my death means that no other innocent person is cursed with a wolf." Hal's lips thinned and the muscle along his jaw twitched.

She'd not shake his determination easily. Nor could she tempt or distract him with sex as she did The Master.

"Do not say such things." Yassimine held a hand over his mouth.

He used the displacement of her grip to pour the wine. It had an odd odor. She sought to separate the scents within the wine from the damp and dust of the cellar and the strong musk of Hal nearing transformation.

"Barley wine? Why barley?"

"Because the barley was rotten when it was fermented."

"A good way to use grain that cannot be eaten."

"My father did not give me much. But he told me a story once. A story of how a great magician used barley wine to see beyond this realm."

"Is that a good thing?" Yassimine had never considered

things spiritual before. She was a wolf, the intermediary between her people and the gods. She transformed into the wolf. By eating people, she aided them in the transformation to the realm of the gods. Nothing else mattered.

But Hal made her look at life differently. She was not sure she liked that. She wanted a comfortable routine again. She wanted absolutes of right and wrong. She wanted to not have to think for herself.

"Seeing beyond reality can be a good thing. Or it can nearly kill you. Depends on how you use the visions." Hal closed the bung and rose from his crouch beside the barrel.

"And the great magician your father spoke of?"

"Dr. John Dee is still trying to figure out what he sees beyond sight. The visions, or maybe the rotten barley in the wine, nearly killed my father."

"I cannot take a chance that you will kill The Master with this wine." She slapped at his hand. The decanter tilted and a goodly portion of the wine spilled onto the stone floor. It pooled in the mortar between the stones then trickled toward the drain at the far end of the storage room.

"You won't stop me, Yassimine. Someday, someway I will succeed in this." His smile chilled her blood.

"Don't you see that if you tamper with the ritual in any way, terrible things will happen?"

"What can be more terrible than turning an innocent soul into a monster?"

"They might become something worse than a werewolf. Something The Master cannot control. Something no one can control."

Hal whispered an incantation in Welsh as he sprinkled ghostweed into the mixture of herbs. Six packets, two for each of the three days of the full moon. The Master would throw the packets, including their cheesecloth envelopes, onto the brazier at precise moments in the ritual of conversion. Ghostweed was hard to find. Most cooks and midwives had weeded it out of their herb gardens. The sedative properties of ghostweed could be very useful in tiny doses.

But it was too easy to overdose. Deirdre used it sparingly in her spells. Betsy used it liberally and had gone insane.

Desperation had driven Hal beyond fear. He'd gladly inhale the smoke from the packets of herbs and take his chances that he'd remain clearheaded enough to do what he had to do. The Master would get the full dosage plus the barley wine he'd added to the heavy Burgundian vintage The Master would drink throughout the ritual.

Hal smiled. Yassimine had caught him in the act of substituting the wine, as he had planned. He allowed her to think he had abandoned his plot.

A step outside the door of The Master's suite sent him into hiding behind the draperies. Three heartbeats later the door opened.

"The sun is almost set," The Master said. Anticipation put an edge in his voice and a quickness in his step.

Hal remained absolutely still while The Master grabbed two packets of herbs at random and his favorite decanter of wine. "We'll do the female first," *El Lobison* said to the guard who accompanied him everywhere. "Might have a go with her myself as soon as she's settled into her new role." He and the guard chortled.

Hal did not join their laughter as he slunk deeper into the shadows behind the silk curtain.

"You want her, too?" The Master asked his guard. "Strength and firm tits. Bet she's a lusty *puta*."

If she's a virgin as you claim, how can she be a whore? Hal thought.

"Like a bitch in heat," The Master mused. "I shall have many bitches, all of them in heat all of the time." His eyes glinted with lust. He was three steps closer to leaving the room before he spoke again.

"Send for the pup. I am anxious to begin." The Master's voice faded away as he left his quarters.

Hal counted one hundred heartbeats, then followed. His bare feet made no sound on the stone flooring, nor did he stir the rushes. Barely a whisper of air among the draperies and tapestries told of his passage through the castle.

At the door to the dungeons, The Master paused. He worked two spells to unbar and open the massive door.

Hal caught up to him then, approaching silently. "You sent for me?" he whispered into The Master's ear.

The Spaniard twitched in startlement. He controlled his reaction well. But Hal noted how his eyes darted to the deepest shadows.

The guard merely stepped away and made the sign of the cross with his back turned to The Master.

Hal almost wished he believed in something strongly enough to make a warding gesture like that. Then he thought a second time and repeated the cross just to annoy The Master.

"The Christian God cannot help you, pup," the Spaniard sneered. "Only I can. I am your god now." He yanked the door open. It banged against the wall behind it and bounced. The sound echoed down the long corridor.

Hal smelled the rise in fear from those imprisoned below. He kept his face bland and followed The Master.

They wound their way around several cross corridors until they came to a single door at the end of a dark tunnel. The ceiling seemed to press down upon them. For the first time, Hal was aware of the tons of earth and stone piled on top of them. Should one of the passages collapse . . .

"Open it," The Master commanded to the guard, waving his hand at the stout iron lock.

Hal eyed the mechanism as closely as he could in the flickering torchlight. Stout, but huge. He could see two levers inside that must turn in order to release. With just a small touch of his mind, he was sure he could open it. He was surprised that the young woman behind the door had not found a way to manipulate the lock if she were indeed a hedge witch and desperate, too.

Keys were unnecessary to magicians. But mundane people like the guard needed them.

The smell of the dungeon rose up to meet Hal in waves. Urine, sweat, spoiled food. Fear. Blood. Woman.

He knew this room as intimately as he had known his own cell back in Paris. In the corner, the woman crouched. She locked her arms around her knees and buried her head the moment the door opened. When she lifted her face after many long moments of silence, she blinked her eyes rapidly.

The single torch must be blinding after days in the absolute blackness of this windowless room.

"Loosen her chains," The Master commanded.

The guard leaped forward to obey. Hal followed him

more slowly, treading gently upon the foul rushes. He kept thinking *Trust me,* as loud and as often as he could.

The woman stared at him. Then she lifted her lip in an almost feral snarl. She trusted no one.

"Good, she already sinks into the role that is to come to her." The Master snapped his fingers. A tiny red spark sped from his hand to the brazier in the corner. A wolf pelt lay beside the heating element. And the magic girdle.

The Master produced his ritual knife from the inner folds of his doublet. The blade glinted sharp and clean in the weak light.

"Leave us." The Master waved the guard out of the room.

The woman remained crouched, chafing the raw skin around her wrists where the manacles had rubbed her almost to bleeding.

"This will heal clean," Hal reassured her. He touched the wounds gently. No magic flowed from his hands into hers. He did not want to startle her.

A tiny core of warmth behind his heart blossomed. He would save one person this night, as Helwriaeth's spirit had saved him many times. Helwriaeth. The source of whatever honor and dignity he had left. Everything he did tonight brought meaning to his familiar's sacrifice.

"Clear the rushes and draw the sigil here." The Master pointed to the center of the cell with his boot.

"I . . . will your control over her be so complete if you do not draw the sigil, direct the magic?" Hal hesitated. If he participated at that level of the spell, he might not be able to master the power that built within him. He had to be able to direct his magic precisely at the proper moment.

"My control over you will be more thorough by forcing you to put aside your reluctance." The Master's eyes narrowed.

Hal suspected the man could see right through his careful plans as well as his mask of obedience.

"Did . . ."

"Yes, Yassimine told me about the barley wine. I tapped a new cask myself." He held up his decanter. "You have not had the opportunity to taint this. Now draw the sigil. You will make clean lines at exact angles with no scuffs or variations."

This time The Master brought a pistol to bear on Hal's chest.

"The wolf within me will heal any bullet wound . . ."

"Not if the bullet is silver and lodged in your heart."

Chapter 60

"I'LL take my chances." Hal lunged for The Master. No time to think. No time for subtlety. The pistol changed everything. He kept his gaze upon the muscles in the man's hand. Half a heartbeat before the trigger finger flexed, he deflected his progress to the left and down. Hot air whizzed past his ear. He hit the stone floor with a thud and a grinding in his knee. Then he heard the explosion of the pistol and felt the searing pain of the bullet where it had grazed his temple. His mind screamed. Fire lanced from temple to jaw and over the top of his skull to the other ear.

Black stars blossomed before his eyes. He kept going. All of his life force concentrated upon felling the Spaniard.

The girl screamed in the corner. Her voice pierced Hal's aching head, robbing him of precious balance.

He rolled to his feet. His fist balled. Anger gave him enough control to keep from clutching his head in both hands and falling to the floor.

The Master retreated two steps toward the door. Eyes wide, jaw trembling, he waved his hand in an opening gesture at the locked portal.

Hal duplicated the gesture in reverse.

The door remained sealed.

Then The Master reached for the silver talisman suspended upon a thong about his neck.

Hal's muscles tightened in anticipation of the additional pain. His skin itched and his joints ached, ready to transform into a wolf.

"Not again. You will not corrupt an innocent again," he muttered through gritted teeth. He slapped the talisman out of the Spaniard's grip.

The Master's hook raked a long slash along Hal's side.

Hal gritted his teeth against the pain.

Yassimine's scent flooded his senses. Wolf. Bitch. She had transformed in response to the moon and anticipation of the ritual. She scratched at the door.

Red magic flared around the edges of the wooden panels. An eldritch green glowed beneath it.

The girl whimpered in her corner.

Hal slammed his fist into his opponent's jaw. The Spaniard stumbled and slammed into the wall.

"The moment the way is clear, run," Hal commanded the girl. "Left outside the door then right at the first passage and left again into the main corridor. Keep heading down. It will take you to the beach at the base of the cliff."

A lessening in her whimpers was the only answer.

Red-and-green magic loosed from the Spaniard's fingertips.

Hal rocked back from the intensity of the energy. His heart stuttered and restarted. He prepared his own spell.

A wall of fire rose up between him and his opponent. The Spaniard backed away, toward the corner with the brazier.

Hal lifted a packet of ghostweed with his mind and dumped it into the fire.

The Spaniard reeled and his eyes blinked rapidly, out of focus.

Yassimine leaped at the door. It nearly buckled. She set up a long and mournful howl.

Pain from the bullet graze began vibrating along Hal's head in sympathy with her protests.

As the howls increased in volume, The Master straightened. He seemed to regain confidence and cast off the drugged smoke. He brought his ritual dagger to his hand without drawing it.

Hal felt the magical power draining out of him. The ghostweed in the smoke!

Out of the corner of his eye he detected movement from the girl. She crept up behind The Master armed with the pistol, held in reverse as a club.

"Do as you will with me, Spanish dog," Hal spat. "But you shall never corrupt another. Never." He swept his right foot into the Spaniard's hand. The knife flew away.

The girl smashed the butt of the pistol against the back of the Spaniard's head.

The door splintered and crashed inward. Yassimine followed, snarling and snapping.

"Keep clear of her," Hal shouted as the girl tried to lunge into the passage and safety.

Yassimine caught her ankle in her teeth.

Screams.

Blood.

The wolf within Hal demanded domination.

He had not the strength to fight the wolf, and The Master, and Yassimine.

The grinding pain in his joints obliterated every thought. He gave in to the demands of his wolf. A long howl escaped his throat as he clamped his mouth on the Spaniard's arm above the hook.

He screamed. Yassimine leaped to defend the man who controlled her every thought and action. Her teeth tore into Hal's side.

Wolf muscles and joints did not move as human bodies did. Hal tried anyway, using his hind legs and claws to fend off one threat while worrying the greater.

And then the girl came to his rescue. She picked up the smoldering coals in the brazier with her bare hands and flung them at Yassimine.

The she-wolf yelped and ran, tail tucked between her legs. She could not fight fire.

The smell of singed fur and muscle, of human flesh seared, and the blood pouring from the Spaniard's arm nearly gagged Hal. But he kept his teeth embedded in his enemy's arm.

At last the Spaniard slumped to the floor in a dead faint.

Hal crept to the far corner and vomited. His belly convulsed again and again. Sweat poured from his brow. His body grew chill.

He became aware of a gentle hand smoothing his hair away from his face. He looked up into the astonished gaze of the girl he had rescued.

They needed no words for a long time, just relishing the moments of inaction before they had to move once more.

"Release the other prisoners. I will dispose of that man's

body." Hal struggled to his feet, stiff, aching, and sick at heart.

"I'm coming with you." She rose with him, keeping her hand under his shoulder.

He seemed to need to lean on her to keep his balance. "Fine. You can help me carry him down to the beach. I'll throw him into the sea. Even if he lives, his fear of the water will make him drown."

"Not that. I'm coming with you when you leave here."

For the first time, Hal looked closely at her. Firm skin, clear eyes—one blue, the other brown. An attractive face, dark blonde hair that might brighten up with a good washing. She looked to be about sixteen. Maybe younger.

"You know what I am."

She looked him up and down several times. "Yes. You are a man."

"I am also a wolf."

She shrugged one shoulder, dismissing the problem.

"My life is not an easy one."

"Neither is mine. Folks around here have no use for a witch with mismatched eyes."

"I am called Hal."

"Zella." She held out her hand in formal greeting.

Hal grasped her elbow, and she his. "We'd best get busy. The guards won't leave us alone for long once Yassimine warns them."

"They will deliberately look away when she crosses their path. They do not wish to attract the attention of a were-wolf bitch in pain."

"Aye. I'd avoid her, too."

"Where do you live, Hal?" she asked as he gathered the Spaniard's body in his arms.

"Nowhere. Everywhere. Mostly in a cave in the Mendip Hills near the Welsh border."

"Travel a bit, do you? Often fancied a bit of travel."

"Then we travel together as soon as I consign this bit of trash to the fish."

He scooped up the magical girdle along with the Spaniard. No telling when it might become useful.

Yassimine watched the straggling line of prisoners climb the cliff face. Hal and the treacherous bitch waited for the others to reach the halfway point before they, too, mounted the rocks.

What kind of spell had the female put upon Hal?

Yassimine wanted to whine and howl her grief at the loss of her love. He was lost to her now. But he had left a bit of him inside her womb.

Finally, she crept from the safety of the cave mouth to the waterline. Waves lapped at her paws in growing intensity. She sniffed the air and the water seeking the one out-of-place element.

There, over by the rocks where the waves crashed, sending spray a goodly way up the cliff. She yipped encouragement to the man who clung to the rough surface with his hook. He grew weaker by the moment. Barnacles cut his chest and face. His hook slipped. The blood pouring from the bite wounds attracted predatory fish.

She had not much time.

The next wave brought the water up to her chest. She bit at the salty foam on its crest. Then she leaped forward just a little. The water buoyed her up. Desperately, she worked her limbs, paddling against the inrushing tide and the strange currents around the rocks.

Whenever possible, she yipped again, letting her Master know that she came.

Chill sapped her strength. Her thick fur protected her better than mere human skin. But she would not last long. She plunged onward, desperate to save the man who guided her, fed her, sated her instincts. Relentlessly, the ocean dragged her back toward the beach and away from her Master.

She pushed her limbs harder, fighting current and tide with every stroke.

At last she reached the rocks. She let the flow of water wash her closer and closer to him. She nudged her muzzle beneath his left shoulder, and he clung weakly to her ruff.

She began the long swim to the beach. Twice, he lost his grip and drifted away from her. She had to paddle back and retrieve him. After a long, long time she felt gravel beneath her chilled paws. She scrabbled for purchase until The Master's limp body wedged into the loose pebbles. Then she grabbed his collar in her teeth and dragged him.

Step by step she pulled. At every third step she had to shift her grip as the cloth tore and slid out of her grasp. By the time she reached the cave mouth, he had lost consciousness. His left arm hung limp and white. The straps that held the hook in place loosened. The metal and wood fell free. The bleeding had stopped. Was there anything left to drain out of him?

Eventually she dragged him into a sheltered nook where the wind could not reach. With one last howl of despair she curled her body around The Master, giving him whatever warmth she could.

But the moon dropped lower and lower in the sky. Soon she would have to become a woman again. Soon she would lose the fur that protected them both from the elements.

She had never prayed before. Her wolf god did not require prayer, only obedience and sacrifice. But she prayed now that someone would find them. Someone with medical knowledge to help The Master.

All her plans to kill the man and become mistress of her own pack of wolves died. Hal had stolen the girdle.

She did not know how to live if The Master died.

Chapter 61

The Crown and Anchor, London, and elsewhere.

WHEN I finally dragged myself to Sir Francis Walsingham's home, two days after my return to London, I told him everything. Everything except the true reason Uncle Donovan had been at Sheffield. I explained away his presence as my own request for soldiers to protect the queen's interest.

Elizabeth accepted my written report with pursed lips and crinkled brow. A few days later she threw Oxford into the Tower. But not for his part in the plot. She imprisoned him for his audacity in an affair with one of her ladies. And when she discovered the lady's pregnancy, she, too, was confined to the Tower—in a different cell.

Everyone remembered too well that a decade before Elizabeth had imprisoned Katherine Grey, her cousin and potential heir, for marrying without permission. The hapless groom, the Earl of Hereford, had also been consigned to the Tower. Katherine gave birth there. Elizabeth confiscated the child and gave him to Burghley to raise. A year later Katherine gave birth again.

Katherine was removed to a remote manor and placed under house arrest. The earl remained in the Tower until Katherine's death from a wasting disease a few years later.

Oxford languished in prison for a few weeks. Then he confessed his allegiance to the Catholic faith and named many coconspirators. First and foremost were Robert Parsons, the radical Jesuit who had organized the plot, and Father Edmund Campion, another Jesuit even more devout and inspirational than Parsons—whom Oxford pointed out as leaders in the newest campaign to rid England and Europe of Elizabeth and the Protestant heresy.

That same summer King James VI of Scotland signed a treaty of alliance with France. Catherine de Médici, as regent of France, and Francis Duc de Guise, the premier noble in France and leader of the Holy League, pledged to support the young Protestant king in the "Ould Alliance." James' mother, Mary, could look for no more support or escape plans from her Continental relatives.

How de Guise reconciled this treaty with the goals of the Holy League, I did not know. He and his father before him had lied and deceived in the name of expedience.

Ambassador Mendoza continued his plots to assassinate Elizabeth and put Mary on the throne. Most never passed beyond my tavern. Mendoza's favored courier had a taste for Portuguese fortified wines. I kept him well supplied. And while he was in his cups, I relieved him of many messages, copied them, and returned some of the originals to his pouch.

I left it to Walsingham's linguists to decipher the codes and take action.

While my baby grew big in my belly, I heard nothing more from Uncle Donovan. Elizabeth told me that he had taken temporary sabbatical from her service, pleading ill health. He sold his home in Edinburgh and returned to Kirkenwood.

From the travelers, I learned that Betsy chafed at the new confines imposed upon her by her father. No more alchemy, no more lovers. No more making the tenants of the barony the victims of her experiments.

Travelers came often to my door. The ones who arrived at the kitchen asking for Lady Dee received a meal in exchange for a few chores. A tavern always needs coal hauled up from the river, vegetables peeled and pared, barrels moved from cellar to tap. The women and children swept and scrubbed the floors or the dishes. Whatever they could do to help. Most of all, they brought me gossip.

I learned more of what the common person in England thought and did in support of Elizabeth than any number of royal commissioners. I heard which secret Catholics would rally to Mary's cause and how many more preferred Elizabeth.

My cousin Griffin, Hal's twin, came to Ide Hill south of London twice a year as his father's deputy to oversee the steward. He had grown into a fine and sensible man. He visited each time he came to London.

At the end of harvest he brought a male wolfhound to mate with Coffa. I offered him one of the pups, but he declined.

"Betsy would kill me if I brought home a pup out of Coffa." He said it soberly and I knew I must take his statement as the literal truth.

I kept searching his face for signs of Hal. So like him, and yet so different. He had not the rough manners or the bulk about the shoulders and thighs I had last seen in Hal. He had not the ready humor and quick memory of shared adventures as children.

When winter grew cold and the year of 1580 came to a close, I departed my snug quarters and retreated to Meg's hut at the foot of the tor. Coffa and I traveled slowly. Though the babe had a few months yet to grow, she weighed heavily against my back and my bladder. We stopped often.

Coffa had just weaned all but one of her pups. They, too, needed to travel slowly. This last female lingered close to her mama's side, waiting to see if she would attach to me or my baby. Giving birth was risky business for women. I had to trust in Meg's skill to keep me and my child safe.

My aunt met me on the path where it branched up to my father's grave or off toward the creek and her home.

We traveled up without a word to each other. She had built a rough shelter using the triad of rocks at the spring source as the back wall.

"Your mum came here to birth you in storm and agony. I pray your delivery will be easier," she said as she ushered me into the warmth of the hut.

"I do not have a demon pounding upon the walls," I replied quietly.

"But you have a few demons within."

"Hal," I gasped.

"Him and others."

"I loved Michael. But . . . if I had loved him more . . ."

"He would still have died defending you from the she wolf and from my brother's treachery."

Not quite reassured, I settled into the round enclosure.

"No corners for demons to hide in," Meg informed me. She built up the fire and set about preparing our supper.

I meditated on the stories and musing of my father's journals. I understood the words. I did not always comprehend the thoughts. But then I had never had faith as strong as my father's.

I wanted more. More stories. More . . . of my father.

I tried prayer. I prayed the rosary. I spent hours on my knees while winter raged about my shelter. I cupped the black crystal from my staff as well as the rosary while I prayed.

The sorrow in my heart was too deep to open up to any god just yet.

A family of Gypsies made camp nearby. The patriarch, Micah, claimed to have known my father. His wife and daughter remained silent, never giving their names. Meg and I were *gadge,* not one of the Rom.

I learned that each of them had both a Christian name and a Rom name. The men revealed only the Christian name imposed upon them by forcible baptism.

Meg and I welcomed the Rom to the shrine. They had come many times in the past. As always, they placed greens and holly berries near the grave. They offered up fire and water and blew air from their lungs as part of the ritual. Then they prayed in their exotic language. Music seemed to lilt across the breeze in accompaniment.

They stayed close by for many weeks. The Gypsy woman and her daughter attended me daily, checking on the babe, preparing to assist in the birth.

From the worried glances they exchanged with Meg, I suspected my daughter would not enter this world easily.

The days grew longer as the sun marched toward the Equinox. Winter storms grew fiercer. The babe grew bigger still. Shortness of breath, lack of appetite, and an overwhelming thirst with consequent frequent trips to the privy plagued the final weeks of my pregnancy.

Micah, George, and Zebadiah left our snug enclave in search of a doctor and a priest. Three skilled midwives might not be enough.

They did not return in time.

A full moon rose on a clear and cold evening. I paced round and round the top of the tor. Each of the stones in the faery circle learned the feel of my hand that night. I learned the unique grain and power trapped within them.

An *other* paced behind my left shoulder. A shade of another person. My father?

No. In this time of travail I knew the one who watched me so closely had to be my demon-cursed mother. Never before had I felt her presence, as if abandoning me at birth, she had forsaken the right to console me after her death. My father had come to me several times, mostly in the quiet time before dawn when the Earth is still, holding its breath, waiting for the new day. He had never spoken to me, just kept the childhood monster beneath the bed and my nightmares at bay.

But now, I faced a time of trial that only women can endure. Roanna kept me company in my vigil.

Coffa and her pup trotted at my side, unafraid of the shade that followed me. They whined and leaned into me, pushing me back to the hut. The women kept the fires burning high. They also hung many charms about the hut, for luck, for release of pain, to ward off any and all evil spirits.

A wolf howled in the distance. I shuddered. Was it Hal? Perhaps another of his kind waited for me.

More than anything I longed for my cousin to comfort me, hold my hand, let me lean on him for a time. But he did not come to me that night.

And then the pains began.

I kept walking as long as possible. My labor progressed quickly. Soon, Meg guided me into the hut, closing the leather curtain in Coffa's face. My dog crawled beneath it anyway. She would not leave me now.

The unnamed puppy remained outside, uncertain.

For a day and night and most of the next day demons clawed at my innards. I screamed. I swore. I flung ungrounded magic to the hills and back. The spells backlashed and made my pains worse. Finally, Meg slammed her fist into my jaw.

Black stars blossomed before my eyes and I lost consciousness. Meg and her helpers never told me how long I drifted in the blessed blackness. Long enough for them to turn the baby so that her head slid into the birth canal instead of her bottom.

I awoke with the need to push. Things happened very quickly after that. I heard a cry that was not my own and felt the gush of warm blood.

Meg and her nearly silent helpers exchanged worried glances. Then they dropped my daughter onto my distended belly without ceremony and began working again.

"What?" I asked weakly. My throat was so raw I could barely form the words.

"Give your daughter suck," came the terse reply. The first words I had heard from the Gypsy woman during the entire procedure.

With the last of my strength I drew my daughter close and guided her to my breast. After a moment of rooting around, she latched on and drank greedily.

Meg packed me with herbs and moss. And still I bled.

The Gypsies shook their heads and departed. "We cannot risk being in the same dwelling when a *gadge* dies. Her spirit will haunt us, make us unclean," the daughter—only a few years older than myself—explained.

As the sun set I heard them break camp and trudge down the hill. Afraid of my death.

Chapter 62

Early spring 1581. A cave barrow, the Mendip Hills, England.

HAL stood at the mouth of the cave he and Zella called home. A lonely wail followed the wind, circled the hills, taunted him, and moved on. Magic followed that cry of despair.

Anxiety built within him. He thought he knew who cried so deep and long. Dared he go to her?

"What ails ye?" Zella asked. She came up beside him and slipped her arms around his waist. Her full breasts pressed against his back. Through his thin shirt he felt them tighten with desire.

His own need for her quivered into life.

In all the long months they had been together, since escaping *El Lobison* in Cornwall, she never seemed to tire of his lovemaking. She liked it best close to the full moon when he was most dangerous. She became almost violent in response to his own urgency.

They had little else in common other than both being outcasts. He had not returned to Walsingham or Paris. He did not know why. His lust for Zella was not strong enough to keep him from his work.

The wail on the wind called to him once more. Any thought of Zella vanished. He listened closely.

"Dee," he whispered.

The wind seemed to call his name in reply.

"Her again." Zella dropped her arms and retreated into the cave. She had enough magic in her to pass through the barriers set long ago. But not enough to do much more. When angered, she could light a fire with a blink of her

eyes. She had no control over where the sparks would land;
the kindling, their blankets, the flour and dried meat
supplies.

Hal had spent hours over the past few months trying
to teach her to control the fire—or her temper. Nothing
penetrated the defenses she had built against witch hunters
and bullies. She'd had a hard life, with no schooling and
few ambitions.

He had renewed the seals on the portal to make certain
she did not accidentally release Tryblith, the Demon of
Chaos.

"I have to go to her." Hal grabbed a small pack from
the stack of supplies just inside the second magic barrier.

"She is no part of your life now. Your life is here. With
me." Zella stood firm, hands upon hips, mismatched eyes
blazing toward temper.

For once Hal did not flinch away from her. Let her burn
everything here.

"Dee is dying." He threw his spare shirt and a packet of
medicinal herbs into the pack. A small cooking pot. Some
dried meat, cheese, bread. And the magical girdle. His
knife he wore on his belt at all times.

"You have not seen her in near a year though you speak
of her nearly every day. You dream of her. And you call
out her name when you make love to me!"

"Her death and my life are tied together. I do not know
how. I must go." He took the first few steps toward the exit.

"You desert me."

"Stay here if you like. The locals know you. You won't
starve."

"And if I carry your child?"

"Do you?" That thought stopped him. But he did not
look at her, afraid to see the truth in her eyes. Not that she
was capable of telling the truth when she chose to believe
otherwise. Perhaps the seal on the demon door weakened
and let the evil trickle into her. Perhaps she had merely
learned to lie quite young to protect herself.

"Can't tell yet."

"I'll come back. Though I doubt you will quicken. I have
it on reliable authority that werewolves are sterile with any
but their own kind."

"Don't bother coming back. I won't be here."

"Where . . . ?"

"Not your concern, I reckon. You never took me to church so the babe is mine alone."

"If there is a babe. Couldn't take you to church when the priests would burn me on sight. You, too, for that matter."

"Any child I bear is mine."

"I'll find you."

"No, you won't. I won't let you."

"How will you live?"

"Same as always. Sell a love potion or a remedy for a cow with the milk disease. Sell myself to men."

She looked at him as if she expected him to protest the last statement.

"You weren't a virgin when I found you. I have no stake in your chasity or lack thereof." He shrugged and began his journey, lighter and freer than he'd been since . . . Since Zella came into his life.

In the center of the faery circle outside the barrow, he turned a full circle, listening for the cry on the wind again.

There. East. He thought he knew the place. He shed his clothes and stuffed them into the pack. Then he fastened the entire burden securely about his shoulders and ran. He gained momentum on the downhill. As the sun lowered, with the moon near to rising full, his strength grew with each step. Across three small rills, over scrubby hills where only gorse and heather grew, around the city of Wells with its great cathedral and choirs singing day and night. At full dark his body shifted seamlessly into the wolf. The pack straps held on his four-footed form.

Only Dee mattered. He had to reach her before she died, had to hold her in his arms one more time, tell her he loved her, apologize for everything he had done to her.

All night he ran. The miles fell behind him.

Two nights and most of the third day he ran with only brief rests and hunted meals. Panting, with sleep dragging at his eyes he came within view of the tor. The small boulders of the faery circle made a crown of the top. The cry on the wind had grown weaker. Barely audible.

Not much time remained.

"Dee!" he cried. "I'm coming." Exhausted, he plodded on, climbing the steep hillside, avoiding the camp of Gypsies he smelled on the other side of the tor.

He crested the tor, gasping for breath, knees trembling and shoulders drooping. He discarded the near empty pack that seemed to weigh as much as three horses. One step closer to the ring. One more and then he came to an abrupt halt. The ring was stronger than he. He had to go around. At the far eastern edge he saw the gateway. Looking through the two gate stones gave him a clear glimpse into the ring proper. A small hut had been added to the three altar stones since his last visit. By moonlight. With the elves.

Best not to think on that night.

He had to step into the creek to pass into the ring. Taking a deep breath against the chill water he accepted the ritual cleansing.

Darkness seemed to lift from around him. His knees grew more secure and the headache pressing behind his eyes lifted and eased.

A wolfhound barked a warning. A puppy yipped an echo.

Hal barked back at them, keeping his tone friendly and free of threat.

The adult dog crawled out from beneath the leather curtain covering the doorway. She snarled and drooled into her beard, in no mood to take any nonsense from a mere human.

"Coffa?"

Deirdre always named her dogs Coffa—Remembrance. Hal held out his hand, palm down for her to sniff. He avoided challenging her by looking directly into her eyes.

The dog backed off from his hand but stood squarely in front of the doorway. He sensed her uncertainty about his identity, human, but not human, wolf but not wolf. She had been bred to hunt wolves, take them down with a single vicious chomp to the throat.

The pup was not so cautious. It bounced over, eager for a new playmate. Hal ruffled its ears. It rolled over exposing a creamy white belly. He scratched and noted that she, too, was female—the successor to the current familiar.

After a few moments of play, the mother's ears relaxed and she stepped closer to receive her fair share of pets and scratches beneath her chin.

When both dogs had accepted him, Hal approached the hut.

"Deirdre?" he called softly. " 'Tis I, Hal."

A moan answered him. Then he heard someone scrambling about. Aunt Meg held the curtain back for him. "Quickly. She must not chill."

Meg barely glanced at him before turning back to her patient. Sweat soaked Deirdre's hair and shift. Fever flushed her face. She thrashed and moaned in pain. She smelled blood. Lots of it. And death.

In the corner an infant whimpered, too weak from hunger to cry lustily.

"You need a wet nurse?"

"I cannot leave her long enough to find one."

"Go. Take the child to the village. Or the camp of Gypsies at the base of the tor. Surely one of them can feed the child. I will stay with her." With a few deft movements he flung a cloak about Meg's shoulders and ushered her and the precious bundle out of the hut.

"Ah, Dee, what have you done to yourself?" he sighed as he knelt beside her.

Her hand fluttered, seeking him.

He held it to his cheek. "I love you, Dee. I always have."

"Hal," she whispered through cracked lips. "I knew you would hear my call. I knew you would come. You must stop the bleeding."

"How? I am no healer. I am barely human."

"You have healing powers in your blood."

He cocked his head curiously, thinking madly. Since the day he had been infected with the wolf, he had not sickened. Wounds healed within days. Minor scrapes and bruises lasted mere hours."

"What do you need?"

"Bind us together, as my father bound himself to my mother." She turned her head away and looked at a stack of leather-bound books thrust into a corner.

"The journals. Which one?"

"The last one. Dark red leather. Only half filled. He outlined his ritual and purpose. Da had to kill my mother to kill the demon that infected her. Every blow they inflicted upon him, she suffered the same. They killed each other. But her demon was defeated."

"I don't intend to kill you, Dee."

"Then save me with your blood." Her strength faded and she relinquished herself to the fever and semiconsciousness.

Hal grabbed a double handful of the journals, swiftly sorting them by binding. The dark red one, only half-filled with entries seemed to fall out of the stack and into his lap of its own volition. Quickly, he scanned the last entries.

A circle. A giant pentagram. Two rings. A long knife slash along each arm, and then lashing the two wounds together so that their blood and their souls mingled.

A powerful spell. Created out of love. Ending in death.

He had not worked magic of this intensity in many years.

"I'll not lose you now, Dee. I need you. I think all of Britain needs you more."

Grimly, he left the hut to trace a circle with the butt end of Deirdre's staff. Then he made a pentagram within the circle that encompassed the hut, the three altar stones, the source of the creek, and the graves of Griffin the Elder and his dubious bride Roanna. They should be a part of this spell that hopefully saved their daughter.

He had to grab his knees and draw long deep breaths to steady himself when he was done. Already, the magic he had raised pulsed within his blood and beat at his senses. Sweat dripped into his eyes and hunger gnawed at his belly.

Creek Water to cleanse his knife. Fire to purify it. The kiss of the Wind to bless it. The metal of the blade had come from Earth.

He reentered the hut. Before he could think of the enormity, the permanence of the magic, he drew the knife the length of his arm. Blood beaded up along the seam of flesh and began to heal almost immediately. A second slash opened Dee's arm. He clamped the two wounds together and bound them with some of the swaddling linen they had used for the baby.

"I love you," he whispered with the last of his strength and collapsed beside his beloved.

Chapter 63

Spring 1581. Rippling Dell Abbey near the faery circle.

I AWOKE in a large feather bed piled high with bolsters and warm coverlets. Rich tapestries surrounded the four posters and canopy. I heard my daughter crying. Instinctively, I parted the draperies to find her. She lay in a cradle three steps away from the bed. I managed one of those steps before my knees gave out.

Aunt Meg and a woman I did not know hurried into the room and helped me back into the bed. Another woman, dressed as a servant or possibly a farmer's wife, followed them. She took possession of a low chair beside the cradle. Immediately she opened her bodice and began nursing my child.

My breasts ached for the lack of holding the baby close.

"You'll hold the babe soon enough," the unknown woman beside Meg clucked. She was dressed in sturdy wool with plain petticoats and only a small farthingale. A bit of modest needle lace circled the neckline of her bodice. A corset kept her posture rigid and thrust her breasts high. She must be the lady of the house.

"Back into bed with you," Meg added. Suddenly her familiar accent sounded coarse and uneducated next to the lady.

"Hal?" I had to know if he had come to me in my extremity or if I had dreamed it all in the depth of the fever.

"Gone. Gone as the wind.
Blow, wind, blow, and go, mill, go!
That the miller may grind his corn;
That the baker may take it,

459

And into bread make it,
And bring us a loaf in the morn."

Meg's eyes glazed over and her mind drifted off into another world, another time.

Was she speaking in metaphor? Or did she merely refer to her own tendency to drift about the country like a will-o'-the-wisp?

"How can he be gone. He . . ." I looked at the healing wound along the length of my left forearm. He had come to me. He had healed me with his werewolf blood.

I owed him my life. If he had been captured or faced harm, I needed to protect him.

"He left as soon as we knew you were out of danger," the lady added. "Your husband was most concerned about you."

"He is not my husband. My husband died," I said flatly.

"Then . . . ?"

"My cousin. Closer to me than a brother."

"Ah," she replied as if that explained everything. But it did not.

"The Rom have blessed him for what he did for you," Meg whispered to me. "They see that he is more than a man, less than a wolf."

That statement puzzled me for a moment. When I formed a question for my aunt, her eyes had glazed over once more and she sang nonsense words to herself.

"You must eat now. Rich broths at first. Meat tomorrow. Lots of red meat," my hostess said. She fussed with the coverlets and prepared to depart.

My mouth watered at the thought of the meat. Red meat still dripping blood.

Zounds! What had I become?

Meg stayed with me only a few days more. Not once in that time did she return to a rational adult state. Her words and songs often as not sounded as gibberish. She was fascinated with my baby, as she was fascinated by all babies. But she did not need to raise this one, as she had raised me.

Then one morning she disappeared into a spring mist, back to her own quiet pursuits where she thought she was most needed. I suspected my father's shrine had become too populated for her and she found a new refuge. I never saw her again and never heard of her death.

We baptized my daughter Margaret Roanna, for my beloved aunt who came and went with the wind and for the mother I had never known. My hosts snorted, believing I should have named her Elizabeth, after the queen who had adopted me when my family deserted me and I stood alone.

Maggie Rose my daughter became as she wormed her way into the hearts of the entire household of my hosts Baron Thorndike and Lady Imogen of Rippling Dell.

With the help of the wet nurse, I offered Maggie Rose my breast. At first, no milk came and I reluctantly returned the baby to her nurse. But I ate ravenously for another week. Mostly red meat, barely cooked. I found myself in the kitchens at midnight, stealing chunks of raw beef. Then my milk came in, thick and creamy and abundant. I could have fed three babes.

The long gash on my arm healed without a scar.

As the moon waxed fat, barely a month after giving birth, I departed the kindness of my benefactors, with the promise of an introduction at court when next they came to London. I dared not linger with them should Hal's wolf curse have invaded my body.

I arrived at Sir Francis Walsingham's home midafternoon on the first day of the full moon. My bones ached and my skin itched. I could not eat enough.

After hearing my tale, Elizabeth's spymaster agreed to house me in the prison cells in his cellar for three days and nights. And have me closely watched. He and his lady wife brought my daughter to me during the daylight hours. But at night, two men with torches and silver knives stood guard.

Coffa and her pup also watched over me, wary of the men, more wary of the change in how they smelled me.

I thanked whatever god looked out for me and mine that I did not transform.

Maggie Rose and I retired to the Crown and Anchor after a four-month absence.

Life in my tavern proceeded much as it had for years. Coffa aged rapidly. Many of her duties as watchdog and familiar fell to her last offspring, Newynog. Her name came from the Welsh word for hungry. The young dog was as hungry as I. We often prowled the kitchens and larders "testing" the joints and roasts intended for the patrons. We had to determine if the meat had gone bad or not. We also satisfied our voracious appetites without arousing the suspicions of those around us.

Sometimes, as the months and years progressed, I sensed Hal watching over me. I never saw him. But I caught glimpses of him out of the corner of my eye. He disappeared the moment I turned my head. I did not need evidence, I *knew* that he watched from a distance. Though my need for raw meat faded over time, my blood responded to his presence. A tingle at the base of my spine awakened whenever he came near. I ached for him, knowing that now, more than ever, we were bound together body and soul. I could never love another, had not truly loved any other but him.

Maggie Rose grew almost as rapidly as Newynog. Her blonde hair curled tightly as a cherub and she looked out upon her world through wide blue eyes as deep and as dark as any Kirkwood scion.

I told her stories of my family going all the way back to the Merlin of King Arthur's time. And when she grew old enough to ask about her father, I told her about Sir Michael Maelstrom. As time passed, my memories of him became fused with my memories of Hal and our childhood. Bit by bit, Michael *became* Hal in my mind and hers.

She and I kept the name Griffin. Not through any dislike of Michael's name and title. More an acceptance of who and what we were.

War and controversy stilled swirled around Mary Queen of Scots. I kept up my spy work for my queen from the safety of my tavern.

Pope Gregory XIII reformed the calendar of Europe in 1582. Within months, many monarchs accepted his new way of reckoning time and moved their dates ahead by ten days. Elizabeth stubbornly refused to change just because a Catholic bishop had an idea. Gradually, England became even more isolated from Europe over the simple refusal to change the date.

In 1583, Sir Francis Walsingham and I ferreted out a French scheme to put Mary back on the throne of Scotland as joint ruler with her son James. Nicholas Throckmorton and his nephew Francis made the mistake of mentioning in my tavern that they had made frequent visits to the French Embassy in London. Careful watching and listening related to all of their activities unearthed the details. Elizabeth squelched that plot very quickly. So did James VI of Scotland. He no more wanted to share a throne than Elizabeth did.

Pope Gregory offered a one-million-gold-ducat reward for the removal of Elizabeth from her throne.

Francis Throckmorton implicated Spanish Ambassador Mendoza in his plot. Further investigation revealed that Philip of Spain had begun his enterprise of England.

The threat of invasion loomed upon our horizon.

Throckmorton met a grisly traitor's death for his part in the conspiracy. Ambassador Mendoza was escorted out of England. I do not believe the queen's men were gentle with him.

At sea, Elizabeth's privateers detained numerous Spanish galleons and relieved them of their treasure from the New World. Philip of Spain demanded the head of Francis Drake, the bold and daring captain of many of these raids. Elizabeth knighted the man instead.

Philip seized all English ships in his harbors and made them part of his fleet. Elizabeth countered by making Drake an admiral and providing him with twenty-two ships and two thousand men. She then dispatched this awesome fleet to the New World to "worry" Spanish shipping lanes and seize Spanish bases in the Caribbean Islands.

Religious wars in France continued to rage. Civil war and rebellion tore the Spanish Netherlands to shreds. Portugal, too, rebelled. Elizabeth sent what aid she could—even the offices of Leicester as her deputy general to Amsterdam. But Spain was rich and tenacious.

Elizabeth moved Mary Stuart from the relatively easy accommodations in Sheffield to Wingfield and then to the castle at Tutbury. Each move reduced the exiled queen's freedom and tightened scrutiny of her correspondence. After the Throckmorton plot, James VI wrote to his mother that he could never ally himself with a "captive in a desert." Mary wrote a new will bequeathing her claim to the English throne to Philip of Spain. The King of Spain published the details of the will for all the world to know.

Elizabeth was livid. Mary's aging guardian, the Earl of Shrewsbury was replaced by a tight-lipped Puritan, Sir Amyas Paulet.

Parliament passed a new law ordering all seminary priests to leave England within forty days or suffer the penalty for High Treason, a grisly death of drawing and quartering after questioning under torture. Sir Francis Walsingham received permission and money to hire more secret agents to keep abreast of the plots and counterplots.

Some of that money came to me. I paid my own informers, the people of the road who heard and saw more than many of the trained observers. Sometimes the wording of the messages sounded as if they came from Hal. He never came himself and never used his name. Yet, somehow, I knew he directed my informers.

I no longer had employees of the Spanish Embassy to supply me with news of plots from that end, but Jesuits and other plotters seemed to think the Crown and Anchor a safe haven because of its former association with the Spaniards. They never realized that all of the conspirators of the *thwarted* plots in the past had met in my taproom.

In March of 1586, Philip of Spain petitioned the new pope, Sixtus V, for the church's blessing on his enterprise of England. The pope's agreement, along with substantial funding, turned the diplomatic jousting into a Holy War.

The next round of plot and counterplot came, not from information gathered within my tavern or from any number of Walsingham's other agents but from the devious mind of the spymaster himself. He made me Mary Stuart's laundress.

Mary was moved from Tutbury to the fortified manor of Chartley. Its bleak and forbidding walls seemed more than adequate to retain one lone woman. Perhaps the most dangerous woman in all of Europe.

I moved to Chartley. The last woman to wash and iron Mary's clothing had smuggled letters in and out of Tutbury in the dirty laundry. My facility with languages and my

ability to observe much while remaining relatively invisible—
as most good servants are invisible to their masters—made
me the best candidate for the job.

The fortified manor belonging to the young Earl of
Essex—Leicester's stepson—near Buxton stood in the center of the Peak District on the River Wye. If Mary should
escape, the rugged country and wild moors offered many
hiding places on the way to either coast and a ship away
from England.

Sir Amyas Paulet knew only that Walsingham had placed
one or more agents among the household. He did not know
that I was among them.

Newynog moved into the manor kennels and became another set of ears for me. This familiar seemed more intelligent than any I had worked with before. Perhaps our bond
with raw meat had brought her closer to my mind at an
early age.

While Maggie Rose and I settled into our new positions,
Walsingham developed a second plot.

Gilbert Gifford presented himself to Sir Amyas Paulet
with credentials from Walsingham. I happened to pass by
the private solar of Mary Stuart's guardian with a pile of
fresh linens at the time.

"Sir Amyas, I am happy to convey the good wishes of
our mutual . . . uhm . . . er . . . friend," Gifford said. His
voice squeaked and wavered as it always had.

Of course I recognized him from his days of loitering
around the Crown and Anchor, talking earnestly to the
Spaniards about religion. He had disappeared about two
years before. I believed he had gone to France to become
a priest.

Since my father had done the same, I could not fault the
man. He broke no English law by becoming a priest in a
foreign land, only by returning as one.

What was he doing working for Walsingham?

"Your plans are in place?" Sir Amyas asked. His thin
lips ground together in disapproval.

I could smell the perfume Gifford used in his hair oil
from my listening post outside the doorway, within feet of
the back staircase. Sir Amyas, with his belief in simple food,
sober clothes, plain speech, and stark church rituals, must
have been highly offended by Gifford's adherence to

French fashion. Embroidery stiffened his doublet and
weighed down the elongated pointed front. Too much
horsehair and bran padded his trunk hose above spindly
legs. His calf padding had slipped on his journey and
sagged awkwardly.

His aura shot streaks of green and yellow out from his
head. This man lied. Did Sir Francis know? Or did he trust
me to ensure he did not develop counterplots to foil those
of the spymaster?

"I have found a brewer, Master Burton, an honest man
but sympathetic to *the cause*. I need only for you to give
the man patent to deliver to your most gracious manor,
milord." Gifford added a deep bow to his fawning attitude.

I did not need to hear the crunch to know that Sir Amyas
ground his teeth together.

"Go up to her now. Tell her your plans. I will have the
written instructions for the brewer when you finish." He
waved Gifford out of the solar.

I ducked back into the stairwell. Then I followed the
messenger, ten steps behind him, with my burden of linens
for Mary's clothespress. He seemed just a little too eager
to reach Mary if Walsingham had truly converted him to
work for England and Elizabeth.

No one paid attention to me as I slipped into Mary's
chambers. Gifford and Mary continued their conversation
in French without pausing. Mary spoke English as well as
I did with only traces of her Scots and French accents. They
used French to keep servants from reporting conversations
to Sir Amyas Paulet.

Apparently both considered servants too ignorant or stupid to learn a second language, and the educated too good
to stoop so low as to pretend to be one of the lower classes.

I listened closely as I folded and refolded clothing. I
hummed while I worked, masking my close attention to
their words.

"You must prepare two letters in response to each letter
I forward to you," Gifford said quietly. "One of those letters must forbid your agents and friends from furthering
any more plots."

"But they must help us. We cannot escape alone. We
have tried!" Mary replied indignantly. She rose to her impressive height, half a hand higher than Gifford. Her hair

had gone gray but she still allowed curls to peek coyly from beneath her cap.

"That letter you will put into the old code, the one Walsingham has broken. We must lull him into believing you docilely accept this latest prison and Sir Amyas' preaching about leading a simpler life, devoid of ostentation."

"And the second letter?" Mary cocked her head prettily. She had never outgrown her need to flirt with men.

Gifford was not immune to her charm. He practically panted as he gazed adoringly into her eyes.

"Put the second letter into this new code." He drew a small roll of parchment from the back of a gaudy pouch at his waist. "Your French friends assure me this code cannot be broken. Even so, I will meet the brewer each time he delivers ale to Chartly. I shall remove the letters from the waterproof box hidden in the casks. I shall make certain the real letter with instructions gets to Paris. Walsingham can do as he will with the other letters."

Chapter 64

25 June, 1586. Chartly Manor, Derbyshire, England.

DONOVAN stared at the high walls around Chartley
Manor. Elizabeth had ordered the old moat redug and
water diverted from the River Wye to fill it. This time, the
queen meant for her cousin to remain locked up.

That fate for Mary Stuart he fully intended to accept.
But, oh, it was hard to convince his heart that this might
very well be the last time he would see his love. Now that
he accepted the continuation of the love spell, he succumbed to it readily, dismissing thoughts of Martha as a
ghost from the past who could never again make him feel
guilty about Mary.

Instinctively, he clasped the locket he always wore about
his neck.

At the guarded drawbridge, Donovan presented an old
letter from Elizabeth granting him the right to investigate
diplomatic matters regarding Scotland at will. He had no
idea if Elizabeth still honored his original commission to
the court of Scotland. He no longer cared.

His family had shattered. His faith had always been as
weak as his magic. Everything he valued had scattered as
dust in the wind. All he had left was his love for Mary.
Even if that love existed only in a magic spell left over
from a woman more than twenty years dead.

Sir Amyas Paulet met him with a sour expression and
skeptical survey of the letter.

"This missive is not dated," he said, meticulously refold-
ing the letter. He peered long at the broken seal. Elizabeth's seal of a crown set within a Tudor Rose had not
faded with time as the ink had.

"My service to Her Majesty is unending. Matters have arisen that require I interview Mary Stuart." Donovan carefully omitted any title surrounding Mary's name. After nearly twenty years in prison all of her honors had been taken over by others. She, too, had nothing left.

"Very well. You may have ten minutes." Paulet turned sharply on his heel and left the small receiving room.

"May I remind you, Sir Amyas, that my title is older than the queen's. My rank exceeds yours by several degrees, and that my mission is sanctioned by Her Majesty. I will take as long as I need for this interview." Donovan puffed out his chest and stared down his nose at the slighter man.

"My commission comes directly from Parliament, milord," Paulet replied, equally as haughty as Donovan. "I wield authority in this house. No other may question me. You may have ten minutes of privacy. Then you must leave, or I must join you to monitor the interview." The little man planted himself directly in front of Donovan.

Donovan tried staring him down, tried pushing him with magic to relent.

Paulet did not waver.

"Very well. I shall take the ten minutes of privacy. If I have not been able to ferret out the information I need by then, you may join us. Lead the way," Donovan ordered as if the man were but a servant.

Frowning all the way, Paulet led Donovan through a series of rooms and up the broad staircase to a suite in the north tower. Donovan scouted every inch of the trek around the manor for holes in Paulet's security. Only the double door to Mary's suite opened off the landing at the top of the stairs. Except for the servants' stair a few paces to the left, this area was completely separate from the rest of the house.

From his exterior survey, he knew that the walls of the tower were sheer with few windows or other protrusions to facilitate a climb.

Two armed guards stood before the door to Mary's suite. They inspected Donovan for obvious weaponry and then patted his entire body seeking any concealed places. He had to surrender his short sword, his cloak, and his riding crop before entering. They even found the stiletto in his boot.

At last, the guard opened the door for Donovan and Paulet. Mary's guardian preceded Donovan into the room despite the protocol of rank and privilege.

"He may stay ten minutes," Paulet announced to the lady-in-waiting who met them in the outer chamber.

"I shall inform Her Grace," the lady dipped a very slight curtsy and retreated to one of the inner rooms.

Donovan knew her to be one of the four ladies-in-waiting named Mary who had come with the Queen of Scots from France all those years ago. Now only two of the women remained, loyal to their mistress to the last.

He had a sudden vision of the two Marys weeping, draped in deep mourning veils. *Please let this be just my imagination,* he pleaded with whatever god listened. *Do not plague me with the visions that drove my twin.*

Paulet departed without further ado.

Donovan heaved a sigh. The man served Elizabeth's purpose diligently. But could he not be more courteous about it?

The Mary reappeared and beckoned him inward. Donovan stepped into the next room, a small, dark parlor with a meager fire and only two chairs. Mary Stuart had added bright cushions and tapestries, probably her own needlework.

The exiled queen stood in the center of the room, tall, straight, and beautiful as ever. Age had rounded out the contours of her long face and figure and dulled the vibrancy in her hair. She still commanded attention just by breathing.

An ill-clad servant stood meekly before Mary Stuart. Her head barely reached Mary's shoulder. Something about the angle of her head and shoulders looked familiar. Donovan was about to ask the woman to turn toward him when Mary spoke.

"This letter is number one. The other is number two." She handed the servant one tightly rolled scrap of parchment for each hand. "Can you remember that?"

"Yes, ma'am. Number one, and number two." The servant mumbled so badly Donovan could barely hear her. Her accent, from the wharfs of London, almost needed a translator.

"Be certain you tell the brewer, Master Burton, which one is which," Mary insisted. "Number one and number two." She pointed to each missive in turn.

"Aye, ma'am." The servant dipped a hasty curtsy and scuttled out. Never once did she turn her face to Donovan. But he caught a glimpse of her hands. Certainly the skin showed signs of redness and cracking from rough work. The fingers were long and the nails well cared for. She had worn a heavy ring on the fourth finger of her left hand until recently. Not the hands of an uneducated woman used to hard work all her life.

The way she clutched the rolled letters to her breast reminded him of . . .

He clutched the locket on his chest to aid him as he peered at her more closely with extra senses. An envelope of magic shrouded her.

"Donovan, my love. How I have longed to see you again." Mary rushed into his arms.

Donovan had no more attention for anything but Mary. He held her close, kissing her long and deep. He could not get enough of her. She sighed and rested her head on his shoulder, content to nestle close to him when all he wanted was to tear off her clothing and carry her to the bed.

After a long moment of silence while he regained control of his emotions, he spoke.

"Are you certain you can trust the servant?" Something . . .

"The laundress?" Mary pulled back enough to look him in the eye, still enclosed within his arms. "Of course, we trust her. She barely has a thought in her head. She is not smart enough to betray us."

Donovan kept his doubts on that matter to himself. Time was too short.

"How fares our son, milord?" Mary asked, still snuggled close to his chest.

"I have not seen James in many months, my love. I have retired from Elizabeth's service."

"So you wrote to me. I did not believe it. You need action. You need to be in the thick of things."

"My family and estates demand my attention." An outright lie.

The silhouette of the laundress still bothered him.

The locket seemed to burn his skin through his doublet and shirt. He touched it briefly. The sensation fled.

"We are always happy to see you, milord," Mary said with another fierce hug before she backed away and seated herself on the closest high-backed chair. "But why have you come if not to give us news of James?" She gestured for Donovan to sit. The habit of the royal "we" died hard with her.

He sat at her invitation. Mary chose a high-backed chair across from him. Not close enough.

"Parliament is determined to put an end to the threat you pose to Elizabeth and her crown," he said bluntly, reaching for her hands to hold them in her lap. "Philip and Pope Sixtus have turned the campaign against Elizabeth into a Holy War."

"A war that will not end with our death."

"But it must. You are the only Catholic heir to Elizabeth with a clear claim to the throne."

"We have assigned our rights to Philip in our will."

"Parliament will never allow a Spaniard to set foot in England."

"Who rules England; the monarch or commoners?" Mary stood up, indignant and outraged.

Donovan was obliged to release her hands and to stand as well. "Our government has evolved out of a long and painful process of civil war, trial, and error. Our monarch rules with Parliament. As your son rules in Scotland with the aid of a Parliament."

"An insult to royal blood."

"Mary, please. I beg of you. For the sake of our love, for the sake of our son, preserve your life. Put aside your plots."

"We cannot. We cannot allow a heretic to continue to taint the good people of this land."

"I wish I could believe in something as strongly as you do, Your Grace."

Sir Amyas Paulet banged on the door. "Your time has expired, Milord of Kirkenwood," he announced through the closed portal. He sounded almost gleeful to cut short the interview.

"Farewell, my love," Donovan said quietly. He turned on his heel and left before she saw the tears that filled his eyes.

"Did you ever truly love me, Mary?" he whispered from the courtyard, staring at one of the narrow windows in her tower. "Or was I merely a convenient friend the night you discovered the depth of your husband's perfidy?"

As he rode away from Mary's prison, he remembered why the laundress had seemed so familiar to him. He slapped his forehead with his fist. Should he go back?

Would she even listen?

His locket burned. He touched it and rode away, his thoughts filled only with Mary and his love for her.

I watched my uncle ride away. With every heartbeat I expected him to turn around and betray me. I should have known that he would penetrate the gloss of magic disguising my features. My head spun with plans to scoop up Maggie Rose and Newynog and flee.

Uncle Donovan rode around the last bend and did not return. I breathed a little easier. I had a little time.

I hastened to the kitchen where Master Burton ate a hearty meal. Roasted boar, bread, cheese, ale. Plain food, but plentiful. As we all ate in this grim and humorless household.

He looked up from his meal at the sound of my step on the flagstones. My shoulders drooped and my chin sagged. I kept my eyes cast down. " 'er Grace said this was number one." I handed him the rolled note in my left hand. "And this be number two." He had no way of knowing I switched the notes. As I had switched all of those that passed through my hands.

Mary kept the cipher on her person. I had not the time or knowledge to break the codes. Walsingham's pet linguist Thomas Phelippes, however, could manipulate encrypted letters quite easily.

"Right on, my girl." Burton took the letters and pinched my cheek in rough affection. "These will get where they need to get. Never you fear." Then he heaved himself off the bench and over to his empty barrels stacked on a cart in the courtyard.

When a sliver of the moon rose that night, Maggie Rose,

Newynog, and I stole a horse from Sir Amyas Paulet's stable and rode post haste to London. I dared stay in Mary's household no longer.

One friend who had also worked with Walsingham had died a horrible death under torture in Spain. Another agent had disappeared without trace. If 'twere only me, I would gladly risk the dangers of continuing at Chartley. But I had to consider Maggie Rose.

I had to remember that as the Pendragon of Britain, more than my daughter depended upon me.

I only hoped my replacement could do more.

Better yet, I prayed that Walsingham had enough information to finally end the Holy War brewing around Elizabeth and her near thirty year reign.

I prayed my father's rosary the entire trip to London.

Chapter 65

17 July, 1586. London, home of Sir Francis Walsingham.

THREE weeks after fleeing Chartly, I still looked over my shoulder for one of Mary's fanatical followers turned assassin. If Uncle Donovan had let slip the least suspicion of me . . .

My hands shook at odd moments and I started at sudden noises. Newynog stayed within reach of my fingers at all times.

I could not sense Hal's protective presence at all.

Only Maggie Rose seemed impervious to the danger. I did not believe Uncle Donovan would betray me deliberately or conspire toward my death. But a chance word to Mary would set a plot in motion. The spell she cast over men demanded total and blind obedience. I could not decide if she wielded true magic or some innate charm invisible to other women. I was not safe if Mary knew that her laundress was a spy for Walsingham.

I spent many mornings with the queen's spymaster. His lady wife delighted in Maggie Rose and spent hours playing with her, teaching her letters and numbers, and brushing her fair hair.

Only here did I feel safe. Everyone here carried weapons, and not the flimsy court ornaments that would barely pierce velvet let alone armor. Walsingham kept a loaded pistol in the drawer of his writing table. He also wore a serviceable short sword that matched his fashionable court dress. I had a stout knife strapped to my thigh, accessible through a false pocket in gown and petticoat. I also carried an Italian stiletto in a special scabbard built into my boot. Newynog was perhaps my best defensive weapon. Her nose and keen ears identified friends and strangers. She "smelled" emotions in people and relayed them to me. Even in the tavern she allowed no one to come too close to me without my acknowledgment.

But my tavern was riddled with Catholic sympathizers. Michael and I had worked hard to cultivate them as customers so that we could eavesdrop and monitor their actions. Any one of them could be an agent for Mary.

"I insist that you take one of my men into your household," Sir Francis said. "One of the stouter ones with a good knowledge of weapons as well as hand-to-hand combat."

"How will I explain a man living in the tavern who is not my husband?"

"Call him your cousin. Hal Kirkwood has been missing so long, no one remembers what he looks like."

"He looks exactly like his father—and my father for that matter. He always has. Any number of people remember one or both of them."

"You will think of something. You always do." Sir Francis dismissed my objections.

As much as I wanted protection, I did not want a man underfoot. Any man who was not Hal.

Before I could voice my next protestation, a discreet knock came at the door to the study. Thomas Phelippes, the code breaker, fairly bounced into the room. His grin stretched his thin face into impossible angles. He carried a piece of loose parchment. On the bottom of the missive he had drawn a crude gallows.

The world went white. I saw a death's-head leering beneath his taut skin.

Cold sweat broke out on my back and brow. My sense of up and down, right and left swirled. Images flickered around the edge of my vision. Nothing coherent, merely impressions of blood and destruction.

Somehow I managed to maintain my seat. My hands ached from gripping the arms of my chair.

"It is done," I whispered.

"Not quite done, my dear. But the jaws of the trap have closed," Walsingham said around a smile.

He handed me the letter Phelippes had copied into plain English from Mary Stuart's coded message to her newest coconspirator, Anthony Babington of Dethick. I had met the young man briefly a year ago. About twenty-five, gently born, his eyes blazed with fervor whenever Mary's name or a Catholic conspiracy was mentioned in his presence. I believed he had served Mary's household briefly as a page when the Earl of Shrewsbury was still her guardian.

In the lengthy letter Mary heartily endorsed Babington's plot to murder Elizabeth.

> *The affair being thus prepared, and forces in readiness both within and without the realm, then shall it be time to set the six gentlemen to work; taking order upon the accomplishment of their design, I may be suddenly transported out of this place.*

"Pen a postscript to the original letter in code, Phelippes," Walsingham said. He grinned and rubbed his hands together. "Ask for the names of the six who will assist Babington so that she might reward them suitably and name them in her prayers."

"Certainly, Mary Stuart incriminates herself in this missive," I said, fighting to keep my senses from reeling again. "Must you falsify the evidence?"

"She gives specific instructions to six assassins poised and ready to take our queen's life when next she walks in the park at Windsor. We must know these men lest they carry out the plot even after Mary's arrest and trial. All of England is grateful to you, Lady Deirdre. Without you, we would not have the evidence we need to end the conspiracy."

Of course Elizabeth would be at Windsor now where Mary's agents awaited her in the forested park. With war in the Netherlands and Portugal, and Philip of Spain planning a campaign against England, Elizabeth had chosen not to go on progress this year. Drafts made the massive stone edifice of Windsor most uncomfortable in winter. She journeyed there by choice, only in high summer when the heat and diseases made the city unlivable.

Mary's assassins knew precisely where and when Elizabeth was most vulnerable.

They came for the queen, not me. This did not allow me to breathe any easier.

For weeks Babington and his coconspirators had openly bragged of their enterprise and toasted their success throughout the inns of London, including mine. Babington had also commissioned a group portrait of himself and his future regicides as a memorial of so worthy an act.

I knew all this. Had known it for some time. But I had not believed in Mary's total complicity in the project until now.

And suddenly the images that had flickered around the edges of my vision became clear. I shared my father's repeated vision of towering waves stained by the blood of thousands and Mary Stuart leading a long line of faithful men to the gallows. He had seen Mary's end.

The vision was clear. Upon Mary's execution, death and destruction at sea must follow. A mighty battle that no one could win. Spain would invade.

I had set the chain of events in motion.

Suddenly I knew, as my father had known, that I had to do everything in my power to prevent Mary's trial and execution. Her guilt was a foregone conclusion.

I had to forget her little kindnesses to me and her other servants. She had no reason to notice any of us, but she remembered to ask after Maggie Rose each morning. I had watched her hold her head up proudly while Paulet belittled her for her religion. I had knelt with her in prayer.

Mary could not be allowed to escape. But she must not die at the hands of an executioner.

Quietly, I excused myself from Sir Francis and Thomas Phelippes. Upstairs, in the private rooms of the house, I sought out Lady Walsingham and my daughter.

Maggie Rose ran to me, squealing in delight.

"Look at my hair, Mama," she ordered as she hugged my knees. "See how we have dressed it. Even Her Majesty has not so gracious a coiffure."

"My Heavens, sweeting, you must have two dozen braids and twice as many ringlets!" How Lady Walsingham had managed to work the fine locks into so elaborate a style I would never know.

We giggled and cooed over Maggie Rose's hair for a moment.

"My Lady Walsingham," I addressed our hostess formally. "I needs must run several important errands for your

husband," The lies tripped from my tongue most easily.
"May I impose upon your hospitality for a few hours and
leave my daughter in your tender care?

"Heavens, yes, child. Go. Take as long as you need."
Before I could curtsy and back out the door, she had taken
Maggie Rose's hand and shooed her into another chamber.
"We shall find ribbands to twine in the curls and pins to
tie up the braids," she said, more entranced with my daughter than with me or my chores.

Before Sir Francis could find any reason to detain me, I
slipped away from his house and returned to my tavern.
Within moments I had swallowed my pride and my reservations. Long before nightfall, I took to the road to find the
only man with enough influence and love for Mary to stop
the coming events.

Mary's trial and execution would make her a martyr. One
dead martyr was worth more than ten thousand armed
troops in the Holy War Spain and Rome launched toward
England.

20 July, 1586. The Great North Road.

Hal stood in the center of the Great North Road. Deep
ruts on either side of his feet had dried and crusted into a
washboard. A single rider must keep to the center to save
the horse's feet. Dee would have to stop in front of him or
ride right over him.

She would stop for nothing else.

The vibrations of pounding horse hooves danced through
the soles of his boots. The rhythm relayed urgency.

Then he saw her silhouette against the sliver of a moon.
Enough light for him to tell that she pressed herself low
against the horse's neck. A breath of her magic urging the
beast to greater speed whispered to him across the still
night air.

"You will press the horse too hard and make him
founder," Hal said quietly.

Dee reared up from the horse's neck. She looked around,

startled and wary before her gaze paused on him. He heard her sigh in relief. And then she parted her lips, looking to him in hope and . . . dared he dream? . . . welcome.

"Hal," she breathed.

"Deirdre."

"Hal, I need your help."

"You never seek me out otherwise."

"I have looked."

"Not hard enough."

"You did not want to be found."

He had no reply to that. He'd spent as much time in Paris of late as he did in England. Upon Walsingham's orders he cultivated the new king of France, Henri of Bourbon, King of Navarre and, for the past two years, of France. Henri IV was a staunch Huguenot, walking a political tightrope. Hal whispered caution and compromise in his ear at every turn.

"What do you need now?" he finally asked.

Newynog, the latest wolfhound in a long line of giant dog familiars lumbered along the road. She must have fallen behind while searching out a stray scent. Now she raced to catch up. But she did not pause at Dee's side. She continued on, coming to an awkward halt directly in front of Hal. She reared up, placed her huge paws on his shoulders and licked his face.

A wave of warmth and well-being washed over him. Not since Helwriaeth had given his life for Hal, had he felt a similar gush of love, unbounded and unconditional.

"I have fed you too well, my friend," he said, ruffling her ears. He pressed his face into her neck and breathed deeply of her doggy scent.

"If she is used to you feeding her, then she would not alert me when you lurked about my tavern watching me." Dee remained firmly ahorse.

Hal desperately needed to hold her in his arms, much as he held her dog.

"Are you taking Newynog north to Kirkenwood for breeding?" He put the dog aside and approached the horse. It flared its nostrils and rolled its eyes at his scent. When it started prancing, Dee curbed its instinct to flee with knees and reins and balance. Hal could almost see the calming thoughts she poured into the creature's tiny mind.

"Your brother brings mates for her to Ide Hill."

"At least one member of the family believes that the dogs have the final choice of Pendragon."

"Hal, we have much to say to each other. I cannot spare the time right now. I must find your father."

"Then you travel in the wrong direction. He abides at Ide Hill these days. Rather, he sulks at Ide Hill."

"And he did not tell me!" She yanked on the reins, savagely bringing the horse around. Newynog leaped to be off again.

"Dee! Wait."

She paused before setting her spurs to the horse's flanks. Newynog raced back to her side to see why she had delayed.

"Dee, what is this urgent mission of yours?"

"Travel with me and I will tell."

"I have no horse. And yours will not support our combined weight for long, even if it would tolerate my wolfish scent." Though Hal longed for the excuse to wrap his arms around her, hold her close against his chest, breathe the scent of her hair.

"Then meet me there. Help me persuade Uncle Donovan to take action."

"I can't, Dee. I can't face my father."

"You must. For his sake. For your own. For all England." She touched spur to horse and pelted back down the road the way she had come. Newynog loped at her side, tongue lolling and drool flying from her beard.

Hal breathed deeply. Then he shed his clothing, wrapping them into a tight bundle, and strapped them to his back with his belt. Within three heartbeats, the joint wrenching pains and burning itches signaled his transformation. As a wolf, he could travel farther and faster than he could as a man. He'd reach Ide Hill almost as quickly as Dee. He need not stick to the roads to find his way.

Chapter 66

20 July, 1586. Early morning, Ide Hill Manor, southeast of London.

TWO wolfhounds barked an alarm as I rode pell-mell up the drive of Ide Hill. We had never spent much time here when I was a child. Uncle Donovan had designated the manor and estates as Hal's heritage from his mother. Griffin, by law, would inherit the entailed title and honors of Kirkenwood. Betsy and I supposedly had dowries.

I had no idea what Uncle Donovan planned for this manor now that he had disinherited Hal.

Robin awaited me at the door with a loaded pistol and two stout footmen behind him. He had the courage to return to England. But his wife remained in Edinburgh with their children. His eyes looked overly dark and sunken in his thin face. He had not slept well or recently.

If Uncle Donovan's secretary did not sleep well, then my uncle must not have slept at all.

"Where is he?" I asked. The wolfhounds backed away from me and Newynog. They recognized dominant females on a mission.

Robin did not. He remained firmly planted in place.

"He wishes to see no one."

"I don't care what he wishes. I need to speak with him. This is important, Robin."

"His health and well-being are important. I will not disturb him."

"Must I go to the queen and order him to court?"

"You could try. He would defy you both."

Some of my urgency deflated. "What ails him?"

"Mary."

"How?" I looked up and examined Robin's face more closely. Worry lines radiated from his eyes and mouth. His skin looked flushed beneath a surface pallor.

Suddenly I began to worry as well.

"He will not speak to me. He has locked himself away since he returned from his last visit to her."

"I was there. I think I know what ails him."

I pushed him aside and ran up the narrow, enclosed stair. Newynog stayed close upon my heels.

Behind us, I heard the other dogs whimper as Robin curbed their natural instinct to follow us.

Uncle Donovan sat slumped in the dark of the privy solar behind the family parlor. A small fire in the grate offered a flicker of light. He stared at it, unblinking, not even acknowledging my entrance. His hair looked ragged and uncombed. He had not shaved in days. His doublet hung open. I did not see the heart-shaped locket he always wore next to his heart. A shift in the light from the fire glinted on the silver chain riding up against his throat. He must have tossed the locket over his shoulder so that it hung down his back.

I had never seen him so unkempt.

Newynog pushed ahead of me and thrust her muzzle beneath his limp hands dangling between his legs. Absently, he scratched her ears but did not move from his dejected posture.

"Uncle Donovan?" I said quietly.

"I do not wish to be disturbed." His voice came out dry and cracked with disuse.

I felt my way to the decanter and goblets that always stood upon a glass tray on a small inlaid table on the opposite side of the hearth. The wine was warm and still filled the decanter. He had not touched a drop. How long had it sat there?

"Drink," I ordered him, handing him a full goblet.

He took it absently. "Your father's friends at Whitefriars made this glass," he said. His fingers traced the graceful curves of the red glass. "You have to add real gold to the mix to get a true red like this. I bought it from them to commemorate Martha's safe delivery of the twins. Did you know she nearly gave birth in the Abbey right after your father married us?"

"I know. I read the journals. Drink." I knelt in front of him and guided the glass to his lips.

He tasted the wine hesitantly. Then he drank deeply. His throat worked each swallow as if in pain. "I truly loved Martha, you know."

"I know. You did not betray my presence at Chartley to Mary or her agents, Uncle."

"I considered it."

"But you did not. Your love for me is a treasure I hold close to my heart."

"Reserve that love for your father. I do not deserve it. I did not deserve Martha's love either."

"Griffin Kirkwood was a great man. I cannot deny that. He sired me. But you raised me, Uncle. You taught me all the things a father needs to teach his children." I gulped back the emotions that threatened to choke me. "You loved me. My father never even met me." Gently, I cupped his face. Several days' worth of beard scratched my palm. "I love you, Uncle Donovan. I can only respect and admire the man who sired me."

"Ah, Dee," he sobbed. "I do not deserve your love or your respect."

"If you have made mistakes, I have not suffered much from them." I conveniently forgot the long years of estrangement. I'd had Michael then. If I'd had my family as well, I might have spent my marriage resenting Michael because he was not Hal instead of learning to rely upon him and becoming friends as well as lovers. I might not have Maggie Rose.

"Your eldest son, Griffin, has turned into a fine man. All of your foster children have prospered—including Robin. We all owe you much, including our love and respect."

"You do not speak of Betsy or . . ." he choked, "or Hal."

"Hal is on his way here. Will you speak to him?"

"Hal?" His eyes brightened a moment. Then his face closed, and he slumped again.

"I broke my promise to your father, and to my Grandmother Raven. I did not love you as my own. I loved you more than my own. I loved the foster children better than my own. I have failed. I failed Hal most of all. All because I held my love for Mary more important than my children, my estates, my duty to England. More important than my *wife!*"

"One does not choose where one's heart settles." I should know that most of all. If ever a love was destined to fail, 'twas mine for Hal.

"My heart did not settle on Mary. A magic spell—demon born—placed it there, then bound it with thick chains and agony."

"Partially." A glimmer of an idea surged forward. "All of the men who have worshiped Mary, the Earl of Bothwell, the Duke of Norfolk, Babington," I named the most notorious and most recent of the men to plot with Mary. "All of those men whom she has led to the gallows or imprisonment loved her blindly. They allowed her to dictate the terms of their love. She used them for her own ends. And they never questioned the tightness, or even the practicality of her schemes. You thought only of her best interest. Your plots with her were for her life, not for power or glory. You questioned everything she did. Those other men were spellbound. You genuinely loved."

"But . . ."

"I think the demon spell merely augmented what was already there. Now you must do one more thing to protect her, as you have always protected her. You must go to Elizabeth and convince her to intervene. Parliament must not bring Mary to trial, nor convict her. They must not be allowed to execute her."

For a few heartbeats, life and love animated his face. Then it fell again.

"She does not love me. She never has."

"She must. You fathered her only child."

He looked at me in astonishment. "How did you . . . ?"

"I guessed. I watched the way you deal with the young king. I read some of your letters to Mary that passed through the Spanish Embassy on their way to her."

"She used me to get that child. Darnley, her husband, preferred boys to women. He could only function with a woman if he beat her. Watching her in pain aroused him."

I shuddered at the images. I had met a few men like that over the years. Fortunately, Michael had shielded me from the worst offenders. But I knew they existed. Some of them frequented my tavern.

"For the sake of James, your unacknowledged son, you must prevent Mary's execution."

"James thrives without her. He fears her. As long as she lives, his crown sits uneasily upon his head. He loves his crown more than anything in this world. He has learned to hate women because of his mother."

"Please, Uncle Donovan, you must act. You are the only one Elizabeth will listen to. If Mary dies, Spain will invade England, there will be terrible battles. My father foresaw it."

"No. England will survive without my interference. I will break the thrall of the love spell once and for all." He might not have heard me for his self-absorption.

"For James, for yourself. For England, you must intervene."

"No."

"My father's visions are coming true. He saw that if Mary dies, then Philip of Spain will invade."

"No, he won't. Philip is afraid of us. Of England's might. Of Elizabeth's cunning. It has been, what—five years—eight years since the pope offered the one-million-gold-ducat award for Elizabeth's downfall. Philip has not acted in all that time." So he had heard me. He did think clearly. He just did not care anymore.

We had all lived with the threat of invasion for so long that it no longer carried urgency or even true fear. Invasion had receded in our memories like childhood monsters under the bed.

But part of Uncle Donovan's statement rang true. "Yes, Philip is afraid of the English. Afraid that if Mary rules England, she will ally with her French relatives and present a united barrier to his conquest of the Netherlands, and in the New World. Philip is as afraid of Mary as he is of Elizabeth."

That jolted Uncle Donovan out of his despondency for a moment.

"If he waits until Mary is dead to invade . . ."

The hairs on the back of my neck stood up. Newynog pricked her ears and shifted to the doorway. She stood there, alert, almost eager for the newcomer.

"Henri IV of France and his mother-in-law, Catherine de Médici, cannot rally support for anything but their own civil war. Catholic against the Huguenots. Regent against the king," I pressed my argument. "Philip feeds the Holy League in France with money and arms so that they will continue the wars against the Protestants indefinitely."

Uncle Donovan must reach a conclusion himself or he'd never act.

"And the Master of Werewolves breeds fear of the Protestants in France by attacking only Catholics," Hal finished for me.

I breathed more easily. The tension between my shoulders relaxed.

"*El Lobison*'s wolves kill hideously," Hal continued. "The families and friends of the victims fear for their immortal souls if they die in the jaws of a werewolf." He stood, tall and strong in the sparse light from the larger room at his back. "A werewolf must always kill more souls, seeking to absorb one because his own is lost."

"You would know." Uncle Donovan tightened his lips in anger or accusation.

"I observed the hideous slaughter. I did not participate."

"How do you know? Lycanthropes have no control over the beast within them, nor memory of their actions. I have read every arcane text written on the subject." Uncle Donovan stared at Hal with a mixture of loathing and despair.

"I have both memory and control. Helwriaeth did not completely die. His noble spirit joined with mine. He has given me strength to use the wolf within me rather than be used by it. I have never killed a human as a wolf. I thought I had killed *El Lobison,* but I failed in that. He lives, manipulating the Spanish and the French through terror. In that, I am more human in my darkest moments than *El Lobison,* even when he was sane."

"I do not believe you." Uncle Donovan turned his face away from his son, so like him in face and form and yet so different in bearing.

Hal held himself tight and wary. Graceful. Powerful.

Uncle Donovan seemed . . . shrunken.

"Then believe Dee. She has been involved in politics all along. Elizabeth trusts her as the Pendragon."

"Then Dee should go to Elizabeth." Uncle Donovan rose

for the first time and retreated to the wine decanter. He poured a full goblet and downed it in one gulp. The refill lasted no longer. He shook the last few drops of wine into his cup and stared at it.

"Robin!" he called. "Robin, where are you? I need wine. Now," he called.

Hasty footsteps in the outer room signaled Robin's rush to comply.

"Wine will not answer your questions, Uncle Donovan. Nor will it grant me the authority you think I should have. Elizabeth listens only to the information I gather, not my opinions. She never asks my advice, never consults me. She only nods at my reports and turns to Walsingham or Burghley."

"Then you are useless as a Pendragon. As useless as I am as a father."

"Agreed." Hal slammed the door and stomped away. His footsteps retreated a long way before I could no longer hear him.

"You are not useless. Elizabeth respects you. She has never given up hope that you will return to your diplomatic work. If you will just go to Elizabeth . . ."

"No. Mary must die."

"Then a large part of you will die with her."

Chapter 67

20 July, 1586. Ide Hill

HAL held me in his arms as we retreated from Uncle
Donovan.

My heart nearly broke with my uncle's.

"You know you have to go to Elizabeth. Make her see
what awaits England if she follows through with this," Hal
said quietly as we lingered in the Hall.

"I can try. I doubt she will listen to me. She did not
listen to my father and she loved him more than a little."

"You have to try. For yourself as much as for England.
You will not rest until you at least try. And if she refuses,
then you have to try again. That is why you are the true
Pendragon and my father can never be. You do not give
up."

"I shall seek audience with her on the morrow."

"Early. Before Walsingham and Burghley have a chance
to poison her mind."

"Maggie Rose is with Lady Walsingham. I sent word that
family business called me away for several days. I have the
time to prepare."

"Do you have appropriate dress?" He eyed my masculine riding leathers skeptically.

It occurred to me that in recent years he had seen me
wearing only these practical garments and no garb suitable
for a lady.

"Of course. I have spent many evenings at court listening
covertly to conversations in Her Majesty's service."

"Then you must seek out the queen as she breaks her
fast."

"I wonder if Robin would have any influence over her?

Come back to the tavern with me, Hal. We have much to talk about. Years to catch up on."

"No." He sounded as resolute and despondent as his father.

"But . . ."

"I said no. I have much control over the wolf. I have none over my heart." In two blinks he had disappeared. A breath of a draft across my hair might have been a kiss. Then again it could have been just a draft.

I sought out Robin in a private solar at Ide Hill.

"Me?" he snorted. "The queen listen to me? The last time I was in her presence she banished me from court for life because I married without her permission and I married a commoner."

"But you are her son!"

"A son she did not raise, does not know. I am more a Kirkwood than a Tudor. Legally, I bear the Kirkwood name since your uncle adopted me. No. Elizabeth will not listen to me. She will not listen to anyone but her own fears and prejudices."

By dawn I was on the road to Greenwich. Elizabeth had vacated Windsor quite hastily as soon as Walsingham had revealed Babington's plot to her. I rode, clad in my bright blue-green velvet riding habit with a high-crowned hat trimmed with an exotic peacock feather that matched the velvet. Newynog walked sprightly beside me, tongue lolling and ears back. She loved traveling. Two servants, who grumbled continually about the inconvenience of travel, trudged behind me hauling a cart with my trunk and a maid to help me dress. One gown with attendant petticoats, farthingale, ruffs, corset, and jewelry filled the entire iron-bound piece of luggage.

Once at Greenwich, I needed an entire hour to dress properly. Then I had to wait another hour upon Her Majesty's pleasure. She had broken her fast long ago. Ministers and councilors and documents surrounded her. Walsingham stood closest to the queen. He glared questions at me that I should appear at court when he presumed me on the road to Kirkenwood, having left my daughter in his custody.

Elizabeth rose from the prison of those documents. "Lady Griffin," she exclaimed, leaving her ministers to collect the parchments from the floor where they rolled once she abandoned the writing table and high-backed chair. "You have absented yourself for too long from our presence." She extended one hand for me to kiss her ring.

I did so, from the depths of my curtsy. "Majesty," I murmured.

"Walk with me," Elizabeth commanded. She lifted me from my obeisance and tucked my hand around her arm. The queen towered above me. Most of her courtiers had to look up to her.

She intimidated most women. Not me. I knew too much about her from my years as her lady-in-waiting. Today, I used court etiquette and a meek demeanor as a means to an end.

We roamed the maze of rooms at Greenwich with courtiers, minister, ambassadors, and ladies in our wake. I let Elizabeth work off some of her restless energy before broaching my subject. She chatted eagerly about the gossip from my tavern and about my daughter.

"Majesty, I have come to you with information from my father's journals."

Her eyes widened in surprise, then softened with affection. "We do miss Father Griffin sorely. He guided us through tricky pathways of thinking to an easier mind." She scratched Newynog's ears absently, as if from long habit.

"My father can counsel you from the grave, if you will but read some of what he has to say."

Elizabeth looked sharply over her shoulder at the myriad of followers. "We wish privacy," she barked at Lady Sidney who led the pack.

That stalwart lady halted and turned to face the others. She stood firmly between them and her queen. The officials and sycophants bunched up together, shoving for better position and muttering curses. I wondered if they would tumble like ninepins.

During the slight confusion, Elizabeth led me through a narrow doorway that gave into a series of small, inelegant rooms, and from there to the gardens.

"We have not long before they catch us," Elizabeth said a little breathlessly. "Speak quickly of Father Griffin's words."

As we traced the paths of the silver knot garden, I related my father's recurring vision. "The images are clear.

If Mary dies, Spain will invade. There will be a terrible
battle at sea with much loss of life. I do not foresee a
favorable outcome for England. Parliament must not bring
Mary to trial or execute her. 'Twill only make her a
martyr."

"Be you victim to the same vision?" Elizabeth halted
and looked deeply into my eyes.

I kept my gaze steady and resolute. "Sadly, God has not
seen fit to bless or curse me with vision. I relate only Father
Griffin's words from his journals."

"And do you share your father's faith?" The queen
dropped my arm and put two paces between us, as if she
feared the papist taint.

"I wish I could share my father's faith. I wish I could
believe in anything as firmly as did he. My loyalty to you,
Your Majesty, is the closest thing I have. I would give my
all for you, as my father gave his all for his beliefs."

"We shall consider your words," Elizabeth said as she
retreated indoors. At the last moment she flung a few
words over her shoulder. "You will sup with us. We would
hear more of your father's adventures."

But not his counsel.

Walsingham waited only long enough to have all of his
evidence in hand before arresting Mary. On August 4, with
the arrest of one of the conspirators, the rest went into
hiding. Walsingham hastily had copies made of the group
portrait of Babington and his cohorts and distributed throughout the kingdom.

August 9 brought Mary's arrest and a thorough search
of her belongings. Sir Amyas Paulet impounded three
chests full of letters, jewelry, and money to fund the
conspiracy.

Whispers spread through the Crown and Anchor. One
of my own scullery maids attempted to steal food to take to
Babington. Walsingham's agents followed her to St. John's
Woods north of London. They found and arrested the man

who had orchestrated the plot to murder Elizabeth. I never saw the maid again.

When news of the arrest reached London, the next day, as Babington was taken to the Tower, all the church bells pealed out joyously. The people lit bonfires and danced in the streets in jubilation. Beer and ale flowed freely. The plot against their beloved queen was thwarted.

As each of the fourteen men now in custody confessed, the Privy Council urged Elizabeth to summon Parliament. She stalled as only Elizabeth could stall, waiting for others to act or change their minds. She cried, she argued, she raged. And still her ministers made their demands. I prayed that my father's words whispered to her through me from his grave had some effect. In the end, she could not hold out against her most trusted councilors.

On September 9, she summoned Parliament.

Babington and his associates stood trial first. Guilty verdicts were a foregone conclusion.

The Privy Council ordered the hangman to defy custom. Babington and his coconspirators must not be dead when cut down from the gallows. They must suffer the full extent of the grisly death reserved for traitors—drawing and quartering.

My reports had helped bring about their arrests. Their actions and attitude of defiance brought them to their torturous ends.

Chapter 68

September 10, 1586. The Port of Cadiz, Spain.

YASSIMINE trotted happily along the rocky strand. A warm breeze ruffled her fur. She paused periodically to sniff the air. Scents of new-cut lumber, tar, fresh twined rope, seawater, fish, and the sweat of many men drifted in turn past her sensitive nose.

Hammers pounded, saws grated, and men swore. Sails hoisted, ropes flew everywhere, and sailors scrambled to complete obscure tasks. She tried to block out the unpleasantness. Everywhere something was abuilding or repairing.

Bright sun warmed her back and made her squint when looking out over the calm water. She basked a moment in the dry heat, so close to home, yet different. She had never seen nor smelled the sea until after The Master purchased her in the slave auction. For many years she had cursed the day Turkish raiders had burned her village, destroyed her altars, and killed all of her kith and kin. Now she appreciated the one thing she could never have in the simple village that worshiped the wolf.

At home, only normal human women were allowed to bear and keep their living children. If one such as she happened to give birth to a live child, especially one fathered by another wolf, the child died—often at the hands of its own father.

Her pup gamboled along behind her. His big paws, fair coloring, clumsy tracking, and delight in the adventure of life reminded her of his father.

Her people might worship the wolf, but they closely controlled the number of them they had to live with.

In her heart she called her youngling Baruckey, "Blessed"

in her mother language. The Master called him "Brat" or, upon occasion, "Lobo," meaning wolf in Spanish.

Since the pup had been sired while she and Hal had been in wolf form, she had had to transform in order to bear him. Now the transition from woman to wolf and back again came easily to her at any time. Like Hal, she was no longer a slave to the pull of the moon when it rose full above the horizon. She needed to remain lupine to nurse Baruckey. Once he was weaned and discovered how to become human, they had spent almost half their time in fur.

Now the boy preferred his wolf form when strangers visited The Master or The Master traveled. Though a true wolf of five years of age would have achieved full adult size and maturity, her son preferred his wolf body to reflect his immaturity as a human.

Yassimine did not object. She enjoyed the child in both forms.

"Come!" The Master commanded sharply. His left arm hung uselessly in a sling. He had abandoned the hook since he could not use it with the withered limb. Instead, he carried a short riding whip in his right hand that might lash out at any moment to punish. His temper remained on the edge of explosion at all times. But he, too, delighted in the pup, thinking it his own.

Yassimine yipped a command to her child, cuffing him lightly with her muzzle. He paced beside her for several long human strides while they caught up to The Master. Then Baruckey found a dead fish in a clump of seaweed much more interesting than obedience.

She thought the fish more interesting than The Master at the moment. The consequence of too much time spent in fur.

The whip snapped. Her left foreleg and paw stung. She bared her teeth, defying the whip.

"Is that safe?" A man approached The Master. He carried a sheaf of parchments, rolled and flat. His clothing, though dark and sober was cut of the finest cloth by expert tailors. His barber had taken pains to keep his hair and beard in precise conformation to court standards.

"Do you question my methods, Don Cordovan?" The Master lifted his own lip in imitation of Yassimine's snarl.

"Never, *El Lobison.*" Don Cordovan made a slight bow.

Three rolls fell to the ground. Two more threatened to spill from his overloaded arms.

Yassimine and Baruckey bounced to investigate this new puzzle.

The man stepped back from them.

"You have no need to fear her. She will not menace you unless you threaten the pup."

"Sí, *El Lobison*." Don Cordovan said, but his wide eyes and the scent of fear in his sweat betrayed him.

Yassimine nosed his boots.

He gritted his teeth but held his place.

The Master laughed.

Then he sobered abruptly. "I see no new keels laid since last week. No stockpiles of supplies. Your work on His Majesty's Enterprise does not progress well."

"Ships cannot be built or supplied or manned in a day, *El Lobison*."

"In Venice, a ship can be built in three days. Marco Polo attested to this in his writings. I have seen it myself."

"The Venetian vessels ply only the waters of the inland sea. They do not face the dangers of the English Channel."

"The fleet must be ready to sail the day news reaches His Majesty that Mary Queen of Scots has been executed."

"We have time. She has not yet been tried." Don Cordovan bent to retrieve his rolls and documents. "The English are unbelievers. They will not hasten with these matters."

Yassimine listened more closely at the mention of the English.

"The English dogs believe in their queen!" The Master snapped his whip against his tall boots.

Yassimine cringed out of the way. She made certain Baruckey also moved beyond the range of the whip.

"To the English, their queen is as important as the Virgin Mary is to you," The Master continued. He leaned forward. A nasty snarl escaped his lips.

Don Cordovan blanched. He attempted to cross himself, but his load got in his way. Two dropped to the strand. Another three threatened to slide out from under his arms.

Baruckey caught one of the rolls in his mouth and shook it as he would small prey.

Yassimine cuffed him and snarled. He dropped it and ran away just as the whip snapped.

"No matter how fast or slow the English proceed in their

case against Mary Stuart, this fleet, the mightiest armada ever assembled, must be ready to sail on time. His Majesty will brook no delay."

"Seems as if he should have built this fleet ten years ago and rescued the Catholic queen from her Protestant jailers before they manufactured evidence to execute her."

"Fool. His Majesty does not want Mary to rule England! He wants England for himself."

"I see," Don Cordovan said as he tried organizing his burden. "He launches the armada only in revenge for Mary's death, and not before."

"Precisely."

"Do I have authority to hire more shipwrights, skilled carpenters, and cannon makers? We must spread our network far afield to purchase gunpowder, food stores, and seasoned barrels for water, *El Lobison*." The man dropped his head and his eyes in deference. Or in fear.

"Do whatever you have to. I will have His Majesty sign the bills of lading." The Master turned on his heel ready to stomp off.

"And where may I find you should I need instructions or other authority?"

"You will not find me. Send your reports to His Majesty. He will contact me if necessary."

The Master stalked back the way he had come, slapping the whip against his boots. "We leave for Paris today, Yassimine," he said as he walked. "Don Bernardina de Mendoza and I must assure that the Duc de Guise and his Holy League are prepared to march on Paris when the armada sails. Civil war will follow. France will not be able to come to England's aid when we crush the unbelievers. Then we go to Amsterdam. I must also coordinate with the Duke of Parma in the Netherlands. He provides the troops that will land in England once we have crushed their opposition at sea. Fresh blood for you and the brat, my wolf."

Yassimine licked her chops. The French ate more sweets than the Spanish. Their blood was sweeter.

"This time we will return to England with an army at our backs, Yassimine. The unbelievers will defy us no longer. I shall have my pack of wolves in England as well as the Continent. Then we will conquer the New World with terror as well."

Yassimine curbed Baruckey's playfulness and began to follow at The Master's heels to signal her approval of his plans.

"Yassimine, remind Don Cordovan how he will be punished if he fails to complete the ships in time," The Master said carefully. Then he grabbed the pup's ruff to keep him close.

Yassimine loped toward the retreating man. His back was to her. His parchments continued to slip and throw him off stride and off-balance. She leaped and pushed him with all four of her paws.

He went down. Yassimine kept her entire weight upon his back. Breath escaped his lungs with a whoosh. He whimpered.

Yassimine opened her jaws wide and placed them warningly against his neck. She sensed the blood pulsing in his great vein. His heart beat loud and rapid. Hunger awoke in her, strong and urgent.

He sniveled.

She pressed her teeth into his neck. Not much. Just enough to taste his blood. The first lick and she wanted more. But she knew what The Master would do to Baruckey if she disobeyed and killed this one.

Don Cordovan cried out.

"Yassimine, no!" The Master called. "I need him alive."

The blood tasted sweet, hot, alive. She needed more. More pressure upon his great vein. A spurt of blood shot into her mouth. She swallowed slowly, savoring the slightly salty, slightly coppery taste.

"Yassimine, off!" The whip slashed across her back.

She reared back her head, ready to snap at the biting coil of leather.

"Off!" The Master brought the whip down again, this time across her muzzle.

Snarling and drooling, needing to taste more blood, she backed away from her prey.

The Master yanked on the silver chain that dangled from her two highest teats.

Burning pain jolted through every joint. Desperate to free herself from the agony, she willed her body back to human form. In an eye-blink the pain increased. Her sensitive nipples shriveled under the pressure. The sea breeze raised goose bumps on her naked skin. The other silver piercings on her body flared and joined in punishing her. She cried out. Tears came to her eyes.

Her joints wrenched back to the wolf. She sat on her haunches, cowed and meek before The Master's domination. He released his pressure on the chain. Her pup slunk to her side, licking at the raw skin where the silver pierced her.

The Master smiled. "Now you will behave."

Don Cordovan scuttled away from her, one hand clamped to his neck. Three times in rapid succession he crossed himself. Possession of the precious documents seemed forgotten, or no longer important.

"And you, Don Cordovan, will remember what will happen to you if you fail me."

"I will not fail His Majesty. The enterprise of England will sail on time." He continued to retreat, slipping to his knees every third step.

"Forget His Majesty. You will not fail me! I rule Spain through my wolves. You will know terror beyond belief if you fail to complete this armada on time."

Chapter 69

20 September, 1586. The Giant's Dance.

SEVERAL days before the scheduled executions of
Babington and his cohorts, I took Maggie Rose and Newynog far away from London. Away from the execution.

Away from the plots and machinations that gathered to
oppose England. Away from the evil that fed off of politics
and war.

We went west toward Salisbury Plain and the Giant's
Dance, the ancient stone monument where my parents
had died.

Death stalked London that day. I wanted to find some
place to celebrate life with my daughter and my familiar.
Instead, I visited the site of my parents' death.

As I traced the outer ditch that defined the Giant's
Dance, I wept for the lives my spy work had brought to an
end. But I could not weep for Griffin and Roanna who had
met here in challenge. Here my father had wed them in a
magic ritual so that whatever wounds they inflicted upon
each other, the wielder suffered the same. Together, they
had killed a demon. And each other.

Maggie Rose and Newynog capered about, picking dai-
sies and chasing butterflies. I stood by the altar stone and
marked where the sun would rise on the morrow, the Au-
tumnal Equinox. The beginning of the end of the year.

Was it also the beginning of the end for Elizabeth's reign
over England?

For many generations my ancestors had given their lives
for peace and unity here at home, for the protection of
these islands we held sacred. I could do nothing less.

War would come. I needed to be prepared.

I had the tools. I had the clear vision. But I could not do it alone.

Like my father, I wanted to be home, at Kirkenwood, for the ritual I needs must perform. The standing stones of the village there were familiar, a part of the family. These stones were larger, more magnificent and orderly. They would have to do.

I began walking my circle on the outside of the blue stones. These rough-hewn monuments were smaller than any of the others. They showed more weathering than the harder stones of the primaries. But they were special. The ancients had recognized the power within them and transported them incredibly long distances for a purpose.

Newynog and Maggie Rose drifted toward the center without having to be told. I needed them close at hand for their own protection as well as mine.

A sparkle of energy sprang from each stone as I touched it. Faint at first, the power grew with each successive stone. A web of blue-green light, the same color as my riding habit and peacock-feathered hat, grew, reached out, began to vibrate.

I had never seen my own magic take on color before. Perhaps today only the guilty would die rather than an innocent because I worked a spell.

At the moment I returned to the first stone the magic snapped closed, forming a dome over the entire ritual ground. I took my place at the center of the web. My daughter and my familiar pressed close to my side, giving me their strength and love.

Echoes of questions passed through me from my web of power. Minds quested to seek me out and marvel.

"Come," I called gently. "Come to my center. Come to be one with this ancient land."

Blood is shed today. You call up dark powers that are not easily harnessed. So many minds and temperaments vibrated along my strands of magic.

I held tightly to my control over the pulsating power.

"You may think of those who die this day as sacrifices. But not for me. Not for my own power."

You will need that power.

"In the days and months to come. Today, I ask for cooperation from you."

I sensed a puzzlement among the Otherworldly creatures who communicated with me from each of their various realms.

"Come forth to this center of power. I declare this neutral ground, hallowed by blood, ritual, and love." I conjured the image of my mother and father locked in mortal combat here. I called forth the memories of other rituals and sacrifices as old as the stones, as old as the land.

Hesitation, bewilderment, and . . . attraction. They could not resist my call.

One by one they came. The faeries came first, for they were my friends. A swarm of brightly colored winged beings flitted around my head like a halo or a crown.

And a raven. One of the blessed ones from Kirkenwood.

Then the elves appeared. They rode their magnificent horses around and around the inside of my ring of power, ever restless and anxious for their freedom. They feared my power but could not resist it.

We knew your father well. The king of the elves separated from his fellows and rode toward me. He galloped his ghostly horse directly at me in an intimidating display.

Maggie Rose and Newynog hid behind me. I stood my ground. If I flinched, even a little, I gave him power over me.

At the last second, he reined in the horse. It reared and pawed the air. Then it crashed back to the earth, sidling and curling its lip. But it never touched me.

The king of the elves doffed his cap to me with a half grin. *You are your father's get,* he almost laughed as he returned to his fellows.

Pixies, brownies, and sprites jumped up from behind stones and tufts of grass. They giggled and danced. With each step they jumped and hopped, tugging at my web of power.

I smiled at them and tightened my control. They shrugged and continued their dance without testing me further.

Then came the demons. I had not called them, yet they also responded to my web of power. Hideous creatures with too many out-sized limbs. Hairy bodies. Lizard bodies. And combinations of both. They all had one thing in common: huge maws with dagger-length teeth that dripped poison.

I gulped back my instinctive fear and wondered which

one was Tryblith, the Demon of Chaos, that had plagued my mother through most of her life. It had cost both my parents their lives in the battle to defeat it. Shapes and shadows these beings remained. Only reflections of their true selves could venture into this reality from behind their sealed portals. Even from behind those barriers, though, they wielded tremendous power.

Each of the demons huddled in its separate nook of the circle closest to its geographical portal. They knew nothing of cooperation. Few could think longer than their own immediate gratification for blood and power.

I feared working with them. How easily they could tempt me with power, with revenge, with knowledge. . . .

And then two ghostly figures appeared beside me. A tall man, a reflection of Uncle Donovan in his youth but without the comfortable padding of an easy life of nobility. Lean and drawn, prematurely gray of hair and beard, with little crinkles about his intensely blue eyes that showed worry, privation, and pain.

"Father," I welcomed him, holding out my hand.

He took it. A frisson of Otherworldly cold coursed through me. I drew it in, warmed it as best I could and passed it back to him. His form solidified a little.

His companion in death came to my other side. A short woman, my height, not quite tiny. Large gray eyes haunted her delicate features. A mass of red hair, the color of maples in autumn, framed her face. A sepulchral wind blew her curls into her eyes. She tossed her head saucily to clear her vision.

"Mother." I held out my other hand to her in equal greeting. She hesitated a moment, looked to my father, then accepted my welcome.

Maggie Rose peeked out from the shelter of my leg. Her mouth opened and closed in mute wonder. Then she placed her own little hand beneath mine and her grandmother's. Newynog nudged my father for the required ear scratch. His eyes danced with joy as he complied.

One of the demons cringed backward. The one with the hairy body, lizard legs, and dragon maw. He tried to leave this reality. My net trapped him. He huddled in his nook, gibbering and making weak slashing gestures at me and my family.

"We are complete," I announced to the gathering.

Not quite, a new voice stated. It echoed of the ages and a multitude of my ancestors.

"Grandmother Raven," I acknowledged her regal presence beside me. "England faces great peril."

We know, the gathering replied with one reverberating bellow.

"We cannot allow foreigners to rule us."

What difference if Spaniards deny our existence or the English Protestants! The elfin king spoke for them all.

"The Spaniards do not deny your existence. But they will seek you out and do all that they can to murder you, remove you from your protected realms as well as from this one. The English may deny your existence, refuse to see you or listen to you, but they know you are there. As they have always known. They will placate you with their little rituals and superstitions though they tell no one of it. With the English, you have a life though it be weak. With the Spaniards and their Inquisition, you have nothing."

Faint murmurs rose around me. Fear. Disgust. Sadness. I felt all of their emotions and shared them.

Why do you summon us to tell us what we already know? a bright green faery whispered as he flew past my ear.

I had no doubt the entire assembly heard him.

"To ask your help."

The crisis is not yet come, Father reminded me.

"But it will come. And I need you all to be prepared. Be ready to heed my summons when England needs you most."

Silence alone answered me.

Release us, the elfin king demanded.

"Do I have your promise?"

Promises are easily broken, lightly kept. Humans, most of all, break theirs without thought.

"I know. Many have broken their promises to me and to you. But I and my kind have always honored their word to you. I give you my word, as Pendragon of Britain, that I and my descendants will honor you all from now until the end of time."

Heed her! Grandmother Raven cried with the authority of all those who had preceded her. *She is one of mine. She has the support of every Merlin of England, from the beginning of time.*

Grudgingly, each of the beings I had called muttered a promise. Even the demons grudgingly vowed to help fend off intruders. With their word of honor, each being faded from view but remained connected to my net of power.

Lastly, my parents alone faced me.

We are proud of you, daughter, they whispered as they, too, faded.

I sighed and began the long ritual to ground and center my massive spell. Fatigue dragged at my limbs and eyes. Yet I felt strangely lighter and freer. Power continued to tingle in my fingertips, ready at my calling.

At last I looked up from my work.

A solitary wolf stared at me from atop the altar stone.

We, too, give you our promise of help. For we would be free of the Spaniard who seeks to rule through terror; who seeks to control us through silver and magic, he said directly into my mind.

"Thank you, Hal."

Chapter 70

20 January, 1587. London.

HAL wormed his way through a crowd gathering before
Whitehall. He edged aside the local blacksmith. He jumped
and started as if Hal had attacked with weapons drawn. So
did the carpenter's wife. Hal worried his lip.

He saw silhouetted figures standing behind the protection
of the glass windows in the palace before the mob. The
people in the palace darted about in a frenzy of unease.
Doubtless, Elizabeth was informed of all that transpired.

Something was terribly amiss here. The crowd smelled
of wolves.

The silver chains at Hal's ear and about his waist burned
in the cold air. He had not needed to claw at them so
deeply since . . . since he had consigned The Master to the
fishes off the coast of Cornwall. *El Lobison* had survived
the impossible and gone on to threaten Europe once more.

No one else living had The Master's powers. No one
else could command the men in this crowd who smelled so
strongly of wolf.

El Lobison must have returned to England.

"Have ye heard the latest?" a man in rough homespun
with a shaggy beard and wild eyes that tended to glow
red asked quite loudly. "The Spanish landed at Hastings at
midnight. Burned the town."

"I 'eard they landed at Portsmouth," another replied. He
was dressed more respectably in fine wool and wore a many
pocketed apron full of tools. He smelled of sawdust and
varnish.

"They freed the Queen of Scots! She meets with French
troops tonight at Great Yarmouth," a woman screamed and

threw her flour-dusted apron over her head. "Oh, my poor wee babes will be roasted alive and eaten by the Catholic dogs," she sobbed hysterically.

"If only Queen Bess would sign the warrant for Mary's execution, the Spanish would retreat," a spindly man in cleric's clothing moaned. He carried a Bible, but he smelled of wolf and wore a silver talisman in place of a cross. The chain seemed to pierce his nape.

Hal thrust him aside. The wolf-cleric stumbled. As he fought for balance, his eyes contracted, turning red, and his bushy blond eyebrows spread across his brow.

Hal gave him a sharp blow from his elbow into the gut. The cleric retched but remained silent.

"No, goodwife," Hal whispered soothingly pushing a thread of magic into her mind. He placed a comforting hand upon her shoulder. "The French shelter on their own side of the Channel. I have it on good authority that Good Queen Bess has spoken long and earnestly with the French Ambassador. There will be no invasion from that quarter."

The woman stared at him blankly.

Then the rough-bearded man who had sparked the round of rumors slapped Hal's hand off the woman's shoulder. "She speaks true. We have to take arms and protect ourselves. We have to burn the outer edges of the city so we have clear ground to see the Spanish coming."

A torch appeared in the hands of a local bailiff almost by magic. "Burn the city and flee. Cain't let the Spanish dogs get us!" he screamed.

Rumor had become a living, breathing entity. It fed on panic like the evil humors that caused disease. Hal could almost see it rising from the cobbles in a miasma of choking illness.

The rough-bearded man grinned at Hal in triumph. His open mouth revealed yellowed and broken teeth with elongated fangs. He wore a silver earring.

"I can't let The Master win," Hal muttered to himself.

As the crowd surged and flowed around him, he took one deep breath, then another. He found calm at the center of his being. With the third deep breath, power was his, available at his fingertips. The wolf within him demanded the element of Fire; huge bolts of lightning to scatter the crowd in fear.

Hal pushed aside the urge. He called up Air, the balancing element to Fire. A light breeze played around his senses. He added the scent of fresh-mowed hay and spring flowers from memory. A faery alit on his shoulder and blew a lilting tune through tiny pan pipes.

We promised cooperation, the green being giggled at Hal's look of surprise.

So you did. And so did I.

Hal thought calm. Gentle waves of peace rippled out from him. First one hysterical Londoner, then another stopped screaming, or crying, or moaning in mid-thought. Worry lines disappeared from their faces. Tension eased from their shoulders. They shook their heads as if to clear their minds of a dream, then drifted back to their normal pursuits.

The rough-bearded man and the cleric tried to rally the mob once more with shouts of new rumors of doom.

Hal concentrated on dissipating their words. A few members of the mob gathered around the rough-bearded man. He led them off toward the old walled city. Every hand among them seemed to carry a torch.

"I can't do this alone," he told the faery as he hastened to follow them.

You do not need to. The little winged being flew off in the wake of the retreating crowd. A handful of other brightly colored faeries joined him.

Concentrate upon the black-robed one, the many tiny voices chimed together.

"Yes, the cleric has many questions to answer." Hal quickly grounded the spell he had worked, then he looked about. A dark shape scuttled away like a wounded animal.

Hal swooped down and grabbed the man by his collar. "Now, Sir Wolf, you will tell all."

"I know nothing. I merely followed the others," he stammered. His heavy-lidded eyes darted back and forth, his gaze never lighting for long.

"Look at me!" Hal commanded. He pushed just a little left-over magic into his voice.

"I . . . I cannot. I . . . am not allowed." The man's shoulders nearly reached his ears and his chin sunk toward his chest.

"Where is your master?" Hal shook the man like a terrier with a rat.

"He'll kill me!" he squeaked.

"Would you rather I killed you?"

"Death at your hands will be clean." The man suddenly crawled out of his hunch and assumed an air of injured dignity. "If he kills me, my immortal soul is in jeopardy."

"By living in that man's shadow you jeopardize not only your soul but all of England. What were his orders?" Hal demanded. He did not relax his hold on the man's garment.

"Elizabeth must be frightened into signing the warrant for Mary's death since logic does not touch her."

"God's blood! They mean to make a martyr of her. The very people who should have rescued her years ago."

"And when she is dead, the entire country will be in a panic and disorganized, ripe for invasion." The cleric wormed out of Hal's grasp and slipped away in an eye blink. His mad laughter lingered after him. "We shall slaughter all those who resist and make a fine meal of them!"

Hal took off at a run. He had to talk to Dee. She had to take this new evidence of conspiracy directly to the queen.

1 February, 1587. London.

Elizabeth refused to see me. I tried sneaking into her presence and was promptly sent away from the palace by Sir William Davison, Walsingham's deputy. Sir Francis himself could not see me because of some ailment, whether real or feigned I knew not, except that he did not wish to be a part of the events about to happen.

Elizabeth signed the warrant for Mary's death. She stalled for months. Finally, she succumbed to pressure from Parliament, her advisers, and the populace. Later, she would deny it. Later, when the deed was done, she would claim that Davison had secreted the warrant amongst a pile of other documents requiring her signature. Later, she would claim second thoughts and request the warrant re-

turned to her, but by that time Sir Christopher Hatton had
affixed the Great Seal to it and the Privy Council—headed
by Burghley—had dispatched it to Fotheringhay Castle.

Elizabeth went so far as to order Paulet to dispatch Mary
by some other means so that she could claim her rival
queen had died of natural causes. Paulet, being an honorable man, refused.

Elizabeth must carry the burden and the blame for
Mary's death.

The execution was supposed to be conducted with utmost
secrecy until after Mary had died. Elizabeth ordered it to
take place in the Great Hall of Fotheringhay rather than
the forecourt to avoid unnecessary witnesses. The warrant
was dispatched to Paulet at Fortheringhay by trusted secret courier.

And all of London knew about each step of the procedure as it happened. We all waited breathlessly for the
news that the deed was done, that this threat to our beloved
queen had been removed by a headsman's sword. Only a
few of us knew that Mary's death would put into motion a
chain of events of even greater threat to England.

I thought about summoning my Otherworldy helpers.
Surely the elves or a demon could whisk Mary away. . . .

Uncle Donovan intervened first. He arrived on my doorstep at dawn of February 16, mounted and packed.

Hal had come, too. His horse pranced and sidled away
from him. Hal tried unsuccessfully to gentle his horse from
the ground. Brute strength kept it from bolting.

"I have to see her one more time," Uncle Donovan said
in way of greeting. His eyes looked like black pits, his
cheeks were gaunt, and his hair much more gray than last
I'd seen him. He looked more like the ghost of my father
than ever.

Within moments I had changed into riding leathers, packed
my panniers, arranged for neighbors to care for Maggie
Rose, and saddled my horse. Newynog whined and paced
restlessly between me and my daughter. She needed to protect us both. Grudgingly, I sent my dog to stand with Maggie Rose. I had defenses of my own, as well as Hal and my
uncle. My daughter had none.

Then we were off, riding as rapidly as we safely could
toward Mary's final prison deep in the Midlands. Hal

fought his horse the entire way. It distrusted his smell and tried to buck him off repeatedly.

Before we had traveled twenty miles, Hal had dismounted and dropped into his wolf form. Thenceforth, he ran beside or ahead of us. We kept the extra horse on a leading rein as a relief mount.

"Why did you bring Hal?" I asked my uncle during one of the many halts necessary to keep the horses running.

He shrugged. He had said little if anything on the journey. All his thoughts centered on his inner pain.

"Griffin should be the one beside you in this time of travail," I suggested gently.

"My son is at Kirkenwood with his new bride. Where he belongs."

"And your other son?"

Again he shrugged. "Robin has left my service. He has settled with his wife in Edinburgh. He has a position at James' court. Peregrine and Gaspar have become excellent stewards in Griffin's service."

"And Hal?"

He turned his face away before he answered. "Of all of my children, you and Hal alone have remained true to the vision of what the Pendragon must be." He did not mention Betsy. We both knew that dark magic had taken her mind. Likely, she would never again be sane. "You and Hal, the two of you are the ones who should witness this terrible tragedy."

"Do you intend to watch your love die?"

"I do not know. My heart is close to breaking already."

I held his hand. What else could I do?

We arrived at Fotheringhay well after sunset on the seventeenth day of February. Lights blazed from every window. People bustled about. Paulet and the Earl of Shrewsbury huddled in a small solar on the first floor of one of the towers. They avoided the Great Hall. The place where the execution would take place. On the morrow. Early.

"I must see her," Uncle Donovan pleaded with Paulet.

Hal, fully human and clothed again, and I remained behind him. Both of us avoided looking in the hall behind us. Grief and dread knotted in my belly. Hal's hand reached for mine. We both swallowed deeply. I looked into his eyes and choked back my tears. He nodded briefly in acknowledgment and squeezed my hand. We needed no words, only the solid presence of the other. For this brief time we could be together before my duties and his wolf separated us once more.

But Uncle Donovan had no one left.

My vision and the world cracked around me. Red blood and black death splashed over distorted images of my family, the heritage of the Pendragon, all the good work we had done in ages past.

I could not see how it would all come right again.

"You have to let me see her!" Uncle Donovan shouted. He rushed toward Paulet, eyes wild, hair in disarray, desperation written over his entire body.

The aging Earl of Shrewsbury, the man who, along with his wife Bess Hardwick, had been Mary's guardian the longest, rose and clasped my uncle by the shoulders. He shook a little sense and calm into Uncle Donovan before speaking.

"She has requested a night of solitary prayer. You'll not deny her the solace of her faith on this night."

"Her faith," Uncle Donovan said bitterly. " 'Tis her faith that caused this. Her faith that kept her from my side all these years."

"Maybe so. But 'tis her faith that has sustained her through all of her failures and disappointments and betrayals. She has been betrayed by those she trusted as much as she sought to betray others."

"If she truly loved me . . ." Uncle Donovan started.

"Give her this night of prayer, Father," Hal intervened. "Leave a message declaring your love until you meet in heaven, but give her the solitude with her God that she craves." Gently, Hal took his father by the shoulders and led him back the way we had come.

A chance for a future for all of us opened before me.

"Mayhap you, too, should spend the night on your knees," I suggested. "We will join you. You have your own ghosts to reconcile with." I fingered the rosary in my pocket.

We found the chapel on the other side of the hall. Mary kept to her prie dieu in her rooms, forsaking the altar she considered profaned by Protestant services that had been held there. Uncle Donovan stumbled most of the way there.

He collapsed onto his knees at the altar rail. I thrust the pearl beads and gold cross into his hands. He stared at it blankly for several moments.

"Pray as your brother prayed," I whispered.

Together, we began the Our Father. By the time we had finished that first prayer, the room was filled with Mary's keepers and judges, the servants who loved her, and the ghosts of those we had loved best and lost. My parents, Grandmother Raven, Uncle Donovan's two wives, and other distant ancestors.

Even Hal remained in the chapel, distant and silent in the corner near the door. But there.

Everyone came but Michael, the one restless spirit I needed most to see and seek forgiveness from.

At the last, as we completed the circle of prayers through all three decades of beads, a new presence joined me. Michael. My husband, the father of my child. But not my true love. He drew Hal to my side and joined our hands in silent blessing.

Uncle Donovan placed his hand atop ours, adding his own reconciliation with who and what Hal and become and that his love for his son had not died.

A sense of completeness, of rightness settled upon my shoulders.

Chapter 71

Spring and summer 1587. London and Kirkenwood.

OTHERS have written far finer descriptions of Mary's execution than I could. They tell of her defiantly-red petticoat. How her pet dogs hid beneath it until her death, how they emerged at the last, whining and keening for their mistress. They tell of the three blows the swordsman needed to complete the job. They tell of how she prayed through the terrible ordeal and lo, when her head finally rolled away from her body, her lips continued to move, completing the prayer.

Most of all, the chroniclers tell of her incredible dignity. Mary Stuart went to her death every inch the queen.

But we did not witness it. Hal and I took Uncle Donovan away before dawn. He never saw the love of his life again. He did not even witness her burial or visit her grave.

"Remember her as she was, Da," Hal consoled him as we rode away. Strangely, the horse seemed to have accepted him this time. "Remember her as young and vibrant and beautiful, as she came to you seeking a friend and solace the night King James was conceived."

Uncle Donovan nodded briefly, then sank back into his grief.

"You truly loved her, Uncle," I whispered. "If 'twas all a demon spell, you would be free of her now."

"I shall never be free of her. She will haunt me as she will haunt Elizabeth and all of England."

His words were true.

The Catholic world rallied together to seek Elizabeth's downfall and claim the riches of England.

London rejoiced with church bells and bonfires and dancing in the streets at the news of Mary's death.

Elizabeth took to her bed and wept for days on end.

Philip of Spain stepped up the pace to a frenzy for constructing his armada. We had a few months' respite only. As soon as winter storms cleared the English Channel, they would launch. The Duke of Parma in the Netherlands gathered an army to join the invasion.

Attacks by werewolves increased in the countryside. The stories of dismemberment and being eaten alive filtered into London only slightly exaggerated by number. The gruesome details remained true.

By late March nearly all of England was in a panic. The terrible deaths must be God's revenge for murdering Mary. Or so the rumors insisted.

Hal tried to hunt down the wolves. He succeeded in killing only two. I shot two more with silver-tipped arrows. And still their number increased.

We suspected that The Master and Yassimine were still recruiting new soldiers for their private war of terror.

Hal and I wondered how The Master achieved this without the magical girdle. Then I overheard Dr. John Dee at court bewail a theft from his home. He lost only a few fine artifacts he'd collected during his years on the continent.

One of those artifacts had to be the girdle.

Oh, yes, Hal stayed with me. He became a part of my household at the Crown and Anchor. His ready strength in completing the heavy work of hauling coal from the river barges and lifting full barrels endeared him to the hearts of the other workers. His quiet ways encouraged the patrons to talk to him unguardedly. Maggie Rose accepted him as if he had always been there. Newynog shifted her focus from me to my daughter. She still loved me. She still was bound to me and my magic, but she did not like sharing me or my bed with Hal.

Hal was always tender with me. Never a hint of the violence the wolf brought out in him showed in his lovemaking. When the wolf became strong, he disappeared for a few days and returned restored. His trips to Paris, cultivating the friendship of the newest king of France, Henri Bourbon, King of Navarre, husband to one of Catherine de Médici's daughters, usually occurred near the full moon when he felt he must separate from me anyway.

One day a young man of the Rom came to our door. He

asked for no work or food. He would speak only to Hal. I stepped away to give them the illusion of privacy. But I kept my ears open.

"A hedge witch has settled near Dover. She has one blue eye and one brown. She asked me to tell you this."

"How fares she?" Hal asked. He gripped the doorframe so tightly his knuckles turned white.

Who was this strange woman? Jealousy flared briefly in my gut. I pushed it away with a great deal of effort. Hal loved me. He always had.

"The witch fares well. Many along the coast seek her potions and charms to ward off strangers. They fear the Spanish will land in the night and kill them, one and all."

"When next you see this witch, tell her I wish her well."

"She also told me to tell you she has no children."

Hal nodded abruptly and ushered the man out into the yard. He closed the door firmly behind him.

I guessed much from this exchange. Hal never told me the meaning behind the strange message. I could only draw a little comfort that he had not sired a child on another.

Our close blood relationship bothered us only occasionally. I took pains to ensure that I did not conceive. Neither of us wished to risk having a child that might be tainted by first-cousin parents and by a werewolf sire.

I tried almost every day to remove the silver earring and the chain about Hal's waist. I tried when the moon was full and when it was dark. I tried during the day and at midnight. I devised new spells and sought old ones in arcane texts.

Nothing worked. The silver repelled my touch and continued to burn Hal. He fought the compulsion to return to The Master with every conscious breath. At times, when he seemed closest to losing control, I held his hand. He calmed almost immediately and resisted the Spaniard's magic.

We spent as much time as we could with Uncle Donovan at Ide Hill. He sank deeper and deeper into despondency. He took joy only in playing with Maggie Rose. Griffin made his usual journey there after the Spring Equinox. He brought his wife and their new son—born on February 18, at midmorning, almost precisely the same moment Mary died. Like all the other firstborn sons of the family, we named him Griffin. Griff also brought a mate for Newynog. The two dogs took off on their own, anxious to be about their business. Maggie Rose pouted that Newynog had deserted her.

The baby gurgled and cooed when handed to his grandfather. At last, I saw Uncle Donovan smile. He confiscated the baby, turning him over to his mother and nurse only for changing and feeding. Just like his sister, Mad Meg, who had latched onto children as her only solace for the mental pain of her childhood trauma. Since she had disappeared, I believed that Uncle Donovan had assumed her archetypal role of addled elder relative.

Insanity thrived in our family, in Betsy, most of all. We all understood that uncontrolled access to magic with no useful outlet had led her down dark paths that led to her own dark obsessions and madness.

Had the same purposeless magic in Meg and Uncle Donovan broken their minds?

We were almost a family again. As long as we did not speak of missing relatives and old griefs.

Then Griffin announced his plans. "I have outfitted a privateer to join the navy Admiral Drake gathers at Portsmouth for the defense of England."

"How dare you squander *my* money on this frivolous . . ." Uncle Donovan exploded at the news.

Baby Griffin started crying from the sudden noise. His mother rushed to soothe him with gentle rocking and reassuring words. Maggie Rose and Newynog gathered round to add their own special blend of calm. I noticed that my dog now shared her attention between my daughter and Griffin's son. As if she needed to decide who would inherit the next familiar.

I nearly choked at the idea. If Newynog settled a pup on one of them rather than me, then my time on this Earth was as limited as hers.

I must have gasped or made some small sound, for Hal took my hand and squeezed tightly. He would protect me at the cost of his own life. I knew that. But I did not want that. I wanted him to live, to carry on, to raise my daughter for me as no one else could.

We had all gathered around the card table after dinner. The servants had withdrawn. Our discussion was private.

"Father," Griffin addressed Uncle Donovan formally. "Elizabeth has given Drake orders to sail to Spain and do all that he can to delay or prevent the armada from launching. She has called for investors. As heir to the barony, and steward of all your properties in your absence, I can do nothing less than heed my queen's call." My cousin presented his father with a clean-shaven chin as stubborn as anyone else in the family. He and Hal no longer looked identical. Separate life paths had etched different scars onto their bodies and minds. The wolf in Hal would always make him appear bigger, shaggier, and more dominant. But Griffin carried a keen intelligence. I suspected he looked a lot like my father and Uncle Donovan in their twin youths.

"I forbid you," Uncle Donovan said. He narrowed his eyes and thrust his own chin.

" 'Tis done. I sail with the ship in three days—before Elizabeth has a chance to rescind her orders. I trust you and my brother will care for my wife and son during my absence." Griffin remained absolutely calm.

Uncle Donovan looked near panic. At last he sat down and shuffled the cards. "If you sail, then so do I. Your mother would want us together in this. I have abdicated my responsibilities to England for too long."

"I have a role in this as well," Hal said quietly. He continued to hold my hand but I suddenly felt terribly alone and very cold.

29 April (Gregorian Calendar on the Continent), 19 April (Julian Calendar in England), 1587. Port of Cadiz. Spain.

Hal stalked the ramparts of Cadiz for signs of hidden cannon. Last night he had spiked two weapons that overlooked the bay. At the mouth of the bay, Admiral Sir Francis Drake had spread his fleet, effectively blocking the escape of any of the ships in the anchorage. Somewhere out there, Hal's father and twin helped coordinate the battle to come. Even though his twin had no magic, Hal had found it easy to maintain mind-to-mind contact. He had used this method to keep in touch off and on over the years.

The little galleys you beat off earlier have retreated to Puental, at the entrance to the upper bay. They are in a position to menace you as you sail in to the anchorage, Hal reported.

A brief mental grunt acknowledged the sending. Griffin received a lot easier than he sent messages.

Hal paced some more. Too many batteries of big guns bristled from the hillsides, aimed directly at the shipping lanes.

He set off through the streets of the city at a meandering pace. If he could neutralize the guns of the old fort above the sea wall, where the galleys anchored, then the English would have an easier time getting into the bay. Natives stared at him in suspicion. With his rough clothing and heavy beard he might pass as a sailor. If he was a sailor, why did he not rush to help his crew escape from the coming fray? He felt their thoughts as an irritation on his skin without having to enter their minds. The wolf in him wanted to bare his teeth and growl. He kept the beast tightly leashed.

As he searched to find access to the old fort, he kept an eye trained upon the activity in the bay. The English approached. The Spanish ships with crew and sail enough scrambled to escape. Galleys and smaller merchants with low draft sought the shallows and shoals where the bigger English race galleons could not tread.

Griffin! Hal nearly shouted. *There's a big one. She's not moving and she's fully manned.* He tried to send what he saw. Griffin knew ships and weapons. Griffin was the warrior.

Questioning emotions only, no coherent reply from his twin.

A levanter, I think you call it. I don't know ships. But she's huge. Crew is loading and aiming.

What . . . kind . . . guns, came the hesitant and weak reply. Not so much words as an image of a pistol with a question mark over it.

I don't know guns. Big ones. Lots of shot. Can't see how many barrels of gunpowder. Again he sent the images as he searched for signs of barrels full of explosives. Powder was expensive. Hal knew that much from his early years of border warfare at Kirkenwood. Would a merchant ship carry enough to feed every cannon, every ball it carried?

Within moments, the levanter fired the first volley. All of the shots fell short. Hal could see the gunners hastening to adjust the range.

Drake's men were better trained. Six ships brought their guns to bear on the monster merchant vessel. Over half their shots found a mark. The levanter continued firing, but the English methodically pounded it to pieces. Three shots left the doomed vessel even as it sank.

Then Drake turned the fleet toward the rest of the prizes in the anchorage.

Shore batteries began firing. Hal hastened his stride. He had to stop those guns.

He pushed his way through a mob of locals trying to get away from the battle. Snatches of conversations flashed past him. He wished for a better command of Spanish. He caught the sense of panic and a fear of landing parties. Images of sailors raping women and murdering children flashed in and out of his mind. But the sailors these people feared were the enemies of old, swarthy Barbary Pirates wearing exotic jewelry and costumes. To the locals, the fair-skinned English were the same as the pirates.

Hal shrugged and forced his way closer to his objective.

The old fort loomed over the harbor. Massive stones piled on top of each other presented a formidable barrier. Strangely, the local soldiers had not barred the gate. Many of them could be seen fleeing the city with the other panicking citizens. Apparently, they had not thought an enemy could approach from land rather than the sea.

Hal crept in, keeping to the shadows. The hot southern sun filled the open bailey of the fortress. There were few, if any, places to hide here. Many men ran about in seeming aimless alarm. The babble of Spanish sounded almost as loud as the cannon fire. If any of them had specific errands, Hal could not determine what they were.

He took a chance that the Spaniards were too absorbed in their own problems to notice a stranger. Six steps across the bailey. Seven steps.

The silver chains at his ear and waist flared hot and demanding. His bones ached with the need to transform.

He caught the heavy scent of Yassimine's perfume.

A heavy fishing net dropped around his head and shoulders. Above him, from atop the walls, he heard The Master chortle in glee.

Chapter 72

HAL fought the net with teeth and hands and magical fire. It wound and clung to him in ever tightening folds. His teeth elongated and his bones ached. If he could just transform . . .

No. He would not stoop to The Master's level. He would not become a mindless beast.

Breathe, Hal. Breathe! he heard Dee whisper into his mind from afar.

Breathe. Control. In on three counts, hold. Out on three counts. Hold again. One long breath. Two. Upon the third he found the center of his magic. Calm spread outward from him.

The net relaxed. He pinched one woven joint of the ropes. The hemp disintegrated in a flash of elemental fire. More of the net seemed to press away from him, as if a living being in fear.

"So, my pup has come home," The Master said. "I knew you would. I knew you could not resist the chance to work mischief behind the scenes in this battle."

Yassimine appeared behind him. She seemed changed. Older, colder, more cautious. She hung back, flexing her fingers and curling her lip as if preparing her wolf claws and fangs.

A third presence circled them. Hal could not see it, only knew another wolf waited for orders from The Master.

Hal said nothing. He just touched three more pieces of the net at his side. They evaporated as mist in the sunshine.

El Lobison seemed too caught up in his own sense of superior triumph to notice. He, like Betsy, had worked one dark spell too many. The evil in the magic had taken his mind.

Yassimine remained the true threat. He could take her in a physical fight, as long as she had no help from her master or that unseen third presence.

Better to flee this time. He'd bide his time and take down this man when he had a better chance. Or was more desperate.

Before he could think of a better plan, he broke through the already severed net and flung it in Yassimine's face. She shrieked and tried to fight free of the writhing ropes. The more she fought, the tighter it clung to her.

Hal turned and ran up to the nearest rampart.

The Master flung something at him. It fell short and exploded in a plume of flame and smoke.

Keeping low, obscured by shadows, Hal sped along the ramparts to the landing above the gun ports. He dropped over the side, clinging to the stone parapet until the tips of his toes found something solid to support his weight. A quick glance down confirmed that he stood upon one of the cannons. Frantic movement behind the gun told him that the crew prepared another shot.

Not much time. What could he stuff into the muzzle to make the thing explode?

A spate of Spanish erupted from the men behind the gun port. Hal dropped until he straddled the cannon, then lunged into the little room behind it. He came up with flying fists. He connected with two jaws. Foot to a chest. Swing, drop, punch, kick.

Pounding footsteps behind the room.

One gunner tried to rise.

Hal kicked him in the ribs.

The door began to glow. Above the smoke he smelled Yassimine and The Master.

Quickly, Hal grabbed the water bucket kept against a stray spark igniting the volatile gunpowder. He tipped the whole thing into the powder barrel. The stuff would not support even elemental Fire now.

He jumped up onto the cannon once more. It gave slightly beneath his weight. He looked at it carefully. He'd altered the aim by a fraction. He bounced upon it again and again. The muzzle now pointed to the shallows of the harbor. The English fleet would need to keep to deeper water. He leaped to the second cannon beside him. That weapon shifted a little, too. Two more bounces and it aimed toward the docks.

The gun crew would waste several shots and inflict a great deal of damage on their own ships and facilities before they corrected the aim. But they could not do that until the gunpowder dried or they fetched a new barrel. He'd bought the English fleet some time.

Satisfied that he had done enough here, he took a deep breath and scrambled down the rough stonework of the fort to the rocky cliff below. He watched the English capture three ships. Already several were aflame farther out in the harbor. Within moments, he was out of sight and headed out of the city. He lost himself among the fleeing mob, aiming for the Puental, the small harbor near the head of the bay, and the monster bronze guns at the mouth of the inlet. He might be able to do something there before Drake decided to go after the little boats hiding in the secondary anchorage.

One year later. London.

I welcomed Hal upon his return from the Continent several weeks before Griffin and Uncle Donovan sailed back into Portsmouth Harbor. He said nothing of his adventures, merely returned to his daily chores around the tavern as if he'd never left.

Men!

Drake appeared at court within two days of anchoring and announced proudly that he had "singed the king of Spain's beard!"

But beards grow back.

Besides the battle at Cadiz and other minor triumphs, Drake managed to set fire to many of the supplies gathered for the armada, among them, all the barrel staves. Without barrels, the ships had no water for the crew. Without water, they would not last three days at sea.

When the Spanish resupplied, they found no seasoned

barrels, only green wood. They held water but did not keep it clean.

Philip had to wait another year before he could regroup and gather enough ships.

We had a breathing space to prepare. Elizabeth dipped deep into her treasury and commissioned ships to be built and supplies stockpiled. Drake designed several new race galleons. Less topheavy than the Spanish castles upon the sea, these ships were based upon the lines of a mackerel. The ships, like the fish, cut through the waves, using the sea to help them maneuver. Spanish galleons merely floated atop the sea and fought it for every turn and shift in the wind.

The next spring, France seemed close to erupting into flames once more with religious wars.

"*El Lobison* sows his seeds of terror once more," Hal muttered. His eyes began to glow red and his fists clenched.

He disappeared in May for a few weeks. I did not think much of it until he returned sullen and angry.

"What ails you?" I asked. I planted myself directly in his path deep in the cellar. He could not run away from me as he had several times that day.

"France will not rise in support of Spain and the armada," he grumbled and hoisted a huge cask of ale onto his shoulder.

"How can you be sure?"

"Because the king of France has made peace with the Duc de Guise. While he talks compromise, he cripples the Holy League at every turn. He actively searches for *El Lobison* with priests and fire and silver."

" 'Tis an uneasy peace at best, I suspect."

"Aye. 'Twill last for a time, but Henri IV will have to execute de Guise if he is ever to sit easy on his throne."

I blanched and grew cold. A generation before, my father had assassinated the previous Duc de Guise to ensure peace in France. I shuddered to think that history might repeat itself so closely.

"What did you say to Henri?" I asked through gritted teeth.

"I convinced him to retire from Paris, regroup, and confront de Guise from a position of strength even if it wasn't in Paris. He had to defy Catherine de Médici to do it."

"You gave him the idea."

"I escorted him through secret passages, dark alleys, and sewers."

"Does he know that he will have to remove de Guise from power?"

"Aye."

"You gave him the idea."

"I gave him the idea. And I hate myself for it. Henri is my friend."

He shouldered his way past me. I had to move rapidly or fall beneath his big feet.

A few days later word reached London that the armada had sailed near the end of April.

Griffin and Uncle Donovan hastened to Plymouth. Drake called in all of his captains and crews that had wintered at home—thus not needing salaries or consuming vast quantities of food at the queen's expense. Stockpiles of powder and shot were loaded. The Earl of Leicester recruited an army and began training them at Tilbury near the mouth of the Thames, the most likely landing spot for an invasion of troops from the Spanish Netherlands.

The rest of England held its breath.

I knew what I had to do. My family had to work together. I needed Hal. And I needed Betsy. I could not merely summon her to London. While the Spanish sailed slowly toward the English Channel, I had to go to her, penetrate the fog of her madness, and make her see sense for a time.

Maggie Rose and I headed north with Newynog at our heels. Hal refused to face his sister. I sent him to the Netherlands. Someone had to keep Parma and his army from joining up with the armada.

Chapter 73

15 May (Julian Calendar), 1588. Kirkenwood.

I STOOD beside the tallest standing stone in the village of Kirkenwood. The remnants of the circle of stones glared back at me moodily. I carefully picked out the faces in the whorls of granite in each. King Arthur was supposed to be in the westernmost stone facing east, the place of new beginnings. His Merlin faced west, the closing of the day and the end of an era. Arylwren, Merlin's daughter stood beside Arthur. Great grandmother Raven I found easily. My father remained elusive. Perhaps because he did not rest in peace. Could not rest in peace until England was safe from the armada he had seen in a vision.

When I had turned a full circle and identified each stone, I faced the castle above me where it perched on the tor like a sprawling demon that threatened to spill over the sides of the great hill. Betsy awaited me up there.

My back itched like a thousand insects crawled over my skin.

"Mama?" Maggie Rose tugged on my leather jerkin. "Mama, who is watching us?"

"Our cousin, Betsy," I answered her, not surprised at her awareness of the presence of magic.

"I like this place, Mama. Newynog does, too. She says this is a good place to have her puppies. Can I have one of the puppies?"

"If Newynog decides to give you a puppy, then it is yours."

"Goody. I want a boy puppy. Boy dogs are bigger and stronger and fiercer fighters."

You have never seen a mother dog defend her pups, I almost said to her.

"Are we going to go to Cousin Betsy, Mama?" My daughter tugged again, impatiently now.

"No, sweeting. Cousin Betsy must come to us."

I had not seen Betsy in many years. But from our childhood I knew her moods, her little rituals, and her priorities. If I approached her in the castle, her own territory, she would dismiss me out of hand. If I waited for her at the kirk, or by the lake she would sweat with fear at treading upon sacred ground.

But here, among the standing stones that had watched over us all of our lives, we could meet as equals. Perhaps the spirits of our ancestors would help clear the miasma of insanity long enough to make her see the necessity of my proposal.

A raven flew to the top of the center stone. It eyed me for many long moments, cocking its head this way and that. At last, it fluttered its wings and settled to supervise the proceedings.

Maggie Rose and Newynog found a fascinating tuft of grass and a butterfly to play with. I watched the heights for signs that Betsy heard my mental call.

At last, a small, dark shape crept out of the pedestrian gate. She flowed around the castle walls and down the side of the tor. She kept carefully to the old processional way, the long path that swept back and forth across the face of the hill and partially around its slopes. In days of old the entire hill, except for that path, was seeded with traps both mundane and magical.

Betsy knew that all of the traps had been dismantled generations ago. But she, in her madness, must still sense and fear echoes of them.

Not for the first time I wondered if my family was doomed to insanity. Aunt Meg and Donovan in the previous generation had both succumbed to the tempting depths of shadows within their minds. Now Betsy of my generation had also fallen victim. And Hal. The curse of the wolf could be called a form of insanity. Protestant theologians did not believe in the curse; they considered werewolves insane and capable of being cured.

Was Betsy's weakness of the mind a curse of demons?

Or was it merely that wielding powerful magic rotted her conscience and blotted out all else?

I almost prayed that an early death would take me before I, too, fell victim to insanity.

"I saw you coming," Betsy whispered from behind me.

I jumped a little in startlement. I had lost track of her from the depth of my musing.

"I knew you would know," I replied.

She had shrunk in stature. Her hunched posture and forward jutting head brought her down to nearly my own slight height. Her black gown hung on her wasted form like so many tattered veils.

"I watched you in my scrying bowl. Da took away all my tools. But he could not take away my scrying bowl and my agate. With them, I can see everything."

"Does the bowl show you the danger that approaches England?"

"Hundreds of ships. They wait off Corunna. They wait to gather more ships. Big ships. Like nothing we have ever seen before."

"We have ships of our own. Better ships."

"The Spanish have a rendezvous with an army. They cannot wait long." Betsy sounded almost sane, coherent at least.

"Elizabeth's agents have disrupted communication between the armada and the Duke of Parma in the Netherlands. The Dutch are sinking the barges to carry troops to the ships." I knew that Hal was working on this part of the plan.

"And while the Spanish dogs wait, they starve!" Betsy danced about. "Their barrels are green and their water and food spoils."

"Betsy." I grabbed her arms and shook her lightly. "Betsy, look at me. We have made certain the armada has problems. They are still a threat."

"Boom. Cannons go boom!"

"Yes. The cannons can still go boom. The cannons can still sink English ships and kill English sailors. The ships can still sail past Tilbury and up the Thames to London. We have to prevent that."

"London. I wore pretty gowns at court in London."

"There will be no more court if the Spanish come."

That sobered her a moment. I grabbed the half moment of clarity and pushed a tendril of magic through her eyes. I could almost see it winding its way through the dark maze of her mind, lighting tiny candles along the way.

Her eyes opened wide and cleared.

"I have to do something," she said in almost a normal voice. "I am the Pendragon. That is why you came to me. Only I can protect England."

I let her think that by my silence I agreed with her. She never had been and never would be a true Pendragon.

She drew herself up into a dignified posture.

"Yes, we have to do something. You and I. We have to work together," I said.

"But I am the Pendragon. Not you. Not Hal. Only me. You must acknowledge me as Pendragon." Betsy sounded petulant and childish in her demands.

"Whatever it takes to secure your help."

One heartbeat. Two. Then three while she thought about it. Her eyes glazed a little and her concentration wandered.

"Betsy, come back to me. Betsy!" I pushed harder on the magic. A number of the candles that I had lit in her mind had snuffed out. Some remained. I closed my eyes and concentrated on lighting more.

As fast as they flared, the shadows extinguished them.

"Oh, Betsy, how do I get through to you?"

She turned away from me. Her gaze rested on the standing stone where our Great grandmother Raven was said to reside.

Gently, I led my cousin to stand beside the towering chunk of granite.

"Touch the stone, Betsy. Touch Raven's face."

She reached out with a single finger and traced the outline of the face in the stone. Golden fire followed her finger until I clearly saw the face etched in the stone

"That's right, Betsy. Learn her face. Our fathers buried her the day you were born. Part of her is in you." For many long moments I talked, as I talked to Maggie Rose to ease her out of her nightmares.

Betsy crooned a childhood nursery rhyme.

> *"Sing a song of sixpence,*
> *A pocket full of rye;*

*Four and twenty blackbirds
Baked in a pie!"*

*"When the pie was opened,
The birds began to sing;
Wasn't that a dainty dish
To set before the king?"*

The last line came out choked and garbled as if a dozen voices tried to use her mouth all at once. Then she looked at me with clear, vivid blue eyes that saw all the way into my soul and reflected the wisdom of the ages.

"Thank you," the voices said. "We have opened her mind and set free the blackbirds of despair. Now we can help."

"Betsy?" I peered deeply at her. Subtle changes had taken place, a softening around the mouth, a pinch to the nose, more care lines around her eyes.

"She is with us." The myriad voices resolved into one, husky like Betsy's but with a resonance that seemed alien. "She is strong and fighting us. Our control over her is limited."

Puzzled, I looked at the stone where her palm lay flat against the surface.

The grain in the granite was mute and abstract. The golden fire now haloed Betsy's face. Raven's face.

"Raven?" I asked, still puzzled.

"She is with us, too."

"Who are you?"

"All of your family. We will help. Britain must remain free and inviolate. The armada must be stopped. Come. We have not much time to reach our destination."

Chapter 74

30 June (Julian Calendar), 10 July (Gregorian Calendar), 1588. Dunkirk, Netherlands.

HAL hoisted a flat beam from the pile of a dozen other similar beams onto his shoulder. A Spanish soldier watched him too carefully. Not many men in this Dutch shipyard could lift a beam by themselves. But a few could.

"You." The Spaniard flicked his whip toward Hal's back. "I don't recognize you."

Hal ignored him, feigning an ignorance of the Spanish language.

"Protestant dog!" This time the Spaniard's lash slashed across Hal's back. It tore his sweat-stained shirt.

The wolf in Hal leaped to the surface. He snarled involuntarily. The moon pulled him. His skin itched, and he longed to tear out the man's throat. He'd had enough of persuasion and subtlety.

He swung around to face his attacker. The beam caught the guard full in the face. He fell. Immediately, six Dutch carpenters and shipwrights jumped on the man. They stripped away his weapons and his fine clothing. His silver crucifix disappeared into a Dutch pocket.

Before another guard wandered in their direction, the enslaved ship builders had trussed their prey like a bird for roasting, weighted him with stones, and tossed him face-down into the canal.

In seconds they all resumed their work with half smiles on their faces. They all appeared busy. They actually accomplished little. In the week Hal had worked alongside them not one shallow-draft flyboat or troop barge neared completion.

Now for a little surprise for the Spanish army when they tried to float on these barges to their rendezvous with the armada.

Once he'd finished here, Hal could go home where he was safe from prying Catholic eyes and the threat of the Inquisition and burning at the stake. Home with Dee and Maggie Rose. Away from this foreign place where he did not know the places to hide from the moon.

He dropped the beam from his shoulder. A quick look around showed all the workers back in their usual routine of too many hammer blows and not enough nails, of endless shifting of bits and pieces, and accomplishing nothing.

Hal pulled a pouch out of his shirt. He'd worked long and hard, talking to every hedge witch from here to Amsterdam to put together the ingredients for this spell. He didn't like depending upon the knowledge of others. But all of the family magic texts were back at Kirkenwood.

"With the power of Earth, I beseech thee." He sprinkled the metallic salts over all the stores of lumber scattered about the shipyard. "With the power of Water, I invoke thee." A quick flick released his codpiece and he pissed at the corner of each load of wood, just like a wolf marking his territory. "With the power of Air, I conjure thee." His lungs ached by the time he blew his powders around. "With the power of Fire, I bind thee!"

At last he snapped his fingers and sent a stream of sparks into the spell. The salts flared. Blue and red lines of power snaked over the wood. A terrible stench rose.

Men coughed and retched and fled the yard. The Spaniards led the way. Hal ran right upon their heels. He'd not be left lagging so they could accuse him of witchcraft.

If everything worked according to plan, the salts would rot some of the wood, drain the seasoning out of some, and weaken the rest with knots and split grains.

None of it would build a sound ship to ferry Parma's army to England.

Hal just wished Dee had compiled the spell. He'd trust it then.

Persuading Parma that the entire enterprise of England was poorly planned and impossible to execute had been easy compared to this.

Friday, 19 July (Julian Calendar), 29 July (Gregorian Calen-dar), 1588. The White Cliffs of Dover.

I paced the cliffs of Dover every morning for a week, wait-ing. Watching. Swallowing my fears. Preparing a ritual. Newynog helped, dragging sticks and boughs to pile upon the ceremonial bonfire.

I had left Maggie Rose with Lady Walsingham. Newynog had clearly been torn between her bonds with me and her need to protect my innocent daughter. I knew we need not worry about Maggie Rose. If I failed, then no one in En-gland was safe. Lady Walsingham would flee to Kirken-wood.

Clear of mind and conscience, I prepared the biggest, most comprehensive spell of my lifetime.

Innocents would die whether I worked this magic or no. I'd best work it and save as many English lives as I could.

Betsy—or rather Raven—paced with me most mornings. More and more often, Betsy surged to the forefront of the personalities in her body. She tore her hair and screamed invective at the wind. I do not think she understood how or why we watched the sea so anxiously. She only wanted to go home to the safe familiarity of Kirkenwood.

The captain of the *Golden Hind* spotted the Spanish Ar-mada preparing to enter the English Channel. He raced with the news to Plymouth with the news for Admiral How-ard, the commander of the Great Fleet, and Admiral Drake, the man all the seamen looked to for leadership. Fitting that the news should come from Drake's former ship; the one he'd sailed on his adventures through the New World harassing the Spanish. Uncle Donovan had joined the admirals at bowls along with a few other senior officers from the fleet. Reputedly, Drake quipped, "We have time enou' to finish the game and beat the Spaniards, too."

I never heard if my uncle had anything to say on the matter. I doubted he said much of anything to anyone anymore.

The fleet warped out of the harbor near ten of the clock that evening. They had about fifty ships to begin with. More joined them later.

The following morning the Spanish Armada, one hundred thirty sail strong, began its slow march up the English Channel. The Great Fleet assembled under Howard and Drake had to prevent their enemy from keeping their rendezvous with Parma and his army. To maintain the wind advantage, they had to stay behind the armada.

I had to find a way to help them. 'Twas the duty of the Pendragon, of all of my ancestors, and descendants. And me.

By the time first shots were exchanged between the two fleets on Sunday morning, I had set my bonfire and drawn my pentagram around it. Betsy/Raven worked with me. Exhausting work, even with two of us. Magic takes more strength and stamina than plowing fields and chopping wood. I hated every moment of it, constantly looking over my shoulder for any sign of *El Lobison* and his werewolves. I knew they would come, attracted by the magic.

Who would die because of it?

We took turns looking in a scrying bowl, monitoring the progress of the battle.

Many shots were fired on both sides. Neither side suffered much damage. The Spaniards had little skill with cannons fired from the heaving deck of a ship. They needed the English to close with them for grappling and boarding by their superior numbers. Their ships were nothing more than floating castles. The English had more maneuverable ships and knew the danger of coming too close. They used their race-built ships as weapons. Their gunners were more skilled, but they had not the length of range of the big Spanish guns.

Monday, the Spanish continued their march up the Channel with the wind behind them. Our ships pursued cautiously, maintaining the advantage of the wind.

"Summon them," Betsy/Raven demanded. She stared westward, as if she could see as far as the running battle.

I did not need to ask who. Those Otherworldly creatures who had promised to guard England needed to take their posts. We could not guard every inlet and harbor against the shallow flyboats and barges filled with troops from the Netherlands. Elves and pixies and brownies and the others could make certain they proceeded no farther than the beaches. Knowing my friends, they could put the fear of God into those soldiers and make them retreat.

A smaller fire, with special herbs from my scrip, and a circle sufficed to send the message to those who had made a promise to me.

By dawn, a dozen Gypsies and vagabonds set up camp about one hundred yards from our ritual site.

"Your summons is more effective than I thought," Betsy/Raven said with one eyebrow arched.

"They will watch over us while we are engaged in our work."

"You expect interference from the English?" Betsy's panic flashed across her face. I watched as Raven struggled to regain control.

"Not from the English," I replied. The hair on my nape stood on end and my heart beat double time. I trembled, wondering when the wolves would attack.

Raven's arched eyebrow queried me without words.

"The true enemy will come," Hal said from behind me.

"I hate it when you sneak up on me like that!" I jumped nearly a foot at his first word. But I should have known he was there. The tingling at the base of my spine had been overshadowed by my sense of the other werewolves approaching.

Betsy surged into dominance of her body. Her eyes blazed amber fire and she tore her hair. She screamed and tried to run away.

I grabbed her.

She slammed a tight fist into my jaw. I saw stars. Reeling, I slapped her. Her head jerked. She kicked me. I bounced back, but I kept a hand on her elbow.

"Monster! He'll kill us. He'll tear us limb from limb," she screeched. She sounded more like a seagull than a human.

"I will not kill you," Hal said mildly. But I sensed his effort to maintain calm.

"You hate me. I hate you." From one statement to the next she changed from hysterical to deadly calm. She narrowed her eyes and stared at him as if she pushed a spell into his mind.

I stepped between them. "Raven, I need you now." I used the same voice I had used to summon the protectors.

Betsy fought Raven's presence. Her face contorted. Her fists punched and she jerked wildly, almost convulsed.

Finally, calm dignity washed over her face and body. Her posture changed and the stubborn chin, common to all Kirkwoods, relaxed.

"She is getting stronger. My control may slip at any moment. We must begin." Raven panted from the effort of maintaining control.

"The fleet is not close enough," I protested.

"We must do it now."

The scrying bowl showed the fleet nearing Lyme on the south coast. Guns blazed furiously, nearly continuous on both sides. We almost could not see what transpired for all the smoke. The wind came from the east, to the advantage of the Spanish.

"We need to shift the wind before we do anything," Raven said.

"If they keep this up, both sides will run out of powder and shot," Hal said. "Without cannon, there will be no battle, and the Spanish will meet with Parma's troops."

"Then we have to make certain the sea and the weather keep them from doing that," I replied.

Raven and I moved to the bonfire. Hal prowled his own circle beyond our perimeter. From his restlessness and hunched shoulders I knew that we were not completely safe. "Hurry," he muttered over and over.

"Light the fire," Betsy/Raven commanded. She stood slightly apart, avidly watching my every movement.

I think she might have been trying to read my mind.

"Not yet. 'Tis not yet time. We will need it later." I stood my ground, outside the pentagram.

"Do it!" she commanded.

Even Hal looked around sharply at her tone.

"You do it. Fire is not my element."

"You have to do it. Now!" Betsy ceased lurking and once more took over the body. "I am the eldest. You must obey me."

"No." I fought to remain calm.

"Winds do blow. Earth, heave and throw. Fire, glow," Betsy chanted. She began walking the circle around the pentagram.

My mind raced, trying to figure out what she truly

wanted. If she started the spell too soon, the wind would drive the ships aground. Our ships as well as the Spanish. We had to choose our moment, knowing that storms took time to brew and followed their own course not ours.

I desperately needed Betsy's affinity with air to accomplish the spell properly.

But now she tried to abort our efforts.

"Hide!" Hal screamed. He pushed me to the ground, landing atop me. "Whatever happens. Stay safe." He kissed my temple and bounded back up.

A quick look around showed ten werewolves facing us. Their red eyes glowed and their fangs dripped ichor.

The Gypsies had deserted their protective posts.

Chapter 75

HAL dropped to wolf form without thinking. He kept a wary eye on the lead wolf while Dee scuttled to the other side of the bonfire. Betsy continued to dance around, chanting as if the fire had actually started to burn. But Hal had kept a tight clamp on the element of Fire and kept it from joining her spell.

Three wolves stood in front of the pack. He found Yassimine by her scent in the center surrounded by her get. If he had not known her so intimately, the males around her would have masked her.

Hal's piercings and chains did not burn.

"Where is he?" he growled at Yassimine.

She did not reply in coherent speech.

Hal sent a tiny probe into her mind. The wolf augmented his magic, made it easier.

The probe floundered around in a fog of hate and blood lust. Whatever humanity Yassimine had ever had was nearly lost.

But an image of *El Lobison* emerged.

The Master lurked nearby. He would watch rather than fight. He would laugh gleefully with each death. He would swoop down to be present at the kill, or he would flee to safety if Hal triumphed.

Run, Dee. Run as far away as you can. And then keep on running.

Of course she did not heed him. She never would. Her sense of responsibility kept her here, the only place where she had a chance to help the fleet.

Newynog stayed by her side, snapping and snarling.

Dee snatched up a stout stick from the bonfire. Fire blos-

somed from its end. She thrust it into the face of the first
wolf to step forward.

That beast yelped and ran. Flames caught the fur and
kept burning, fueled by the Air that flowed around him.

Another creature lunged for Hal. He met Hal's teeth on
his throat. They must be young to the wolf form. Otherwise, they'd be more canny.

Yassimine still hung back. Her eyes blazed and her tail
bristled. She lowered her head into stalking mode. Two big
males remained in front of her.

Hal took the offensive. If he could take out Yassimine,
they had a chance to send the rest of the pack scuttling
away in fear. The Master would follow them rather than
face Hal without Yassimine.

Hal circled looking for a weakness, an opening.

Dee circled the other direction, thrusting her torch
toward any that swung a head or ventured a paw out of
the pack. Newynog kept the others at bay.

Hal was reminded of the double circle they had traced
in the dirt back in the convent at Montmatre outside Paris.
A glimmer of an idea formed. If they could complete the
circles . . .

Betsy began singing:

> *"Rain, rain, go away,*
> *Come again some other day."*

Over and over she sang a song, keeping a storm at bay
to the west. Opposite to what Dee had planned.

Hal sensed the magic streaming from Betsy's fingers. It
grounded uselessly. But the scent of power permeated
everything.

Yassimine broke free of the pack. She sped toward
Betsy, low to the ground, nose out, tail fully extended. A
furry arrow with a target.

Newynog followed. She leaped to land upon Yassimine's
back. Missed. Regained her feet and continued the pursuit,
jaws snapping.

A second wolf, smaller than the rest with similar, but
paler markings to Yassimine spun and leaped with the precision of a juggler, directly for Dee.

She waved her torch at him. He kept coming.

Newynog abandoned Betsy to rush to Dee's defense. Fur bristled, she stood squarely between the little wolf and her mistress.

Hal continued around his circle and launched into the flank of the arrogant pup.

His jaw locked on a clump of fur. The young wolf twisted out of his grasp.

Dee flung something from her scrip into the midst of the pack. An eerie sulfur cloud burst out. Red-and-black lightning shot from the center of the yellow mist. Hal thought he saw two black eyes glow with Otherworldly fire in the midst. Then the demon, or his imagination, disappeared.

The pack scattered.

Betsy screamed.

The pup snarled at Dee, leaped toward her with snapping jaws. Newynog rose up on all fours and batted her enemy to the ground. The wolf landed hard upon the ground, gasping for air. Recovered. And followed the rest of the beasts into the woods.

Newynog pursued.

The yellow cloud spread.

Numbness infected Hal's joints. Sleep made his eyes as heavy as lead.

"Betsy!" Dee moaned. She ran right through the cloud toward the fallen and bleeding figure of Hal's sister.

Yassimine awaited her. She seemed as vibrant as ever, unaffected by Dee's spell and magic powder.

I cradled Betsy's limp form in my left arm. All the while I fended off the persistent werewolf with my torch. But the fire was burning low. It would not last long.

"I knew Hal and his kind would kill me eventually," Betsy gasped. Pain contorted her features. One arm hung uselessly. Copious amounts of blood poured from her chest and belly.

" 'Twasn't Hal," I sobbed. "Hal would never hurt you. He's your brother."

"I tried to kill him. 'Tis only fair," Betsy whispered.

The wolf came closer. Blood flecked its muzzle. Its red eyes flared with Otherworldly fires.

I thrust the torch at it. A spark landed just behind one ear. The wolf did not flinch.

The heavy lethargy of inevitability weighed on my joints and muscles.

"Hal wanted to kill me. So I drove him from Kirkenwood. I wanted to kill him. But he was too cunning for me. The scrying bowl does not lie. I saw him kill me and so he has," Betsy continued to ramble. Her words grew weaker with each phrase.

I could do nothing to staunch her wounds and keep the wolf from killing me, too.

" 'Twasn't Hal," I insisted. "Hal wouldn't."

She did not listen to me. I heard only broken phrases as she slipped away from me.

The world was growing white around me. I grew hot, though I know my skin felt cold and clammy. The light swirled around me.

I needed to follow Betsy toward the light, guide her. . . .

The wolf came closer.

I jerked back to reality. But the light still drew me. I was too hot. Too cold. Could not think.

The wolf enclosed Betsy's dead foot in its massive jaws and pulled.

"You will not dismember her!" I flung the torch and the last of my magic into the wolf's snout.

In wolf form, Hal leaped upon its back. His jaws clamped upon the spine, just beneath the skull. Yelps. Fur flew. They tangled and growled. I could not distinguish one from the other in the fury of their wrestling. A terrible sound erupted from both their throats.

Wild shouts in Spanish erupted from the shelter of a line of rocks behind me. A slight man with a pointed beard and useless left arm rose from a crouch. He flung fire balls at Hal.

"Hal!" I screamed as I flung a weak wall of magic between *El Lobison* and my beloved.

The swirl of white grew thicker, more enticing.

I forced myself to stay awake. I could not let the whiteness take me. If I followed Betsy into death, I did not think I had the strength to return on my own.

I heard a crunch of bones breaking.

Screams from Hal and his prey. An eerie wailing from the Spaniard.

The wolf beneath Hal grew limp. She shed fur. Her limbs lengthened. *El Lobison*'s mistress, the exotic woman who had walked at his side the one time I had seen them. She collapsed. A wealth of silver dropped away from her. A spate of words in an ancient tongue I did not know flew from the Spaniard's mouth.

Waves and waves of magic surged off the woman's corpse. Almost visible ripples in the air backlashed into *El Lobison*. It swirled and whipped into a glowing storm. Leaves, rocks, sand, and other debris caught up in the cyclonic winds.

The Spaniard continued to shout words of defiance. His voice became weaker. He shrank and withered and finally collapsed into a puddle of fine black velvet and blood.

I stared at him in horror for many long minutes.

Quiet eventually penetrated my mind. Quiet.

The fighting was over. I opened my eyes cautiously. The woman lay dead or near to on the ground at my feet. Blood pooled everywhere, turning black, attracting flies.

"Hal?" I struggled to come to my knees.

"Whst," he murmured in my ear. "You are hurt. Stay still." He cradled my head and shoulders in his naked lap.

"You live," I breathed.

"And so do you." He kissed the top of my head. "But one of the wolves bit you. I need to dress the wound now. I need to draw out the poison."

"Poison." The word took a moment to penetrate my mind. Then the hurt did as well. My left arm burned from wrist to shoulder. Some of the blood was mine.

As I tried to think what we must do next, the Gypsies crept out of the woods. One by one they emerged. Seven men each carried a wolf pelt.

Newynog dogged their heels. Blood flecked her muzzle and spattered her chest. She limped. No satisfaction radiated from her.

My heart cried out to her. But I could not move. Could not think.

"Ye're safe now," Micah, the head of the tribe proclaimed. "We beg forgiveness that we let them slip past us. We had to get the women and children to safety."

Not all of the women and children had fled. One boy, about the same age as Maggie Rose hung back behind the last of the men. He peered out from behind them with wide eyes and half opened mouth.

He looked familiar. Where had I seen him before? He had the dark coloring of the Gypsies but resembled none of the men. Who was he?

"You missed one," Hal said. "There were ten. Dee killed one with fire. I killed this one," he spat at the limp form sprawled at our feet. "That makes nine. Where is the tenth?"

"Only these seven fled past us. We got them all," Micah insisted.

The boy turned so that the light hit his brilliant blue eyes. Then I recognized him. But the poison stole my words and my will.

Chapter 76

Monday, July 29 (Julian Calendar), August 7 (Gregorian Calendar), 1588. Just after midnight, off Calais Roads.

"TRUST me, Griffin, the ships will burn hot and they will burn long," Donovan reassured his son.

Griffin tossed a barrel of tallow to a seaman aboard one of the vessels selected to burn.

"Without men at the tillers, the ships will go adrift afore they reach the Spanish," Griffin insisted. He frowned and gestured for the sailors to pack the combustibles tighter.

"The tide is with them. And so am I."

"You don't mean . . ."

"No. I will not man the boats to my death." Donovan shuddered at the thought. But then . . .

"I have never known you to use your magic so blatantly," Griffin said sotto voce.

"I have never had to before. I always had Hal, or Betsy, or Deirdre when I needed a spell. Their talents were always so much greater than mine, I felt . . . inadequate. Here, I am the only magician. Magic is the only way we can be certain these ships hit their target."

"And now, you have only me." Griffin sounded terribly disappointed as he gestured the sailors to take to the boats.

"I have you, a fine son who is intelligent, responsible, and who has given me a grandson to carry on as Baron of Kirkenwood . . . when I am gone. Your mother would have been proud of you. I am proud of you." He clapped Griffin on the shoulder in affection. "Get you gone. I'll join you in the boats as soon as I have lit all eight boats."

"I take that as a promise."

"I promise."

Even before the last man had jumped down to the waiting ship's boats to carry them back to the main fleet, Donovan concentrated hard on what he must do.

He drew a pentagram in the air. Faint green fire followed
his sigil. Then a circle around the glowing lines. A word or
two to invite all four elements to participate on all eight
boats. Then he punched his fist through the center of the
pentagram.

Sparks flew. A few landed on a line of gunpowder at
Donovan's feet leading to some rags soaked in tallow. The
rest of the flamelets scudded across the short gaps between
this ship and her seven sisters. In less than a heartbeat all
showed signs of burning.

Donovan jumped over the rail onto the rope ladder and
dropped quickly to the waiting boat.

"Loose the lines!" Griffin yelled.

Sailors dropped the stout ropes that kept the ships
together.

The ships began to drift inland with the swelling tide.

"Keep them in line, Da. Just like we planned. Two
abreast and close together," Griffin coaxed.

Donovan kept his mind linked to the fires. "Lines of
Fire, Seek to join your brothers. Form ropes of flame. Lash
yourselves to each other."

All of his concentration remained on the ships. He became the fire, breathed the smoke, lived the moments of
ecstasy as each new bit of fuel joined in the dance of heat
and light. His spirit cavorted along the decks and rails. He
raced along ropes, up the masts and into the sails.

He was not even aware of Griffin hauling him back
aboard their own ship, *Golden Griffin,* a merchanter of
about ninety tons converted to a war vessel. He did not
feel the solid deck beneath his feet as he stood at the taff
rail watching the ships enter the Spanish anchorage below
the cliffs of Calais.

"You did it, Da." Griffin slapped his back. "The Spanish
hauled off two ships. But the rest got through."

A mighty explosion turned the sea and sky red. Hot air
blasted Donovan. He rocked back on his heels, struggling
for balance.

"The heat is so intense the guns are exploding!" Griffin
jumped up and down in excitement.

Hastily, Donovan released the elements and grounded the spell. His mind rose up as if surfacing from a deep, deep dive. "The armada is scattering," he breathed.

"Aye, Da. They fly before the wind, anywhere to avoid the fireships."

"They'll be a long time regrouping."

"Before then, we will pick them off one by one."

"Aye." Donovan relaxed and found his knees decidedly weak. "Parma will not march overland and join with the armada here."

Someone thrust beer and bread into his hands. He ate it blindly, seeking only fuel for his body after the tremendous expenditure of magical energy.

For hours, he and Griffin watched the havoc they had wrought with the Spanish. More damage than any of the three or four battles they had fought along the length of the English Channel. The English had precious little munitions left. They had to take out as many of the enemy as possible this way.

As dawn crept up behind the cliffs of Calais, Donovan spotted the first two fireships, smoldering hulks on the beach. The other six burned near the water line deep within the harbor.

"Look there!" Griffin pointed to the shallows below the cliffs.

The *San Lorenzo,* the biggest and most formidable of the Spanish galleasses, had run aground. The more the galley slaves worked to free her from the soft sands, the more the ship canted, turning her shallow bottom toward the English.

The signal came from Admiral Howard. Small boats, muskets, attack and take the prize.

Griffin lowered the first boat. Common sailors followed him eagerly. Each man carried a musket with as much powder and shot as he could carry, and a cutlass, sword, or dagger.

Donovan found himself swept into the tide of enthusiasm and into one of the boats. He was too tired to protest. Much too tired to be of any help.

The moment the small boats came into musket range of the grounded galleass, Spanish sailors began firing upon the boarders. Griffin and his men fired back. Six rounds later three men reeled, crying in pain. They clutched gaping wounds that spouted bright blood.

"Griffin!" Donovan could not see his son.

The men in his boat let loose another volley.

More cries of pain and dismay. This time from the *San Lorenzo.*

"Griffin," Donovan called across the water separating him from his son's boat. He pushed his voice with the little magic left to him.

The next round of shots exploded in his ears. Near deafened, he slumped down in the gunnels. His legs went numb. Heat drained from his body.

"Milord," a sailor leaned over him. Worry creased his eyes. "Milord, where are you hurt?"

"Hurt?" The words came out slurred to Donovan's still ringing ears.

"There's blood, milord. On your back and legs."

Donovan reached a hesitant hand behind him. It came up sticky with blood.

"My son?" he asked, not too certain how to proceed.

" 'E took a hit, Milord. Can't tell how bad from this distance."

All around them, men sprouted wounds. The boats drifted, put a little more distance between them and the grounded ship.

A grinning Spanish face peered over the canted rails of the galleass. The man sported an elegant befeathered cap. The captain.

"Get me a musket. Loaded," Donovan said between gritted teeth. "I'll end this once and for all."

Anger, despair, the sense of nothing left to lose, brought magic to Donovan's hands. He channeled it into his eyesight and along the barrel of the gun.

One shot. He had one chance.

Roanna, Deirdre's mother, had used this same spell once to send a fire arrow a great distance to crash through the glass window of Donovan's bedroom. It took the life of his first wife, Betsy's mother. Now the spell brought his life full circle.

Never take a life with magic. Was that Grandmother Raven's voice?

I have to, he replied and pulled the trigger. He stayed

conscious long enough to see blood blossom from the grinning captain's forehead.

Within moments the Spanish deserted their ship. Without a captain to lead their defense, they lost the will to fight. Hundreds of sailors leaped into the shallows and swam or waded ashore. They left their dead and wounded behind.

The citizens of Calais had gathered on the beach to watch the fray. They jeered the Spanish sailors for cowardice.

Donovan's crew boarded the ship and claimed it as a prize of war. He watched from the safety of the little boat. His body grew cold. Numbness crept up his torso and down his arms. His vision blurred.

Before his hand went completely numb, Donovan reached to clasp the locket suspended from a silver chain.

"Milord, your son lives," a sailor cried. " 'Twas only a flesh wound to the arm."

Donovan sighed. "My son is safe."

He let go his fading determination. His vision dimmed. Among the shadows a figure appeared, clad in a red petticoat. She held out a hand to him in welcome greeting.

"Mary!" He reached to touch her. She retreated.

"Mary, you never loved me," he cried. Despairing at his incredible loneliness, he yanked upon the locket. The silver links parted. His hand fell away, fingers opened. The locket fell into the sea.

The ghost of Mary shifted, changed, became a determined and diminutive blonde. Martha. His second wife. Mother to the twins. "Martha," he whispered. "Martha forgive me."

"You were always more stubborn than sensible, Donovan," she replied, smiling. They clasped hands and the shadows swirled around them both.

"Hang on, Da. I'll get a physician," Griffin cried.

"Martha," Donovan breathed. He cast off the burden of his body and followed her. "Martha, my love."

Chapter 77

Monday, 29 July (Julian Calendar), 8 August (Gregorian Calendar), 1588. Before dawn. The White Cliffs of Dover.

"DEE, wake up," Hal called to me, seemingly from a great distance.

I think I moaned. My joints burned and every muscle in my body ached. I had a sudden craving for raw meat stronger than I had experienced in many years.

"You are weak, love. Feverish." He propped me up and held a cup of water to my lips.

I drank thirstily.

"We can wait no longer, Dee. We have to send a storm to scatter the Spanish Armada."

"The fireships?" I vaguely remembered discussion around the fire between Hal and some of my Gypsy friends. Even now, the strange boy with the piercing blue eyes peered at me from behind a nearby clump of gorse.

"The Spanish fled their anchorage at Calais in panic. They reformed out to sea."

"Our fleet?"

"Reinforced and in hot pursuit. But the armada is dangerously close to the rendezvous with Parma. I cannot be certain Parma will not launch his troops if he thinks he has clear passage to the protection of the armada. They could land at Great Yarmouth by tonight. I don't think either side has much munitions remaining. We might not be able to stop Parma if he reaches the protection of the armada." Hal held a new cup to my lips. This one smelled of broth and herbs.

I picked out feverfew, wild parsley, and willow bark by scent. A few others remained elusive. I hesitated.

A Gypsy woman—the females never gave their names—nodded approval at me. I could safely drink the brew.

I sipped tentatively. They had laced it with honey to make it palatable.

"Drink it all, Dee. You have to get back on your feet. Now," Hal instructed. "I cannot work the spell."

"I do not know that I can either." I slumped back into his arms, too weary to think. If I expended any of my strength working magic . . .

Newynog whined and nuzzled beneath my limp hand. I could not even scratch her ears. She was content just to have me touch her.

"You have to try, Dee. We cannot allow the armada to rendezvous with Parma. You are the only one who can do this, Dee." He shook me to keep me conscious.

"But Betsy . . ." Then I remembered the wolves. Betsy dying in my arms. The attack.

My magic had attracted the werewolves.

Suddenly I thought my entire left arm aflame. It itched with preternatural fierceness. I stared at the offensive limb. "How long have I been lost to the fever?"

"Two nights and a day," Hal replied.

I shuddered.

"Will I become . . ." I could not voice the possibility of becoming a werewolf.

But Newynog had made it clear that the next familiar would go to Maggie Rose or baby Griffin. Very soon, I would die, or . . . shudder again . . . worse.

"No. You will be spared," Hal said. He hung his head.

"Tell me the truth," I demanded with more strength than I thought possible. Strength began to tingle in my feet and hands. The potion began working, abating the fever. Soon I might be able to stand on my own. Or sit at least.

"There was no ritual. No preparation. No—intercourse. You received a bite. You should be dead."

"You healed me once with your blood, Hal." I touched his face tenderly, wondering how much longer I would be able to do that. "Did you do that again?"

"No. You fought the fever on your own. Some of my wolf lingers in you."

Upon occasion, at the full moon, I craved raw meat and

never sickened with a cold or other ailment that plagued the citizens of London, especially in summer.

I thought I heard cannon booming in the distance.

Everyone looked up from their activities and stared to the north and east.

"Dee, you have to do it. Now."

I breathed deeply.

"Yes, I must." A sense of inevitability settled around me. I could push myself beyond my limits. I would not recover. But England must be safe.

"Tell Maggie Rose I love her," I whispered to Hal as he heaved me to my feet.

"You tell her. When we are done. Now, can you walk to the bonfire, or must I carry you?"

I looked across the distance from the Gypsy camp to the stacked wood and pentagram. My knees sagged at the thought of walking the fifty paces.

Before I could form an answer, Hal swung me up into his arms and marched the short distance.

"Whatever happens, Hal, I want you to know that I love you, too. I have always loved you, since we were small children."

"I will not let anything happen to you." He kissed me soundly as he set me on my feet beside the pentagram. Newynog offered her shoulder to prop me up.

"Hal, you have to let me finish the spell even though it kills me." I clung to his shirt, pleading with my entire being.

He stared at me in stony silence.

"Promise me, Hal."

"I will not break a promise, especially one I make to you. So I will not promise."

He stalked back to the line of Gypsies, silent observers of the miracle I needed to work.

A freshening breeze heartened me. The element of Air seemed anxious to get from here to there. Something pushed it. Good. I had something to work with. As I took my three deep breaths, I concentrated on the heaviness that pushed Air around like a bully in a tavern brawl.

"I will need you to light the fire, Hal," I said quietly. The bully in the Air fought my subtle hints for control. I could not conjure a storm, light the fire, and remain conscious, too.

Hal stepped up beside me. He took my hand as he also centered his magic with three deep breaths.

Suddenly, a wreath of faeries filled the rapidly chilling air around me.

What can we do to help? they cried in one voice.

"Entice Air to fight the cold water of the North Sea," I suggested. Like all bullies, this air mass needed to feel superior. Air and Water opposed each other in the circle of elements. I was Earth, the complement of Water. In fighting the sea, the Air was fighting me, another bully, but less dangerous.

Hal added his silent encouragement to Air. He was Fire, an ally.

The faeries giggled at the dangerous game we played.

"Circle," I said quietly. "Opposites."

He nodded and began tracing the circle drawn in the ground deasil, along the path of the sun. I broke away and followed the white chalk markings that shone through the broken turf along the opposite path, widdershins. We passed each other and then met back at the beginning.

"A double circle, just like at Montmatre?" he whispered.

"Three times." Speaking became difficult. All my concentration had to remain on the circle. On the magic I expended.

The faeries circled us both. Wider and wider they drew their own sigil. I heard a thunder of galloping horses. The elves joined the faeries. Pixies, sprites, and brownies followed the circle as well. Air followed them, blowing stronger with every passing heartbeat.

By the time Hal and I met for the last time at the beginning of the circle, I was panting, leaning heavily on Newynog. Air had become a strong wind. It circled us, growling at our tricks to corral it.

"Fire!" I commanded.

Almost before the words were out of my mouth, Hal flicked his fingers. Sparks landed in the dry kindling at the heart of the bonfire. Flames ate greedily of the fuel Newynog and I had provided. It climbed rapidly. Air sought to join with it. Lightning flashed between them.

Below the cliffs, the sea churned.

Air grew stronger.

I let it gather power as it circled us. Again and again, it

fought my control. Again and again, I reined it in until the very ground shook with the thunder it commanded.

Or was that the boom of cannon fire traveling across the water?

With each moment, strength drained from me. I think I fell to my knees. All of my concentration centered on the duel with Air and Fire against Earth and Water.

Heat climbed up my limbs from the fever that reasserted itself.

I poured more and more magic into my control of the brewing storm.

My heart stuttered, stalled.

My breath left me.

Hal slapped my back.

I jerked back, gasping for air.

The storm broke free.

I pushed it away, in the direction of the merging fleets.

"I need to see." I could not hear my own words for the howl of triumph released by the wind.

Someone thrust a bowl of water in front of me and a pebble into my limp hand.

For a long moment I could not think what to do.

Hal guided my hand up over the bowl of water. He squeezed my fingers until the pebble dropped. Water rippled. Smoke swirled. Images appeared.

Faster than events could transpire, I watched Drake's ship *Revenge* close upon an enemy and fire the first salvo. The Spanish fired back. All the ships opened fire on both sides. Hundreds of cannons belched flame and smoke and death.

Hour after hour the guns blazed.

The seas heaved and took their own toll.

Slowly, the English pushed the Spanish farther and farther north, away from their rendezvous with Parma.

The guns fired slower and slower. Fewer and fewer Spanish responded to the English salvos. I watched the Spanish flagship falter. Two men argued on the castle deck, Medina Sedona, the Captain General of the Spanish Armada, and an admiral. They pointed and gesticulated and finally settled on one last salvo of cannon, broadside into Drake's *Revenge*.

I think I screamed.

Then, just as I thought Drake would haul around and present his vulnerable flank, the storm hit.

Both fleets scattered. Air pushed and pushed and pushed. The Spanish passed out of range of the shorter English guns. But they were also out of range for any meeting with troops from the Netherlands. Neither side had much, if any, powder and shot. Drake could only follow the fleeing armada and prevent them from landing on British soil.

As the vision in the scrying bowl evaporated, so did my mind. I had nothing left to give the spell or my life.

Chapter 78

Tuesday, 31 July (Julian Calender), 1588. City of Dover.

"BREATHE, Dee. Breathe, damn your eyes." Hal pressed hard upon her chest, forcing her heart to keep beating. Then he breathed into her lungs, giving her the air she needed.

Three times since yester'eve her being had just . . . stopped. He had barely been able to revive her on the long slow journey to the home of a physician in the city. The good doctor had thrown up his hands in despair. Short of applying leeches, he knew naught what to do.

At last, Dee's chest rose and fell on its own, painfully slow and ragged.

"God's wounds, Dee, you have to get better. You have to live. I can't do it on my own. I need your help. I need you!" he sobbed. His tears fell on her face. He left them where they fell. Too tired to think, he rested his head beside her on the counterpane.

And then he prayed. As he had never prayed before, with fervor, and honesty, and faith. A measure of peace . . . or was it merely sleep? . . . settled upon his shoulders.

After a long, long time her eyelids fluttered open. She looked about, dazed, uncertain, clearly puzzled.

"I'm alive?" The words came out on a single breath, barely heard.

"Thank God and all his angels, you live." He hugged her gently, afraid to crush the life from her once more.

Weakly, she lifted a finger to the tears on his cheeks and in his eyes.

"You cried for me."

"I prayed for you. I'd cry a lot more if you died on me."

"You should have let me go."

"Never." He kissed her temple and lay back. Perhaps now he could sleep.

"I . . . I don't feel . . . whole." With a puzzled frown on her face, she ran her hands the length of her body.

"You are all there. Everything works. Life nearly left you with the end of the spell." He watched her carefully to make certain she did not succumb once more to the deep sleep of death.

"Hal, I am not all here." Her voice sounded panicky.

He sat up and held a hand over her. He pushed a little magic into his fingers, questing, scanning for dangers to her health. She pushed his hand away.

"You should have let me die." She rolled away from him.

"Dee?" He pulled her back to face him. "What ails you?"

"The magic." She spoke so quietly he almost did not hear her. "My magic is gone."

"What?" He pushed himself to a sitting position. With that extra little bit of distance he scanned her aura. Compact layers of yellow and pale green surrounded her head and shoulders.

"You used a lot of magic . . . maybe it's sleeping. You slept a long time."

"No, Hal. 'Tis gone forever," she sobbed. "I gave it all, to the spell."

"You gave it to save England." He gathered her close, letting her spill her tears.

"All these years I have fought using my magic, sought other choices, wished I did not have the talent. Now that it's gone . . . I guess I am not the Pendragon anymore."

"You have lived without using your magic. You can continue without it."

"A last resort, but sometimes very necessary. Would we have won the last battle without it?"

"Maybe. Maybe not."

"Betsy is dead. I have no magic. You must be the Pendragon now, Hal. As Grandmother Raven predicted. Donovan's son would inherit." She lay within his embrace limp, nearly inert.

"Da died, too," Hal said quietly.

She drew in a sharp breath. Tears formed in her eyes.

Her hand reached to hold his. "Not Uncle Donovan. He was a truly good man."

"I heard Griffin's cries on the wind after the storm passed. Da died honorably in battle. He saved a number of lives." Hal paused a moment to control his own grief. "You can't give up being Pendragon now, Dee. Not until Maggie Rose grows up to take your place."

"The Pendragon must have magic," she insisted.

"Dee, I am a werewolf. I can't be the Pendragon."

"There is no one else." That stubborn chin thrust out. She would live now.

A chill of inevitability stabbed his chest. Responsibility weighed heavily on his heart.

"I can't do it alone."

"You have to. I . . . I'm not whole." She sounded tentative. Perhaps he could persuade her yet.

"Neither am I. You have love and wisdom to give to me in guidance. Our fathers learned that the job is too big for one person. The world has grown too complex and frightening for one person to do it all. You have to help me."

A smile started at one corner of her mouth. His heart swelled in response.

"I am truly human now. Mundane. I can learn to understand humanity. And I need not fear that magic will take my mind as it did Betsy's and Meg's and even your da's. I want to see my friends again. I need to see them, make certain they fare well. I want to hug them and laugh and cry with them."

"The Pendragon needs many friends as well as compassion and understanding. What about your friends, the Gypsies?"

"Them, too. Did Micah find the tenth wolf? Were any of them hurt? Are they still here?"

"The tenth wolf is still missing. The Rom await you just outside Dover City. They love you as a Merlin. They need you as much or more than any other citizen of Britain."

"Can we take to the road together?" She stared into his eyes, eager now to love and to live.

"Aye. The Pendragon needs to roam Britain, learn the heart of the land and its people."

"Then we will roam it together. With Maggie Rose and her familiar."

"What about Newynog?"

"I think she knew I'd lose my magic."

"As soon as you are able, we will travel to Kirkenwood to find a mate for your dog."

"I think she already did, when I went to fetch Betsy. We must take her back there to whelp. With Maggie Rose. Then we must go back to France. We have to make sure the peace between Henri and the Holy League lasts."

"Will you keep the tavern?"

"Let Walsingham have it. He needs to hear the gossip there. So he can run it."

He kissed her then, long and hard, anxious for her to be truly well so they could begin their new life together.

"One more thing," she said hesitantly.

"What, my love."

Before he could protest, she reached over and touched his silver earring. It fell into her hands. A tremendous weight seemed to lift from his head and shoulders.

"How?"

"The silver reacts to magic. I have no magic left." They both stared at the chain and ball in her palm. As they watched, it began to turn black.

She dropped it onto the rush-strewn floor and shook her hand. With a whoosh it disintegrated into dust.

"Surely, if breaking the spell were that simple, the other werewolves would . . ."

"The other werewolves lose a great deal of their humanity during the ritual. Ever after that, they shun their friends and family. They would not think to remove the thing," she said, still staring at the wispy ashes.

"If you wouldn't mind, can you take care of the other chain as well?" His breath came in anxious pants. To be free of the constant burn, the insidious compulsion to return to The Master, to the place of his death, left him almost dizzy with relief.

The ring at his navel and its accompanying chain about his waist resisted Dee. It took a few moments of prying to open the silver link and slide it free of his skin. But she succeeded.

They both lay back for a long moment, relishing the separation from his past.

"I'm still a werewolf," Hal admitted at last.

"I can live with that."

"Then I guess I can, too. I found the second girdle at *El Lobison*'s camp. Maybe we can find another female werewolf. In Eastern Europe, I think, a priestess of her kind who will free me of my curse."

"Hal, I think we need to take one of the Gypsy children with us. The one with the intense blue eyes. He is going to need our guidance. I think he will need you to teach him to manage his wolf and grow into a man."

"Two children roaming with us. We'll have no home."

"All of Britain is our home."

Epilogue

Sunday, 26 November, 1588. St. Paul's Cathedral, London.

ALL of England celebrated the thirtieth anniversary of Elizabeth's accession to the crown for a full week. Pageants and processionals, tournaments and masques, plays and music and bonfires.

Hal and I waited in a place of honor near the steps of St. Paul's on that chill but clear Sunday morning. Maggie Rose held her new male puppy tightly. Helwriaeth squirmed and wiggled to be set free. She let him drop to the ground, but kept a firm hand on his collar and lead. They made a happy pair, even though the dog had not the intelligence or magic to become a familiar.

Newynog had bequeathed the female familiar to baby Griffin, Hal's nephew.

I think I breathed a sigh of relief at that. Maggie Rose was destined to fulfill a quieter, less dangerous role in history than that of the Pendragon.

Baruckey, the strangely silent Gypsy boy, watched my daughter without envy or resentment. He had refused a dog of his own from Newynog's litter.

Both Hal and his son fidgeted, uncomfortable in their new finery. Stiff ruffs and boning in their doublets confined them in ways neither liked.

"Stand still," I admonished them both.

Hal cringed. Baruckey looked at me with his piercing blue eyes, Kirkwood eyes. Hal's eyes.

Even without magic, I knew what he intended to do. I stepped on his foot to break his concentration. "Not here and not now!"

"But . . ."

"Later. After dark, you and your father can run the heath."
We glared at each other a moment. Baruckey did not take discipline easily. But he recognized both Hal and I as being more dominant than he in the family that had become his pack.

I did not have to have magic to know that he would challenge us constantly. I hoped we could instill a measure of civilization and manners into him before we could no longer dominate him.

"Is that man not the actor we saw in the play yester'eve?" Hal asked. He nodded toward a handsome young man off to our left.

"Yes, I believe so. A brilliant performance. Do you remember his name?"

"His name is Will," Maggie Rose said. "He wrote the play, too, though the theater owner will not admit to it."

"Ah," I replied. Maggie Rose seemed to know much more about life in London than I ever did, even during the years I ran a tavern.

"Look, Mama, the queen comes." Maggie Rose jumped up and down in her excitement. "Isn't she pretty with all of her jewels and pearls? And her red hair as bright as yours."

"She looks sad," Baruckey muttered.

Maggie Rose pouted at this negative comment. She wanted to paint the world to suit her own mood, not Baruckey's.

"The queen is all alone," I explained. "The man she loved above all others died two months ago. She misses the Earl of Leicester terribly." I reached for Hal's hand and held it tightly. A miracle had brought me back to life. I prayed every day that he and I might share many long years together and never again be separated. As Elizabeth and her beloved Robin Dudley had been separated.

A mighty cheer swelled through the crowd as Elizabeth disembarked from her special coach. She smiled and waved to them. Ribbands and banners flew through air, along with green boughs and . . . Could it be?

"Yes," I sighed. "The faeries have come to celebrate with her." Dozens of brightly colored beings flew marvelous spirals and looping patterns around her head.

Newynog lifted her head and snapped at one of the audacious creatures that came too close to her nose. Helwriaeth leaped and frolicked in turn.

"Ah, our Merlin has joined us." Elizabeth held out her

hand. I curtsied and kissed her rings. I had to jab Hal with an elbow to remind him of proper etiquette. Maggie Rose curtsied prettily. Baruckey glowered.

"Thank you for inviting us," I replied as I straightened.

"We owe you much. More than this little token can convey." She pressed a medal into my hands. I looked at it. On one side was the queen's portrait. On the other a race-built galleon. Inscribed around the molded images was the legend that had become the motto of the victory over the armada: "God blew with His winds, and they were scattered."

I handed the piece to Hal for his inspection. We had heard about the victory medal. Both of us grinned. God may indeed have had something to do with the wind. He just needed a little help now and then.

"Join us for the service." Elizabeth gestured for me and my family to follow her into the cathedral.

"Thank you again, Majesty," I said. This time I had to step on Hal's foot to keep him from running away. "We are all honored to join you."

"We are grateful that our message found you in London."

"Yes, Majesty. We have just returned from Oxford. It seems a distant cousin, one Christopher Marlowe, has begun signing his name Christopher Merlin. He quite openly claims descent from the original. We had quite a long and involved conversation with him."

The young playwright, Marlowe, had nearly soiled his nether garments when Hal described the consequences of drawing too much attention to our relationship to our esteemed ancestor. He vowed to be more subtle in the future.

As we talked, Baruckey dropped into fur without warning.

"And where are you off to next?" the queen asked as she nodded her head and waved to more of the cheering crowd. "You really should wait for our passport to travel abroad. But we know you will not heed our restrictions."

Hal smiled at her, letting just a little bit too much fang show.

I jabbed him again.

"Paris next. We have unfinished business with the Duc de Guise and the Holy League."

Elizabeth sighed. "Just make certain you leave no trail back to us."

"That is why we travel without passport."

The organ swelled to greet the queen as she entered the church nave. The choirs lifted their voices in polyphonic hymns of Thanksgiving and praise to Gloriana.

My family and I slipped out the back, unseen, anxious to be about our business. The business of England.

Irene Radford

Merlin's Descendants

"Entertaining blend of fantasy and history, which invites comparisons with Mary Stewart and Marion Zimmer Bradley" —*Publishers Weekly*

GUARDIAN OF THE PROMISE
This fourth novel in the series follows the children of Donovan and Griffin, in a magic-fueled struggle to protect Elizabethan England from enemies—both mortal and demonic. 0-7564-0078-3

*And don't miss the first three books
in this exciting series:*
GUARDIAN OF THE BALANCE
0-88677-875-1
GUARDIAN OF THE TRUST
0-88677-995-2
GUARDIAN OF THE VISION
0-7564-0071-6

To Order Call: 1-800-788-6262

Melanie Rawn

"Rawn's talent for lush descriptions and complex
characterizations provides a broad range of drama,
intrigue, romance and adventure."
—*Library Journal*

EXILES
THE RUINS OF AMBRAI	0-88677-668-6
THE MAGEBORN TRAITOR	0-88677-731-3

DRAGON PRINCE
DRAGON PRINCE	0-88677-450-0
THE STAR SCROLL	0-88677-349-0
SUNRUNNER'S FIRE	0-88677-403-9

DRAGON STAR
STRONGHOLD	0-88677-482-9
THE DRAGON TOKEN	0-88677-542-6
SKYBOWL	0-88677-595-7

To Order Call: 1-800-788-6262

Curt Benjamin

Seven Brothers

"Rousing fantasy adventure."
—*Publishers Weekly*

Llesho, the youngest prince of Thebin, was only seven when the Harn invaded, deposing and murdering his family and selling the boy into slavery. On Pearl Island, he was trained as a diver—until a vision changed his life completely. The spirit of his long-dead teacher revealed the truth about Llesho's family—his brothers were alive, but enslaved, living in distant lands. Now, to free his brothers, and himself, Llesho must become a gladiator. And he must go face to face with sorcerers...and gods.

Book One:
THE PRINCE OF SHADOWS   0-7564-0054-6
Book Two:
THE PRINCE OF DREAMS   0-7564-0114-3
Book Three:
THE GATES OF HEAVEN   0-7564-0156-9
(hardcover)

To Order Call: 1-800-788-6262

Kristen Britain

GREEN RIDER

As Karigan G'ladheon, on the run from school, makes her way through the deep forest, a galloping horse plunges out of the brush, its rider impaled by two black arrows. With his dying breath, he tells her he is a Green Rider, one of the king's special messengers. Giving her his green coat with its symbolic brooch of office, he makes Karigan swear to deliver the message he was carrying. Pursued by unknown assassins, following a path only the horse seems to know, Karigan finds herself thrust into in a world of danger and complex magic....   0-88677-858-1

FIRST RIDER'S CALL

With evil forces once again at large in the kingdom and with the messenger service depleted and weakened, can Karigan reach through the walls of time to get help from the First Rider, a woman dead for a millennium?   0-7564-0209-3

To Order Call: 1-800-788-6262

DAW 7

Tanya Huff

Smoke and Shadows

First in a New Series

Tony Foster—familiar to Tanya Huff fans from her
Blood series—has relocated to Vancouver with Henry
Fitzroy, vampire son of Henry VIII. Tony landed a
job as a production assistant at CB Productions, iron-
ically working on a syndicated TV series, "Darkest
Night," about a vampire detective. Except for his
crush on Lee, the show's handsome costar, Tony was
pretty content...at least until everything started to fall
apart on the set. It began with shadows—shadows
that seemed to be where they didn't belong, shadows
that had an existence of their own. And when he
found a body, and a shadow cast its claim on Lee,
Tony knew he had to find out what was going on, and
that he needed Henry's help.

0-7564-0183-6

To Order Call: 1-800-788-6262